"I have never watched the Super Bowl. I consider football even more boring than computers. Nevertheless, I found THE FRANCHISE vibrating with energy, wonderfully well written, compelling, and dear—altogether a Christmas-morning sort of surprise."

> Carol E. Rinzler
> *Cosmopolitan*

"Pulses with savage humor!"

> *Chicago Sun-Times*

"If the characters in this book are thinly disguised fictional counterparts of real-life pro football people, the law ought to move in right now and arrest just about everybody in the game!"

> *Sports Illustrated*

"A violent and conspiratorial vortex of madmen and money worthy of Nathanael West's *Day of the Locust* or Robert Stone's *A Hall of Mirrors*...THE FRANCHISE is a tough, insightful and sometimes darkly humorous novel."

> *Texas Monthly*

(more...)

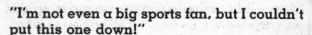

"I'm not even a big sports fan, but I couldn't put this one down!"

Liz Smith
New York Daily News

"The muse has said to Pete Gent, 'Go long. And it'll be there.' The muse was not just woofing."

Roy Blount, Jr.

"THE FRANCHISE, like the rough and profitable business it is about, is full of blood, pain, sex, drugs, and hush-hush secrets. A real page-turner."

Larry King
Author of *The Best Little
Whorehouse in Texas*

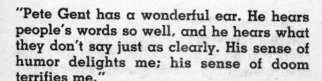

"Pete Gent has a wonderful ear. He hears people's words so well, and he hears what they don't say just as clearly. His sense of humor delights me; his sense of doom terrifies me."

Dick Schaap

"Extraordinary. Once I started I couldn't put it down."
Ted Nathanson
Coordinating Producer, NBC Football

"Masterfully dances among parody, exposé and fantasy...combines hilarity with cynicism, thoughtfulness with supense."
San Francisco Chronicle

(even MORE...)

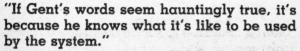

"If Gent's words seem hauntingly true, it's because he knows what it's like to be used by the system."

Milwaukee Journal

"This wickedly funny and extremely violent novel virtually wipes the floor with professional football.... Gent depicts in searing detail an America gone completely football-mad.... A wildly imaginative, daring performance, this novel may change the point of view of many pro football aficionados."

Publishers Weekly

"Lots of fine, raunchy dialogue and gritty inside-atmosphere."

The Kirkus Reviews

Also by Peter Gent
Published by Ballantine Books:

NORTH DALLAS FORTY

THE FRANCHISE

PETER GENT

BALLANTINE BOOKS • NEW YORK

This book is dedicated with love to my son, Carter Davis Gent, a brave boy who did his job, kept his promises, did not quit and was still made to pay in pain for the mistakes and greed of others.

Texas
1983

A society, most of whose members spend a great part of their time, not on the spot, not here and now and in the calculable future, but somewhere else, in the irrelevant other worlds of sports and soap opera, of mythology and metaphysical fantasy, will find it hard to resist the encroachments of those who would manipulate and control it.

ALDOUS HUXLEY

THE FRANCHISE

PART ONE

"Lately it occurs to me,
what a long strange trip it's been."

THE GRATEFUL DEAD
"Truckin'"

THE PENTHOUSE

TAYLOR Jefferson Rusk moved into the hotel a week ahead of the team. He took the key to his assigned room on the ninth floor, dropped it into his back pocket, then checked into the penthouse suite as E. Fudd.

The huge twenty-fifth-floor suite had a 360-degree view of Park City, and access was limited by a special key to the private elevator. Taylor's plan was to stay hidden.

"You guys going to win the Super Bowl, Mr. Rusk?" The bellman unloaded Taylor's bags from the dolly. "We got it on pay TV here in the hotel. Every room'll be filled at triple the rate."

"My name is Fudd. E. Fudd." He handed the bellman a fifty-dollar bill. "Mr. Rusk is registered into a room on nine. Anybody wants him, send them there." He handed the bill to the uniformed man. "General Grant will arrive every day the identities of Mr. Fudd and Mr. Rusk stay separate."

The tall quarterback pulled back the curtain to view the city skyline; the sun was high, casting hard shadows through the light smog. The Pistol Dome was humped up far to the south, dark against the horizon.

"You gonna beat 'em by sixteen?" The bellman slid the fifty-dollar bill into his green jacket pocket. "That's the latest line outta Vegas."

"I don't gamble." Taylor stared at the giant growth on the horizon. "Too much like believing in God, banking on a miracle to keep the corn growing or the dice rolling. . . . Too much ritual, not enough substance, to show *He* has chosen *you*." The quarterback pointed at the Dome. "There's your cathedral, one hundred and sixty million dollars of veneration. The Opium of the Masses. OPM. Other People's Money."

The bellman's pointed face pulled into a wolfish smile. "I was just wondering if you heard talk? Sixteen points is a big spread."

Taylor turned to the pockmarked, nervous, rumpled man. Dirty gold braid decorated his dark-green outfit.

"Well, what do you think?" The man was looking for an edge on life. *Any edge*.

"What do *you* think?" Taylor tossed back.

— 3 —

"I think you can do it. *If* you got a reason."

Taylor hadn't expected that reply. "Winning is reason enough."

"Winning is *one* more, not sixteen more." The bellman stood his ground, probing, poking around. "Sixteen points is a big spread. Sports writers and handicappers on TV, they say you've made the Franchise a Super Bowl power. They say Denver really isn't as good as their record, what with computer scheduling, parity, the playoff system and the competition committee. But," the bellman waved away the media obfuscation, "in January everybody's a football expert. I want to know what *you* think."

"I *can't tell you* what I think. It's against the rules." Taylor returned his gaze to the outside, looking down at the University.

"You been around. . . ." The bellman pressed. "Your opinion means something, Mr. Rusk."

The six-foot-five-inch, 225-pound quarterback of the Texas Pistols turned from the window and looked at the bellman. Taylor's voice was soft. "You insist on confusing me with that guy down on nine." He stuck his big hand out. "Gimme back the fifty dollars."

Reluctantly the man in the green jacket placed the bill in the huge palm. Taylor tore it in half and handed one piece back to the bellman. "You get the other half tomorrow *if* no one else confuses me with the guy down on nine."

"It won't happen again," the agitated little man said.

"Quarterbacks are either in the penthouse or the shithouse." Taylor tossed the remaining half bill on the dresser. "I want to be undisturbed in the penthouse."

The bellman disappeared out the door.

Taylor Rusk moved back to the glass, watching the course of the river as it slid brown beneath the ancient iron Red River Street Bridge. He didn't remember the water turning dirty this early.

Taylor looked back out to the giant hulking shape crouched fearsomely south of the city. The Pistol Dome was a sleeping dragon that he would have to fight soon.

"Gamble or die," Taylor said aloud with a slight resignation. "Or change games."

Turning away from the glass wall and the hazy skyline, Taylor wandered around the penthouse suite, ending his perambulation in the bedroom. He began unpacking.

Winning is one more, not sixteen more.

But Dick Conly promised that salvation was beating Denver by the purposely, insanely, high spread. Salvation from *what* was never quite clear; nevertheless Taylor and Red Kilroy had worked to preempt espionage and sabotage ordered by the Cobianco brothers, Suzy Chandler and A. D. Koster. Taylor hoped they had worked effectively.

It could be done. It had to be done. Beat Denver by *one point more than the spread*.

Taylor stripped naked, laid a bath towel on the soft thick beige carpet and did thirty minutes of Yoga poses, ending cross-legged, eyes closed, arms resting on his legs, thumbs and index fingers forming circles.

The circles. The power.

Next, stretched out flat, he ordered each muscle to relax, turn loose. He let the blood flow, breaking the dam of tension. Forgotten sore spots quivered, jerked, twitched. Breathing deeply through his nose, Taylor began concentrating on the red spot growing between his eyes.

Awakening at dusk, Taylor *knew*. They could deliver the Super Bowl. Whatever was necessary, he would create. The great joy of exceptional talent was knowing what was needed. Taylor Rusk needed *not to beat himself*. That he knew.

Sixteen points behind at the gate required a fast start, acceleration, high-speed thinking and looking far ahead, over hills, around corners.

It seemed impossible. Almost.

He would succeed, he decided then and there, using whatever it took from horseshoes to handgrenades, going fast and hard, craving the *action*, the adrenaline, the movement and the velocity of his life and the game. An athlete's life: destructive and creative, invincible and frangible; each day a battle, a race that *must* be run, always going faster and harder. Yet, Taylor Rusk also knew he was reaching the finish line, reaching the end without a way to slow down. Twenty years of acceleration just to hit the wall. And sooner or later everybody hit the wall. Taylor knew the finish was close, so the crash would be less startling—not any less destructive, just not quite the surprise.

Life as demolition derby. The athlete's life. Taylor wouldn't have it any other way. He couldn't.

Simon hadn't been ready to hit the wall. He didn't know about it.

A.D. crashed early. While others lost it in the curves, he picked up the pieces and the loose change. But he still crashed.

Red Kilroy skidded along the wall for years, tearing up his family and his insides.

Dick Conly built the Franchise for Cyrus Chandler, and they

pushed each other to the wall, yoked together by a deathbed promise, a bond of hate and greed. Their poisonous feud raced through the economic and social fabric of Texas, putting lots of people into the wall. The crashing and burning boggled Taylor's mind.

During the Franchise's building years, even fans hit the wall. Too many times, Taylor Rusk had opened the Monday paper to face orphaned children and a fat widow. Father had hit the wall, leaving a note blaming his suicide on "the Pistols' constant turnovers and their inability to move the ball in sustained drives." In those days, Taylor's voice echoed through the ancient, nearly empty Colony Stadium as he called snap numbers and audibles.

"Four-three . . . set."

Ghostlike, his voice would return from the empty seats around Lamar Jean Lukas, the First Fan. One of the few survivors.

"Four-three . . . set."

The rats in the locker room used to eat the leather earpieces out of headgears, and scorpions joined the players in the showers. Now fans fought and killed to get possession of *the ticket*. Big-bucks fans. Five-thousand-dollar-bond fans. One-hundred-thousand-dollar luxury skybox fans. Now divorce settlements hinged, not on custody of the children, but on custody of the Pistols season tickets. One woman successfully pleaded, "What's the use of having the goddam kids if he's got the football tickets?"

The Pistol Dome and the Pay-Per-View TV were Dick Conly's parting brainstorm. The monument to his fiscal and creative genius. Commissioner Burden had wanted Dick to wait until the League got complete antitrust exemption through the Congress, but Dick Conly didn't wait on anybody, the League or the Congress.

Dick didn't make money, he created value—and he wanted to have his legacy in place before the rules changed and somebody got a hand in his pocket. For the ten Pistols home games the past season, Channel Thirty-three Pay-Per-View drew a hundred thousand households at forty dollars apiece, paid by Electronic Funds Transfer.

Four million dollars for every home game, collected at the speed of light.

Forty million dollars a season *unshared*. There was no League provision for the sharing of home-game pay-television revenues. And with their own pay-TV broadcast hardware and brand-name software, there was no limit to the Pistols' market. A truly national football team.

Beat the spread. That was Taylor Rusk's part in Dick Conly's last great scheme for the Franchise. It finally came down to that.

Taylor stood at the hotel window and watched the night overtake the city. The sun sank behind the ridgeline, lights twinkled, the sky glowed pink. The Pistol Dome turned darker as the daylight faded. Soon it was hidden in the growing shadow of the rock scarp, crouched out in the dark south of town. Waiting. It was waiting for him, waiting for the Franchise.

Taylor Jefferson Rusk had come a long way and traveled such a short distance. It seemed like yesterday.

Now the kingdom was in disarray.

THE HEAT

IT was the heat that awed Taylor Rusk as he played football in central Texas, watching the surf of hot air rising up off the baked earth, a gauze curtain rippling the blazing rising sun that greeted the morning workout. The hot waves distorting, wobbling the orange ball as it climbed, growing hotter.

The heat. Taylor Rusk would play football in Texas for twenty years and was continually amazed when it got so damn hot he could see it.

He first noticed it his freshman year, the first morning practice at Park City High School.

Taylor's parents didn't live in wealthy Park City. They lived in Two Oaks, a small hill-country town between San Antonio and Austin. The Park City coach flew in and recruited Taylor his eighth-grade year. His father told him it was an opportunity to "advance," and so Taylor Rusk advanced down out of the hills and moved in with his aunt and uncle in Park City.

Taylor spent the early morning of his first high school practice watching the waggling sun tottering up into the blue clear sky.

Later Taylor would be described in his Park City High senior yearbook, *The Wildcat*, as "a popular and friendly transfer who led the Cats to consecutive state championships. He plans to attend the University." He didn't remember being all that popular or friendly, but he did know it's what's on the paper that counts. *The statistics.*

"We exist only on paper," Simon D'Hanis, another transfer, said. "We are the stats."

D'Hanis came from Vidor, near Beaumont, in East Texas. Hard folks, swamp people from the Big Thicket. His father was a mean drunk; his mother, Silsbee trash, was kind and cowed and beaten. "It's a way out, Simon," she said, signing papers making the Park City coach Simon's legal guardian. He never saw his parents again.

Simon D'Hanis lived in the locker room.

Taylor also got to know A. D. Koster, a wise guy, whose house slipped into the Park City school district by one of those bureaucratic accidents that make life worth living. Abraham Dwight Koster had been in the streets since he was nine, when his mother married a merchant marine in Los Angeles and sent A.D. back to live with her mother in a tiny bungalow backed up against the toll road. All through high school Koster drank and dealt pills and weed. Abraham Dwight Koster also was kind and attentive to his senile old grandmother, forging her shaky signature so he could cash her personal and Social Security checks long after she had died.

Abraham Dwight Koster had great natural athletic ability, with good bone and muscle structure. He had a quick mind, always probing for weakness, looking for the edge. A.D. was a natural football player, drunk or sober, and by his senior year at Park City he had played both ways an equal number of times.

By then Simon D'Hanis was All-State guard. He worked every summer, changing tires at the truckstop on the traffic circle, and turned hard.

A. D. Koster discovered amphetamine sulfate and was an All-State back. Second team.

A.D., Simon and Taylor Rusk were friends by acts of omission. At preppy, sophisticated Park City they really didn't belong to any group and so became a group themselves.

Strangers in a strange land.

Taylor was an exceptional athlete as a freshman. Simon and A.D. became really great football players as juniors.

Taylor possessed great athletic ability and the willingness to work and develop his skills. He grew four inches, put on twenty pounds between his sophomore and junior years and at the same time increased his agility, playing basketball and drilling five hours a day. Every day. Taylor never drank or smoked and was beginning his athletic blooming at exactly the right time, in exactly the right dimensions. And at Park City he filled a very necessary slot in the Three-Deep charts.

He advanced. He looked good on paper and on the field, breaking school and state passing records the next two years. By Taylor's sophomore year the Park City coach had nothing left to teach, so the coach, a strict disciplinarian, became frightened of Taylor, spending most of Taylor's junior year trying to convince him he wasn't *that good*. It was the first lesson Taylor learned about coaches' mind games, and by then it was too late for the coach. Their relationship was never more than a business deal.

Park City, behind the quarterbacking of Taylor Rusk, won the state championship twice. A.D. and Simon were also stars, and with their support Taylor controlled the team.

"I was just testing you as a junior," the Park City coach told Taylor his senior year. "To see if you could take the pressure."

"I was testing you too," Taylor replied. "And you graded out prime asshole."

The Park City coach's face tightened and he stomped away yelling, "Jocks! Prima donna sons of bitches!"

"The man loves the game," Taylor told Simon. "Loves the game—hates the players."

Taylor, Simon and A.D. went to the University together. They were recruited by Lem Carleton, Jr., the University regents chairman. Lem took them to the Spur Club dining room, bought them steaks, got Simon and A.D. drunk, then pointed out that the most important people in the state, including himself, had gone to the University and the *real important* ones were tapped into the Spur Club.

"You gúys are real blue chippers," Lem said. "You think I'd bring *any* football player up here? This is the *Spur dining room*. Right, Taylor?" Lem asked cannily, preempting Taylor's response. Taylor had forced Lem to invite A.D. and Simon.

"Yeah." The quarterback was not enthusiastic. "Real blue chippers."

"You said it, bubba," Lem junior gushed.

"I guess I did." Taylor watched Simon twist nervously in his ill-fitting suit while A.D.'s head swiveled, eagerly devouring the expensive wainscotting, the furniture, the lovely hostess, the elegance of quiet wealth and power.

Later, Regents Chairman Lem Carleton, Jr., took Taylor Rusk, Simon D'Hanis and A. D. Koster from the Spur Club over to a whorehouse in an apartment building just off campus. Simon, Lem and A.D. grabbed women and went upstairs.

Taylor Rusk stayed in the kitchen and talked to Madam Earlette.

She told him about the moonlighting wives and mothers picking up a few bucks with their bodies.

"We're all on scholarship here, sonny." Earlette gestured up with her head, making her heavy jowls wobble. "I ain't even got my first team here tonight." Her rheumy brown eyes narrowed. "They all spend one night home with the family in Park City."

It was a momentous occasion. At the whorehouse Lem junior signed the three to NCAA National letters of intent and A. D. Koster discovered amyl nitrite.

THE MAKING OF
THE TEN-CENT DOLLAR

As Taylor, Simon and A.D. were bagged by the University recruiter in a cheap off-campus apartment house, another meeting was beginning in the sanctum of the Spur Club.

"In twenty years every poor son of a bitch up north that can afford it is gonna head south before the lights go out and the niggers take over," Cyrus Chandler said in his amiable drawl. Cyrus was convincing his business associates that the city needed a professional football franchise. His full head of black hair was streaked with gray, his jaw was firm. He was sixty years old. "We want the next franchise in the South to come here, and I can get it. I am asking will you support the Franchise when I bring it in?"

Everybody around the table said yes.

"I'll bring Red Kilroy over from the University as head coach and general manager," Cyrus continued, to convince the already converted. Red Kilroy had the best record of any coach left alive. A lot of them had died young.

The people around the table represented banks, newspapers, radio and television stations and politicians. Cyrus sold them on supporting the Franchise and the big-league-city image. They were all members of Spur.

Before the war, during his senior year at the University, Cyrus had been president of Spur. During the war Daddy, Amos Chandler, had gotten Cyrus "deferred" to work as an assistant to Amos's lawyer, Dick Conly, who was "detached" as a civilian adviser to the Department of the Navy. The Navy used lots of oil, and Amos

Chandler had discovered oceans of it. Conly arranged for the Navy to buy it. Dick Conly and the war made the Chandlers richer.

After the war, brilliant young lawyer Dick Conly showed wealthy oilman Amos Chandler how to do all his deals, from pipelines and refineries to airlines and racetracks, oil fields and uranium mines, on other people's money. OPM. Opium.

"We are going to have god-awful inflation, so put every cent of cash in gold and real estate," Dick Conly advised. "Borrow up to the eyebrows and pay it back in thirty years with ten-cent dollars."

After Amos died, Dick Conly had remained as Cyrus's adviser, the guiding genius behind every profitable Chandler Industries enterprise. The Franchise was Dick Conly's idea. It wasn't easy. Trying to get the Franchise, Cyrus Chandler had threatened everything from lawsuits to underwriting another professional football league. Conly's suggestion to bribe Senator Thompson swung it. For twenty-five thousand dollars the senator's communications subcommittee came down on the football league and the FCC.

The senator was Spur and Spur was the wedge, but the twenty-five thousand dollars was the hammer. There was also the promise of five percent when pay-TV became feasible. The teams were already cutting up a hundred million yearly in network television money alone.

"Gambling thousands against millions," Dick Conly said to Cyrus about the bribe. "A measly twenty-five thousand."

The Franchise price was thirty-eight million dollars to buy into the cartel, while special tax legislation allowed straight-line depreciation of those millions over five years, a sizable write-off against Cyrus Chandler's other income.

Dick Conly's same thinking got Chandler Industries two hundred million dollars in government tax credits to build offshore oil-field equipment during the Crisis. As well as one-hundred-percent write-offs during the Glut.

It took four years to get the Franchise, and Dick Conly had finally had to bribe a United States senator. It had all cost large amounts of time and money.

OPM. Other people's money. The taxpayers' money.

Not other people's time, though. Dick Conly's time. The Franchise had cost Dick Conly too much time. It was all he had and all he valued; there was no way to write it down against someone else.

Everybody does his own time.

* * *

Taylor Rusk had done his own time since the day he left Two Oaks to make his first "advance" in the world.

"Can't stay here, boy," his father had said, and he was right. "A country boy can fall *way* behind, and most Texans are already a generation off the pace. Change is inevitable, but growth isn't. You need a place to grow."

Taylor grew, almost as fast as Chandler Enterprises. When television finally came to Two Oaks, Taylor Rusk was on it and Chandler Communications owned it.

Taylor Rusk's family had been in Texas since the war for independence, living on the small remains of a generous land grant for service to the Republic; the pitiful ridge-running remnants of a once hopeful family of yeoman farmers worn down by taxes and richer men.

Men like the Chandlers.

The Chandler family established itself in Texas from Virginia before the close of the Civil War. In fact, only moments before.

Racing the news of Appomattox west, their saddlebags bulging with Confederate money, five Chandler brothers started buying land the minute they crossed the Sabine River into Texas. Using the worthless scrip, they bought thousands of acres of prime East Texas timberland, which naturally led the family into the exploitation of natural resources. When gas and oil were found under the timberland in 1917 by a one-eyed driller from Pennsylvania, the Chandler Timber and Oil Company was founded. The combination of the basic criminal inception of the Chandler family enterprise, coupled with the fact that East Texas was probably populated by the meanest people in all of Texas (excepting several strips along the Rio Grande), led to a series of feuds between the Chandlers and the Others.

The Others were usually made up of the people or their kin, heirs and assigns who had been swindled with Confederate money, plus a continually changing cast of newcomers seeking profit in promoting turmoil.

It can be said that the Chandlers were victorious, since it was from Chandler Timber and Oil that the billion-dollar conglomerate Chandler Industries descended. But the mortality rate was high, and Chandlers were a limited resource. The Others drew on an endless supply of manpower, especially in the tumultuous years between the end of the Civil War and the First World War.

The day Amos Chandler Number Three blew in—at three thousand barrels a day—Amos Chandler's only child, Cyrus Houston Chandler, was born. The last male heir in the Chandler family. When Number Three blew in, it also killed the one-eyed driller. Amos thought it was a small price to pay.

The Chandler Field helped the Allies win the War to End All Wars. Amos got a medal for helping. He took the medal and the cash.

In 1939, Chandler Drilling brought in the Big Tex Field. Amos found that oil himself using a witching stick, soaked in crude oil, dangling from the dashboard of his Model-A Ford.

In 1941, Amos "detached" Dick Conly to Washington to help the Department of the Navy build an oil pipeline from Chandler's latest oil field to the East Coast. Amos sent twenty-five-year-old Cyrus to DC with Conly "to learn the ropes." Chandler Pipeline did the general contracting and all of the river crossings for the Navy on a cost-plus basis. When the war ended, the government sold Chandler Industries the pipeline for one-fifth of the cost of construction. Nice rope work.

While in Washington, Cyrus Chandler met and fell in love with the glamorous and infamous Gatlin twins, Wanda Jane and Wanda June, two stunning brunettes who had come from a vague Virginia background to wartime Washington to catch themselves rich husbands.

Cyrus Chandler spent most of the war in the Mayflower Hotel with one or both of the twins, plus assorted congressmen, admirals, generals and bureaucrats. The Gatlin twins waged an intense battle for Cyrus Chandler. Wanda June won her war on VJ Day.

Wanda June Gatlin, at two A.M. on the day the Japs surrendered, landed Cyrus Chandler, Texas oilman's son, in his Mayflower suite. Cyrus's last gasping lurch on the overstuffed couch was the final punctuation to a great war effort.

During the war Amos Chandler moved Chandler Industries from Tyler in East Texas to a small city in Central Texas, knowing this new city was destined to grow along with the rest of urban Texas. He quickly purchased large ranches and cotton farms on the edge of town directly in the path of the as-yet-to-be-announced interstate highway system that would connect the city to everywhere.

Gas was twenty-five cents a gallon, and the US Geological Survey swore to the Congress that US reserves of five hundred billion barrels would last forever, but Amos and other independents began drilling in the Middle East with great success. The big oil companies wanted Chandler's cheap independent $1.50-a-barrel Middle Eastern oil put on a quota "for reasons of national security" and the fact that big oil was selling domestic oil at $2.50 a barrel. The government responded with the Import Allocation Allowance. Imported oil was held at twenty percent of the total crude in the US market, even though it was one dollar a barrel cheaper than the big oil domestic. Amos called it the "Drain America First" law. The law stayed until the Crisis and oil-price explosion. The import allocation was rescinded. Quietly. The USGS revised its US reserve figures down tenfold. Oil was forty dollars a barrel. OPM.

Amos Chandler bought a bank and built a high-rise office building of black glass and steel right in the center of town. All on borrowed money. And then he died.

Dick Conly took over as CEO of Chandler Industries. Cyrus and Wanda June Chandler took a trip around the world, then returned a year later to Texas to hold court as social butterflies and second-generation money.

Wanda June gave birth to a girl they called Wendy Cy. As Wendy grew up and Junie old, Cyrus began to look for new interests. The Franchise was Dick Conly's idea, but Cyrus quickly claimed paternity to the tax advantages and shelters that the Franchise offered and waited for the phenomenal projected revenues.

The toughest part was getting the Franchise. Cyrus Chandler approached the League and was rebuffed, so he turned over the problem to Dick Conly. The League had a monopoly on professional football and wasn't anxious to cut the pie any thinner. Dick Conly baked a new pie.

Dick Conly was a problem-solver.

THE LEAD SINGER

"WHO the fuck cares what the New York Athletic Club thinks?" Taylor Rusk said to Vic Hersch, the University director of sports information.

"The New York *Downtown* Athletic Club," Vic corrected the quarterback. He had hailed Taylor in the hallway and asked for a moment of his time.

Taylor was on the dodge from T. J. "Armadillo" Talbott, the

University athletics director. If T.J. could corral Taylor in the athletic complex, he would drag Taylor back to his office, senile, shaking, sad, and repeatedly tell the stories behind his medals and trophies, team pictures and championship plaques. All the funny, angry and incomprehensible anecdotes led to the same conclusion: ten years earlier a conspiracy involving Regents Chairman Lem Carleton, Jr., had moved Red Kilroy into T. J. "Armadillo" Talbott's job as the University head football coach.

Armadillo was right about the conspiracy but wrong about the conspirators. The real leader was T. J. Talbott's chief assistant and best friend, who was angling to be head coach. The first thing Red Kilroy did was fire the whole staff, including the chief assistant.

"Lem Carleton got to feeling guilty," Armadillo said, "so they give me this job of motherfucking, cocksucking, ass-kissing, flatdick, ball-busting, shit-hole, scumbag athletics director."

T.J. put it eloquently; *athletics director* sounded dirtier than any of the adjectives.

The way Armadillo Talbott put it could last for hours. T.J.'s great football teams won national championships in the fifties and sixties; so, figuring an hour for each decade, plus open-ended raving on T.J.'s conspiracy theory, Taylor Rusk took momentary refuge in Vic Hersch's Office of Sports Information.

"It could mean the Heisman Trophy," Vic pleaded. "Just take a look."

"Fuck the Heisman Trophy." Taylor checked out the hallway, peering left and right. Armadillo Talbott had such a nasty habit of appearing out of thin air that Taylor suspected the building contained secret passages. Nothing about major college football would surprise him anymore. Not after those two guys from Houston got away with drowning the fag in the bathroom of the athletic dorm.

Taylor checked the hall again. "Is Armadillo in the building?"

"He ain't even on the planet, Taylor." The sports-information director sniggered at his own joke while digging behind the metal desk in his narrow, windowless office. "Just take a look at this thing, then write something nice and humble to go with it. I'm mailing it to sportswriters and broadcasters all over the country. We can't crank this campaign up too early."

"You should have started when I signed my letter of intent. The New York Athletic Club: a bunch of bald stockbrokers who think that racquetball and shuffleboard are sports."

"It's the goddam Heisman Trophy, Taylor!" Hersch continued

— 15 —

to dig through the pile behind his desk. "I suppose you don't want the Heisman."

"You can't spend the son of a bitch." Taylor leaned out the door, checking the hall for the ever-roaming athletic director. "So who needs that fucking millstone?"

"Here it is!" Vic yelled, and straightened up.

Taylor jumped backward at the sports-information director's cry and sudden move. The quarterback was edgy. He checked the empty hall again.

"Ain't this a beauty?" Vic Hersch held up a green-and-white-striped envelope, legal size and half an inch thick. "It's a die-cut mailer. We are going to put out about five thousand of these. You got to write a little note, something personal. Christ, you're in communications. Communicate."

Taylor took the heavy envelope and opened it. Inside was thick, one-hundred-pound, cast-coated white paper intricately printed in five colors, folded, blind-embossed and gold-stamped with the University seal.

"Just slide it out here on the desk. It's great, Taylor. Every sportswriter in the country and the membership of the New York Downtown Athletic Club will get one," Vic said. "I'll get you the Heisman."

Taylor Rusk dumped the contents of the envelope. The folded cast-coated paper lay flat, then slowly seemed to come alive; the edges peeled back, more edges and shapes appeared, unfolded, and then the whole thing bloomed into a scale model of University Stadium filled with printed people. The goalposts and team benches grew into place. The green midfield turf opened up and slowly telescoped like a time-lapse beanstalk growing into a three-dimensional, scale-model, lithograph die-cut, arm-cocked-to-pass Taylor Rusk.

It was a wonder of printing and design genius. It was very expensive.

"I'm not writing anything to go with that," Taylor said. "I'm not having *anything* to do with that."

"Taylor, you owe it to the University. If you get the Heisman, we get the press." Vic was disappointed; it didn't stop his pitch. "I can show you figures on alumni donations directly relating to schools producing Heisman Trophy winners. You *owe* us."

"I owe you shit, Vic. You get the season and probably a Bowl Game out of me. Your share from the television revenue of that Bowl Game alone is four hundred thousand dollars. Don't tell me

I owe the University. I'm not writing anything." Taylor turned to leave.

"You know," Vic said, "that means I'll have to write it."

"Vic, c'mon . . ." Taylor stopped with his hand on the door-knob. "I come off looking so dumb. . . ."

"Goddam, Taylor, these things cost five dollars apiece . . ."

"And you got five thousand?" Taylor turned loose of the knob and slapped his own forehead. "Give me the goddam twenty-five thousand dollars, I'll go to New York and jack off everybody in their goddam Downtown Athletic steamroom."

"Jesus, that's disgusting. . . ."

"And that's not?" Taylor pointed at the waving figure in the center of the pop-up stadium. He turned back to the door and jerked it open.

"Taylor! Where you been?" Athletic Director T. J. "Armadillo" Talbott was standing in the hallway. "I got some things I want to tell you. . . ." He grabbed the quarterback's arm and pulled him toward his office.

"But, T.J. . . . ah . . . I got to study." Taylor tried to resist; T.J. pulled harder, digging in, the reason for the nickname Armadillo. Taylor protested more. "No fooling, T.J., I got exams."

"Fuck exams." T.J. hauled him down the hallway. "I'm talking *football,* mister."

Taylor let the athletics director drag him off to spend hours spinning tales of manic success and paranoid woe.

Sports Information Director Vic Hersch looked into the hall and waved as the unhappy quarterback was dragged around the corner, out of sight.

"Goddam, Taylor, this is big-time football." Hersch walked back into his office and quickly composed a paean to sportsmanship by Taylor Rusk. They had his signature on file. The mailing would be finished before October first.

Hersch leaned back in his wooden chair and looked at the opened mailer.

The die-cut pop-up Taylor Rusk quivered like a brand-new pecker.

Hersch started a harsh, loud laugh. It echoed through the halls of the sports complex all the way to the Athletic Director's office, where it interrupted T.J.'s story of how sick the society had gotten now that beating up and drowning fags was against the rules.

Armadillo looked out his door. Hersch's laugh was getting louder and he was pounding his desk.

"What the fuck is that little asshole laughing about?" Armadillo Talbott asked.

Taylor shrugged but he knew. It was what he liked about Vic Hersch.

THE HEISMAN

TAYLOR Rusk was sensational his senior year, despite the five thousand pop-up peckers Vic Hersch sent out with a forged message. No one was a better quarterback than Taylor Rusk, either statistically or as a leader of his teammates.

And no one outcoached Red Kilroy that year.

Red had reached a stage where the opposing coaches were not challenging him mentally. His game plans and preparations, his practices and meetings, were all precise, exact, lean, with no extra mental fat to slow up a player.

Red no longer recruited players. "Why recruit?" he said. "I'm the kind of coach who can take mine and beat your'n and then take your'n and beat mine."

It was almost true. It was absolutely true that as a result of this policy the slush-fund money still poured in, but little of it went out anymore.

Red Kilroy reached his peak with Taylor Rusk and he knew it, and he knew Taylor knew it. Red Kilroy already had plans to move when Taylor Rusk won the Heisman Trophy.

Taylor's acceptance speech consisted of three words: "I deserve it."

THE CORN PICKER

THE New Orleans Bowl committee and the television network had promised six hundred thousand dollars to each school. The Bowl Game would feature Taylor Rusk. Red Kilroy and the university team ranked number one nationally against the team ranked number two.

"A true national championship game" was how the Bowl committee and the network promoted it. They paid Taylor ten thousand cash to make certain a nagging hamstring pull wouldn't keep him out of the game.

Taylor took the ten thousand dollars and kept quiet about the hamstring, which was never more than a rumor, let alone an actual pull. The rumor alone affected the spread by seven and a half points.

"Jerry Ball, *The Denver Post*," announced a balding reporter who approached Taylor in the French Quarter before the Bowl Game. He was covering the college scene, waiting on the guy who had the pro football beat to have a heart attack. "What about Red Kilroy?"

"Well, Jerry . . ." Taylor noticed how Jerry had carefully placed his remaining hair across the dead zones of his scalp. The New Orleans dampness had defeated his purpose, sticking his few remaining strands together, plastered flat. "Red Kilroy always felt players should want to play for him. He has a good pro system and is a good judge of talent. He can run them around his desk in their street clothes and know everything he has to know." This was the same story Taylor told anyone who asked about his coach.

"How would you describe"—balding Jerry seemed to be dissolving in the humidity—"winning the Heisman Trophy?"

Taylor thought for a moment, furrowed lines dug between his eyes across his thick brow ridge.

"Well," Taylor said, walking off, "it's a lot like getting caught in a corn picker."

It was a rare cool, sunny, dry day. After an easy stroll up Toulouse he turned down along Royal Street, heading for Rampart Street past Bienville. Ahead near Rampart a big white Victorian house with three stories of bay windows, verandas and porches was set back off the street behind a wrought-iron fence. The windows were all draped in bright red velvet.

As Taylor passed, the front door opened and Dick Conly stepped out; he didn't notice Taylor until he reached the gate. They passed within six feet of each other. Taylor said hello and stopped; Conly just nodded and moved rapidly down the street. Looking at the house, Taylor saw a swarthy face in a second-story window. Then the red velvet closed.

In the Bowl Game, Taylor Rusk threw twenty-nine for thirty-four and five touchdowns. Simon D'Hanis and the rest of the line protected him like a pack of Dobermans. A. D. Koster intercepted two passes, running one back thirty-six-yards for a touchdown.

They won forty-five to seven.

Later, walking from the locker room with Simon and A.D., heading for the bus back to the hotel, Taylor Rusk was hit in the face. Launched out of the darkness of the Bowl, a Grapette bottle smashed into Taylor's nose, tearing and dislocating the septum. He needed ten stitches to close the gash between his eyes.

Taylor healed fast with little discomfort or scar. He wondered where the Grapette bottle had come from. *And why*.

Taylor Rusk figured he had a loose sleeve flapping near the corn picker.

THE RENT

THE phone rang.

"If it's Cobianco about the rent," Abraham Dwight Koster said from the back bedroom, "tell him I'll bring it down in the morning."

"Dammit, A.D.," Simon D'Hanis said, "we gave you the money two weeks ago!" D'Hanis was hunched down in front of the old console television, trying to tune in the afternoon movie. He twisted and turned the rabbit ears covered with aluminum foil. A face appeared on the screen amid the static snowstorm. The face spoke with a thick accent.

"Akim Tamiroff." Simon pointed at the television and settled back on the worn green couch. Simon watched a lot of movies, proud of his vast store of old movie trivia; he always named the actors as they appeared on the screen.

The phone continued to ring.

Taylor Rusk entered from the outside. He was returning from his journalism class and heard the ringing from the stairway up to the second-story apartment. Knowing his roommates would never answer it, the quarterback took the last steps two at a time and caught the phone on the sixth ring.

"If that's Cobianco, tell him I'll be down with the rent in the morning," A. D. Koster repeated.

Taylor frowned and looked at D'Hanis, who shrugged, then pointed at the screen with a thick finger. "Akim Tamiroff."

Simon stretched his six-foot-four-inch, two-hundred-fifty-pound frame out on the green couch. The springs and wooden frame groaned, the plastic squeaked.

"Hello?" Taylor Rusk held the phone and began to shuck his tan jacket with his free hand. There was silence on the line. "Hello?... Hello?" Taylor was aware of his own heavy breathing. He dropped his jacket across the back of the white wing chair, waiting for sound on the line.

"Is this Taylor Rusk?" The voice was deep and mysterious.

"Yeah."

"Listen very carefully. Follow the instructions I give you and do not reveal the contents of this phone conversation to anyone."

"What?" Taylor looked over at Simon to exchange a quizzical glance, but a new actor had appeared on the TV screen, and the big man was trying to identify him in the blizzard of static. "What is this?" Taylor spoke into the phone with irritation.

"Just be quiet. Listen and learn. The Brotherhood has been watching you."

"The Brotherhood?" Taylor said sharply. "What Brotherhood?" *Another goddam crank call*, he thought, frowning, and the pull of the skin made his recently broken nose hurt. He continued to frown despite the ache.

"I told you to be quiet and just listen." The voice tried to take command. It was a strained sternness.

Taylor Rusk rolled his eyes, let out a long slow sigh, hooked the phone with his shoulder and began to look through the mail left on the phone table. There was a letter from his mother. Mail from Two Oaks, Texas. A long way away.

"Tomorrow night at midnight, come to the Tower dressed in old clothes..."

"All I got is old clothes, buddy."

"Remain silent," the voice snapped.

Taylor detected the East Coast accent. A rich kid sent to learn Texas, help keep it colonized, and look after Daddy's investments.

"Now, wear old clothes to the Tower. Bring one large onion, a bra, panties and a length of twine at least two feet long..."

A. D. Koster stepped out of the back bedroom and looked at Taylor, his eyes expectant. Freshly showered, shaven and lotioned, A.D. was slipping into a brown sport coat that set off nicely against his white shirt and brown tie, gray slacks and new brown alligator shoes. A.D. liked to dress. He did a pirouette for

— 21 —

Taylor to get the full effect of A. D. Koster on the make. It was pretty impressive.

Taylor pointed at the phone and shrugged his shoulders. He made a twirling motion at the side of his head with his left index finger.

"... and two Marks-A-Lot felt pens in green and white." The mysterious voice continued, droning out of the receiver. "Be sure to be at the Tower at exactly—"

"Look, buddy," Taylor interrupted. "I'm busy, I don't have the time."

"I told you not to interrupt—"

"I'm not interrupting. You go right on talking through your nose." Taylor grinned at A.D. "But I am hanging up."

"No, wait, you don't understand!"

"Sorry, but a very beautiful boy has just walked in, demanding my attention."

"No, wait!"

Taylor hung up.

"Who was that?" Simon asked from the couch. The movie was off and a commercial was on the TV screen.

"Some guy wanted me to bring an onion and women's underwear down to the Tower at midnight tomorrow." Taylor picked up the letter from his mother.

"Send him instead." Simon looked at A.D. straightening his tie and shirt cuffs. "He looks dressed for it."

A.D. smoothed his hair down, using the window as a mirror. It was getting dark outside.

"No." Taylor pursed his lips, trying to organize his thoughts. "The guy said to wear old clothes. A.D. doesn't have any, do you, A.D.?"

"Not if I got anything to say about it." A. D. Koster watched himself in the darkening window. He turned and looked back over his shoulder at his rear view.

Taylor watched A. D. Koster admire his own reflection. "What's this about owing Cobianco the rent money? I thought we paid two weeks ago." Taylor turned to Simon, who pointed at A.D.'s reflection and went back to watching television. The commercial was over.

"I just haven't taken it down there yet," Koster said. "I been busy as hell. I'll get it in the morning. Don't worry."

"I'm not worried," Taylor said. "It's your name on the lease if you lost our money gambling. I figure those brown alligators are my size, and for his satisfaction Simon will jam your bare feet up your ass."

D'Hanis nodded, his eyes on the screen.

"God knows *what* the Cobiancos will do, though," Taylor added.

"You guys, knock it off." A.D. spoke a little too hard. "I just forgot, that's all."

"As long as you didn't forget at one of those poker games over at the Deke house," Taylor said. "Scared money never wins, A.D."

A.D. laughed too hard and hit Taylor on the shoulder. "Put your coat back on and come with me. I wanna show you my new girl."

Taylor picked up the letter from his mother. "I'll read this instead."

"C'mon, you can read it later." A.D. grabbed Taylor with one hand and his coat with the other. "Besides, there isn't anything interesting in there."

"How do you know?" Taylor moved along toward the door.

"No checks or anything; I already looked," A.D. said. "You coming, Simon?"

"Buffy's on her way over from the Pi Phi house," Simon grunted, staring at the TV.

"Just you and Buffy and Akim Tamiroff," A.D. said. "How cozy. Come on, Taylor, wait till you see this one. Besides, I got a favor to ask."

The alarm went off in the back of his brain, but Taylor allowed himself to be pushed along. The quarterback shrugged back into the tan jacket.

Simon heard them go down the stairs, followed shortly by the sound of Koster's blue Chevrolet convertible starting, rattling and squeaking out of the parking lot.

The phone began to ring again. Simon never moved.

The familiar square face appeared on the screen.

"Akim Tamiroff," Simon said.

The phone rang fifteen times and stopped. Simon never took his eyes from the snowy screen.

THE CARHOP

"D'HANIS and his goddam television."

A.D. was shivering like a wet dog, talking fast and bouncing on the car seat. Taylor figured he was speeding.

"I talked to Red today about going with the Franchise. I already know his system. I could help the team a lot. Maybe player-coach. Pro management as my life plan could be a big break."

"Save it for Red, A.D." Taylor leaned back and stretched, relaxing for the first time since he had hit the floor running at six that morning. Taylor Rusk always took a double load of classes in the spring to make up for the light loads he carried in the fall, when he was playing ball, and in the winter, when he was coming down and healing up. That spring he carried a triple load in order to graduate on time.

"Jesus, Taylor, this could be a big break for me. Couldn't you talk to . . . ?"

"I'm not going to Red. Now forget it." Taylor wanted to relax and tried not to think about the rent money he was certain A.D. had again lost gambling. A.D. always lost at cards. Driven by the dangerous combination of greedy ambition and fearful machismo, he was a lousy gambler.

Simon D'Hanis and Taylor Rusk sublet from A.D., who leased from the Cobianco brothers. Housing close to the campus was difficult to find, and A.D. charged Simon and Taylor three-quarters of the rent. A.D. paid only one-quarter, although they were high school friends and college roommates.

"Doing business," A.D. called it. "I'm going to be a businessman with an office, a big desk, a huge salary and a secretary with giant *chalugas.*"

A.D. overestimated executive joy and underestimated the Cobianco brothers. All financial transactions went through A.D. The good news was that neither Simon nor Taylor were listed or liable on the lease. The bad news was that A.D. was handling other people's money.

"Football and doing business is all I know, Taylor. You see the guys they got running Houston? Idiots." A.D. was outraged. "I'd be a hell of a general manager."

"What worries me, A.D., is the possibility that you believe what you're saying."

Taylor watched the campus roll by, the treeline snaking behind the stadium and field house, marking the river that wound through the school. Orange bulldozers and earth movers were scattered across a giant slash covering Regents Hill, where another twenty-story dormitory was going up: Amos Chandler Hall.

"The campus has really grown since we came here." Taylor frowned. "Dormitories. . . . Goddam, do I hate dormitories. They are full of people."

A.D. was still bouncing on the seat and tapping a rhythm on the steering wheel with his fingers. He leaned over and turned on the radio. The Rolling Stones whined and moaned from the speakers.

> I'll be in my basement room
> with a needle and a spoon
> and another girl to take
> my pain away.

Taylor peered out the window at another generation of students, heads down, trudging to some building to learn something.

"You know"—A.D. jumped in the seat—"when you talk to Red . . ."

"I'm not talking to Red, A.D."

"Thanks a lot, buddy."

A.D. headed his convertible toward the city.

Red Kilroy had been at the University for ten years. To be head coach of a winning program at a major university, *the University*, took more than the sense to draw the X's and O's. Red Kilroy controlled a multimillion-dollar enterprise with hundreds of employees producing some of the best football in the country. He was cunning, with incredible endurance and the amazing ability to size up players physically and psychologically, predict what they would be in four years, then demand the player make Red's predictions come true.

"You won't make a liar out of me!!" he would scream, cuffing the player alongside the head. "I said you were gonna be goddam good this year, you bastard. If Red Kilroy says a piss-ant can pull a plow, you hitch him up." Then he'd kick the player in the ass. The player got better or quit.

"If Red Kilroy says it's gonna flood champagne, you load the boat. If Red Kilroy says . . ."

Red was a mean son of a bitch. Of course he lied all the time. It came with the job. But who was going to call Red Kilroy a liar? Nobody, Taylor Rusk knew.

Taylor liked the old bastard. He was a genius. Not just a football genius but a genius genius. Taylor figured that was what made him so crazy. It was his junior year before Taylor noticed that Red was drunk most of the time.

A.D. was still tapping his fingers on the steering wheel but had quit bouncing in the seat. "Wait'll you see this little split tail." A.D. was talking about the latest in a long series of girl friends, all attractive. A.D. was always in pursuit of women and style, action, money, class, winning.

"How old is she?"

"Old enough to know better, too young to resist." A.D. laughed, an uncontrolled spasm. "How the hell should I know? Who cares? Old enough to bleed, old enough to butcher; you taking the census or something? Wait till you see her."

The convertible sped past the last campus building and down Central Avenue to the city. A.D. only dated girls from the city.

"I got nothing in common with these college girls. They either believe that all this college horseshit is real or they got senior clutch and wanna get married. I don't want a wife. My old man told me, 'He travels swiftest who travels alone.'"

A.D. squealed the convertible into the Central Avenue Sonic Drive-In. Taylor turned and sat up. His nose ached, his jaw was sore and his shoulder muscles hurt. He had worked out hard that day, but it hadn't made him feel better. He threw too much and ran too little.

A.D. pulled into a stall. The menu hung on the metal rack below the intercom.

"Can I take your order, please?"

"Yeah." A.D. finished cranking down his window. "Have Suzy skate us a couple of giant Cokes."

"I don't want a Coke."

A.D. held up his hand for silence.

"I don't want a Coke," Taylor repeated.

"Who cares, man? We're here to watch Suzy skate the Cokes, not drink the fuckers."

"Awww, shit, another waitress?" Taylor ran his hands through his long black hair and felt oil on his fingers. He had showered only two hours earlier.

"You have bad luck with waitresses, A.D."

Leaning back in the seat with his greasy fingers clasped behind his neck, Taylor closed his eyes, wondering if he had the energy to study that night and still be up at seven to make Doc Webster's eight A.M. test on the Civil War. He took every course he could from Doc Webster. Taylor enjoyed and liked him; he often went to him for advice. Doc had a law degree but hated lawyers—perfect credentials for Taylor's adviser.

"You can't figure where you're heading if you don't know where you've been," Doc said. "So study history or repeat it."

A.D. was tapping on the steering wheel, watching the skating waitresses in tight tank tops and shorts.

"I'll admit Doris was unfortunate," A.D. said grudgingly.

"Unfortunate is an understatement." Taylor didn't move or open his eyes.

Doris, a waitress at the Clover Drive-In, told A.D. she was pregnant and needed five hundred dollars for an abortion. A.D. stole six televisions from the athletic dorm to get the money, only to discover later Doris wasn't pregnant, *was* a hooker, and had a pimp in the Charros, a Mexican motorcycle gang from the East Side. When A.D. went over to her house to get his five hundred back, the pimp and three others hammered the dogshit out of him with pick handles. A.D. missed three weeks of classes before his face and ribs healed enough to act like nothing happened. People assumed he had lost the teeth in football.

"Here she comes." A.D. leaned forward.

Taylor peered over the leather dashboard at the flowing blond hair, beautiful little-girl face, succulent woman's body, long legs, tight white shorts and red satin jacket open over a blue tank top. Tray over her shoulder, breasts out like a '60 Cadillac, taking long strokes with her lean, tan legs, Suzy Ballard skated the Cokes like the queen of the Roller Derby.

"Can you believe it?" A.D. whispered. "She's only sixteen."

Taylor was silent; he had stopped breathing.

"Two Cokes." Suzy Ballard skidded alongside, hooking the tray on the window. She wasn't wearing a bra, and thimble-size nipples strained against the blue tank top.

Taylor hadn't taken a breath since Suzy wheeled out the door. He finally reacted to the carbon dioxide overload, exhaling long and loud, lying back in the seat, aroused and perplexed.

"Why, A. D. Koster, I didn't see that was you." Suzy smiled, her teeth white and straight. She bent into the window, kissed A.D. on the cheek. Her satin jacket hung open, and Taylor glimpsed an exposed nipple of one startling breast. She astonished and beguiled him. From outside the car, or half outside, she was enticing him, draining him physically and emotionally.

"You may be overmatched here, A.D.," Taylor said quietly.

"And who are you?" Suzy's blue-green eyes glittered, her teeth sparkled. Wrigley's spearmint crackled wetly in her red mouth.

"I'm Taylor." He smiled carefully, working his eyes gently over her full lips, flawless teeth and high cheekbones—a stunning, angelic, perfect face. "The local voluptuary." He held out his hand.

"I'm Suzy." Her eyes bore into him. The blue had faded, the green turned dark. Menacing.

Taylor found himself frightened of a sixteen-year-old girl.

Her eyes seared into him without a hint of friendship. They shook hands. Her vernal flesh was soft, yet Taylor was surprised at the firmness of her grip. It was the kind of handshake he got before a coin toss.

"Hand me my Coke, will you? I'm gonna need the caffeine."

"That's seventy-five cents," Suzy said, her voice hard, dark-green eyes still on Taylor, driving him into the seat. "Everybody knows you get the money first, sonny."

"Taylor, get it, will you? I haven't got anything smaller than a twenty." A.D. had moved up in the seat and his face was against Suzy's cheek. He was whispering to her. She traced A.D.'s hard jawline with a long fingernail while Taylor dug out a dollar and handed it to her.

"A.D. says you're gonna get him on with the new pro football team." She slid the dollar into her apron.

"He did?"

"Yeah. Sounds great. A.D.'s real smart." Pressing the Coke into Taylor's hand, scraping the palm with her nails, she kept her eyes on him and her free hand on A.D.'s face. "They need any young blondes with good bodies?"

"They'd have more use for you than A.D. Keep the change." Taylor dropped his hand to the seat.

"Thanks, sonny," She released him from the cold, hard stare. "But I go with A.D. We are a team. He's got the brains, I got the body." She looked at A.D. for the first time. "We got what he needs, don't we, A.D.?"

"I been telling him."

Taylor tried to analyze what took place there at Stall Nine of the Central Avenue Sonic. The contradictory beauty of Suzy, angelic and tough. The sight of the carelessly exposed nipple, the heavy smell of Jungle Gardenia. The malodorous mix of French fries and gasoline, ketchup and exhaust. Food and petroleum. He tasted it in his Coke. The sound of a loud roaring, like the ocean, the traffic on Central Avenue or blood pounding through his ears.

She was sixteen and she called him sonny. A senior in college, Taylor Rusk was six foot five and weighed 225 and she called him sonny. The memory always looked, smelled and tasted good. The roaring sound bothered Taylor. It was the sound of fear.

"Didn't I tell you she was something?" A.D. was bouncing in the seat again, tapping the steering wheel. They were headed back up Central Avenue to the University.

"She's something, all right," Taylor said. He was slumped down in the seat. "I'm just not sure what. Why did you tell her I was getting you a job with the Franchise?"

"You're just jealous, man, admit it. Come on, admit it. You're jealous." A.D. took both hands off the wheel and turned to look at Taylor. "Is she a knockout or what? You should feel those *chalugas*." A.D. made squeezing motions. Doing fifty-five miles per hour in three lanes of heavy traffic back out Central toward the University, A.D. had neither hands on the wheel nor eyes on the road.

"Yeah, I'm jealous. Now, why did you lie about the job? You owe her money too?"

"Listen, Taylor, I'll fix you up with her—talk about sport fucking. Just help me out with Red—"

"Goddam, A.D.," Taylor cut him off. "Just shut up and watch the road." A. D. Koster never did watch. He was running too fast to see where he was going or notice where he'd been.

Suzy Ballard didn't care. She had plans.

"You ever had a horse eat oats out of your hand?" A.D. pressed his case. "I mean, this gal can suck a dick. Now, if you and Red could get me . . ."

"Knock it off, A.D." Taylor closed his eyes and, looking back into tomorrow, heard the clackety-clack of roller skates on concrete.

BUFFY

LOUISE Buffy Martin sat on the floor next to the green plastic couch. Simon was still stretched out and was watching another movie on a different channel. Buffy clutched Simon's big-knuckled right hand with her small fingers. The foiled rabbit ears had been recontorted and the picture was much clearer.

When A.D. and Taylor returned to the apartment, Simon pulled his hand free and pointed at the screen. "Harry Carey," Simon said, "*junior*."

Buffy quickly clutched Simon's hand back. Her red face twisted into a tormented smile; she said hello to Taylor and A.D., keeping her wet eyes on Harry Carey, Jr., and her hands on Simon.

A.D. went to his room to change again. Taylor stretched out on his bed and read the letter from his mother. A.D. was right; there was no mention of money or anything interesting, other than the fact people were dying like flies in Two Oaks. Taylor's mother's letters were more like casualty lists. She certainly hoped "your poppa and I will see you again. We always wondered whether sending you off to the city in the ninth grade was the thing to do."

Taylor Rusk knew moving was change. He just didn't know what change meant. That was why he stayed with A.D. and Simon. He watched them change, then figured from there.

"I don't think life gets any *better* than this," Simon said when they won the first high school state championship. He had been right. It all changed, but it didn't seem to get better, just faster and different.

Taylor put down the letter and curled fetuslike around his pillow and wadded quilt. He pictured Suzy Ballard on roller skates, then Buffy Martin clutching Simon D'Hanis's big scarred hand. He wondered why she was crying.

"Do you want to have the baby?" Simon asked, his eyes on Harry Carey.

"I don't know," Buffy said. "What do you want?"

"I asked first." He felt the pulsing of her heart in her desperate grip.

Louise Buffy Martin was the eldest daughter of a South Texas rancher who owned sections of Bee County in the high double figures. He also had a seventeen-room house in Kingsville and was married to the daughter of the bank president. Louise Buffy Martin was the first issue of that dandy union of land and liquid capital.

Buffy met Simon when they were freshmen; they had dated ever since.

"I want it if you want it." Buffy's voice was weak and cracked. She dabbed at her eyes with a handkerchief. She had red hair and pale skin with freckles and was a stocky five foot five. Her face was pretty but too full. When she cried, it bunched up rather than breaking into wrinkly patterns of pain.

"I want it." Simon slowly broke into a grin: he laughed, suddenly excited. "Goddam!" Simon had wonder in his voice. "I never had a kid." He no longer saw Harry Carey or cared about him. "Goddam, *my kid.*" His eyes unfocused a moment and then snapped back clearly. He sat up and looked at the sad South Texas rancher's redheaded daughter.

"Let's go to Oklahoma and get married."

"Tonight?" Buffy's question was a yelp of joy.

Simon nodded. "That's why God made Oklahoma."

"C'mon . . . wake up." Simon D'Hanis shook Taylor Rusk roughly out of his dream. "I'm getting married and I need a best man."

Taylor pulled away and rolled over sleepily. "Get A.D. He's got the wardrobe."

"I want you. Now come on." Simon grabbed the mattress and flipped Taylor out onto the floor. "Buffy has gone to get Wendy Cy Chandler to be her best lady."

Taylor curled up on the floor. His eyes still closed. "It's called maid of honor, not best lady."

"I don't give a shit." Simon came around the bed and started pulling Taylor to his feet. "Come on, we got a long drive to Oklahoma."

"Jesus! Oklahoma?" Taylor Rusk realized he was going. "Isn't there some place a little closer than goddam Oklahoma?"

"They're expecting us to pick them up in an hour," Simon urged Taylor as he dressed. "Hurry up."

Taylor stopped at the telephone and dialed history professor Bertrand Webster. Into his fifth martini, Doc Webster slurred his hello.

"Doc? This is Taylor Rusk." He spoke loudly and slowly,

knowing that at this time of night the professor was half, maybe totally, in the bag. "I can't make class tomorrow."

"Well, Taylor"—the professor spoke like he was trying to walk the line for a traffic cop—"I have a test scheduled for tomorrow." He made *scheduled* sound like it had ten syllables. "Is it important, Taylor? Not some goddam football thing?"

"No, Doc, this has to do with women and sex and probably getting falling-down drunk and crossing a few state lines or international borders, where adventures follow one another like little duckies about to perform immoral acts on sorority girls."

"Well, then," Doc said thickly, "you may go, but take notes."

"Good night, Doc." Taylor looked at the phone. Simon was hovering next to him. "Doc's about the only professor I ever had who was worth a shit. Him and that economics professor that Lem junior and the regents tossed out for smoking dope and screwing coeds in his office."

"Let's go." Simon took Taylor's arm and pulled him out the door, down the stairs and into Simon's purple and white four-door 1957 Pontiac hardtop.

"It was boys." Simon started the car.

"What?"

"The economics professor was screwing boy students." Simon put the car in gear.

"Boys?" Taylor slouched in the seat. Simon nodded. "Well, I told you he was likeable."

In the apartment the phone began to ring. It rang twenty times, then was silent for ten minutes, then rang twenty times more. A. D. Koster sat in the back bedroom, smoked cigarettes and pretended not to hear. He assumed it was the Cobianco brothers about the rent money he had lost to them betting on baseball games. A.D. was wrong.

The calls were for Taylor Rusk about the onion.

THE WEDDING PARTY

"You sure this is what you want to do?" Taylor Rusk asked.

"Yeah, I'm sure. Look for the turnoff and shut up." Simon D'Hanis was hunched over the steering wheel, squinting into the oncoming headlights. He was hunting for the back alley to the Pi Phi House. The girls would be waiting outside by the dumpster. "I've been on my own since ninth grade, living in the Park City coach's basement or with you and A.D., two weirdo tramp athletes, high school transfers." Simon spit *transfers* out like a dirty word. "I want more. I'm making my stand. I'm gonna have my *own* family." Simon looked at Taylor Rusk. "Could you throw out the woman that was carrying your kid? You couldn't do it."

"Well, fortunately for me, which does not necessarily mean unfortunately for you, I don't have to make that decision." Taylor looked for the alley. "I am just along to add my moral weight to this great event. I'll live and die a tramp athlete. I like it. It's how I relate to the world." Taylor caught sight of the break in the curb line. "Okay, fatso, there's the alley."

Simon turned and cut off the lights. His heart hammered and his mouth was dry as he drove in the shadows behind the Pi Phi house.

Taylor saw two figures pick their way toward Simon's car through the parking lot filled with Cadillac convertibles, Porsches, Jags, the less exotic Triumphs and MGs. A couple of Fords and Chevys. All the Pi Phis had money or at least acted like they did. Buffy was the only Pi Phi Taylor knew.

Just keeping up with Red Kilroy and chasing paper before his NCAA eligibility and the money ran out was all Taylor Rusk was able to maintain. He *needed* that degree. Someday he would *have* to get a *job*. Fit in. Get along. Go along. He wasn't sure he could do it. He was an athlete. Always. It was going to be difficult, and adding anyone to his life greatly increased the chances of the catastrophic. Especially adding a Pi Phi, they believed absolutely in divine wealth. They deserved it all, expected it to be provided. He never could figure out how Simon did it and still watched all those movies on TV. But then, Simon never did worry much about the catastrophic.

At the Pi Phi house Louise Francine Buffy Martin was crying again. She and Wendy Cy Chandler got in the rear door on the driver's side. Taylor had gotten out on the passenger side, thinking Buffy would want to sit with Simon. She didn't. She wanted to sit in back and cry. Wendy tried to comfort her. Simon headed the Pontiac north into the night.

The interstate was almost finished, but suburbs didn't yet sprawl all the way from the Rio Grande to the Red River, and they got out in the country pretty quickly. After about an hour Taylor looked into the backseat and thought Wendy Chandler glared at him, although he couldn't be sure in the bewitching light. He stole more glances with only moonlight to help him. All he saw were two shadow shapes.

Buffy sobbed all the way to the Red River.

Taylor slouched in the seat and tried to sleep. It gave him a stiff neck that nagged him for the next forty-eight hours. His nose still hurt when he frowned, and he was frowning plenty.

Wendy Cy Chandler calmed Buffy and talked up the positive side of elopement: "It cuts through all the bullshit." Taylor wondered what bullshit and how Wendy knew.

At daybreak in Hugo, Oklahoma, they found a justice of the peace at a cafe. He waived the blood test and married them right there at the table. He also served them breakfast. All for fifteen dollars.

Buffy stopped sobbing when the food arrived.

The honeymoon seemed to start when Simon and Buffy began making out in the cafe over coffee. Wendy Chandler relaxed and Taylor saw her for the first time.

It was as if she had been able to keep him from *really* seeing her until she was ready. That was what he had seen inside the moonlit car—the warning not to see.

The justice of the peace went to get more biscuits; the friendly middle-aged man with six kids also ran the self-serve gas station next door. The door to the kitchen banged shut. Wendy Cy Chandler took one long last look at Buffy and Simon, then turned to Taylor.

"They are each other's problem now." She managed a weak smile.

"I guess that's what it's all about." Taylor slouched as he always did and kept his head low. Furniture was not designed for people six feet five inches tall. He leaned with his elbows on the table and peered over the lip of his coffee cup at Wendy. She was smaller than he had thought. Her presence had seemed much larger in that dark car under that huge moon and sky. In a lighted empty cafe, sharply defined against the blue-and-white-checked wallpaper and tablecloths, chairs and tables, salt and pepper shakers and of course Buffy and Simon, Wendy seemed small and pale. Her dishwater hair was pinned up in a hurried twist, wisps floated weightlessly out from her face. Her skin was transparent. She almost wasn't there. At five-foot-three and one hundred pounds there was a certain amount of will involved in being seen. Wendy Chandler was of strong will, like her grandfather, Amos, and she had willed herself to be delicate and beautiful.

She was.

Her eyes were the palest blue as she fixed them on Taylor. She looked like a porcelain figure in faded jeans, a red and yellow plaid flannel shirt and squaw boots. She sat cross-legged in the chair; her spidery fingers rested on her knees—a finespun, perfect miniature.

Taylor kept his head below her eyeline and smiled at her.

"Look what I found." The JP came out of the kitchen, clutching a large industrial mayonnaise jar full of a light-purple fluid. "Mustang grape wine—made it myself. We'll toast the bride and groom. Ought to be plenty good." He had a fistful of water glasses. One for everyone but himself. "I just make it for the hell of it. I haven't had a drink since the big war," he explained. "I almost killed an MP in Oakland." He placed the glasses and poured. "I was a twenty-one-year-old Marine back from eighteen months in the South Pacific. I promised the good Lord if he'd let the MP live I'd never touch another drop. Now I don't drink and I drive a Jap car. Kinda makes you wonder. . . . Maybe I should have kept drinking and let the MP die. What do you think?"

"I don't think," Taylor said. "I react."

"Me too," the justice of the peace said. "It's how I damn near killed the MP."

"Well," Wendy announced, "if I'm having a drink before eight in the morning, I'm sure as hell going to take out my contacts first. Last time I passed out and welded them right to my eyes."

She leaned forward, her slender fingers working quickly, deftly. She popped out the contacts and tossed them onto her tongue, kept them in her mouth while searching her purse for her lens case and glasses. She found her gold-rimmed glasses, put them on and looked at Taylor again. Her eyes were an even paler blue. It took Taylor a long time to realize the contacts were tinted.

They all had two big glassfuls of mustang grape wine, toasting the bride and groom. The JP made them eat more biscuits and drink coffee before he would let them leave.

They all felt great. It was spring and they were young. Taylor paid the bill as the others walked out into the day.

"Have a nice day." The JP's shirt hiked up, exposing a pistol butt.

Taylor nodded, pushed the screen door open and stepped outside.

Just across the Texas line they stopped at the Armadillo Ranch and Gift Shop. Simon and Buffy walked in back by a scroungy lonely buffalo in a wire pen. Taylor went into the gift shop and bought Wendy a Picasso print silk scarf. "A gift for the maid of honor," he said.

They walked out to the caliche parking lot. Wendy leaned against the post supporting the red and white sign offering free looks at the forlorn buffalo. She held the scarf up and the North Texas warm spring wind rippled bright Picasso colors. It reminded Taylor of watching the heat rise at a morning workout.

Taylor struggled to think of things to say, but Wendy, her face turned to the late morning sun, beat him to it. "My father intends to buy you. Did you know that?"

"Who's your father?" Taylor feigned ignorance. He didn't know why.

"Cyrus Chandler. He's going to get the new football franchise and he intends to buy you first. He says you won the Heisman Trophy, whatever that is, and you are good local box office." She looked flatly at Taylor, watching him intently through the round gold-rimmed glasses. The print scarf flapped in the wind.

"And?" Taylor turned into the sun and closed his eyes. He let the sun soak his face.

"And," Wendy said, "how do you feel about it?"

"Don't know yet. I haven't heard his price. Besides, he doesn't have that franchise yet. The League isn't anxious to share."

"They will be after Dick Conly finishes with them." Wendy smiled. "Well, how do you feel about being owned?"

"Just like any old dog, I guess. It ain't the being owned; it's the owner that matters."

"Does Daddy pay well?"

"For me he should," Taylor said, "if the Franchise takes me in the first round. They all want to sign their number-one pick or they look stupid. After the third round it's like being taken prisoner. I've got a guy negotiating for me. I've never been injured. I'll do all right and your daddy'll do terrific. Quarterbacks have been known to play ten or fifteen years, depending on the line and the system. Owners can play forever; it's their ball. Which I guess means it will eventually be yours. Do you want it?"

Wendy smiled. "Do you stay in the bargain?"

"Only if we use my balls," Taylor replied, "and I get to keep them both."

"What if Daddy and Dick Conly get them first?"

"Lots of folks have tried." Taylor tried to look back into Wendy's pale blue eyes, but the sun's afterimage blurred the vision. "They may well have succeeded. It gets to where you can't keep track of the rules. Fortunately for me, the University doesn't follow the rules, and six hundred dollars shows up in my mailbox on the first of each month with no return address. Does that mean they've got me?"

"They *pay you* to play for the University?" Wendy was surprised. "You don't think that's immoral, an insult to your integrity?"

"Immoral? No. I have discovered that what most people consider to be their moral code turns out to merely be their budget. I'd be insulted only if the cash fails to arrive: Only a fool would put up with all the shit for nothing. Amateur sports ends as soon as you pay the coach, and his morals are limited strictly by *his budget*. I know a basketball player who finds money in his street shoes after every game."

"But..."

"Look, for four years the University used me like a rent-a-car. Criminal Conspiracy 101 should be a phys-ed class. I've been a professional since high school, and I want to end up with more than mythical titles and a few thousand from the University slush fund. If you want to protect your daddy's investment, I guess you better go ahead and search me." Taylor held his arms out. "Make sure Red Kilroy or the Park City coach didn't get something you want."

"No, thanks." Wendy's expression changed to disapproval.

"No, really, frisk me for scars, soft spots, unexplained lumps, sores, swelling, missing parts. Stigmata. Report to Cyrus that I am a fine specimen who demands only a continuing illusion that sports is a rite of passage and big bucks to convince me I'm getting close to the top." Taylor looked over at Wendy and enjoyed her puzzlement. "I want to be an athlete, which is not always compatible with being a football player."

"What is that supposed to mean?"

"It means your daddy can learn to like me as a tax exemption."

"*My* daddy's favorite exemption happens to be me."

Taylor still faced the sun.

"You have a boyfriend?"

"I'm engaged."

"In what? I didn't see any ring."

"We're going to Neiman's to get it next week." Wendy's tone changed. She was irritated. "We were going to get the ring to-morrow, but Lem is going to be at the Tower tonight. He's been tapped by Spur."

"Spur?" Taylor picked up a limestone pebble and bounced it off the billboard.

"You don't know Spur?" Wendy couldn't believe Taylor Rusk was that simple. "You've never heard of it?"

"Vaguely," Taylor said. "I heard of it somewhere. . . ."

"Well, it's *the* club to belong to. Every spring they pick only the top ten senior men." Wendy looked closely at Taylor. "Once in Spur, lots of doors open—not just at the University, but down-town too. All over the world. My father was president of Spur back in 1939. The governor was a member then. Senator Thomp-son and Harrison H. Harrison." She looked at Taylor's blank face. He smiled. She did not and he detected pity in the look and in her voice. "Well, they're being tapped tonight at the Tower at midnight." Wendy smiled. "I'm not supposed to know, but Lem can't keep anything from me."

"Tonight, huh?" Taylor said.

"Tonight."

"And your fiancé will be there? What's his full name?"

"Lem Carleton III. Everybody calls him Three. His daddy, Lem Carleton, Jr., is regents chairman. Lem Three is president of the IFC."

"The IFC?" Taylor saw no reason to reveal his peculiar rela-tionship with Lem junior. Lem Three was a better subject. "IFC?"

"The Interfraternity Council," Wendy explained. "Don't you know *anything*?"

"You think it helped ol' Lem getting into Spur because his daddy is the regents chairman?"

"Maybe in the short run." Wendy was irritated by Taylor's question. "But they're the ten top men, and being one of them means guaranteed success in the long run."

"You talk like everybody *gets* a long run. Some people have very short runs. The ten top onions," Taylor said, laughing, "on a short run."

Wendy gave in and they both laughed hard. The wind blew

— 38 —

caliche dust clouds around them and the spring sun baked them. They felt good and strong, almost content. "Are you the kind of person who forgives but never forgets? Or forgets but never forgives?" he asked.

"I don't know." She reached up and touched the red welt between Taylor's eyes. "How did you get that scar?" Gently she stroked the violet slash between his eyes. Her touch enfeebled him.

"The corn picker got me."

"The corn picker?"

"Actually it was a Grapette bottle." Taylor's voice quivered. "It's a long story." His insides shivered and he leaned against the billboard for support.

"The kind of person who forgives but never forgets?" She repeated his question. "Or the kind who forgets but never forgives?"

She didn't answer.

Taylor drove south from the Armadillo Ranch and Gift Shop. Buffy and Simon were in the backseat. Wendy sat fragilely against the door. Taylor constantly kept her in his peripheral vision and studied her movements. He watched how at times she surreptitiously studied him.

The sky was cobalt blue. Herds of fluffy cumulus clouds were skidded by the hard spring winds, covering and uncovering the sun. The plains rolled endlessly in all directions. It was a long drive to the city. Simon and Buffy fell asleep. Simon snored.

"I wonder if she knows he snores?"

"Does it matter now?" Wendy stifled a yawn. She held the back of her delicate hand against her full lips, her slim fingers curled out. The tendons stood out from her long slender neck, accentuating its length and the long sweep from her erect shoulders to her slightly pointed chin.

"I think everything matters now. It's live scrimmage for the rest of their natural lives." Taylor quickly shrugged himself out of his tan jacket as Wendy began to drop off to sleep. "Here, use this as a pillow."

"No. No. I'm okay," she said, yawning and stretching. Catlike.

Taylor's eyes were dry and sore. He folded his jacket and handed it to her. She held it against her chest, stared straight ahead vacantly, then placed the jacket across Taylor's thigh, lay her head down, pulling her legs up on the seat, pushing her stockinged feet against the door. She was instantly asleep. She looked even smaller curled up next to Taylor. The weight of her pressing on his leg was pleasant.

Taylor turned off the main road and followed the Trinity Bottom riverbreaks, where in the 1860's Sam Bass and his Denton Mare hid from the railroad law. Finally betrayed and gut shot from ambush in Round Rock, Sam took two days to die. One hundred years later they still had a week-long celebration of the bush-whacking, complete with rodeo and barbeque.

Been dead over a century and still good for business, Taylor thought. Another notch on the Sun Belt.

The Pontiac rolled south from Oklahoma with Simon D'Hanis and his new wife, Buffy, in the backseat and Cyrus Chandler's daughter, Wendy, curled up with her head on Taylor's jacket, the jacket on his thigh. Taylor wanted to stroke the fine-boned face, but he kept his big hand on the wheel. Add a Pi Phi to the load he was carrying now and it was almost certain disaster. The cat-astrophic.

But Taylor did decide to take one extra chance that warm spring afternoon of his senior year at the University. The big quarterback decided to take an onion to the Tower at midnight.

The ten top onions were expected. He had to take a look and see.

THE COBIANCO BROTHERS

A. D. KOSTER was leaving the apartment when the Cobianco brothers drove their black Lincoln into the parking lot.

"Hey, little buddy." It was Don Cobianco, at forty-four the oldest and biggest of the three brothers. His six-foot-four-inch, two-hundred-fifty-pound bulk was stretched out on the black leather backseat behind the driver, twenty-eight-year-old Johnny, his baby brother. Johnny was about six foot two, two hundred twenty. Roger was on the passenger side and was somewhere in between Johnny and Don in size and age.

The Lincoln full of Cobianco brothers cut A.D. off from his car.

"We want to talk to you, little buddy," Don continued. His electric window hummed down and out of sight. Johnny's window was already open.

A.D. thought a moment about running but dismissed that as unbecoming and most likely unsuccessful. Like the Comanche, the Cobianco brothers loved a man on the run. They were keen on the smell of blood.

A.D. walked slowly up to the car.

Sitting in the backseat, Don Cobianco ran his index finger back and forth across his thick dark eyebrow while keeping his thumb on his stubbly cheek, effectively hiding his face.

All the brothers had the same facial features. Thick, dark hair curling all over huge square heads; heavy beards with constant five-o'clock shadows; small, black, deepset eyes flashing dark under heavy brows, aborted Roman noses, fist-flattened and scarred. The bulbous, fleshy dimpled chins were especially sinister. Full red lips. Capped very large teeth. Hard, mean men in ill-fitting polyester leisure suits.

The Cobianco brothers had started out as Teamsters, then had moved in on the building trades and small real estate developers around the University. They carried the book for the city and ran most of the prostitution and drugs. From union trouble on down to shylock deadbeats, the Cobianco brothers handled it. A. D. Koster fit in there somewhere; now he was about to learn exactly where.

Next to Don sat Tiny Walton, a Cobianco "associate" who did their wet work, most recently a nineteen-year-old coed hooker that an ambitious US attorney had been squeezing against the brothers.

The US attorney had subpoenaed her in front of a grand jury, immunized her and taken away her Fifth Amendment rights. The coed prostitute had to either testify or go to jail for contempt. The judge gave the pretty young girl the weekend to think it over.

Tiny arrived that Sunday, cut her up in the bathtub of her efficiency apartment and used the trash compactor to reduce the teen-age carnage to a neat, square plastic-lined brown paper bag. Tiny left her in the dumpster behind the apartment house. The trash collector picked her up promptly at six the next morning.

The US attorney said she had fled and issued a warrant for her arrest. Two months later he was appointed a federal judge and completely dismissed her from his mind. A busy man, he had politicians to protect.

The coed prostitute was never missed, and Tiny Walton didn't have to use his alibi. The killing was a favorite of Tiny's, and he often recounted to the brothers how he had explained to the hooker what was planned and how she had reacted.

A. D. Koster's confrontation with the Cobianco brothers that morning in his apartment parking lot was "about various financial obligations assumed on Mr. Koster's part that were not forthcoming as promised." That was how Don put it, and it sounded very sinister coming from inside a black limo full of thugs.

"Listen, I know the rent is late," A.D. started saying, "but you got to remember the two guys I live with ain't the most dependable sons-a-bitches in town. They're jocks, for Chrissakes! You can't image what it's like to get money out of them, but I'll get on it." A.D., hunched up like he was cold, was shifting from foot to foot with his hands jammed in his pockets. Don held up his hand for A.D. to stop talking.

"You owe us money on baseball, you cocksucker," Johnny, the youngest, snapped and accidentally spit on himself.

"I'll get that money too." A.D. leaned over and helped Johnny brush his own saliva off his coat. Johnny knocked his hands away. Tiny smiled at both of them.

"What we heard, A.D.," Don said, "was that you lost all your money, plus another grand you don't have, playing cards all night with fraternity boys. Isn't that what you guys heard?" Don asked his brothers. They both nodded.

"Well, that's all bullshit!" A.D. started shuffling again. The three Cobianco brothers watched and smiled. "I didn't lose the money in no card game. It's those two turkeys I live with; they just won't come up with the money."

"Do you think we should speak with them?" Don said quietly. "Maybe we can impress on those boys the necessity of honoring commitments. We are doing business here. They can't be exempted just because they are big football stars. Maybe our associate, Mr. Walton, should talk with them."

Tiny's smile was unchanged. He looked at his manicured hands. Big, thick fingers and knuckles, the perfect fist.

"No! Wait!" A.D. stepped back; he again considered flight. "They aren't here. But I'll get them today for sure and make them pay up."

"That's fine, A.D.," Don smiled. "I know I can count on you for the baseball money too. I wonder how that story about you having a thousand dollars in IOUs over at the Deke house ever got started?"

"The price of fame, I guess," A.D. said. "People like to make up stories about you and include themselves. You know how it is." He tried to smile.

"No, we don't know how it is," Don said. "We're just three flat-nose Italian guys who had to work downtown for their money.

We don't know about Park City or the University, the big time or fame or being a big celebrity. Do we, guys?"

The two other Cobianco brothers shook their square heads.

Tiny was studying his heavy gold, twelve-carat diamond pinkie ring. The setting was in the shape of a gold horseshoe. He had taken it off a bookie who disappeared down a Fort Worth well in 1968.

"We're so stupid, we believed the fraternity boys' story about your IOUs," Don said. The eyes stayed on A.D., who kept his head down and shuffled from sneaker to sneaker. Don Cobianco's voice rolled and filled with anger.

"We were so dumb, me and my two brothers, that we let those fraternity boys sell us those IOUs. That's how stupid we are. I don't mind the money," Don Cobianco said, "but I can't stand to look that stupid. You know what I mean, A.D.? Like letting some fast nigger beat you in front of eighty-five thousand people. You got to intimidate him. Right on the next play. Show whose field it is, you know? When somebody makes us look that stupid, they are gonna get intimidated. You understand that, don't you, A.D.?"

"Ah. Yeah. I understand that." A.D. shuffled and shivered like he was cold.

"I didn't hear what you said, A.D.," Don said loudly. "Did you guys hear him?"

The brothers in the front seat shook their heads again.

"What did you say?" Don leaned forward, gripping the window frame with his thick fingers. The huge knuckles were white from the tension in the grip.

"I said I understand," A.D. said slightly louder. He kept his eyes on his blue sneakers.

Tiny smiled at his huge horseshoe ring.

"Now we got to go make those fraternity boys understand. Let's go, Johnny." The window started up and the Lincoln roared out of the parking lot.

A. D. Koster never moved from the lot. It took the Lincoln one and one-half minutes to circle the block and pull back into the parking lot of the apartment building.

Johnny wheeled up alongside A.D. and rolled down Don's window. Don stayed back in the seat and said, "You want to get in and talk about it?" The voice was soft and disembodied.

A.D. nodded his head, but did not move.

"Better help him, Johnny."

Johnny Cobianco got out from behind the wheel and pulled at

A.D.'s arm. A. D. Koster peeled free from the pavement and stepped woodenly into the big black car.

Johnny closed the rear door and got back behind the steering wheel.

"We got some jobs for you to do, A.D.," Don said.

"What kinds of jobs?" A.D. found his voice. "How long will they take?"

"All kinds, A.D., and they'll take a long time. A long time."

Taylor Rusk steered into the parking lot two hours after A. D. Koster had ridden out in the back of the Cobianco brothers' Lincoln.

A.D. had not returned.

Taylor stopped the car; everyone began to come awake.

"This is where I get out," Taylor said. Wendy Chandler lifted her head from the pillow of his jacket. She leaned over against the passenger door and kept her eyes closed.

"Bye," she said softly, her face finely wrinkled and red from sleep.

Buffy stretched out in the backseat. Simon slipped behind the wheel and Taylor clapped him on the shoulder.

"You and Buffy can live with us if you want. We pay three-quarters of the goddam rent anyway."

"Thanks, we may do that for a while," Simon said. "But first I'm dropping Wendy back at the Pi Phi house. Then Buffy and I are going straight to the Longhorn Motel and get some *sleep*." Simon turned his head to check traffic, then drove away.

THE TEN TOP ONIONS

AT midnight that night Taylor walked across the deserted drag and onto the campus, tossing a small onion from hand to hand. Reaching the statue of an Indian warrior of undetermined tribal affiliation, Taylor heard something behind him.

A giant apparition, at least seven feet tall, lunged out of the shadows of the new economic-geology building, scuffling and snickering, with a long loping stride, closing on Taylor quickly.

Taylor squared off, tensed himself and waited.

The seven-foot-two-inch-tall apparition was Terry Dudley,

grinning and laughing at Taylor. He had been All-American center on the University basketball team five years before and had played professionally for San Antonio.

A B.S. in poly sci, Terry Dudley was back at the University to finish his law degree.

"Jesus, man, you sure got a small onion." Dudley ruffled Taylor's hair and slowed his seven-foot gait so six-foot-five-inch Taylor wouldn't have to strain to match it.

"You mean how big the damn thing is matters?" Taylor shook his head. "What the hell . . . ?"

"Bigger onion is sweeter." Dudley reached up and casually plucked leaves off a branch that was at least nine feet off the ground. "I imagine we're gonna have to eat it, don't you think?"

"I *didn't* think. I don't think." Taylor was becoming doubtful about the whole evening.

"Oh, that's right. You never joined a fraternity." Dudley was a Sigma Nu. "You and your two Park City pals have your own little group."

"They never force me to eat onions," Taylor said.

"Tonight it'll be the same old frat-rat bullshit," Dudley said. "You bring the bra and panties?"

"No." Taylor looked up scornfully at Dudley, who let out a long sigh.

"Aaah. The big boys are out tonight and the whole campus is tingling with energy," Terry Dudley teased. "Can't you just feel the whole contact high? Thirty-five thousand other students waiting on tonight's ritual. Who? Who is somebody? Tonight we find out. Little hearts a-pounding . . . loins inflamed . . ."

"What's this guy Lem Carleton like?"

"Three?" Dudley seemed surprised. "They picked Lem Three?" Taylor shrugged. "I heard that."

"He's Junior Carleton's kid. That's probably why they picked him. He's IFC. Lem Three just wants to get along with everybody." Dudley pointed at the Tower. "He's a fair politician. Not as good as I am, though. Not as good a compromiser as me . . . get along . . . go along."

"You are misinterpreting Sam Rayburn and the value of a good fight as a negotiating device," Taylor said. "I prefer to fight rather than agree."

"What if the other guy agrees with you?"

"Then I'll change."

Terry Dudley was the player who kept finding the money in his shoes after games. The cash totals always worked out to five dollars a rebound and two dollars a point. Terry figured the ratio out quickly. What he couldn't figure was how the money got in his shoes so fast.

"I had to call the campus police last night again," Dudley said. He was tearing a leaf into strips.

"Another girl?" Taylor tossed his onion and looked up at Dudley.

"Two," Dudley said. "They were already nude and in my bed when I got home. They came in through the bathroom window." Dudley looked down at Taylor. "That's *never* happened to you?"

Taylor shrugged. "I've always lived off campus and I keep my windows locked."

"I live on the fourth floor."

"I'll bet that cuts down on the fat girls."

"You'd be surprised. I've met some determined fat women. It drives me crazy," the basketball player said. "I mean, shit, one of those gals last night was pretty good-looking. I *know* this has to be wreaking terrible damage to my sensibilities as a human being, not to mention as an artist."

"I know what you mean." Taylor flipped his onion behind his back and caught it over the opposite shoulder.

"No you don't." Dudley stopped. "You didn't even know about eating the onion. We have different souls and destinies, Taylor."

"Yeah." Taylor nodded slowly. "And you are a lot taller."

"And I'm a lot taller," Dudley agreed.

Dudley walked again, turning thoughtful. He snatched another leaf out of the upper branches of a live oak. They passed the big statue of the Old Cowboy, heading toward the iron bridge.

"Anyway, it'll be the usual hazing horseshit. I know most of the guys who are in Spur now. They aren't *too* bad. I don't think any of them are dangerous." He paused. "But of course they never are at this stage, are they, Taylor?"

"Ask me a question I can answer, for Chrissakes." The quarterback was getting progressively hostile. He didn't like surprises, but he was prepared to deal with them. He rolled the onion over his heavy knuckles.

They reached the bridge. Taylor stopped, held his long finger to his lips and leaned over the rail, listening to the water run over the rocky riverbed.

"Beautiful sound, isn't it?"

"Comes right out of the ground like magic." Terry Dudley began walking again. "The Comanches thought it *was* magic."

Dudley suddenly made a gentle fake and took a short jump

shot at an imaginary basket. He retrieved the imaginary ball from the net and dribbled over to Taylor. "Did A.D. lose as much money playing cards at the Deke house as I heard he did?"

"Probably." Taylor pressed his thumb and forefinger against the scar tissue between his eyes, making his nose ache. "Don't tell me how much you heard. I don't want to know."

"It was big, big, *big*, I heard." Dudley took another fake and hooked toward the basket, which had mysteriously moved. Dudley made a swishing sound. He seldom hit the rim.

"I told you not to tell me," Taylor moaned.

"I didn't tell you. There's big and there's big."

"You said big, big, *big*."

"I know, man." Dudley moved into Taylor's face but kept the imaginary ball on his fingertips, low and away. He wanted the drive.

"Christ, where's he gonna get that kind of money?"

"I'm just telling you because the president of the Deke house will be here tonight. I didn't want him to know more about it than you. A.D. lost *big*." Terry Dudley dropped his shoulder, dribbled off the bridge and slam-dunked into the crotch of a tree twelve feet off the ground.

"I was afraid about the rent money. It was more than that?" They walked along together again.

"The rent, the milk and egg money, Grandpa's watch, Grandma's silver and the baby's shoes," Terry Dudley said.

"Shit. What am I doing here? A.D. is in trouble and on the loose. We're talking Richter-scale disaster looking to happen. I better..."

"Too late." Dudley grabbed Taylor's arm. "Much too late. You may need tonight for an alibi and these Spur assholes are witnesses."

"I was never a joiner...."

"Come, Taylor. Your fate is waiting over in that green dildo."

The Tower, lit up with green lights for the special occasion, glowed above the trees directly ahead of them. It was a few minutes after twelve. "Let's just stick together," Terry Dudley said, "and let me do all the talking when we get there. I'll get you out of a lot of the shit. I do believe my future will eventually be in politics, you just watch." Dudley grinned.

"We'll do a lot of pick and roll and short dump-offs on these guys. Okay, Taylor?"

"I follow you," Taylor agreed. "You're the tallest."

"Hold it *scum*!" a voice bellowed from the interior shadows of the Tower. Green lights glowed against the monolith.

"See what I mean?" Dudley whispered. "Let me do all the talking."

"Did you bring your onion, *scum*?" said the voice from inside the Tower. Terry Dudley grinned; he recognized the voice. The ornate heavy oak door was opened slightly.

Normally the Tower was kept locked, because it was such a favorite spot for suicides and snipers. That night the door was ajar and the reedy, vicious voice demanded to see the onions.

"Let me see that onion, *scum*." The voice attempted strength but broke. Taylor could see a flickering of candlelight through the arched granite doorway. Taylor Rusk held up his onion.

"Where are the bra and panties, *scum*?"

"We are wearing them," Dudley said. Then he whispered to Taylor, "There isn't a son of a bitch in there gonna want to check on *that* after I do my entrance. Now, key on me."

"You are two and one-half minutes late, *scum*. Stop whispering."

Terry Dudley paused, then said slowly, "We were discussing psychotic behavior and obligations."

The voice didn't quite know what to do with that, and there was some loud whispering inside the glowing, throbbing Tower.

"Okay, *scum*," the voice finally said, "you may pass to join your fellow scum already gathered and waiting above. When you pass through, keep your eyes down and don't look in our faces."

Taylor was thinking there would have to be some pretty tall faces inside for him and Dudley to look down and not see them. But before he could think more, Terry Dudley grabbed the first person he saw inside the Tower, the student commander of ROTC—who topped out at five feet eight—and went berserk. Seized by his uniform lapels, the ROTC student flopped around like a rag doll.

"Don't you ever call me *scum* again, you little sawed-off Nazi dog turd, or I'll kill you." Taylor could hear the guy's brass rattling. "I got *pride*, you hear me? *P–R–I–D–E*." Feigning madness, seven-foot-tall, 250-pound Terry Dudley shook the student soldier like a dirty mop.

In the flickering candlelight Taylor Rusk squinted into the dark corners of the octagonal first floor of the Tower. He could see humanoid shadows, motionless, stunned to inaction, paralyzed by the immense ferocity of the angry giant, the nine other outgoing members of Spur turned to furniture.

"You understand, Jack? Pride is why I'm here." Dudley stopped shaking the man as suddenly as he had begun, his voice flat, calm. "Now, I assume you are going to want to discuss other virtues, like dedication, loyalty, honesty."

"Don't forget height," Taylor added, still watching the motionless nine look at their shoes.

"Well, I'll be glad to talk about them rationally upstairs." Dudley was now brushing off the man's coat and straightening his medals. "I'm sorry, buddy. I sort of lost it there . . . *pride*, you know?"

Dudley pointed up the winding staircase. "You say the other scum are up there?" The small shattered man nodded dumbly. "Hey, you okay? I'm sorry. You just sort of got to me. Let's go, Taylor." Dudley strode over and mounted the staircase. "Geez, man, I'm *really* sorry, but it's like a trigger with me, my pride. I'm thoroughly embarrassed. I hope this doesn't mean we can't be friends, maybe do this more often."

As soon as Terry Dudley and Taylor Rusk disappeared above the first level of the Tower, frenzied whispering broke out on the ground floor.

"I doubt they'll be fucking with our pride anymore tonight," Dudley snickered. "What are they going to do, throw us out? I imagine we'll be exempted from everything, especially having to swim in the fucking river in the dark."

Terry and Taylor stood off to the side and watched that night as the Spur initiates were tormented by the outgoing ten: ritually humiliated, tossed fully clothed into the river, forced-fed onions and generally degraded until the morning sky turned pink.

It was a wonderful ritual to watch. It had a lot of little nuances that Dudley was always quick to point out. The outgoing ten were particularly cruel to Wendy Chandler's fiancé, Lem Carleton III, reminding Three that since he was a freshman he had run for some office and lost every year. The insult made Lem cry.

At Shelter Oaks, by the Union, they made Lem strip, then made fun of his genitals.

"Gives you a real sense of brotherhood," Taylor said to Terry Dudley.

THE DEAL

DICK Conly was angry.

Senator Thompson was keeping Dick waiting purposely. The senator did not want to appear too eager to snatch the twenty-five thousand cash Conly had brought from Texas in the crocodile briefcase. Conly was slightly drunk, but the obvious sham would have irritated Dick Conly drunk or sober. He hadn't even wanted to bring the money.

"Goddam, Cyrus, it is such a piss-ant little amount," Conly had complained to Cyrus Chandler. "Send one of your hard-peckered boys. I was planning to go up in the New Mexico Pecos Mountains."

"I want Senator Thompson to *think* that twenty-five thousand is a lot of money, and I do that by sending someone important—the president and CEO of Chandler Industries. He'll be suitably impressed and it will only cost twenty-five thousand."

"Plus *my time*. Jesus." Conly was disgusted. "The bastards sell out so fucking cheap. Twenty-five thousand measly dollars."

Once, when Amos Chandler was alive, Dick Conly had carried two million dollars in cash to some Arab in the same crocodile attaché case. Conly and the Arab got so drunk in New York celebrating the deal, they left the crocodile attaché with the two million in a cab. The driver hunted them down at the 21 Club at four A.M., hours later; they were still oblivious to their loss. The cabbie returned the case and the two million. Conly ended the evening by ordering separate ambulances with nurses and attendants to take him and the Arab back to their hotels and tuck them in bed.

No, $25,000 wasn't any money at all, but Dick Conly would let Senator Thompson find that out on his own. That was known as legislative experience. On-the-job training with OPM. OJT/OPM.

A cruel curve drawn at the right corner of Dick Conly's mouth gave every expression a sneer; his face was at an angle to the world. Dick Conly knew the world without its fashion. Long ago as a young lawyer in DC, fighting World War Two for Amos Chandler, Dick Conly saw the bear. Hell, he brought the bear to

Cyrus's suite at the Mayflower and drank Nelson Rockefeller *and* the bear under the table. He won, but now he had a drunk bear on his hands. He figured it was better than having a Rockefeller puking on the carpet. So Dick Conly learned to smile—but first to sneer, and the mark never left his face.

"What kind of fucking country we have here?" Conly mumbled. "Idiots." It saddened him that a US senator was so stupid as to think making Dick Conly wait in the expensively paneled outer office made Thompson seem less greedy. All it could do was piss Dick Conly off. Which it did. That was seldom a good idea. He despaired for his country. Sort of.

"The senator will see you now, Mr. Conly." The slightly fleshy, attractive, fortyish secretary stood in the open doorway to the senator's inner office.

"It's about goddam time." Conly lurched out of the chair and snatched up the crocodile briefcase. "Does the son of a bitch want to take a goddam bribe or not? I have important people to corrupt." Conly brushed past the secretary and into the office, confronting the small white-haired man, the senior United States senator from the solid South. Bailey Bradley Thompson chaired several important committees and subcommittees. He had been in the Senate since before the war and had access to the Mexican vote in San Antonio, El Paso and South Texas to the Rio Grande Valley. They *all* voted for Bailey Bradley Thompson. Alive or dead. Several times.

"You want the payoff or you just want to jack off?"

The secretary's mouth dropped. She looked quickly at the senator for some indication of how to react.

"Don't look so shocked, honey," Conly said. "If he ain't laying pipe on you and keeping you up-to-date on his business, I don't want to bribe the son of a bitch anyway." Conly leered at her. "I'm at the Mayflower."

"Dick, you old joker." Senator Thompson stood to his full five-foot-eight inches and stuck out his hand. He motioned the secretary out with his eyes. "And hold my calls," he yelled after her.

Conly didn't even bother with the senator's extended hand. He just flicked the latches on the attaché and dumped the twenty-five thousand dollars out on the senator's desk.

Dick Conly had figured the exact combination of small bills that would not only total twenty-five thousand but would fill the briefcase. It spilled out onto the senator's desk and looked like *a lot of money*.

"Goddam," Senator Thompson gasped involuntarily. "Goddam." His eyes grew large and he ran his hands over the pile of old bills.

Conly watched the little man and wondered how in God's name the government worked if senior senators were this overcome by such piss-ant little amounts of money. Dick Conly had special contempt for a man who so obviously hungered for the actual bills, the pieces of paper with the meaningless denominations printed on them. An IOU from a government a trillion dollars in debt wasn't money. Not *real money*. Real money was a concept, a brilliant scheme, seizing the opponent's weak point, taking the high ground in an elaborate power play. *Power*—that was wealth. Changing the rules, changing the game. Not pieces of paper.

Senator Thompson began stuffing the paper into his desk drawer.

"We get the right ruling out of your subcommittee on this bill, Senator," Conly said. "That's the deal. The money for the ruling and the votes."

"Yes, certainly." The little gray senator never took his eyes off the bills. "I'm a man of my word." He kept shoveling the bills into the drawer. "Couldn't be a US senator if my word wasn't my bond." He put in the last packet and locked the drawer, using a key he carried on a gold watch chain tucked into his waistcoat pocket. "Now, how about a drink, Mr. Conly?" Senator Thompson looked up to find an empty room.

Dick Conly was already gone.

"Well . . . I'll be goddamned." Senator Thompson was puzzled. It was like Conly hadn't been there at all. Bailey Bradley Thompson's confusion slowly turned to action as the senator took the key from his vest pocket and reopened the drawer to make certain that it all *had* happened. The paper bills were still there; he called his secretary to count them and fill his briefcase. He thought again about Conly's abrupt departure.

Senator Thompson looked around the richly appointed office, then spoke to his secretary.

"Hell, you'd think Conly thought he was too good to drink with a United States senator."

The secretary smiled, nodded, and lost count. Ten-cent dollars. Later she met Conly at the Mayflower.

Two weeks later a Senate communications subcommittee, chaired by Senator Bailey Bradley Thompson, ruled the Football League must accept the franchise application before it from a certain Texas city or run the risk of being investigated by the FCC and possibly being found in violation of antitrust laws.

The franchise application at the League office had been filed by Dick Conly for Cyrus Chandler.

The League didn't like antitrust threats. They didn't much like Dick Conly either.

In a hastily-called owners meeting, Commissioner C. Robinson Burden advised the franchise be granted immediately to Cyrus Chandler. Just in time for the draft.

Conly sent fifty thousand dollars and an override on two wells in the Wanda June Field to the League commissioner. A greedy young comer, more expensive than a senior US senator, but Robbie Burden was cheap at twice the price.

Dick Conly wouldn't drink with the commissioner either.

The owners pooled their old and used-up players and offered them for sale to the Chandler Texas Franchise for $38 million.

Cyrus Chandler and Dick Conly bought the players and took straight-line depreciation for five years, allowing $7 million plus per year in tax-free income. Until the Franchise began to show an "unavoidable" profit, Dick Conly applied the paper losses against Cyrus Chandler's oil income.

Dick expensed players differently, depending on base salary, deferred payments, and bonuses, but usually wrote off the player's total salary immediately, even if deferred clauses delayed payment of substantial sums for twenty years.

The players wore out pretty fast. Football was hard on inventory. An average career was 4.6 years. New players were drafted and purchased with multiyear deferred-payment contracts, assigned dollar values and expensed currently in a never-ending cycle. If a player was getting $75,000 a year with another $100,000 deferred for 20 years, the Franchise expensed the whole $175,000 while collecting interest on the $100,000. Million-dollar contracts with deferred payments into the twenty-first century gave the Franchise huge tax breaks. It was all in how it was put down on paper. The stats.

The Franchise had purchased the right to create values and then expense them. Dick Conly assigned players big contracts, then released them, writing off the full contract value as loss.

The Franchise scheduled their first season for the following fall.

Taylor Rusk was the first player chosen in the draft. The Franchise bought him. Dick Conly put a big dollar value on Taylor. People would pay to see someone worth large sums of money, Conly knew.

Even if they were only ten-cent dollars.

WATER CARNIVAL

THE last major social weekend of the spring term at the University was Water Carnival.

Four consecutive days and nights celebrating water; the river magically gushing from the faultline and flowing through the campus, crystal clear and seventy-two degrees year-round. Millions of years-round.

Fraternities, sororities, honoraries, dormitories and other campus factions spent the three weeks prior to Water Carnival building floats to run down the river, through the campus and into town. The riverbank lined with crowds of students, parents, alumni, townies, the University and the city elite, plus the bums from under the Red River Street Bridge. Only during Water Carnival did people give much thought to the river.

It was a big event ranking second only to the A & M game.

Lots of parties. Drinking. Sex. Lots of changes.

At Water Carnival the new members of Spur were announced and launched down the river on a floating party barge of folding chairs covered in purple and white crepe paper. The ten top onions awash.

Terry Dudley drove his latest demonstrator over to give Taylor Rusk a ride to Water Carnival rehearsal.

The basketball player was singing as he stooped through the doorway to Taylor's apartment.

When the morning comes and you gotta get up
How you gonna find your shoes . . .

Dudley accompanied himself on an imaginary guitar, making all the necessary sounds with his nose, throat, mouth, and tongue. He was particularly good at imitating the sound of a steel guitar with his nasal cavities.

In an empty bed with an aching head
You know, it's gotta give you the blues . . .

The giant man turned, twisted and strummed that imaginary guitar while Taylor looked for his tan jacket. Dudley finished his song, took one last strum with his huge fingers and set down his imaginary guitar against an imaginary amplifier. "Let's get going, Taylor. The Big River waits."

"Why rehearse floating down a goddam river?"

Taylor was wearing an athletic department T-shirt, jeans and A.D.'s alligator shoes; he had taken the shoes when A.D. admitted he'd gambled away the rent money. Simon had moved out.

"What's to practice?" Taylor dug through scattered piles of newspapers and dirty clothes, looking for his jacket.

"Let me handle this," Dudley ordered. "Didn't I get you through the initiation? Christ, what sort of social life do you have? At Varsity Club meetings, you're known as the man who isn't here. And you're vice-president."

"I'm not a joiner—"

"You told me," Dudley interrupted.

"—people join *me*," Taylor finished.

"Yeah, I can see." Dudley glanced around the empty apartment.

Taylor found his jacket wadded up under the rubble; it had been missing a couple of days. He pulled it on, slapping at the wrinkles, trying to smooth out the big ones. He followed Dudley down the stairs and outside.

"I go get drunk a couple of times a year with the sales manager and the dealer and give them my season tickets," Terry explained as they drove across campus to the river. "I remember their kids, their wives, their girl friends, and keep them straight, which is something neither of them can do. In return I try out a new car every year."

Taylor tried to straighten the collar and brushed out the deep lines in the front of his jacket. The effort released a sweet familiar smell mingled with the sour of his own sweat. Taylor savored the fragrant trace, the pleasant essence, trying to identify the scent.

"You testing the air?" Terry asked.

Taylor ignored him but lost the scent. Roses?

Terry Dudley wheeled the big Cadillac demonstrator into the lot behind the aquatic station and parked right beside a Chevrolet convertible full of girls from the Pi Phi house.

Stepping out next to Taylor Rusk, Wendy Chandler was wearing jeans, boots and a madras blouse with cardigan sweater tossed loosely over her delicate shoulders. Her left hand carried a five-carat diamond ring. Taylor's nostrils flared as the air filled suddenly with the haunting fragrance of roses, crushed roses. Wendy smelled of crushed rose petals. Taylor took deep draughts of the sweet air.

The others walked toward the crowd gathering on the riverbank.

"Where's Lem Three?"

"He won't be here until later," Wendy said. "He's learning what his future holds."

"How's he doing that?"

"My daddy is telling him."

Taylor couldn't tell if it was sarcasm, resignation or contentment. He didn't really care. He only cared that Wendy was there alone right then.

THE ASSISTANT PR MAN

"YOU'LL start out in the public relations department as an assistant to the PR director, Rickie Dixon," Cyrus announced as Dick Conly poured himself a drink. "From there on, the sky is the limit, Lem. We'll probably work you into the scouting combine in a few years."

Lem Carleton III was meeting with his future father-in-law, Cyrus Chandler, and Dick Conly, Chandler Industries' CEO. They were sitting in Cyrus's penthouse office, discussing the football franchise and Lem's place in it.

Dick Conly drank quietly and watched from the corner. Whatever Cyrus said, Dick Conly had to make happen. He had promised old Amos that he would look out for Cyrus. Dick Conly would do it. Cyrus would resent it and never understand it. Conly derived very little pleasure from working with Cyrus. Amos Chandler was a giant. Cyrus paled by comparison and Cyrus knew it. And he knew Dick Conly knew.

"Well, Dad Chandler . . ." Lem leaned back and took in the luxury of Cyrus's penthouse office. "You don't mind if I start calling you Dad, do you?"

Cyrus shook his head. Conly rolled his eyes back and laid his head on the soft leather of the corner loveseat.

Conly pegged Lem Carleton III as someone merely chasing legitimacy. His father, Lem Carleton junior, the University regents chairman, had been born to minor wealth, but because Junior and Cyrus were Spur '39, Dick Conly made him major-league wealthy with one deal in the Wanda June Field. Junior remained wealthy, burying himself in regents' work after Cyrus squeezed him out of any further deals when Conly showed Cyrus his share increase on future ventures—without Junior. Now Cyrus would force Dick Conly to accept the task of carrying the guilt for Junior, weaning his future son-in-law on to *real life*.

It wasn't difficult to run a professional football franchise and make a good profit. The IRS bookkeeping gymnastics—plus the guaranteed television money—did that. The TV contract currently paid each team $5 million a year and was soon up for renegotiation. On the business side the Franchise would run on a $3 million budget efficiently, even paying Lem Carleton III and other front-office cronies huge salaries. Then there was a $1 million shell game they played with the scouting combine.

Additionally if they won, the Franchise would sell lots of tickets and make a *huge* profit. That was Dick Conly's long-term plan: build the Franchise into the mechanism of the League to ensure winning continually. Programming the whole system so whatever mergers and playoff systems develop, Super Bowl efforts would be more a matter of fine-tuning—the League, not the Franchise.

One reason Conly insisted on hiring Red Kilroy was because Red had placed ex-players and assistants throughout the League from the playing field to the Commissioner's office. Red had a network. Conly wanted it.

The *fix* would be built into the system.

Cyrus told Lem Three about the joys of being an assistant PR man, while Conly sipped his drink and tried to think of a positive use for him—for either of them. *The kid couldn't even be a US senator*.

"I was sort of hoping for something a little . . ." Lem groped for a word, confident in the face of his own ignorance, ". . . a little nicer. . . ."

"Jeezus—" Conly blurted out. Cyrus held up his hand, and Dick Conly drank his glass dry. The whiskey burned back the disgust.

"It is control of the League that I am going for." Cyrus explained Dick Conly's plan to Lem as if it were his own. "I want my people everywhere in the League and I want the best people, and I don't mean just on the field. I'm going to make professional football the best show for the money. Pay-TV is going to be in place in a couple of years, and that is why you need to start out in PR and learn it. Learn about media and communications."

"Buy yourself a stable of sportswriters and broadcasters," Conly interrupted.

"But," Lem protested, "don't you think public relations is rather common?"

"You bet your ass, sonny," Dick Conly roared. "Common as cowshit. We're making money, not playing games." Conly splashed more whiskey into his glass. "Mass media is *supposed* to be common—the *more* common the better. We're trying to attract an audience of millions. Those are common people and we want them. All of them."

Lem looked confused and disappointed, his eyes traveling nervously from Cyrus to Conly to the floor. "You just want me to be assistant public relations man?" Lem was hurt. "No executive title? Wendy told me . . ."

"Damn boy!" Conly roared. "Wendy Chandler doesn't run this business; I do!" Lem winced back into the chair. "I run this son of a bitch, and if you want to go to work for me, you do what I say."

"Now, Dick, calm yourself," Cyrus interrupted. "Lem, you're among friends here, and remember, all my daughter is going to be is your wife. Do you want the job or not?"

Lem was stunned by the sudden ferocity of Conly's attack and had no idea what he had done to deserve it. After all, he was third-generation money. It wasn't like he needed the job. He couldn't help it if he *wasn't* common.

"I . . . ah . . . well . . ." Lem tried to find his voice. "Yes, certainly I want the job, but . . ."

"No goddam *but*'s," Conly said abruptly. "Don't chase it if you can't kill it, boy, and don't kill it if you can't skin it. Either way you end up with a stinking mess." Conly drained and sloshed still more bourbon into his glass. He looked at the door as Lem Carleton III skulked out of the sumptuous office, Cyrus following him.

"Take it easy, Lem," Cyrus soothed. "We can't make it look like marrying the boss's daughter is all it takes in this business." The elevator opened at the end of the hall. A teen-age boy got out.

"I guess not." Lem dug his toe in the thick carpet. "Well . . . I'm supposed to meet Wendy now."

"Go on," Cyrus said. "Kiss her for me."

Lem smiled when he left, but he was angry and humiliated and brushed past young Luther Conly without a nod.

"Mr. Chandler," the boy asked, "is my dad finished yet?"

Cyrus frowned and looked puzzled. "Why, Luther, I'm sorry, Dick just left. He must have forgotten."

The boy's face fell; his eyes misted and his body trembled.

"He's been busy as a one-armed paperhanger," Cyrus smiled.

The boy nodded and walked back to the elevator. Cyrus returned to the office.

"You better quit drinking so much, Dick." Cyrus watched Conly gulp down the whiskey. Cyrus's small pointed tongue flicked across his front teeth like a reptile's, tasting the air.

"You quit giving me shit jobs like raising your future son-in-law and carrying twenty-five thousand to that jerk-off Senator Thompson. Then, I'll quit drinking so much." Conly looked at his watch. He was expecting his son.

"Hell, Dick, it isn't just for Wendy." Cyrus leaned back and put his feet up on the desk, looking out at the fast-darkening skyline. "Lem is Junior's boy, don't forget. I have known him since he was that high." Cyrus held his manicured hands two feet above the plush light-purple carpet. "He and Wendy Cy were the two cutest kids . . ."

"Since when did who had the cutest kids make a shit, Cyrus?" Conly banged his glass on the solid teak coffee table that Cyrus had brought from China on the company plane. "You squeezed Junior out of the Wanda June Field when Lem was only five years old and a lot cuter. And I'll be goddamned, but my kids are cuter than yours or Junior's and I don't even get to see them." Conly poured himself another drink. "Where the hell is Luther? We had a movie date." He checked his watch. "It's always been too easy for you, Cyrus. I make it too easy and it's hard on me and mine."

"Maybe so, Dick. Maybe so." Cyrus looked over at Conly and shrugged. "Maybe I feel guilty." He suddenly changed the subject. "A guy told me I can put over two million tax-free into my pocket when we get to the Super Bowl. So let's move. We scalp the Super Bowl tickets, only pay taxes on the face value and pocket the rest. It's foolproof."

"It's stupid. A guy told you? What guy?"

Cyrus didn't answer.

"Nothing is foolproof," Conly reminded Chandler. "The word

does not apply to you. You attract an inordinate number of fools."
He pointed at the chair Lem Three had occupied. "We have fools
marrying into the business and the family."

"We can use Don Cobianco's operation to help move tickets,"
Cyrus urged. "He's been anxious to do me some favors."

"Is that where you got this harebrained idea? I'll *bet* he's anxious to do you some favors. Listen, Cyrus, don't ever put us in
bed with the Cobianco brothers. Ever. They're penny-ante thugs."
Dick Conly spent a lot of his time protecting Cyrus from people
like the Cobiancos. He had killed a couple, protecting Amos.
"Scalping tickets involves the IRS. It's stupid. Don't ever do deals
with people who got less to lose than you."

"I like the idea, that's all. It's fun." Cyrus laughed. "Now,
what about the Anglo-Bahamian Bank in Freeport? I need a stash
for the scalping money."

"We have to get to the Super Bowl first." Conly decided to
stall. "By then we'll be making so much money, we'll have no
reason—"

"Scared, Dick?" Chandler cut him off. "I have a plan. If you
can't . . ."

"Everybody has a plan, you asshole," Conly yelled at Cyrus
Chandler. "Now listen to me. I already checked and the Anglo-
Bahamian Bank is a CIA front."

"Oh, Jesus . . ." Cyrus turned white. "What'll we do? We can't
use that bank."

"It's the safest place to be. You stupid bastard, the CIA isn't
going to tell *anybody* what they're doing, especially the IRS."

"They won't?" Cyrus had broken into a fine cold sweat.

"No."

"They can't turn me in?" Cyrus giggled.

Conly shook his head. "They might *threaten* to tell the IRS . . ."

"But they're illegal too!" Cyrus began a high-pitched cackle
as the sweat ran from his armpits. "They won't endanger their
own operation over a couple of million, right?"

"Yeah, but don't do it. The Cobianco brothers could leave your
ass hanging out between them and the CIA. You're gambling
billions against a few million."

"We'll see," Cyrus said. "A million here and there adds up."

"Don't do it. I'm warning you. This could hurt Chandler Industries; Mob and CIA connections are not the best of international
associates."

Dick Conly checked the time again and sighed. "I gave Luther a thousand-dollar watch for his birthday and he's half an hour late."

"I'll bet he just forgot, Dick. You know these kids nowadays." Cyrus grinned, his eyes small and mean.

"No, I don't, Cyrus. Thanks to you, I never see my kid. Well, I better get Red Kilroy in here: We have a franchise to build."

Dick Conly drank far into that night and many other nights, carrying out his plans and thwarting Cyrus's disastrous schemes.

Conly never did figure out how he and his boy, Luther, missed connections that night on the movie. Neither did Luther. They missed others, many more.

Finally all.

ESCAPE FROM REHEARSAL

TAYLOR Rusk watched Lem Three arrive at the Water Carnival rehearsal while Terry Dudley listened raptly to the guy in the blue blazer, white pants and shoes who was using a bullhorn to assign numbers to floats.

"Number twenty-six, that's the Dekes. . . . Number twenty-seven, the Kappa Sigs. . . . Number twenty-eight. . . ."

Taylor Rusk watched Wendy Chandler and Lem Carleton as they began to argue.

"Number thirty-two is the ROTC Queen's float. . . ."

Lem took Wendy behind the bleachers, erected strategically for the University and Park City officials and honored guests to see the floats while also being seen themselves. Taylor watched as the tide of the argument turned quickly against Three.

Suddenly Wendy Chandler snatched the engagement ring from her finger and threw the five-carat diamond into the tall grass of the riverbottom.

Lem was devastated. Horror-stricken, he chased the glittering arc carved by the huge diamond in the fading skylight. He got several twinkling fixes on the trajectory and quickly triangulated a swatch of tule as the touchdown zone, where he fell to his knees and began searching.

Wendy spun around and began a furious march up the sloping riverbank toward the aquatic station and the parking lot beyond, leaving Three scrambling desperately in the tall grass.

"Keys in your demonstrator?" Taylor asked Terry Dudley, who was entranced by the guy with the bullhorn.

"Okay, the Canoe Club will serve as parade masters and carry walkie-talkies. . . ."

"The keys in your car?" Taylor bumped Dudley, who nodded but kept his eyes on the guy with the bullhorn.

"Number forty will be the Sigma Nus. . . . Number forty-one will be the Spur float. . . ."

"Save me a seat on the float."

Taylor turned and jogged after Wendy, catching up with her in front of the oil rig that had punched out the first oil on University property.

"Can I give you a ride somewhere?"

"Only if I can drive." Wendy didn't break stride.

"The keys are in that blue Cadillac four-door."

They sped off.

It took all night—he was eaten alive by mosquitoes and nearly bitten by a cottonmouth—but Lem Three found the flawless diamond ring.

Taylor sat silently while Wendy squealed the big blue car through the campus and city, up over the faultline and into the hills. Finally he asked, "What were you and Lem fighting about?"

"He didn't like the way the future looked." She kept her eyes fixed on the darkening road; her small hands and thin arms wrenched the big wheel of the car. They wove their way onto the limestone plateau. "So I changed it."

"Can you do that?"

"We'll see, won't we?"

Taylor Rusk nodded and remained silent for several wild miles.

Wendy wrestled the car and kept the gas pedal to the floor. They left the road several times. She kept the car accelerating, slowing only for the switchbacks and caliche hairpins.

The Cadillac clawed its way up the scarp and the cedar breaks stretched ahead in the twilight.

"How come we never met before Buffy's wedding?" She took her eyes off the twisting road.

"I don't get out much." Taylor said. "Don't know what to do. Mostly I play ball, study, eat, sleep, play ball and play ball."

"Real good-timer, huh?" She turned back to the road. The Cadillac ate away the pavement.

"If you like playing ball."

"A. D. Koster was such a dreamboat in high school," Wendy

said. "All of us thought he was some sort of animal, like—like James Dean."

"He was . . . still is. . . ." In high school A.D. rolled his Camels up in the sleeve of his white T-shirt and rode a Harley Electra Glide he had stolen in Galveston.

"So it was you and that fat guy D'Hanis that were always with him," Wendy said. "Your cuffs were always too short on your pants and you wore sweat socks."

"I still wear sweat socks. They're free and clean and I sweat a lot. You want me to introduce you to A.D.? Hell, if you're into shoes"—Taylor pointed at his feet—"these shoes once belonged to A. D. Koster."

"I already saw them. They're nice with those sweat socks."

The Cadillac slowed noticeably. The plateau was sinking into darkness.

"I'm taking you to a friend's place," Wendy Chandler announced as the car climbed higher. "He won't be there. You'll like it. I have to get away from campus and think."

"Me too. If we take long enough, I'm certain I can think of *something*."

Taylor knew where she was going as soon as she turned off the Ranch Road pavement onto the county caliche road past Dead Man Hill. He kept quiet as she followed the roughly graded road through the rocky pastures and through the gates and cattle guards and across the fords of the shallow-flowing Dead Man Creek.

"I was a freshman at the University and I decided to have my first affair," Wendy explained as she drove across the third ford of the creek. "I picked this professor who was kind of old and married. It made it seem safer or less involved or something. His wife had cut him off years before over some other beef about another student, I think. Imagine that. Anyway, their kids were grown and gone. So I took a shot at him and he brought me here."

"Was it safer?" Taylor asked. "Less involved or something?" They topped Coon Ridge, dropped down and crossed the creek for the final time.

"I don't know. I guess it was *or something*. He's still my best friend at school."

They pulled up next to the old stone farmhouse set back in the live oak motte on the bluff above Dead Man Creek.

"He only comes up here on weekends. You'd like him."

"I do," Taylor said.

"Doc Webster? You know him?" Wendy looked at him quizzically. "He never mentions you."

— 63 —

"Everyone mentions you," Taylor said.

"Then you've been here before?" Wendy opened the car door; the interior light immediately attracted several varieties of flying insects, some quite large.

Taylor nodded and swung halfheartedly at the bugs invading the car. "Let's get out and into the house before the big ones come."

"How are Simon and Buffy?" Wendy led the way into the stone house.

"I haven't seen them. Simon called from the Longhorn Motel when he found out A.D. had lost the rent money again. He just came over and got his stuff and vanished into the night. Haven't heard a word since. You talk to Buffy?"

"We're not that close. She was a loner and spent all her time with Simon. I was president of the house and nobody else wanted to make that horrid drive to Oklahoma." Wendy opened the back door to the cabin.

"You never answered my question that day." Taylor knocked down a moth that was flying straight for his eyes. "Do you forgive and not forget..." They stepped inside, walked through the kitchen into the living room. "...or forget but not forgive?"

"Maybe I forgive *and* forget. Build a fire." Wendy set her cloth shoulder bag on the table with a familiar clunk, then walked into the south bedroom.

"I find that hard to believe." Taylor looked into the cloth bag. A pearl-handled, nickel-plated, five-shot, snub-nosed .38 fit snugly in a specially sewn pocket. Grip, handle and trigger quickly accessible, she could shoot the gun without removing it from the purse. "Very hard to believe. I personally forgive but never forget."

"That's nice," Wendy called from the bedroom. "You would make a great pet elephant."

"The idea is to not make the same mistake twice."

"You'll be easy to paper-train."

Taylor found kindling in a brass woodbox and began constructing a fire in the rock fireplace.

Taylor Rusk and Wendy Cy Chandler spent several days at Doc Webster's ranch, while back on the river their places on the floats drifted lazily, conspicuously empty in front of everyone on campus and in town.

Hardly anyone forgot or forgave.

RED KILROY

"I want coach *and* general manager." Red Kilroy sipped his Scotch and looked into the glass while he made his demands of Cyrus Chandler and Dick Conly. "I need complete control and autonomy just like I have over at the University. I will want to bring my whole staff. I want a lot of money and a part of the Franchise, stock options based on an incentive program indexed to wins and losses. I'll want dental, medical and a slush fund. Otherwise, why should I leave the University?"

"We'll meet most of your demands," Dick Conly said, "because you are quite honestly worth it. But you can't own any stock in the Franchise. The League prefers one owner. It eliminates the chance of public fights. Besides, I don't want you as a stockholder. You'll try and squeeze in deeper. I just want you to worry about wins and losses of football games, the evaluation of talent and the development of long-term program strategies and short-term tactics. That's the job description. It pays four hundred thousand dollars base. We can work out the incentives and bonuses. You'll like the numbers, but no, you would make a dangerous business partner. You can never be allowed to own. You don't understand the concepts of balance and order. You always want more, to win, to have."

"Then why should I leave the University?" Red leaned back smugly, dealing from a certain strength. The University job paid $200,000 plus oil-well overrides, a free house, a television show and endorsements that added another $150,000, three free cars and a slush fund—kept in his office safe—that was estimated at about $300,000, of which $100,000 went straight into Red's pocket as cash, untaxed, yearly. There were free trips, million-dollar life insurance policies and scholarships for children. His total income with all the unlisted perks was over $600,000.

"You'll leave," Dick Conly replied. "If you don't the NCAA and the FBI are going to be in your office the first thing tomorrow, going through recruiting files and opening your safe. Try explaining three hundred thousand dollars cash. Not everybody in this state went to the University. It just seems like it. Now, do we have to get down to ear-biting?"

"Bullshit," Red said. "*You're* in those files. You can't turn me in and stay clean yourself."

"Can't we?" Conly said. "Are you certain? Well, I certainly hope we don't have to go to all the trouble to find out. You'll be an employee, a valued but replaceable technician—not an owner or partner, just an employee. We will pay you well, but don't ask for an ownership position again."

"Maybe," Cyrus interrupted, angering Dick Conly, "if you get us into the Super Bowl . . . maybe then we'll talk about an ownership percentage. Until then . . ." Cyrus let it hang.

"I'll think about it." Red stood and left quickly.

"Well, Cyrus," Conly sighed, "you have done it again. You just gave Red Kilroy the one thing that I wanted that ambitious bastard stripped of completely before we hired him—*hope*." Dick's aggravation was apparent.

Red Kilroy, with the fine survival sense developed as a major-college football coach, knew he had finally met his match in Dick Conly. But when Cyrus dangled the hope of percentage or stock options if they got to the Super Bowl, Red Kilroy had what he needed. The hope that he would own his *own* franchise.

Red Kilroy took the job.

They kept it secret until after the big alumni catfish fry and beer bust, when the "boosters" showed up with cash and catfish, coleslaw and Pearl beer.

There Red announced he was leaving the University to coach the Franchise.

The athletic director, T. J. "Armadillo" Talbott, gave him a plaque and launched into a rambling speech about commies infiltrating the Cotton Bowl committee and the NCAA.

Red Kilroy left the fish fry late that night, opened the safe in his office and took the whole football slush fund with him in a duffel bag.

He got away with close to $300,000.

How could the University report the theft of something that wasn't supposed to exist?

Hardball, Red called it.

The University had many lean years after Red Kilroy left; the fans were certain it was because the great Red Kilroy had gone to the Franchise, and in a way they were right.

One Red Kilroy Era ended and another one began.

* * *

Once at the Franchise, Kilroy determined priorities.

Red's goal of Super Bowl was servant to his desire to become Franchise owner. Think *win!* Every day, all day.

Red's system was simple. Offense and defense were based on the same primary concept: the control of territory.

Many had broken the game down into various concepts of controlling territory. Lombardi did it at Green Bay based on excellent personnel and an infectious desire to excel under pressure, causing dams of emotion to burst forth into winning efforts; crazed men momentarily became superhuman, made no mistakes, executed. Lombardi was power and execution. Landry, a defensive expert at New York, had borne the 4–3, created the flex defense and adapted the multiple-formation offense to answer the questions of controlling territory. He perfected the scanning, retention and recall methods of the computer to construct models of future battles for turf. Landry was the general of the electronic battlefield. The prediction and adjustment capabilities were phenomenal. There was little or no need for emotion, but rather exquisite technical control.

Red Kilroy combined both, with an evangelist's ability to convert or kill.

"Never be afraid to be human and make mistakes," Red told his players. "Just don't *ever* do it on a football field."

DOC WEBSTER'S RANCH

"THERE'S no phone here," Wendy announced. "That's what I love about it. People really have to *want* to find you." They were at the ranch, missing Water Carnival. Taylor had the fire burning when Wendy returned from the south bedroom of the stone house. She had changed into loose-fitting corduroy pants, a Peruvian wool poncho and rabbit-fur-lined buckskin squaw boots.

The stone house was cold, and the sputtering fire was making slow progress against the chill radiating from the cold rock. The roof was tin. The floor and walls were of thick odd-shaped limestone blocks in beige and pink hues. It was the native stone. The country was littered with it and it lay two miles thick below the thin topsoil.

It was the plateau. Old sea bottom. Skeletons and sea shells forty million years old.

The house was four rooms with a long porch running the length of the south side, facing the creek. The kitchen in the northwest corner had an ancient white enamel sink with a hand pump on the west wall with accompanying drain and butcher boards. A four-paned window was punched into the rock over the sink. The only light in the kitchen was a bare bulb hung from the center of the ceiling. The north wall was covered with white-painted metal cabinets surrounding an old white electric stove and a Coldspot refrigerator with the round motor humming and vibrating on the top. Next to the refrigerator, a door opened directly outside to the oak motte. A full rain barrel stood next to the outside door. It had rained heavily in the hills all week.

The kitchen table was heavy plank and set in the middle of the room. None of the eight chairs matched; two were handmade wooden captain's chairs, three were from different Formica dinette sets and three were stolen from the University cafeteria. There was also an old tall wooden stool in the corner. The south wall was all pantry shelves filled with foodstuffs and kitchen equipment; on the top shelf sat a big box of D-Con.

A heavy post-and-lintel archway led through the south wall into a living area, twenty-five feet square, with Indian rugs hung on the rock walls and laid on the rough stone floor.

The fireplace took up the west wall of the living room; on the hearth was an umbrella stand full of old hand-whittled canes and a Confederate cavalry sword and scabbard once carried by a captain in Hood's Texas Brigade.

Four tall eight-pane glass windows in the south wall overlooked the porch. Two hammocks hung from the smooth cedar posts that held up the tin roof. There was a nice view of the crest of the hill, dropping straight to the creek. Nestled into the south side of the ancient protective grove of live oaks, the cabin commanded the high ground north of Dead Man Creek.

Two doorways off the living room led to separate bedrooms. The brass double beds were piled high with down comforters and hand-sewn quilts. The walls were hung with blue-and-gray paintings, black-and-white photographs and bookcases; books were scattered everywhere. The main subject of almost every book was the War of Rebellion. Doc was an antisecessionist—Sam Houston—Jacksonian—Democrat native Texan.

Wendy Chandler crept over to the fire silently and knelt on the red and black Indian rug, holding out her hands to the flame.

"You build a great fire," she said.

"They offer a course in this at the University." Taylor tossed on the twisted piece of oak. "It's for jocks. Helps us with hand-eye coordination, keeps our grade points up and we get warm." He stopped talking and watched Wendy for a moment as she looked into the fire and nodded slowly, lost in the flames.

Taylor felt a chill.

"These damn rock houses are cold. It's colder in here than outside. Let's go outside and warm up, give the fire a chance to get burning."

Taylor held the door onto the porch open. Keeping her eyes on the fire, Wendy backed outside under a clear night sky.

"You have a girl at the University?"

"I had one, sorta. Turned out she was a person who *forgot* but *never forgave*. She ended up mad at me for all sorts of things she couldn't recall. We broke off after she"—Taylor hesitated—"pulled a knife on me."

"Pulled a knife on you!" Wendy was startled.

"Yeah, well, she carried a Buck knife. She was afraid of men, she told me. I knew she had the knife but there was just something about the way she snapped it open, that"—Taylor paused—"scary sound when the blade clicked, locked open. She was a pretty girl too. Somebody must have scared the shit out of her. . . . Maybe I made a sudden movement. It is sort of like why you carry the nickel-plated thirty-eight in your purse." It became a direct question.

"I carry it to shoot anybody I think needs shooting," Wendy said. "So don't press your luck and stay out of my purse. My mother gave the pistol to me when I left for the University." That was all the explanation Wendy volunteered.

"Do you sleep with it?"

"If I have to."

"Maybe tonight you'll get lucky and won't have to sleep with the big iron."

"Maybe tonight I'll get lucky and hit what I shoot."

JUNIE INTERRUPTS
INVENTORY

"CYRUS!" Junie stepped down into the sunken work area of the mammoth den.

The walls were covered with trophy heads ranging upward from the tiny dik-dik to second largest water buffalo ever recorded killed by a rich man. There were around fifty head-and-shoulder mounts, four types of big game cat fully stuffed, an upright Kodiak bear and two elephant tusks crossed above the marble fireplace mantel.

Cyrus Chandler, Dick Conly and Red Kilroy were down in "the Pit," the sunken center of the huge room. They were studying the teletype lists of the unprotected players that the other franchises were tossing into the For Sale pot known as the player pool.

"Cyrus!" Junie was insistent as she handed her coat to the maid, Isabelle, who disappeared down a long hallway. "Listen to me!"

"Goddammit, Junie, what the hell do you want now?" Cyrus glared at her for a moment, but then his eyes began creeping back toward the player list.

"Wendy wasn't on her throne."

Cyrus let out a long, slow sigh. "What throne?"

"At Water Carnival on the Pi Phi float. She's president of the sorority, you know."

"I know, Junie, just like her mother before her," Cyrus said. "You two are a grand tradition. Now, what am I supposed to do about Wendy not being on her throne? Is there a usurper that I can squeeze out economically? Maybe ruin her father with incriminating financial or sexual innuendos—questions of paternity?"

"It was empty," Junie moaned. "*No one* sat on the throne. I asked some of the girls when I went over to take pictures; they hadn't seen her since Tuesday's rehearsal. She had a fight with Lem." Junie was anxious and unhappy. "I saw Lem." Now Junie's voice quivered. "They have broken their engagement. She threw that perfectly lovely five-carat diamond away."

Conly laughed and caught Red's eye; both grinned and continued to scan the lists of available players.

"It's not funny, Dick," Junie moaned. "The poor boy spent all night in the riverbottom, looking for it." Junie sighed. "Luckily he found it."

"Wait until he tries to sell it," Dick Conly said. "That'll really break his heart."

Wanda June Chandler looked around the room at all the dead animals and shuddered involuntarily. She hated the mounts; that was one reason why Cyrus filled his den with dead animals. Junie would not stay long in a room with glass-eyed and sawdust-filled carcasses. This revulsion did not carry over to the cedar closet where she kept her dozen or so fur coats. Questioned once about the contradiction, Junie didn't see any connection.

"They don't have faces on them, darlin'," Junie explained.

"I'm worried, Cyrus," Junie whined. "She's never done *any-thing* like this before."

"She does it all the time." Cyrus's eyes moved back to the Chicago list and he made a mark next to a wide receiver. "Have you forgotten the time she went to Paris on my American Express card because she got pissed off at Lem?" Cyrus looked at Conly. "She brought back that frog clothes designer. I had to throw the fag bastard out."

"As I recall"—Junie turned snotty—"Dick threw him out." She glanced at Conly, who kept his eyes on the player list, and she continued with urgency, "But that wasn't during Water Carnival." Junie's eyes welled with tears. "The president of the Pi Phi house just doesn't do that. I'm so embarrassed. I'm going to call Lem's mother and see what she knows."

"That's fine, dear." Cyrus looked over at a name that Red Kilroy had circled on the Cleveland list. "Tell her to have young Lem call me. We have business. Tell him to call anytime; we'll be up here all night. He might as well start earning a living. His father never did."

Junie nodded and disappeared down the hall to the master bedroom. Dick Conly watched her go, her forty-year-old-plus body still firm and supple. Cyrus watched Dick watch Junie. It pleased him to have things Dick Conly wanted.

Red Kilroy tapped his pencil on the name that he had circled on the Cleveland list. "This Bobby Hendrix son of a bitch is trouble, a regular clubhouse lawyer. But he can catch a football. I swear his peripheral vision is so good, he can see his goddam ears."

"Do you want him?" Conly asked.

"As a receiver, you bet, but he's a Union man, a real pain in the ass. The commissioner wants to blacklist him. He was one of the ones who threatened the antitrust suit, and now he's after Charlie Stillman."

"Can he play football?" Conly asked.

"He and Speedo Smith are about the best there are around," Red said. "But Smith's on the Blacklist too. He was Dallas's player representative. Hendrix got to him at all the Pro Bowl games, I figure. They say he was a lot of trouble."

"Do you want them?" Conly watched his head coach's eyes.

"I sure do." Red didn't pause. "Team them with Taylor Rusk in a couple years . . ." Red whistled and grinned. "These guys are player's players. They know *how* to play and win and they can teach the young guys. We could make a big move here . . . *cheap*." Red glanced at Cyrus.

"Don't worry about finance," Conly warned. "Do you want them as players?"

Red nodded, his eyes cutting from Conly to Chandler.

"Hold on, now, do we want troublemakers on our team?" Cyrus interrupted, directing the question to Conly.

"Cyrus," Dick Conly said patiently, softly, "you will cause more trouble before dawn than these two niggers will in their whole careers."

That seemed to satisfy Cyrus momentarily.

"Hendrix is a white guy," Red Kilroy said.

"They are all niggers, Red," Conly replied. "Fuck their blacklist, we'll get them both."

"It'll make Cleveland and Dallas mad," Cyrus warned.

"I'll worry about Dallas," Dick Conly said. "Nobody worries about Cleveland."

PRACTICE

"My first couple of years at the University, I used to schedule my classes two hours apart. Then I could walk back to my apartment and be alone for at least one hour." Taylor watched Wendy Chandler's face. They were back inside; the fire had knocked the chill out of the rock house. "I was in culture shock, but I knew I'd make it."

"What made you so sure?" she asked.

"No choice," Taylor said. "I'm an athlete."

"And you can't fail?" Wendy was not being inquisitive.

"No." Taylor tossed a chunk of mesquite on the fire. "Failure is inevitable, but an athlete can't quit."

"Can't? Or won't?"

"The difference is academic. The General Rule of Life says anyone can get whatever he wants out of life if he is willing to work unceasingly with discipline and dedication. If he refuses to accept defeat, he will achieve his goal."

"Sounds frighteningly familiar," Wendy said. "Very American. It certainly supports the Protestant work ethic. Dreadfully middle-class."

"It is." Taylor nodded. "More dreadful for those of us in the lower classes. What's worse is The Specific Rule of Life."

The mesquite chunks began to pop and burn in blues and greens, he stared at the fire.

"Well?" Wendy was impatient. "What's the Specific Rule say?"

"That . . ." Taylor nodded; his face vacant, enchanted by the varieties of color that consumed the mesquite. "Everybody is an exception to the General Rule."

"That's it?" Wendy was slightly astonished. "That's all? But you said . . ."

"That I *knew* I would make it at the University," Taylor interrupted, "because I was an athlete."

"Yeah." Wendy's sarcasm changed to confusion. "I believe this is an exercise in sophistry."

"Everything is an exercise in something. Just don't quit," Taylor said. "But I should point out that I *did* make it . . . just like I *knew* I would."

"Because you're an athlete." Scorn tinged Wendy's voice.

"I'm a poor white agnostic American post-industrial border warrior . . . just waiting on the broadsword and family crest. I am an athlete, I do not *quit*, that's all I know. Everything else I work out daily."

"I'm glad you told me."

"You *should know* before we get too deeply involved." Taylor's voice was soft, strangely distant. He kept his eyes on the blue-green flames and the mesquite, and he spoke as if by rote. "My life is intense, boring, violent, temperate, creative, destructive, vital and irrelevant . . . and I am indestructible, frail, competitive, cooperative, selfish and generous." Taylor paused for breath and Wendy's comments, but she only stared at him silently, her face enigmatic.

"My fate is determined by meticulous planning and heedless happenstance," he went on, "ingenious strategies and wild swings of the pendulum. I flip for both sides of the coin and get the edge."

The mesquite popped and snapped, crumbling to glowing coals. Taylor was rambling, entranced.

"Every day I confront unlimited contradictions with limited skills. I *must* succeed, though failure is inevitable. I keep on, each day expecting victory in the face of insurmountable problems, ever-increasing humiliations. I accept pain, fear, defeat as due. I do not expect any luck but bad and know that if gods or spirits exist, they are arrayed against me. But each time I'm beaten down I get up and start over, reinforced only by my ignorance."

Wendy was stunned by his passionate words, spoken in a passionless monotone like a pubescent Boy Scout reciting the Gettysburg Address.

"I refuse to quit the hopeless battle against chaos and darkness. My commitment is to life and man's place in an endless war with death. I never quit and will die hard."

He looked up from the fire and saw her watching him. His face was drawn but calm, his eyes black.

"I'm an athlete." He spoke with the resignation of a man facing the gallows. "It's my curse, my hope, my dream, my nightmare . . . my *excuse*."

His eyes, black holes in his face, radiated intensity from a spectrum beyond the visible. Wendy could feel his energy converging on her, exhilarating, electrifying, galvanizing, full of life and power. Terrifying.

"I thought you should know," Taylor said, "I'm just waiting for my broadsword."

"Thanks." Wendy's voice was weak, cracked, dry.

"I'll tell you one thing." Taylor watched her profile against the stone. "If that sword does show up? I don't have a thing to wear with it. The damn cleaners lost my chain mail."

Wendy laughed with relief and a new humor. "My poor little warrior. You have to dress impeccably to wear a broadsword. Slacks and a sweater won't do."

Taylor watched the changing shadows and angles of firelight on her face. She continually looked different and the same. It wasn't the fire. It was her.

"You know," Taylor began suddenly out of the quiet crackling of the oak and mesquite, "they have this show on television for old people. They give great advice for football players. I watch it a lot. The other night the subject was learning to cope with the death of your mate."

Wendy saw the sadness pass from eye to eye, then a smile turned up his mouth and Taylor laughed.

"It was too insane." He kept up the slight laugh. "They had an expert guest, of course, and the expert told everybody to take time now while your mate is still alive and *practice living alone*. Sort of make a game of it, he advised; every time one leaves the house, the other pretends they are dead."

"Nawww." Wendy began to laugh, "That's a lie...they wouldn't...."

"I swear, the expert said it. *Practice living alone*. The guy was an expert, this was television...Think about it....It makes sense."

"Maybe too much sense."

"Want me to close my eyes and hold my breath? Let you get the feel?"

"No!" Wendy was suddenly angry and hurt and frightened.

"Good. 'Cause the expert is wrong," Taylor said. "I've been practicing living alone almost ten years. It does not get easier. All I get is increasingly numb."

SCORPIONS

THAP!

It sounded to Taylor like exactly what it was: a scorpion falling off the ceiling and hitting the pillow next to his head. It brought him out of a sound sleep and off the bed in one quick movement. It wasn't until he got the light on and saw the scorpion scampering off the pillow under the covers that Taylor was certain he had not dreamt the sound.

Thap! He had heard it a lot when he was a kid.

Taylor killed the scorpion with his shoe, put it in the ashtray and slept the rest of the night on his side.

He dreamt first about the time his brother Billy was stung by a scorpion. Billy was allergic and the flowers were blooming. He slept on his back with his mouth open ... wheezing ... snuffling ... gasping for air.

Thap!

Right off the ceiling into Billy's mouth, the scorpion stung about ten times before Billy got it spit out. Billy was in a lot of pain for a long time with his tongue torn up and throat swollen almost shut. He almost died. Poor Billy. Taylor dreamt about his little brother. In the dream he cried about Billy's pain. He hadn't in life.

Thap!

Another scorpion fell, but this one hit at the foot of the bed and crawled off onto the floor, skittering across the rock and into a crevice in the wall. A big scorpion, a couple of inches long. Taylor barely noticed it.

He was starting a dream about Wendy Cy Chandler.

In the other bedroom Wendy wrote in her diary long after Taylor had killed the first scorpion and gone back to sleep.

It's like he expects me to like him, she wrote.

He's not romantic at all . . . he just stands there and expects you to like him and do anything he says . . . not that he has any ideas about what to do. If you don't like it, then it is not simply a matter of taste but evidence that you have a flaw. He is so rough and smells of sweat. His hair is dirty and unkempt . . . fingernails are broken and dirty. It would take a lot of work to carry on a relationship. I would have to keep him up, like the yard.

Wendy stopped writing, laughed quietly, then began writing again.

He would be like a favorite dog that was always around, with all the problems attendant to owning a long-haired showdog. If you left it up to him, you never get to the show. He says he is an athlete and that is all. I wonder what my father thinks of him.

She would soon find out.

Taylor would have enjoyed reading the entry. It showed that Wendy understood what he was doing a hell of a lot better than he did, and she put a better gloss on it. Almost made it seem honest and real.

Wendy wrote about Taylor until late that night. She also wrote about herself. Once she thought she heard Taylor at her bedroom door, which she kept open to the fire. He wasn't there.

"My problem is I'm out of sequence," he had told her earlier. "I learn the wrong things first. I have my illusions destroyed before they get created. It is less painful but confusing, because everything *isn't* an illusion or a metaphor; some things *are* real. Apparently I don't get *to be anything* when I grow up, since we are dragged through life by our illusions, and I won't have any left by the time I'm thirty. Lately I have been basically motivated by the constant urge to lie down. I would like to perfect the *nap*."

Wendy fell asleep trying to imagine the perfect nap.

Thap!

Another scorpion woke Taylor at six A.M., and after beating it to death with his shoe, he dressed and found Wendy in the kitchen. She was sitting at the table, her face freshly washed in cold water, her hair pulled back severely and pinned. Wearing a loose-fitting chamois cloth shirt, jeans and boots, she was staring into her teacup.

"Morning." Taylor stepped to the doorway and gripped the rough wood lintel. Wendy looked up to see him hanging in the doorway like an orangutan, dumbly concentrating on releasing tension from his spine.

"Do you want coffee? Tea?" Wendy looked into the living room at the glowing coals and fresh wood of the morning fire. "Or should I just check you for nits and lice?"

"Coffee first." Taylor swung from the crosspiece. "Then the complete grooming ritual."

Letting go of the door frame, Taylor touched his toes and began his stretching exercises.

"I was just sitting here, thinking about my father." Wendy filled the percolator with coffee and water from the hand pump. "We are *both* his property, the way he sees it. You know what I mean? He looks at me like I'm the Thanksgiving turkey. I think he still believes in feudalism and marriages of state."

Taylor was doing other stretching exercises as he listened; Wendy watched the coffee pot on the white Kelvinator and talked about her life.

Taylor's neck was sore. The falling scorpions had added tension to his degenerating cervical vertebrae. He had cracked two in high school, but the coach had pronounced the injury "a stiff neck" and Taylor played the following week in a cervical collar. He threw for two TD's and ran sixty yards for one. He had no conscious memory of the game or injury. He just knew his neck hurt.

"I met Three because his daddy and Cyrus did business in an oil field named after my mother. Can you imagine?" She frowned. "Is this a boring story?"

"Hardly." Taylor rolled his head on his shoulders. "It's giving me a stiff neck. You gonna marry him?"

"Nope. I'm running off with the circus to be a bareback rider." Wendy glanced at him, her eyes downcast, strangely shy. "I appreciate that you didn't hit on me last night."

"I figure everybody else must. I wanted to...but last night was for creating illusions before I destroy them, contrary to my usual order and style of life. Besides, the scorpions held me prisoner until daylight."

Wendy laughed, showing her teeth: even, white, delicate, almost translucent.

"All night I kept waiting for you to creep into my room with some lame line." She covered her mouth with slender fingers.

"I was waiting in my room for you to rescue me," Taylor said. "A metaphysical standoff."

"Were you scared? Because I was Cyrus Chandler's daughter?"

"I was scared of the nickel-plated thirty-eight. I have a fear of technology."

Wendy led him out into the cool morning air toward the oak motte and blue Cadillac.

They sat on the hood of Terry Dudley's demonstrator, listened to the birds and watched the sky turn pink. The clouds, dark dirty wads of cotton, bleached whiter as the sky turned from pink to brilliant red. The ridgeline etched clearly against the sky. The hollows and canyon were growing out of darkness into dark green shadows. The creek bubbled, still in the dark.

They kissed when the sun crawled into view.

"Is our romance against the clock with an absolute end?" Wendy asked, "Or is it based on ever-increasing, expanding loving of one another?"

Taylor's eyes widened in a confused, pleasant surprise. "Choice? You want me to decide?"

Wendy nodded. "It seems pretty life-enhancing to me; love according to your athletic ideal. Dedication...desire... commitment...technique, execution, strategy, tactics, style. They're all part of loving someone."

"Don't forget practice. Hours of practice. I'll go first." He moved massively, swiftly. Taylor gripped her shoulders, pulling her to him and she was suddenly aware of his pure physical presence, the grace of motion, the enormous size and inordinate animal elegance of his body. A thoroughbred smelling of sweat, slightly crazed, high-blooded, powerful and erotic.

Thrilled, eager, terrified, Wendy grabbed his thick hair and drew his lips to her mouth. She kissed hard; he slipped his arm across her back and gripped her right thigh gently. His hand encircled her slim leg. He lifted her. She pressed her soft, pliant, moist lips against his chapped flesh. She was soft, gentle, and smelled of crushed rose petals. His lip bled as she mashed her mouth against his.

"This morning your eyes are the most exquisite green I have ever seen," he said, cradling her face with his hand. "Can you change eye colors?" She leaned away slightly and studied his expression.

"In time," she said warily, "I will let you see more." Closing her eyes, parting her lips, Wendy Chandler kissed him again, long and deep, with much urgency and a confused, lingering fear.

Taylor Rusk found choice wrenched from his soul.

SECURITY

CYRUS Chandler had several phone lines in the Pit of his den. The room showed the signs of the hectic work done the past days, building the Franchise. Cyrus, Dick Conly and Red Kilroy seldom left the Pit during days of negotiations, five-way conference calls and secret deals. The Franchise purchased most of the players they wanted from the player pool; the worn-out, used-up, cast-off human capital of the League. Fifty players, for approximately $750,000 apiece, totaling the $38 million price for the Franchise.

By the end of Water Carnival, Wendy Chandler and Taylor Rusk were conspicuously missing. Junie, Lem Three and Lem's mother, Pearl Mae Carleton, connected them, and Junie told Cyrus.

Cyrus called security.

Taylor and Wendy were sitting outside the stone house on the Cadillac's hood when a white four-door Ford with a whip antenna drove up. There were two men in the front seat in narrow-brim cowboy hats and gray Western suits.

The window on the right side hummed down.

"Everything all right, Miss Chandler?" Bob Travers, the passenger, asked. The driver looked Taylor over.

"Everything is perfect, Bob."

"Toby and I'll be around," Bob nodded.

"Fine. Tell Momma not to worry," Wendy replied.

"Wilco." Bob rolled up the window. The white Ford drove back across Dead Man Creek, up Coon Ridge, and disappeared over the top, leaving a billowing white cloud trail of caliche dust.

"Who is Bob?" Taylor watched the car disappear.

"Security." Wendy's face hardened, tiny lines eroding the brightness from her eyes.

"Who is Toby?"

"Security."

"Whose security?"

"Not yours."

"I would just like to own a new Ford," Taylor finally said.

"I'm sure my daddy will help you get one." Wendy tossed the dregs from her coffee cup into the small patch of prickly pear and walked into the stone house through the kitchen door.

"Anything I can do? You seem upset."

"Choose." She took his hand and pulled him toward the bed. "You can choose."

They made love slowly, searching each other out in soft, tender places, taking a long time. Wendy felt so small beneath him as she shuddered and heaved.

"Please" she began to cry, her tears mingling with his sweat. "Please." Wendy convulsed and thrashed, clawing his shoulders. "Please . . . choose me."

PANTHER HOLE

AT the east edge of Coon Ridge the land falls away to the north and the creek makes a turn following the slope of the ground. In flood this sudden turn becomes a churning, boiling, grinding whirlpool. The violent currents, eddies and torrents have, over the last several thousand years, carved out a deep hole in the limestone canyon wall and riverbed. The much harder granite outcrops form a perfect swimming hole about twenty feet deep. Above are boulders, good places to sunbathe and dive into the cold clear water.

Taylor and Wendy spent the last afternoon at the swimming hole, doing both and watching the bass swim around the rocks.

Panther Hole was deep blue compared to the shallower water running along most of the creek. It was called Panther Hole because the old rancher who sold the place to Doc Webster swore he saw a jaguar there on Easter 1902. He called it "a Meskin panther."

Wendy and Taylor were stretched out on an oblong granite chunk stuck out over the water when Doc Webster appeared on the opposite bank. At his side was a short, dark, kinky-haired young man.

"People are laying bets all over campus on where you are and if you're together. I'm right proud that you chose my scrabbly ranch to consummate this notorious liaison. The Franchise and the daughter—it has the sound of a stage play. A hill-country drama. This is Tommy McNamara." Doc Webster ruffled his hand through the dark, curly hair. "Tommy is a soon-to-be-famous Texas author financing his first novel by doing a government study of the effects of sleep deprivation on chickens."

Wendy and Taylor turned over on the rock, watching the two wretched men on the far bank. The dark young man with the tight curly hair kept hopping from foot to foot like the ground was hot; then he would shiver all over. Doc Webster drank from a bottle of vodka and handed it to his friend, who gulped it down like water. They hadn't slept in days.

"Oh, Doctor," Taylor said, "please tell us how Tommy deprives those government chickens of their sleep. Wendy and I really really want to know."

Wendy elbowed him in the ribs. "Don't encourage them."

"At first I yelled at the chickens a lot," Tommy said, "but they took it personal, so now it's rock 'n' roll music twenty-four hours a day." Doc took the bottle. Tommy stumbled backward, then caught his balance and continued. "Plus all the amphetamines in the chicken feed. Keep a bunch of chickens awake three, four days on speed and rock 'n' roll and you will really see them pushing back the frontiers of science."

"The guy has got values," Wendy said to Taylor.

"I *knew* you two would be here," Doc yelled across the water. "When I saw those two empty seats! The vacant throne, the absent

Spur. I knew you came out to my ranch and fell to fucking just past the first cattle guard."

Wendy sighed, laying her head on her arms, while Taylor watched the crazed men.

"A very fecund point, Doctor." Tommy munched his chicken feed and looked across Panther Hole at Wendy and Taylor. His thick glasses only discerned two separate blurs; his goggle eyes rolled wildly in his head. "Our quest required both of us to unlawfully consume great quantities of the US government's chicken feed, and to cover our tracks, I'm stepping on the rest with cracked corn. I hate to do it, but the government don't let people steal chicken feed. Money? murder? okay, but any chicken feed gone and they'll get your ass."

"Tommy used to edit *The Iconoclast*," Doc boasted.

"*The Iconoclast*?" Wendy asked. "You were against a lot of stuff, weren't you?"

"Goddammit, you name it, this boy is against it." Doc drunkenly bent and hugged the small, dark, kinky-headed boy around the neck. "This is the Kinky-Headed Boy. As my only other client, he's going to do great things." The professor pointed a rolled-up paper at Wendy. "I have her father's absolute final offer for you."

"Fine, Doc," Taylor said, "I'll look it over later. I just want my fair advantage. Six hundred thousand dollars a year in cash."

The two men stumbled up the path toward the stone house, passing the vodka bottle, munching the government's chicken feed and singing:

> *If only John Lennon had packed a .44*
> *The eighties would not have become such a bore . . .*

Wendy and Taylor stretched out on the towel on the hot granite and let the sun bake them. They could hear Doc Webster and Tommy McNamara after they went inside the house.

"Doc is your lawyer?"

"Uh-huh. That's your father's sixth absolute final offer he's got."

"Is Doc any good?"

"Who knows? He's a lawyer who can still feel shame; that's something."

"I'll bet the Kinky-Headed Boy doesn't live long enough to do great things," Wendy said.

"He's already lived long enough," Taylor said. "I just wonder what he thinks is a great thing? A rooster that crows for Yellow Sun Records?"

"Is six hundred thousand dollars a great thing?" Wendy asked.

"Six hundred thousand dollars is just a price tag. You're a great thing." Taylor pulled Wendy to him. She curled up against his hot chest. He kissed her, liking the taste and feel of her sweat. She placed her fingers behind his neck as Taylor pulled back to gaze at her fine-boned, sun-reddened face.

"I haven't let you see me at top form yet. Maybe someday . . ." Wendy rolled over on her stomach.

Taylor began to massage her neck and shoulders and trace the fine line of tiny blond hairs that followed her spine.

"Maybe . . . soon . . ." she murmured drowsily. "I'll let my angels go dancing with your demons . . . Then we'll see if you know a great thing when you see it. We may have a major love affair. *If* you have the nerves to make the just and courageous choice."

THE WATER
CARNIVAL BURGLAR

A. D. Koster spent Water Carnival burglarizing sorority and fraternity houses to come up with the money he owed the Cobianco brothers. He got the money, but it took all four nights and by then he was The Water Carnival Burglar, being hunted by the law and "crimestoppers" on the TV news.

The last night, armed frat rats lay in ambush. Two drunken Phi Delts were shot and wounded by a squad of Sigma Chi vigilantes.

Meanwhile, with Suzy Ballard driving, A.D. hit the black and Jewish fraternity houses. The pickings were slimmer but much safer. A.D. knew about people; that was his strength. He just didn't know about himself; that made him weak and dangerous.

Taylor thought A.D. was The Water Carnival Burglar. Since coming home on Simon's wedding day with a black eye and stitches in his lip, A.D. had been desperate for money. After Water Carnival he never asked Taylor for money again. Taylor assumed it was for the Cobianco brothers. He never asked. A.D. never volunteered.

After Water Carnival nothing was ever the same.

The Sigma Nus dyed the river purple, killing all the fish and amphibians for three miles downstream.

CYRUS MEETS
THE CORN PICKER

AT sun-up the clattering, backfiring rattle of Doc's old pickup driving round and round in circles in the rocky side yard woke Taylor.

Wendy Chandler was gone and he was in bed alone.

"Goddam, Doc," Taylor grumbled to himself sitting up. "What the fuck are you doing out there?"

"Nothing," came Doc's voice from the living room. "I'm in here, looking at your contract. That's Tommy getting ready to go in and cover a symposium on 'The Electronic Revolution in Mass Media and Its Effect on Relations Between Business and Government.' It's being held at the University School of Economic Communications."

"Why go?" Taylor fell back in the old bed. It seemed too large without Wendy. Taylor ran his hand across the place she had slept.

"He has to do a story for the paper about it," Doc answered from the next room.

"I mean, why go after hearing the title?" Taylor lay on Wendy's pillow and found the scent of her hair. "What's left to say?"

"Plenty. Your friend, Terry Dudley, fellow Spur and lawyer-jock, is a speaker on the effects of the revolution on professional athletes and their unions. Terry Dudley is a brilliant young man," Doc continued, "and will go a long way. He has a great future ahead of him."

"He's studying to be a talking head." Taylor ran his cheek along the pillowcase, then buried his face in the pillow, searching for a further sense of her presence.

"He is definitely more of a team player than you."

"He was in a team sport." Taylor lifted his head and spoke sourly. "I'm a command officer fighting limited war."

"Well, my little containment fascist, you may do well in the future. Much better if we get this first contact right."

From outside came a peculiarly frightening screech as Tommy McNamara banged the truck into the stone wall near the bed.

"What the fuck . . . ?" Taylor jumped. "He's mashing cats against the house."

"Just getting up momentum," Doc said. "He doesn't *want* to go, but he's like the rest of us, always doing things for the money."

"I thought he lived on chicken feed."

"That's what you'll be working for if you don't get up and out here," Doc snapped. "We have a Standard Player's Contract to negotiate. Oh, yeah, Neely Johnson from Chandler Communications will be at the symposium today, talking about advocacy advertising as an alternative to handing the money directly to senators, regulatory-board members, congressmen and presidents."

"Who's representing the masses at this mass communications thing?" Taylor stretched and yawned.

"You have a degree in communications and graduated with honors. How about you?"

"I just learned it, Doc, I never said I believed it. Besides, they change the rules so fast, I couldn't keep up if I wanted." Taylor swung his legs off the bed and sat up. "Now what is all this shit about my contract and Terry Dudley's future?"

Doc, his back to Taylor as Taylor walked into the living room, was reading the papers spread out in front of him. A Standard Player's Contract.

"I'm leaving Tommy the ranch. He'll do great work here." Doc leaned back, away from the papers, and stared sightlessly at the wall.

Taylor didn't speak, listening instead to the distant commotion as the Kinky-Headed Boy's truck roared up behind Coon Ridge and away, finally leaving the ranch in silence.

"Yessir." Doc leaned back. "Tommy will do fine here. You, on the other hand . . ." Doc's voice trailed off as his interest was drawn to a particular clause in the contract in front of him.

Taylor rebuilt the fire, uncovering the coals, still glowing hot remnants of the light that had played across Wendy Chandler's face. The new flames grew as Taylor stripped cedar bark and piled on oak chips. He stared into the fire. *Choose me . . . Choose me.* Did he and Wendy have a relationship? Did she want one? Did he? Were they as connected as last night's fire to this morning's, a common glow that could grow quickly into flames? And if they were, could she stand the heat? The pain? Or had it been just one fire from the start to be purposely doused, drowned, scattered— once the flames had driven away the chill from the soul, a momentary warmth of heart to replace the five-carat fire she had tossed into the tules.

"Wood shavings take a long time," Taylor said aloud, stepping away from the increasing heat of the fire. "I wonder if she knows or cares."

"The future, Taylor. It's your decision, and it's all the time you have left." Doc said, "Wendy may not understand how fast your future arrived."

"Is that why you're comparing it with Terry Dudley's?"

"No. Lem Carleton III's." Doc eyed Taylor. "Shouldn't forget the future of a man you just put horns on."

"You don't know that."

"I took a calculated guess. I also compared your future with the rest of this year's batch." Doc added, "Just 'cause Wendy's at the track . . ."

"Batch of what?"

"Why, Spur, Taylor. Spur." Doc was amused and stroked his chin slyly. "How do you think you were chosen? By all the paper you so deftly chased? The NCAA records? Your Heisman Trophy?"

"Well . . . fuck, I don't know . . . I figure they didn't hurt." Taylor was puzzled.

"They didn't. They helped quite a bit; in fact, they got the attention of the folks who count, but in your case that was the dilemma. As the people who counted watched you closer and closer, they noticed that you had acquaintances but, other than A. D. Koster and Simon D'Hanis, you had few friends. Were you a team player? No. You had the stats. You were the perfect paper man with the grade-point average and the passing percentage to prove it. All you lacked was *one friend* among the people who counted. You appeared to have no systems potential, no networking abilities."

"Well, I didn't know anything about that shit." Taylor was irritated. "I didn't have time to go around kissing asses to join a group I never heard of. . . . I don't join groups. I didn't give a shit if I got in Spur. I still don't."

"Wasn't that how you met Wendy Chandler?" Doc asked. "Wasn't it worth meeting her?"

"I met her before. She was in Simon D'Hanis and Buffy Martin's wedding party. The two of us *were* it."

"Oh, so Spur made no difference to Wendy?"

"Don't you remember, Doc? I called you about missing that Civil War test and..." Taylor stopped as he stumbled across a thought. "Jealous, Doc? Are you jealous of me and Wendy? I never thought..."

Doc Webster burst out laughing.

"No...no...hardly that. I couldn't be happier for the both of you. I just thought Spur played a bigger part in your relationship."

"It played a part. I wouldn't have gone to Water Carnival rehearsal, watched her throw Lem Three's diamond into the river-bottom. Spur played a part."

"Good." Doc smiled and picked up another page of the contract. "Maybe a bigger part in *her* case than in yours. I'd hate to think I wasted my efforts."

"What efforts?" Taylor was bewildered.

Doc smiled; his eyes twinkled. "Among the people who counted, no one else knew you more than casually. I was your only friend."

"You're in Spur?" Taylor looked at the history professor with renewed amazement.

"The class of '39." Doc nodded. "Some real scumbags in that one. Cyrus Chandler, Harrison H. Harrison, Senator Thompson. Our gang of war profiteers. During the selections I spoke up for you. It was lies, all lies, but you're in now and they can't put you out."

"How did Terry Dudley get chosen? He's five years out of school."

"Special case; he had a lot of juice." Doc dropped the contract and looked at Taylor. "In 1940 I went on to law school and got my degree, only to realize *if* I expected to get rich, I would spend my life around lawyers, judges, politicians and criminals." Doc sighed slowly. "So I joined the Army, the Texas thirty-sixth. After the war I gave up on being rich, relearned history and became a teacher. I have never regretted the decision. I have my tenure and a vast store of inside information that makes me almost invulnerable and quite possibly dangerous. Most of the time I just lay around, but every now and then I piss in the soup."

"Like getting me into Spur?"

Doc nodded. "And this contract."

"What about it?" Taylor tossed a log on the new fire. "It's the standard contract; every player in the League has to sign one."

"Well, if Jefferson Davis had signed his niggers to the Standard Player's Contract, we might have avoided the Civil War. You can be the line command officer for this franchise, but unless you look forward to a life of involuntary servitude, I better handle this contract and all your financial affairs," Doc said. "It will allow me to piss in the soup more frequently, which will make me happy, can make you rich and will quite possibly improve the taste of the soup."

The two men worked on the contract for five days before Doc went into town for the first negotiating session with Cyrus Chandler.

It was the only contract Cyrus negotiated, and Doc ran him through the corn picker.

Doc's first demand was a "golden handshake" clause worth one million dollars. Cyrus agreed finally, then began his spiel about the advantages of deferred payments. Doc stopped him with a demand for six-month money-market interest on anything deferred and the use of the money to deal margins in the commodities market.

They finally agreed on a two-year contract at $600,000 per season with an additional signing bonus of $400,000, of which $300,000 was deferred. Using the deferred money as collateral, Doc optioned 200,000 bushels of wheat for three dollars a bushel. An ex-student who was in the State Department had leaked him the word on a Russian wheat deal. After the Russian wheat deal was announced, Doc sold at six dollars a bushel.

After that, Doc went into silver at five dollars an ounce, again paying the minimal five percent margin on futures contracts. He contracted one hundred thousand ounces, which he continued to roll over until he sold at $18.80 an ounce. Adding the silver and the wheat profits, the quarterback's total was over $2,000,000, which Doc locked into five-year government securities at eighteen percent. During the intervening years Doc seldom mentioned financial transactions to Taylor Rusk.

On the other hand, he mentioned them to Dick Conly and Cyrus Chandler at every opportunity.

Conly just gritted his teeth and tried not to look as foolish as he felt for allowing Cyrus to handle Taylor's first contract. Dick Conly knew that a good negotiator should bury a player on the first contract with deferred money, incentive and performance bonuses, houses, cars and insurance policies, all combined to keep the base salary low. Keeping the base low made future raises insignificant.

Cyrus Chandler was angry because he looked foolish. He would have been furious had he known that no one was surprised.

When Cyrus Chandler was initiated into Spur in 1939, Doc Webster nicknamed Cyrus The Cockroach. "It ain't what he eats or hauls off but what he falls in and messes up." The same personal qualities that earned Cyrus the nickname before the Big War continued unabated throughout his life. It was why Amos Chandler had left Chandler Industries in Dick Conly's hands.

Cyrus "The Cockroach" Chandler had signed Taylor Rusk to the largest *real money* contract in League history and lost his first and best chance to rob the quarterback with a fountain pen.

Pissing in the soup.

PLAYING WITH PAIN

USING the $10,000 paid by the Bowl committee for keeping his hamstring pull a rumor, Taylor bought a "previously owned" yellow Lincoln four-door. He drove the huge car to the Pi Phi House, stopped by unannounced and picked up Wendy. She was irritated and pleased simultaneously.

They drove slowly through the campus; it was late and the traffic had eased. They passed the Union building, an eclectic creation of exotic granite quarried near Enchanted Rock. It was a beautiful setting with a boulevard flanking a long row of oak trees that were once part of an exceptionally large motte called Shelter Oaks. The original motte had been used as a refuge by the Indians because its gigantic size offered protection. The ancient oaks formed a perfect canopy. No Comanche would fight in the Shelter Oaks for fear his spirit would be lost.

Wendy turned and watched the huge, wide, gnarled live oaks, the massive, drooping, twisting, arching limbs. During her college years Wendy came to know each tree intimately. There weren't many left between the bulldozers and Oak Decline.

"I spent hours lying around those trees," Wendy said. "They're like old friends."

Taylor let the Lincoln idle along; he rolled down all the electric windows. Air rushed in with heavy, damp force.

"Smell." Wendy inhaled deeply. Her tiny nostrils flared and her soft pale eyes sparkled as the air rushed into her lungs. Her cheeks flushed. "Don't you just get high on the air?"

Taylor flared his nose and tensed his neck to inhale, but his displaced septum caused whistling noises. Wendy laughed at him.

"Shouldn't laugh at another's misfortune."

"It's the price you pay for the privilege you earn," Wendy mocked. "Which in your case is a distinctive profile."

She gazed at the live oaks, passing slowly, shimmering, a defiant green.

"Okay, tell me . . . what did you guys do at the Shelter Oaks the night of the Spur initiation?"

"I didn't do anything. Lem took off his pants and they all made fun of his dick. . . ."

"Stop!" She slugged his arm.

"That was about it." Taylor watched as the last oak passed and they left the Union and the boulevards.

"It's a beautiful place." Taylor watched the strange purple granite building and the surviving oaks in the mirror. He pictured the young beautiful girl next to him on the grass with her girl friends.

The front wheel of the Lincoln hit the curb.

"Ooops." He began paying closer attention. The driving angle began to get steep; he planned to cross the river on the low-water bridge. Taylor pointed up to the footbridge. "Simon D'Hanis threw an ROTC student commander from up there for demanding a salute."

"Oh, my God." Wendy held both her hands to her mouth. "Was he trying to kill him?"

"I got that impression at the time. The river is rock bottom and four inches deep everywhere else, and this lucky SOB, falling backward with no idea where he was going, hits in the *one hole* that was about six feet across and six feet deep. He screamed a long time, I remember that." They bumped over the low-water bridge through the Canyon Cut.

The Canyon Cut was a popular place on campus. Students sat around on blankets; the smell of tobacco and marijuana filled the canyon. There was laughter and movement up and down river. Radios played rock 'n' roll, country, Chicano and Tex-Mex. The road and bridge were built so the campus police could patrol from squad cars.

Suddenly a Grapette bottle careened off the hood of the Lincoln. Taylor quickly put up the windows and accelerated across the bridge and up the hill.

"That was a Grapette bottle," Wendy said. "Wasn't it a Grapette bottle that hit you in the face after the Bowl Game?"

"It was." Taylor grimaced. "By God, I think you're on to something."

"No. I'm serious . . ."

"Well"—Taylor accelerated to the ridgeline—"the guy with the Grapette bottle is serious too. He's stalking me across the country."

Taylor took her to the stadium. The night watchman let him drive right out onto the middle of the field. Taylor had a blanket and a picnic basket in the trunk.

"Now, it's from out here that I do my serious work."

Taylor sat on the blanket, leaned against the side of the car. The hot catalytic converter was melting the artificial turf; the smell was nauseating and most likely toxic.

"Let's walk the field." Taylor held out his hand and helped Wendy to her feet. "The moon has risen over the press box."

"You say such romantic things." Wendy pulled loose and began to run down the sideline. The moon provided enough light, and Taylor watched her move like a wisp of smoke. She waited for him on the five.

Taylor crossed into the end zone, following Wendy. She reached the goalposts and swung around one white upright with both hands laced together. Her cotton dress clung against her as she swung.

Taylor watched her swing, feet planted on either side of the pole, leaning away, holding with both hands, her head thrown back, hair waving down, her blue and white cotton dress pressed against the delicate form of her body. The slim legs and hips, small well-formed breasts against the cotton. The looseness of her dress swinging with her motion. She moved like a butterfly.

"My God, you are a beautiful woman."

Wendy flowed around the goal. "Do you really think I'm beautiful?"

"Increasingly beautiful every moment."

"Do you love me?"

"Do you love me?"

"I asked first."

"Does what is happening anyplace but right here really matter?" She stopped swaying and looked at him. He began to shiver like he was cold. Wendy could look deep into him when she decided to take the chance and reach for the center, probing for soft, empty places. She found them quickly.

Wendy moistened her lips. She knelt down and ran her hands across the bristled artificial turf.

"Maybe you better go get that blanket." She began to unbutton the front of the simple cotton dress. "Hurry now. We'll see if we can make the Polyturf move."

The walk from the end zone to the car at midfield and back, in the bright moonlight, in the empty stadium, was the most memorable yardage Taylor Rusk ever covered.

"Why the end zone?" Taylor pulled off his boots and socks.

"It seems like the best choice. It'll be something to compare with other experiences you've had or will have in the end zone."

"Sort of a baseline?"

"Gives us both a common denominator. We got some heavy decision-making to do, so we had best get to work on our data base." Wendy unbuttoned his shirt and pulled it off. She was always surprised by the size of his powerful upper body. "We should both pay close attention to any transferable type of behavior. Or is there no comparison?"

"There is only one way to find out," Taylor pulled her to him, dragging her slender soft ankle across the Polyturf, causing a small burn. "First we choose up sides."

"Choose me," Wendy said again. "Choose me."

They gripped and stroked each other, his big hands covering her small smooth body. They kissed and she pressed herself against his naked chest, ignoring the sting of her ankle. She played with pain. It was the big leagues.

"There is a certain enchantment about the stadium," she said later. They were both covered with sweat. "All those dark empty seats."

"Fill them full of screaming people and you really focus the mind."

A slight breeze blew the length of the field, down one tunnel and up and out the other.

"This is the end zone, huh?" Wendy sat up and looked around. "I'm going to try harder to learn about football."

"It takes a long time to learn your way around a football field. A long time."

"That's why I'm here."

THE DEMOCRATIC SPIRIT

CYRUS wanted a contest run on television to choose the new Franchise name.

"I want something subtle but Texan," Cyrus told Conly, who had suggested "The Texas Pistols." "Not something as obvious as The Texas Pistols, for Chrissake, Dick. Where's all that goddam imagination you're supposed to have? We'll let the fans decide. We'll do a promotion tie-in with all sorts of consumer products."

"By vote," Conly said. "The American way."

"We'll let them pick the *colors* too." Cyrus snapped a look at his sardonic CEO. "Purple and white. Great choice, Dick."

They, too, had been Conly's suggestion.

The *Name the New Franchise* and *Pick Your Favorite Team's Colors* contests ran simultaneously. Over a hundred thousand entries were recorded. The decision was strictly a democratic one: the most votes for the name and the most votes for the colors.

The new Texas Pistols would wear white at home and purple on the road.

When he heard the fans' choices, Cyrus Chandler stayed visibly angry for two weeks and fired his accounting firm.

THE SIGNING

"EXCUSE Taylor and me, will you, fellows?" Cyrus Chandler steered a course through the assembled press and club and league officials. The TV lights were still on; cameras rolled and shutters clicked. Taylor Rusk had just signed his $1.6 million two-year contract with the Franchise.

At the edge of the crowd was Simon D'Hanis. Cyrus had requested he attend Taylor's signing ceremony. Simon had signed two days earlier. Cyrus signaled for the lineman to follow him and Taylor away from the press and into his office. Dick Conly, Lem Three and Richie Dixon stayed outside and got drunk with the press. It was Lem and Richie's job; Dick Conly did it for the hell of it.

Taylor sat on the couch as Simon shut the door.

"Happy with your contract?" the owner asked his big lineman.

"Yeah," Simon nodded.

"We didn't have much left when Doc Webster, Taylor's agent, finished with us," Cyrus said coldly. "You should have gotten a better deal."

The implication was clear: Cyrus Chandler hoped to confuse Simon—embarrass him—and teach Taylor Rusk a lesson.

"Did you read it?" Cyrus's eyes glittered with cruel expectation.

"Not all of it, but Charles Stillman explained it to me." Simon smiled. "It's a fair three-year contract. I'm grateful."

"We didn't come here to talk contracts," Taylor interrupted, sensing Cyrus's intent.

Cyrus Chandler sat behind his desk and leaned back. He glanced at Taylor, then focused on Simon D'Hanis. "You *got* yours, Taylor, but Simon..."

"Simon," Taylor argued, "don't you see what he is doing here?"

"A number-two choice"—Cyrus frowned—"should have done better. Stillman? Why did you choose Charlie to be your agent?"

"I don't know. I've known him for a while," Simon said, squirming, glancing from Taylor to Cyrus. "He works for the Players Union."

"You mean he hangs around the locker room a lot." Taylor immediately regretted the remark.

"I guess so." Simon looked angrily at Taylor; his palms were wet.

"Incidentally"—Cyrus stuck Simon hard—"you don't have a three-year contract. *We* have the three-year contract. *You* have three one-year contracts. You never even noticed. And of your $125,000 bonus you took $100,000 as deferred payments, right?"

"Yeah." Simon's eyes dropped to gaze at the carpet beneath him; he absently pulled at his lower lip. "Stillman said that and deferring half my salary for fifteen years would keep my taxes simple."

"It should keep them real simple." The owner laughed. He enjoyed this big man's discomfort; he couldn't help acting smart, bragging, beating the giant down to his knees. "You have any idea what those dollars will be worth? When and if you get them? Stillman took his ten percent up front on the gross amount, so you even got fucked by your own lawyer. You aren't rich, you're broke." Cyrus paused. "And apparently dumb."

Taylor thought Cyrus had overplayed his hand—fatally. Simon *did not* like being called dumb. It always discomposed the Big Thicket white-trash giant to be called dumb.

Except today.

"Jesus." Simon sat down hard like he had been shoved. Taylor watched Cyrus strip D'Hanis bare.

"All those big numbers, the $400,000 that we just batted around out there for the press. That's *for* them. Makes you *look* more valuable."

"Simon, don't listen to this," Taylor pleaded. "These guys are slime."

Simon sat frozen, staring blankly at his hands in his lap.

"Stillman was so anxious to fuck you and make us happy that we didn't have to buy him off." Cyrus grinned and saliva formed at his mouth's corners. "He wants to do more business with us, and we are going to be around for a long time. *You* are just passing through."

"Simon," Taylor interrupted, "come on, let's get out of here. You don't have to take..."

"He damn well does!" Cyrus yelled. "And you are next, Mr. Hotshot Crotchkey. I'll get to you after I finish with the boy here."

Simon flushed red, embarrassed, frightened. He clutched the arm of the chair. Knowing they suckered him so easily scared him.

I am dumb! Simon thought as he looked at Taylor slouched on the small couch, watching from the corners of his eyes. Simon hated him for being there.

Cyrus continued, "I'm telling you these things now because I like you and I expect great things from you as a football player. Taylor is going to be the Franchise. It's good PR, but building blocks like you are the reality. I will take care of you, but we don't deal with agents. We'll renegotiate your contract next year. Just you and me."

"Simon, don't you see what's happening here?" Taylor said to his confused, distraught friend. "He and Conly and Stillman have been lying to you from the beginning. He screwed you then and he's lying to you now. Take your lumps and walk; don't make him another deal. Fuck him."

"You got yours, Taylor," Simon said softly. "I want mine."

"I didn't get mine out of yours, Simon, so don't let him."

Simon stood to leave. The movement caused Taylor to tense. "Whatever you say, Mr. Chandler." Simon walked out.

"Jesus! Simon!" Taylor knew his friend's mind was made up. Further arguing was useless.

Cyrus looked sourly at Taylor, then smiled at the closing door, elated by the ease with which Simon was intimidated, scared and humiliated.

"That was nice, Cyrus," Taylor said. "You should carry a cattle prod."

"You're next." The owner turned to Taylor Rusk. "Your order is just as simple. You stay away from my daughter. I have plans for her and do not want the kind of grief you would cause my family. You are property of the football franchise, that is *all*. Junie goddam near drove me nuts during Water Carnival. I already told Wendy. Now I'm telling you."

"What did Wendy say?"

"None of your goddam business. My plans for her don't include you. It's my family and my franchise. Do you understand?" Cyrus pointed at the door. "We can just as easily step right back out that door and pop your little bubble quicker than we pumped it up. You understand the bottom line? I want your word or you are through with this football team."

"Well, Cyrus, I have plans that don't include you or the Franchise." Taylor smiled slightly. "So let's go back out there and tell the newspaper and TV folks you have changed your mind and I'm *not* the Franchise nor the greatest quarterback ever. It was a mistake giving me the Heisman Trophy. See what Red Kilroy says when you tell him what you just did to Simon D'Hanis. You don't know anything about football or the men it takes to play and win. Simon's supposed to keep killer niggers off me and you fuck him into resenting my salary!"

"It's a tough life, kid. This is show business. Guys like him are cheap."

"Well, guys like me aren't, as you well know," Taylor said. "Your inability to judge talent is astonishing."

"Stay away from my daughter!" Cyrus looked at Taylor. "You fuck up on this and you'll never work in this business again."

Taylor glimpsed something missing in Cyrus's lined face, something dangerously absent: *discipline*. Not even the slightest trace.

"Since my first day on a football field," Taylor said, "people have been threatening to stop me from playing. It comes with the turf. Threats are the language of sports. You don't scare me."

"It's true." Cyrus's voice rose to a screech. Flecks of saliva flew from his mouth. "You fuck with me and you will never work again."

"Are you going to *get me* for dating Wendy?" The quarterback looked around the richly furnished office. "A cement overcoat? I doubt it. You *might* be able to carry out your threats, but *first* you got to get out of this room. So you better just get Dick in here before your alligator mouth overloads your hummingbird ass."

"I can put you on the *list*!" Cyrus's squawl broke to a whine. "We can keep you from ever playing again!" His hand shook as he mashed the intercom call button.

"I've heard that before." Taylor turned toward the sound at the door. "Damn, this is the big leagues; let me see you actually do it."

Dick Conly walked into the office and headed for the wall concealing Cyrus's alcohol.

"Precisely, Taylor," Conly said. "It's the big leagues, and you are so damn good at it." The general manager banged at Cyrus's wall until the hidden wet bar swung out. He held up the brand-new eight-ounce Texas Pistols – logo tumblers, purple and white, crossed Walker Colt .45 single-action revolvers. "Drink?" Conly looked to Taylor.

Taylor waved off the alcohol. "I'm on drugs."

Conly nodded. Cyrus frowned as Dick poured four ounces of whiskey and drank it down in a long continuous gulping motion. He poured another. "Lots of people can play football, but only a few can make big money. Do what the man wants," Conly said. "You could be making a big mistake. Expensive. Wendy and Lem Three are getting married this July. It's been set for a long time. You won't be able to make the wedding because you'll be in camp early with the rookies and the centers. We're going to train in your part of the state, just up the road from Two Oaks at Ben T. Milam Junior College up in the hill country." Conly was painting the air with his hand. "Bluebonnets and bluestem grass, Indian firewheels. Beautiful country. God's country. Cool breezes."

"You a chamber-of-commerce lyricist?" Taylor looked up at Conly's face. His long fingers were laced tightly together and his palms were dry. So was his mouth. "You can't interfere with us. I'm not afraid of you and I sure as hell couldn't be the Franchise if I were afraid of Cyrus."

Taylor unlaced his fingers, clenched his fist and held it in front of Dick Conly's face. Conly drank another glass of whiskey and watched with dead-fish eyes.

"That's me in there. I can hold me in one hand." Taylor's jaws were tight; the muscles flexed and made his cheek quiver. His eyes cold, narrow; his lips, stretched to a thin crease, barely moved. "If I trust you and open my hand, I will float away, I know it. You know it. But you need me. Where would the Franchise be with Red Kilroy as coach and any other quarterback? Red is a raving lunatic."

"The man is a football genius," Cyrus protested.

"Sure, he's a genius," Taylor agreed, "but that doesn't mean he isn't a raving maniac. You have any idea what it is like to control and play a football game in front of seventy thousand people with a full-blown bozo on the sidelines as head coach? Against Ohio State he shit in his pants in the third quarter and didn't leave the field until the game ended. He stunk like a shithouse and was crazier than a shithouse rat.

"You bring in your number-three choice, that hotshot quarterback from Florida State." Taylor smiled. "Red will eat him for breakfast, bones and all, and then walk around asking everybody where the quarterback from Florida State went."

"Red Kilroy knows more football than you'll ever know." Cyrus wasn't looking at Taylor.

"There is no first place in the mad house, Cyrus."

"Red wants to trade for a good quarterback." Cyrus was still at him. "We got Bobby Hendrix from Cleveland; now Red wants that guy that threw to Hendrix, Kendall Adams."

"Kimball," Conly corrected, "Kimball Adams."

"Right," Cyrus said, "Kimball Adams."

"He's almost forty and has had four knee operations." Taylor sighed, sensing a long war ahead. "How long do you think he'll last behind the kind of offensive line we're gonna have? You might get one good year out of him. Red knows that, I know it. We're gonna have to run sprint-out passes for the first three years at least. How's Kimball Adams gonna run a sprint out? He's good, but he won't put up with Red going crazy on game day. He needs ten shots of Novocain a half to play for Cleveland, and they've *got* an offensive line. Sorry, Cyrus, but you need *me*. And you can't make me do anything I don't want to do, on or off the field. That's *why* I'm the quarterback."

Taylor looked at both men, then extended his hand. "If you fellows want to say good-bye, let's have that one-million-dollar handshake Doc had you put in the contract." He stared at the two men; neither reached for the million-dollar hand, so Taylor walked out into the lobby.

"Asshole. College kid asshole," Cyrus said. "I give him a great contract; then, when I try to keep him happy and wise him up, he walks out acting like the Franchise."

"He *is* the Franchise," Dick Conly said. "What the hell did you do to Simon D'Hanis in here?"

"I took him down à notch or two for Mr. Rusk's benefit." Cyrus smiled. "Now, what will Taylor Rusk do about my daughter?"

"Whatever he damn well pleases." And this time Dick Conly drank from the bottle.

"Fellas . . . say, fellas . . ." In the outer office Simon D'Hanis called to the various writers and cameramen, sound technicians, assorted press and Franchise officials who were drinking free whiskey and looking at the hostesses dressed in black-net stockings, skintight purple-and-white hot pants and T-shirts.

Taylor stood next to the door and watched.

"Fellas, if I could have your attention again . . . ." Simon walked up to the podium and the bouquet of microphones taped there. "Charlie, could you come here a minute?" He waved at his agent, who was near the back of the room, talking to Lem Carleton III and one of the hostesses.

"Charlie Stillman and I have one more announcement," Simon insisted, and people began to move back toward the podium, turning on tape recorders, cameras and klieg lights. Charlie Stillman, a tall, thin man with a pointed face, was a graduate of the University law school and had been recommended to Simon by the athletic director, T. J. "Armadillo" Talbott. It was a mystery to Taylor why Simon believed Armadillo. Taylor had tried to get Simon to let Doc Webster handle his contract, but Simon said Doc was a drunk with a bad reputation. Taylor wondered where Simon D'Hanis, from Vidor, Texas, learned to worry about Doc's reputation. Taylor guessed Dick Conly.

"What is it, ol' buddy?" Charlie Stillman said to Simon, who had the agent in a shoulder grip and was avoiding his gaze, concentrating his efforts on reinspiring the press.

Finally all the lights and tape and film were running.

"I just wanted to tell you about Charlie." Digging into Stillman's shoulder with his strong fingers, Simon turned, looked into Stillman's eyes and saw a man who knew he'd been caught. "He sold me out like a sneaking dog, and if I had my two-seventy, I'd show . . ." His eyes catching sight of Taylor, Simon suddenly stopped. ". . . show . . . and . . . I'm . . . I'm . . ." He looked at Taylor again. "I'm sorry." Simon released the vise grip on Stillman's shoulder and shoved him over the podium and crashing through the crowd.

Simon stormed into an open elevator. Two writers trying to follow were tossed gently off, only bouncing a couple of times. The TV sound man was screaming that his leg was broken.

The doors closed on Simon, all alone in a descending elevator.

Taylor watched it all. Nobody had won and Simon had lost. It was so pointless.

CALLING THE PLAYS

TAYLOR and Wendy went up to Doc's on Dead Man Creek and watched the moon rise big and red, climbing rapidly into the sky, getting smaller, finally turning white.

"You remember the Bowl Game when A.D. got hurt?" Taylor closed his eyes. "It was near the end of the game . . . remember?" Their separate hammocks creaked slowly in rhythm, the white nets of cotton cord stretched between the skinned and jointed cedar poles that supported the porch's tin roof. The crickets and hammocks made the only noise for a while.

"No. I didn't watch." Wendy didn't want to talk about the Bowl Game.

"Well," Taylor continued, unaware, "A.D. was flopping like a fish, screaming, moaning and groaning. Simon wanted to call a priest instead of the trainer." To keep his hammock swinging, Taylor pushed off the stone floor, his long leg crooked, his foot flat. "So now everybody is scared and the trainer says, 'A.D.! Where are you hurt?' and A.D. acts like he's taken bullets in the chest. He groans finally. 'Don't worry about me; how are my fans taking it?'"

Taylor began to laugh. When Wendy did not respond, Taylor's laughter quickly died off. They lay silently in the hammocks, listening to the whippoorwill in the oak motte.

"You going to do what my father wants?" Wendy asked finally.

"No. I try never to cooperate with the system. How about you?"

"I don't know. Are you proposing?"

He shook his head. "Don't ask for forever if you don't want it."

"Maybe I want it."

"Maybe don't have a pay window."

"Life isn't always metaphor for sports."

Taylor said nothing for quite a while; then quietly, carefully, he said, "It takes management and coaching to win consistently, but to do it *quickly* the Franchise needs a great quarterback—me. There are plenty of good players for the other positions, all mass-produced by the colleges, all available. But great quarterbacks are rare."

"You make it seem that way," Wendy said.

"That's the reason Red's in a hurry," Taylor went on. "Me too. I'm a lifelong tramp athlete with one chance in a million to turn some big money. If your father stays clear."

"He won't," Wendy said. "He never will."

"I know, and that means skating on thinner ice than usual. I still want you with me, but I can't think about a wife and children. It's going to be full speed through the fog, with me calling the turns. I have to pay attention."

"How about a simple yes or no," Wendy said impatiently.

"It doesn't work that way."

"You're backing down from my father," Wendy accused.

"Not an inch, nor am I purposely pushing him. I don't need any additional bends in the road. Speed and time are important."

"You're just going to let real life go by while you play games for my father."

"This *is* real life." Taylor pointed at himself. "I have to control the playing field or I am gone, replaced by a technician who becomes the coach's pawn, showing great skill but no magic."

"Now you're a magician?" Wendy was sarcastic. "You definitely are an escape artist."

"Keeping my eyes on the road ahead is not the same as ignoring you. My life is what it is," Taylor said. "You're welcome to make this insane run; you can get off or back on anytime, but don't grab the wheel."

"No wedding? Or children?" Wendy spit the words angrily. She was unused to being denied.

"Why risk the first few laps," Taylor replied. "I have the skills, knowledge and power to survive the business. With your help I could win at it, on and off the field."

"What am I supposed to do?" Wendy asked warily.

"Understand."

"What do you mean by that? Understand what?"

"Three things are important." Taylor frowned. "Don't lie, never make a promise you can't keep, and never quit.

"I fight for control every day, against more than Cyrus. I trust no one, especially people who believe in Spur, team, and University. I thrive against the system."

"What does that have to do with me?"

"Be on my side . . . trust me . . . and . . ."

Wendy interrupted unhappily. ". . . And let you call the plays."

Taylor nodded and remained quiet.

The whippoorwill started up again, and they both looked off into the darkness toward the sound.

Finally Taylor spoke, "What power I have, what control I exercise in the world, has its source in *the game*. On the field I must have complete *control*. . . . No plays from the bench or suggestions from the press box, because those bastards aren't out there. Only the players are . . . only the players count. I have to deliver on demand at the right time. Timing. It does no good to do magic tricks on Monday . . . if the game was Sunday. Timing and winning are power and control."

"Timing what?" Wendy closed her eyes. "Winning what?"

"All of it," Taylor said. "All the way to the Super Bowl. And *fast*. It's possible in three to six years, if they build the Franchise around me. And if I deliver." Taylor continued, "I force your father, Conly and Red to deal with *me* because on game day they need me more than I need them. That is *power*."

"Do you love me at all?" she asked quietly. "Are you always this cold and calculating? My stomach is a broken Slinky and you just swing there, passionless, blank-faced."

"I get nervous when people start tossing passion around like a Frisbee. There are two sides to the goddam Frisbee and chaos is one."

"My father is not going to stop my marriage."

"Well, he's not going to force me into *mine*. Passion is not what we need right now. We need patience, calculation, time to figure our next move. Logical decisions are catastrophic in an insane situation, and your father . . ."

"How can you humiliate me like this?" Wendy stopped the hammock and stepped onto the rock porch floor. She walked to the west end and peered around the ranch house. "All my friends think we're getting married."

"I didn't tell them. Let's just ease on down to training camp and see how the first season goes. . . ."

"Son of a bitch!" Wendy leaned against the stone wall and stayed at the west end of the porch. "Dumb son of a bitch. You've got no idea what's important—"

"I've got one idea," Taylor interrupted. "Love hurts, passion hurts. And I'm in a business where, during the important times, I cannot allow pain, mental or physical, to interfere." Taylor stared at Wendy's back; she was hugging herself like she was cold. She looked small, alone and abandoned.

"I ignore pain," he went on, "but I never forget it, because then it runs loose. Forgotten pain is the most destructive kind."

"Bullshit!" Wendy turned. "One person isn't enough: You have to have hordes of fans. And you're afraid of my father and Dick Conly. You're afraid to chance it."

"I'm less frightened of your father than I am of you."

"Why? Why me?"

"You're used to looking at other people as parts of your life." Taylor stood up and stretched his fingers pointing skyward. "You'll want to choreograph parts of my life. You actually think you can make me do what you want to do whether I care or not."

"Tell me"—keeping her back to Taylor, Wendy leaned forward and braced her chin on the back of her hand—"is that what it is about *me* that enchants you so that marriage is out of the question? Take a chance."

"You don't even know what you're asking . . . *Forever!* Forever is one of those no-changing-your-mind jobs." Taylor frowned. "It's a son of a bitch. Chance has no meaning relative to forever."

"Come on, marry me!" Wendy was suddenly pleading.

And Taylor was suddenly frightened. A man with the talented desire for command—thriving on conflict, violence and danger, executing tactics and strategy under extreme pressure—he had delivered two national championships, rewritten record books and always delivered. Yet, he was frightened at the thought of caring for someone, even himself. Forever.

"Wives and children aren't all that bad, for Chrissakes," Wendy said. "A lot of people do it."

"We're not a lot of people. I'm on the fast track, trying to survive."

"But I have money. You don't have to do this." Wendy was tired, desperate.

"Don't you see," Taylor said, "I *want* to do it. At least in this game I call the plays. What am I if I'm not the quarterback?" Taylor frowned at what he was saying. It wasn't coming out like he wanted. "If we get married now, it's like I'm confronting Cyrus, and there's no way to guess what he'll do. He has some other plans for you. Well, let him think what he likes. We'll do what *we* want and need. He can't *make* you marry Lem, for Chrissakes. This isn't the twelfth century."

"No," Wendy said, and her voice suddenly fell, resigned. She watched the moon. "It's not the twelfth century, and I don't know what you are if you're not the quarterback."

Just as Dick Conly had promised, Taylor *was* in camp when Lem and Wendy flew to Puerto Vallarta and got married.

Taylor got drunk and went crazy, ending up in a fight with A. D. Koster over who was the greatest all-time Comanche chief, Quanah Parker or Buffalo Hump.

Nobody thought it strange. All sorts of weird things happened at *that* camp.

CAMP

"YOU coming?" Simon D'Hanis looked down at Taylor Rusk on the small dormitory bed. It was the team's first night off since camp began. It was also the first time the big guard had said more than "Hello" to Taylor since the camp began.

There was a big yellow school bus idling in the parking lot, waiting to take the players to the weekly dance at the Crystal Palace Dance Hall.

"No." Taylor lay on the small bed with a paperback in one hand. His other hand rested behind his head. He was barefoot and wore khaki shorts and a Texas Pistols practice T-shirt.

Simon was freshly shaved and showered, wearing a red Ban-Lon shirt, black slacks and loafers. His face was slightly flushed; his oversize muscular body seemed to pulse with anticipation. He smelled like English Leather.

"You just going to stay here and mope about Chandler's daughter marrying Lem Carleton III? Marriage ain't all that easy." Simon started to turn away. "I ought to know."

"I'm just going to read and rest," Taylor said. "I thought you were still mad at me."

"What?" Simon turned back. He wanted Taylor's company.

"You've been acting pissed ever since the day Cyrus tacked our dicks to the floor."

"Buffy explained to me about Wendy and you and Cyrus. I figured out the rest."

"He got us both."

"I know. I'm sorry."

"You're a lineman, you're forgiven."

"Well, c'mon, let's go, then."

"I'm still tired. Simon, you're a born curfew breaker; you like the thrill. As long as your wife sets a curfew, your marriage will last."

"Why don't you go get Wendy back? You could do it," Simon urged. "That's why you're the quarterback."

"Maybe I don't want to be quarterback anymore."

"You got something you want more?"

Taylor was silent for a long time. He wanted Wendy Chandler back.

"So . . . what do you want me to do? C'mon, man." Simon sat down. The tiny bed groaned and creaked. "It won't be as much fun without you tonight," Simon complained. "It's going to be history in the making."

"You'll have plenty of fun. Find Kimball Adams and Ox Wood." Taylor kept his eyes fastened on the book.

"Isn't it amazing?" Simon said. "I'm playing in the same line with Ox Wood. The guy is my idol."

"It's not healthy to have idols, Simon," Taylor warned, "especially when you're supposed to be one yourself. It's the guys you play with and the money you leave with. . . . That's all."

"You are a cynic and you would be no fun." Simon left. Howling and beating on doors, making his way down the hall and out to the idling bus in the parking lot.

Taylor tossed the book onto the empty bed. He roomed alone; he demanded it in his contract. His privacy was important to him.

He heard the school bus roar and rattle out of the parking lot, drowning the howls and yelps of the oversize crazed men who hadn't been anywhere since training camp began on July fifth.

Red Kilroy weeded them out fast and early.

The ones in the school bus, Taylor and others around the junior-college campus were the survivors. On the first day of practice there had been one hundred and fifty football players. Seventeen days later Red Kilroy, his staff and the Texas sun had reduced the number to ninety. Another ninety men would come and go before camp ended and the roster was set. Red had his scouting network searching the colleges and the pros around the country, checking waiver lists, keeping him posted on more available bodies.

After seventeen two-practice, three-meeting days, with just enough extra time to eat, tape and sleep, the survivors were at the breaking point. So Red turned them loose on the Crystal Palace.

Red would continually need replacements: more bodies and more skill. He would find them, too, because he never stopped looking. Never. After coaching twenty years, he had spies out everywhere. He kept track of everybody, everything—all in his head. The others were going to computers, but not Red. He never thought about anything but football and winning. And connections. His network. Red's boys. Techniques, strategies, personnel, weight, and nutrition programs; he never stopped trying to improve, to increase, to grow, to conquer, to win, to succeed and achieve his long-term strategic goals. Ownership. Possession. Control.

Red developed methods and measurements of achievement and success, then committed it all to memory. He chose assistants and scouts on the strength of their memories, drove them all as nuts as he was and made them devoted geniuses. Technique, tenacity and good people—that was Red Kilroy's system. So was alcohol and manic depression, fear and anger; but mostly it was genius. Damned genius.

Winning took exceptional men and ate them.

"Hey, Taylor? You still crazy?"

A. D. Koster stood in Taylor Rusk's dormitory room doorway. His cheek was bruised and his chin scabbed over.

Taylor turned over on the unmade bed and looked at the damage he had done.

"I'm still crazy, A.D. I'm just not mad anymore." Taylor absently rubbed the knuckles of his right hand. "How you feeling?

"Terrific. There's something about being sucker-punched that really clears your head."

"Simon's on the school bus with the rest. They plan to sucker-punch the Crystal Palace Dance Hall."

"Kimball Adams called it a search-and-destroy mission. He went off in his own car."

Twenty-year veteran Kimball Adams, the much-traveled, controversial, study-by-the-jukebox-light quarterback, had been purchased from Cleveland to go along with veteran receiver Bobby Hendrix.

A.D. was in the room next to them. Red was keeping A.D. because he knew the system and was working his way to starting at free safety. A pure hitter rather than a complete defender, A.D. would often separate a receiver from the ball *and* his ribs. Fearsome on the field, he took between fifty and seventy milligrams of Dexedrine for games, earning the name Footsteps by hitting anything that moved.

The safety had been passed over in the draft and signed as a free agent for a $6,000 bonus and a good contract—a calculated gamble by Red. "I'll sign you, A.D., if you'll just run a slow forty for the Scouting Combine," Red had promised. And Red delivered. A.D. was already collecting on his contract. He'd done better in real dollars than Simon D'Hanis, the number-two choice. Simon wouldn't start collecting until the season started and was already having trouble making ends meet. Buffy, beginning to show her pregnancy, had rented a nice expensive apartment in Park City.

"Did Hendrix go with Kimball?" Taylor worried about Hendrix, one of the only two good receivers. The other was Speedo Smith.

A.D. shook his head. "No, Kimball was going to his drinkin' place. Hendrix said he might join him later. He was studying his playbook. They are sure a strange pair." A.D. rubbed his hands together. "I'm in, Taylor, I'm in."

"How deep?" Taylor asked. "I heard you lost more money to the Cobianco Brothers."

"I'm clean. Besides, even Cyrus Chandler gambles with those guys."

Taylor just shook his head.

"I'm telling you, those guys Adams and Hendrix are real antiques," A.D. said. "They were in the Old League."

"They have seen the elephant and watched it die," Taylor agreed. "Come on, A.D., sit down. I forgive you."

"You forgive me? You hit me five times before bothering to even mention that we were having a disagreement!" He pointed to the bruises and scabs on his face. "Luckily I fell under the table, where you couldn't get at me."

"It was a bad time of the month. Wendy Chandler married our PR assistant and Simon was treating me shitty. I'm sorry."

Before A.D. could accept the apology, Taylor's phone rang.

"That's for me," A.D. grabbed the phone. He was right. It was Suzy Ballard, the roller-skating carhop, who had just driven up from the city in A.D.'s car.

"I'll be right down, babe." A.D. hung up and stared down at Taylor. "Tonight the fire, Taylor, is in Suzy's eyes." He dug in his pocket and pulled out a roll of one-hundred-dollar bills, peeled off two and dropped them on Taylor's bed, then glided out the door.

Taylor listened as the distinctive click of the taps on A.D.'s alligator shoes faded. The evening was silent.

Two crisp one-hundred-dollar bills lay on the bed and the rent was finally paid. Taylor decided A.D. would survive everything but the fire in Suzy Ballard's eyes.

Taylor turned his thoughts to Wendy, recalling her delicate features and pale blue eyes.

Choose me. . . . Choose me.

THE OFF NIGHT

"Well, there they go." Red Kilroy stood at the window with a double Scotch and watched the yellow bus head off for the Crystal Palace. "Let's hope none of the good ones get hurt."

"I haven't seen that many good ones." Cyrus Chandler, dressed in white shirt, white pants and canvas shoes, was stretched out on a couch. The dormitory room was an exact duplicate of the room that the players lived in, except the small beds were replaced by a brown corduroy couch, several chairs, a low wooden table and a portable bar. Cyrus, Dick and Red had meetings and drank in this room.

Red kept his assistant coaches, trainers and equipment isolated in another wing of the dorm with the players, away from management and press.

"Cyrus . . ." Red took a deep drink. ". . . what you know about football talent don't amount to a fart in a whirlwind."

"Maybe." Cyrus was strangely unperturbed. "But I own this team and can say whatever I please. . . . Most people can't tell."

"I can"—Red bristled—"so keep it to yourself."

Dick Conly just drank. He was familiar with the scene.

"Well, lookie here." Red pointed out the window. A blue Chevrolet convertible rumbled into the lot; behind the wheel was Suzy Ballard. All three men looked out the window as the beautiful young girl wheeled the car through the white caliche lot and stopped right by their window. She was so close, they could see her breasts, unencumbered and jiggling delightfully as she brought the car to an abrupt halt by jamming the transmission into park.

"I'll bet two hundred dollars she's here for A. D. Koster." Red watched the other two men gape as Suzy got out of the car and stretched and yawned, straining and rippling. She wore tight white shorts and a T-shirt. The late afternoon sun stretched her shadow across the dusty parking lot. She was barefoot with brown, tough little feet. She disappeared inside the lobby and shortly emerged with A.D. Red Kilroy turned and held out his hand.

"Give him two hundred dollars, Dick," Cyrus growled. Cyrus never handled cash.

"Do I know my players," Red said, "or do I know my players?"

"Are we going to keep him?" Cyrus said, watching A.D. steer Suzy and the Chevrolet convertible out of the lot.

Red did not respond. He never told anyone his plans. All Red had to sell were his plans, his program, from expansion team to world champions. He wasn't giving it to Cyrus Chandler or Dick Conly over drinks. It was Red's system, his program, his people. He was going to keep A. D. Koster, because A.D. was a Red Kilroy man. At least for the moment.

"Red, I've given a lot of thought to the idea of you being both head coach and general manager," Dick started slowly, "and I just feel that the two responsibilities are beyond the capacity of one man."

Conly was building a backfire against Red's blazing ambition—ownership—fanned by Cyrus's vague promise to consider a percentage for Red if the Pistols got to the Super Bowl.

"I'd like your input on who you could work with," Conly continued. "We were thinking about bringing a man over from Chandler Communications. It seems logical."

Red had been expecting this move—Chandler and Conly pushing to see if he would shove back. It was wasteful, ultimately costly to all of them.

"I guess it all depends on your definition of terms," Red finessed. "I think we can work that out as long as I retain all game and field control and final say on player personnel. Who goes, who stays, is up to me. And I pay the players and coaches. I *hand* them their checks. Or I walk now, go back to the University and sue you for breach of contract."

"I'll give you player personnel, Red," Dick said. "Calm down. Quit all this talk about lawsuits and contracts."

"A man writes a contract," Red frowned, "with the eye to breaking it, not keeping it."

"Don't tell them ballplayers that." Conly laughed. "We'll both be looking for work."

"I have tenure back at the University whenever I want, Dick."

"You going to give back the slush fund?" Conly asked.

"Dick, I want you to be general manager," Cyrus suddenly interrupted.

"Well, shit," Conly said. "That's the first I've heard of this. I don't want to be general manager. Damn you, Cyrus! I've got other responsibilities. . . . I don't have the time for your whimsical bullshit. Neely Johnson is ready to move over from Chandler Communications. We had everything settled. With his broadcast experience . . ."

"I've changed my mind." Cyrus was firm.

"You're going to push me once too often," Conly threatened, but he realized he had been mousetrapped. Cyrus was becoming enchanted with his new toy and wanted Dick to make it work.

"Red," Dick said, "if I *have* to be general manager, you will have complete field command. And the paychecks of the players and coaches will be delivered to you before each game."

Red pointed at Cyrus. "Dick negotiates, but he signs everyone I want, for whatever they want, and makes every trade I say. Cyrus, *you stay out*. I know what you did to Simon D'Hanis just to keep Taylor Rusk away from your daughter." Red's forehead was already flushed and anger spread across the coach's face. "*You keep your hot-pants daughter away from my players!* You mend your own damn fences and I'll build a football team—the best money can buy—but it is going to cost you plenty and you are going to stay away from player personnel and game plans. We will have separate offices and office personnel. *All communication* is through me to players and assistants."

"Instead of me giving more money to the players"—Conly toasted toward Red with his glass—"how about I just give it to you? Then you decide what to do with it."

"Now *that* is how to run a football program." Red smiled thinly. "You aren't *always* doing those boys a favor by giving them money."

Dick Conly did what Cyrus asked. Right then and there he agreed to become general manager of The Texas Pistols Football Club, Inc. It was a compound mistake.

"You'll run the show, Red," Dick explained. "My son, Luther, is here as a ball boy and I want to spend time with him; it'll be simple for me to stay out of your way."

"Nothing *stays* simple," Red, still flushed, warned. He was right.

The teletype machine began chattering, disgorging names and

information. The TWX machine was connected to the other team camps and the League office and spit out the waiver list names of players: rejects, failures, crazies, normals and of course *bait*.

"This young kid from Utah, Whippett—can we get him onto the taxi squad?" Red asked, fingering the teletape.

"He won't pass waivers," Conly said. "Goddam Cleveland is claiming every guy we put on waivers."

"They're still mad about us taking Hendrix after they blacklisted him," Red said. "They'll get over it."

"Or tired," Dick added.

"Dallas didn't seem mad when we picked up Speedo Smith," Cyrus said.

"Don't let that fool you," Conly told him. "Nobody holds a grudge like Dallas."

"What do we do in the meantime about Whippett?" Red asked.

Conly wasn't surprised that Red immediately asked his advice. The head coach was confident within his system, and could size up men quickly. He recognized Conly's worth better than Cyrus did. The more difficult the problem—the more complicated, devious, obtuse—the better Dick Conly was at solving it. Dick Conly knew how to do business. His personal life was a mess, but he could solve Cyrus Chandler's and Red Kilroy's problems.

"What do we do about the kid from Utah?" Red Kilroy repeated to Conly. "Whippett."

"Simple," Dick Conly said, "If we can't get him past waivers, put him in the National Guard and have him called up for six months. . . . See what Cleveland thinks of that."

The two men smiled. They knew they would get along.

When young Luther Conly arrived to go to the movie, they were making the deal for Whippett with the Texas National Guard.

"I'm ready, Dad." The boy burst into the room. The head coach and Dick Conly were both on telephones.

"Just a second, General," Dick said. "My boy just walked in." He cupped his hand over the mouthpiece and dug his other hand into his pocket. "Say Luther, you want to talk to a *real* general?"

"No, thanks, Dad, I want to see the movie."

"Yeah . . . well. I know. Say, Red." Conly dug a wad of bills from his pocket. "Any of your assistants going to the movie tonight?"

Red shrugged. Dick looked back and Luther was gone.

"Huh . . . he must not have wanted to go very badly." Conly uncupped the phone. "Sorry, General. Now, Whippett has got to find a vacancy in a guard unit. El Paso? Jesus, that's a long way, but . . . all right. If we can't make a deal for him, I'll call you back and you get him activated. Great." He hung up the phone and looked at Red Kilroy. "Now, what do you suppose got into that dumbass kid of mine?"

Luther Conly listened outside the room, tears running down his face. It was beyond his understanding that his own father would rather do *that* than go to a movie with his own son.

That dumbass kid of mine.

Luther walked all the way back to his room, crying and hitting his leg with his fist. He was a very unhappy ball boy. He was positive he was doing something wrong.

Luther collapsed on his bed, sobbing and wondering why nothing was simple and everything was so boring. He smoked a joint and played records, falling asleep and dreaming his father didn't like him because he didn't play football and was only a kid. He didn't know what to do about either.

TYPICAL
AMERICAN BOYS

"Hey, kid." It was Bobby Hendrix at Taylor Rusk's door. The dormitory was dark and quiet. Taylor had fallen asleep. Hendrix, the tall, thin, freckled-faced redheaded veteran of eighteen professional football seasons, leaned against the doorjamb, the ever-present toothpick in his mouth. He talked in a slow East Texas-Louisiana drawl.

"You awake, kid?" Hendrix called again.

"I'm semiconscious; it's the best I can do," Taylor sighed. "How do you keep going? You've done eighteen years of training camps."

"I just keep getting up—off the bed, or the ground. They get tired of hitting me before I get tired of catching the ball." Hendrix placidly pulled the toothpick from his mouth. "I got knocked down in bars a lot, and there they whistle *you* dead, not the play. I learned quick about getting back on my feet; can't run if your feet aren't on the ground." He stuck the toothpick back and studied his new young passer, letting the conversation abruptly die, gauging the effect of the growing silence.

Bobby Hendrix had caught more passes in high school, college and professional football than any man. He lacked speed and strength, but he had patience and will. He was the first man on the field for practice and the last one to leave, often driven off by darkness. And when they knocked him down, Bobby Hendrix *always* got back up.

"Okay if I turn on the television?" Hendrix asked. "The Prez is gonna be on; I want to watch his act."

Fixing his gaze on Taylor's face, Bobby searched for the impatient anxiety that haunted many young quarterbacks. It was not there. Deeply, strongly centered in the game, Taylor had no doubts about his skills. Hendrix found Taylor enigmatic—detached and calm yet weirdly intense and caring. He was a good one and they would be friends, he decided. Their mutual success depended on it.

"You're married," Taylor announced abruptly. "It seems like having a family would be hard."

"Insane." Hendrix nodded absently, pushing the toothpick with his tongue. "Completely insane. I got four boys." He flashed four bony fingers. "Four. Count 'em." A smile flickered across the cadaverous face, the toothpick motionless. "In-fucking-sane."

Taylor studied the ghostly face. "How old are they?"

Hendrix laughed. "How the hell should I know? Two are little tiny and two are somewhere in their teens. Why are you asking? You plan on . . . ?"

Taylor shook his head.

"Well"—Hendrix repositioned the toothpick—"then let me ask you another question: Do you know Terry Dudley?"

"Yeah. He was a basketball player."

"Well," Hendrix continued slowly, "I called the national union office today. They put me on hold, then disconnected me four times; real jerk-offs up there. I finally talked to this friend of yours, Terry Dudley. He's a staff lawyer for us now and he told me some pretty interesting things."

Taylor was surprised at the news of Dudley's job.

"Right now," Hendrix drawled slowly, "Charlie Stillman is the director of the Players Union."

"That guy was Simon D'Hanis's agent." Taylor's voice hardened. "How did that happen?"

"Charlie Stillman sent out the signature cards and the clubs made the players sign them before they gave them their game checks. It was really Robbie Burden, the commissioner's, idea. Pretty damn smart. You got a lot to learn, kid." Hendrix continued,

"What we got is an owner's operative surrounded by a staff loyal to him. The officers and player reps are systematically traded or cut. The commissioner isn't dumb, and the owners are around long after any player. We have no continuity, so Stillman steps in and runs the Union. Stillman calls for a show of Union solidarity so the owners can see who stands up, then they start taking names and kicking asses.

"Burden has lots of power for a hired gun. The owners are always fighting and Robbie plays politics, putting himself into the power vacuums. Dick Conly may be the commissioner's match, though." Hendrix, six foot two and 180, turned his red head slowly and looked at Taylor. "Unless they're on the same side."

The television bathed the room in soft light.

"It's control of the League that they all fight about. The Franchise was only the first step. There's revolution coming, and we're either the soldiers or the software. Robbie blacklisted me for trying to get Stillman fired from the Union—made Cleveland put me on waivers," Hendrix said, "but Red and Conly took me anyway. It sure pissed Cleveland off at Robbie Burden. So Conly accomplishes two things: weakens the commissioner with Cleveland, while Red gets me for the one-hundred-dollar waiver price." Bobby Hendrix laughed. "I'll play my string out here. We'll win some games; we'll surprise some people. Red's got a good system. This business isn't exactly overflowing with geniuses. He'll outsmart a lot of coaches."

"I'm glad to hear you say that."

"I guess I might as well elect myself player rep." Hendrix grinned. "What kind of guy is your friend Dudley? At least he was a *player*, even if it was roundball."

Taylor shrugged and frowned. "He's well known and smart. One of the top onions at the University. Got his law degree while he played pro in San Antonio, had his own TV show, political science degree, a good media man—semicelebrity."

"Well," Hendrix said, "now he's on the Union staff. He handles contract grievances. In this league the first mistake you make is reading your contract. The second is reading the Collective Bargaining Agreement. Did you sign the licensing release they passed around yesterday?"

"No."

"Good; me neither. Your friend Dudley told me that the commissioner has promised those people they can use our pictures on their bottle caps and they've already started distribution. Stillman promised that the Union would deliver the releases from the players." Hendrix moved the toothpick from one corner of his thin mouth to the other. "The commissioner has promised something that he and Stillman may not be able to deliver. Dudley says we can sue the bottling companies if they use our pictures and the commissioner's office doesn't have individually signed agreements. That's why they're on us to sign them, just like the union cards." Hendrix laughed softly. "I'm calling other guys around the league about this licensing agreement. We might be able to get rid of Charlie Stillman over this. Maybe give your boy, Dudley, a shot at the job."

Hendrix sat at the foot of the extra bed and turned up the television volume. The face of the President appeared.

"My fellow Americans," the President said, and proceeded to explain the necessity of the "lender of last resort," the Federal Reserve, to pick up the greater portion of the bad paper in the Third World to show American resolve to defend democracy wherever threatened.

"Revaluation," he called it.

"Ever' dollar you got just turned into seventy-five cents," Hendrix said. "They turned on the presses to bail out the banks."

The Prez, bathed in sweat and shaking, said good night.

"Academy Award all the way, Mr. President. You saved the picture." Bobby Hendrix turned down the television and said, "I got to go meet Kimball, Margene Brinkley and Darryl Wood. You better come and spend those dollars before they turn to pesos."

On the silent screen a newsman stood in front of a chart that showed revaluation as a series of progressively smaller silhouettes of dollar bills.

Bobby Hendrix picked up Taylor's phone and dialed four numbers. Red Kilroy answered in the other wing.

"Red, this is Bobby. I want to borrow your car.... The keys?... Thanks. Bye."

Bobby Hendrix looked over at the rookie quarterback. The Franchise. Red had already talked to the creaky, wise outside receiver. "Take Rusk and make him a passer, watch his doses of Kimball Adams... and teach him to *read*. Bobby, teach him to read those defenses!" Red had pleaded. He was on a tight schedule to the Super Bowl.

"Kid"—Bobby Hendrix put down the phone,—"come on with me. It's time you met life from the Old League, two real dinosaurs. You have the rare privilege to learn at their feet," Hendrix drawled, slowly moving the toothpick around in his mouth. "You just got to be careful it don't kill you."

The television was still playing.

The Billy Joe Hardesty *All-American Evangelical Hour* began. Hendrix turned up the volume. It opened on a medium close-up of Billy Joe, his fat red lips, wattle-strewn face and neck. Billy Joe pointed a short, thick finger at the two football players.

"I want to save *you* from eternal damnation," Billy Joe announced. The camera pulled back. "And I am going to do it tonight."

"Let's get out of here," Hendrix said. The All-American Youth Choir was humming softly, and the camera continued to pull back, showing Billy Joe resplendent in a dark-blue polyester suit with a red tie, white belt and white loafers with gold buckles.

"The End Time is near," Billy Joe ranted. "The anti-Christ walks among us! The economy is collapsing and a giant computer called The Beast is preparing to fulfill the prophecy of Revelations Thirteen, verses sixteen to eighteen . . . coming up right after this message!"

"I grew up with Billy Joe Hardesty in Orange," Bobby said. "When he was in high school, he stabbed my friend's dog, set several of his sister's cats on fire, and just after he strangled a goose at the golf course, he found Jesus." Bobby Hendrix talked as they walked through the silent dormitory. "It seems to keep him happy."

"It must have pleased all the small animals on the upper Texas Gulf Coast too," Taylor said.

KIMBALL ADAMS'S DRINKING PLACE

"WHEN Kimball Adams found out that he and I had both gone to Texas in the expansion, he came down here and searched out a drinkin' place." Bobby Hendrix steered Red Kilroy's car down a two-lane caliche road. "He insists on one that's too mean for the local law. I think he outdid himself this time."

Taylor Rusk slouched against the door, fascinated by the deodorizer that hung from the rearview mirror of the head coach's car. It was a cutout of a nude woman. The car smelled like a clean public restroom.

"Kimball always calls it a drinkin' place, like Br'er Rabbit had his laughin' place, but Jesus, a cedar-chopper bar . . ." Hendrix glanced at Taylor. The young quarterback was listening and looking at the erotic stinking car deodorizer.

"I know." Hendrix frowned and nodded. "It's weird, ain't it? Red's a good man. He's a player's coach." Hendrix absently put his eyes back on the caliche road. The high country twilight was quickly turning dark.

"Yeah, I know." Taylor nodded. "He doesn't fuck with your head much unless you don't produce. Then he just hits it."

"Kimball finds him a drinkin' place and that's where he spends his time. He tries to find one close to camp on low-traffic-density roads. He went to insurance school for a while, and the drunk driving deaths and/or loss of a major limb percentages really shook him up. He found this place after three intensive days of looking. He'll stay drunk most of camp."

Hendrix steered the car up to a crossroads, both roads leading nowhere into the canyons clotted with cedar brakes.

On one corner was a limestone block building with a tin roof and a screened-in porch. OLD LEADVILLE was painted in black on a white sign that hung from the porch. POST OFFICE, BEER AND WINE was painted in smaller black letters.

Kimball Adams's convertible was parked alongside a couple of ancient pickup trucks, one brand-new welding truck and three flatbed trucks stacked high with fresh-cut cedar posts. Big double-bit axes and large McCullouch chain saws were piled on the cedar logs.

Bobby Hendrix pointed at the white Lincoln with the blue leather interior, covered in a fine glaze of caliche dust. It was a beautiful car, top peeled back to let in the night sky.

"Kimball has rented a Lincoln convertible every year for camp and *never has once* put the top up," Hendrix said affectionately. "That is the Old League—lots of lunatics in Lincoln convertibles. Now rookies got Porsches and Mercedeses. Used to be no self-respecting football player would buy a small car. 'Park it like a ball player' was our motto. These new cars are like driving your watch."

"Adams is a real country-clubber," Taylor observed, staring at the limestone building. "And Old Leadville looks like a helluva town."

They went in, stooping down to enter the low stone building. The floor was cedar blocks and sawdust. A bar ran along one wall, and a shuffleboard game was in progress along the opposite wall. The jukebox was silent, an ancient tall round Wurlitzer dead in the corner next to the cold rock hearth. The shuffleboard game produced most of the sounds. The hiss of the puck sliding along the highly polished wood. The click of metal. The muffled thumps of too much strength.

It was a warm night and the room was hot and stifled. There were three men at the bar, all dirty and sweat-stained, with heavy arms and broad backs. They were big-bodied men with dull, flat eyes, suspicious faces. They had spent the day filling the flatbed trucks with cedar posts. They were cedar cutters.

Kimball Adams sat at the corner table opposite the dead jukebox and next to the cold fireplace. There was a purple and white Texas Pistols duffel bag at the ancient quarterback's feet. Sitting at the table with Kimball was Darryl "Ox" Wood. Wood had played in college at the University of Michigan, had been an all-pro guard in Philadelphia for two years and had been traded to Cleveland to protect Kimball. Which he did well. Ox, covered with tattoos and scars from surgery and combat, stood about six-foot-nine and weighed 320. He ran the forty in 4.6 as a rookie and refused to ever do it again. Ox was smart and studied at his trade. He greased his jersey with Vaseline so the defensive lineman couldn't jerk him around, and he sharpened the screw heads on his headgear so that anybody that head-slapped him would come away with hand lacerations.

"The last zeuglodon, a fine example of prehistoric whale," Hendrix called him. "The man is a different species."

"I have two rules," Ox said to anyone who listened. And when Ox spoke, *everyone* listened. "First, protect the quarterback; second, avoid any sort of repression or negative vibes. All you *need* is love, but if you got an extra pocket and it doesn't hurt the drape of your coat, go ahead and drop a thirty-eight in there. What the hell."

Red advised Ox to avoid the press and police whenever possible.

Ox came to the Texas Pistols to protect Kimball Adams. "Unless you get me Ox Wood's protection, you'll have to play Taylor Rusk," Kimball had said. "Be a terrible thing to happen to a young quarterback to have to play behind that line, particularly a thoroughbred like Rusk, one you want around long enough to build the Franchise. A once-in-a-lifetimer who does not drink or believe in God, can run the hundred in 9.5, is built like Time and throws from end zone to end zone."

Red had been waiting twenty years for a good bird dog; he wasn't going to waste a quarterback. Red traded for Ox.

"Let's go out on the porch, Kimball," Bobby Hendrix said as he and Taylor approached the table. "It's too hot in here."

"You ain't here two seconds"—the old quarterback's voice was a deep growl—"and you are trying to organize something." Kimball slouched in the heavy wooden chair. Ox smiled at both Hendrix and Taylor.

"Siddown a second." Kimball kicked a chair toward Hendrix. Hendrix shook his head and pointed toward the porch.

Kimball, the forty-year-old quarterback, wore a sweat-stained and crushed silver-belly Resistol, severely creased, down on his forehead, shading his eyes. A cigarette burned unfiltered from the corner of his mouth. The smoke curled up past the burst blood vessels of his nose and cheeks and eyes. Kimball Adams looked at Taylor by cocking his head slightly and peering from beneath the brim of the dirty, sweaty hat through the cigarette smoke.

"Hey, Ox, lemme have your tongue." Kimball jerked the short cigarette butt from his lips. "I imagine ol' Bobby here's been givin' you his union speech. Well, take it from me, the Union will just elbow up to the trough with the owners, and the players will still suck hind tit. Nothin' will really change but the split."

Ox made a sound like "Ahhhh" and Kimball ground out the glowing cigarette on Darryl "Ox" Wood's tongue. Ox did not flinch. Taylor Rusk did. Hendrix grinned. It was an old trick.

"Ice, glasses, beer!" Kimball yelled. "And bring it out on the porch." Kimball picked up the duffel bag and headed outside. Ox ate the cold cigarette butt and followed Kimball and Hendrix.

Kimball Adams's duffel bag was full of bottles of Johnny Walker Scotch. He paid the bartender a hundred dollars a week to make sure he never ran out of glasses of ice.

Kimball fell silently into a chair, glaring angrily off the porch, lighting and smoking Camels. He put out two more on Ox Wood's tongue for Taylor's benefit.

"You ever bet on games?" Kimball asked Taylor Rusk.

"No," Taylor said. "I don't understand why people gamble."

"The real gamblers aren't gambling," Kimball said. "You think Cyrus Chandler bets on football games?"

"I never thought about it," Taylor said, embarrassed. He never had thought about it until that moment.

"Well, think about it, kid," Kimball said, "This is a magic show and we are all involved. Everything is based on making something look like something else. Cyrus Chandler owns racehorses and a track in Florida. You think he knows the difference between us and his ponies?"

A big black Lincoln drove up outside, and Kimball instantly walked off the porch to the parking lot. Taylor Rusk recognized the driver as Johnny Cobianco, the youngest of his landlords at the University.

"Is he talking about fixing games?" Taylor asked Hendrix. He tried not to seem shocked.

"I don't know if games are fixed or not," Hendrix said. "I just run the plays that are called."

"One day I'm gonna have to call those plays," Taylor said.

"Not right away, I don't imagine. No matter how much they talk about you being the Franchise, you don't know anything compared to Kimball."

"Apparently." Taylor shook his head in surprise.

"Unless he gets hurt bad, Kimball will play a couple more years; then it'll be your job and we'll see if you're the Franchise or not. No sense getting beat up at the front end of your career. Just hope when you get in there that you have Kimball Adams's knack."

"Knack for what?"

"Calling the right play at the right time."

Kimball returned to the table. Taylor watched through the screen as Johnny Cobianco drove away and was swallowed up in a red glow of caliche dust and taillights.

"Well," Kimball said, sitting back down and digging into the duffel bag for a fresh bottle of Johnny Walker Red, "I just learned the score of our opening game. We're gonna almost win."

And Kimball was right. The Pistols were six-point underdogs and lost by ten. They were as close as a field goal on the twenty going in late in the fourth quarter when Kimball threw an interception. Hit the linebacker right in the chest. The guy caught it in self-defense. Walking up to Taylor on the sidelines, Kimball sang, "Welcome to my world. . . . Won't you come on in?"

Kimball Adams told Taylor at the Leadville Bar and Post Office that night that his greatest play with Cleveland had been when they were beating Pittsburgh by more than the spread and he had to throw an interception and then block Ox Wood to keep him from tackling the interceptor. Kimball sprang the defensive back for a touchdown and made the block on Ox look like a missed tackle. Won the game but didn't beat the spread. Kimball was an old pro from the Old League.

"It's great moments like that that was what the Old League

was about," Kimball said, holding up his Scotch glass and looking at Taylor. "You'll never have that. In a few years they'll have the whole season figured out by computer in advance and have the bets already placed, charging the losers interest. In the Old League they needed a great quarterback to fix a game. Winning and losing meant something. Soon they'll fix it so they'll call the plays by satellite and you won't even know what they are. It'll be coaches, officials and extraterrestrials. You'll see I'm right." Kimball drank his Scotch until the ice clinked against his big, white capped teeth.

Middle linebacker Margene "Meg" Brinkley drove up in his pickup truck. Three-year veteran Margene was also a rodeo cowboy, a calf roper and bulldogger. Backs and receivers tackled by him found themselves in a real wreck. He called it "grabbing their slack."

"All right!" Margene was chewing a thick wad of Red Man; his bald bullet head shone. "Let's talk about who is gonna run this here football team." He spit a thick brown stream on the floor. "I'll run the defense. Any objections? Good, I'll get me a beer while you boys fight over the offense."

"Let's see what kind of offense we start the regular season with before we argue about who runs it," Kimball growled. "It might run itself."

"It might run away," Hendrix added. "Taylor, we need to stop by the Crystal Palace, check on the rest of the boys." Bobby Hendrix stood and stretched. "Let's go."

"Don't ever let 'em call your plays for you, kid," Kimball advised Taylor before he got out the door. "Once they do that, you're lost."

THE CRYSTAL PALACE

THE Crystal Palace was a barnlike pavilion that opened for summer dances when the dude ranches in the river valley were doing peak business. For a century, dances were held every Saturday there on the chalk bluff overlooking the river. A row of unshuttered windows about four feet tall opened the dance hall on all four walls. Kids crawled in and out and sat on the sills, kicking their feet against the unpainted sideboards. The older people danced to the country band while the young couples sat at the long tables and chattered and preened and posed and drank beer and whiskey. Everyone went to the Crystal Palace: local valley ranchers and residents, the young local toughs, the dude-ranch owners and employees, the chamber-of-commerce types, real estate men, developers, the dude-ranch guests from Dallas, Houston, San Antonio and Austin. And tonight, for the first time, professional football players from the Texas Pistols' training camp.

Hendrix pulled Red Kilroy's car up next to a green Nash Metropolitan. "Is there any curfew tonight?" Hendrix asked. The nude cutout deodorizer twirled and spun from the mirror.

"No, no curfew," Taylor said, looking at the green Metropolitan. Then he slowly studied the complete outside layout of the Palace and the major characters hanging around. "It seems under control."

"That is not always a good sign," Hendrix said.

The young quarterback moved inside the crowded dance hall. Hendrix followed behind, watching Taylor's intimidating physical presence. The crowd parted; the receiver hobbled pleasantly in the wake.

Inside the Crystal Palace, Suzy sat at a table with Simon D'Hanis and watched A.D. dance with a counselor from El Río Frío Camp for Girls. Taylor and Hendrix joined them. Suzy was watching, looking bored. Simon was strung tight as a drum, tapping on the table and shuffling his feet restlessly. His eyes roamed the building.

Everybody seemed to be paired up, a social system already in place. The football players seemed to stand out in the crowd. They were breaking and bending the Crystal Palace Dance Hall social system. A. D. Koster was leading the charge as he bumped up against the counselor from El Río Frío. This not only pissed off Suzy but also the local bull rider, who had brought the counselor to the Crystal Palace in his new welding truck. He was planning to have himself a couple more drinks of Wild Turkey and then feed the faggot his brown alligator shoes. Taps and all.

Suzy watched A.D. and the counselor for a few more bored seconds, then looked slowly around the table at the pulsating Simon, the redhaired laconic Hendrix and finally at Taylor Rusk. She leaned over and grabbed Taylor firmly by the knee. "C'mon outside and buy me a beer. I'm tired of watching A.D. dry-hump."

Taylor was again impressed by the strength of her grip.

"I'm staying here to make sure Simon don't explode," Hendrix said.

Taylor followed Suzy through the crowd outside to the barbeque stand, where Suzy ordered a chopped-beef sandwich and two beers. Taylor paid and carried the beers while Suzy ate big bites of the sandwich and walked over toward the river. Taylor followed, weaving through the people sprawled out on blankets, watching the tight white shorts and sipping from both beers. They passed two deputy sheriffs and a game warden passing around one cigarette.

Suzy found two outcrops at the bluff edge overlooking the river. They were back in the shadows, out of the lights strung from the beer and barbeque stand.

Taylor handed Suzy her beer. "You drank out of it!" She noticed the light weight of the beer can.

Taylor nodded.

"Jesus, well, goddam help yourself."

"I bought it," Taylor defended.

"Nobody held a gun to your head."

"I couldn't be sure your shorts weren't loaded," Taylor said.

"Hey, sonny, don't go pulling the pin like that." Suzy looked at him and sipped her beer, "It could go off in your hand." She still called him sonny.

Taylor sat on a flat ledge. "Are you serious about A.D.?" he asked.

"About as serious as he is about me. You want to know if my intentions are honorable?" She wadded the barbeque into her cheek and chewed. The last of the sandwich disappeared into her pretty mouth and she crumpled the waxed paper, washing the sandwich down with beer and tossing the waxed paper off the bluff, down into the shallow white-blue water of the river.

Suzy looked around for something to wipe her hands on. They were greased with barbeque sauce. She settled on Taylor's T-shirt and reached over and wiped her small hands clean, staining his shirt with red sauce.

"Help yourself."

"Thanks." Suzy bent over and wiped her mouth on the shirt.

"Code of the West."

"I see where Cyrus Chandler's daughter married Lem Carleton III." Suzy frowned at Taylor. "A.D. told me she was your girl."

"A.D. was wrong." Taylor looked down at the river. The waxed paper was still visible.

"Sure. Sorry. Why'd she get married? Pregnant?"

"How should I know?"

"The papers said she was beautiful and looked great in Mexico on their honeymoon. The wedding cost two hundred thousand dollars. They flew everybody to San Antonio for a reception in the old brewery, then on to the South Texas ranch for a catered trail-drive breakfast."

"She'd been engaged to the guy for a long time."

"You were just a last desperate swing before she settled into the complacency of her wealthy early twenties?" Suzy mocked. "Oh, I see now."

"I was just a stop on her highway of life . . . another town along the road."

Suzy smiled and slowly scrutinized the shadows of Taylor's face, trying to discern his intentions.

"What about you?" Suzy took a long swallow and finished her beer, absently crumpling the can in her strong, slender hands and tossing the metal wreckage into the river. "You want to be something when you grow up?"

"Not if I can help it."

Suzy and Taylor Rusk ended up drinking several more beers, then climbed up in a live oak to neck and escape the ticks and chiggers. They were only partially successful. Suzy got tick bites on the insides of her thighs, and Taylor had at least fifteen chiggers burrowed into his armpits. They got the ticks off Suzy by heating Taylor's pocketknife blade. Suzy painted over Taylor's chigger bites with her clear nail polish, leaving them to suffocate.

"It's a better fate than they deserve," she decided.

About midnight the Crystal Palace Dance Hall went up for grabs when the welder hit A. D. Koster right on the point of the chin, knocking him loose of the El Río Frío counselor. A.D. sailed across the dance floor and into the band, hopelessly entangled in the drum set. Simon D'Hanis hit the welder. Bobby Hendrix dove out an open window. The two deputies and the game warden charged inside.

After that the versions of the Crystal Palace Massacre vary widely. But like the Alamo, San Jacinto and the Spindletop Oil Boom, it marked the start of an era. The Franchise had arrived.

After the dance hall had been cleared out and the band finished loading their van, Hendrix called Suzy and Taylor down out of the tree. They went in search of A.D.

Everyone else had been accounted for and were long gone on the yellow school bus. A.D. was the only MIA.

They eventually found him and the welder, both battered and bruised, sitting behind the bandstand with their arms over the other's shoulder, drinking from the same bottle of Wild Turkey and cussing women. The counselor from El Río Frío Camp for Girls was nowhere to be seen.

A.D. called the welder a "goddam nail-eatin', ass-kickin', woman-fuckin', good ol' son of a bitch." The welder proposed a toast to A.D.'s "noble ancestor and famous Apache, Quanah Parker."

"Quanah Parker was a Comanche," Suzy said, picking through the wood of a broken table. "There *is* a difference. It was in the way they fought and treated their women." She hefted a three-foot-long two-by-four and hit A.D. across the shoulder blades as hard as she could. The blow knocked him face-first in the welder's lap. She had aimed for A.D.'s spine and hoped for paralysis.

"Hey," the welder-bull rider yelled, "that's my pal!" He struggled to rise. Suzy drew back the yellow pine stud.

"Well, say hello to him for me." She hit the man a sideways blow across the forehead that sounded like extra bases in a game of sixteen-inch slow-pitch. The welder-bull rider went flat on his back and joined A.D. in the ozone.

It would be another seventeen days before Red gave them a second night off. It was soon enough for some and too late for others.

TRYING OUT

THAT first camp was a never-ending parade of bodies passing through the Franchise like grease through a goose. Every day saw new kickers, tackles, guards, ends and defensive backs. This was a world of hemorrhaging receivers and crippled running backs.

Names were written on adhesive tape and stuck on the front of the headgear so coaches and other players could identify the man. It was impossible to keep up with the faces.

Texas was the last stop on the inevitable drop out of professional football. An expansion team got to look at all the rejects, and they came in all colors, sizes, shapes, religions and states of mind. They were scarred, tattooed, crazed, addicted, broken, bashed, worn out, blown out, fucked up, fucked out, scared, mad, friendly, kind, courteous, loyal, trustworthy, brave, selfish, selfless. There were sadomasochists, homosexuals, heterosexuals, bisexuals, a-sexuals. They all had one thing in common: they were football players, and Texas was the last bounce.

After Texas it was the netherworld, the god-awful "out there" of the dead silent civilian world. They had all spent years and tremendous amounts of energy to avoid that inevitable, final fall from grace. This gave them a special kind of shared desperation in their lives, a fear of professional death that burst out in odd uncontrollable ways. Some extremely funny, some not so funny, some downright horrible.

An exceptional few combined all the traits with brotherhood, human love, courage, strength and a sense of justice. It was in those men Taylor glimpsed the greatness that would coalesce under Red's obsessive genius. The Franchise would soon overflow with skilled, talented technicians. Red kept all the artists, the weirdos, the crazies, the lunatics.

This was all the result of Red Kilroy's game plans and nose for talent and Dick Conly's scheme to build winning into the system. Their tactics and strategies—combining short-term methods with long-term goals—created a timetable to the Super Bowl. It was a fast track and there were lots of wrecks. Players crashed and burned and needed replacing.

Red Kilroy looked at everybody that didn't belong to anybody. There was only one criterion: *Could he play?*

INVESTICO AND OTHER
DIRT

"OKAY, boys," Mr. Smith, the tallest of the two security men, said. "First, let's run down the list of places the commissioner's office has placed off limits in Texas."

The other agent, Mr. Jones, had assembled a flip chart and stand. He held a long wooden rubber-tipped pointer in his right hand and slapped it lightly against his leg. He was wearing a dark-blue suit and brown oxford shoes with thick soles.

"Turn over to the Texas list, J. Edgar," the tall security man said. He, too, was in a dark-blue suit, but his shoes were black wingtips with tassels. J. Edgar Jones flipped through the ring-bound cards, quickly finding the one headed "Texas."

"Now, these are the places that *known gamblers* frequent," the tall security man said. "And the commissioner expects you all to steer clear of these places year-round. You'll each get a mimeo with the off-limits lists of all the League cities. Keep them with you when you travel and do not frequent any of the establishments listed." The tall man looked around the room as if he expected questions or confessions from the players. A few coughed and shuffled their feet. Kimball stared blankly at the blackboard, ignoring the whole proceeding.

"Know the places in your city by heart."

The phrase startled Taylor Rusk. *"By heart?"*

"And don't frequent those places. Gamblers can use any piece of information that comes from inside the locker room to give them a little extra edge. Injuries especially, but personal things, like family trouble or who is drinking too much. . . . That can all help the gambler to increase his edge and we don't want to do that."

Taylor nodded absently and wondered who the gambler increased his edge against. And why the League sent these two particular security men to explain it to the Franchise.

"Now, tonight we've got a special treat for you fellows . . ."

"Treat?" Taylor whispered to Hendrix. *"Treat?* Who the fuck are these guys?"

Hendrix hunched over to Taylor and whispered, "Investico. A private security company hired by the League. They come around to every team every year. Investico's owned by Casino International and they specialize in gambling security. They usually hire ex-FBI and CIA men, guys who can keep things secret, covered up. They're the ones who'll tap your phone if you ever get out of line."

". . . one of the all-time great defensive linesmen, Leroy Weller. Ten years in the Pro Bowl. . . ." J. Edgar Jones got his job by catching the eldest daughter of the LA franchise owner with two ounces of cocaine packed in a condom and inserted in her vagina on a return trip from Peru. J. Edgar saved her from a major bust and his reward was half of the coke and a job in League security. The commissioner personally placed him with Investico.

The incident gave Robbie Burden the hammer he needed to force the Marconi family to put the Los Angeles franchise on the market, eventually to be purchased by the Portus family, allies of Commissioner Burden. J. Edgar liked his work. It paid well.

". . . We're talking a class guy and Hall of Famer . . ." J. Edgar was stem-winding. He loved this part of the job. ". . . I give you a real man of courage: Leroy Weller." The agent led the light applause.

"Jesus, Taylor, you know what this sounds like?"

"An AA meeting. No wonder Red and Dick Conly aren't here. What the fuck are *we* doing here?" Taylor put his head down.

Leroy Weller walked stiffly to the front of the old junior-college classroom with its black chalkboard and old heavy wooden chairs and desk with thirty years of grafitti.

"Hi, fellas. I'm Leroy Weller and I'm suffering from the disease of chemical dependency."

"Jesus, this is pitiful."

"So who gives a shit?"

"Give the poor bastard a break," Taylor hissed. "Confessing drug and alcohol dependence is his gig now."

"The lousy asshole," Hendrix whispered. "He made big dollars. Anyone in the Pro Bowl ten years made big bucks."

Weller told the whole gory story of his fall from success and wealth in pursuit of illegal marijuana and two-thousand-dollar-per-ounce cocaine, finally running afoul of the law when "a friend" informed on him. "It saved my life," he said. "I spent ten thousand dollars a week on cocaine alone. So don't none of you hotshot rookies think you can handle it. I couldn't handle it and I'm a hell of a man. I spent everything I had. I ran my home, car and children's clothes up my nose. I started free-basing, fucking white women. I was thinking I was a big-time football player. Well, I was *shit!*" Leroy Weller began pacing and ranting like a revivalist. J. Edgar Jones stood grinning like an approving deacon.

Leroy's reputation as a maniac on the field, plus his pure physical size—six feet six inches, 275 pounds—plus his obvious intensity about the subject, tended to dampen any of the more vocal dissent. Kimball Adams, however, was not impressed.

"Aw, shut up, Leroy, and go on home. And take the fucking narc with you," he growled. "We want to go get a beer."

"I can forgive that; I can understand that," the big black man said, his face giving the lie to his words. "You can't admit that . . ."

"I don't want no forgiveness or understanding, Lee-roy," Kimball mimicked angrily. "I want a fucking beer. I don't see no coaches or management, except for dickhead over there, who took roll." Kimball pointed to Lem Three, sunburned in his white shorts, holding the roll clipboard. "I'm going for a beer."

"Now, wait a damn minute, Kimball. You think you're man

enough to go through this weak, God-fearing man?" Leroy slammed his huge fists into his chest. The rib cage thundered.

"Nigger, please," Kimball said, not backing off, "you're making an asshole of yourself."

"I am not."

"Come on, Leroy." Hendrix stood up and pointed at the bewildered agent. "You are helping people like him. After years of being the rooster, you're turning bird dog. If it wasn't for assholes like J. Edgar Jones, cocaine would still be eight dollars an ounce. You wouldn't have snorted your life away at eight dollars an ounce."

"You ain't listening, Bobby."

"You aren't remembering, Leroy."

Taylor interrupted: "Speaking for low nigger on the pole, I'm leaving. I know I'm weak and Leroy's weak and J. Edgar seems like a real turd. You guys don't tell me how to think and feel and I'll do the same."

"What the fuck kind of meeting is this?" Simon D'Hanis wanted to know.

"I still ain't seen the man that can get past me!" Leroy thumped his chest.

"Jesus, what I would give for a thirty-eight Special," Kimball mumbled.

"Do you want . . ." Ox began, but Kimball touched his arm and shook his head.

"Did this guy go to Notre Dame?" Taylor hissed to Hendrix, who nodded. "I should have known. Notre Dame, UCLA and the Big Ten. They really put weird backspin on these guys."

"Look, turkey"—Speedo Smith gathered up his gear and started toward the door—"I don't know what you are, but what you *aren't* is gonna lay your hands on me. The law is supposed to protect us from people like you, not force us to listen to you talk. You ain't no man—you are back to slaving nigger, slaving for owners. Everybody dies, man. So die, nigger. Don't change sides at the end, just die."

"Grab his slack, Speedo," Margene Brinkley said.

"I'm with you, Speedo." Taylor followed the small, belligerent wide receiver's lead. "I have the horrible feeling that these guys' salaries are just added on to my phone bill. Let's get out of here."

Speedo pushed by Leroy Weller, but Weller stood between Taylor and the door.

"I don't know what Speedo has planned in this event," Taylor said, "but I plan a very large lawsuit."

Weller stood his ground. "Oh, yeah, man?"

Taylor glared into the big man's small eyes, "You fucking touch me and I'll sue you, Mr. Smith, J. Edgar, Robbie Burden, the League and Investico."

At the sound of his own name J. Edgar bolted into action. He grabbed Leroy's arms. "Well, fellas, why don't we break it on up now. Okay?"

Ox Wood walked up to J. Edgar and Mr. Smith and Leroy Weller. "If I see you guys around my house, I'll kill your kids."

J. Edgar and Smith turned white.

"I can dig where you're coming from," Leroy Weller said.

Dick Conly looked stupid on purpose to aggravate representatives of the League Owners Council, Boyton Kink and Don Jackson, attorneys-at-law.

"If you have any specific questions . . . ?" Kink asked.

"How much is this costing and do I have a choice?"

"The money is already paid as your franchise's share of each assessment."

"I was afraid of that."

"Besides house counsel, the League Owners Council keeps a Washington, DC, law firm of antitrust lawyers." Jackson sold like it was Electrolux.

"The lawyers are working with the commissioner on their latest antitrust laws. We plan to move first on the Senate side, attaching a rider to a black-lung bill," Kink continued his update. "The US Senate allows 'non-germane' amendments. Senator Thompson is to carry the ball for us—"

"Well," Conly interrupted, "Bailey Thompson is about as non-germane as possible, and with all three of you working on it, I expect you will all shortly disappear up your own assholes."

The two East Coast lawyers smiled thinly and continued their spiel, laying out the schemes agreed to in the latest Council meeting.

Conly slid his eyes around the room. Lem Carleton III was listening raptly, his mouth ajar. Lem was slightly drunk. Alcohol insulated him from the monstrous violence of the Franchise and the League.

Red Kilroy's grin caught the general manager's eye. Red had invited himself to the meeting and was also drunk. Dick liked his head coach, a man who dealt in real politics with no illusions about the League, which was why he let him attend. Red would do whatever was necessary to win. He was a gutter fighter and didn't quit, and Conly found it hard to oppose him in order to protect Cyrus Chandler's interests. Conly winked at Red and the head coach blew him a kiss. It was right in the middle of an explanation of the latest IRS ruling on whipsawing, the practice of declaring different tax values on the same transaction so that both the buyer and seller show big tax losses. It was particularly tempting in sports-franchise bookkeeping. The head coach blowing a kiss to the general manager startled the handsome young lawyer, Jackson. He lost his place, blushed and stammered, his eyes cutting from Red to Dick.

"You were talking about whipsawing the value of player contracts and franchise fees," Conly said sternly, enjoying the ambitious man's discomfort. "We know all that. Tell us about how the commissioner fucked up by asking for complete antitrust exemption like baseball on the grounds it *wasn't* interstate commerce."

"Right. Right." Donald Jackson, Harvard Law, collected himself. "On antitrust we're going to have to settle for a piecemeal approach," the lawyer said. "You have to remember we need the Union on this on the Hill. We need organized labor support for antitrust exemption. This guy Charlie Stillman is valuable."

"Union? Organized labor?" Red Kilroy roared. "We don't need no union or no lawyers. You're a staid little shit. Get some real dirt under your fingernails and blood, not rhetorical blood, not flesh in the abstract, but the real gore," Red said. "You're getting a big fee that I could use to buy several good running backs. You want to whipsaw your intangible? I'll goddam whipsaw your intangible, you little puny chinless Harvard fart!"

The lawyer was stunned. Red stumbled toward him, scattering chairs, finally falling.

"Aw, fuck it. I don't want to be an owner if I got to hang around with you guys." Red banged furniture and walls, heading out the door.

"The hell you don't," Conly said softly after Red had gone.

THE STING

TAYLOR Rusk shuffled down the hall of the dormitory, wearing a Texas Pistols T-shirt, gray basketball shorts and moccasins. The afternoon workout had just ended; he was heading for his room to nap before dinner and the night meeting.

"Hey, fool," Speedo Smith called out from his room as Taylor passed. The big quarterback stopped and looked at the black man stretched out on his bed, arms back, his head resting on his hands.

All-Pro Speedo Smith had been blacklisted by Dallas for getting involved in the Union. Bobby Hendrix had recruited him at the Pro Bowl to help get the Union back from Charlie Stillman. Alfred "Speedo" Smith then compounded his error by trying to help his teammates deal with the bureaucratic chaff of the Union and the team. He made waves and appeared to have lost a step, so Dallas placed Speedo Smith on *The List*. It was a big mistake.

Dick Conly let Dallas think that the Pistols were just going through the motions of claiming Speedo for the one-hundred-dollar waiver price "to help get that wiseass jungle bunny out of football."

Dallas explained to the local press the wisdom of getting rid of a receiver who had just caught seventy-nine passes for eighteen touchdowns and over two thousands yards in offense.

"Smith is lazy," Dallas's general manager said. "He had nine-flat speed but twelve-flat hands." The press bought it and wrote it. Several laughed at "twelve-flat hands."

Taylor leaned against the door frame of Speedo's room.

"You know, fool," Speedo said, "we need to get Red to put in a system of automatic checkoffs on blitzes. The wide-outs run quick in-routes to the hole. The quarterback uses a three-step setup . . . a short pass, then a footrace." Speedo smiled. "My fans will love it. We all take our keys from the linebacker movement *after* the ball is snapped. There is no way they can defense it."

Taylor walked in and sat on the empty bed that belonged to veteran defensive back R. D. Locke. Locke hadn't returned from the practice field. Speedo's roommate was a quiet, peculiar man. Big, silent, seething anger.

"You better talk to Kimball Adams; he is the starting quarterback. I'm the understudy."

"I already did," Speedo said. "He likes the idea. If you two tell Red, he'll do it."

Taylor nodded. Speedo was right; dump-offs would take some pressure off the line to pickup stunts and blitzes. Now Speedo just had to control his blazing speed; otherwise he would outdistance Kimball Adams's arm. Taylor thought he could take full setup and still overthrow Smith on a full speed-up route. He was wrong and he never did. Alfred Roosevelt Smith was the greatest wide receiver since Bobby Hendrix, and in Dallas, Speedo had revolutionized passing. Red Kilroy knew he would again. Speedo may have made waves, but he hadn't lost a step.

SCRIMMAGE

"BUFFY is coming up for the scrimmage tomorrow," Simon said. "I haven't seen her since camp started. She didn't want to come because she's beginning to get real big, but I told her I had to see her. Boy, will I be glad when we break camp."

Taylor had his eyes on the playbook.

Red Kilroy kept his team hitting and scrimmaging because he needed to see a lot of bodies in head-to-head competition and game situations. He kept lots of "live dummies" around to hit and practice blocks and tackles against.

Five exhibition games just weren't enough to judge the number of men Red ran through that first training camp. The Texas Pistols would continue to hit and scrimmage into the regular season. Players would come and go all year long based on performances in practice as well as games. It violated the League rules, but Red had violated the college rules; he sure wasn't stopping now.

"These are a new kind of anabolic steroid," Simon said to Taylor, lifting a big, dark-brown thousand-tablet bottle from the forest of bottles and pill vials that covered D'Hanis's dresser top. Simon took twenty-seven pills a day—from megadoses of vitamins to steroids.

"I got these from Melvin Wilkins, the assistant track coach at school," Simon continued to explain as he shook several large pink pills into his hands. "He got them from a Russian weightlifter at the Tokyo Games. They really build the muscle tissue." Simon popped the pills and washed them down with water, then began picking over the rest of the bottles. "Red told me I'm gonna need to weigh at least 265 to play guard in this league and they got me on a power-lifting program. I usually have hell keeping my weight over 250." Simon picked out another brown bottle. "But these Russkie steroids have already got me up to 260 and climbing."

"I heard those things made your balls shrink." Taylor sat at the small built-in desk, still studying the playbook. He had stopped at Simon's room while returning from the QB meeting, where Red had just added the new sting adjustment against blitzes— exactly what Speedo Smith had wanted.

"No, they don't make your balls shrink," Simon said. "What makes your balls shrink is all the stuff in the mashed potatoes. The Russians give steroids to their woman athletes," Simon grinned. "Those gals got balls the size of Rio Grande grapefruit."

After the snap, his first key was the middle-linebacker. Martha. Red designated the linebackers with women's names.

"Have you noticed"—Taylor kept his eyes on the playbook— "that all defensive maneuvers are described in a shorthand code vocabulary that is decidedly feminine? Red must have new psychological theories." Taylor paused. "Maybe pathological. We didn't do this in college." He turned to the glossary at the front of the book.

A pass-rush stunt with the defensive tackles crossing was a *Tit*; the tackle-and-end stunt was *Tits* and *Ass* or *T/A*. It was easily remembered and quickly communicated. There were several pages in the glossary, which included a definition of the term *Clothesline*: raking the forearm across the opponent's throat, face or head, so as to bring tears to his eyes or otherwise obscure his vision and give him reasons to worry about his physical well-being. *In the Hole* was a clean shot at the QB with the intention of testing his manhood and durability. It *meant* kill or cripple.

"Euphemisms do take the edge off." Taylor went back to studying his keys on the sting routes.

At the snap, Martha was his first key; then, as he backpedaled, he checked the strong side backer, Sara, finally checking the weak side, *Wendy*.

It *would* be *Wendy*.

Taylor quickly turned back to the playbook glossary, but Wendy's delicate face began to materialize among the X and O patterns of a 93 sting against a full blitz.

It was useless: Her face was in his head. Always on his mind, throughout his body—her voice, the touch of her soft, transparent skin, her long, slender fingers slowly crawling up his back like a daddy longlegs.

His eyes scanned the pages of Red's football terms. Desperately.

His life was whirling through time out of control. He was the quarterback and had committed the cardinal sin: He had lost it. He had known better than to even consider a Pi Phi. It was too much. He used every ounce of his skill, guile, courage and physical ability to quarterback a team, deal with Red Kilroy, first the NCAA and the University, now the League. It was all he could do, yet he'd added Wendy Cy Chandler. It was burying him.

"Okay, Simon." Taylor found a term from the playbook glossary and the panic eased. Wendy faded for the moment, though he knew she would return. She always did. "Okay, Simon, this is a tough one."

The big lineman continued to shake bottles and vials, extracting tablets and capsules. "Yeah, I'm ready. You been fucking around in here forever."

"Okay, what's an outside Garterbelt?"

"A pass-rush stunt," Simon replied. "The defensive end pulls the offensive tackle outside, opening a hole for Sara or Wendy to blitz. A double outside Garterbelt is done on both sides for Sara and Wendy." Simon perused his bottles.

"And when Martha comes, too, along with the free safety?" Taylor asked.

Simon picked up a bottle and dropped it in the waste can. "A double outside Garterbelt with a Duck in a Sailor Hat."

Red designated all defensive backs as different fowl.

Taylor closed the book, pushed up to his feet and shuffled out. He was tired and didn't lift his legs.

Simon continued through his daily pill ritual.

Taylor had noticed a definite change in the size and shape of Simon's body during training camp. At a time when most guys lost weight, Simon was putting it on—hard, strong muscle tissue. His shoulders tapered into his head, and his neck had disappeared into the bulging knots of muscle.

Taylor had also noticed a change in Simon's personality. His mood swings seemed to be much greater, from euphoria to deep depression, but that could be from all the weeks of training-camp confinement. Taylor's own mood swings were fearful. There were days when he *knew* he couldn't get out of bed. He was not tired. Just scared and lonely.

Everybody was getting cabin fever, anxious to break camp and get back to the city. There were arguments and fights. Damage was done.

Early in the next day's scrimmage, Kimball Adams had Ox Wood at right guard and a rookie from Ohio State at the left. Kimball audibled a quick trap and the rookie missed the call; he pulled full speed the wrong way, hitting Ox Wood pulling full speed the right way. The two men hit head to head directly behind the center. The enormous crash knocked both men out cold.

Ox came around shortly.

The rookie was still out of it when Luther Conly walked him to his seat in the plane. Five months later he came to as a Delta steward trainee in Atlanta.

At that scrimmage Lamar Jean Lukas sat directly behind Buffy Martin D'Hanis. Lamar assumed Buffy was a player's wife since she was young and pregnant, so he carefully kept his comments to himself. But Lamar Jean thought the Texas Pistols looked only fair, even for an expansion team.

The scrimmage was sloppy. The defense generally outplaying the offense, not unusual early in the year. It was a low scoring scrimmage—generally dull, uninspired play by the offense, with lots of penalties and missed assignments.

Lamar had played a little football in the Marine Corps, but he wasn't good enough to keep from getting sent into action. If he hadn't had most of his right calf muscle shot away in a small firefight in Cambodia, Lamar Jean Lukas would have walked out on the field that day and asked for a try-out.

Lamar had seen Taylor Rusk in the Bi-District championship game and the quarterback did it all. He scored every way: pass, run, kick—hell, *fly*, thought Lamar. Park City went on to beat Wichita Falls in the Cotton Bowl for the state championship. Taylor Rusk was the greatest athlete Lamar had ever seen. Taylor Rusk was Lamar's hero.

That's why he'd taken a year's worth of savings and gone to the Texas Pistols ticket office. Lamar Jean Lukas bought a season ticket on the forty-five-yard line. There were plenty of seats to pick from, and Lamar Jean Lukas was one of the first paying customers to support the Franchise. The ticket-office people promised him that buying one of the first season tickets meant he would *always* have first consideration on ticket sales.

What they told him was true.

Until the Pistols began to win.

Lamar sat quietly behind the pregnant woman, studying her

reactions, and figured out she was Simon D'Hanis's wife. Two rows down was an old man with a young blonde in shorts and halter on his arm. Lamar recognized the old man as a United States senior senator and the chairman of the armed-services subcommittee.

Dick Conly, dressed in a Texas Pistols T-shirt and white shorts, his spindly legs glowing red from too much sun and his face flushed from too much alcohol, sat down beside the small, wrinkled senator.

"Is this little honey taking good care of you?" Conly asked the senator. He rubbed his hand too vigorously on the girl's naked back.

"So far so good," the senator laughed. "But it's early yet. We have to see if she lives up to her potential."

"Potential has ruined more lives than I'd care to count." Conly sipped from a white plastic cup with the crossed purple pistols on the side. "Potential," Conly repeated, continuing to rub the girl's bare shoulders. "You make certain the senator goes back to Washington happy, you hear? He's one of the Franchise directors, and in DC he's got to keep the government on an even keel and off our back. Right, Senator?"

The senator nodded.

Lamar studied the forces of the American way as the first fan.

Taylor Rusk had been alternating offensive series with Kimball Adams. Taylor threw the only two scoring passes. One was to Speedo Smith against a weak-side blitz using the new sting adjustment. As Taylor backed out after taking the snap, he saw the weak-side linebacker crashing toward him, so the quarterback just flipped the ball over the line. Speedo Smith had keyed on the blitz, adjusted his route from a zig out to a quick slant and the ball hit him in the chest. He split the seam between the two safety men and raced sixty yards to the end zone with the defensive backs running a poor chase ten yards behind.

Taylor connected on the same adjustment with Bobby Hendrix from about twenty-five yards out. The safety dragged Bobby down from behind, but the skinny redhead fell into the end zone.

The only other player to score was a running back from Central Michigan. Danny Lewis had only fair speed but incredible balance and the ability to bounce away from tacklers, wriggling free, continuing forward. Margene Brinkley, the middle linebacker who had begun to run the defense, said hitting Danny Lewis was like trying to tackle silk.

Lewis's secret was simple: "I'm scared to death out there. Fear is a hell of a motivator when you add to it the ability that goddam football has for attracting a crowd of snarling maniac speed freaks."

Every time Taylor called a play to Danny Lewis, the running back would blanch and look down at the ground. As soon as Lewis's hands touched the ball, he would start screaming and running.

As the defense pursued him, Lewis's screams increased the closer and the bigger the man.

Late in the scrimmage Kimball Adams was at quarterback and called a quick pitch to Danny Lewis. Kimball tossed him the ball and Lewis headed for the sideline, screaming, bouncing, wiggling and twisting. He turned the corner, shaking off tacklers, using his free hand to keep himself off the ground after being hit by defensive backs.

The screaming never stopped until Danny Lewis crossed the goal line fifty-five yards later, where he dropped the ball and continued out the back of the end zone.

Not counting the ten yards of the end zone or the additional twenty yards to the track, where Lewis finally stopped and looked back for pursuit, it was the longest run from scrimmage that day.

It was also how he ended up with the nickname Screaming Danny Lewis and won himself the halfback job.

Taylor Rusk rolled on the ground, laughing so hard he ruptured a blood vessel in his eye and knocked over one of the assistant coaches.

Something inside snapped, and it felt good to laugh spasms of maniacal laughter. Taylor hadn't laughed since Wendy married Three. He couldn't recall laughter before Wendy. They had certainly laughed together.

Taylor lay flat out on his back, arms stretched out. He laughed both sadness and relief into the clear blue hill-country sky.

Wendy was in the gray Mercedes stretch-parked in the near end zone. The passenger compartment was secreted behind mirrored glass.

Taylor had been stunned when the German limo arrived, though he shook it off. He always played well hurt, but he worried about playing confused and unhappy, continually losing at life. The white lines changed all that, as usual. It was a different world inside those lines. It was his world; he blazed the trails. He didn't get left behind and lost. In there he got what he wanted and hunted for more. Outside those lines he had been careful about his wants. At least until Wendy Chandler.

Lem Carleton III had been drinking with the senator and Dick Conly throughout the afternoon; now he staggered to the Mercedes and rapped on a darkened window. There was no response. Lem Three, assistant PR man, cupped his hands and tried to peer through the shaded glass. Off balance, leaning down, Three lurched forward, banged his head on the window and fell sideways into the end line. White clouds exploded out of the grass. Three pulled himself to a sitting position, his face and chest covered with chalk. Regaining his feet, Lem tried the door. It was locked. Three stood there looking at himself in the mirrored window, a chalk-whiteface clown in his base makeup. The limo pulled away, leaving Three alone in the end zone.

Red Kilroy decided that day he needed to get himself a fullback. He knew right where to look—Canada. Toronto. The player was Amos Burns. Red told Dick Conly to go get him Amos Burns.

"I've got a good contact in Toronto, Knuckles Nelson," Red said. "He'll help us."

"Why should he?" Conly was skeptical.

"He wants to coach in the League . . . someday."

"Someday ducks will tap dance," Conly said. "I'll call Knuckles."

On the far sideline Luther was packing away footballs and equipment. Dick was suddenly sad, inexplicably unhappy. "I need a drink." The general manager searched for the ice chest.

"Here." The head coach handed him a half pint of 101-proof Old Crow.

Taking a deep gulp, Conly watched his son proudly and fearfully. In this sweet, slender boy, all knees and elbows, the general manager saw his own mortal dilemma: he loved Luther with an intensity that could consume him. He took another long swallow.

Dick avoided losing by the simple mental gymnastic of never wanting to have. He enjoyed and loved his wife and girls, but Luther he had *wanted*.

He had never expected to want, to have. It was the problem he couldn't resolve, and as he proudly watched Luther, he kept a football field between them.

"Hey, boy," he called out gruffly. "I'll catch you later tonight. I have to call Canada and shaft Toronto out of a blocking back."

Luther kept his head down, working feverishly. He waved "Okay" and mumbled, "Yeah, sure." He would never comprehend that his father was frightened of him.

It turned out that it wasn't Toronto that got the shaft but a college All-American named Jimmy Jackson, who graduated the following year. In return for Amos Burns, Dick Conly promised Toronto that Texas would grab All-American Jackson next year in the draft.

"We just won't offer him any money," Conly told Knuckles Nelson. "The only other place he can go is Canada. You guys draft him. Put Amos Burns on the next plane. Jimmy Jackson is your meat."

And that's how All-American Jimmy Jackson ended up playing professional football in the Canadian league for twenty thousand dollars. He had no idea how it happened.

Amos Burns did several years of good journeyman's work as a blocking fullback for the Texas Pistols. Amos really blocked the three girls—Martha, Sara, and Wendy, the Duck in the Sailor Hat, the Garterbelt outside or inside, single or double, the Chicken Lips, the strong safety. Amos Burns hit them and they stayed hit. Sometimes for days.

After the scrimmage Red gave the team the night off with no curfew.

Kimball Adams and Ox Wood took A. D. Koster and headed for the Old Leadville Bar and Post Office. The yellow school bus hauled about forty players back to the Crystal Palace.

Simon D'Hanis checked into a local motel with his pregnant wife, Buffy. Simon was hyperventilating a little when he grabbed his toilet kit and headed out of the dorm room.

Bobby Hendrix wrote a long letter to his wife, Ginny, and his four boys.

Bobby Hendrix told his wife to tell her father they could move on a Venture Capital Offshore drilling deal with H. Harrison when they sold the property in Cleveland and resituated themselves in Texas. The VCO oil-well investment would be the biggest investment Bobby Hendrix had ever made. It was certainly the biggest gamble. Bobby Hendrix rubbed his cramped, sore hands before folding and sealing the letter. The freckled, aching, stiff fingers did fold the letter, but Bobby was out of saliva.

Taylor Rusk took a nap.

Speedo Smith and Screaming Danny Lewis climbed a small mountain behind the practice field and drank beer and wine and smoked dope.

Red Kilroy worked on some new offensive wrinkles. All night the TWX clattered people's fates back and forth across the country.

The blonde in the shorts and halter lived up to her potential and sent Senator Thompson flying back to the nation's capital happily deluded about his sexual prowess. Cyrus Chandler's helicopter picked the senator up in the parking lot and took him to the airport. Cyrus picked up with the blonde where the senator left off.

Suzy Ballard got off late at the Sonic Drive-In, and when she arrived at the dormitory, A. D. Koster had gone off with Kimball Adams and Ox Wood. Two zeuglodons and a garden variety, common-as-cowshit rat.

Dick Conly watched Suzy arrive. He staggered out of his room and down the hall to meet her as she was putting down the house phone.

"He's gone off with Kimball Adams," the general manager said.

"Where?"

"I don't know." Dick Conly looked over the young girl, again barefoot, dressed in white shorts and a tank top. She bit her lower lip in anger. She was about the same age as Luther.

"Damn him," Suzy said. "I told him I would be a little late."

"Can I take you somewhere?"

"I got a car, thanks."

"Good." Dick Conly weaved slightly. "You take me somewhere."

Suzy Ballard just looked at the florid-faced middle-aged man.

"You want a drink?" Dick Conly held up his plastic glass with the purple team logo on the side.

"Yeah." Anger tinged her voice. "Do you own this team?"

"Honey, I just run it. I run everything."

Suzy giggled. "Let's go get that drink."

"Good, they have a bar at the Sahara Motel."

Suzy knew what that meant and decided it might not be all bad. It was a way to get even with A.D. Besides, Dick Conly would probably pass out before he got around to dragging her into bed. He didn't, but it still wasn't all bad.

Luther watched from his window as his father drove off with the carhop that everybody from Park City High cruised the Sonic to see.

Suzy performed sexually like an Olympic gymnast. Dick Conly just lay back, grunted, groaned and fell hopelessly in love. Before dozing off, Dick Conly offered Suzy a job with the Pistols.

Back at the dormitory Luther tried to masturbate, but his father and Suzy kept popping up. Luther quit in despair when his arm began to ache. He felt guilty and depressed, his balls ached and he'd skinned his dick.

POST-SCRIMMAGE
WITH LAMAR JEAN LUKAS

"HEY, Taylor. Taylor."

Taylor Rusk felt someone shaking him awake. The dormitory room was dark and the only light came from the hall.

"Taylor, wake up, I got to talk to you."

The quarterback slowly came awake and looked into a shadowy face he had never seen before. Lamar Jean Lukas was standing over the bed, shaking him.

"Come on, Taylor, wake up. We got to talk."

"Who the hell are you?" Taylor asked, too tired and sleepy to really care.

"Lamar Jean Lukas. I'm a season ticket holder." Lamar Jean grinned and sat back on the extra bed. "I want to talk to you about the scrimmage this afternoon and about the team's prospects."

"Go find the other season ticket holder and talk to him about it, for Chrissakes, and let me sleep." Taylor rolled over, putting his back to the man. "I'm tired. Leave me alone."

Lamar was momentarily angry but let it pass and gained control of himself before he spoke again. "C'mon, Taylor, I'm a big fan of yours and the Pistols. I just wanted to tell you a few of the things I noticed out there today. I used to play in the Marines."

"Everybody has played somewhere." Taylor didn't turn back. "Now, go back to the Halls of Montezuma and let me sleep."

"Hey, man," Lamar flared and grabbed Taylor's shoulder, jerking him over in bed, "don't turn your back on me. While you were screwing off, being a star, I was getting my ass shot off to keep the goddam commies out of Vietnam."

Lamar had Taylor awake. The big quarterback sat up and rubbed his eyes. "I don't care if the commies are in LA. When they get to New Mexico, come and tell me. Now goddam . . . ah . . . what did you say your name was?"

"Lamar. Lamar Jean Lukas." He stuck out his hand. "Pleased to meet you."

Taylor took it without enthusiasm.

"How did you get in here?" Taylor asked. "Civilians are not supposed to be in this dormitory."

"I'm not a civilian. I just wanted to give you a little advice. I drove up here from the city to watch the scrimmage. I just wanted to help out."

"Well." Taylor just wanted this nut out of the room. He knew the type; delay and future promises were usually the best approach. "Listen, Lamar, I appreciate the interest, but I'm just too tired to concentrate right now. Why don't you put it all in a letter or something and mail it to the team offices. We're breaking camp soon." Taylor Rusk wanted Lamar Jean Lukas to go away fast but not mad. An angry, embarrassed fan might lay out there and ambush you one day. If fans killed each other over football games, how long before they started killing quarterbacks?

"A letter? You think so?" Lamar asked.

"Yeah. Yeah." Taylor lay back, checking Lamar over for suspicious lumps in his clothing, a pocket or belt knife. "A letter. Then I can study it. Make sure you get everything down. That's the way Red does it. Now, you better get out of here before one of the coaches comes by."

"Why don't you give me your address?" Lamar said. "Or phone number. We could talk and become friends."

"I don't have a place yet." Taylor began to get nervous about Lamar. His eyes seemed to shine in the dark. Taylor never thought shiny eyes were a good sign. Middle linebackers had shiny eyes. "Listen, put it in a letter and mail it to the team office. They'll get it to me. Now, you better get out of here. If the coaches catch you, they'll file trespassing charges on you."

"But I got a season ticket."

"They'll still do it, man," Taylor said. "You know coaches."

"Yeah." Lamar nodded his head. "The assholes."

Taylor grabbed and shook Lamar's hand. "It was great meeting you, but you better get going." Taylor indicated the door with a nod of his head. "The coaches are always sneaking around."

"Those bastards," Lamar said. He paused and looked at the floor. "A letter, huh?"

Taylor nodded. "You better get going. I'll talk to you later."

"Okay, man, that's a *promise*." Lamar slapped his knees, stood up, walked to the door, checked the hall and was gone.

Taylor shook his head and tried for sleep, chasing the frightening specter of a world full of nameless, faceless fans nursing private grudges against Taylor Rusk. He drifted into unconsciousness.

Early that morning Simon came in to Taylor's room and slammed the door so hard it sounded like a gunshot. Simon's mood swings were getting easier to discern.

COMMIE STEROIDS

SIMON sat on the edge of the bed and glared at Taylor, forcing the quarterback's eyes open by will. Simon's pupils were dilated, making his eyes look almost black.

"Simon?" Taylor sighed. "Before you say anything, I have already been threatened in the dark by a lunatic Vietnam-vet football fan."

Simon's breathing was rapid and shallow.

"If whatever is making you crazier than normal can be solved by simply fine-tuning your drug intake, I beg you go do it without further complaint."

"What makes you the authority on sanity around here? Because Doc Webster got you all the money?"

"Simon, I don't sign your check. We've been through all this."

"You and Doc Webster wrecked Conly's budget for salaries, so there was nothing left for me. Cyrus said so. Charlie Stillman did too."

"Simon, there *is* no player's salary budget. Cyrus jerked us both around that day. It was over Wendy, not money. Cyrus doesn't know about money. Dick Conly and Red run this team, not Cyrus." Taylor closed his eyes. "Charlie Stillman sold you out; accept it, learn from it. Relax, Simon, and quit worrying."

"I am not crazy." Simon puffed up red, clenching his fist.

"You're not *crazier*. You should cut down on the steroids. Talk about lousy credentials—a drug thirdhand from a Russian. You might as well go to the team doctor."

"You have never been injured. You have no understanding of pain. It is *my* pain. Mine! Not Buffy's. Not Red's. Not yours to dismiss at will. You need some broken ribs. You don't know what it does to get broken." Tears sprang from Simon's eyes. "Each one is worse." He wiped a great paw across his face. "You've *never* been hurt, you just don't know." Simon D'Hanis's red face was now wet with smeared tears and he was trembling. He paced into the bathroom and back out, cracking his huge knuckles. The chemical change in Simon was more than Taylor could bear.

"She don't understand why I love playing!" Simon slammed his palm on the side of the dresser. "I don't *like* injuries. Sure, I get hurt, but if you can't stand the heat—"

"Don't crash and burn," Taylor interrupted. "Even though people pay to watch us crash and burn, that doesn't mean we have to."

"She wouldn't understand." Simon furrowed his brow. "Buffy thinks everything is just fine."

"Well, isn't it?"

"Is it for you?"

Taylor did not reply. The question stopped him dead.

"See what I mean?" Simon chewed on this thumbnail.

"Lay off the steroids, Simon," Taylor mumbled.

"I should have known you'd side with her." The door closed with an explosion. Down the hall another door slammed shut.

Taylor was crossing the parking lot, heading for the training room; Simon and Buffy D'Hanis sat in her car. The Mercury had been a wedding present from her father. Her mother just cried daily until July. Taylor walked over to say hello to Buffy.

"Hello, Buffy. How's the bride?" He put his hands on the door and leaned down.

Buffy turned away from Taylor and said nothing.

"She's fine," Simon growled. "She's just goddam fine."

Taylor moved back at Simon's anger. The big lineman squirmed from behind the wheel. Taylor still leaned against the passenger side. He could feel the car rise when Simon stepped out. The springs groaned.

"Mind your own business, Taylor."

Simon walked quickly off toward the dormitory.

"I got the parking concession, Smiley." Taylor turned back to the car. "What's bothering the founder of the Akim Tamiroff Fan Club?"

Buffy slid over to the steering wheel, keeping her back to Taylor. The child she was carrying made the maneuver difficult and awkward. She said nothing.

"That's twice he screamed at me, and it isn't noon." Taylor noticed Buffy's struggle and came quickly around to the door on the driver's side.

"Let me help."

"No. No, Taylor I don't need any help. Please leave me alone."

It was too late; Taylor was already around the car and leaning in to help her get behind the wheel. She turned her head away, but Taylor had already seen.

"My God, Buffy, what happened?"

"Nothing. Nothing. Nothing happened." She began to cry.

Taylor eased into the car, took her head gently in his hands and turned her face to him. Her lips were bloody and swollen and one eye was purple-black, puffed almost shut. Buffy looked at the horror in Taylor's face with her one good eye.

"Is it that bad?" she sobbed.

"It's pretty bad," he told her. "You can't go back in the game and you are doubtful for next week. Jesus Christ, did he do this?"

Buffy broke into racking sobs and Taylor held her, laying her head on his shoulder. She cried for about five minutes, completely soaking his shirt. When she calmed down she began apologizing.

"I'm sorry, Taylor. This isn't your problem. I'm sorry. I'm sorry." Then she began to cry again, softly this time.

"Did Simon do this?"

She nodded her head. "He just went crazy," she sobbed. "He's never laid a hand on me before." Her lip split open again and began to bleed. Taylor dabbed at the blood with his shirt.

"You better see a doctor," he said. "Or at least come with me and let the trainer look at you."

"No. No. Don't you dare tell anyone about this." Buffy lifted her battered head and glared with her one good eye. "I'll never speak to you again. If you're my friend and Simon's friend, you won't ever tell anybody about this. You stood up at our wedding."

"If you call that standing. You can't drive back to the city in this shape." He pushed her head back to his shoulder and stroked her hair. She started to wail.

"I kept telling him he was gonna kill the baby. He was crazy. What's happened to him, Taylor?"

"I don't know, Buffy. Maybe it's the pressure. This is Fruitcake City, the last bounce. Maybe he hit too hard. It's a mean game and the sidelines are vague. Nobody is sure and it's that way on purpose."

Taylor checked her eyes and ears for blood while Buffy sobbed softly.

A. D. Koster's convertible roared into the lot in a cloud of white dust. Suzy Ballard was at the wheel. Dick Conly staggered from the passenger side around to the back entrance of the dormitory. Suzy checked herself over in the rearview mirror and put on some lipstick.

"Wait here, Buffy." Taylor eased out of the car and Simon's wife lay back against the seat. Taylor jogged over to Suzy.

"Say, Suzy, can I ask a favor?"

"It depends," Suzy said coldly, putting the lid back on her lipstick. "What's in it for me?"

"How about I don't tell A.D. you been fucking the general manager."

She narrowed her eyes and returned the lipstick to her purse. She grimaced, shook her head and checked it in the mirror, studying the fall of her hair. "That's a lame threat, sonny, but you got spunk. Okay, what do you want?"

"I want you to leave A.D.'s car here and drive Simon's wife back to the city in her car."

"Then what'll I do for a car all week?"

"You'll think of something," Taylor smiled. "You can always roller skate."

"Shithead." Suzy pushed out the door, shoved Taylor aside and crossed the lot to Buffy's car.

"Jesus Christ." Suzy saw Buffy's face. "Did you get the guy?"

Taylor leaned across to Buffy. "Suzy will drive you home." He turned to Suzy. "Don't you leave her until somebody gets there to look after her."

"Oh, Taylor, please," Buffy cried, "don't call my folks, please."

"Don't worry, Buffy, it'll be just fine," Taylor soothed, then turned to Suzy. "Get her on home."

"It'll be just fine," Suzy mimicked. "Is that right? Men are usually fools or assholes, but you could be both." She drove the car off toward the city, leaving Taylor with a multiple-choice expletive.

Taylor went inside and called Wendy Chandler Carleton. She answered on the third ring.

"Wendy, this is Taylor."

"Yes?" Her voice turned distant and cold.

"Buffy's on her way home. Can you get over there and meet her?"

"Well, I suppose I can."

"Good. Do it."

"Why?"

"Because she needs help and you're a goddam Pi Phi."

"Is it the baby?" Wendy's voice was suddenly urgent, frightened.

"I don't know what it is, Wendy. I don't know anything at all."

"You never did," Wendy said, and hung up.

THE RIOTS

THE riots had been going on for several days and the game had been postponed from Saturday to Wednesday.

That was the good news.

The bad news was that it was now Wednesday and the city still burned and people had been murdered around the stadium.

"We have to play." Simon was scratching his head with his massive hand. Simon and Buffy had made up and his mood was better. He didn't seem as much like the old Simon, but there had been an improvement.

"Why do we have to play, Simon?" Bobby Hendrix asked. The lanky redhead was stretched on his bed, watching the live television coverage of the riots. "We're not getting game checks; we're playing for free."

A black man was televised live dashing from a looted store with a table-model TV. The TV camera was in a helicopter and a woman announcer was doing play-by-play as the man dashed over the rubble around burning buildings until he disappeared into a warren of still-standing slums. Then they did the replay.

"Look," Taylor said. "Stop-action looting."

"Well," Margene "Meg" Brinkley, sitting at the desk, said, "it's a charity game, isn't it?" The defensive leader was, due to a lost rodeo weekend in Bakersfield, covered with tattoos. Sitting cross-legged and barefoot, he was now picking his toenails and smelling them.

"Can you really smell?" Taylor looked at Margene's nose, smashed across his wide face.

"Sorta." Brinkley sniffed at a toenail.

"Don't mind him, Taylor," Kimball Adams said. "Meg is the result of years at a school that uses the same system developed in Yuma to escape the territorial prison in the 1800's."

"What system is that?"

"You pay big bucks."

"What's wrong with that?" Simon asked.

"Nothing, if you don't get caught," Hendrix said. "Get caught and there is a peculiar process. The college slaps its own wrist.... Coaches deny any knowledge, then move to better jobs with $200,000 salaries and $500,000 Bowl Games with schools that haven't been caught lately. And of course they *nuke the jock.* The NCAA makes an example of someone who is really no one. Big bucks for everybody but the twenty-year-old who let some scumbag recruiter buy him a sport coat. The jock is still wearing the same sport coat ten years later in the unemployment line."

"That's the beauty of cash," Kimball said.

"Bullshit," Hendrix shot back. "There's no beauty in a system that corrupts young athletes for nickels and dimes while the NCAA and the networks make millions. They give players room and board, books and laundry, and call the split even."

"Here comes the Union speech," said Kimball. "Bobby you're still pissed 'cause you weren't smart enough to get extra money in college."

"Smart? It don't take smart," Taylor Rusk added. "Just turn your umbrella upside down, 'cause it is raining money."

"I'll tell you how dumb I was," Margene Brinkley said, his eyes on the televised riot. "The first school I visited offered me money, which frightened me and I left. But when the second school offered me money and I left, they chased me outside, apologizing for such a measly offer, and began to up the ante. The faster I walked, the higher the price went. Finally, when I reached the car, it was ten thousand dollars cash, a new car, university jobs for my parents and sister, plus a rent-free house. So my advice to this year's high school blue-chipper is park a *long way* from the coach's office and don't talk."

"Is this a charity game tonight or not?" Simon watched the live riot.

"Yeah. It's a charity game," Hendrix sneered. "They give *our* salaries to charity, otherwise the split is the same. We have to get the Union to get us paid for exhibition games."

"I'm gettin' paid," A. D. Koster said.

"You're getting paid out of your regular season money," Hendrix said. "They must figure you're gonna make the team."

A.D. grinned.

"I don't see what you're so happy about," Hendrix said. "They're getting five free games a year out of us. They sell tickets and TV rights to those games. They make money off the games, but we all do it for free. We should at least make them put exhibition-game money into the pension fund."

"Did I tell you?" Kimball looked smugly at Taylor.

"You ain't made the team until training camp is over," A.D. said, "so why should they pay you?"

"Because, asshole, people pay to see *us*, not Cyrus Chandler."

"Ignore A.D., he's already management," Taylor said. "Got his beady little eyes on a job with the Franchise. A player coach? No chance. Maybe assistant PR man. Lem Three smell of blood, A.D.?"

A.D. crossed and recrossed his legs, checked his fingernails, then glanced at the televised civil war, which showed a complete city block disappear in flames and smoke. It was a time-lapse replay with background music.

"Jesus," Simon said, "is that the stadium there?" He leaned forward for a closer look.

Everybody else was watching A. D. Koster's face.

"Take the drop to management, A.D.," Taylor said. "You're the kind that belongs there. Red won't keep you much longer. But Cyrus Chandler will have all sorts of jobs for a guy that don't mind getting his hands dirty up to the armpits in other people's bowels."

"And one of those jobs, you asshole," Bobby Hendrix interrupted, "is convincing people that management is the show. Well, the players and coaches are the game and the game is the show! No one can *own* the game. If we give up that fight, then the game will become whatever Cyrus Chandler, Dick Conly and the Macaroni family decides."

"It's Marconi, and remember, Mr. Union Man," Kimball Adams said, "if the Union gets to decide who the players are, there ain't much difference."

"I heard the Marconis were being forced out by the commissioner," Margene Brinkley said.

"Giving up Los Angeles without a fight?" Kimball Adams flicked the remote control and ran through all the channels. "I doubt it." The television flashed up two car ads, a game show, two soap operas, a catfood ad with a celebrity cat, another game show, a skinny fag who used to be a fat fag explaining the difference and a mail-in life-insurance policy that seemed tailored for a person who thought this was his last trip to the post office.

"Give up LA without a fight?" Kimball brought back the riot. "What's Burden got on them?"

"I heard it was a drug thing, a border bust," Brinkley said.

"Come on, the players?" Kimball was highly skeptical. "Nobody on the West Coast steps across the line in their right minds. Do they? The last guy that went out there alone was Gary Cooper in *High Noon*."

"A family problem. Daughter," Meg explained. "Well, they got it quieted down. The guy that sold her the coke snitched her down. It was that Investico guy, J. Edgar."

"No shit?" Bobby Hendrix sat up on the bed. "He set her up for the commissioner?"

"Nobody knows. But the Marconis are forced to sell to a fella named Portus—a crony of Cyrus Chandler, as well as the commissioner."

Kimball seemed stunned. He had spent one season in Los Angeles, then was traded suddenly in the off season. "You sure it was Betsy? The daughter?"

Margene nodded. "J. Edgar set her up and they were waiting. She had two ounces in her box. They skin-searched her."

"Only two ounces?" Kimball frowned and exhaled through his nostrils. "I can't believe they found it. I lost a Pro Bowl wristwatch and a championship ring in there one night."

On the screen the television camera had picked up on the progress of an upright freezer. It was a pastel blue and picked up sharply as an electronic image.

"Look at that." Taylor Rusk pointed at the television. "That guy has got a freezer all by himself." Everyone watched the progress of the lone black man and the upright freezer as he started up the front steps of an apartment building with the blue freezer. It was a mighty struggle between that black man, eight narrow, crumbling red brick steps and the great pastel-blue freezer.

"Just to teach you a lesson, I'll bet ten dollars," Kimball said to A.D., "that the nigger whips the freezer and gets it up those steps."

"It's too heavy," A.D. said. "He can't make it alone."

"Bet?" Kimball wanted to know.

A.D. nodded.

It took the black man about twenty minutes, with a lot of yelling and screaming at the television from the ball players, before the blue freezer disappeared into the apartment building with a last-gasp effort and exceptional body English from Kimball, who was up off his bed, yelling, "Get mad, nigger! Get mad!"

"Did you learn something?" Kimball asked as A.D. paid off for the second time that morning.

"Yeah. I learned not to gamble with you."

"Anything else?" Kimball put the second ten dollars with the first.

A.D. shook his head.

"This ten dollars is why we'll go in tonight and play that game." Kimball put the money in his pocket. "It is a point of honor and trust. The bets have been laid, and there are lots of folks depending on this action."

"You make it sound like Mom, hot dogs and apple pie," Hendrix said.

"As American as bootleg whiskey, horseracing and whorehouses."

"And unions," Hendrix added.

"And show business," Kimball retorted and sipped at his beer. He always liked to have several beers before a game. "It will be business as usual at the stadium tonight, gentlemen. The show must go on. Angry niggers or not. I have it from the Man."

"Who's the Man?" A.D. asked.

"If I knew, do you think I would tell you?"

Bobby Hendrix ran his freckled hands through his hair, then picked up his wad of Nutty Putty and began his finger exercises. Bobby Hendrix carried his Nutty Putty with him constantly, continually working his splendidly sure hands through a series of exercises to increase strength and cut down on dislocations of the fingers.

Kimball finished his second beer of the morning. The game had been scheduled for seven P.M. The old quarterback looked over at Taylor Rusk, the young quarterback, and laughed.

"You just stick with me, kid, and I'll make a star nigger out of you." Kimball opened another beer.

"Kimball, slow up on the beer. This is a night game," Hendrix cautioned. "Don't get on the wrong schedule."

That afternoon at three they left the hotel for the stadium. Shots were fired at the bus as they left the freeway at the stadium exit.

Nobody was hit.

They played the game and, from the pressbox, fires could be seen burning all around the stadium. Texas lost by more than the point spread after Red Kilroy sent in a rookie center in the fourth quarter and on the next two possessions Kimball Adams fumbled the first snap, leading to fourteen points for the opposition.

After the game Red stopped Kimball on his way to the bus. The two men walked away from the others.

"I'm cutting the rookie in the morning," Red said.

"Naw, Red," Kimball said. "Those fumbles were my fault."

"I know. But I'm covering for you because you're getting too careless. I don't know who owns you and I don't care. You're a great quarterback on the take, and I need you to make us look respectable and to keep Taylor Rusk from getting killed. I need time to get to the Super Bowl. It's my chance to be an owner." Red narrowed his eyes. "You teach that boy how to be the quarterback you used to be. I don't have the time to bring him slow. Conly's all right, but Cyrus Chandler is a time bomb. I have to win right away or I am gone. Teach Taylor Rusk what it took you twenty years to learn, and do it this year, and I'll see you always have a job in football."

Kimball looked straight ahead. "And?"

"Nothing else. Try to win when you can and don't introduce Taylor Rusk to whoever owns you." Red paused. "I'll try to keep you from getting caught."

"What do Chandler and Conly say?"

"I doubt that they've noticed yet. Besides, I'm in charge of player personnel. It don't make a shit what they think. You bring Rusk along. You help make Taylor Rusk a quarterback who will win me a Super Bowl and I'll send you out of football a hero and make sure you work when you retire at the end of next season."

Kimball Adams turned slowly and looked at Red. "Retire?"

Red nodded. "You have two years left, Kimball. I need that much time to build an offensive for Rusk. Linemen and backs. I can't let him get hurt so young. He's a phenomenon, but we need more to go with him. . . . I can't wait for the draft. I'm gonna start swapping bodies."

Kimball stared at Red for a long time; then, taking a drag off his cigarette, he flipped the butt off into the burning night. "I ain't got much time. I guess I better get started making Taylor Rusk the Franchise."

Off in the distance was the sound of automatic-weapons fire. The sky glowed as the city burned.

CABIN FEVER

"EVERYBODY is going crazy." Taylor was sitting on R. D. Locke's bed, talking to Speedo Smith. R.D. was out.

"Don't worry, turkey," Speedo reassured, laughing. "It's cabin fever. Everybody gets it by the end of camp."

"Simon has turned into Godzilla." Taylor leaned against the dresser.

"Get off my bed, motherfucker." The voice came from behind, and Taylor looked up into the glaring black eyes of R. D. Locke.

The broad-shouldered, muscular veteran defensive back had come in the expansion from Pittsburgh. He was six-foot-three and was reviving the bump and run. He developed the punishing coverage style to hide his lack of speed. The rules allowed only one "bump," so R. D. Locke made it count, often making the "run" unnecessary.

Once behind R.D. you could beat him bad deep, but it was painful exercise. R. D. Locke also forced end runs better than any defensive back in the League, crashing into pulling guards and blocking backs with a crazed enthusiasm that bordered on the degenerate. R. D. Locke was fearsome but vulnerable, which made him all the more violent, sometimes out of control.

In practice Taylor had seen R.D. cover a hotshot All-American receiver from Clemson. At twelve yards downfield the rookie started his move, which remained forever unfinished. Anticipating the break, R. D. Locke planted both feet and lunged, smashing the kid's face with a thick forearm. The rookie crumpled in a heap. He never again beat Locke on a pass route and was released early in camp.

"I said get the fuck off my bed, white boy!" R.D. walked over, took Taylor's arm and jerked him to his feet.

Speedo stopped laughing.

"Hey, R.D.," Speedo said, "calm down, man. I . . ."

R.D. turned on his roommate. "Shut up, nigger, 'less you want to wake up dead in the morning."

Taylor Rusk wrenched his arm free. "Okay, okay, R.D., I'm sorry I sat on your bed." Taylor, not yet afraid, started for the door. "Ill-mannered son of a bitch."

R.D. yelled after the quarterback, who was now out in the hall.

"Your momma!" Taylor yelled back.

Locke's face contorted in black fury, and he started after the quarterback. Then he stopped, turned to his dresser and jerked open the top drawer.

Taylor continued on down the hall, scuffing his moccasins, angry and confused. He had gotten about three doors down the hall when he heard Speedo Smith yell.

"R.D., you crazy nigger! Stop! Taylor, look out!"

Taylor Rusk looked back just as R. D. Locke stepped out into the hall with a .38 Detective Special in his hand. Time slowed as the angry black man brought the small, lethal pistol up to firing position and squeezed off a shot.

Boom!

Taylor ducked and felt the breeze from the slug ruffle his hair. The barrel of the snub-nose looked bigger and bigger.

R.D. leveled the gun with both hands. Taylor backed away but was afraid to turn and run. Taylor couldn't take his eyes off of the pistol, as if he could dodge the bullets by watching for them. R.D. sighted down the short barrel at the center of the big quarterback's chest and began to squeeze off another round. There would be no missing this time. The hammer was already raked back. R.D. grinned crazily and squeezed.

A blur lunged out the doorway and tackled the insane defensive back.

Boom!

The shot went wide of Taylor, blowing a wad of plaster out of the wall. Speedo Smith drove R. D. Locke across the hallway with the force of his tackle. R.D.'s head and right elbow hit the door molding. He dropped the gun and Speedo kicked it toward Taylor. R.D. slid to the floor, dazed.

The hall quickly filled up with players emptying out of their rooms. Simon D'Hanis, Meg Brinkley and Ox Wood helped Speedo keep Locke on the floor. R.D. was foaming at the mouth. Taylor Rusk stood paralyzed, staring at the pistol in his hand. Then he began to shake.

One of the assistant backfield coaches came running down the hall.

"What's going on here?" he demanded, looking at the three men holding Locke on the floor. "I thought I heard shots."

"You did, man," Speedo said, his breathing shallow and rapid. "You did."

Taylor held up the pistol.

"Oh, my God!" The coach's eyes grew. "Whose is that?"

Taylor looked down at R.D., who was rolling his eyes, still foaming and struggling futilely against the mass of Simon D'Hanis, Meg Brinkley and Ox Wood. Speedo Smith got up and walked over to Taylor.

"Thanks," Taylor finally said. He looked glassy-eyed at Speedo and then back down at Locke.

Speedo's breathing had begun to slow. He nodded and walked back toward his room without looking back.

The backfield coach's mouth hung open. Finally he said, "Okay, nobody move. I gotta go see Red." He took the gun from Taylor. "Was he shooting at you?"

Taylor nodded, his legs rubbery. He thought he was going to be sick.

"Okay, okay! Jesus Christ! Goddam! Hell!" The coach looked at the gun in his hand. "Nobody do or say anything until I get back here with Red. That's an order."

The coach looked at the men holding R. D. Locke. "Don't let *that* son of a bitch up." The coach ran off, carrying the pistol. He had to push his way through the crowd of players gathered to see what all the noise was about.

On his way to Red's room the assistant stopped at the dormitory office. He had the telephone switchboard shut down and ordered all the outside doors locked.

"You're doing this to me 'cause I'm black," R.D. yelled, struggling vainly in the grip of the three mammoth men.

Taylor looked down at R. D. Locke. The black man's eyes blazed with a hatred that was generations in creation. Taylor turned, walked to his room and lay down. As he listened to the buzz of activity in the hall, he suddenly felt strangely calm. Twenty minutes later he heard Red Kilroy and Dick Conly arrive.

"All right, the rest of you back to your rooms. Simon, Margene and Ox bring R.D."

Taylor listened as the players returned to their rooms. Several of them looked in on Taylor. He waved them off.

Two hours later Simon came by the room. Taylor was still staring at the ceiling.

"Well," Simon said, "he's gone."

"The police come and get him?" Taylor asked. His voice cracked; his throat and mouth were still dry from fear.

"No, Red said it was just a case of cabin fever." Simon went into the bathroom and splashed water on his face. "We just put him on a plane. Red traded him to Denver."

Taylor nodded his head slowly. "Cabin fever, huh?"

"Yup," Simon said. "Worse goddam case I ever saw."

SON OF THE
SOFTWARE

"CALL Robbie Burden," Cyrus said "and tell him I want a spot in his office for Lem Three."

"Why?" Conly said. "He isn't bothering anybody here. He just sits there, drinking whiskey in his coffee cup, and tries to think of catchy things to write on banners and bumper stickers."

"I want him to get an idea of how the League office operates and get firsthand experience dealing in broadcast from production to advertising. There's a revolution coming."

"I know, Cyrus. I told you about it."

So Lem Carleton III and his pregnant wife, Wendy Cy Chandler Carleton, moved to New York City, where Lem worked as assistant to Commissioner Robbie Burden for telecommunications and special projects. He spent his time at the League office, trying to comprehend the size and velocity of change in broadcast technology, regulations and profitability. He learned how to market football. He saw them building the barricades for the communications revolution that Dick Conly said was coming.

It failed to stir him, but it fascinated his wife.

Wendy Chandler Carleton was exhilarated by the struggle for control of the telecommunications industry. She had an interest in the software. One in particular.

"Software is my life," Taylor had told her.

Dick Conly's plan for the software was a football-league network broadcast direct by satellite to a football-league decoder. The viewer would be able to watch any league game on a twenty-five-dollar pay-per-view basis, plus the cost of the dish antenna (six hundred dollars) and the League decoder (five hundred dollars).

Chandler Communications Research and Development had already perfected "addressibility" capabilities for the Direct Broadcast Satellite project. Chandler Aerospace was test-firing satellite launch rockets and had space reserved on the shuttle. They planned to be kicking satellites out of the shuttle like hay bales, and by the mid-eighties approximately forty million homes would be connected—with $1.25 billion potential each of twenty weekends, not counting doubleheaders, Thanksgiving, the playoffs, or Super Bowl.

Dick Conly figured the Super Bowl broadcast would gross $2.5 billion.

$2.5 billion.

One game.

Dick Conly thought like that, betting millions against billions. Chandler Communications subscription television would gross eight million dollars per game on local pay telecasts of Pistols home games that were blacked out in Park City and a 150-mile radius. Eighty million a season for the Franchise before one ticket was sold.

The stakes were going up fast.

THE BOTTLE-CAP WAR

HENDRIX was complaining about the Union.

Kimball was needling him out of boredom.

Taylor was resting on his back with the playbook over his face. He was thinking pass routes while his receiver ranted.

"The pension plan promised lots but guaranteed little. We don't even control or have access to the money. Owners' pension contributions are voluntary and teams are just not paying. Stillman keeps saying it's a great deal, but he gave the owners control of the pension in return for dues checkoff."

Spurred by his anger at Charlie Stillman, plus his eternal war against Commissioner Burden, Bobby Hendrix had generated a fair amount of resistance among older players throughout the League against signing the bottle-cap licensing agreement.

Robbie Burden found himself in legal jeopardy and pressured Charlie Stillman to get the Union in line.

In Bobby Hendrix's room the phone rang, and the redheaded man answered.

"We've got to be reasonable, Bobby," Stillman was pleading

over the phone. "The Union could look bad. This could hurt a lot of people."

"Name two, besides you and the commissioner?"

"We need not get personal," Robbie Burden interrupted. It was a conference call. "This is business and we're merely trying to rectify an oversight."

"Fire Stillman and make that ex-basketball player, Terry Dudley, the new Union director," Hendrix demanded.

"What?" Director Stillman lost control momentarily. "You little cocksucker . . ."

"Shut up, Charlie!" the commissioner ordered. "Just shut up!" Robbie Burden's tone softened for Hendrix. "Listen, Bobby, it's *your* union—"

"Don't give me that shit," Hendrix cut the commissioner off. "You go tell your owners to tell their reps to fire Stillman and hire Terry Dudley or you are going to have Dr Pepper's legal department all over your ass." Bobby hung up.

Charlie Stillman was fired.

Terry Dudley was hired and the Union took control of their own pension and health funds.

The bottle-cap war ended.

The revolution had begun.

PLAYING IN THE DARK

DURING exhibition season Taylor Rusk worked hard to improve and develop his skills at quarterback. Taylor planned on being *the Franchise*. He planned to control the players, to deal with Red as he had done at the University. Then start learning to deal with Cyrus and Conly. Cyrus proved to be merely willful and spoiled, but Dick Conly was a lifelong hired gun. Power struggles were Dick Conly's business; smelling out an ambush was his unique talent. Taylor would build his power base between the white lines on the field. They couldn't reach him there.

Red pushed Kimball Adams to spend extra time teaching Taylor to play major-league quarterback. What took Adams years he taught Taylor in months. How to read defenses, when and where to expect them and what to do, how to take his keys from the linebackers and the weak and strong safety. How to call a game, probing for weakness and strength; how to play the field like a chessboard and basketball court. When to audible and why. How to use the clock. How to control his offense. "The best information comes from your teammates on the field, not some asshole on the sideline.

"Keep control," Adams said. "That's the bottom line."

Taylor had a good feel for sensing a blitz and continued developing the skill with the sting system of automatics. All backs, ends and linemen had to learn to key without any call. They expanded it eventually to automatic adjustments for every defense. Pass patterns changed in midroute. The angles on the field. Kimball taught Taylor the geometry of the game to combine it with Rusk's strong arm and touch, the exquisite patterns and fingertip catching of Bobby Hendrix and the devastating threat of Speedo Smith.

The weak offensive line tried to protect the quarterback, and Ox Wood harangued the lineman about pride and courage, the savage man-on-man wars between the tackles, the shame of a quarterback sack.

"These boys represent all that is good." Ox had his arms draped over Taylor and Kimball. "Womanhood, motherhood. And *we* must protect them. We must win the war in the trenches. Goodness needs time to flower, and it is up to us to bite, kick, slug, cut-block and trap-block for our offense to blossom. It can be a beautiful spiritual feeling. We must stand. *They shall not pass*."

Tears streamed down Simon D'Hanis's face. "Goodness shall triumph over evil! They shall not pass!"

About all that *didn't* pass was Kimball Adams's kidney stones.

But they never quit. Humiliated. Beaten. Exhausted. They never quit.

"You're fifty percent of the way," Red said after a disappointing loss. "You're *not* quitters."

It was that particular night exhibition game when Simon D'Hanis developed his raging hatred for combination football-baseball stadiums.

The pregame ritual included a flag ceremony with the stadium lights out. Old Glory was led by a single spotlight to center field. Everyone sang "The Star-Spangled Banner" except Red, who forgot the words.

The stadium remained dark as the starting lineups were introduced. From inside the tunnel each player ran out in the spotlight—alone. The stadium was a dark, roaring maw.

"Just follow the spotlight, men," the guy with the walkie-talkie said. He slapped Ox Wood on the shoulder and the big All-Pro lumbered out into the stadium. The crowd howled and roared out of the dark. Ox just thumped his way through the tunnel, out the dugout and into the spotlight. The brilliant beam seemed to carry Ox over the warm-up circle, past the pitcher's mound, across the infield and out to the football field. The darkness yowled. Unaffected, fearless, steady, gliding in the spotlight, his short legs skating the yellow circle of light, Ox Wood stopped at midfield and waited. He stood alone in the swirling, dusty stream of light.

Simon D'Hanis was terrified, frightened, confused and lost. His legs felt rubbery. Could he make the run? Suddenly darkness swallowed the great hulk of Ox Wood and the crowd squalled like some wounded animal as the smoke-filled, swirling, filthy stream of light crawled toward Simon. An electronic voice was calling him out into the void. "Number Sixty-three, Simon D'Hanis."

"Just follow the spotlight, son." Someone slapped Simon's pads, and the frightened young man staggered from the tunnel into the spotlight's glare.

Simon D'Hanis was not ready for the spotlight.

He couldn't seem to get his balance, running fearfully, surrounded by blackness in the bright-yellow vacuum, with eighty thousand people screaming damnation, hurling their fury at him from the darkness. Simon was weightless, senseless, and could only blindly stagger, watching the lighted spot on the ground, twice almost falling, to the vocal pleasure of the Cleveland fans. But Simon battled back, struggled, analyzed his problem, focused his effort at staying erect. By the time he was passing the on-deck circle, he was getting his feet back under him. He was feeling good and running fine.

The crowd roar was losing its fearsome quality. Simon's eyes began to adjust; his running rhythm smoothed out nicely.

"Just follow the spotlight."

A few more steps past the batter's circle, then across the infield, on out to the football field. Eighty thousand sets of vocal cords running vibrations at him, and Simon D'Hanis was pumping up and sending some vibrations out himself. He began screaming, joyously, angrily, ecstatically.

Word was being passed to Simon D'Hanis's adrenal glands. The surge of adrenaline pushed Simon into a full barbarian warrior running naked from Gaul to Rome. Simon, the naked warrior, was accelerating well when the pitcher's mound leaped up in front of him out of the darkness. The cleats on his right shoe hooked on the pitching rubber. Stumbling, staggering, showing the quickness of mind and body that made him such a great athlete, Simon kept his feet until he reached the outfield, then fell, bounced and did a complete somersault, flipped back to his feet and continued to Ox Wood's side.

Taylor heard the audience catch its breath. Simon heard a funny little click in his knee.

The crowd began cheering for Simon D'Hanis, who finished his run to midfield like a Tennessee walker.

"It's those goddam Russian steroids," Taylor said to Bobby Hendrix. "He's turning into Olga Korbut."

THE REGULAR SEASON

THAT first season Bobby Hendrix, Kimball Adams and Taylor Rusk shared a three-bedroom apartment out by the airport, close to the practice field. Hendrix was afraid to move his family and pull the boys out of school, since he was on the Blacklist and might be out of football at any moment.

Kimball called his wife for the first time since he had arrived in camp six weeks before.

"Aren't you coming down, honey?" Kimball asked.

"You asshole!" she screamed. "I would rather stay in Cleveland and watch Lake Erie die and the river burn than be in goddam Texas with you, you drunk, potbellied, obnoxious, rag-armed son of a bitch."

"Honey . . . honey. . . . We were busy . . . two-a-days into the regular season. They didn't have phones available. You know you love me."

"Like I love vaginal itch, you schmuck!" She slammed the phone down.

Adams looked at Hendrix. "She may be a while."

Mrs. Kimball Adams stayed in Cleveland and sold Kimball's clothes and car. They never got back together.

Simon D'Hanis and Buffy, the proud parents of a baby girl, lived in a duplex in Park City.

"It's a good place to raise kids," Simon said.

"You don't have to tell us, Simon," Taylor said. A.D. started laughing while nodding in agreement that Park City was indeed a good place to raise kids.

A.D. stopped laughing long enough to say, "Especially somebody else's kids."

Simon was irritated, and he always remembered his two old roommates laughing at him for saying that Park City was a good place to raise kids. Later he would begin to believe they laughed at him about a lot of things, and when Taylor tried to tell Simon they had been laughing with him and not at him, it was too late. Simon D'Hanis had ceased laughing altogether.

A. D. Koster moved in with Suzy Ballard over by the University in the apartment complex he, Taylor and Simon had shared in college.

Suzy got a few modeling jobs and was in one national beer commercial before she took a job with The Texas Pistols Football Club, Inc., and began an open affair with Dick Conly. A.D. encouraged Suzy's liaison with Conly. Suzy could help promote A.D.'s career in the Franchise. It was part of A.D.'s plan. A.D. and Suzy became more partners than lovers. They were a good team.

Red Kilroy also had a plan. It was Red's plan to trade away Texas's top three draft choices every year for the next five years. He would bring in good players who could win. All Red cared about was *winning now*.

Red Kilroy demanded his players be smarter and stronger. If they were, he made Dick Conly pay them more. As soon as they realized this, they made fewer and fewer mistakes.

"You can't overpay good players," the coach said. Conly agreed. Cyrus didn't.

"This foolishness must stop." Cyrus was in Dick Conly's office. "I read in the paper that you gave Kimball Adams a ten-thousand-dollar bonus. What for?"

"He's coaching Rusk, putting in extra hours, working hard," Conly defended the bonus to Kimball.

"I have it on good authority that Mr. Kimball Adams has very unsavory friends."

"Of course, Cyrus." Conly was losing patience. "He plays professional football."

"He's friends with the Cobianco brothers," Cyrus said.

"So are you. Kimball Adams isn't a problem, *you* are." Conly stood and pointed. "*You*. If I turn my back on you, we get turds in the punchbowl. So he shaves a few points; Christ, the man is forty years old and crippled. He puts on a marvelous show. This *is* show business and he sells tickets."

Cyrus was not swayed. "He already is under contract. He's paid a fair wage."

"Who are you all of a sudden, Henry Ford?" Dick yelled. "Don't give me that shit. I'm the guy who negotiates these contracts, with the singular exception when you nearly gave the whole store away, trying to outsmart Doc Webster and Taylor Rusk."

Cyrus ignored the general manager. "There is, furthermore, to be an internal investigation started. And if Kimball is keeping company with unsavory characters..."

Dick Conly picked up his tumbler of warm Scotch and tossed it into Cyrus Chandler's face. Cyrus shut up immediately and took on the puzzled look of a man slapped across the mouth with a wet squirrel.

"What is this *furthermore* shit?" Conly slammed his empty glass down. "I don't take *furthermore* from God himself. I run this franchise and Chandler Industries. You know nothing about how it all fits together!" Conly suddenly slugged the window glass with his fist. It didn't break: Conly had long ago had glass put in that you couldn't drive a truck through.

"Easy, Dick." The blow startled Red.

Cyrus was still stunned, Scotch on his face, soaking his shirt.

"No, it's too hard for you. So I have to do it!" Dick slugged the window again, harder. The window boomed and rattled and Conly's knuckles went numb. "Traveling the world in your DC-9 and being chauffeured in limousines to the sources of *your wealth* and attending Chandler Industries' yearly off-site planning sessions is just too tiresome. Instead you jet to the Hot Springs Ranch with your pals from Spur 1939. Ten wrinkled dicks with the young cookies attached, swimming naked in the hot springs.

"I have to go commercial during the airlines strike and have stenographers pick me up in their Toyotas and don't get home for two fucking months, to do what you could have done in two weeks while also learning something about why you were born rich. Something I already know because I put it together. . . .

"So now, after tiring of private jets and limos, you have come to advise me on how to compensate Kimball Adams. Well, you screw with Adams and he'll hit you so hard your house pets will die."

The mention of potential physical pain seemed to give Cyrus a start; he took his handkerchief from his breast pocket and began to mop his still-dripping face. He was still dazed.

"Now you are getting to be a serious pain in the ass. You fucked Taylor Rusk around so your daughter will marry that congenital idiot Carleton kid and in the process you scramble the very delicate mind of Simon D'Hanis, our best young offensive lineman. Now you accuse Kimball Adams of the horrible crime of hanging around with *your* gambling buddies." Dick Conly tried to kick out the window. His boot boomed against the pane, but it didn't crack. Dick was getting Cyrus's attention.

"What you fail to understand, Cyrus..." Conly walked back to his desk and threw a five-pound brass duck paperweight at the window. The bang was deafening, but the glass remained unmarked. "... is that professional football is about to take a quantum leap in revenue. Billions of dollars! It is not a business that you can run because you're rich and played high school ball at least one year. This is becoming real gangster territory, not small-time bookies.... I'm talking oil, broadcast and film companies. Real thugs." Conly picked up the heavy brass duck and threw it again. It whirled end over end. The crash was nerve-shattering.

"I thought we had this settled a long time ago, Cyrus." The duck bounced across the floor, Conly retrieved it. "You stay out of the Franchise operation or I hit out for the Pecos Mountains and you go to hell in a handbasket."

"Well"—Cyrus spoke softly, for the first time since Dick's tirade had begun—"I just thought I might..."

Cyrus flinched and stopped speaking as Dick Conly again hurled the duck, slamming the brass into the window.

"You think about what you want for dinner, Cyrus. That's *it*!" Conly walked over to the paperweight, which had picked up some nicks on the bill. The glass was unmarked. Dick ran his hand across the smooth surface. "Amazing." Then he turned back to the owner of the Texas Pistols. "Right now, Cyrus, we need Kimball Adams. He can help Taylor Rusk and in return he gets something for his old age, which started this year. You didn't buy the use of Kimball's courage, you purchased only his body and the minimal motor skills necessary to collect his money. So if he shaves a few points and still puts on a show that pays the tab, then all I would advise you to do is to quit betting with the Cobianco brothers."

Dick tossed the paperweight from hand to hand. Cyrus looked at the head coach, silent in the corner, studying a file folder.

"Red?" Cyrus said. "What do you think?"

"I think my contract reads that I don't even have to talk money other than to insist the player gets treated right. You can't overpay a good player."

"You can't overpay a good player." Cyrus repeated it like a catechism. It seemed to please him—a good cocktail-party answer.

"Well, if that settles everything . . . I'll be heading out." Cyrus started for the door. "I'm flying to the Big Bend. I promised Junie and Wendy a trip to the Hot Springs Ranch."

Dick Conly scowled at the closing door.

"That guy needs a ring job or a new head gasket," the coach said when Cyrus was gone. "Does he have the power to take over here?"

"Without the knowledge the power is useless."

"Or dangerous." Red Kilroy laid the file folders on the desk. "I say we cut all those guys. Losing seems to agree with them."

THE CUT

WHENEVER Red Kilroy's secretary called Jack the Equipment Man to clean out a guy's locker, it fell to Jack to be the bearer of rather distressing news to men of generally larger than usual size with a high threshold of pain, a low flash point and all the resultant incumbencies, including free-floating desperation and disrespect for the human body, particularly someone else's.

Jack often locked himself in the equipment cage to escape the rages of men "released outright" from professional football. *Released outright* was such an innocuous phrase that, to really understand what it meant, you had to be in a position like Jack the Equipment Man.

Another job that shared a certain equivalency with Jack the Equipment Man was that of the business-office receptionist—especially when a particularly incensed giant covered with tattoos and surgical scars came to the office, cursing management in a loud twang through his flat nose, searching out Red Kilroy or Dick Conly over a broken promise or an unpaid plane ticket or hotel bill. The receptionist had orders that the head coach and general manager were never to be found, and the ex-player was never to be admitted to the inner offices.

A. D. Koster got Suzy Ballard the receptionist's job by hustling Lem Three, who, after returning from the League office, was in charge of hiring secretaries and receptionists.

"It'll be a good image for the team." A.D. had brought a bottle to Three's office. They both drank while Suzy acted like she was a nineteen year-old Apache Bell from Tyler Junior College, a high-kicker. She did fine.

"I man, goddam, Three, lookie there." A.D. had his arm around Lem. "If she's the first thing that hits the customers' eyes when they step off the elevator, they see style."

Suzy had surprising success that first season compared with Jack the Equipment Man. Jack lost three teeth and had his nose broken twice. Invariably Jack would have his arms full of the guy's equipment when the punch came.

Suzy Ballard, on the other hand, was always polite and firm in denying entry to the angry player, insisting that neither Red Kilroy nor Dick Conly were even in the building. The door was locked and could only be opened from within.

Only Abdul Jamail Willie, a 335-pound defensive lineman from southern Illinois, ever gained entry into the inner offices. Willie put his fist through the solid oak door and unlocked it from the inside. He was after Lem Three, who had weeks before relayed Red's promises to pay Abdul Willie's airfare and hotel bill, a total of $1,650, while Willie tried out for the team. Red then refused to pay when Abdul was "released outright." Since Lem had made the promise, Willie planned to kill him first.

Fortunately Willie got his arm stuck in the door, allowing time for Lem Three, Red and Dick Conly to escape down the service elevator.

Willie never did get his money.

FREE LUNCH

TAYLOR came to the team offices to meet with Red and pick up the offensive plans for the first division game.

Kimball Adams didn't bother to get out of bed for the quarterback meeting.

At first Suzy denied that Red Kilroy was in his office. She offered to take a message.

"C'mon, Suzy, it's me, Taylor," the quarterback spurned the message offer. "Red is at the office at six-thirty every morning except Sunday, when he waits until seven o'clock. He's deeply religious."

"I'm sorry." Suzy kept her eyes on Taylor's face and smiled. "I have my orders."

"I haven't been released or cheated out of any money. I have a meeting"—Taylor pointed to the small gold watch on Suzy's slender wrist—"and Red is never late. Red is on schedule." Taylor gazed down at Suzy's watch and took her slim hands in his thick, long-fingered grip. "You have beautiful hands." He turned Suzy's hands over and over, enjoying their delicate sensitive shape. "Beautiful hands."

"Thanks very much." Suzy withdrew from his grip. "They came with the arms. I just looked down and there they were."

"Good, use one of them to dial Red and tell him the heir apparent, the man they call the Franchise on a slow news day, is here for the quarterback meeting and to take any messages back to Kimball Adams, who has a terrible hangover and a fat, ugly girl lying unconscious across his thorax, making attendance, as well as breathing, next to impossible."

"Buzz off, Taylor." Suzy turned her eyes on the message pad, her slender fingernails drumming the desk top.

"*You* ever try to get out from under an unconscious fat lady?"

"It isn't that hard." She looked up. "You *really* have a meeting?"

"Doesn't Red *have* visitors? I'm not kidding, I'm here and Kimball isn't. You can't imagine how tough a fat woman can be to move when she's out cold." Taylor ran a finger across his lip thoughtfully. "I can't figure how Kimball got under there."

"Somebody probably dropped her on him." Suzy began dialing Red Kilroy's office number. Red answered and told her to buzz Taylor right in.

Dick Conly passed the quarterback in the hall. Suzy replaced the receiver just as the general manager reached the reception area.

"How about letting me take you to lunch?" Conly asked the pert young blonde.

"The coach says not to date players," Suzy told him.

"What player? I'm the general manager."

"I'll let you know later." Suzy released the button on her desk and the inner door stopped buzzing. "You look a lot better than you did at camp."

"I was sick—all those two-a-days. What about lunch?"

The phone began buzzing.

"Okay, okay, just let me work." Suzy snatched up the receiver. "Texas Pistols. Mr. Conly? Certainly, let me ring." Dick Conly went back to his office.

Suzy had her sights on Dick Conly. She had a nose for power, and Dick had power. He would share it with her, but Suzy Ballard was not certain he had *enough* power. She was young and she, too, had plans. Big plans.

"Can't be too careful, Taylor." Red remained seated, marking up a paper gridiron as the quarterback entered his office. The coach was noting what the defense did on the field, where and when, down and yardage. "You heard about Abdul Willie putting his fist through the door?"

"Something about you reneging on a promise to pay his bills," Taylor said. "He called Bobby Hendrix to see what the Union could do; Hendrix called Terry Dudley, who . . ."

"Don't." Red held up a hand. "I don't want to hear the word *union*."

"Then you might hear Abdul breathing down your neck again."

"It wasn't me." Red dropped his felt marker and opened his arms. A gesture of innocence. "It was that goddam Lem Three who promised him."

"Just like Jack the Equipment Man decides who to cut?"

"Why?" Red looked up at Taylor. "Why do you always attack me, try to undermine my command?"

"I can't stop myself; the coach is best who coaches least. It's an old Chinese Ping-Pong axiom." Taylor walked around the desk and peered over Red's shoulder at the gridiron marks. "You're staff and I don't trust you as far as I can throw Ox Wood."

"I guess you have your reasons"—Red played sad—"but I'm telling you"—tears welled in the head coach's eyes; he was good at command tears— "you misjudge me. That's what worries me."

"Worries you. . . ." Taylor laughed, again amazed. "Worries *you*?"

Dick Conly took Suzy out to lunch. They went to the Jewboy over off Houston Street. It was a Mexican-food place.

"Why do they call a Mexican restaurant the Jewboy?" Suzy asked. They were seated in a corner booth.

"Trying to keep the food faddists and Mexicans out."

The main dining room was small and dark. The floor was either earth or soft dirty wood. A large white refrigerator stood next to the jukebox, which featured nothing but Little Joe en La Familia, "King" Carrasco and the Jack-A-Lope Brothers with Kimmy Rhodes. The Jack-A-Lope boys were on Rude Records, Conly's favorite label.

"You want a beer?" He reached into his pocket and pulled out a pack of brown Sherman's cigarettes.

"I better not."

"You're with me." Suzy took the slim natural tobacco cigarette Conly offered and Dick fired his gold Dunhill. "I wanted you to have the day off to help me get that fat woman off Kimball Adams. Red thinks Kimball's feet may not be getting any blood."

Suzy put the brown cigarette down. "Is he kidding?"

"I don't think Red kids. If he does, we're all in serious trouble. There are large amounts of money riding on the assumption that the one thing Red Kilroy is not is a joker."

"What does that mean?" She held up the Sherman's and puffed daintily.

"Nothing. Except you get the afternoon off to have lunch. I'll bet the fat lady gets off Kimball under her own steam and both quarterbacks will be at the practice field bright and early tomorrow."

"That's all?" Suzy looked down at the ashtray, knocking ashes.

"Enjoy yourself. I'm not dangerous unless I have an investment of time, money or emotion." The general manager looked at the young girl. So young. "I'm powerful but seldom ruthless because I plan ahead. Now, how about that beer?" He didn't wait for a reply but stood and walked over to the big white refrigerator. The floor felt mushy under his boots. He took two Bohemian Club beers from the refrigerator and returned to the table. Suzy was finishing her Sherman's and putting it out in the ashtray.

— 170 —

"I have always considered that a paper trail is fatal." Dick set the beers on the table. "I never write the important things down; I remember. Thinking ahead and a good memory are always worth something in cold cash or career trajectory." He paused to watch her face. "And I'm looking for an executive secretary."

"I can't type," Suzy said quickly, turning suspicious. He was moving faster than she expected.

"I don't need a typist, I need someone who can think," Dick replied. "You are very perceptive, ambitious . . ."

"And I have a good body."

"That, too, plus an excellent memory." Dick smiled, his offer genuine and his manner disarming. "Think about it."

"I will." Suzy drank her beer. Conly watched her slender hand carry the bottle to her lips, her head tilting back, her neck pulsing slightly as she drank. She set her bottle down and licked her lips. "You people are nuts," she said, then belched.

"Professional football is for misfits and crazies," Conly replied. "But I'd rather be a misfit or a crazy than somebody who fits in and gets along. God, I would hate to be a person everybody liked."

There were no other customers in the small dining room. The waitress, in a white uniform, sat at the table closest to the cash register and talked to the cashier, a tall woman with red hair piled into a multistoried beehive.

"I wonder if she's going to come take our order?" Suzy absently peeled the label off the wet brown beer bottle.

"She's waiting to see if we're serious." Dick got up, walked over to the refrigerator and returned with two more beers. The waitress watched him all the way, wrote something on her pad, then went back to talking with the cashier.

"You've definitely got her interested," Suzy said. "She's taking notes."

"What we need are a couple more customers. Get her a little more motivated. Otherwise we might have to drink three beers apiece."

"Why don't you just go tell her we want to order?"

"I don't want to cause any trouble."

"High school doesn't prepare you for stuff like this," Suzy said, starting her second beer.

"I never even finished high school, but I still got my law degree." Dick Conly waved at the waitress, who ignored him.

"You must be one of those natural geniuses."

"Sort of," Dick said. "I cheated and lied a lot. Still do."

"Me too," Suzy said, excited at their particular communion.

— 171 —

"I talked to Lem and just sort of lied my way from roller skates to receptionist in one leap." Suzy giggled.

"Well, from now on, Hot Wheels, you work under me."

"I've had experience in that position. . . ." Suzy let her voice trail off, smiling at the general manager. She put her elbows on the rough wooden table and held her beer bottle to her mouth with both hands, then glanced at the waitress.

"We have plenty of time."

"For what?" Balancing the beer on her lower lip, she peered the length of the bottle at Conly, then tilted the bottle. The beer wet her lips. Her slender throat moved slightly.

Conly nodded. "You can really drink beer."

"I can really do a lot of things," Suzy said. "I plan to do them too. Model, actress, things like that. A.D. says he'll get me modeling jobs and, with Texas increasing film production, finally work into the movies full-time. I can do it. Maybe you could help."

"Hey, Reba," Dick yelled, "get off your butt and get us two of Pedro's dog-meat dinners."

The waitress wrote on her pad, then slowly got to her feet and made her way toward the kitchen. "You want them mild or hot?"

"I want them mild, and I mean *mild*."

"I want to be in show business," Suzy went on as if Dick hadn't spoken, "and you and A.D. are my first contacts. Contacts are important."

"How important?"

"Real important."

"Well," Conly backed off, "all I know about Hollywood is what I see in the movies."

Dick Conly had excellent contacts in Hollywood, as Cyrus had financed several low-budget westerns and horror films. He had been executive producer on the films, which had been shot in Texas and Los Angeles, though Dick purposely kept this information from Suzy.

No sense in helping her cheat and lie to me, Dick thought.

THE CHARTERS

THE first season Dick Conly hired charter planes at inflated cost from a small regional carrier owned by Chandler Industries. The inflated charter fees offered the Pistols additional expense write-offs while helping finance the rebuilding of Tex-Mex Airlines to take advantage of deregulation and the regional-feeder airline boom in Texas.

Unfortunately that first year Tex-Mex Airlines consisted of old propeller-driven craft, mostly DC-3s and -4s and a couple of DC-6Bs.

The team flew the best 6B, while Red and his staff, Cyrus Chandler and Dick Conly took their families and friends in the Chandler Industries' DC-9.

The Franchise had flight insurance on all its players except Bobby Hendrix, Kimball Adams and Taylor Rusk, who refused to sign because the policies named the Franchise as beneficiary.

The charter pilots had all come from South American countries where Chandler Industries had operations. Pleasant, polite fellows with little grasp of the English language or North American geography, they had been pilots for military governments that had since fallen from favor.

On the Cleveland flight the Nicaraguan pilot mistakenly landed in Toledo, and the Dallas flight ended at Meachum Field in Fort Worth. In the rain, coming into Green Bay, the Colombian sloshed the ancient plane to a halt in the mud one hundred feet to the right of the concrete runway.

After that Bobby Hendrix flew commercial, paying his own way.

"Bobby's always been scared of flying," Kimball Adams explained to Taylor.

"You call this flying?"

Taylor grew accustomed to the sobs and whimpers of his teammates as they waited in airport lounges or aboard the plane.

After the Minnesota game, the Nicaraguan was trying to take off in a snowstorm, overloaded with gasoline, football equipment and players. The plane crashed off the end of the runway. Its wheels never left the ground.

By radio from the DC-9, Cyrus ordered Jack the Equipment Man, the highest-ranking member of management on board, to have the plane towed back onto the runway. He wanted them to try again.

"The Pistols don't give up, Jack," Cyrus said. "Understood? Besides, they're insured." Several players cried openly.

On the second try into the teeth of the storm, the lumbering overweight plane got off, bouncing once in an open field, where the landing gear yanked a quarter mile of barbed-wire fence out of the ground.

A beer in his bandaged hand, Kimball turned to Taylor and yelled over the engines' scream, "Hey, *amigo, qué pasa?*"

WINS AND LOSSES

THE Texas Pistols were not successful their first season, and Taylor Rusk played sparingly. Mercifully.

There wasn't a whole lot to be picked up out there by Taylor except bad habits and broken bones.

Kimball Adams played battered behind the porous offensive line, anchored only by All-Pro Ox Wood and the intense All-Rookie Simon D'Hanis. Kimball was the last quarterback to play with a single pencil-bar face mask. He was often bloodied and he played mad, always mad.

Ox couldn't protect Kimball from everybody. Enlisting help from middle linebacker Margene Brinkley and others on both defense and offense, Ox devised a strategy of massive retaliation, sometimes to the complete disregard of the final score. Horrible revenge was exacted from those teams Ox thought were overly zealous in the inevitable sacking of Texas Pistols quarterback Kimball Adams.

The word got around the League quickly that Ox was protecting Kimball Adams.

Swift, sure punishment—that was the protection. Deterrence theory in action. Only the purely crazy or the heavily drugged continued to try and punish Kimball Adams. Unfortunately the League was filled with plenty of both. Ox and Margene and the rest stayed busy all season, breaking jaws and ribs, rupturing spleens and kidneys, tearing up knees and ankles.

It was slight satisfaction to the devastated Kimball Adams to hear Ox constantly repeating, "We'll get that cocksucker for that, Kimball."

"Get him *before* he gets me, Ox," Kimball said, waiting for the cobwebs to clear. "*Before.* . . . Now, get me up."

"They'll be stopped," Ox promised.

They *were* stopped, but not soon enough, and Kimball Adams was hammered all season, taking his beating like a quarterback, standing up in the rapidly collapsing pocket.

Against Pittsburgh, after a six-foot-seven-inch, 270-pound rookie tackle missed his man, Kimball got up off his back, walked slowly to the huddle and kicked the rookie right in the crotch. He then called time out for the trainers to come haul the tackle off the field.

"The name of the game is pain," Red said. "It's the only test of manhood our country offers, short of war."

"What about a big killing on the commodities exchange?" Taylor asked.

It was one of many agonizing Monday meetings, and Red ignored the remark.

"Pain. Pain. Hit. Bleed. Pain. Do you want to take it or inflict it?"

"You act like I got a choice," Kimball replied, his eyes black, his nose ajar, nostrils packed with bloody gauze.

"They do!" Red pointed around the room. "They can *inflict* it. I want guys who hit, hit, hit, *hit, hit, hit.* That's how you win football games, not with fancy plays or computers or elaborate scouting systems. You take the guy across from you on Sunday afternoon and you kick his ass all over that field for three solid hours. If each of you does that, nobody is going to beat us."

Red paused strategically and looked around the room for someone foolish enough to ask a question or look dubious. Red had cut guys in meetings for not looking attentive.

"We hit. We are hitters and will not be denied."

"It sounds great in the meeting." Bobby Hendrix was sitting by his locker, rubbing analgesic balm all over his bony, freckled body.

"Unfortunately"—Kimball pulled on his rib pads—"lots of teams got fancy plays, computers, elaborate systems, plus bigger, better, faster, meaner guys who love to hit and inflict pain while they win."

"It's sort of a hobby with them," Taylor added. "Testing Kimball Adams's manhood."

Taylor developed a peculiar respect for a quarterback so courageous with so little to gain.

He loves the game, Taylor decided. *And wants the control, the power.*

So did Taylor Rusk.

Years later, as time did one thing possible with pain and dulled it, forgot it, confused it, the Texas Pistols' debut seemed funnier. The stories definitely gained in the telling. It had been embarrassing, humiliating misery. Maybe it was fun.

Mostly it was painful.

PRAYERS

I⊤ was before the Cleveland game that Red Kilroy knelt and offered this prayer:

> *We thank thee Lord for the world so sweet*
> *We thank thee Lord for the food we eat*
> *We thank thee Lord for the birds that sing*
> *We thank thee Lord for everything.*

"That was a strange prayer, Red," Taylor said as he followed Adams and the head coach to the field. "It was a little early, too, don't you think? Before warm-ups?"

"I got a few things on my mind, Taylor, do you mind?"

Taylor shook his head.

"How about asking for fewer birdies next time," Kimball said as they walked the tunnel, "and get me a fucking center and a couple of tackles?"

"Get your own, asshole." Red walked off.

"Red always wanted to be a quarterback," Taylor said, "but he can't call a game. It's making him crazy. Now he wants to be an owner."

"Being an owner *is* crazy," Adams said. "Ranching hard dicks to show your friends."

"In college Red started a pregame prayer with 'Now I lay me down to sleep . . .'" Taylor said. "He's at his worst on game day."

"'Now I lay me down to sleep'?" Adams repeated softly and

— 176 —

stared down a moment. "What a way to live." He looked over at the strong young quarterback he was grooming for the New League. The New Age.

"What about the turf here?" Taylor asked.

"It jumps up and smacks you in the face a lot." Kimball climbed up into the dugout and groaned, straining to make the long step up to the field. "Well, Taylor, keep your eyes on me. I might do some shit out there that only you can see."

The aged, battered quarterback started to jog across the infield; his movements were stiff, knees and ankles hurting with each jolting step on the hard baseball infield. He *was* the elephant.

Taylor stayed in the dugout, watching Kimball Adams enter his old home stadium alone. The stands were still half empty; it was over an hour to kickoff. These were early warm-ups for punters, kickers, passers, receivers and the injured—anyone who had a specialty or problem that required extra attention before team drills.

Taylor watched Kimball Adams limp across the baseball diamond to the football field to join the eight or ten other Pistols already out there. A spattering of applause rippled through the crowd and moved around the bowl. The cheering started loudly in the near end zone, then progressively lost volume up the sideline to the fifty-yard-line seats, the high-dollar tickets. The applause picked up again going in, regaining its intensity and reached a crescendo in the far end zone. The reception died ambiguously as it moved up the far sideline. By midfield it stopped.

Kimball Adams was welcomed back by the fans. He picked up a ball and threw a few warm-ups to Speedo Smith, who had come out earlier to catch punts.

"The niggers like you here." Speedo pointed to the end zones.

"They love me." He tossed Speedo the ball. "A legend in my own mind."

"Mine too." Speedo practiced a one hand catch.

"You don't have to say that."

"I do if I expects the ball."

Taylor pulled on his warm-up jacket, zipped it tightly, stepped out of the dugout and walked slowly to join Speedo and Kimball Adams. He heard Bobby Hendrix's footsteps behind him, recognizing the receiver's gait. Taylor slowed and they soon walked side by side.

"Well, Taylor, this here is what it's all about."

"*What* is all about?"

"If I knew *that*, you think I would be doing *this*?"

"Well . . . at least"—Taylor pointed to the seats—"a crowd seems to be gathering."

"Yeah, that's all Jesus was trying to do; draw a crowd." Bobby dug into his pants and pulled out his can of Nutty Putty and began working it with his fingers, strengthening, loosening, toughening.

"He sure did it the hard way," Taylor said. "That still doesn't mean it's *about* anything."

"You're the complete cynic, Taylor. You have to learn to enjoy the struggle more. The fight." The long, white, spidery freckled fingers walked and ran through the thick multicolored wad. "I had to steal this stuff from my kids; I lost mine. I took all they had—all sizes, colors. Still not enough. I stopped at two shopping malls on the way to the airport. Nothing. Electronic games everywhere. No Nutty Putty." He handed the rainbow-hued amalgamation to the quarterback.

"Did you try room service at the hotel?" Taylor took the spongy wad and worked it with his hands and fingers. "You let your children play with this stuff?" Taylor held his fist up and squeezed; the plastic colors oozed between his fingers. "This is sick." Taylor's fingers dug and squeezed through the resilient blob. "Does Ginny know your children use this?"

The two men walked to join their teammates; the stadium began to fill. It was a beautiful day for football, but the League had chosen to play a night game.

It was their ball.

After Cleveland's middle linebacker smashed Kimball's nose on a blitz, he called a time-out to let his line collect themselves and concentrate on the game. Blood running down his throat from the broken nose, Kimball stepped back and looked at the crowd. They caterwauled and snarled, barely in control, smelling blood, wanting more. Kimball decided he would drown them in it.

Kimball sniffed back blood, stepped in his huddle and plotted not victory but revenge. Texas reduced the Cleveland defense and offense and special teams to smoking ruins in less than three hours. The Pistols lost 3–0 but Cleveland never recovered.

The battle was expensive to the players; serious casualties were inflicted. The Pistols' offense was sometimes threatening. The defense was devastating.

The Cleveland middle linebacker speared Bobby Hendrix in the back with his headgear, sending the flanker to the hospital for X-rays and morphine shots. The skinny redhead pissed blood for three days and missed two games.

The Pistols' team doctor called his bookie immediately with the injury report to be sure he got down before the spread changed. The X-ray technician got down for two hundred dollars against both teams for the following week, since they'd been bringing those guys in to his emergency room at such a phenomenal rate and in such bad shape.

Neither noticed the hairline fracture of Bobby Hendrix's cervical vertebrae. Not that it mattered. Bobby didn't notice it either, his low back was hurting so much.

Ox Wood got the middle linebacker just after the final gun.

Cleveland wound up with two broken legs, a dislocated shoulder, a variety of facial injuries, nine undiagnosed concussions and two jammed necks, the result of wide receivers being pushed by strong safety A. D. Koster headlong into the goalposts. The Cleveland fans booed both receivers as they were carried off the field semiconscious, spilling blood from every orifice in the skull and complaining of burning pains in their legs. Violence spilled out of the stands onto the field a couple of times. Taylor kept his helmet on and watched the crowd.

The Cleveland doctor diagnosed one of the two broken legs, but everything else he called a strain except the head and neck injuries, who were told: "You just got your bell rung."

If the player complained that his injury was possibly worse than the doctor diagnosed, the Cleveland doctor would agree with the player, call for nurses and aides and ask for rubber gloves; then, with meticulous procedure and surgical precision, he would mortify the injured athlete by taping one five-grain aspirin to the player's body.

The Cleveland doctor's practice consisted of the Cleveland team and rich widows with bad habits.

THE COMMUNICATION
ARTS

THE final week of the season Dick Conly was alone in his office, thinking about the problem of the season and beyond. He had to find them before they found him. He studied a copy of the Collective Bargaining Agreement, then dialed the phone.

"Yeah," Cyrus Chandler answered Dick's call to his lake house.

"I'm looking at the CBA," Conly said into the phone. "The next one won't be so easy. Stillman couldn't handle Bobby Hendrix, and if Terry Dudley starts listening to Hendrix about free agency, we could have a problem." Conly paused. "Dudley's a friend of Taylor Rusk, and I don't have to tell you if Hendrix, Rusk and Dudley get to thinking . . . they could end up stealing our software."

"You worry too much," Cyrus replied. "Terry Dudley will be okay."

The delicate hands unbuttoned Cyrus's shirt and the woman reached inside, scraping her fingertips across his thin chest. Cyrus covered the phone. "Stop. Jesus." The woman continued.

"This is serious. We need to be sure." Conly was angry; he could hear the woman's teasing presence throwing Cyrus into confusion. Cyrus was breathing hard.

"Don't worry," Cyrus panted, "I've kept tabs on him. He's in Spur . . . oathbound to other Spur members."

"If it ain't the Yakuza or the Comanche, it ain't no oath, Cyrus," Conly said. He could hear giggling over the phone.

"You're right," Cyrus replied. "Better keep a closer eye on Terry Dudley. Jocks are always jocks."

Cyrus Chandler rang off with the promise to call the next day.

"Terminal dumbass." Conly replaced the receiver. He looked out his office window, then dialed Suzy Ballard's number. He let it ring twenty times before he slammed the receiver down.

"Goddam whore, where are you?" He didn't want to know. And he knew he didn't want to know. Dick Conly was not stupid; he was just growing old and lonely, wanting to have something, someone.

He called home and Billie, the housekeeper, answered.

"Your wife and the girls has gone to the ballet," the fat black woman said, "to watch some Russian fag defector jump around in tights and a codpiece."

Dick laughed; he loved Billie.

Amos Chandler had found Billie in New Orleans with the Man in Louie's Joint on Rampart Street, trying unsuccessfully to sing. A punk sailor started heckling her and Billie took out his front teeth, laying him low and cold with her bare knuckles. The Man had Louie send her to his Royal Street house; Amos hired her on the spot and brought her to Texas to run his household. When Amos died, she came to work for Dick Conly, refusing an offer from Cyrus. She never lost her punch.

"What about Luther?" Dick asked. "Is he home?"

"In his room."

"Put him on; I got time to catch a movie."

"He's asleep." Billie was stern. "He don't need to catch no movie. He needs somebody to talk to besides the reefer man."

"Oh, Christ. Meaning I don't spend enough time with him?"

"You should come home more," Billie said. "Not for your wife or me—we both know what you look like—but these kids won't be here forever. 'Specially Luther. The girls got their momma, but him, he need a man. Hell, I need a man."

"Is he doing anything besides smoking dope?"

"A lot of jerking off, but that's okay. Drinks a little, that's all I know. He's a good boy, but he's lonely at a time in your life you ain't s'posed to be lonely. He needs you."

"I've been so damn busy."

"Save that shit; this is Billie Jean, Queen of Rampart Street, you talkin' to. Just 'cause Amos treated Cyrus good and he grew up to be a peckerhead don't mean that ignoring Luther is gonna make him the tall dog."

"But, Billie..."

"Uh-uh, I'm tellin' you to come on home and spend time. We're all just passin' through, Mr. Conly. There ain't none of those instant foreplays in life."

"Replays," Conly replied. "Instant replays. Unfortunately there *are* instant foreplays in life."

"Well, I gotta go. Those toilets won't clean theirselves. Now, get on home." She hung up without waiting for a reply.

Dick Conly sat on his desk and looked out at the night, missing his youth and the wild times with Amos Chandler.

"I'll set up a big hunting trip," Conly said to himself, and stared at the skyline. "Luther and me, maybe Taylor Rusk and some of the other players. He'll love it."

Luther Conly didn't like hunting or football.

Dick Conly dialed Suzy Ballard's number. It rang and rang. Finally he called Taylor Rusk. Taylor answered on the third ring.

"Taylor, this is Dick Conly, your general manager. Let's go drinking and fucking."

Taylor held the phone away and looked at it, slightly shocked.

"Frankly, Dick, I've got practice tomorrow, and Terry Dudley is here now."

Conly knew that before he called. "The basketball player?" he replied, acting surprised.

"I believe he now prefers to be known as the new director of the Players Union, which he has been since Bobby Hendrix forced out your old pal, Stillman."

"Does he drink?"

"Ask him yourself." Taylor handed the phone to Terry Dudley.

"You bet, Mr. Conly," Dudley said. "Conflict? Hell, sounds like a major breakthrough in labor-management relations. Come on over." Dudley replaced the receiver and began rubbing his hands together.

"Today is our lucky day," Terry said, staring at the phone like it was a magic lamp. "Conly has political contacts all over San Antonio and South Texas. This could move my timetable for the Union way up."

"You better walk soft with Conly," Taylor warned. "He wants something."

"Jesus, Taylor, this guy could help us. Where's Hendrix?"

"Gone to Houston to be with Ginny and the boys at his father-in-law's. Gus Savas has one of those River Oaks mansions."

"Did Bobby fly? I thought he was scared of flying."

"He flew scared," Taylor said. "He had to talk to Savas about an oil deal with VCO."

"Harrison H. Harrison's company? The father-in-law must be rich, huh?" Dudley began pacing the room.

Taylor nodded. "Gus is a damn successful independent, a wildcatter. He found some big fields at the right time and sold them to the majors for the right price. That's how the business works: Wildcatters find and sell oil to the majors and they hide it again."

"Somebody ought to kick the majors' asses!" The seven-foot man struck out with his long sinewy leg and size-seventeen shoe. "Might be a good political position for the Union. The fans could dig that, and we'll need the fans if we strike."

"Fuck the fans," Taylor said, "and the strike."

"Kick the majors' asses," Dudley repeated. "How many owners are oil men?"

"Too many. We'll run out of feet long before they draw down their stock of asses."

"I saw A.D.," Dudley said suddenly.

"Speaking of asses. Where'd you see A.D.?"

"He came to Union headquarters with a couple of walking garbage compactors. We had some drinks. They wanted to talk about Union pension insurance." Dudley wrinkled his forehead as he moved birdlike around the room. "They kept talking to me about a big-term life-insurance-policy scheme. Not only would I not have to pay a first year's premium, but A.D. would give me a twenty-thousand-dollar finder's fee."

"Twenty thousand dollars for finding yourself?"

"I know, Taylor, I'm not as dumb as you seem to think. Christ, the guy is *your* fucking friend. I was *nice* to him because he was a friend of *yours*, but after *that* offer and a second look at the two jukeboxes..."

"The Cobianco brothers."

"One was Cobianco, the other was a Tiny something." Terry shook his head, arms and hands. "I think it was Tiny Mind. Nice friends you got."

"They aren't my friends."

"They did have one good idea about the next bargaining agreement between the Union and the League... *residuals*... like actors get... a piece of the action." Dudley stopped pacing and looked at Taylor. "Do you think Conly would go for that?"

"He'd love it," Taylor replied, "because he knows none of us have a clue *how much* action there is, and Conly doesn't have to tell us." Taylor was irritated at Dudley's sudden obtuseness. "The Union would have to *define the action* and the League wouldn't have to open the books. Forget it. Dick Conly will pick your pocket. You'll never get rich."

Terry wasn't listening. "I'm gonna ask Hendrix and Speedo ...they've been around and they're the player reps. Right now I got to take a shit," Dudley announced.

"Well, take it home with you."

"Come on, I'm waiting to meet Conly."

"He'll have his own."

Dudley disappeared down the hall just as the door opened and the Texas Pistols' general manager stumbled inside Taylor's apartment, holding out an empty glass.

"You drank it," Taylor said without moving.

"Hell of a place, Taylor," Conly said. "Hell of a place, but with what we're paying you, you could afford better."

Down the hall the commode flushed and Terry Dudley returned, buckling his belt. Dick Conly still held out the empty glass.

"Bloody Mary," he said.

Dudley took the glass without saying a word and disappeared into the kitchen. He fixed the Bloody Mary and returned. Conly took the glass into the dining room.

"Well?" Dudley looked at Taylor. "Are you going to introduce us?"

"I know Dick Conly. You want to meet him? Go fucking meet

him. What the hell kind of a Union politician are you? Get in there and let him beat your brains out."

Returning to the room, Conly held out his empty glass for a refill. Dudley took the glass from Conly's hand and returned to the kitchen. The general manager watched the new Union director intently as he walked away.

"What the fuck does he want?" he asked Taylor.

"His fair advantage, Dick, just like everybody. He just wants what he's got coming."

"He ought to be careful; he just might get it," Conly said. "You, too, Taylor."

Taylor got to his feet. "Well, Dick, you can be certain *you* won't get it."

"Let's go to Hollywood," Conly said. "Get a bungalow at the Beverly Hills, play with the stars and starlets."

"I am a star," Taylor replied, "and I'm going to Colony Stadium and play with myself."

Dudley returned with the Bloody Mary.

"You want to go to Hollywood, fella?" Conly asked.

"Sure, but I just wanted to meet you and sort of listen to what you had to say."

"About what?"

"Politics, business, government, labor, stuff like that."

"It's all the same; what can I possibly tell you?"

Dudley shrugged. "Inside stories, secrets . . ."

"Here's my only secret: You live in a country where wealth is its own reward. Money means freedom, and freedom means no rules, and man cannot live without some rules. Even if only to break them. Get me another drink."

Dick found Taylor's phone and dialed Suzy Ballard's phone number. She answered on the fourth ring; she had sat next to her phone and watched it ring the first three times. She told Dick to come right over. He was gone when Terry Dudley returned with the Bloody Mary.

"Aw, shit." Dudley drank the tomato juice and vodka in one long gulp. "Shit, shit, shit, shit, *shit*."

MOUSE FOOD

COLONY Stadium, an ancient, crumbly cement structure, was used for the black high school south of Park City. The blacks lived south in a small clump of houses between Park City and the redneck cotton-gin town-soon-to-be-suburb of Clyde. The black area wasn't incorporated and didn't provide city services, but it did have a football stadium. The area was called the Nigger Colony, and the Texas Pistols used Colony Stadium for practice the first year in the League. It was one reason why the Pistols had such a large black following in the early years, much to Cyrus Chandler's dismay.

Dick Conly had originally made a quiet arrangement with Lem Carleton junior to lease some extra space from the University for a practice field and locker-room facility, but when the issue came before the athletic board for routine authorization, Athletic Director T. J. "Armadillo" Talbott vetoed the plan.

Armadillo demanded that Red Kilroy return the University football slush fund. "You tell that sneak thief Kilroy we want our three hundred thousand dollars back," Armadillo ordered.

"What three hundred thousand dollars?" Red had replied.

So the first season the Pistols practiced in Colony Stadium. The final practice of the season was extra long and hard. Red wanted to win the final game against New York.

"A win will give us momentum for next season," Red claimed.

"Only if the first game is by Groundhog Day," Taylor Rusk said sourly.

"You'll be out here till then if you don't shut up and throw some more decent passes," the coach shot back.

"Goddammit, Red, we've thrown too much already. My arm hurts."

Red kept them working another forty-five minutes before sending them to shower.

"I'm afraid Harlowe's going to get rattlesnake-bit," Simon said to Taylor as they walked off. "She's a good retriever. She's ready to work quail and I got twelve thousand acres leased up past Childress. But until Harlowe's snake-trained I'm not taking her out. A damn shame, too, 'cause I got bobwhite and blue quail out the old whazoo up there."

Small rivulets of sweat worked their way through Simon's heavy whiskers and dripped from the underbrush that covered his brow ridge without break from side to side. He had stripped his six-foot-four-inch frame to Pistols practice T-shirt and jock. His body had grown hulking with muscle definition.

Taylor unlaced his shoe and noticed a slight twinge in his elbow. "Goddam Red. I told the son of bitch we were throwing too much today." He worked the sore arm, trying to feel the nature of the ache.

"Let's go kick his ass." Simon was dead serious. "It'll make him easier to handle later on . . . make him flinch a little."

Taylor shook his head. "Red is nuts enough. He might start flinching too much."

"That's what worries me about Harlowe." Simon returned to the danger of rattlesnakes while quail hunting up near the Oklahoma border. "This guy from Dallas who's on the lease with me has a German shorthair. He's lost two dogs already. Diamondbacks bit their heads while they were on point."

Taylor pulled off his second shoe and worked his arm. The ache had lessened and so had Taylor's anger and panic. "What's a lease cost now?"

"I don't pay," Simon said. "I couldn't afford it. You get the whole year for a dollar an acre with a limit of six guns. I get it for practically nothing 'cause they think I'm gonna win Rookie of the Year."

"Jesus, twelve thousand dollars to go hunting." Taylor dropped his shoe and stared openmouthed into the tiny locker; a small mouse was hunched in the corner chewing contentedly on Taylor's chin strap. The quarterback wiped his face with a dirty towel and yelled over his shoulder. "Any hot water in there yet?"

"No!" came Bobby Hendrix's reply, echoing from the shower. "But it's only December if you want to wait."

"Taylor . . ." Simon stopped and stared into the quarterback's ancient locker. "Taylor, Taylor," Simon was whispering, "there's a mouse eating your chin strap."

"I know. I think he likes the salt from my sweat."

"Yeeech . . . that's disgusting!" Simon tossed a sock into the locker and the mouse disappeared into a hole in the back.

"Hey! Simon! Leave my mouse alone!"

The old stadium locker was cold and dark and dank and was home to creatures with little interest in professional football. They cared only about the Pistol Franchise as a source of food. Rats, mice, scorpions, spiders, mosquitoes, lizards—creatures that scurried noisily through the walls or sat quietly, eating the leather ear pads out of a helmet or sucking the blood out of players and staff.

"Anyway"—Simon kept his dark hooded eyes on the locker—"I want Harlowe ready for next quail season up there. She's a great dog—soft mouth, hell of a nose, and she already follows hand signals. She is that once-in-a-lifetime dog, and I don't want her sniffing up to some six-foot diamondback and getting bit in the head."

"I don't blame you."

"So I want to take her out and snake-train her after the season. You wanna go?" Simon asked. "Harlowe likes you and I could use some help."

"If you quit harassing my mouse."

"Deal," Simon said. "Now I gotta go pump up." He headed for the weight room.

Bobby Hendrix, pale white and freckled, topped by a shock of red hair, hobbled heel-and-toe out of the shower, dabbing at his shivering naked body. He moved gingerly but stiffly on the cold cement. His movements belied the grace with which he controlled his battered body on the football field.

"Bobby?" Taylor was working his complete arm. "Didn't you think we ran too many routes today? We had skeleton, one-on-one, full-team passing, and then ended with individual routes."

"Way too much." Bobby limped over. "Red can't keep me on my feet that long. I'll leave my game on the practice field. Does your arm hurt?"

"Elbow aches; not bad, it just pisses me off. He kept us out there because he knew we didn't think he was right. One of his fucking mind games."

"I'm walking off next time," Hendrix announced. "If I can walk."

"Well . . ." Taylor's next few words were drowned out by the explosion. Everybody tensed, ready to run if the stands began collapsing into the locker room. Dust boiled out of the weight room, followed by a string of profanities screamed in rage by Simon D'Hanis.

"What was that?" Hendrix was calmly rubbing his hair dry. He had been in the League too long to be surprised by anything.

"Sounds like Simon." Taylor worked his fingers. "Here he comes. Ask him."

— 187 —

The pulsing hulk of Simon D'Hanis, covered with sweat and concrete dust, walked toward the two men and the mouse gathered at Taylor's locker. Simon's face was contorted in fury and disgust.

In the middle of some arcane power-lifting exercise that the weight coach had devised for the ever-willing, increasingly narcissistic lineman, Simon had torn the complete weight machine from the low-grade Colony Stadium cement. The resultant momentum had thrown the machine through the cinder block wall and destroyed the hot-dog stand in the tunnel.

Fortunately it was not a game day or there would have been deaths and injuries. The machine blasting through the wall caused a large section to collapse, tearing loose stored weights and bars. Thousands of pounds of metal had cascaded onto the concrete floor.

The noise was deafening and the dust heavy, but once it was learned no one was injured, everyone except Simon returned to their previous tasks, including the mouse chewing quietly on Taylor's chin strap.

It would not have been surprising that first year if old Colony Stadium had been ordered demolished with the Pistols inside.

Although Taylor thought Simon overdid the steroids and biomachine approach, Simon D'Hanis did make the All-Rookie team. Pumped up and powered by Russian hormones, a high-protein diet and hours of intense working with weights, Simon had grown to a monstrous 275 pounds.

"Goddam, Simon," Kimball Adams chided as the dust swirled around him, "tear down the stadium and put all us niggers out in the cold."

"It's warmer outside," Bobby Hendrix noticed. The skinny redhead shivered, his face pinched together in pain as the cold knifed right to his damaged joints and scar-tissued muscles.

"I don't feel like a nigger." Simon stomped up beside Taylor.

"You're just on a different diet," Speedo Smith said, walking to his locker, where he found a scorpion waiting in his shoe.

Simon pointed at the pale, white, freckled Hendrix. "I'm sick of your Union bullshit and old-pro wisdom."

"He has seen the elephant," Taylor said. "He pushed the owner to give Terry Dudley Charlie Stillman's job. I figured you'd like anybody that got Stillman fired."

"That motherfucking Stillman sold me out!" Simon raged, and cement dust rose off his gigantic body like smoke. "Fuck Stillman, fuck the elephant, fuck Stillman with the elephant."

"Calm down, Simon." Taylor pointed into the locker. "You're keeping the mouse from eating."

The mouse was back on its haunches, head swiveling, watching Simon move about angrily. The big guard was not angry about anything specific, just angry—chemical aggression, synthetic fury on the loose. The mouse sensed trouble and ducked into the hole.

The mouse understood Simon D'Hanis chemically and instinctively and got the hell out of there.

THE WRONG NUMBER

THE New York–Pistols game was one of those contests when both teams are unconcerned about the final score and are simply bent on destroying each other.

The game was so vicious, so violent, that at halftime, Taylor watched Kimball Adams sit and bleed by his locker . . . knocking back straight shots of whiskey while snorting a gram of cocaine. Leaving to start the second half, Kimball carried two more grams with him.

The officials lost control of the field and the coaches their players, and the teams rioted within the confines of the game.

There were fundamental rules that Taylor assimilated in his years of athletic competition and hostile relationships with crowds. This was obviously one of those situations.

That's why Taylor refused to go into the game.

"What? What? What?" Red always did that three times when someone responded with an answer he didn't want. He felt three gave the offender time to figure out the correct answer. If the next response was wrong Red would scream *"What?"* four times. By then the player better be right or gone.

"Gimme a fucking break, Red. I am not going out there." Taylor pointed as Kimball Adams took a headgear in the chest. The Pistols' tackle had missed a stunt by the defensive end and tackle; the end hit Kimball going full speed. Kimball's head snapped and he crumpled.

"There isn't a thing for me to learn out there except how to bleed and recognize the sound of broken bones and my own screams," Taylor said. "C'mon, Kimball, buddy, get up!" he rooted. Adams staggered groggily to his feet.

A glint caught Taylor's eyes, pulling them away from the coach's face. He resisted, not wanting to be off balance against Red's counterattack, but Red's eyes fell sadly to the telephone in his hand. Cyrus Chandler was on the other end—on the line direct to the New York owner's private air-conditioned suite where Cyrus Chandler was a guest. The suite had a wet bar, white-coated bartenders, carpeting, heavy leather swivel chairs. It was extremely civilized.

Surrounded by his well-fed and -wined friends, Cyrus told his head coach to put Taylor Rusk in the game because he wanted to show what the Pistols planned to build the Franchise around.

On the field the New York–Texas game was a war of attrition; destruction and vengeance the game plan. There was no winner, only survivors.

"Goddam, can't somebody get the middle linebacker?" Bobby Hendrix pleaded, dabbing his bleeding nose and mouth. "That's the third time he's clotheslined me."

"I could send Amos," Kimball said. "What do you think, Amos?" The huddle turned to the blocking back. Amos Burns's dark eyes looked out from under his black, wet, deeply wrinkled brow.

"I can get him, but if I don't put him out, he's gonna know *you* sent me." Amos looked at Kimball. "I'll hurt him, Kimball, but I can't promise he won't be back, looking for you."

"I'll get him," Simon D'Hanis said. "We'll see how bad this joker wants to bump heads. Gimme a pass-over block with opposite influence."

"Okay! Ninety-three opposite G pull influence!" Kimball ordered. "On two."

The huddle broke. The teams took up their positions.

"I'm making an inside handoff, Amos," Kimball told the big back. "After I give you the ball, you veer. I'm getting the hell away."

Amos Burns grinned.

Kimball called the defensive set; the Pistols' center called the line blocking odd; the New York lineman played the gaps. The linebackers came around, faking a blitz. Kimball knew they weren't coming, though—the safeties were too deep—but he called out a dummy audible so they'd wonder if he bought the fake.

On the snap Kimball Adams whirled quickly, slamming the ball into Amos Burns's stomach. The ninety-three opposite-influence blocking worked well against defenses that read and pursued. New York read pulls, and both of their tackles were chasing the pulling Pistols linemen, leading Danny Lewis flaring on what could be either a pitchout, power sweep or screen pass.

It was none of those.

Amos Burns was through the holes left in the line of scrimmage by the New York pursuit.

The middle linebacker took the influence fake and the two steps necessary to remove him from the play. A furious competitor, he knew Amos had beat him through the hole, but he reached desperately to grasp at the stocky back.

Dig down, he was told over and over. *Dig down.* The middle linebacker dug down.

He never saw Simon coming.

Simon saw the opening under the helmet cage and, using his own headgear, hit him high, trying to tear his face off. The collision echoed across the field, and players on both teams turned to see. It was a familiar sound: demolition.

The middle linebacker was sprawled out on his back. His helmet flew off and it looked like his head was still in it. His face had bones sticking out of it. Every time he exhaled, blood bubbled from a hole beneath his eye.

Simon staggered back to the next huddle.

Burns had gained six yards.

Up in the air-conditioned owner's suite, Cyrus was on the phone, instructing Red Kilroy to put Taylor Rusk in the game.

"Have him throw some to the nigger speed-burner," Cyrus said. "Then tell him to hit Hendrix with a few so I can show these assholes up here what we stole off the blacklist." Cyrus Chandler laughed and rolled the big cigar around in his mouth. Dick Conly sat tight-lipped next to him. Wendy sat next to Dick.

Lem Three was drinking double martinis, trying to forget how Cyrus had screamed at him in the hotel lobby because the buses were late at the airport and the room keys were not sorted correctly.

Wendy poked Dick Conly. "Stop him, Dick."

"Why?" Conly said, "There's always the chance he'll step on his own cock and break his neck. Can't stop a man from making an ass of himself. All you can do is refuse to kiss it."

"Please stop him," Wendy urged. She turned to Lem. "You tell him, Lem."

Lem rocked forward and almost fell to the floor; Wendy helped him regain his balance. He looked down at Dick. "She's right, Dick, do whatever she says. I'm telling you, she's always right. This is the best woman . . . person . . . the best in the world . . . but how was I supposed to know that those dumb fucks can't check into a hotel on their own or that the bus drivers would get lost? Christ! I did my best." Lem's eyes reddened.

"Hush now, Lem." Wendy patted his leg. "Lean back." Then she turned back to Conly. "Tell him or I tell him."

"You think he'll listen?" Dick stared at the field, watching Red and the quarterback standing by the phone. "To me? To you? Shit, he didn't listen to Amos! Every son of a bitch in the Southwest listened to Amos Chandler except his own son."

"*Whaaat?*" Cyrus's voice quivered, a sign of real strain. "He said *what*?" Cyrus quickly regained his voice control. He switched the phone to his right hand, knuckles white. "Put that son of a bitch on the phone."

Wendy looked down to the field. Taylor Rusk in his spanking-clean uniform was taking the phone.

"Now listen to me, mister!" Cyrus began yelling. His grip on the phone caused it to shake.

Dick elbowed Wendy to make certain she saw that Taylor now had the phone to his ear. She nodded. Conly's nose flared as he suppressed a grin; his eyes rolled. They both watched the quarterback in the bright white uniform standing at the phone table, holding the receiver.

Wendy put her binoculars on Taylor. His face was totally devoid of emotion, like a man refusing a telephone magazine subscription.

"I own this ball club, fella, and . . ."

Wendy watched as Taylor reached out and snatched the tape shears from the trainer's scabbard. The quarterback held up the receiver and cut the cord. He took the receiver with him back to his spot on the bench between two big linemen. They had saved him a lined parka.

"Goddam you! . . . Goddam son of a bitch! Football-player asshole!" Cyrus raged into the dead line. "I own you. . . . I'll bury you!"

The New York owner laughed until he cried. A reaction that drove Cyrus almost crazy.

Dick winked at Wendy, then leaned over. "Cyrus," he asked, "you sure you dialed the right number?"

Taylor Rusk didn't play that day; he kept the telephone receiver and hung it over his dresser mirror in the bedroom where he used the Heisman Trophy as a doorstop.

THE AQUARIAN

WENDY Chandler Carleton's labor pains began at midnight. One hour and thirty minutes after arriving at the hospital, she gave birth to an eight pound eleven ounce boy.

Cyrus and Junie wanted to name him Cyrus Junior Carleton or "Bubba," while Lem junior, Lem Three and Pearl Mae Carleton were holding out for Lem IV or "Four."

Wendy named the boy Randall Ryan—the last names of the maternity nurse and her aide, who were more helpful and supportive the last hour and a half than were all the rest combined during the whole nine months of Wendy's pregnancy.

Randall Ryan Carleton was Aquarian.

Cyrus claimed Aquarians were good lawyers and politicians. Junie was convinced they were pessimistic because her sister, Wanda Jane, had married a very pessimistic Aquarian.

Junior and Pearl Mae thought he would probably be an artist or musician.

Dick Conly saw the Aquarian as a way out of his own dilemma.

Red Kilroy told Taylor about the boy when he called him in to play a few off-season mind games.

"My reading of the zodiac," Red explained, "says this boy's got good legs."

THE MAN FROM
NEW ORLEANS

IT had rained hard around Sam. Now the Quarter glistened black and gray in the mist and clouds of dawn. He liked the wet darkness of the swamp, the city squatting on the ooze. Pulling the heavy red velvet drape from the window, he hooked it over the bronze gargoyle, then sat in his heavy oak straight-back chair with hand-carved elaborately scrolled arms and claw feet.

The chair and drape and most of the interior furnishings of the grand house were from the French Period.

The house, built during the American Period, was Victorian, painted white and green, three stories with bays and extended verandas and second-story porches. The wrought-iron fence and gate were forged during the Spanish Period. The help was African. The Man was Lebanese.

New Orleans was his place in the world. He knew it the moment he arrived from the desert through Mexico. Years ago with Amos Chandler. Hard years but good years, well worth the effort.

He stared out the bay window down Royal Street at the dismal morning, dripping wrought-iron balconies and peeling white paint. The mist came and went. He wanted hard rain and black clouds all day; then he would sit in the chair and stare from dawn to dawn.

She was the city in the swamp.

He was the Man from New Orleans.

And there was a knock at his door.

"Sir, Mr. Kazan?" He heard Cisco rap lightly again on the door. "It's Mr. Conly on the private number."

"Fine, Cisco, put him through." The Man picked up the phone. "Yes, Richard, my dear friend?" He paused, listened and nodded. "This has to do with Marconi's problem. I hate to see those kinds of fights, but all is not lost if you get *some* gain. Memphis and Phoenix are the core of Marconi's support. You'll have their proxy at the owner's meeting. When they go with you, the handwriting will be on the wall."

The Man listened and smiled.

"Always my pleasure, Dick."

The rain picked up and the call ended.

The League Owners meeting at La Coste Country Club had two major items on the agenda. The question of the LA franchise and the awarding of the next three years' worth of Super Bowls. After the presentation of evidence against Marconi's daughter by J. Edgar Jones of Investico, the owners talked and smoked and conferred. Dick Conly broke the stalemate by providing the proxies of the Memphis and Phoenix teams, helping Commissioner Burden and the West Coast owners finally force the Marconi interests completely out of the Los Angeles franchise. They then voted to secure it for one Richard Portus, a twenty-one-year-old graduate of the University. Portus's father was an oil-man friend of Cyrus Chandler, and Conly helped to secure the LA franchise for Portus.

In return the Texas Pistols were named to host the Super Bowl in three years.

Now all Dick Conly had to do was build a stadium for the game.

DICK'S DOME:
THE TEN-CENT DOLLAR REVISITED

"ONCE we amortize the player costs of the purchase price of the Franchise and lose the depreciation, we're going to show a positive cash flow unless we do something," Dick Conly said. "The television money is going to be unbelievable. We've got to find some shelter."

"Any ideas?" Cyrus Chandler sat behind his half-full glass of bourbon.

"A couple." Dick Conly dug a shaking hand into the stainless-steel ice bucket, then dropped the cubes into the whiskey. "We form a trust for your new grandson and move ten percent of the Franchise in every year. We would appoint and control the trustees. It would reduce the tax exposure and it'd allow you to offer Red the ownership position that he wants. Give him two and a half percent and he'd have a reason to help keep down player costs."

"Whoa!" Cyrus sat up. "I told him maybe if we got to the Super Bowl I would reconsider."

"He would be easier to control if he had something to lose besides his job."

Cyrus shook his head. "Go ahead and set up Randall's trust, but hold off on Red. I want to think."

"Every time you think, it costs us money."

"I want to . . ."

"You go ahead and think, Cyrus. Meanwhile in three years we host the Super Bowl," Conly explained. "And between now and then we build a stadium."

"We just got University Stadium," Cyrus protested. "Why spend the money to build one?"

"We'll be spending someone else's money, first of all. And second of all, with our own stadium we are vertically integrated. We can move the money around a lot easier, without even considering our radio network and the television plan," Conly said. "Depending on where we want the income to show up, we charge rent and split parking and concessions accordingly. We'll finance it through bond sales too. They have to buy bonds before they can buy season tickets. We pay the bondholders about three percent interest with an option to buy the bonds back at face value in thirty years."

"With ten-cent dollars," Cyrus added.

Dick Conly often used inflation in player negotiations, deferring large contract payments into the twenty-first century, expensing the full amount currently. Now they were planning to do it to the fans.

"We'll put it outside the city in one of those little suburbs to the south—maybe Clyde."

Cyrus was puzzled but interested in the plan. It was another Dick Conly money-making scheme using OPM.

"South to Clyde for two reasons." Dick had poured another drink and was sketching out some rough figures on a cocktail napkin. "First, the city is going to grow south when the new airport is built out past Clyde. That means expressways and accessibility to the stadium. Next, the mayor and city council of Clyde have already promised us free municipal services and exemption from property taxes. I've already optioned a thousand acres on both sides of the freeway for a thousand dollars an acre. In thirty years that land will be selling by the square foot and we will exercise the option to buy the bonds back from the ticket holders at face value. The Franchise owns the land, the stadium and all improvements and won't have a tax problem with property for thirty years." Dick looked at Cyrus Chandler. "You won't be here."

Cyrus blinked and jerked back.

"Do the math. This is for your grandson, that's why I'm moving assets into the trust as fast as possible—for *him*." Dick tossed the paper with the hastily figured stadium-financing plan. "The least you can do for the kid is protect him with the trust." Conly smiled. "Not that I enjoy planning your estate, but the assumption of your death is *so* attractive."

Cyrus didn't smile. "What makes you so certain this'll fly?"

"Two things," Conly replied. "We get the Super Bowl in three years. Robbie Burden is willing to go along as long as the commissioner's office gets its share of tickets. And Red Kilroy and Taylor Rusk just might take the Pistols to the Super Bowl by then. Since the blackout rule includes *all* local games, that means my Pay-Per-View television plan will include the Super Bowl Game."

"What's the Super Bowl worth?"

"How does a hundred-million-dollar gate strike you?"

MIND GAMES

BEFORE Red met with Cyrus Chandler and Dick Conly to discuss the draft, he had Taylor stop by his office. He wanted to lever his head a little.

"Taylor, you know this is pro ball, and . . ."

"It certainly is, Red."

"What?"

"Pro ball. You said this was pro ball. I was just agreeing with you." Taylor walked away from the coach's metal desk to the window. "Geez, Red, what a shitty view."

"What?" Red bit through his cigar in frustrated confusion. "Siddown, Taylor. I've gotta meet with Conly about the draft, and . . ."

"I *guess* you got a draft." Taylor ran a hand around the window. "They not only gave you a bad view, you're on the north side of the building. I'll bet you freeze in here on cold days."

"What are you talking about now?" Red swiveled his leather swivel chair around and spit part of the cigar into the waste can.

"Red, I didn't invite myself over here. I figure you called me up here to threaten me with all the quarterbacks available in the draft."

"Taylor. Taylor. How can you say that?"

"Bull's-eye."

"I have to think ahead."

"And I don't?" Taylor turned quickly from the window and advanced on Red. The size of the movement was intimidating. Red pulled back into his chair.

"I don't have to think ahead? Is that it, Coach?" Taylor's wide, long hands splayed out on the metal desk as Taylor leaned across it. "Now"—his voice was soft, but the man towering over Red Kilroy was visibly angry—"I don't like mind games. I thought we got all that shit straight at the University. So far you have told me that this is pro ball and the draft is coming. What advantage do you think that gives you over me?"

"Look, Taylor, I'm just the coach. Conly and Chandler have their own ideas about what we need in the draft." Red tried to look sincere. "They want more quarterbacks. Cyrus doesn't like you much."

"And?"

"Well, they want to use our number one to get Jacobi from Notre Dame."

"And?"

"Jacobi?" Red went on. "The quarterback from Notre Dame? Doesn't that mean anything to you?"

Taylor moved back to the window. He looked north to where the new expressway fed out into cotton fields and gin towns.

"Notre Dame, Taylor, Notre Dame." Red slapped himself on the top of the head as if pounding a stake into his brain. "Catholics, Taylor. Do you know how many Catholics there are in the world?"

Taylor shook his head. "How many?"

"How the fuck should I know? But they watch a fucking lot of TV football. Dick and Cyrus think they'll watch Texas if we get Jacobi. And frankly, Taylor, it's a sound theory."

"But you're willing to stick with me."

Red nodded grimly.

"Well, Red"—Taylor glanced over his shoulder—"your whole scheme is so obvious as to be patently absurd, starting with the fact that this *is* pro ball and Jacobi couldn't carry my jock. Hell, he can't carry his own jock." Taylor looked back north. The city was sprawling up the expressway, devouring the rich black land. "What do you *really* want, Red? What's the tradeoff to keep this vile papist conspiracy from usurping my quarterback's job?"

"Let me call the plays." The words rushed out, betraying the desperation Red was trying to conceal.

Taylor laughed softly out the window. He didn't answer.

"Well? Taylor?" The coach swung his chair left and right. "What about it?"

Taylor stayed silent, staring toward Oklahoma, recalling the wedding trip and Wendy Chandler. The campus was to his right, the spring-fed river snaking, glittering through the trees. He watched the bums under the Red River Bridge. "I heard Lem and Wendy had a baby," Taylor finally said.

Red spoke coldly, hard. "Big deal. Now, what about me calling some plays from the sideline?"

"Maybe Jacobi'll let you do it. 'Course with Jacobi, you may also have to do the running and passing."

"I take that to mean no?"

Taylor nodded.

"Son of a bitch." Red slammed his hand flat on his desk.

"Red, control is the quarterback's job. Creativity under stress is impossible without control. Otherwise I'd play wide receiver— less strain and pressure." Taylor's eyes glittered; he loved this argument. "That's reality out there. The other players must talk to me and me to them. We must communicate completely. They must trust me and believe in me. On the field and off. You are noise—interference. The game is not a bunch of separate plays, it's one continuous process. And no matter what else, on Sunday I am willing and able to create the whole process. The power and control have to stay on the field."

"You know what I'll get for you?" Red added. "The guys who never make a mistake."

"Nope."

"I'm talking a team of mistake-free lunatics. . . ."

Taylor shook his head. "You find 'em and train 'em. But I'll communicate with 'em and run the team."

"I want more," Red pleaded.

"Red, we're all in this alone, and if you take power from the field, I lose it. And that makes the difference between great football and magic." Taylor grinned. "Perspective, Coach, keep your perspective."

"Fuck perspective—" Red began.

"I am the passer," Taylor interrupted. "When I put the ball up, only three things can happen, *and two are bad*. I won't accept that risk unless I choose when and where I throw."

"This is my *chance*," Red pleaded. Sweat beaded on his upper lip; droplets ran down his forehead from his hairline.

"You don't have a choice, Red. It's my chance too. I'm not

changing, and if you don't let go, I'll break your fingers. I want no mistakes on game day.... That includes you."

"Let me call some plays, Taylor! Just a few!"

The quarterback shook his head.

"Christ! You are some Frankenstein's monster," Red growled. "Greedy bastard."

"I gotta go." Taylor started toward the door. "You will call no plays during the game. If you try, I'll call time out. You just get me a team of lunatics who can execute, teach them what to do and where to be, and I'll win the games."

Red watched his quarterback cross the room in a quick, supple move. His physical size, strength and grace never ceased to awe the coach. Taylor was not just a smart, skillful quarterback; he was a genius, and Red's system required a genius at quarterback. Taylor Rusk was so mentally and physically durable that Red suspected he was a different species of man. The coach watched the door close as Taylor Rusk left.

"If you weren't so fucking good..." Red growled, then sighed, "...then we would really be shitty."

He flicked the projector back on and watched the middle linebacker from Chicago tip off the coverage every time.

SNAKE-TRAINING

SIMON had just washed and waxed his new red Bronco the day he loaded up his dog, Harlowe, a new electric collar, and a defanged rattlesnake. He bought the five-foot diamondback snake hot from a herpetologist at the University.

Simon decided to drive past the Pistols office and look for Taylor's car since the offices weren't that far out of his way. He drove slowly through the lot, looking for Taylor's long four-door yellow Lincoln. While cruising slowly and looking, Simon almost ran over one of the ball boys.

Luther Conly, Dick's boy, was stumbling through the lot, blinded by tears. Simon swerved the Bronco; Luther banged right into the side and fell to the asphalt. Harlowe fell off the seat and banged her head against the dashboard, heavily padded with the Leather Cowboy Interior Package. Harlowe wasn't hurt; neither was Luther. Simon was scared to death.

He jumped out and scooped up the young boy, who continued to sob. Simon held him gently; boys at his age were eggshell fragile.

Luther continued to sob, his face against the massive chest. Simon did the only thing he knew and hugged the teen-ager to him. Luther hugged him back and began to cry harder.

Harlowe whined from inside the new Bronco.

"Take me with you," the boy sobbed, "please take me with you." He continued to cry. Simon held the boy and looked bewildered.

"We're just gonna snake-train old Harlowe. You wanna go?"

Luther nodded his head rapidly, his face still buried in Simon's chest.

"Here's how it works." Simon had stopped the Bronco in Taylor's apartment parking lot. Luther and Harlowe were sitting side by side in the passenger seat. The snake was curled up, cold and quiet in his cage in the back. "First I put the electric collar on Harlowe." Simon followed his own directions. "Then when we get her and the snake out in the field; I let her get a look, a smell, and maybe the sound of the rattles. Then I punch this button here on my remote control and give Harlowe a good jolt of electricity."

"Aversion therapy?" Luther asked.

"Snake-training." Simon looked at the remote dials and button. "I better make certain this thing works before we get way out in the country."

Simon slid his fingers beneath the electric collar around Harlowe's thick gold neck. She was a big, beautiful golden retriever, with a shiny coat and long feathers of hair streaming from her legs and tail. A once-in-a-lifetime dog—bright-eyed, friendly, alert and smart—Simon wasn't going to lose Harlowe to some fucking rattlesnake. He kept his fingers under the collar and turned on the remote, dialing the power output to Low. Harlowe didn't move and Simon's fingers felt nothing. He slowly turned the dial and pushed the button, still getting nothing as he reached Medium. By the time he got to High, Simon knew the remote was broken.

"Let's go inside and see if Taylor's got a screwdriver." Simon stepped out of his new Bronco. Harlowe sat upright and alert in the front seat.

"Maybe it's the batteries," Luther offered, walking around the Bronco. "This sure is a great car."

"Just got it."

"The upholstery work is beautiful." Luther followed Simon toward Taylor's apartment.

"For two grand extra it better be beautiful." Simon rapped on the door and walked inside. Taylor never locked his door. It was a habit he would break as things got going faster and growing bigger.

"Hey, Luther." Taylor sat on the floor, doing yoga stretching exercises. "How's the old ball boy?"

"He's great, Taylor, just great," Simon answered. "Except I banged into him with my new Bronco."

"I banged into you, Simon." Luther turned to Taylor. "Simon said I could come along."

"It's okay with me." Taylor assumed the lotus position, breathing deeply, trying to align his spine for more power.

"My electric collar is fucked up." Simon held up the remote control. "You got a screwdriver?"

"In that drawer there." Taylor stood up and took several deep breaths. The quarterback walked over to the table where the big guard had begun to disassemble the remote control.

"The kid was crying like a baby in the parking lot." Simon opened the remote and looked in bafflement at the colored wires and copper connections. "I went by the offices to see if you were still there. He'd gone over to meet his dad and Dick wasn't there."

"Do you know what you're doing?" Taylor watched Simon tinker with the wires, then push buttons and turn dials.

"This is basic research. I got no idea what I'm doing." Simon shook his head and turned the output dial up to High and punched the shock button about ten times.

Taylor watched Simon twirl the dial from High to Low, punch the shock button again, wiggle a few wires.

Taylor looked at Luther, who seemed smaller, frailer, than in training camp. Luther walked over to watch Simon work on the remote for the electric collar. The long antennae wobbled and whipped as Simon applied the larger-hammer theory of repair.

Taylor walked to the kitchen and filled his glass from the spigot. "You want a drink of water?"

Luther shook his head.

"What's the trouble between you and Dick?" Taylor asked.

"I just want to know him. I like him and we're never together. It's always going to be later. He pushes me farther from him."

Simon looked up from his tinkering with the remote. "You got any D batteries? These are brand new, but I'll try anything."

Taylor put down his glass and dug through a drawer, finally

tossing Simon a blister package of batteries. Simon replaced the batteries, continuing to twirl the dial and punch the shock button.

"Being a teen-ager is tough, Luther." Taylor didn't know why he was giving Conly's kid advice. "But you have to keep on."

"It's funny. I couldn't wait to be sixteen and I've never had a more miserable year in my life."

"Things go along like this for years and then get worse. Everything comes," Taylor said. "All that happens to survivors is they get old. Your father understands that better than most. This business is about age and infirmity. Too soon old, too late smart. Dick is frightened, like everybody else. He's frightened of loving you, frightened of the pain of loving and committing to transitory things."

"Like his own son?"

"The most transitory of all. You won't be sixteen forever—one true thing in life. Things change with increasing speed." Taylor walked to the table where Simon tinkered. "It takes forever to be born, an eternity to reach five years old, and a millisecond later you're sixty-five, getting a gold watch for a job you never liked." Taylor kept his eyes on Simon's work. "I haven't felt young since seventh grade." Taylor looked outside at something and his eyes narrowed. "Say . . . ah . . . Simon? Did you get your new Bronco?"

"Yep." Simon spun the dial and pushed the shock button on the remote control. "You should see that Leather Cowboy Interior."

"I *can* see it. I think you oughtta come have another look."

"Why? I gotta get this thing fixed or I'll never get Harlowe snake-trained."

Taylor frowned, his eyes still fixed outside the window. "I think you got that fixed."

Simon sighed and turned in his seat, continuing to twirl the dial and punch the shock button. "How do you know?"

"Did you take the electric collar off Harlowe before you came up here?"

"Oh, my God!" Simon raced to the window.

The red Bronco sat in the lot, shiny beautiful and new. Simon's eyes widened. "Oh, my God!" The inside of the Bronco was a Green Bay blizzard of stuffing from the leather seats, headliner and side panels whirling like snow before the wind, impenetrable to the eye. Inside, somewhere in the storm, was Harlowe, exhausted and terrified, no longer reacting to the senseless jolts of electricity that had suddenly begun shortly after Simon entered Taylor Rusk's apartment. Before the fear and pain and confusion had driven Harlowe into nervous shock and exhaustion, she had tried wildly and vainly to claw her way through the two-thousand-dollar Leather Cowboy Interior and out of the car. Only the body metal and the seat springs stopped her.

"Oh, my God! Harlowe!" Simon raced out of Taylor's apartment. "Harlowe, Harlowe..." The big man lumbered down to his Bronco and opened the doors. The leather interior was shredded. The stuffing floated out into the wind and blew through the apartment complex. On top of the snake, Harlowe lay panting with her eyes rolling wildly.

The snake was dead.

Harlowe, the once-in-a-lifetime dog, underwent a year of treatment by a dog psychologist but was never the same. She seldom left the house and was terrified of red cars the rest of her life. And, of course, couldn't ever wear a flea collar.

Taylor and Luther Conly watched the red Bronco careen out of the lot, throwing off a rooster tail of leather bits and stuffing as Simon raced to his vet. Taylor turned to Luther. "You need a ride somewhere?"

Luther shook his head. "If the snake-training is over, I don't have anyplace to go."

RED'S PLAN

BEFORE he entered the meeting, Cyrus Chandler had the secretary hold all calls. Cyrus didn't tell either Red or Dick he had cut off the phone. Dick was expecting a call from Luther. Red had scouts out with contracts, deals on the burner.

"I will *not* give all my number-one draft choices for five years," Cyrus yelled.

Conly sat silently at his desk and watched Red and Cyrus argue. Red and Dick had thrashed the plan out the night before in the basement of Red's house.

"No draft choices above third for five years. We'll be gutting ourselves." The owner's hands shook and his voice quivered as he continued to rage. "You can't just give away my draft choices. This is my money. My draft choices."

"We won't need 'em." Red leaned back with his feet up on the coffee table. "You trade for these guys this off-season listed here, get them for a total of fifteen to twenty draft choices over five years, and we will get to the playoffs in two, maybe three, years." Red spoke softly, explaining. "Taylor Rusk will be ready to take them."

"Everybody builds from the draft," Cyrus argued.

"Bullshit," Red said. "Besides, I don't have time."

"We promised you all the time you needed." Cyrus seemed hurt that Red would recall broken promises.

Red looked over at Cyrus. "You also gave me complete control on player personnel."

"We're not interfering or breaking our promise," Cyrus moaned, "but we certainly have the right to question a decision that could be detrimental to the long-term prospects of the Franchise. What about my idea about Jacobi and the Catholics?"

"Knute Rockne died," Dick Conly said.

"The guy can't carry Taylor Rusk's jock. Besides, I'll find plenty of good ballplayers after the third round." Red stabbed a finger at a name on his list. "This guy we'll get cheap from Oakland. He raped his white girl friend and she may file. They want him out of the Bay area. We'll be signing lots of free agents. The colleges are turning out plenty of good football players. We pay off the college coaches to steer players to us from all over the country."

Cyrus looked over Red's list of college players. "I don't recognize one name."

"They are all great college players with what I consider necessary to make it in the pros."

"Which is?" Cyrus demanded.

"Can't explain."

"Why do we pay one million dollars a year into the scouting combine if we don't take their advice?"

"Because the combine is a front to create nonexistent expenses," Conly sighed. "The money is hidden; it's a scam. Most of our combine money is in tax-free industrial bonds. The million is really just bookkeeping; it's all accounted for and we can get it if we want it. As long as we don't need it, we expense it to the combine. Every team does, except some of them actually use the information."

"The losers," Red added.

"How many of those big-money guys pay off? The percentages are low. We'll have a number-one draft choice again in five years."

"But you . . ." Cyrus continued with the argument he had rehearsed the night before.

Red looked to Conly for support.

"Cyrus, Red is right. Besides, it's his prerogative. It's in his contract and it's what you pay him for, anyway. Let him do his job and let me get back to mine."

"Well, I'll be a son of a bitch." Cyrus threw his pencil clear across the room. It bounced near Red.

Conly strode over and banged the latch that swung the walnut wainscotting back, revealing the fully stocked wet bar. "We can get those players on that list. We can *steal* them. We are not dealing with geniuses here, Cyrus." Conly took a long gulping drink from a bottle of Jack Daniel's Black Label. "We can have an experienced, talented team. Overnight." He slammed the bottle down on the bar, suddenly looked puzzled and checked his watch. "Wonder why Luther didn't call?"

"Back to business," Cyrus said. "We got a job to . . ."

"Give the goddam job to Red." Conly pointed at the coach with the neck of the Jack Daniel's bottle. "You can probably trust him. He can do it and he won't steal much. I'm getting back to the real world for a while."

"C'mon, Dick, calm down. Since when were you the big family man? This *is* the real world, you know?"

"It's *your* world, Cyrus." Conly started for the door.

"Don't leave," Cyrus said. "We have other decisions to make."

"Let Red make 'em. I'm taking the whole spring off to become friends with my boy, who has spent the last year in his bedroom alone, smoking dope and waiting for his father."

"You can't," Cyrus protested.

"Watch. It's simple." The door whooshed shut behind Dick Conly.

It *seemed* simple.

Red never moved. Cyrus stared at the closed door.

"Well," Red said, "I'll just keep this list and make the deals." Red got to his feet and walked to the door, the list dangling at his side. "I'm pretty good. You don't recruit high school kids for twenty years without learning how to be eating Momma's chicken-fried steak and be lying through the cream gravy to her boy." Red began to laugh at his own words. He laughed harder and hurried out to find an assistant coach to tell.

Cyrus Chandler sat alone in the office and listened to the re-treating giggles of the head coach. He buzzed A. D. Koster's office, looking for someone who would tell him what he wanted to hear.

A.D. was out but would oblige the moment he returned.

THE LAST OF
LUTHER CONLY

DICK Conly went home and found his sixteen-year-old son, Luther, in the closed garage. The soft-faced boy was sprawled across the backseat of his mother's brown Rolls-Royce Corniche. The engine was running and the boy was dead.

Inside the house, on his freshly made bed, there was a note: *"I'm sorry, Dad. I can't figure out why. Luke."*

The newspaper called it a tragic accident. Cyrus Chandler saw to that. It was his newspaper.

"It was the least I could do," Cyrus told his wife, Junie.

"It was also the most," Wendy said. She stood in the open doorway with Lem Three. "You didn't even go to the funeral." Wendy walked into the living room. Her parents sat in the Pit and were drinking martinis. Wendy and Lem were dressed for the funeral. "Your absence was conspicuous."

"Now, Wendy..." Lem Three tried to quiet his wife from several steps behind her and was having luck commensurate with his comparative mobility.

"His family needs him." Wendy was angry. "And you keep him at your side so Red Kilroy wouldn't outsmart you. He is a brilliant man. Why did he have to become general manager of your goddam football team? He was busy enough cleaning up all your other business deals—"

"Now, Wendy," Junie Chandler interrupted without much enthusiasm. She really didn't know what Wendy was mad about. "I won't allow you to use that tone of voice to your father."

"Is *he* the only one that gets to use this voice?" Wendy shot back. Cyrus watched his daughter's face with passionless eyes. He took a cigarette from the silver case on the round marble table. He lit the cigarette with a lighter in the shape of a gold goose.

"Well..." Junie was trying to reply to Wendy, "well..."

Wendy glanced from her mother to her father. Her unsteady, confused mother and her calculating, confused father.

"Well," Junie finally said, "well, yes, your father can talk like that because he is a man. Right, honey?" She nudged her husband. Cyrus closed his eyes slowly and nodded.

"Lem?" Junie continued, "Isn't that right?"

Lem stammered slightly.

"Don't answer, Lem," Wendy said.

"Wendy. Wendy," Cyrus said in low, soothing, loving tones. "You are letting this get all out of proportion. I didn't force Dick Conly to do anything he didn't want to and I'm certainly not responsible for the death of a boy who was known to be on drugs. He smoked marijuana in his bedroom. Dick told me. He did it for over a year. He was addicted to marijuana and I personally plan"—Cyrus had just thought this up, hoping to placate his daughter—"I plan to start a fund to go after all the dealers of drugs and pornography and I am going to endow the fund in that dead boy's name. What do you think about that?"

"I think it sucks. You don't even *know* the kid's name."

"I do too," Cyrus shot back angrily. She had spurned his gift.

"Well?" Wendy kept her hands on her hips and looked at her father.

"Well what?"

"The kid. Dick Conly's, the one who killed himself in his mother's Rolls. What is his name?"

"I know it," Cyrus protested. "I know it . . . it's . . . I know it . . . don't tell me." Cyrus held up his hands and a frown dug in along his brow. "It's ah . . . Richard . . . Dick junior!" Cyrus smiled at the logic of his guess.

Wendy stared at her father. The guess had been wrong. Things were worse.

"Luther, sir," Lem said quietly. "Luther James Conly was his name." He nodded and smiled wanly.

"Oh, yes, sure," Cyrus grabbed the sides of his head with both hands. "How stupid. Sure. Yeah. Luther."

"You were his godfather," Wendy sneered.

"I was?" Cyrus was startled. "I mean, I was. I know I was."

"I didn't know until we got to the church," Lem said, smiling.

Wendy turned around and hit Lem right above the ear with her black beaded bag. It had her pistol in it. Lem hit the floor cold, cutting his chin.

Wendy didn't even stay around to watch Lem bleed on the parquet. She left the front door open.

Junie fretted and Cyrus said nothing until Wendy's car started and the sounds of her driving rapidly away died in the distance.

"She'll get over it," Cyrus told Junie, who was on her knees beside the still-unconscious and bleeding Lem. A servant called an ambulance. "He'll be all right. They have people to take care of this sort of thing." Cyrus got up out of the Pit and retired to his bedroom. Junie waited by Lem's side until the ambulance arrived and carted him off to the hospital. Junie called Lem's mother and told her. They both agreed to keep it quiet.

The story was all over Park City by nine the next morning. The mailman inquired of the butler at Cyrus Chandler's house whether it was a shooting, stabbing or just another beating. The butler pleaded ignorance, having been off that day, but according to the maid it was a pistol-whipping. The mailman liked that story and that's the one he carried.

HORSESHOES
AND HAND GRENADES

THE day they buried Luther Conly, Taylor Rusk was ushered to an unfortunate seat in the church balcony that looked directly down into the casket containing the handsome, dead sixteen-year-old boy. Taylor kept his eyes closed throughout the ceremony as the young people around him broke down, confronting death in their midst. The young girls started first, some already sobbing when they arrived in the hot, crowded balcony. Some were jolted by the sight of Luther James Conly in a three-piece suit, looking the same and terribly different. It seemed he could open his eyes and lift his head off of that small silk pillow and step out of that casket. Almost. That got the last ones crying: the horror and nothingness of *almost*.

Taylor closed his eyes and thought about offensive adjustments against various zone defenses and Kimball Adams's instructions on keys to those defenses. Taylor kept his eyes closed and reran pass-defense adjustments until the service ended, the balcony emptied and the body was closed in the casket and wheeled to the hearse. He stayed until after the procession had left for the cemetery with the dead boy.

Sixteen, almost seventeen.

"Only counts in horseshoes and hand grenades," Kimball Adams always said about *almost*.

Taylor drove out to Doc Webster's ranch. Wendy drove up after dark. The meeting was accidental. They had both gone to Doc's ranch for refuge after the funeral.

"I would have married you," Taylor said, "if you'd insisted. But you didn't. You listened to my side and then you disappeared. It was *our* relationship choreographed by *you*."

"If all I was going to get was somebody who would back down from my father and make me like it, I would rather have Lem; he's bred to it. "

"Well, you got Lem. We are all players in your game. You wanted me as a husband to hit your father over the head," Taylor argued. "Why should I let you use me?"

"You were . . ." Wendy said, "you were something special."

"I still am," Taylor smiled wryly. "Just because you have changed, doesn't mean I have."

Taylor stood on the porch and watched Wendy's taillights disappear over Coon Ridge. He rocked in the chair until dawn, then went swimming in Panther Hole.

Returning up the bluff, he could hear the Kinky-Headed Boy's stereo.

> *Well, I'm sittin' down in San Antone*
> *waitin' on an eight o'clock train*
> *my woman left me here last night*
> *and things ain't been quite the same.*

Up from Panther Hole, chilled, refreshed but still confused, Taylor rubbed his hair vigorously, shaking out the water. The morning sun dried him.

As he passed the bunkhouse, Tommy McNamara, the Kinky-Headed Boy, stepped out the screen door. His eyes looked red and tired; he'd been working all night on his book.

> *I gotta get back to Dallas to tie up a few loose ends*
> *work a week, make a hundred dollars*
> *ahhh and hit the road again.*

"You two get back together?" McNamara rubbed his eyes, holding his thick glasses in one hand. He was a small man, compared to Taylor. He had a pleasant, open face that always seemed happy no matter how care-worn his eyes. His big, sad brown eyes. He put his glasses back on and magnified the sadness in his eyes.

"Almost." Taylor pulled on his shirt and watched the tired young man looking for answers and solutions to insane questions.

Tommy McNamara looked up. "Almost?"

"Almost."

The Kinky-Headed Boy frowned vacantly, lost inside his own head. "Well...what the hell." He turned and walked into the bunkhouse. Taylor started for the back entrance to the house.

The stereo continued in the bunkhouse. Driving, cocky guitars, fiddles, steel and wire and electricity, fingers and picks, flutes and drums—the new country music. The soaring rhythms denied the sadness of the song. The singer continued to whine in false bravado.

> So I don't want you to think you're the first one
> to leave this old boy out here on his own
> 'cause this ain't gonna be the first time
> this old cowboy spent the night alone....
> No, this ain't gonna be the first time
> this old cowboy spent the night alone.

DICK AND RED
BUILD THE FRANCHISE

DICK Conly returned to work at the Franchise the Monday following his son's funeral. He no longer wanted the spring vacation Luther wasn't there to have with him. Dick never worked harder or better, saying work was the best tonic. How much more he drank was hard to quantify, since he already drank so much. But Dick Conly was a consummate general manager. He quickly built a contender.

Dick went right to work on Red Kilroy's plan to trade draft choices for proven veterans and sign college players in their undergraduate years. He drove hard bargains and made good deals. He swapped away eighteen draft choices for twelve tried-and-proven veterans. He conferred frequently with Red, seldom with Cyrus.

Red and Dick worked some magic themselves and Conly allowed Red to gradually increase his power. The GM no longer wanted to have anything, with the single exception of Suzy Ballard. Dick made Suzy his assistant and she convinced him to hire A. D. Koster after Red cut him.

The second season, the Texas Pistols went nine and seven with Kimball and Taylor alternating at quarterback the first seven games. As the pass protection began to improve, they became a true team offensively, and Taylor Rusk became the starting quarterback for the last seven games. Texas was 7–0 with Taylor at quarterback. He was sacked only six times.

It was all part of the plan, though exactly whose was debated for years.

Taylor never doubted his ability, and his confidence was contagious. They were beaten five times by better teams and beat themselves twice against inferior opponents. They were never outcoached. Red covered details and gathered intelligence from the network of Red's boys throughout football, from junior high to the New York pros. The diligent, plodding head coach spent his life building his network, and it was paying big dividends. His people were in place from coast to coast and from the Canadian league to the Mexican border.

Dick Conly the Ingenious created fail-safe schemes. And now they had the personnel. They were on schedule.

Kimball Adams retired to become a travel agent and New York's quarterback coach. After the last game of the season Red got him the coaching job. They stayed in touch—bits and pieces, rumors, gossip, game plans. Kimball stayed drunk, but his New York travel agency did well, mainly handling Las Vegas junkets. Kimball had played drunk and the alcohol didn't dim his motor skills as a coach, only his pronunciation. And his perception of life.

The Cobianco brothers began to use Kimball's travel agency for casino junkets to Vegas, Atlantic City and the Bahamas.

"The less you get beat up in the front end of your career, the more years you get at the back end," Kimball Adams had told Taylor that first night at the Leadville Bar and Post Office.

Kimball got beat up at both ends and in the middle. And it wasn't over yet.

"All we need now," Red told Conly, "is seasoning and tempering from the heat of battle. The hotter the better."

"Then let's stoke the fire, Coach. I want a white-hot flame and a football team that can stand a holocaust."

Training camp the third season was thermonuclear, and the Texas Pistols were welded into a winning team.

It was hellfire. It worked.

THE PLAYOFF BOWL

RED Kilroy gazed out the team-plane window and watched the flat coastal plain of Florida rushing up at him. Ahead he could see the guidance lights directing them to a long shimmering strip of cement. When the big plane bumped down, Red took a small adrenaline rush and toasted himself silently. He had done what he said he could do and had brought a third-year expansion franchise to the Playoff Bowl. The trades had worked out perfectly and Taylor Rusk had been a phenomenon.

During the week before the Playoff Game, Red felt like the time was right to speak again to Cyrus about ownership percentage. Cyrus had turned him down before, but Red wasn't planning on giving up. Ever.

What kind of a guy could survive in this world if he gives up? Red thought as the team plane taxied to the terminal. *If you give up even for a minute, you are lost. You can't ever grab on again. It's the fast track.* He wanted an ownership position with the Franchise that he was building or he might just quit building.

The plane interior was beginning to heat up.

The players were beginning to stir back in the tourist section.

Suzy Ballard, Dick Conly's assistant, handed the head coach his hat.

"Thank you, my dear," Red said, trying to sound old and feeble. He didn't want to offer the slightest attraction to the girl. He knew her by her eyes, the same way he sometimes picked defensive backs and linebackers. A crazed, angry glisten, a sense of focus, as if Suzy saw into you, searching for soft, hollow, blood-gorged organs. The vitals. Those eyes often meant great linebackers and defensive backs, but Red Kilroy had never witnessed anything positive about them in women.

The team plane jostled across the hot Florida airstrip. The Texas Pistols had arrived to meet Miami in the Playoff Bowl.

Red considered the advantages of Dick Conly as an ally. There was a growing distance between Conly and Cyrus Chandler. If Red could lever that gap into an alliance between Red and Conly, maybe they could both demand ownership positions with options. They were running the club. Cyrus didn't know his ass from a thigh pad.

Will Conly be a good ally? Red wondered as the plane pulled up to the terminal. He looked over at Conly and saw Suzy Ballard watching.

What is she up to? thought Red. *What in God's name is she up to?*

Red Kilroy was the first person to consider that Suzy Ballard had a plan of her own.

It was cold in Florida the whole week before the game. The wind blew and it rained a lot. The team didn't practice much. Since there was no second place, the Playoff Bowl was meaningless. The League had organized charity Bowl Games between the second-place teams from each division. It all seemed pretty imaginary. Red Kilroy told them that it was good practice for the Super Bowl, but it wasn't the Super Bowl and there was no sense confusing it.

Winners got $3,000, losers got $1,800. Everybody got a free room plus twenty dollars a day. Twenty dollars didn't go very far so it was *easy* not to confuse it with the Super Bowl. When Bobby Hendrix complained to the Union about the players being forced to play the charity games, Terry Dudley, the director, told him it was good for the players' image.

Taylor and Bobby were sharing a third-floor room. Rain had canceled that afternoon's practice. Hendrix dialed the phone as Taylor walked to the window. The rain had since stopped, but it was still windy and cloudy. Threatening weather. Red never practiced during threatening weather in Texas because he always watched the complete practice from his metal tower, which stood above the practice field like a lightning rod.

"I don't believe in God," Red said, "but why give the son of a bitch a free shot? He may not believe in me either. You never know: God might think he's Vince Lombardi."

Taylor looked out the hotel window down at the abandoned swimming pool. Rows of empty wooden chairs waited for greasy, fat, old people to come stretch out in the promised Florida sun, bake themselves juicy-brown and talk through their noses about New York and New Jersey.

Hendrix lay on his bed in his underwear, talking on the phone to his wife, Ginny. The first season, Ginny had moved the whole family to her daddy's Houston place in River Oaks. They had lived there ever since, with Bobby joining them in the off-season.

Ginny Savas had been born and raised in wealthy River Oaks and met Bobby when he came to play scholarship football for Rice. Ginny Hendrix's father, Gus Savas, a Houston wildcatter with a River Oaks mansion, was the son of Savas Savas, which in Greek means Sam Sam, a name given by some immigration bureaucrat who was baffled by the number of letters in Pouloupodopoulus.

Ginny was Gus Savas's only child, and Gus doted on her. After her mother died, she often accompanied her father to the elaborate parties of the oil-rich. The parties were dazzling and fascinating, always interesting, sometimes scary. There were always a few European counts and chinless ladies doddering about in jewels by Cartier. There were sleek, handsome South Americans and Mexicans, the wickedly exciting sheiks and shahs and princes. Ginny Savas watched the antics of her friends and neighbors with fear and delight. She saw power and what it did and she was afraid of it. She knew she would never marry among her friends and she didn't. She refused to debut in Houston society. She married Bobby Hendrix their senior year at Rice. They moved to Cleveland, where he caught passes and she raised children. She *liked* Cleveland.

Bobby and Ginny had four boys. The two oldest were sixteen and nineteen. The two youngest were four and six. Bobby reminded Ginny of her father. He was gentle and subtly powerful through the command of his skills. It thrilled her to watch that combination of gentleness and power work on a football field. It thrilled Gus too. Ginny was correct in assessing the similarities of her husband and father and they became a family. Gus brought Bobby into the oil business and made him a little money. Guys like Bobby from the Old League didn't get much from the new pension plan. It was for the new players. Though he had played eighteen years, only six of the years came under the new pension. Bobby could never quite understand how the pension fund seemed to be getting smaller.

"Now that the Cleveland property is sold," Hendrix said into the phone to his wife in River Oaks, "tell Gus to go ahead and talk the drilling deal with Harrison H. Harrison at Venture Capital

Offshore.... You too. ...Okay.... Ginny, kiss the kids for me. I'll try and get to Houston right after the game. This damp, cold weather here is killing my knees, and the goddam Butazolidin keeps making me sick."

Harrison H. Harrison? ...VCO? ...Spur? ...Taylor thought he had better warn Bobby as he continued to listen, dropping his gaze down to the empty pool.

A small child in jeans, tiny cowboy boots, a rough-cut jacket and a silverbelly hat toddled out. A woman followed the child into the pool area. A plastic partition mounted on the sea wall protected the pool and patio from the direct blasts of the ocean wind. The child slowly made his way toward the pool, winding in and out of the rows and rows of empty wooden chaise longues.

"I don't even know if I'll play Sunday," Hendrix was saying into the phone. "If Gus can push Harrison's VCO deal through, I don't think I'll play after next year. I'm taking a lot of shit from Conly about being the Union rep. I'm tired and lonely and want to come home." Hendrix crossed his stringy red-haired legs.

Taylor looked over at the freckled man for a moment to see if he meant all that. Hendrix nodded he did.

Taylor looked back down at the woman and child wandering in the slick desolation of the rain-blown pool area. The blue-green pool rippled with the wind. There was something familiar about the woman—in her movements and how she carried her body. She followed the boy slowly to the far side of the pool, then directed him into one of the cabanas, out of the threatening weather. The ocean was gray and white-flecked. Taylor tried to focus on the woman. He wiped the window glass clean. It was too far to see. The boy ran in and out of the cabana, then began jumping from one wooden chaise to the next. There even seemed a familiarity about the boy.

"Red wants me to come back as player-coach." Hendrix had the phone hooked on his shoulder. "But the commissioner and Cyrus don't want me around because of my Union work. It won't be much money and I'd have to take their shit."

Hendrix suddenly stopped talking and raised his eyebrows. His wife was giving an argument. Looking at Taylor, he pointed at the phone and smiled. "No... no..." he interrupted, "Red could protect me, sure, but that's not it. Playing on Sunday is the only real protection from the shit, and I won't be playing much on Sunday anymore." Hendrix stopped. "No. No," he said finally.

Taylor looked back down at the woman and child out in the weather. He stared at the woman, now partially hidden in the shadows of the green-and-white-striped cabana. The boy had taken off his cowboy hat and seemed to be looking directly up at Taylor. He had long black thick hair. Taylor waved and the child waved back.

"Since when do you need a blood test to buy insurance?" Hendrix interrupted his wife on the phone as Taylor snatched up his purple and white rain jacket, which had the crossed Walker Colts silkscreened in white on the back above the four-inch letters reading TEXAS.

"Okay. Okay. Tell Gus I'll have a blood test as soon as I get to Houston," Hendrix said. "Ginny, tell the kids . . ."

The closing door cut Hendrix off in mid-sentence. Taylor was heading down to the pool.

RAIN

"I hate it when it rains." Suzy Ballard looked out on the rainy Atlantic from Dick Conly's penthouse. "It makes me sad."

"Not me," the general manager called out from the bathroom. "Rainy days always make me feel like I don't have to do anything. My daddy was a cotton farmer on a small scale." Conly was shaving with a straight razor, a habit he had picked up from his father. "We were so poor, Daddy had to slice the fatback so thin, it didn't have but one side." He chuckled. "He farmed on a scale so small as to be downright painful. We'd get a quarter for skipping dinner, then Daddy'd steal the twenty-five cents while we slept and make us go without breakfast for losing it." Conly had a towel wrapped around his waist. His skin was white and pale; his abdomen was flabby, almost swollen and blue-veined. "I love rainy days." Conly smiled and continued shaving. "But then, I enjoyed World War Two."

"Well, I hate rain." Suzy poured another glass of champagne. She was angry at the rain and at Conly for liking it. She was just generally angry. "It's true, you know? We're ninety-eight percent water like the rain and that miserable gray ocean. Why shouldn't it affect us?" Suzy snapped.

"I didn't say it shouldn't," Conly said. "I just said it made me happy because on rainy days I don't do anything but what I want, and what I want is you." He finished shaving and looking in the mirror. He sucked at his protruding stomach with muscles that existed only in memory. He pulled the towel up higher and brushed his teeth.

"All I want is you, too, honey," Suzy deadpanned, and stuck her tongue out at the bathroom wall. "A.D. says all the players are mad because they're going to lose money down here and can't afford to bring their families. The Jew guy that owns Miami is paying for everything and letting the players pocket the twenty dollars a day. And he flew the wives down free."

Sprinkling aftershave in his palm, rubbing his hands together and slapping lightly at his face, Dick winced as the alcohol found and burned each nick of the razor. "What else does A.D. say?" Dick Conly held a hand mirror up behind his head and carefully placed his remaining hair over the growing baldness.

"He says Eddie Dolan is a shitty defensive coach."

"And A.D. is better, right?"

"Right," she spit back. It infuriated her when Conly so quickly uncovered her motives and plans.

"I told you, Suzybelle"—Conly shrugged into a thick blue terry-cloth robe—"Don't try and shit a shitter. I got him the job in the front office, and Cyrus likes him, but Red won't take him as a coach. Red doesn't trust him. That's why he cut him."

"He'd make a good assistant GM," she said.

Dick laughed. "I'll have to think about that."

Conly's laugh made Suzy mad and want to hurt someone, something. Dick Conly, maybe herself. She walked over and plopped down on the bed and went through Conly's wallet. She went through his wallet a lot. Sometimes she took things; sometimes she just looked. She found a new business card:

R. T. TINY WALTON
CONSULTANT

It listed a post-office box in Fort Worth and an 800 number.

"Who's Tiny Walton?" she yelled in to Conly.

"You going through my wallet again?"

"Yes. Who is Tiny Walton?"

"What does it say on the card?" Dick Conly took one last look at himself, denied what he saw and walked into the bedroom.

"Consultant."

"Then he must consult." He went to the bar and poured a glass of straight whiskey. He drank it down like water.

Suzy was curled on her side, Conly's wallet open on the bed.

The general manager walked over to the window, looked down for a moment, then pulled the drapes. The room turned dark.

"Time to quit reading and go to bed, children." He walked to the bed and took the card and wallet, placing them on the bedside table. "Some real jerks in this world."

"Who? Tiny Walton?"

"No. Nobody calls Tiny a jerk." Conly pulled the bed covers back, jerking them from beneath Suzy, who sucked her thumb in the darkness. "There's two people and a little kid down there by the pool. Got that kid out in this weather. I can't believe some parents." He pulled at the knotted cord of his robe and crawled, naked, into bed, groping at Suzy's gown, pushing it up her legs.

"I can't believe it, the Father of the Year is groping me," Suzy said as she lay there. It was the meanest thing she could of think to say, but Dick continued as if he hadn't heard a word. He drank constantly to blot out the picture of his dead son in the back of the car. He had almost succeeded. *Almost.*

He rubbed himself against Suzy while she lay motionless.

"I'm not in the mood." Suzy pushed his hands away. "You want to know what A.D. said about Bobby Hendrix?"

"No, I don't." Conly scrambled after her across the large bed as she pushed and evaded him.

"He said Hendrix knows about Cyrus Chandler scalping tickets and not reporting the income."

Conly immediately lost what were the beginnings of a pretty good erection. He sat up and said softly and too calmly, "What?"

"Bobby Hendrix told A.D. that Cyrus scalped tickets with the Cobianco brothers."

"Did Hendrix say where he heard that?"

"No." Suzy tried to look thoughtful and helpful, even if the room was dark. "But Hendrix is going to bring it up at the Union Negotiators and the Management Council's next meeting." Suzy smiled in the dark and was feeling better, less angry. She had hurt someone, she thought—Dick Conly. It was a lie. Not the part about scalping and evading taxes: That was true because A.D. had brought the Cobianco boys' scheme to Cyrus. Suzy had seen the proof—notes and lists of tickets and package deals, including charter planes, block-booked hotels and tickets. It was all done through the Kimball Adams Travel Agency in New York City.

The lie was that Bobby Hendrix knew.

Suzy knew both Cyrus and Conly disliked Bobby Hendrix's work as player representative to the Union. She felt the energy go out of the naked man next to her. He lay back and crossed his arms behind his head. Dick Conly was worried. If Cyrus Chandler *was* scalping tickets, after Dick had warned him not to, it was almost certain the Cobianco brothers were involved. He had cautioned Cyrus about them many times.

Suzy crawled back over to him and began to kiss and caress him.

"Come on, baby," Suzy whispered, "don't let it worry your old head. Let's you and me have some fun." She rubbed and licked and sucked, but as she had expected, nothing would happen now. Dick Conly lay impotent on the big bed. Suzy loved every second of it. "You should quit this job. Look what it's doing to our sex life."

"Are you sure?" Conly said weakly at one point.

"That's what A.D. said Hendrix told him." Suzy crouched between his legs and reveled in various vain attempts to rouse him. She stopped. "You quit this job, give it to A. D. Koster and we'll go off together to your mountain place in New Mexico."

Conly's eyes unfocused. "The Pecos Mountains," he said wistfully.

They were silent for a time. "You don't do that, do you?" she asked suddenly.

"What?" Dick snapped back from his daydream refuge.

"Scalp tickets? Evade taxes?"

"No . . . no, of course not."

"Good. Good," she said, cupping his genitals. "Otherwise it would be Bobby Hendrix who'd have you by the balls instead of me."

In the long run that might have been a better alternative for everybody.

RANDALL AT THE POOL

WENDY recognized Taylor as soon as he stepped out into the pool area wearing the purple and white rain jacket.

"Randall Ryan Carleton, get down from there," she said, keeping one eye on Taylor as he approached and the other on her son, who was climbing everything he could reach. "Randall, get down from that table."

The boy jumped to the ground and skidded on his hands and

chest. He bounced up seemingly none the worse for wear, his front covered with sand blown onto the patio from the beach. Randall Ryan Carleton climbed the back of a wooden chaise longue and rode it like a horse. Taylor shuffled around the pool, keeping his chin buried in his rain jacket. The boy faced away from Taylor, riding the chaise longue out to sea. Wendy looked directly at him.

"Hello, Wendy." Taylor stuck out his hand. "It's been a long time since I've seen you."

"Hello, Taylor." Wendy took his hand unenthusiastically. "Well, I have been kind of busy with Randall and all. . . ." She looked at the ground and gestured at the boy, who kept his back to them and began spurring the chaise longue with his tiny cowboy boots.

"Where are your folks?"

"Mother's having her hair done. Lem and Cyrus went over to the owners meeting." Wendy sat back in the canvas director's chair.

"I thought I recognized you from up there. Your boy waved at me so I came down."

Wendy shrugged. "I guess he can choose his own friends."

"This is the first time I've ever seen him," Taylor said. "You both looked so familiar from up there." Taylor pointed up toward his window. "It was weird, it was like I had seen him before. He must be the spitting image of you."

"No, he's not," Wendy said, her voice tired. "Randall, this is Mr. Rusk."

The tiny cowboy continued to spur away from them in hot pursuit of the bank robbers.

"Randall, huh?" Taylor looked at the small boy's back. "Come here, Randall, and let's have a look at you and see if you are as pretty as your mother."

"Or as ugly as your father," Wendy added.

He reached out and lifted the small boy off the chaise, turned him around and looked him full in the face.

Taylor Rusk almost dropped the boy in shock.

The boy did not recognize Taylor, but Taylor certainly recognized him.

Taylor held the boy for a long time, gazing into his face, waiting for a sense of recognition from the big brown eyes. There was none, and after allowing Taylor to stare at him, Randall wriggled free and ran over to his mother. He stood behind her chair and they both stared up at Taylor. Taylor stared back.

The boy lost interest and remounted the chaise longue horse, continuing the desperate ride.

"Jesus," Taylor said finally, "this only happens in the movies."

"And in nightmares." Wendy brushed blowing sand off her cheek. "Welcome to the nightmare."

"Welcome to real life. Why didn't you..." Taylor began, but cut his words off.

Taylor put his hand on Wendy's hand and sat beside her. She sat erect in the lounge chair, gripping Taylor's hand and watching their son play cowboy on a wood-back chair against the gray, hateful sky in another world. Tears streamed down Wendy's face and she began to shake.

"Well," she said finally in a cracking voice, "we sure did fool my father into thinking he won."

Randall Ryan whipped his chaise longue unmercifully in pursuit of bad guys while his mother cried softly and his father stared in shock.

The wind picked up and the clouds turned darker; the relentless ocean slashed and exploded against the breakwater.

Then the hard rain began to fall.

THE SAME
OLD COCKROACH

IN the Playoff Bowl against Miami, with less than forty seconds remaining on the scoreboard clock, Taylor Rusk hit Bobby Hendrix on a forty-five-yard zig-out for the winning touchdown. On the same play Simon D'Hanis lunged out to block a stunting end and caught his cleats in the turf. His right leg twisted but the foot didn't move. His ankle taped, the stress was transferred up and his knee was torn apart.

The team ran down to line up for the extra point. At midfield Simon lay screaming. Simon D'Hanis was flown back to Texas right after the game for surgery at the University hospital.

Bobby Hendrix flew immediately to Houston and rejoined his family at his father-in-law's house in River Oaks. The VCO deal was in the works and Monday morning he took his physical for the corporate insurance. That afternoon Bobby Hendrix and Gus

Savas finished negotiations with Harrison H. Harrison for a joint drilling operation with Venture Capital Offshore. It called for three to five oil/gas wells in the Gulf plus $250,000 in dry-hole money.

Dick Conly and Suzy Ballard flew to Albuquerque and drove to the Pecos Mountains.

A. D. Koster took a cab from the Orange Bowl to the local yacht club and paid a kid two dollars to row him out to the sixty-five-foot yacht *Momma*. He carried an alligator attaché case filled with one-hundred-dollar bills and stayed two hours.

Cyrus Chandler took his wife, Junie, his daughter, Wendy, his grandson, Randall, and Wendy's husband, Lem Carleton III, to celebrate in New York. They spent a week shopping, seeing plays and dining in a different restaurant every night. Their limousine met them at the airport and took them to the apartment they kept on upper Fifth Avenue off Central Park. The long, sleek Lincoln ferried them to all their engagements and brought them back with an elegance and ease that made New York City quite nice.

They went to art exhibitions and museums. Lem and the women also shopped relentlessly.

Cyrus found it distasteful that Lem enjoyed shopping as much as the women. He preferred staying at the apartment with his grandson, Randall. He played with the boy while the nanny watched.

The last day in town, Cyrus stayed behind with Randall as the others piled into the limousine for a last desperate grasp at the wonderful bazaar that is New York City.

Cyrus left the boy with the nanny and took a short walk down Fifth Avenue to Venture Capital Energy Plaza. Cyrus rode the elevator fifty-seven floors to the executive suite of Venture Capital Offshore. He had a pleasant chat with his longtime friend, college classmate and fellow member of Spur '39, Harrison H. Harrison. Mr. Harrison was president and CEO of Venture Capital Offshore, a wholly owned subsidiary of Venture Capital America. Mr. Harrison's father controlled the parent company. Cyrus and Harrison talked briefly about Bobby Hendrix and Gus Savas. It didn't take much. "Still the same old cockroach," Harrison said.

Cyrus was back in the apartment, playing with Randall, by the time the shoppers returned.

Lem and the women insisted on modeling and displaying all their purchases. Cyrus held his grandson on his knee and wondered at the jerk that was his son-in-law, who was doing a slow turn in his new full-length mink coat to the squeaks and applause of the women. They flew back to Texas the next day.

Taylor Rusk went back to his apartment and stared at the wall, waiting for Wendy to return from New York City. It was generally agreed in the sporting press that he had made Texas a Super Bowl contender.

Virtually overnight.

Texas Pistols season tickets sold out the first day they went on sale. People camped out in front of the ticket offices for days to be the first in line. The Franchise finally had its fans. Things were changing fast. Too fast.

THE FAN

It would be unfair to characterize Lamar Jean Lukas as your average fan. Unfair to the average fan and unfair to Lamar Jean. Lamar Jean Lukas had followed the Texas Pistols from the day Cyrus Chandler announced he was bringing the Franchise to town and was signing Red Kilroy and Taylor Rusk from the University. Lamar Jean struggled with the Texas team through that first difficult 4–10 season when Kimball Adams was the quarterback. It was a hard season on Lamar Jean, but the second season at 9–7 was a little better. He was joyous when they won, despondent when they lost. Lamar spent a lot of those first two seasons feeling pretty low. It was tough to go to the gas station on Mondays after a loss. But when the Pistols won, he was a ball of fire. That made the final half of that second season pure joy. Working at greasing a car or changing a tire, he would also be describing and redescribing the game highlights. A great catch by Bobby Hendrix, an awful sack on Taylor Rusk or Kimball Adams and the subsequent retaliation by Ox Wood. A good lead block on a sweep by Simon D'Hanis. And all the time Lamar would say, "When Taylor Rusk is ready, he will take the Pistols to the Super Bowl. Taylor Rusk *is* the Franchise. We're friends, you know."

The year Red Kilroy traded away the top three draft choices for the next five years for old veteran players, Lamar argued long and hard in favor of Red. It had not been a popular move with the press and the armchair quarterbacks. But what did those guys know? Lamar Jean Lukas really paid attention. He kept track. He knew.

"These guys got experience. They are proven men," Lamar said, "not some glamour college kid who ain't had his back broke yet. You'll see. Me and Red know what we're doing. We are getting Taylor some protection, and when we get enough, we are going to the Super Bowl."

And Lamar was right.

The television was on in the boss's office at the Exxon station, and the noon news was showing film of the lines of season ticket buyers in front of the Texas Pistols office.

"Hey, Lamar," the boss asked, "how come you ain't down, waiting in line?"

"Because," Lamar grunted, struggling with a double-rim truck tire, "I already got my season ticket. I went down and bought one the first day they come to town." He grunted, sweated and struggled with tire and rims. "Now I get preferential treatment." With a mighty heave he broke the tire free and pried it from the metal.

"There." He puffed a little. "They already sent me my season tickets in the mail, 'cause I was one of the first fans. I been with 'em since the beginning and I'm gonna be with 'em at the Super Bowl. I told you Red and I were right about trading off them draft choices and getting us some experience."

"Did Red call you before he made the trades?" the boss teased.

"You know what I mean," Lamar shot back. He wiped the sweat off his forehead with his shirt sleeve. "You were all pissin' and moanin' about how Red done screwed up the whole thing and I told you he was right back then. And I'm the kind of guy who tells you I tol' ya so. And I tol' ya so."

"Okay, Lamar," the boss said, "so you told us. Big deal."

"It *is* a big deal," Lamar said. "You're sittin' there watching television pictures of people waiting to buy tickets. That is a big deal."

It became a bigger deal when Lamar Jean didn't get his ticket to the Super Bowl.

Lamar Jean Lukas had only two real passions. The Texas Pistols and target shooting. He was on the base shooting team in the Marines before he got sent to Vietnam for slugging a captain.

Lamar was an old fan. The old fans were working people, lower-class blacks and whites. The new fans were more middle class and went more for the spectacle, the chance to identify with some approved mass movement. They knew less about the game and many went drunk. Lamar Jean Lukas didn't like the new fans. He called them Nazi fans.

"Where were all those Nazi assholes when Kimball Adams was calling signals? The stadium was almost empty that first year." Lamar was telling all this to his boss while he tightened the spark plugs on a white Chevrolet. He tightened the final plug and came out from under the hood. "There." He slapped the fender. "American cars since 1968 have become real junk. Detroit would be Fat City if they were still making 1958-through-1968 cars."

"I been working on 'em forty years," the boss said. "I watched 'em change. If they made 'em good, where would you and I be?" He was sitting in his office, still watching the television. "I fixed enough of 'em that I made enough money to hire you and buy me this TV set." He paused and then growled, "Now goddam Exxon is fucking me on my gas allotment, raising the cost on my lease. They're trying to get my TV set."

"They want you to have your TV set, boss." Lamar grinned. "Don't you know that yet? They want to keep tuned in on your brain waves so they can control you."

"Boy," the boss said, "you are crazy."

The boss sneered as a Datsun pulled up to the gas pump. The driver waited patiently, then honked his horn. Both men ignored the Japanese car.

"I'm going target shooting." Lamar went back to wash his hands.

The boss turned and glared at the driver of the Jap car, who finally got the message and drove off.

General Motors, the IMF, the networks and Exxon be damned; the boss would go broke before he would work on a Jap car.

THE BAD WHEEL

WHEN Simon D'Hanis came to in the recovery room, Buffy was standing over his bed. She smiled at him and brushed his hair back from his thick brow ridge.

"How do you feel, honey?" She smiled her chubby smile. She hadn't lost the weight from their first child, Dianna, before she'd gotten pregnant with the second, another girl they named Donna Mae. Donna Mae was born in August of the second season. During the third season their sex life was almost nonexistent, but now, somehow, she was nearly five months pregnant with the third child. But she hadn't told Simon yet and he hadn't noticed. She decided to wait until after he was out of the hospital. She wondered if she would ever lose the weight, and if she did, whether Simon would treat her better. Something had changed him, made him hard, cold.

Buffy had watched him while he slept, his right leg swathed in thick wraps and elevated by a series of slings and sandbags. His face was unlined and peaceful. He looked like the Simon she remembered from college, the man who watched television movies and memorized old actors' names. She remembered when they married in Oklahoma; the biggest problem was dragging him away from the old Harry Carey movie on television. Now, as he regained consciousness, the lines began to reappear on his face. Some invisible force was drawing a mask of fear and anger on the face of a child.

It took Simon a few moments to organize his thoughts and become coherent.

"How bad was it?" Simon finally mumbled, his tongue thick and his eyes rolling in his head. He tried to move and pain slashed across his face. "Aaaahh," he groaned involuntarily, and lay back. The haunted look returned to his once soft blue eyes; a deep line dug down from his hairline across his forehead, splitting his face between his eyes and dragging the corner of his mouth into the perpetual scowl that appeared during his rookie year.

"How bad?" he growled. "I asked you a question." He looked down at his bandage-swathed leg. "I hope it ain't as bad as it feels." He glared at his leg like an old enemy. "Son of a bitch."

"The doctor didn't say." Buffy brushed his hair absently. "He told me he would look in on you when the anesthesia wore off."

"Well, the goddam anesthesia has worn off." Simon's tongue was still thick and the words came out disjointed. "Where's the doctor?" He raised his garbled voice.

"I don't know, honey."

"Well, goddam. Go find out."

The doctor walked into the recovery room, still in his green scrub suit with paper covers on his alligator loafers. He was a big fat man who perspired constantly. He had been the team surgeon for three years and had gotten rich on his Monday-morning calls to his bookie, giving the injury status of the Texas Pistols and several other teams where his friends were the team doctors. That gave the bookie a three-day jump on the point spread before the official injury reports came out of the commissioner's office on Thursdays.

"Well, how are we doing, Simon?" the doctor asked.

"That's what I want to know, Doc," Simon said. He was respectful, almost obsequious, to the doctor. Buffy noticed the difference in Simon's tone toward the doctor compared to his treatment of her. Tears welled in her eyes.

"Well," the doctor said to the bandaged leg, "you had a total blow out: cartilages, ligaments, the whole smear. I did a hell of a reconstruction job, but the rest is up to you. If you work hard and you want it bad enough, your knee ought to be better than before."

Better than before? Buffy thought the doctor's arrogance was outrageous, but she kept quiet and stood back as the doctor continued to look at the leg and talk to her husband.

"I did a hell of a job," the doctor said. "You have to carry the ball from now on. It's just a matter of how badly you want to get well."

"I want it bad, Doc." Simon sounded pitiful. Buffy cried silently as she watched her husband pleading for reassurance from this fat man wearing a sweat-soaked scrub suit and paper covers on his two-hundred-dollar shoes. "I want it real bad, Doc. I don't know what I'll do if I can't play again."

"Well, go for it, Simon," the doctor said, turning to leave without ever looking at the big lineman's face. "The operation was a complete success. I've done everything I can. The rest is up to you."

"I'll do it, Doc. I'll do it." Simon's hands gripped the sides of the hospital bed. His knuckles turned white.

"That's the spirit." The doctor looked at his watch. "I have more surgery scheduled this morning. I better hurry if I expect to get through and still get in some golf. I'll come look in on you tomorrow and see how you're doing."

The doctor nodded at Buffy without noticing, or caring, that tears streamed down her fleshy red face.

"He'll be fine," the doctor said, and disappeared out the door to complete a schedule of five surgical interventions of which Simon's was the only one actually necessary. He had botched Simon's operation by stapling the ligaments too tightly, then sweating into the open wound. This resulted in a staph infection, but nobody would ever find that out, and the doctor would always blame Simon for the failure to recover full usage of the knee.

"He just didn't want it badly enough," the doctor would tell Red Kilroy and Dick Conly, because Simon had failed to rehabilitate. The staph infection alone stretched the hospital stay from one week to a month and a half, as the incision refused to heal and continued to drain pus and blood.

Buffy dried her eyes and blew her nose after the doctor left.

"What are you bawling about?" Simon turned angry. "Didn't you hear what the doc said? I'm gonna be fine. He said the operation was a success."

"What was he going to say, Simon? That he failed?" Buffy stepped back to the bed and touched her husband's forehead. "He's a mechanic and he is sure not going to tell you that anything that he did went wrong."

"I can't believe I'm hearing this." Simon pushed her hand away. "Don't you want me to get well?"

"I don't want you to believe people like him," Buffy said. "He wears alligator shoes just like A. D. Koster and I never trusted A.D. Why don't you stop playing now, Simon, before you get hurt any worse? Daddy'll help us. I've got some money. I can't stand to see you hurt."

"Well, quit watching, then," Simon said. "Now leave me alone. I want to sleep."

She didn't tell Simon that she was pregnant with their third child until after the staph infection cleared up and he came home from the hospital almost two months later. He was weak and pale and took the news without much emotion. When a boy was born that spring, Simon's spirits picked up and he renewed his efforts at rehabilitation, hoping to make it back.

They named the boy Simon Taylor D'Hanis, and Buffy asked Taylor Rusk to be the boy's godfather and Wendy Chandler Carleton to be his godmother.

THE STANDARD
PLAYER'S CONTRACT

"YEAH?" Taylor had barged through his apartment door and snatched up the jangling phone. He had been out running the golf course.

"Taylor, it's me, Doc. I'm in Canada."

"That's great, Doc," Taylor said, "but I don't need you to phone me every time you cross an international border." He looked around the apartment. The maid hadn't come and it was in the usual disarray. Taylor had kept the three-bedroom apartment that he and Bobby Hendrix and Kimball Adams had shared the first year. It was too big, but Taylor was just too disorganized to move.

"This is business," Doc Webster said.

"What kind of business?"

"Football, Taylor. Football."

"I don't want to talk about football."

"Well, actually it's about money. One of my old students has a proposition for you."

"What kind?"

"Strictly legitimate. He knows you're considering playing out your option this year."

"I am?" Taylor was beginning to get cold. The air conditioner was set at sixty-five and he was still in his shorts and T-shirt. His sweat was drying stiff on his skin.

"As of May first you're a free agent. Last season was your option year," Doc replied, "and this boy wants you to come and play for him."

"In Canada?" Taylor asked. "No way, it's too cold."

"In California. He's Canadian, but his daddy bought him the Los Angeles franchise for sixty million dollars."

"That's a lot of money," Taylor decided. "How much do I get?"

"A whole bunch," Doc Webster said. "Five million for five years. A million a year."

"Tell him I accept." The quarterback sat down, reached over and grabbed his shirt. He had begun to sweat again. "Five million?"

"This is straight. He flew me up here because he knew you and I were friends."

"How old is this guy?" Taylor asked, pulling on the shirt.

"Twenty-two."

"Goddam, Doc. Are you sure he's old enough to sign contracts?"

"I have the Standard Player's Contract right in front of me," Doc Webster said. "He already signed it."

Taylor laughed in amazement. "With what—a crayon? Jesus, doesn't he know about the commissioner's compensation rule? Robbie Burden'll try and stop this by giving Texas all the LA draft choices and this guy's firstborn child."

"He knows and says his daddy'll handle Robbie Burden."

"Bring the contract, Doc. Catch the next plane. I do believe we have Cyrus Chandler over a barrel."

A BRAND-NEW CLOWN

"Cyrus, I'm quitting," Dick Conly announced as soon as he had fixed a drink and sat down in the owner's office. "The trust for Randall is all set up and Chandler Industries is in the best shape ever."

"Why, Dick, this is a shock." Cyrus did not sound shocked.

"I'm tired. Everything is on line with the Pistol Dome project and the Franchise." Conly picked up Cyrus's fake surprise but let it drop. He didn't care. "I'm taking a vacation for the rest of my life with Suzy Ballard. The sooner I quit, the better she'll like it. She's up in Taos, looking at furniture to buy for my ranch."

Cyrus raised his eyebrows slightly, then nodded. "Gosh, Dick, I'm sorry to hear this."

"I want out as general manager." Conly drained his glass and poured another. "You can give the job to your son-in-law or Red Kilroy. A. D. Koster is Suzy's choice. I would watch him, though, Red's a better pick, but that's your decision. I want my severance and profit-sharing money sent to Santa Fe. It's about a million five."

"That's an awful lot of money, Dick." Cyrus suddenly tried to become a negotiator. "I'm not sure I can get it that quickly or even whether you're worth that much." His eyes were flat, his voice dead.

"You may be right, Cyrus." Conly took a drink and rattled the ice against the side of his glass. "Make it two million five and I want it in Mexican gold, fifty-peso pieces, in Santa Fe by the end of the week. If you even blink I'm going to three five, you dipshit."

The phone buzzed and Cyrus pushed the intercom button. His secretary said, "It's a call for Mr. Conly from the commissioner."

"I'll take it here." Dick picked up the phone. "This is Conly. Yes. Yes. How much did they offer him? Is it written down anywhere? Well, goddammit, Robbie, find out. What do you think we pay you for? To drink with Howard Cosell, for Chrissakes? If they made the offer in writing, it could be big trouble. And Robbie, when you call back, ask for Cyrus. I just quit." Conly's eyes flicked up to look across the desk at Chandler. "None of your goddam business!" Conly slammed the receiver down and turned back to Cyrus Chandler. "Well, this problem you'll have to handle yourself. I *told you* to sign Taylor Rusk last year, but you said playing out his option would teach him what he was worth."

"Damn right. Doc Webster wanted a million a year." Cyrus leaned back in his chair, still preoccupied with the decision to pay Conly the profit-sharing and severance pay. "Nobody gets that kind of money."

"Remember that Canadian oil-man buddy of yours?" Conly grinned. "The one you insisted I vouch for at the owner's meeting so he could buy the LA franchise for his son when we squeezed out Marconi, and I told you we shouldn't sell the LA franchise to a kid?"

"Richard Portus. We did some joint ventures on the North Slope," Cyrus said. "He's a hell of a guy."

"Maybe so, but his kid just offered Taylor Rusk the million a year that you said nobody gets to play for Los Angeles next season."

"Son of a bitch!" Cyrus fell back into his heavily padded leather swivel chair. "That ungrateful little bastard." Chandler looked wildly around his office for a few moments. "Well, you can't leave now until we settle this. I'll teach both those ungrateful..."

"The hell I can't leave." Conly swirled the ice and whiskey around in his glass. "When I go out, that doorknob won't hit me in the ass and you'll never see me again. Unless my centavos don't arrive in Santa Fe on time, then you'll *wish* you never saw me again."

"You little pissant! Are you threatening me?"

"As plainly as possible. I told you to stay away from the Cobianco brothers, but now you scalp tickets and God knows what else. I can ruin you."

"Dammit, Dick, you can't leave me this fix. I'll teach Rusk and that Portus kid a lesson they'll never forget," Cyrus wailed.

Conly drained his glass and left it on Cyrus's desk.

"Let Robbie Burden handle it through the commissioner's office." He got unsteadily to his feet. "Don't threaten anybody and wait until the commissioner finds out if the offer was verbal or in writing. You've got the compensation clause to fall back on. The commissioner will put such a high compensation price on Rusk that Portus kid'll feel like somebody ran a hot poker up his ass."

"I'm not letting them get away with this." Chandler's face turned red. "Rusk did this to me purposely. The ungrateful bastard hates me because of Wendy."

— 232 —

"So what? I hate you too. Most people hate you. This is business: Don't let your feelings get involved." At the door Conly stopped. "This is your first big test without me, Cyrus; don't fuck it up. There could be antitrust implications. Wait until the commissioner gets all the facts. There's plenty of time. You could get a tampering ruling, so don't panic." Conly stared. "And get your greedy ass loose from the Cobianco boys, Cyrus, before . . ."

"Get the hell out of here!" Cyrus turned on Dick Conly. "You're just like the rest of them—out to get what you can from me. I don't need you. I'll run this club myself."

"You have a short memory, Cyrus. If I had wanted the money, I could have taken it all years ago. But I kept thinking we had more between us—maybe not friendship, but something; maybe part of what I shared with your father. I guess I was wrong."

"You are damn right you were wrong," Cyrus said. "There is nothing between us. There never was. Amos liked you 'cause you would drink with him and listen to him and laugh at his jokes. Well, I hated him and I used you. Now I'm through with you and so is Suzy Ballard."

Drunk and tired, Dick Conly's mind still snapped to the implications of Cyrus Chandler's last statement. He stared at Cyrus for a long time, then shook his head. "I guess I know what you are saying is true, but I won't believe it until I get to the Pecos and she isn't there. She's given me enough to deserve the benefit of the doubt. You should have listened to your father. He was a funny, smart, caring man. I'm just smart and mean. If the money doesn't arrive by the weekend, two and a half million in Mexican gold centavos, I'll bring this whole operation down around your ears. You'll spend the rest of your life in front of congressional committees and grand juries and IRS investigators. You understand?"

Dick Conly stood florid-faced, ramrod straight, his swollen stomach pushing out his shirt. Cyrus tried to meet Conly's stare but failed. He knew Conly meant what he said. He didn't know if Conly could actually do it but wasn't in any position to find out. His eyes dropped and the anger left his voice.

"It will be there," Cyrus said, "but Suzy Ballard won't."

"I'll probably live longer if she isn't. But will you?" Dick turned and left Cyrus Chandler's office. He knew Suzy would talk Cyrus into making A.D. Koster general manager. He realized he didn't care.

It's not my job anymore, he thought. *It's not my job.* Dick Conly smiled at the sense of relief that filled him. *I'll show them;*

I'll outlive the little rat. Conly laughed aloud as he walked to the elevator. He didn't even bother to clean out his desk.

In the elevator the Muzak was playing.

You took my little heart and ran it 'round this town.
Now you're gonna find your circus needs a brand new clown...
...y'all can get me drunk, but, baby, I'm sober now...

Suzy Ballard was not waiting for Dick when he reached his house in the Pecos Mountains. She was with A. D. Koster, making plans to take over the Franchise.

THE BOSS

CYRUS was upset by Dick Conly's abrupt departure, but the longer he thought about it, the better he felt. It would never have been the same once Conly found out that Suzy and Cyrus were lovers and would be married. Cyrus hadn't planned on getting married, but Suzy had convinced him that he was still young enough to start a second family. She convinced him of many things.

That first night he flew out to meet her at the Hot Springs Ranch, he thought about the genius of Conly's last creation: the Pistol Dome.

The Domed Stadium Authority Bond Issue and the two thousand acres in Clyde and all the property tax exemptions had been a brilliant scheme to vertically integrate the Franchise: a money-making machine that would stage football games. The yearly twelve-million-dollars-per-team network television revenue already put the Pistols and every other franchise in profit before the first stadium ticket was ever sold. Complete control of all revenue sources from parking and concessions to rental and other fees at the new domed stadium would allow the Franchise to shift income around, depending on the tax status of each of the individual enterprises.

What worried Cyrus right after Conly resigned was that Dick was the only one who knew how and why it all worked. Cyrus had no idea but decided he would spend some time with Suzy Ballard out at the Hot Springs Ranch and think things through.

He would sit down and figure the whole thing out. If Dick Conly could do it, so could he. *I'm the boss now*, he thought.

And as Cyrus's big two-engined brown and white King Air was winging its way to the Hot Springs Ranch, Cyrus really was glad that Dick Conly was gone. He was tired of Conly always looking over his shoulder. He never understood that the man looking over his shoulder was also protecting his back.

It was a very serious mistake.

Suzy was waiting at the lighted concrete landing strip north of the ranch headquarters. She wore tight jeans tucked into red ostrich boots, along with a red and green flannel shirt with the sleeves rolled up and the front unbuttoned below the mounds of her cream-white breasts. Her blond hair was braided, tied with a red ribbon in a thick pigtail that hung down her back to the diamondback rattlesnake belt. An old, battered, sweat-stained two-hundred-dollar beaver-hide cowboy hat sat tilted slightly forward on her head. Her eyes glowed with anticipation. She held her lips in a slight pout.

When the plane touched down, Suzy stepped into the big black Ford four-wheel drive pickup. She had the truck idling on the runway beside the plane when the pilot dropped the stairs and Cyrus climbed out, beaming, flushed with excitement and anticipation.

"Tell him to take the plane back," Suzy said as Cyrus opened the truck door.

"Why?" Cyrus stepped into the richly appointed cab.

"I want us to be alone," Suzy replied, licking her lips. "Tell him. Come on. Then let's get out of here."

Cyrus slammed the truck door; the window was already down. The pilot stepped down beside the plane.

"Tell him," Suzy urged. "We can have him come back anytime. You're the boss around here, so tell him to fly back to the city."

Cyrus nodded. "Take her back to the city," he said to the pilot.

"You're the boss, Mr. Chandler." The pilot saluted.

Suzy stomped on the gas and the heavy-duty tires squealed. The pilot watched the pickup disappear down the runway, off to the south and the big fortresslike ranch house hidden by darkness and the rough country.

The first night Suzy convinced Cyrus to replace Dick Conly with A. D. Koster. It wasn't particularly difficult. Suzy already had A.D.'s employment contract filled out, which Cyrus didn't even bother to read before signing.

"Now that that is out of the way," Suzy said, unbuttoning the few remaining buttons on her flannel shirt, "I want us to take a long vacation. Let A.D. and the commissioner worry about Taylor Rusk's five-million-dollar offer."

"Can you believe that?" Cyrus said. "After I spoke up for the guy at the owners meeting."

"That's gratitude," Suzy agreed, shucking the shirt. She was naked to the waist in a battered hat, red ostrich boots and tight jeans.

"Should never let a kid be an owner," Cyrus growled. "We should have a League rule, like we used to about foreigners."

"Let A.D. and the commissioner worry about it, Cyrus," Suzy said. "You come here and help me with my boots. We are going on a long vacation."

Cyrus crossed the bedroom. "I need a long vacation."

"All we have is time and each other," Suzy said. "That's all I want."

Suzy didn't mention the five hundred million dollars that Cyrus was worth. She figured it was included.

"A long vacation, honey." Cyrus pulled at her red boots.

"Forever." She fumbled with his belt. "Forever." She pushed against him and guided him into her. "Forever," she said as her hips heaved to meet his short, quick thrusts and he shuddered to a climax.

The next morning Suzy started using Valium and Lasix on Cyrus.

They stayed isolated at the Hot Springs Ranch for weeks. The hands and domestic help were all wetbacks and spoke no English. Only Suzy spoke Spanish.

Cyrus Chandler was never the boss again.

THE REHABILITATION

"How's my godson?" Taylor asked Simon as the big lineman limped into the training room.

Simon didn't answer. He just grunted and walked on through to the weight room. In a moment Taylor heard the sound of the pulleys and cams, the groans of Simon's futile efforts mingling with the clang of metal against metal and the squeak of flesh twisting and turning against leather pads.

Although the rest of his body bulged with muscle tissue, Simon was pale white and his right leg was noticeably smaller and weaker than his left. A purple welt started several inches above the knee, snaked around the kneecap and ended in a grotesque lump alongside his shinbone. The lump of scar tissue had formed around the tube inserted during his hospital stay to drain the wound, ravaged by staphylococcus. The bacteria had raged through the big man's system—weakened by cortisone and Butazolidin—and the prolonged sickness, temperature and forced idleness had forever weakened the leg and damaged the joint. The doctor told Red Kilroy and Dick Conly that the prognosis was not hopeful and the best chance was to try to get Simon healthy enough to trade. The doctor told Simon that his knee was as good as new.

Better than before.

When Simon finally escaped from the hospital and began his recovery and rehabilitation, he found his whole body was flab and fat instead of the hard muscle tissue he had built so steadily over the years. He worked at his comeback with a passion that was madness, coming to the training room at eight o'clock in the morning and staying until the trainers forced him out at night so they could go home. He finally got his own key. He increased the weight he lifted as well as his dosage of steroids, and his body rapidly responded. Except for his right leg. He took megadoses of vitamins, desiccated liver, calcium, vitamin C and iron. He stayed in the weight room every day, all day long, inventing exercises of his own to break loose the adhesions that had formed beneath the ugly purple scar. He cried in pain and frustration as the leg failed to gain in size or strength and continued to hurt. The pain was constant, but he convinced himself that the more it hurt, the faster it was healing.

He tore at the weights, the levers, the camshafts. The pain racked his body and mind. He worked and cried and cried and worked, but the leg would not respond. It would not even straighten out completely. The ravaged joint had lost about ten degrees of flexibility. The *last* ten degrees, the most important ten degrees. The knee would be forever unstable, but no one told Simon and he would not have accepted it if they had told him. He struggled mightily against impossible odds, immovable objects, irresistible forces, but the leg stayed weak and sore. He never stopped limping. And although his body would be soaked with sweat and red with blood-gorged vessels, his skin had a gray pallor and his eyes were dull. He never smiled. He no longer laughed.

"How's my godson?" Taylor Rusk asked Simon again. He had followed him into the weight room. Simon bent over, adjusted the Nautilus machine and glared over his shoulder at the quarterback. Taylor was leaning against the big weight rack by the wall mirror.

"He's all right," Simon growled, turning back to the machine. "He cries all goddam night because Buffy dried up and had to put him on formula."

"How'd that happen?" Taylor asked, surprised at his own concern. "She nursed the girls okay."

"How the hell should I know!" Simon said without looking up. He crouched down, hooked himself into the machine and began doing squats. Taylor could see that his left leg was doing most of the work. It was a bad sign.

"Yeeaahhh! Yeeaahhh!" Simon screamed with each ferocious effort.

"What's the boy got?" Taylor asked. "Colic?"

"Why the hell do you care?" Simon limped and puffed to the next machine, setting it up for quadriceps exercises, and attacked it with fury.

"He's my godson." Taylor watched his friend groan and strain against the blue-and-silver metal-and-leather machine.

"I don't remember you ever mentioning God in all the time I've known you," Simon said angrily. He moved to another machine, approaching it like it was a lifelong enemy. "You found religion now that Buffy named the baby after you?" There was no humor in his voice. "The little bastard don't shut up pretty soon, you may find him on your doorstep some morning."

"Jesus, Simon, calm down. You're not the first guy who got his knee tore up in this fucking business, and you aren't gonna be the last."

"What the hell do you know about it, pretty boy?" Simon whirled and glared at the quarterback. "I did this keeping people from messing up that face that Buffy thinks so much of."

"Everybody appreciates your sacrifice, Simon, but it isn't like you got killed. And Buffy doesn't like my face."

"If you don't shut the fuck up and get out of here, you ain't gonna have a face."

"This is horseshit, Simon, and you know it," Taylor said, weariness creeping into his voice. "You're acting like a complete fruitcake."

"You lousy son of a bitch!" Simon lunged toward Taylor, snatching up a five-pound weight and hurling it at his head. The flat metal disc smashed into the mirror as Taylor ducked back. Simon kept coming at him, his eyes black with fury, his face twisted in anguish and hatred.

Taylor leaned away from the first punch. Simon began flailing roundhouses, his huge fists rippling the air as Taylor stayed on his toes and danced away. Simon's lack of agility was so apparent, he looked more foolish than dangerous.

"Calm down, Simon, for God's sake. Calm down before you hurt yourself." Taylor kept moving away from the raging, limping man, whose punches struck out at nothing but air. The frustration at failing to connect drove him to greater fury.

"I'll kill you, you son of a bitch! I swear to God I'll kill you!" Simon kept coming, his right leg failing and buckling, his left leg only partially compensating.

Taylor began to get frightened as he saw the madman his friend had become. Simon took a wild swing, stepping out with his bad leg. Taylor stepped to the side and hit the big man twice on the chin—hard. The big square head snapped back twice. Simon's right leg buckled; he dropped his fists to regain his balance, and Taylor drove a right across his cheek. Simon fell to the ground, sobbing. Taylor stood back a moment, watching the pitiful heap of broken, quivering muscle that was his friend, Simon D'Hanis.

The trainers both came into the weight room and Taylor moved over to Simon.

"Come on, Simon," he said. "I'm sorry. Let me help you up."

"Don't come near me," Simon sobbed into the purple carpet. "If I get my hands on you, I'll kill you. I mean it: I'll kill you. I'll rip you into pieces." The big man quivered, screamed and sobbed. "You bastard. You ungrateful bastard. After all I did for you. You're no friend of mine."

"Well, you'll always be my friend, Simon. A bad knee just doesn't change things that much for me."

"That's because it ain't your knee," Simon spit. He had stopped sobbing. His voice again turned cold, passionless. "You'll see one day. I swear to God, you'll be sorry."

"Simon, this is stupid. . . ."

"Don't call me stupid!" Simon screamed, pushing himself to his knees. One of the trainers grabbed Taylor by the shoulder and pushed him toward the door to the training room. Ox Wood walked into the weight room. He looked at Simon on the floor and then at Taylor. Taylor shook his head and walked out.

"Ox," the trainer said, "give us a hand here. Simon fell down."

Taylor didn't even bother to dress; he just grabbed his clothes and drove home in his shorts and T-shirt. He felt sick. Simon had needed help and understanding and Taylor had only succeeded in humiliating him in front of others. They could never be friends again. Taylor arrived at his apartment and decided to call Buffy and explain to her what had happened. But when he got his door open the phone was ringing. It was Doc Webster calling from his ranch.

Taylor never did make that call to Buffy. He regretted it the rest of his life.

THE EXXON
CONNECTION

THE stories puzzled him slightly as Lamar Jean Lukas read the news of the proposed bond sale by the Domed Stadium Authority, which was already building the Pistol Dome in Clyde, Texas, south of Park City, north of the new Regional Airport. "All our season-ticket holders will get preferred treatment because they were the ones who stuck with us when the going was tough. Now that we are a playoff team, it is a sacred trust to remember their loyalty." The article quoted A. D. Koster, the new general manager.

Lamar believed him.

The article didn't mention the financing details that would be required as a prerequisite for the purchase of a season ticket: the buying of a five-thousand-dollar revenue bond with a buy-back clause paying two percent interest for thirty years, one percent less than Conly had suggested. A.D. failed to mention the secret agreement with the mayor and city council of Clyde, promising to exempt the Domed Stadium Authority and its two thousand acres along the proposed Airport Freeway from property taxes for twenty-five years while providing municipal services at reduced rates.

The mayor and city council of Clyde considered themselves big league and pro-growth rather than stupid.

Those facts would be totally unsatisfactory to Lamar Jean

Lukas, who believed in honor, trust and fairness, which was the reason the facts had been omitted from the morning paper Lamar Jean had under his arm when he arrived for work at the gas station. The boss had his car parked under the canopy and was shoving his television set into the backseat.

"What's the trouble, boss? TV broke?" Lamar Jean slapped the newspaper across the fender of the red Chrysler. "A. D. Koster said the Pistol Dome down in Clyde is gonna have a roof and air-conditioning and theater seats." Lamar thought a moment. "I wonder if they'll call them the Clyde Pistols? Naw . . . naw." He shook his head.

The boss said nothing and continued to wrestle the television onto the red and white plastic backseat cover. Lamar Jean looked around the station. Something was wrong with the morning routine; several things were amiss.

"Hey, boss, you ain't put out the tires or the oil cans. Hell, you ain't even turned on the pumps. Jesus, your TV set breaks and you go all to pieces." Lamar laughed, rolled up the sleeves of his blue work shirt and limped over to the door to turn on the pumps and pull out the tire and oil display racks.

Lamar reached for the knob. The door was locked.

"The TV set isn't broken, Lamar," the boss said, watching Lamar wiggle the doorknob.

"Well, then why are you taking it away?" Lamar turned. "And you haven't even unlocked the station. What's the matter, boss?"

"I'm not your boss anymore, Lamar." The boss slammed the passenger door of the big red Chrysler.

"Am I fired?" Lamar's face went white. He had never been fired from a job and always considered himself a hard worker. "I gave you a good day's work every day, boss." Lamar limped toward the boss.

"No, you ain't fired, Lamar. I guess if anybody got fired, it was me. Exxon finally got me." The boss stared at the cement drive that he had swept and cleaned for over twenty years. "They doubled my lease and halved my gasoline allotment."

"What are you talking about?" Lamar began pacing, limping. "They got more gas now than a dog's got fleas. It says so in this morning's paper."

"That don't mean they have to sell it to me, Lamar," the boss said. He reached into his coverall pocket and withdrew a folded envelope. "There's a week's pay here, Lamar, and a letter of recommendation. I wish I could do more." The boss held the envelope out and shrugged his shoulders.

"No! No!" Lamar slapped the envelope out of the boss's hand and it fell to the pavement. "They can't get away with this."

"They already done got away with it, Lamar. They are Exxon and they can pretty much do what they damn please." The boss pointed to the envelope lying on the concrete. "Now pick that up and calm down. It don't do no good to try and change things you can't change."

Tears ran down the old man's rough, unshaven face. The sight shocked Lamar Jean Lukas to silence. He hadn't seen a man cry since the yellow Communists shot his calf muscle to shreds.

Lamar stood openmouthed as the boss jerked at the Chrysler door.

"There's . . . a . . . fella's . . . card . . ." The boss wiped away the tears and tried to sniff back the mucus that began to run from his bulbous red nose. ". . . inside." He pointed at the envelope, which Lamar was now slapping angrily against his thigh. "I already called him. . . . He says . . . to . . . come . . . see him."

The boss suddenly ducked into the red Chrysler, cranked the engine over and pulled slowly from beneath the canopy, leaving behind twenty years.

Lamar Jean Lukas stood next to the unleaded pump, slapped the envelope against his leg and watched the red Chrysler crawl slowly into the traffic and lurch out of sight.

"Well, goddam Exxon," Lamar said, opening the envelope, taking out the cash and stuffing it in his jeans pocket. "Goddam Exxon ain't heard the last from Lamar Jean Lukas."

Lamar unfolded the letter of recommendation. It said that Lamar Jean Lukas was a loyal, hardworking employee who always kept his promises, was honest and dependable and would be a welcome addition to any company that wanted loyal, hardworking, dependable employees. A business card was folded inside the letter. It was from the man the boss had called about Lamar.

"I guess I better go see this feller," he said to himself; then suddenly Lamar Jean Lukas whirled and, using his good leg, unleashed a devastating series of kicks against the unleaded pump. The metal dented and bent, the glass broke out, the numbers shattered.

Lamar shook for a while after he stopped kicking. Standing by the ruined pump, taking long, slow, deep breaths, Lamar finally stopped shaking enough to read the name and address on the crumpled business card.

JACK PATRICK "PAT" GARRETT

SECURITY SERVICES, INC.
200 HOUSTON STREET   347–8899

*Security Guards; Attack Dogs; Burglar Alarms; Complete Security
Services for Home and Business; Polygraph Tests; Brain-Wave
Reading; Detection Dogs: Drugs, Alcohol, Explosives; Electronic-
Security Specialists: Freearms Experts; Escape/Evasion Driving School;
Survivalist Training; Executive Protection; Shotgun Training*

Lamar looked at the card in wonder; a short narrative of the
progress of the American Dream.

"Well," Lamar said to himself, as he often did, "a job's a job."
He jammed the letter and card into his work-shirt pocket. "Drop
your cocks . . . grab your socks." He patted the ravaged gas pump
apologetically and limped away.

SECURITY
CONSCIOUSNESS

LAMAR Jean Lukas changed buses twice, then hitchhiked the last
miles to the far edge of Amos Chandler Industrial Park.

A small one-story beige brick building had thick opaque glass
block windows which allowed the passage of specific light rays
and only very heavy-caliber slugs. Beside the entrance a small
white and black sign read:

SECURITY SERVICES, INC.
Pat Garrett, President.

The heavy-gauge steel door was locked. Lamar pushed the
white button on the call box built into the door frame. Ten feet
above the doorway a small TV camera was aimed down at Lamar.

"Can I help you?" It was a woman's voice.

Lamar Jean looked up at the camera and said nothing.

"Can I help you?" the woman's voice repeated.

"Hey, am I on that thing?" Lamar pointed up to the small
camera.

"Yes you are, sir."

"Well, doggies!" Lamar grinned into the camera. "I never been on television except one time this guy from the network interviewed me." Lamar cocked his head at the camera. "But he and the cameraman and all the film caught a friendly mortar round. Blew 'em to smithereens, film and everything." Lamar paused. "I guess *this* is the first time."

"Can I help you, sir?" The woman's voice was more urgent this time. Lamar looked away from the camera and down at his feet. He didn't hear the woman. He heard the mortar round exploding.

"Sir, can I help you?" The voice was insistent and loud. "Please, sir, what do you want?"

Lamar Jean was jerked back across the Pacific.

"Oh? Ah? Yeah . . . sure . . . yeah . . ." Lamar dug into his work-shirt pocket for the business card the boss had given him. The card was damp and wrinkled; Lamar's shirt was soaked with sweat.

"Damn hot out today, ain't it?" Lamar said as he tried to return to the present, gather his jumbled thoughts, read the card and ask for a job. Any job. "I'm here to see a Mr. Garrett. My name is Lamar Jean Lukas."

"What is the nature of your business?" the voice asked.

"I'm looking for a job. The boss sent me here to see Mr. Garrett." Lamar double-checked the name on the card. "Mr. Jack Patrick 'Pat' Garrett." Lamar shook his head and frowned at the small camera now panning up and down the length of Lamar's sweat-soaked body. "Can you let me inside? It's kinda hot out here."

"Just a moment, sir."

Lamar leaned on his good leg and heard the whine and heavy crunch of a mortar round. He thought about the ARVN mortar crew and the dead network guys. Then he thought about Exxon. Lamar Jean Lukas ducked up against the building.

"Sir? Sir?" the voice from the call box was coaxing him back. "Sir? Are you there? Please step out where the camera can see you." The voice floated out of the black iron grillwork built flush with the burglarproof door frame. Lamar backed out, looking up at the camera panning around in search of him.

"Ah, there you are, sir."

"Yes." Lamar nodded slowly at the camera. "Here I am."

"Mr. Garrett says to come right in." The voice had a friendly lilt to it now. A raucous buzz from the door made Lamar flinch. He grappled clumsily with the door, finally pulling it open about three inches. He had underestimated the weight of the heavy bullet- and blast-proof steel. It began to close under its own weight.

Off balance, Lamar propped his bad leg against the doorjamb and jerked hard with both hands, opening the door wide enough for him to slide sideways into the entryway.

The entryway was a long hallway that ended at another door, monitored by another camera.

When Lamar reached the second door, it also began to buzz. Leaning back and gripping the knob with both hands, Lamar Jean yanked as hard as he could. He grossly overestimated the weight on the second door, slinging it wide, banging into the wall, skinning his knuckles.

Lamar stepped onto the tile floor of the brightly lit reception area. Red and black straight-back imitation-leather-and-steel chairs lined the white walls. In the center of the room was a red six-cushion steel-framed sofa. The plaster walls were covered with pictures of Security Services, Inc., in action: armed guards in group photographs, attack dogs ripping at heavily padded arms, close-ups of snarling Dobermans and German shepherds. There was a large photo of the complete contents of the security services personal survival pack, including a year's supply of freeze-dried food, a water purification system, a tent, a sleeping bag, a .22 rifle that fit inside its waterproof floating stock, an AR-15, a .45 automatic and fifteen thousand rounds of ammunition, plus reloading equipment.

Directly across from the door was a small window in the wall with sliding bulletproof glass. Through the thick glass Lamar could see a young woman at a telephone switchboard. She held up one finger at Lamar.

Above the window was a color photo portrait of Jack Patrick "Pat" Garrett dressed out as a major in the Green Berets. Lamar Jean Lukas had never had much use for Green Berets. He had liked their boots, but he had thought their manner, like their hat, was silly. He had never seen many dead Green Berets, though; mostly he had seen dead draftees. Not that any of that mattered to him now; Lamar was just looking for a job, and Security Services, Inc., President Pat Garrett was looking for bodies to fill an armed security service contract. SSI had just signed with Apartment Management, Inc., a Canadian firm that had taken over the Seasons Apartments from a bankrupt dentist whose apartment manager had taken the rent money and run off with two Delta Airlines stewardesses. Apartment Management, Inc., wanted Security Services, Inc., to protect their property.

The Seasons Apartments were eighty-five percent full, but only thirty percent of the tenants were current with their rent. Texas

Pistols quarterback Taylor Rusk was one of the few who always paid it in full and on time; he had ever since he'd moved into the Seasons as a professional football rookie.

Lamar Jean Lukas almost turned the job down; he didn't want to carry a gun, but he needed the money for his season-ticket payment. The full price was due six months before the football season began, giving the Franchise interest-free "float money." This year the Pistols had also added two exhibition games to the season ticket, making it eleven games at twenty dollars a game. The Texas Pistols ticket office let Lamar pay in "two easy equal installments."

So Lamar Jean Lukas got back into guns because he owed the Franchise $220.

THE MAJOR

"CALL me the Major or just Major if you like." Pat Garrett led Lamar into his office. A fierce-looking Doberman stood at parade rest in the corner, eyeing Lamar Jean's throat. Lamar sized up the time and space between him and the ferocious dog, then scanned the Major's desk, deciding on the trench knife that the Major used as a letter opener. Lamar knew he would win and the beautifully vicious two-thousand-dollar attack dog would just be 115 pounds of dog meat. But Lamar knew he would never get hired by an ex–Green Beret who called himself the Major if Lamar killed the Major's favorite attack dog with his bare hands and the Major's letter opener while the Major was deciding whether to pay Lamar the minimum wage to shoot people with a heavy-caliber pistol. Lamar Jean Lukas had been a good soldier who understood the military system. If Lamar killed the two-thousand-dollar dog, Major Jack Patrick "Pat" Garrett would write *Overqualified* on the application.

"You can call me Pat." Garrett was dressed in a khaki leisure suit and ankle-length zipper boots. A small star embroidered with gold stitching sat on the upper lift flap of the four-flap patch-pocket jacket. Over the small gold star were stitched the small white letters *SSI*.

Lamar didn't notice how Major Pat Garrett dressed or look too closely at the plaques, certificates, pictures and neatly boxed and framed gold- and silver-plated special-edition pistols that hung on the office walls. Lamar mainly kept track of the dog and the trench knife that lay across the Standard Employee's Contract with Consent to Take a Lie Detector Test that Lamar would have to sign before he was ready to go out and work.

One steamy afternoon at Tan Son Nhut, Lamar saw an attack dog eat its handler. They kept dogs out by the aircraft all the time. Mean fucking dogs. This dog just went nuts and ate a complete air policeman, who was able to draw his .45 but never got off a round. Dogs went nuts over there just like people.

Lamar had always heard that seeing a horse go crazy on the battlefield was the most unnerving thing to soldiers in the horse wars. Lamar would put that dog that went berserk guarding F-4s up against any horse. Anyplace. Anytime.

"I'm actually not even named Patrick," Major Garrett continued, seating himself in his wooden swivel chair. He motioned for Lamar to sit on the wooden stool across the desk from him. There were no other chairs or seats of any kind in the spacious if rather Spartan office. If the Major had many visitors, they stood.

"I really didn't have a middle name," Garrett went on. The dog rumbled low in his throat. "I just took Patrick after I got out of the service. It fit in well with the Security Service. You know? Pat Garrett? The famous marshal?"

Lamar nodded and listened to the dog.

"You'd be surprised the number of calls I get just from putting Pat in my Yellow Pages ad."

The hair along the back of the dog's neck began to stand as the rumble turned to a growl.

"Louie Deal tells me you're a good worker, you're dependable, you got an honorable discharge and you got skragged in 'Nam."

Lamar flinched when the Major said *skragged*, but then nodded and watched and listened to the dog.

"I wanted to go there myself," the Major said. "It would have looked good on my record. . . . Well, it actually *does* look good on my record. . . . You know what I mean? Just before I retired, my record went to Vietnam, but I didn't actually go. One of those little bureaucratic creations one learns about."

The Major leaned forward and the hair on the dog's neck turned straight up. The Major didn't notice. He had the dog on a "tryout loan" from a service buddy who got them off the Air Force base in San Antonio. The guy's job was killing the crazy dogs.

He sold them instead.

"Anyway," Major Pat Garrett droned on, "I would have liked

to have gone there . . . seen it . . . you know, felt it . . . smelled it . . . you know what I mean?" The dog was onto all four feet, baring its teeth. Lamar Jean moved forward on the stool. The growl was quite audible.

"I saw *Patton* twelve times." Major Pat Garrett's eyes became unfocused and he seemed serene. The dog relaxed and sat back down. It never took its eyes off Lamar's throat.

"We do a lot of rock shows and concerts," the Major said. It had seemed like a long silence. "So you got to have a high shit tolerance, you know what I mean?"

Lamar nodded.

"I mean the shit you got to take from these kids." The Major looked over at Lamar. "Are you up to taking a lot of shit?"

"Yessir, been takin' it all my life." Lamar spoke low and tried to smile. He moved as little as possible. The dog again began a deep, rumbling growl.

"Little assholes!" the Major said. The dog was back on his feet, teeth bare. "Okay, I can use you. You got to take a pistol course and buy your own uniform. Seventy-five dollars. I supply it and take the money out of your first three paychecks. You can buy your own pistol or I'll supply you with a weapon and take it out of your first six paychecks. You got to have a physical. You got a doctor?"

Lamar Jean Lukas sat on the edge of the stool, watching and listening to the dog. Major Pat Garrett was a distant drone, unseen, unnoticed.

Lamar Jean Lukas had his own pistol, a six-inch-barrel Smith & Wesson Model 19 .357 Magnum with black rubber Pachmayr grips. It had been his choice when the time came to buy himself a pistol. Lamar preferred a revolver to an automatic because every time you pulled the trigger the hammer slammed down on a fresh cartridge. That is important to a man who understands a misfire.

His first day on the job, Lamar Jean was assigned to the Seasons Apartments. He noticed right away that Taylor Rusk was living there. The quarterback had a three-bedroom apartment all to himself.

"I'll have to drop in on Taylor," Lamar said to himself. "Surprise him sometime."

FREE LUNCH

TAYLOR'S phone rang. It was Kimball Adams in New York City.

"Hey, Fresh Meat," Kimball rasped into the phone, "it's me, the man who taught you everything worth knowing."

"And some things I'd rather forget," Taylor said.

"Don't forget 'em, Fresh Meat," the ex-quarterback growled. "Those are the most important things. The rest of it is the magic show. How are my old teammates?"

"Waiting on training camp, I guess," Taylor replied. "Hendrix is in Houston with his father-in-law. They closed a big offshore deal with VCO. Bobby may get rich and retire."

"Old Gus Savas?" Kimball growled. "I like that old bastard. He put me into some good oil deals when Bobby and I were in Cleveland, but then oil wasn't bringing but three dollars a barrel."

"Well, they have that problem solved," Taylor said. "This VCO deal looks like a chance for Bobby and Ginny to hit big. They got a lot tied up in it."

"I just talked to Terry Dudley. He plans to run for governor down there in four years," Kimball said.

"A dead man can get elected if he spends enough," Taylor replied. "What else did our seven-foot Union director say?"

"Plenty. He's got big plans. A big network deal. How's Simon and Ox and Speedo?"

"Speedo's helping Hendrix and Dudley with the Union here. They're talking about residuals now," Taylor answered. "Which is causing plenty of trouble since nobody understands anything. The last I saw Ox, he was helping Simon up off the purple carpet in the weight room. Simon's leg isn't healing right. I don't think he's going to make it back."

"How's he taking it?" Kimball wanted to know.

"Not too well, and he don't even know it yet." Taylor sighed. "Generally everybody's gone nuts. The shithouse to the penthouse and back. The elevator doesn't make any stops in between. And don't say I told you so."

"What was it Speedo always says?" Kimball asked.

"'Almost about the same,'" Taylor quoted Speedo Smith. "'Everybody is almost about the same.'"

"Sounds like you all could use a vacation."

"You mean *this* isn't a vacation?"

"I mean a trip," Kimball replied. "How about a few days in the tropical sun, all expenses paid? I got me a travel agency here in New York and I got some airline and hotel packages that are free for promotional consideration, as we say in the business. How does a Caribbean island sound to you?"

"Too small."

"Other than that?" Kimball pressed. "Lay around in the sun, do a little fishing. I got room for ten to fifteen people. The network is doing one of those sportsman shows. They asked me to handle the travel package. Terry Dudley is coming to help coordinate the players with the network. He thinks this is one way to get a better image for the Union." Kimball shook his head. "I think he means a better image for the Union director, but what do I know? Anyway, can you make it?"

"Where?"

"Cozumel. Off the Yucatán on the Caribbean side. Most of the tourists there come from Texas. Good airline connections out of Houston. I'll already be down there. Bring a date if you want, Fresh Meat. There's always room for more. Talk at you later. I'm going to call the others now. Have you got Bobby's phone number in Houston?"

"No, but it's Gus Savas on River Oaks Boulevard. Bobby's still living at his father-in-law's place."

"He ought to: the place is the size of the Astrodome." Kimball laughed again. It was a gargling sound.

"Who else is going?"

"Who do you want?" Kimball replied. "I was thinking of Bobby and Ginny Hendrix and their kids."

"What about Speedo?" Taylor asked.

"Fine. It'll do them Mayans good to meet some niggers." Kimball laughed his rusty laugh. "The network wanted a club official. The only one we could get was Lem Carleton and his wife, Wendy. She's Cyrus Chandler's daughter, you know."

Wendy would be in Mexico.

SIMON ON FILM

SIMON finished his workout and soaked his swollen sore knee in ice water for twenty minutes. His whole leg ached from the cold water. The joint was degenerating. The loss of complete range of motion would cause the quadriceps to remain underdeveloped. The whole leg would slowly deteriorate and atrophy. The resulting limp would misalign Simon's spine and the lower discs would begin to wear. Favoring the weak leg would result in too much strain on Simon's good leg, causing joint problems in the hip and ankle.

Then, finally, would come arthritis.

Simon could see it all in the future. He knew it was coming, inevitable. He had made a study of the science of kinesiology and his own body in particular while a physical-education major at the University. Simon D'Hanis was hurt badly, and although he knew it, he desperately refused to admit it. His mind and body lived in contradiction and it was driving him mad. He flared angrily at any innuendo that his recovery was slow, his injury not responsive. He had tried to fight with his oldest friend, Taylor Rusk, because he had misinterpreted and resented Rusk's concern about his knee. If he wouldn't admit it, he had to keep others from admitting or discovering that the knee was not responding, that the leg was not coming around. Simon forbade Buffy even to mention the injury or talk football around the house. He kept his pain and fear suppressed and hidden, but at weak moments it would burst forth in violence. He had attacked his quarterback in the weight room. At home he had beaten Buffy into submission. When he was home they avoided each other. She kept the children away from Simon while he rested on the couch, his knee elevated and packed in ice, reading the newspaper or watching television. They seldom talked or touched. Simon was wound so tightly that he gave off vibrations. He fulminated, pulsed with fury, desperation, despair, anger and desire. *He could not learn to be a cripple.*

The ice water had turned his leg into a dull aching log while the big man did forearm curls with barbells. He ground his teeth, making his head and neck hurt from exertion and unreleased tension, doing permanent damage to his teeth and jaw.

The phone rang in the trainer's office. A few minutes later Clint, the trainer, came out. Clint was dressed in his whites and ripple-soled shoes.

"That was Red on the phone," the short, heavyset trainer told Simon. "The line coach wants to look at some range of motion pictures of your leg to see if he can count on you for this season. Dry off and let's go to the weight room. The video tape is already set up."

Simon pulled his cold, reddened leg from the ice water and dried it, rubbing the knee scar gently with the towel. The joint seemed to feel better and the swelling wasn't as bad that day. Simon would show them range of motion if that is what they wanted to see; he would move like Fred Astaire.

The trainer had the camera set up and the VTR on when Simon got to the weight room.

"Just get up on the friction table, Simon," Clint said. "I have the dial at zero. We don't care what you can lift yet, we just want to see if you can get full extension and what sort of endurance you have. If you can get it straight and do ten repetitions, I'll be satisfied."

Simon tied his foot into the friction machine and sat on the padded bench with the machine arm paralleling his leg from knee to strapped-in foot. While the trainer fooled with the movie camera on the tripod, Simon switched the controls on the machine so that it would provide reverse resistance to knee movement. The machine would then assist in straightening the leg while Simon would only have to force it back to a ninety-degree angle. The machine would be forcing his knee to full extension, making it appear that Simon had full flexion and extension of the knee joint. The machine would actually pull his leg straight those last ten degrees. The most important ten degrees.

"Okay, Simon." The trainer flipped a switch and the VTR began to whir. "Start straightening that leg. Don't worry about speed, it's range of motion we want to see here."

Simon began to work, appearing to force the machine and his leg straight out, flexing his knee to full extension. The weight of the machine was actually pulling the knee straight, but the trainer didn't know and Simon made it appear as if he were straining and pushing the friction arm. The joint pain was searing, making D'Hanis nauseous. He ground his teeth and his jaw popped.

"Goddam, Simon, that is great!" Clint said from behind the camera. "You got full extension that time, full range of motion. That's the first time I have seen you do that."

"It's been doing a lot better the last couple of days, Clint," Simon lied through gritted teeth, letting the machine pull the screaming knee to full extension. Simon would force the friction arm back down, then let it pull his leg straight out again through the knee's full range of motion.

Ten times.

"That is great, Simon." The trainer flicked off the camera and removed the small spool of tape. "Red'll be glad to see this. Come on, let's go get a shower." Clint started out of the room.

"In a minute." Simon knew he could not stand up; the pain was too great. "I want to sit and do a few more."

"Okay, but don't overdo it," the trainer said as he left the room. "Red will love this tape."

Tears trickled out of Simon's eyes; the pain throbbed the length of his leg. It was another twenty minutes before he could limp out of the room, using weight machines, the wall, doors and lockers to assist himself.

That night the knee swelled so large that it ripped the seam in his trousers. Simon spent the entire night on the couch, crying, with ice packs and wet towels packed around the tormented joint.

The trainer was right. Red loved the tape, showing it to the Los Angeles scout before they finalized the deal for Simon D'Hanis. Then the film went into the Pistols' files in case Simon came back at them with an injury grievance. It was an unnecessary precaution; by then Simon was too crazy to even comprehend the injury grievance process.

THE LOS ANGELES SPC

TAYLOR drove out to Doc Webster's ranch. He built a fire in the cold stone fireplace. It was late and Doc was asleep in the south bedroom. The flames soon blazed in colors as the mesquite burned hot.

Thoughts raged through his mind like the fire.

It seemed like the few years since he'd left college had been a complete lifetime.

Someone else's lifetime.

He had become a great professional football player, the centerpiece of a team that had the ability to reach the Super Bowl.

He knew it was management, systems built by Red and Dick Conly, that kept continuity and created teams with the ability to win championships. But it took *great players* making *great plays* on one specific day to win the Super Bowl. Taylor never doubted his ability to perform, to make those plays and inspire his teammates to the same efforts. Texas would get to the Super Bowl and win.

But now Taylor wondered if he cared. Everything had changed.

It seemed like a hundred years ago but hurt like yesterday. Wendy was married to Lem Three and Taylor's child belonged to someone else. A. D. Koster was gone to the front office and Simon D'Hanis was going steadily crazy.

Taylor stared into the flames. He wasn't aware he was crying until he felt the tears drop on the back of his hand. He cried without ever making a sound or moving. The flames blurred as the tears filled his eyes, poured down his face and soaked his shirt front. When the fire began to die down, Taylor got up and added more wood. He was cold and lonely. The tears stopped, but he felt no release, no easing of the conflict that clutched his soul. All his life he had sought control of situations. He played quarterback so he could call the plays, control the game. He limited his friendships so they could be kept on track and understood, controlled. Performance and grace under pressure, never losing one's grip on a situation no matter how difficult, frightening or painful—Taylor Rusk had always kept control; he yearned for control, he struggled for it, but it was only now that he began to realize he had never been in control of anything. It had always been someone else's world. He had learned to react instantly to someone else's needs and desires and had convinced himself that it was control when it was all merely reflex honed to a razor's edge. And he walked the razor's edge better than anyone. What he had taken for control in his life was merely excellent reflexes combined with robust health, physical size and skills in a business where those assets were highly prized by certain people for various reasons. The most important reasons being "economic rents and profit maximization," as Doc Webster said the next morning when he walked out of the bedroom with the LA Standard Player's Contract to find Taylor staring into a dead fire.

"Your skills provide a surplus of economic rents, which go to the owner instead of the athlete because of congressional antitrust exemptions and the structure of the League, namely the commissioner's compensation and the option-year clause." Doc Webster waved the contract around. "Well, I convinced *my* boy, Portus, that you deserve your fair share of the rents. That boy was always a good student."

"Then he'll make a lousy owner," Taylor said. His eyes felt gritty from a night of staring into the fire and trying to come to some sort of understanding about his own life.

"They shouldn't let kids be owners," Doc agreed. He waved the contract again. "But it's already signed."

"The commissioner will never let it happen," Taylor said. "They merged the leagues just to stop this sort of bidding for players. The free agent system is a standing joke. Nobody moves unless the owners want them to move. Robbie Burden will invoke the compensation rule."

"Who cares? That's a problem between Burden and Cyrus Chandler and the LA Franchise," Doc Webster laughed. "And of course A. D. Koster."

"A.D.?" Taylor frowned at the professor's grin. "What's A.D. got to do with this?"

"Cyrus Chandler made him general manager. Dick Conly quit. It was on the radio yesterday."

"A.D. is general manager?" Taylor scoffed. "That's insane."

"There you go, making a psychiatric diagnosis when we are merely trying to test economic theory." Doc grinned. "Now, let me tell you what I think and then you go check with your friend Dudley and see what the Union thinks. I don't expect the League will let you move either. I imagine they'll do just about anything to stop this, but there are certain laws in this country. I think that Chandler and the commissioner will force my boy to withdraw the five-million-dollar offer either by the compensation clause with threats of taking all his number-one draft choices until the twenty-first century and all his active players over 150 pounds or by having his daddy give him a good spanking." Doc laughed at his hyperbole. Taylor Rusk stared at him. "But that doesn't matter because with this contract we can show in a court of law that the League has illegally conspired to reduce your salary from five million dollars. We'll let somebody else settle the free agent movement question. Our antitrust argument is that LA, Texas and the commissioner's office illegally conspired to deprive you of five million dollars."

"And I spend the next ten years in court," Taylor said.

"Maybe but not likely, even less likely now that Conly is gone. The timing couldn't be better. I don't think anybody in the League wants to risk this in court and have the courts setting antitrust precedents while the League is lobbying Congress for complete exemption."

"They'll settle?"

Doc nodded. "You'll stay in Texas, but they'll have to pay you five million dollars over the next five years. Nothing deferred, no big insurance policies, just plain old inflated American dollars. A million of them a year. I imagine the commissioner will make the LA franchise pay part of the cost and they'll pay it." He held up the SPC.

Taylor took the contract and studied it. It provided for a base salary of one million dollars beginning in May of the next year. At the end of the contract, just above the twenty-two-year-old boy's flourishing signature, was a "Special Provision":

> That the entire sum of $5,000,000, which represents the price of Taylor Rusk's services for five years, is *guaranteed* and will be paid regardless of Mr. Rusk's ability to perform as a professional football player.

"I made him put that in especially," Doc Webster said with a huge grin. "I believe it is what is called a no-cut contract. Have you ever seen one before?"

Taylor slowly exhaled loudly. "Well, I'll be damned—the mythical no-cut contract."

Doc Webster went to the kitchen and returned with a bottle of Herradura tequila.

"How about a toast? First, to Razmus, the economics professor that the University fired five years ago for screwing and smoking dope in his office. He advised the Portus kid." He held the bottle out to Taylor.

Taylor uncapped the bottle of distilled maguey. "Thanks, Doc." He took a small drink. The professor took the bottle and held it up.

"To you, Taylor. Now that you have five million dollars, I hope you can get what you really want." Doc tilted his head back and let the tequila run over his lips and tongue and down his throat. He drank several ounces and handed the bottle back to Taylor.

The big quarterback held up the bottle.

"Here's to life, real control, the razor's edge, Wendy Chandler Carleton and my son, Randall. I want them all and, by God, I'll have them." Taylor Rusk took great gulping drafts of the burning tequila. "This is only the beginning."

By noon both men were roaring drunk and swimming fully clothed in Panther Hole.

Wendy Chandler Carleton stood up on Coon Ridge and watched the two men howling and laughing and falling into the cold creek water. Randall Ryan stood silently at her side, holding her hand. Finally she pulled him gently back toward the car.

"We'll have to come swimming another day, Randall," she said.

The small boy trudged along obediently. When they reached the car he asked, "Is it because of those two crazy men that we can't go swimming?"

"Yes, sweetheart. It's because of those crazy men. They're nice men, but they are crazy."

"I know that big man, don't I, Momma?"

Wendy nodded.

"He waved at me when we flew in that big airplane down to that hotel that had the big swimming pool. We didn't get to swim then, did we, Mom? Does that man always keep us from swimming?"

"No, not always."

Wendy Chandler Carleton started the car and drove back down the caliche road across the pasture and through the cattle guard.

"Mom," Randall said when they reached the highway, "the next time I see that big man, I'm going to ask him to let us go swimming. Okay?"

"Okay, sweetheart." Wendy's eyes welled with tears.

"Mom? Why was Daddy so mad at Grandpa Chandler this morning?"

"What mades you think Daddy was mad at Grandpa?"

"He yelled at him on the phone. I heard him. He said bad words to Grandpa."

"Well, sometimes men yell at each other."

"Like those two crazy men in the water?"

Wendy nodded.

"I like that big man, Momma. I wish I could go swimming with him."

"Maybe you can someday, Randall." Wendy took a hand from the steering wheel and wiped her eyes quickly.

"Mom?" The small boy stood in the seat and leaned against

his mother's shoulder. "You are my sweetheart. I'll never yell at you."

The small boy wrapped his soft arms around Wendy's neck and pulled himself against her in a hug. The tiny fingers tickled her neck as he rubbed his soft cheek against hers.

QUALITY TIME

KIMBALL Adams convinced Bobby Hendrix that he should take Ginny and the kids to Cozumel. Adams told his old receiver about his new travel agency.

Kimball couldn't keep from bragging. "The Cobianco brothers put up the money for junkets to Las Vegas and the Super Bowl. I made a ton on the Super Bowl last year." He trusted Hendrix; they had been friends for twenty years. Hendrix wished Kimball wouldn't trust him quite so much. "We took five chartered DC-9 jets to Los Angeles at two thousand dollars a pop, including hotel rooms and game tickets. I had one thousand tickets and they all went for five hundred dollars apiece in the package. Jesus! The travel business is great. It's like stealing."

"It *is* stealing," Hendrix said. He didn't really want Kimball telling him those things over the phone. He had already heard most of it from Tommy McNamara, who was writing a newspaper story on scalping, but it worried Hendrix that Kimball was telling him because now Kimball knew that Hendrix knew. "I don't want to know about it. This is Texas down here, not America. You should be careful who you tell. There are government agencies like the IRS who might not look so kindly and might begin to ask where you got the tickets and whether all the taxes were paid."

"Hey, roomie," Kimball protested, "if I can't trust you, who can I trust?"

"You can trust me," Hendrix said, "but I don't know anybody else you can trust. So get out of the habit of talking about it." Hendrix changed the subject. "How's the coaching job working out in New York?"

"You know these guys in New York, Bobby. We won our last game last year, so the owner is keeping Bradley as the head coach. I guess he figures he's on a hot roll. A one-game win streak. I just put my time in with the quarterbacks and draw my check.

— 258 —

The guy wins one more game than a dead man and they renew him for five years," Kimball laughed. "This is a tough team to gamble on: The point spreads are almost insurmountable in either direction. Our last game against Dallas we were twenty-point underdogs. Tell me how you can bet a twenty-point spread?"

"I have no idea and I don't want to know, Kimball," Hendrix said. He was certain that Kimball had figured out a way and wanted to brag about it. He knew that Kimball had kept his bargain with Red Kilroy and always mailed the Texas head coach the New York game plan every time the two teams played. Kimball was part of Red's network.

"Guess who I saw yesterday?" Kimball said. "Charlie Stillman."

"I heard he went to New York after we forced him out of the Players Union. He still delivering the flesh for the owners?"

"By the carload. And all with multimillion-dollar contracts deferred about thirty years." Kimball laughed. "It's really funny, the niggers all believe their own newspaper clippings, buying themselves fur coats, houses for their mommas, rhinestone collars for their Yorkies."

"We are all niggers and should read the contracts instead of the newspapers," Hendrix said.

"Hell, Bobby, all of Stillman's clients signed within ten days of the draft." Kimball laughed his raspy laugh. "And he just signed a big contract with the network. He's going to bring some of his clients to Cozumel."

"What?" Hendrix was surprised. "I'm not sure I want to be on the same island with that son of a bitch."

"Come on, you'll be in different hotels," Kimball pleaded. "Taylor'll be there, and Dudley too. He claims it'll be good for Union solidarity and image."

"Taylor always told me that Dudley was a smart guy. It was one reason we chose him as director," Hendrix said. "But he hasn't shown me much except ambition. It's stupid for the Union to cooperate with Stillman. He's the owners' man."

"He's their *boy*. Robbie Burden is the owners' *man*." Kimball coughed a short spasm of laughter. "The way Dudley tells it, the Union will eventually sign a hell of a contract with the network to use players as commentators for football and other sports, including the next Olympics, plus TV movies and a production company."

"So the Union can steal everything they don't get paid?" Bobby sighed.

"Yeah, well, it's not like it was real money."

"What's the story on Dick Conly?" Kimball changed the subject. "Why did Chandler make that asshole A.D. general manager?"

"You remember that knockout teenybopper blonde that used to come to camp in Koster's car that first season?" Hendrix asked.

"Oh, Jeeezus, the one that wore the tight white shorts and the T-shirt with no bra and was barefoot all the time?"

"That's the one," Hendrix said, "Suzy Ballard."

"Goddam," Kimball rasped, "I always wanted to stick my tongue in her bellybutton . . . from the inside."

"Apparently Cyrus had the same idea, 'cause she tossed Conly over for him. Now it's Cyrus Chandler's turn in the barrel. I think making A.D. general manager was part of the deal. Conly's gone off to New Mexico to the mountains. Suzy's moved with Cyrus out to Chandler's Hot Springs Ranch. The word is," Hendrix said, "that Billy Joe Hardesty is going to marry Cyrus and Suzy on his TV show with only close friends, which means they can broadcast from a phone booth and still have room to use the phone."

"Well, it sounds like that little blond carhop is mo-*bile*, hos-*tile* and ag-*ile*. We get the Billy Joe Hardesty show up here on cable about two in the morning," Kimball rasped. "It's great to watch when you're really drunk."

"I'm afraid old Cyrus is in deep shit, and A.D., Suzy and the reverend are about to hand him an anchor." Bobby Hendrix exhaled and flexed his slender freckled hands. "Family and office politics. Shit." He felt vaguely frightened.

"You know, Junie Chandler ain't exactly bad pussy," Kimball said. "She ranks among the top three of all the owners' wives I ever fucked. It just goes to show you what young girls do to old men."

"It just goes to show something, I'm not sure what."

"How's the arthritis, Bobby?" Kimball asked, as if he sensed the pain in Hendrix's fingers.

"No better, maybe a little worse." Hendrix moved his hand gently. "I'm getting it bad in my neck from those chunks knocked out of my cervical vertebrae going across the middle after those wounded ducks you threw."

"I knew you'd get them, Bobby. I'd put you up against the biggest and meanest defensive backs in the League any day of the week."

"You already did, thanks."

"Hey, don't thank me, man. It was all part of the job." Kimball laughed his evil laugh. "Have you talked to Fresh Meat lately? I heard he played out his option and is going to Los Angeles for five mill. You hear anything about that?"

"I know he was on his option, but I didn't hear about any five mill," Hendrix said. "Why didn't you ask him when you called about the fishing trip?"

"I didn't figure it was any of my business."

"Well, that's the first thing you've ever admitted to me wasn't any of your business," Hendrix replied, knowing that Kimball Adams was lying. Red wanted to know about the five million dollars and had delegated Kimball to find out.

"Find out what you can, will you, roomie?" Kimball said. "I'll see you down in Cozumel. You'll love it, Ginny will love it and the kids will love it. Get in a little quality time with the family. Talk at you later." Kimball hung up.

Quality time? Bobby thought. *Quality time*?

"There's a fucking catchphrase for you," Hendrix said aloud, slamming the phone down so hard it hurt his hand. "Never trust a man who talks about 'quality time.'"

Bobby Hendrix, the aging receiver, stared at the phone in his father-in-law's house in River Oaks. He had missed quality time with his older boys, who had had to endure the craziness of early pro ball. The oldest was already gone off to college and seldom returned, anxious to be free.

Soon Bobby and Ginny's second son, James, would be graduating from high school. He was already talking about the Army as an alternative. Ginny had panicked at the suggestion, but Bobby kept her calm, convincing her that Jimmy's decision was a direct result of the movies *Stripes* and *Private Benjamin*.

VCO PULLS THE PLUG

BOBBY Hendrix was worried about telling Ginny that he'd lost almost all their money. Gus Savas, Ginny's father, was a gambler: that's what Bobby liked about him. Gus was willing to gamble right down to the last turn of the card or drill. And that's where

Venture Capital Offshore got them. Harrison H. Harrison just kept pushing money out there on the table and Gus just kept matching it.

Then, one day VCO just closed the well and called it dry.

They knew there was oil and gas down there. So did Bobby and Gus. But meanwhile VCO got a huge tax write-off, still controlled the lease and knew the oil and gas were there for the taking later.

VCO even reneged on the dry-hole money and told Bobby and Gus to sue them.

"I got ten, maybe twenty, years left," Gus laughed and pulled out one of his big cigars. He and Bobby were riding down in the elevator after their meeting with Harrison H. Harrison. "That is an awful lot of time for an old tool pusher to get his revenge." He grinned at his son-in-law. "Big company like Venture Capital Offshore will forget all about the fucking they gave Gus Savas in a few months. But I'm going to spend the rest of my life getting even. What are you going to do, Bobby?"

"Guess I'll have to play another season," the redheaded receiver said to his father-in-law. "Then maybe work for the Union."

Gus frowned. He didn't have much use for unions, having gotten his first job as a tool pusher in the East Texas field by climbing up on the drilling platform and whipping the current tool pusher. The fight ended when Gus hit the other man with a length of chain and knocked him off the platform twenty feet into the mud.

"You and your union," Gus laughed. "What does it get you? Or them? A man's gotta fight for whatever he gets."

"It's not what *we* get, Gus," Bobby said, "it's what we can get for the next generation of football players. There's sharks in these waters, and they have been eating my teammates for twenty years. Football's been good to me, Gus; it educated me and brutalized me at the same time. I don't want to see players cheated . . . by anyone. The Union should stand for what football should be: players looking out for each other. Football isn't *about* life, it *is* life. So I'll stick around and help."

"What do you get from it, Bobby boy?" Gus looked puzzled. "More important, what's in it for Terry Dudley? I know about unions, athletes and football. I know most are selfish, greedy. When Red Kilroy was coaching high school he would come to guys like me for money. 'You want a football team to be proud of?' he'd say, and I'd give him money in cash and he would get football players and win games." Gus puffed thoughtfully on his cigar. "Then one day I decided I don't even know how to be proud of a football team. You know what I mean?"

Bobby looked at his father-in-law's sparkling dark eyes, the perfect match for Ginny's, and nodded.

"I quit giving them money and never watched another game until you came along to Rice and married my Ginny. Now I'm back watching Red's football games again and my son-in-law's a union man." The elevator stopped and Gus clapped a heavy arm around Bobby's shoulder. They walked into the lobby, a structure of giant steel Tinkertoys and smoked glass.

"I never thought my Ginny would ever get married. She didn't like the River Oaks boys or any of them fag South Americans or fake princes. God bless you for that. You been good to her. She loves you very much. You give me four grandsons. But what you gonna do with this union? We busted out in oil, but I can get us a new stake. I'm a promoter. I don't know geology from creekology, but I can raise money to punch holes in the ground. There's plenty of oil left out there. You're a pretty old guy to be playing football. What's in the Union for you, Bobby?"

"I guess the same things that you'll get from whatever you do to Venture Capital Offshore," Bobby said. "A sense of purpose and the possibility of satisfaction. I seldom get mad, Gus, but I always get even. A linebacker cheap-shots me and before long I come out of nowhere and tear his knees off. There have been some pretty cheap shots over the years."

"Just don't get clipped," Gus warned, and rubbed Bobby's shoulder. The answer apparently pleased him. "You are a hell of a boy, Bobby, but you be careful; you got my daughter and grandchildren. Unions can cause trouble; sometimes people get hurt and killed. Cyrus Chandler is a greedy son of a bitch, and the rich don't share without a fight. I know, I used to be one." Gus laughed and beat the redhead's shoulder black and blue.

At the next negotiating session Union director Terry Dudley told the Owners Council that he would file another antitrust suit and consider calling a strike if they didn't bring a residual offer to the negotiating table.

"In order to be fair," Bobby Hendrix suggested, "we would like a look at books."

That request was absurd, but what knocked Robbie Burden backward in his chair was Dick Portus suddenly claiming he could not afford the Union demands.

Terry Dudley immediately filed with the National Labor Relations Board to have Portus's claim ruled bargainable—which meant a look at the books. The owners immediately filed an appeal. The commissioner threatened to fine Portus $500,000 for any more remarks.

"You'll burn in hell before you see the books on any franchise!" the commissioner screamed at Hendrix.

Bobby almost felt sorry for him, he lost it so completely. Robbie Burden hadn't been the same since Dick Conly left Texas. The loss of Dick Conly's genius threatened League stability.

Bobby Hendrix argued that the players had the right to view the books because football was a quasipublic monopoly, like the phone company. That made Burden furious. The commissioner and the rest of the Owners Council got up and left Terry, Bobby, Speedo Smith, the other player reps and the federal mediator alone in the meeting room. The mediator suggested they adjourn until later. Dudley announced that the next player rep vote would probably take the players out on strike. Bobby said privately that they couldn't afford it: There was Union financial problems. Dudley told him not to worry, it was being fixed. The network fishing show in Cozumel was going to bring in big money.

Commissioner Burden knew Hendrix meant it about looking at the books. Bobby knew they were setting up for pay television to take over professional football and that the collective bargaining sessions were the players' only, maybe last, real chance to get information. They were the Information Poor versus the Information Rich.

But Bobby worried about football players; they were greedy and selfish and it would be difficult to sustain a strike. Speedo and several other player reps liked Hendrix's idea of striking only Monday-night games.

"That way," Bobby argued, "you only have to put one team on strike. The other team can go out on the field, ready to play. We pay the striking team, the owners have to pay the other one. It's simple and cheap. But," Bobby warned, "we need to check our own finances before we start talking strike."

Dudley frowned and adjourned the meeting without answering Bobby's questions about the Union finances.

Bobby knew the Union never had enough money. But maybe the Mexico trip and cooperation with the network would *really* bring in some big bucks.

Dudley said it was going to be a good deal for the Union. That had to mean money.

HEADING TO
QUINTANA ROO

BOBBY Hendrix took his wife and two youngest boys fishing in Cozumel. Bobby hadn't told Ginny about the VCO bust out.

The Hendrix family left early for Houston Intercontinental Airport so Ginny could stop by the bank and pick up her diamonds and gold jewelry. It seemed odd to Bobby to take diamonds and gold *out* of your safe-deposit box and *into* Mexico. He let his consternation show a little too much because Ginny said something about it in the car, sitting beside him, her slender legs crossed, fumbling with the catch of the small gold and diamond bracelet that all the wives got for the playoff.

"Are you sure we can afford this?" Ginny asked, sitting back, the bracelet fastened. "Can you afford the time away from the company?"

"Yeah. I need the time away."

The two youngest boys were arguing in the backseat over who got to stand in the middle of the seat. They were four and six years old and fought about everything and swore they never got to do anything.

"I hope Jimmy will be all right." Jimmy, the teen-ager, had elected to stay behind. He had just discovered sex in the form of the seventeen-year-old daughter of the owner of Trans-Texas Energy.

"He'll be fine. Gus adores him. And Jimmy's getting his first steady pussy."

"Hush," Ginny said, and punched his arm.

"Gus will look after him. Teach him to rough it."

Ginny looked at her husband and then out at the Houston skyline.

"We ought to think about this joint venture deal," she said. "Gus is rich, but VCO is *rich*. Not a good match."

Bobby couldn't figure out how to break the news about their loss. Gus had suggested he wait until they returned from the fishing trip.

"They could just suck you under. You have to be careful," she said.

"I don't like to fly and I don't mind admitting it," Bobby changed the subject. "Anybody who thinks that stuffing a couple of hundred total strangers in a tube and shooting them across the Gulf of Mexico is normal ain't normal."

"Just try not to think about it."

Bobby dropped Ginny and the two boys at the airline entrance, found a place to park and wrestled the bags to the terminal.

Ginny loved airports. She used to be with the airlines as a ticket supervisor. She had taken the job when they needed money in Cleveland. She was in her element at the airport. So Bobby took his two young boys while Ginny got the tickets and checked the bags. Bobby watched the boys fight over who sat on his left side. He tried not to think about flying or the money lost down a hole.

"I never get to sit there." Billy, the four-year-old, was crying and pointing at his father's left side where Bobby junior, the six-year-old, was snuggling gleefully. His joy was in direct proportion to his younger brother's misery.

"You can sit there on the way back," Bobby junior said, grinning malevolently. "Can't he, Dad?"

"Yeah, sure," Bobby said, patting Billy's tiny chubby arm and thinking about his financial condition. Now he wished he had left his money in Cleveland real estate.

He was broke and rapidly wearing out.

The team doctor had been giving him increasingly larger doses of Butazolidin and cortisone. He had to take the Bute on Thursday because it made him sick for at least one, sometimes two days. It was a rough drug, used mainly on horses. It sure did knock out that joint pain, though, better than painkillers like codeine or Novocain.

He wanted a shot in the wallet.

"What are you frowning about?" Ginny stood over him, holding their plane tickets. Bobby and Billy were slapping at each other. He grabbed their little hands.

"I'm thinking about whether I can play next year or not," he said, "We'll probably need the money."

"We are getting ready to leave for five days in Cozumel and you want to talk about football. I don't want to hear about football. I don't care. I just want *now*." Ginny sighed and sat down next to Billy, who crawled up in her lap and asked if she liked him or his older brother better. She kissed him absently and ran her hands through his rumpled red hair, straightening it.

"Let's go have a good time, please, Bobby," she pleaded.

"Okay." He smiled and kissed her. "As of now we forget that I'm over forty and an arthritic Union rep and small-time oil man. We are gringo tourists in Mexico, doing a little fishing for the network off the shores of Quintana Roo."

DIXIE FRIED

THE series of five articles by Tommy McNamara ran in the Dallas and Houston papers. The articles were entitled "The League and the Mob." Taylor Rusk bought a paper at the Houston airport.

The government had canceled McNamara's grant to study sleep deprivation in chickens, sending the remaining amphetamine-laced feed and chickens to Texas Garbage Disposal, Inc., a firm owned by the Cobianco brothers. Texas Garbage Disposal, Inc., took a fee for disposing of the chickens, but instead sold them to the Dixie Fried Chicken fast-food chain. For a short time, customers of Dixie Fried Chicken began talking more, sleeping less and finding Dixie Fried Chicken a short-term cure for depression.

Tommy McNamara went to work writing sports.

Taylor Rusk had given him several interviews and introduced him to college and professional players and coaches, helping him establish contacts as a sportswriter. But Tommy made the mistake of writing a column critical of Cyrus Chandler, which cost him access to the Franchise. After that, only the most adventuresome and older players dared talk to Tommy McNamara, limiting him to Taylor, Bobby, Speedo, Screaming Danny Lewis and Ox Wood.

The sports editor said McNamara had lost his objectivity and credibility and gave him two weeks severance pay and bad references. It was, after all, Cyrus Chandler's paper.

That was over a year ago, and Doc Webster had said at the time they were going to be sorry they made the Kinky-Headed Boy mad.

Now, walking into the Houston Intercontinental Airport, Taylor held one piece of that prophecy in his hand. The article was headlined:

TICKET SCALPING AT THE SUPER BOWL
BY TOMMY MCNAMARA

Before Taylor could start the story, his eyes were drawn to another headline farther down the page:

TEXAS TRADES D'HANIS TO LOS ANGELES

The Texas Pistols announced today the trade of veteran guard Simon D'Hanis to Los Angeles for an undisclosed draft choice and an unspecified amount of cash. The club would make no further comment regarding the trade.

A three-year starting offensive guard for the Texas franchise, D'Hanis was injured in the Playoff Bowl against Los Angeles and underwent corrective knee surgery which the Texas team doctor called an unqualified success.

Simon D'Hanis was unavailable for comment.

Taylor folded the paper, stuck it under his arm, picked up his bags and headed for the ticket counter. He knew the trade was to make it difficult for Simon D'Hanis to file an injury grievance against Texas by putting another corporation, the Los Angeles franchise, between Simon and the Pistols. The commissioner and Cyrus Chandler had probably forced Portus in LA to make the trade as part of the beating they were giving him for offering Taylor five million dollars in writing. Simon's betrayal wouldn't be the only price exacted, but it was the first public sign that the full force of the League was being brought to bear on the kid that Doc Webster had gotten to sign the SPC.

Taylor tossed his bags on the scale and gave the ticket agent his name and flight number to feed to the computer. He asked for the No Smoking section as the agent hammered on the terminal keys.

Outside, Speedo Smith got out of a taxi wearing an eggshell linen suit and a white high-crowned Panama with a broad red paisley band set on his delicate head. Speedo carried a big French leather suitcase and matching shoulder bag. The handsome, muscular black man smiled at the whole idea of himself. The tan nose flared and the white teeth showed. He was a beautiful sight.

Taylor looked around the waiting area. Bobby, Ginny and their two youngest boys sat together near the glass wall, looking out onto the plane-lined concrete apron connected to the terminal by umbilical jetways. Aircraft of various sizes and colors taxied in and out of the area. In the distance, planes could be seen taking off and landing in an unending stream. They appeared and quickly disappeared in the dirty white sky.

"There you go, sir," the ticket agent said, stapling the baggage claim checks to Taylor's ticket envelope and inserting the boarding pass. "We'll be boarding in about forty minutes. Have a nice flight."

Taylor stuck the ticket in his jacket pocket and walked over to join the Hendrix family. The two boys were fighting over a candy bar that the older boy had divided unevenly and then eaten down to parity, a deception that did not go unnoticed by the four-year-old.

"I hate you," the four-year-old said.

"We don't hate people," Ginny said quietly. She threaded her arm through her husband's thin freckled one and rested her head on his bony shoulder. The six-year-old retaliated by taking another bite out of the four-year-old's share of the candy. The younger one began to cry.

"Bobby!" Ginny said to the older boy. "I saw that. Now you give both of those pieces to Billy. Right now, mister."

Bobby reluctantly handed the candy over to his younger brother, who responded by sticking his tongue out at him.

"Billy!" Ginny said hopelessly but with force. "You be nice."

"That's not fair." Bobby junior began to cry over his loss of the candy.

"Life's not fair, son," his father said.

"Don't tell him that," Ginny whispered.

Taylor walked up behind them and dropped the newspaper on the bench next to the thin redheaded receiver.

"There's proof that life ain't fair," Taylor said, "and that there are certain people who need hating."

"You shush, Taylor Rusk," Ginny hissed back. "Those boys listen to everything you tell them. Last night Bobby asked me if you and his daddy really killed Hitler."

"What did you tell him?" Taylor eased down beside the couple. The two boys were still busy fighting and hadn't noticed Taylor's arrival.

"I told them the truth: that their daddy and you never killed anybody, including Hitler. I told them that nice people don't kill each other."

"I'll tell them I was just kidding. It was Mussolini."

Ginny Hendrix reached around her husband and punched Taylor

Rusk in the chest. "You'll tell them no such thing, not even as a joke. They don't understand killing."

"Who does?" Bobby Hendrix finally spoke. He took a slender freckled hand and opened the Houston paper to the sports page. Tommy McNamara's headline for part one of his exposé on the League and the Mob glared out in bold type.

Taylor pointed to the article announcing Simon's trade. Hendrix read it quickly.

"He hasn't recovered from that knee surgery yet," Taylor said.

"The doctor said the operation was a success," Ginny noticed.

"That means the doctor got paid," Taylor replied. "I don't think he'll ever recover."

"Then why would LA take him?" Bobby asked.

Taylor pulled the Xerox copy of his Standard Player's Contract that Doc Webster had brought from Canada and tossed it in Hendrix's lap.

"The original's in my safe deposit box," Taylor said.

Hendrix looked the SPC over quickly. He laughed softly and shook his head when he reached the no-cut provisions. "This Portus kid must be a real bozo." He handed Taylor back the contract. "I had heard rumors about this from Kimball. I'll bet the commissioner and Cyrus are shitting bricks. No wonder Dick Conly quit. Somebody is going to have to pay you that money. They won't let you move to LA and they'll want to keep it quiet, but they'll pay," Hendrix laughed softly and shook his head. "They will *have* to pay."

"I'm afraid Simon's part of the quid pro quo," Taylor said, watching as the two boys walked to the glass wall and leaned against it, leaving little chocolate handprints.

"They'll pass him on the physical and then cut him before the season starts," Hendrix said, smiling at his boys. "The commissioner will rule that Los Angeles is responsible and Texas no longer liable because he passed the LA physical. It's standard procedure. I'll tell Dudley about it in Cozumel and see Simon when we get back if he wants to file a grievance."

"He won't," Taylor said. "Simon has hit the wall. I would advise talking to him over the phone."

Hendrix looked at Taylor and raised his eyebrows in question. "Too many of those Russian steroids?"

"Who knows?" Taylor shrugged. "I didn't help him any. I punched him out in the weight room. It was pathetic. He can barely move on that knee."

"I guess not. If *you* punched him out."

"You're talking to the guy who killed Mussolini."

"Uncle Taylor. Uncle Taylor." The two little chocolate-covered boys ran at the quarterback and jumped into his lap, their little pointed knees just missing vital organs. They got chocolate all over his shirt and jacket before giving him kisses and settling each under an arm.

"Momma said you didn't kill Hitler, Uncle Taylor," the six-year-old said. "Tell her how you and Daddy drove the tank to Germany and machine-gunned him when he tried to escape."

As the plane lifted off the ground north of Houston, Speedo Smith sat down next to Taylor Rusk.

"I saw the new general manager," Speedo said. "Your old college roommate. What do you think about him?"

"I think A.D. will be a real pain in the ass. Hopefully Red'll be able to handle him; otherwise there's no telling what will happen. He's a thief and a liar; he is stupid and runs round with gamblers and thugs. . . ." Taylor stopped. "This list is endless."

"Just your regular old general manager," Speedo grinned. "Did you see that we play Denver in exhibition season?"

Taylor nodded.

"Well?" Speedo Smith looked at his quarterback.

"Well what?"

"R. D. Locke is still there." Speedo stared at Taylor. "You do remember the crazy nigger that tried to shoot you during the first training camp?"

"R. D. Locke . . ." Taylor mulled over the name. "How could I forget R. D. Locke?"

"I don't know, Taylor, but those kinds of oversights will most certainly shorten your life span."

They both sat silently and watched smoky, smelly Houston disappear beneath clouds of water and petrochemicals. The plane climbed, then leveled off. They were out over the Gulf of Mexico, heading for the far side of the Caribbean, the Yucatán and the island of Cozumel.

"My great-grandfather, he turned a hundred and ten last week. . . . He was born and raised near Jacksonville and has never been more than ten miles away. His parents came as slaves to East Texas when the Civil War turned after Gettysburg and East Texas was the last stand of the Old South." Speedo smiled. "Last week I went to his birthday party. You ain't never seen so many niggers in your life, Taylor, and all of them descended from *him*. He just sat on the porch of his old shack and rocked and smiled and patted the little babies. He never talked. Everybody else did, but he never talked. I just stood and watched him. Finally he crooked a finger at me and waved everybody else away. He told me that he was proud of me and had seen me play on television and expected me to be the one who brought honor to the family name."

"Smith?" Taylor asked.

"Yeah, I know." Speedo cackled his peculiar laugh. "I thanked him and told him how proud I was to be descended from him and that I was working with Bobby Hendrix and the Players Union to better life for all football players, black and white." Speedo smirked. "Imagine saying that to a man who picked cotton for sixty years as a sharecropper. I *had* to ask him how it felt to be one hundred and ten years old." Speedo imitated the old man's movements and leaned to Rusk's ear, speaking in a whisper, "'Well, son,' he said to me, 'I feel just like a twenty-year-old . . . with something *real bad* wrong.'"

They broke into laughter, Taylor's deep rumbling laugh punctuated by Speedo's high-pitched cackle. They laughed for almost one hundred miles.

"Speedo," Taylor said after they had laughed themselves out, "you be careful with the Union stuff, okay? You already got Dallas pissed off at you and you're still in Texas. It's like Hendrix says: Red Kilroy can only offer so much protection. With A.D. as general manager, anything can happen."

"Don't worry, Taylor, I can take care of myself. Besides, what can they do besides blacklist me, and they already did that."

"I don't know what they can do, Speedo, but Dick Conly was a brilliant man. Add ten points to A. D. Koster's IQ and you have a plant. He's just as dangerous as R. D. Locke."

LITTLE TAYLOR

BUFFY D'HANIS got the kids down for a nap and took the phone off the hook. She slept restlessly, fearfully, and awoke near dark in a sweat, deeply frightened, breathing hard, her heart thumping against her ribs. She did not recall a nightmare or frightening dream . . . just a free-floating terror . . . night terrors. She touched the bruise on her cheek and lay scared, waiting for Simon to return from another fruitless day of raging and straining to rehabilitate his ruined knee. She gave up trying to talk to him about it and just hoped he worked himself to exhaustion and quickly fell asleep when he returned.

She heard a small cry, then a wail, echo through the small Park City apartment. Simon Taylor D'Hanis had awakened from his nap and was hungry, and Buffy's breasts were withered and dry. The small boy's squall was a ringing accusation rebounding off the walls.

Buffy dragged herself from bed and stumbled into the kitchen to start the bottle warmer, then straightened her shoulders, pasted a smile across her face and went into the baby's room. The little boy lay on his back and wailed in hurt and fear. The sound caused Buffy physical pain and she picked up the baby to try to soothe him.

"There, there, little Taylor, Momma's here." She sat down in the white wicker rocker and cooed to her youngest child, hoping he wouldn't wake the others. She wasn't sure she could deal with them all. "There now, Taylor, everything's going to be all right." She held him against her dry breasts and rocked. "There, there, Taylor . . . there, there." She started to hum a song when she heard the timer on the bottle warmer go off. She walked into the kitchen, cuddling and talking to the baby boy.

"There, there, little Taylor, Momma's got a bottle for you." She shook a few drops against her wrist, then popped the nipple into his searching mouth. He sucked contentedly and Buffy walked back to the rocking chair.

"Little Taylor . . . there . . . there . . . Taylor . . . there . . . there . . ." Buffy drifted off continuing to drone comfort to the baby in her arms. "There . . . there . . . Taylor . . ." A noise at the bedroom door jerked her awake. Simon stood there, glaring at her. His face was red, flushed, his eyes bloodshot.

"His goddam name is Simon. Taylor Rusk just got my ass traded to LA," the giant man yelled, and then disappeared down the hall. Buffy's stomach knotted up. The baby began to cry. A door slammed down the hall and the other children woke up, crying and scared. The baby began to spit up the formula. Buffy cried softly and wiped at the baby's mouth with a diaper. She could hear glass breaking in their bedroom as Simon broke the dresser mirror with his fist.

THE ZEUGLODON

KIMBALL Adams was waiting at the Cozumel airport with two VW vans and four Mayan Indians to carry the luggage. They drove quickly from the airport, turning north when they reached the downtown waterfront. The road was little more than a single lane of concrete or asphalt, depending on the materials available. The vans roared north at top speed, dodging the *turistas* in the striped and fringe-topped Jeeps. They hurtled up the newly constructed road until it abruptly ended.

A dark man waved the vans to a halt with a small red flag where a slow-moving construction gang labored with the most primitive of implements. The lead van screeched and squalled to a stop, and the second van bumped it slightly. The swarthy, sullen Mayans worked in the hot Caribbean sun, prying rocks up with wrecking bars, pickaxes and shovels. They smoothed out the roadbed with sand shoveled from a big pile and leveled it with a two-by-six board with handles nailed at each end. The pavement was mixed in a small portable cement mixer. The road-building process was purposely slow to keep people employed. Modern machinery was neither wanted nor needed.

While they waited for the Mayan flag man to wave them through, Kimball turned from the front seat.

"There's no unemployment on the island," he said to Bobby and Ginny Hendrix. Taylor and Speedo sat in the far back of the van with the two Hendrix boys. The second van carried the luggage. "If a guy loses his job, they throw him off the island. The mayor says it's better than paying welfare and they have no crime."

"Depends on your definition of crime," Speedo said.

An explosion suddenly lifted the van off the ground and tossed the occupants around like rag dolls. Rocks and dirt rained down on them. Ginny and Kimball both screamed while Speedo and Taylor dove on top of the small boys.

"What the fuck was that?" Hendrix yelled.

"Dynamite," the driver said laconically. He pointed at a gaping hole smoking in the center of the roadbed about fifteen feet in front of them. "All rock, very hard. Sometimes use dynamite for big rock."

The young Hendrix boys squealed and laughed after the first moments of shock.

"That's just how we got Hitler, boys," Taylor whispered to them as he crawled back to his seat. Speedo's mouth hung open, eyes wide.

The driver steered around the fuming hole and continued north on the unfinished road, which ended at a tall white hotel sprawled out to the water's edge. The beach sand was white and the Caribbean rippled a cobalt blue.

The van lurched to a stop in front of the hotel.

The Hendrix boys piled out first and ran screaming through the hotel lobby out to the pool area and the beach beyond.

While the Mexican drivers alternately unloaded the luggage and held their hands out for tips, Kimball excused himself.

"I have to call downtown and tell them you have arrived." Kimball disappeared into the hotel lobby.

Ginny quickly pursued her children to the beach to make sure they didn't drown one another. Taylor and Bobby crossed the marble lobby floor to the registration desk, leaving Speedo to deal with the drivers and bellboys, all of whom acted as if they had never seen a black man before.

Kimball returned while Bobby and Taylor were signing the register.

"The phones are out," Kimball announced. "The road crew blew down a telephone pole earlier today. Everybody else is staying at one of the downtown hotels near the harbor. You're the last ones to arrive. They've been scouting out the fishing for the last few days. It hasn't been too good around the island and they're thinking about going to a place on the mainland. Bobby, why don't you come with me and we'll find out what's happening. We'll leave Fresh Meat in charge here. Okay, Taylor?"

Taylor nodded and finished filling out his registration form.

Hendrix paused a moment, looking out toward the beach and his wife and kids. "Keep an eye on them, will you, Taylor?" the tall, thin receiver asked. "Tell 'em I'll see them in a little while. We might as well get this show on the road."

"Don't worry, Bobby, I'll look after them," Taylor said, listing his occupation as quarterback on the registration form, just to see what the grinning desk clerk did with the information. "Say hello to Dudley for me." Taylor Rusk signed his registration card. "And push Charlie Stillman overboard the first chance you get."

Kimball and Hendrix had reached the door, but Taylor could hear his redheaded friend laugh. Then Bobby clenched his fist and held it over his head. Though he didn't turn around, Taylor knew he was smiling.

GINNY AND THE BOYS

SPEEDO Smith walked up to the desk, pushing a wad of bills back in his pocket. "Where are they going?"

"Downtown to get the itinerary," Taylor replied. "Come on, I already signed you in." He tossed Speedo his room key and grabbed up two others, his and Hendrix's.

"Thanks." Speedo snatched the key out of the air. "I'm going up to my room and vomit, then I think I'll take a nap." He stripped out of his linen jacket and held out his muscular coal-black arms for Taylor's inspection. "Then tomorrow I'll work on my tan." Speedo walked over to the winding staircase that led to his second-floor room, which overlooked the brilliant blue sea. Taylor walked outside, stopped at the bar by the pool and bought two Cokes and two tall glasses of planter's punch.

Taylor handed Ginny a tall glass and set the Cokes on the rock next to her. She was watching the boys, who had shucked their clothes and were splashing around in their underwear.

"Where's Bobby?" Ginny asked without taking her eyes off the boys.

"He went off with Kimball."

"Damn!" Ginny sipped on her drink, then set her glass next to the Cokes. "I hate Kimball Adams. Can you believe Bobby wanted to name one of our boys after him?"

"Kimball isn't so bad," Taylor lied, trying to soothe Ginny's obvious discomfort. "He's from the Old League."

"Bullshit," Ginny said. "He's from under a rock. *Bobby*'s from the Old League. When we were in Cleveland, the gamblers used to take our games off the board about half the time, Kimball was so obvious about shaving points."

"Kimball said nobody ever noticed," Taylor replied.

"Well, everybody always noticed. Shit." Ginny kept her eyes on the two boys wrestling in the Caribbean. Taylor had never heard Ginny swear before. Now, talking about Kimball Adams, she swore continually.

"Bobby's sick," she said.

Taylor looked out at Bobby Hendrix junior. "Maybe you shouldn't have brought him down here."

"Not Bobby junior," she said, "Bobby, my husband and your most dependable receiver. He's real sick. Something about his blood. I don't know exactly; I heard Gus talking about it to the doctor. They found it when he got his physical for the company insurance before they went in on this VCO drilling deal, which I also think is sick if not dead."

"Are you sure?"

"No. I'm not sure about anything. I never have been, but I watch and listen." Ginny sipped her drink and watched her youngest boys in their dripping, sagging underpants. "I've lived in that big River Oaks house most of my life except the time we spent in Cleveland. I can tell when things aren't right under the roof of that house." She took a long, gulping drink. "And things aren't right. Why did he go off with goddam Kimball?"

The six-year-old pushed his younger brother under the water.

"Bobby! You stop that or I'll whip your ass right here in front of everybody," Ginny yelled. The boys were shocked by their mother's cursing outburst; so was Taylor.

"Bobby's such a roughneck," Ginny said. "But then, so is Billy. He worships his brother no matter what he does to him. I can't remember the older boys acting like this . . . but I was younger and stronger then."

"Me too. What's this all about, Ginny? I've never seen you like this."

"I'm sorry, Taylor, it's not your problem."

"It is as long as I'm sitting on this rock. Now, come on, tell me."

Ginny watched her two boys for a while and sipped her drink. The shadow of the hotel crept up behind them. "I think VCO pulled out of the drilling deal with Gus and Bobby, reneged on the dry-hole money and broke them," she said. "Gus and Bobby don't know I know, as if they could keep it from me. I guess they wanted me to enjoy this trip. All I wanted was for Bobby to enjoy the trip and forget about the money, football and the Players Union. I thought he might get to feeling better, but instead goddam Kimball Adams hauls him off the minute we get here." Tears filled her eyes and her hands shook. "And goddam Kimball Adams is up to no good and never has been. If something happens to Bobby, I'll kill Kimball with my bare hands."

"Bobby's a grown man. He can take care of himself."

Ginny turned and glared at Taylor. "I told you he was sick, and one thing I know is that being around Kimball isn't going to make him feel better. It never did. If it hadn't been for Kimball, Bobby wouldn't be near as broken up as he is now. Half the passes Bobby caught, Kimball meant to be intercepted. Bobby's taken enough Butazolidin and cortisone in the last years to kill a horse, and now he's got something wrong with his blood and you tell me not to worry, he's a big boy. Well, if you believe *that*, you are a jerk." Ginny wiped her eyes with the back of her hand. "You can't even claim your own son because Cyrus Chandler won't let you and you tell *me* not to worry."

"How did you know about Randall?"

Ginny shook her head and looked at Taylor. "There aren't any secrets on a football team." She turned away from Taylor, who sat with his mouth hanging open.

"Boys!" Ginny Hendrix yelled. "Boys! Uncle Taylor brought you drinks. Come on out of the water." The two thin brown boys stopped splashing and looked at one another.

"Yippee," they yelled in chorus, and struggled ashore, racing each other to the rock and the waiting glasses of cola. The boys drank greedily.

Ginny looked hard at Taylor Rusk. "Now, tell them that you and their daddy didn't kill Hitler."

TERRY AND
THE NETWORK GUYS

BY nightfall Bobby and Kimball failed to appear and the phones were still out, so Taylor rented a Jeep. He didn't know what he expected to find or how, but it was better than sitting around the hotel.

The Jeep's candy-striped top was down, but it was too much trouble to put it up. The latches had rusted off and baling wire hung from the hooks on the windscreen. The night was warm and the moon was bright. The road was visible without the weak flare of light from the one good headlight.

The road widened into a boulevard as it wound past the harbor, and Taylor slowed to look at the boats at anchor. There were several sleek sailing ships, several big cabin cruisers and a replica of an old Spanish treasure galleon. The harbor was quiet; the only sound was the water slapping against the hulls of the various ships. Taylor sat quietly and thought about Ginny Hendrix, angry and frustrated, alone and a long way from home. Taylor planned to ask Terry Dudley about Harrison H. Harrison, president of VCO and member of Spur. Terry would know; he kept track of those sorts of things.

Taylor was about to start the Jeep when he heard A. D. Koster's voice so plainly and clearly he thought A.D. was standing next to him. But the new general manager was out on the water, talking from the deck of a big cruiser moored near the galleon. Taylor saw the lights but could not make out who else was aboard. A.D. seemed to be doing all the talking.

"Tiny solved the problem this afternoon. I'm certain that's where McNamara was getting his information. Come on, Charlie, we got to get back to town."

Taylor watched the two shadows go over the side of the big cruiser and into a small rowboat. He sat in the Jeep and watched the rowboat creak toward the shore in the full moonlight. When the two men stepped out, Taylor started his Jeep, flipped on his one headlight and roared up next to A.D. and Charlie Stillman.

"Hey, A.D., what you up to?" Taylor said, stopping the Jeep right beside the two startled men. "I see you still aren't careful about who you associate with." Taylor looked toward Charlie Stillman, who was terrified. "A.D., now that you're a general manager, you can't let people see you hanging around with players' agents like Charlie here. The fans will begin to think something's wrong, and the next thing you know, they'll quit believing you and Charlie and the commissioner. And once they quit believing, it's a short drop to where they'll quit watching; then we'll *all* be out of work."

A.D. tried to speak several times before finally regaining his self-control, which had drained away the moment Taylor had roared up in the Jeep, out of the night.

"Taylor. Taylor. I heard you were on the island. Good to see you. Hell of a place, isn't it?"

"It's okay if you like water and rock."

Charlie Stillman started easing away from the Jeep.

"Where you going, Charlie?" Taylor asked.

"Uh . . . I was gonna get the car."

"Good idea," A.D. interrupted. "You go on ahead and I'll ride into town with Taylor. You *are* going into town, aren't you, Taylor?" A.D. began to climb into the Jeep.

"Yeah. I'm going to get Bobby Hendrix," Taylor said. "His wife and kids are waiting for him back at the hotel."

Taylor saw Charlie Stillman grimace, then quickly turn and walk away. A.D. almost lost his grip on the Jeep.

"You haven't seen Bobby, have you, A.D.?" Taylor watched his old roommate's face. It looked set in stone. A.D. fell into the passenger seat and stared straight ahead. He said nothing.

"I asked you if you saw Bobby Hendrix, A.D. He was with Kimball when he left the hotel this afternoon." Taylor nudged A.D. with his elbow. Koster seemed lost in a trance. Taylor nudged him again.

"Ah, no, I haven't seen him, but if he was with Kimball, they're probably with Dudley and the network guys at the hotel. I'll show you the way." A.D. continued to stare through the windscreen. The wind blew warmly off the water and the ships groaned and creaked at their moorings.

"Whose boat were you on out there?" Taylor asked, watching A.D.'s face.

"Ah, friends of Charlie's. I don't know their names." A.D. stared straight ahead. "Come on, let's get going if you want to find your buddy Hendrix."

"Who's Tiny?" Taylor asked. The Jeep was idling roughly. "Tiny Walton?"

"I don't know any Tiny," A.D. said. "Come on, let's go. I got another appointment."

"I thought I heard you say something about Tiny taking care of some problem with McNamara," Taylor said. "Would that be Tommy McNamara, the Kinky-Headed Boy?"

"I don't know what you're talking about." A.D. finally turned and looked Taylor Rusk in the face. Even in the moonlight Taylor could see what he had to see.

"You're lying, A.D."

"Believe what you want, Taylor. Now, either take me to town or I'm gonna get out and hitch a ride." A.D. looked back to the windshield. "If you want to find Hendrix, I can show you Kimball's hotel. I'm sure he's there with Dudley and the network guys, planning tomorrow's shoot. They're planning to go over to the mainland, I hear."

Taylor Rusk let the clutch out slowly and the Jeep lurched ahead.

"Who'd you hear that from, A.D.?"

"Charlie." A.D. looked back at the harbor as they pulled away. "Charlie Stillman told me."

Taylor watched the harbor in the rearview mirror and marked the lights of the cruiser that A.D. had been aboard. "Terry Dudley has gone soft in the head to think he can make deals with Charlie Stillman."

"Stillman got a hell of a deal with the network," A.D. said. "Big bucks, Taylor, big bucks."

"You always liked those big bucks, didn't you?"

"Look who's talking." A.D. laughed. "You and a college professor sucker a kid into signing a five-million-dollar SPC. You don't call that big bucks?"

"Well, you better be careful." Taylor steered the Jeep along the waterfront into town. "You're playing with the big boys now, not forging your dead grandmother's Social Security checks."

"You think you're a big shot now, Taylor?" A.D. suddenly turned angry. "You think your five million is big bucks? It's nickels and dimes. It's nothing. I'll spill that much before I'm through."

"I'll bet you will, A.D." Taylor smiled. "And I bet you get it all over you."

They reached the center of town and the crowded streets. Young people dressed in bright colors, tanned and burned, lined the seawall and filled the shops and restaurants. The traffic had slowed to a crawl; motorcycles, scooters and bikes weaved around cars, exotic new four-wheel-drive trucks, rented Jeeps and ancient taxicabs as they crept along the boulevard.

"That's the hotel over there." A.D. pointed up the street and hopped out of the slow-moving Jeep. "See you later, Taylor. I got other business. Tell Hendrix I said hello." A.D. disappeared quickly into the crowd.

Taylor drove the rattling, rusted Jeep up to the front of the hotel and parked next to the two VW vans that had carried them all from the airport to their hotel. A brown man in a uniform walked over with his hand out.

Inside, Taylor quickly found the bar and, in the candlelit shadows, could make out the hulk of Terry Dudley surrounded by several smaller figures in odd native garb: the network guys. The network guys huddled around the towering figure of Terry Dudley as if they were searching for warmth and protection.

Taylor walked up to the table and stood behind Terry until one of the network guy looked up.

"Oh, my God." The guy slapped himself in the forehead. Terry turned around and jumped to his feet.

"Jesus! Taylor! How are you?" Dudley hugged him. An unusual greeting. He kept Taylor in his embrace, hugging his arms to his sides. "Goddam, Taylor, we were just trying to get up the nerve to come out there and tell you."

Taylor wriggled free and looked at the upturned faces of the tiny network guys.

"Tell me what?"

"Bobby Hendrix," Dudley said. "He's dead."

ONE MORE
OVER THE MIDDLE

Bobby Hendrix and Kimball Adams rode in the Volkswagen van when they left that afternoon. As the grimy little bus ground away from the white hotel, Bobby craned his neck to catch a last glimpse of his wife and two youngest boys on the beach beyond the pool; the boys already in their underwear and running full blast into the gentle blue-green surf. He hoped Ginny was watching them and laughed at his worries. She raised and took care of all four of the boys—five, including him.

Bobby Hendrix was often awed by the complexity, reality and mortality of his life, his wife and four boys. The Hendrix family. Six human beings bound in life and death to past and future, yet always now, making their way in the universe.

During his childhood Bobby Hendrix learned about the myths, the fears and the broken dreams of the Great Depression in the stories that his parents carried to the dinner table. The horror of poverty. The humiliation of unemployment. The lost dream of a marketable craft.

Tales of struggle and defeat.

To avoid the humiliation of poverty, Bobby's father had advised him to get "a good, steady job, even if you hate it . . . hire on with the government or a big corporation with good insurance and a pension program, put in your thirty years and then get out."

Bobby's parents both retired after thirty hardworking years, thirty years of fear. The Depression hovered over them the way the bomb kept Bobby's generation at bay.

They grew old as gracefully as one can on a pension. "So we won't be a burden on you children," his mother always said. They had kept their end of the long-term promise to a faceless bureaucracy.

Bobby would never do it. His father couldn't believe he made his living playing football.

"Better get a real job," he'd say.

"I don't want to be a millionaire, Pop," Bobby would say back. "I just want to live like one."

What his parents' Depression folktales taught Bobby Hendrix was that people survived. No matter how greedy the corporations or foolish the government or crazed the individuals, humans survived and some carried the spark of a just life—of decency, spirit, myth and dreams—to the next generation.

"It's always been Ginny's job," Bobby spoke half aloud.

"Huh?" Kimball was smoking a cigar and talking to the driver in Spanish. "What did you say?" The roar and rattle, the bounce and lurch, of the German van being maltreated by the Mexican driver on the rather casual road made hearing difficult. The van bounced violently and jerked from side to side, dodging, weaving.

"I was just thinking about my family," Hendrix said loudly. "I always assumed I would get to spend time with them later."

"Christ. You spend a lot of time with your family." Kimball puffed on his cigar and yelled in Spanish at the driver. "I couldn't spend that much time with a wife and kids," Kimball said. "It would drive me out of my mind."

The driver made a hard right onto the airport road.

"Hey, Kimball, he missed," Hendrix said. "I thought town was straight ahead."

"It is." Kimball looked at his aging, freckled, redhaired friend. "I told the driver to take us to the airport. Now, just give me a chance to explain. . . ."

"I'm not getting on a plane." Hendrix wasn't surprised by the old quarterback's deception. It was what made Kimball Adams a good leader. Deception. He had done it before; sometimes Hendrix had gone along and sometimes he had refused.

"You know I hate airplanes, Kimball, and I just got off one. You're wasting gasoline, taking me to the airport."

"Gas don't cost nothing down here," Kimball said. "Government owns the oil companies. I knew I'd never get you away from the hotel if I told you where we were going."

"You mean the phone wasn't even out?"

"The phone *was* out," Kimball explained. "That's why we have to go to the airport instead of the hotel. The flight isn't definite and I was supposed to call Charlie Stillman at his hotel and check the status. He's the producer on this thing."

"Well, let's go to the hotel first."

"Can't."

"Why not?"

"We're losing the light." Kimball pointed out the window at the countryside flying by. "They want to shoot some film of the ruins at Tulum."

"Whoa!" Bobby protested. "That's over on the mainland. That's the Yucatán. I don't want to go to the Yucatán."

"That's why we go to the airport. If the trip is on, the network guys'll want to leave immediately to get over there in time to shoot some film." Kimball paused and puffed a long time on his cigar, acting as if the matter was settled.

"I'm not going on any plane." Bobby shook his head.

"It's just a short hop." Kimball pointed vaguely in a direction with his cigar. "You'll love it."

"I'll hate it."

"Please, Bobby," Kimball pleaded. "It could be a good deal for me with the network."

"Geeezzz . . . Kimball . . ." Bobby didn't want to fly, signaling Kimball he wanted out with his whine, but Kimball didn't back down.

"Look, most likely we'll get there and Charlie Stillman won't; then the flight is off and we go back to your hotel."

"But what if Stillman is there?"

"Then I'm asking you as a favor to me to get in the plane, fly up into the blue and take the pictures." Kimball faced Hendrix. The old quarterback's nose was swollen and reddened from drink; tiny blood vessels had shattered across his cheeks beneath the red-rimmed, rheumy eyes. "I *need* the favor, Bobby. The network guys mean a lot of money to me. They book a lot of trips and they can book through me. Charlie Stillman's in their pockets up to his armpits and he asked me to talk you into flying there today. You'll shoot some film flying over the ruins, spend the night and shoot fishing footage tomorrow. It's only for one night. Charlie says they need you over there tonight with Terry Dudley. It would be a big favor to me." Kimball concluded his heavy plea: "What are friends for?"

Bobby exhaled loudly. "Are they already over there?"

"Yeah, yeah," Kimball pressed, sensing Bobby's weakening resolve. "Look, Bobby"—he kept the pressure on—"Stillman says the network guys'll do business with me if I can perform for them, and I think this is the kind of thing they'll remember: me delivering you on schedule to help them out of a bind. They're all assholes, Bobby, but I can't refuse to do business with assholes or I wouldn't have any business at all."

Bobby frowned at his long-time teammate and friend. "I can remember when you spit on Charlie Stillman."

"I remember when I spit on Mean Joe Greene too." Kimball Adams grinned and rasped his raucous, evil laugh. "I never made that mistake again. I'm trying not to make this one at all. I don't like Charlie Stillman either, but damn, man—"

"Give it a rest, Kimball," Bobby interrupted. "Let me think." Thoughtfully Hendrix stared out the side window; finally his eyes cut back to Kimball and his freckled face split wide, showing good teeth and some gold. "I guess watching Mean Joe chase you all over the field that afternoon was one of the *real funny* things I have ever seen." Bobby began to laugh.

"Does that mean my old target's come through again? You'll go?" Kimball leaned over and took his arm.

"I'd rather not be thought of as a target anymore," Bobby said. "But I guess I can fly over to the Yucatán. Let's hope Stillman fails to come through as usual. I don't even have the right clothes."

"They got brand-name stuff over there to wear on camera." Kimball reached into his shirt pocket and pulled out a toothbrush and a comb and a small tube of Crest. "I brought this for you. You'll only be there overnight. You'll fish in the morning, then they'll fly you back tomorrow and pick up Fresh Meat Rusk."

"Okay, Kimball, you call Ginny." Bobby reluctantly stuffed the toilet items in his shirt. "If I never see Charlie Stillman, it's too soon."

"He probably won't even be there." Kimball relaxed. "This will all be a false alarm."

Charlie Stillman was waiting outside the terminal. He wasn't hard to spot in his white shirt and shorts and white straw hat, chainsmoking, pacing up and down the pavement. His skinny white legs lacked muscle tone and his walk was a controlled stumble.

The VW pulled up and Kimball and Bobby got out.

"Come on, boys, we're losing the light," Stillman said. Charlie sent a boy scampering ahead through the small terminal and out onto the runway apron, where a blue and white twin-engine plane waited. The boy yelled at the pilot, who quickly began his preflight check.

The heavy man sitting in the shade of the wing lifted the sixteen-millimeter Arriflex camera and climbed into the plane through the huge gap left where the door had been removed.

"Where's the door?" Bobby slowed his pace.

"They took it off to give the cameraman a better field of vision to shoot," Stillman said, climbing in ahead of Bobby and taking the copilot's seat. The thick man with the camera took the seat farthest from the opening, leaving Bobby Hendrix the seat next to the door.

"Come on, we have to hurry," Stillman said to Kimball, leaving it to him to prod Bobby Hendrix into the plane.

"You sit there by the door, Bobby," Stillman said. "That way you'll be in the pictures of the Tulum ruins. Crank it up, Gonzolo." Stillman made a twirling motion with his finger.

"Damn, Bobby, I didn't know they were gonna make you ride on the outside." Kimball helped him into his seat by the open doorway. "Hey, Stillman, why don't you ride here? Bobby ain't that crazy about flying."

"We want *him* in the film, Kimball." Stillman was curt, rude. The pilot turned over the port engine. It roared quickly to life. "The network guys want faces, famous faces, not pretty pictures of old rock buildings." Stillman turned around and asked Bobby, "You ever see the ruins at Tulum?"

Bobby shook his head. The starboard engine growled to life, blasting Kimball Adams with air. The plane lurched forward and Kimball was quickly left behind.

Bobby considered jumping out of the plane, but the runway pavement was flashing by. Bobby tightened up his seat belt and looked over at the fat cameraman, who looked vaguely familiar. He wore dark glasses, baggy white pants and a red and yellow floral-print shirt.

The frightened, arthritic, aging receiver smiled and nodded at the man behind the glasses, who was holding the big black Arriflex across his lap. The man smiled and nodded.

"I'm Bobby Hendrix." The slender, freckled man extended his hand. His stiff red hair whipped his face and neck as the wind ripped through it. They shook hands. Bobby was certain he had seen the man before.

"Just call me Tiny," the cameraman yelled over the roar of engines and wind.

The runway flashed beside Bobby Hendrix, then the plane lifted off. The island quickly fell away and there was nothing beside him but the sky.

Cars, vans, trucks and Jeeps became toys and people turned to insects. Hotels looked like whitewashed alphabet blocks. They were quickly out over the spectacular blue-green Caribbean sea. The water's tones and shades varied with the sky and the contour of the reef and coral. A giant stingray was flying through the crystal-clear water. The bottom sank from sight, the water turned a deep, dark blue and the Caribbean was a profound sapphire.

The Yucatán peninsula loomed ahead; the ruins of the ninth-century Mayan city of Tulum stood gray and brooding at the ocean's edge.

The photographer spoke to the pilot in Spanish.

Gonzolo, the pilot, put the plane into a tight turn, and Bobby could see *turistas* scrambling over the ancient ruins like ants. The plane swung in over the jungle and then back out over the ocean. The photographer yelled more instructions, making hand signals for the tighter, steeper turn.

Grown over, Tulum was a good-size Mayan city, and Bobby could see where the white bones of exterior city walls stuck up farther out in the jungle, up along the coast and inland.

The pilot began another tight turn over the ruins. The photographer held the camera to his eye and leaned toward the door.

Bobby could feel the force of gravity pulling and sucking him toward the open door and the temple five hundred feet below. He held on tightly to his seat back and eased the strain on his seat belt. He wouldn't depend on the belt to keep him inside the plane.

Holding the big camera, the cameraman leaned fearlessly toward the open door, trusting his seat belt totally. The pilot turned even tighter. The engines roared and the airplane was up on its side.

"Goddammit," the cameraman yelled, "the son of a bitch is jammed." He looked quickly around, then held the big heavy Arriflex out to Bobby. "Here, hold this for a second, would you please?"

The camera thrust into his chest, Bobby automatically turned loose of the seat back and grabbed it.

The photographer let go.

Bobby Hendrix felt the camera's weight pull him toward the open, sucking door. Bobby's seat belt groaned, creaked and strained. He could not hold the big Arriflex long. It was too heavy, the angle of the airplane's bank too steep.

Bobby strained to hand the camera back as the cameraman leaned toward him. Then the large man reached out with one hand and flipped the latch on Bobby's seat belt, while his other hand gave Bobby a hard shove.

The big black Arriflex sixteen-millimeter and Bobby Hendrix sailed out of the plane and into the white silence of free fall.

It took a long time to fall.

It took the rest of Bobby Hendrix's life.

A FULL
FIVE HUNDRED FEET

BOBBY HENDRIX certainly hadn't expected to die this way. That was his first thought.

His next thought was a simple acceptance of the end: he was soon to become ill-defined.

He made a speed of light decision to make it a full five hundred feet of life and did not waste time on screaming or any other distracting activity.

The quick ease of this decision was due to his knowledge of the seriousness of the blood disease discovered in his insurance physical; it would have killed him in another eighteen months to two years. So he reduced eighteen months to five hundred feet at thirty-two feet per second and found the difference a metaphysical question that was pointless to consider, since he had already been pushed out of the plane.

He wondered why.

Who wanted him dead?

Kimball? Charlie Stillman? The Cobianco brothers? Had someone decided Kimball Adams had talked to him too much? Was this union trouble?

He knew it was all of those and none of them.

He knew it didn't matter.

His death was somebody's desire for a neat solution to a complex question.

A pretty primitive solution, Bobby thought, seeing the ancient altar of the sun rushing up to smash him to pulp.

Then Bobby Hendrix realized it was supposed to be.

MEANWHILE,
BACK AT THE RANCH...

INSIDE the Hot Springs Ranch house the phone rang. Outside, Suzy and Cyrus were walking up from the hot springs. Wearing identical sandals, they both had their hair wrapped in blue towels and wore blue terry-cloth robes. They were about the same size, and to the nearsighted wetback who answered the phone they looked identical.

"*Señora*..." The maid held out the phone; Suzy strode quickly over and snatched it up to her ear. She knew who it would be.

Cyrus admired his young girl friend. Her taut nude body had excited him down at the hot springs, but after the walk up the hill he was too tired to do anything. It had been a nice experience while it lasted. While Suzy talked on the phone, Cyrus decided to buy a golf cart for trips back and forth to the Indian hot springs.

The Hot Springs Ranch was one of the best swaps Cyrus Chandler's daddy ever made. He swapped five thousand acres of leases, expected to be the middle of the biggest oil play since the East Texas field. The oil play turned out to be five wells that pumped two barrels of salt water for every one of oil, while the ranch covered 507,000 acres and fronted on thirty-five miles of the Rio Grande and some of its more spectacular canyons. Cyrus's daddy had made a good trade.

The international operator left the line; Suzy turned and grinned widely at the old man. "Go ahead, sir." The international operator returned to the line.

"Suzy?" It was a weak, shaky voice.

"Yes," she said, smiling to Cyrus and pursing a kiss on her lips.

"Bobby Hendrix is dead." A.D.'s voice cracked. He couldn't say it fast enough.

Suzy looked at her nails and decided that they needed a manicure before she and Cyrus flew in to Presidio to a party to meet some Mexican nationals. They were friends of the Cobiancos and wanted to discuss export/import. Cyrus's divorce was going through quickly; Junie had found a decorator she wanted to marry.

"Well?" A.D.'s quavering voice crackled with static.

"That's fine. Bye-bye." Suzy hung up, picturing A.D. coming out of a phone booth, looking like Peter Lorre in some dismal foreign country, covered with sweat and flies. She laughed and walked to Cyrus, who stared out at the distant mountains.

"Who was that?" Cyrus didn't turn away from the glass wall and the spectacular view.

"Girl talk." Suzy walked up behind him, wrapping her arms around him. She lay her head on his blue terry-cloth shoulder. "What a nice stomach you have, Mr. Chandler." She left the comparison to Dick Conly's hard, protruding abdomen unsaid but understood.

Dick Conly would have quickly ferreted A.D. out of that phone call and drawn his connection to events in Mexico. But Conly was up somewhere in the Pecos Mountains sitting on a pile of Mexican gold pieces. Cyrus Chandler merely wondered how to ship a golf cart to far Southwest Texas for a good price.

THE EMPEROR OF
THE WESTERN HEMISPHERE

TAYLOR Rusk and Terry Dudley were the last two left in the hotel bar, very drunk on many double Herradura Silver tequilas on the rocks. The network guys had all disappeared, first coming by the table, nodding their individual little heads at Taylor and asking Terry, "Is he okay?"

"Yeah, he's okay," the seven-foot man answered each time, weaving in his seat and nodding at Taylor.

"Are *you* okay?" the network guys would then ask the totally drunk union director, whose upper-body wobble was quite noticeable.

"Yeah," Taylor Rusk growled at them. "He's okay."

When all the network guys were gone and the tequila was almost gone, Taylor looked at Terry Dudley and said, "They killed him."

"Who?" Dudley was skeptical.

"I don't know who and I don't know why, but I do know they killed him, Terry. Bobby wouldn't go anywhere with Charlie Stillman, especially on an airplane. He hated airplanes almost as much as he hated Charlie Stillman, which is as much as *I* hate Charlie Stillman." When Terry didn't answer, Taylor asked, "So what do we do now?"

"Cancel the show and get quickly and quietly out of town. There's nothing we can do for Hendrix. The network's already been in contact with the embassy and the consul. We can clear Bobby's body through at Mérida, which may not sound like a big deal, but it gets complicated when a man enters Mexico alive in Cozumel and tries to leave dead from the Yucatán."

The waiter relentlessly replaced the empty glasses in front of the two big men, who relentlessly emptied them of tequila and banged them down on the wooden tabletop. Taylor drank several glasses in silence. Thinking. Wondering.

"What do you know about Harrison H. Harrison?" he finally asked Dudley.

"Harrison H. Harrison was a '39 graduate of the University with a degree in geology," Dudley rattled off. "Spent a while wildcatting in South America and Libya, screwed around helping to get a Republican party going in Texas. He had mixed success, mostly around the big rich cities like Houston, Dallas, Midland and Tyler. Then he went to work for his daddy at Venture Capital Offshore. The family is centered in New York. He is presently president and CEO of VCO, a company that specializes in putting together offshore joint venture deals."

Taylor was amazed by Dudley. "Why and how do you know all that?"

"He belonged to Spur in '39," Terry Dudley answered quickly and surely. "I keep track of everybody who was ever in Spur unless they're dead or listed as missing in action." Dudley laughed in a series of hisses that convulsed his shoulders and head. "It's a big organization, Taylor. Did you ever keep up with any of the guys that were in Spur with us?"

"The ten top onions?" Taylor's eyes were red. "Not really. I see some names pop up in the news, like yours and mine. That's all."

"That was what it was for, you know, Taylor?"

"What?"

"Spur," the seven-foot man continued. "Making and maintaining contacts with smart, ambitious, motivated people from your university. The whole *idea* is to stay in contact, to communicate consistent goals and plans for the future, not just to our generation or college but to all Texans and all Americans. We have powerful members, influential, like Harrison, Senator Thompson, the governor, Cyrus Chandler . . . the list goes on. The initiation just began that night at the Tower, Taylor. It continues for years, hopefully for generations . . ."

"Terry?" Taylor interrupted, "are you trying to tell me that there is an old-boy system?"

"It's more than just an old-boy network, for God's sake. It's a long-term plan and you were asked to *be* part of it. You can *still* be part of it. Once a person's been taken into Spur, he only loses his membership when he dies."

Taylor Rusk shook his head. "List me among the missing."

Terry Dudley hunched his huge frame over the table, pushing his long, melancholy face next to Taylor's. "I'm going into politics, Taylor. Finish up the Union work, do some network television, get good name exposure . . . but I've got to be careful. First I'll run for San Antonio mayor, then a statewide office—maybe railroad commissioner." Terry leaned back and locked his long fingers behind his head. His arms jutted out like giant wings. "A couple of years regulating the oil companies on the railroad commission will give me enough in campaign contributions to run for governor or the US Senate . . ."

"Then president," Taylor interrupted, "and finally election for life as emperor of the Western Hemisphere."

"I'm tall enough to be emperor."

"How did you ever get tied up with Charlie Stillman?" Taylor wanted to know.

"He brought the deal to me. The network package. Everything." Terry shook his head. "I know you don't like him. Hell, *I* don't like him, but it's goddam big bucks they're paying, and they are paying today. We need TV exposure and the money."

"If you are ever going to be emperor."

"Well," Terry Dudley announced, banging his empty glass, "I am steering my course for the biggest spectator sport of all: politics." Terry's eyes twinkled in a sudden rush of humor. "And Spur has paid off in real-world contacts."

"What real world? Hendrix is dead and the show's canceled."

Taylor stared at Terry. "You should be very nervous with the idea that Bobby Hendrix just happened to fall out of an airplane during labor-management talks," he said. "You better be prepared, because if you're wrong about Charlie Stillman or the network, you could be *dead* wrong." Taylor stood and stretched. "Now I've got to go tell a woman and two little boys that Daddy isn't ever coming home again."

Taylor left the bar to tell Ginny Hendrix the awful news.

Terry Dudley, his body scrunched into a tiny straight-backed wooden chair, watched his old college friend leave, then signaled the waiter for another double Herradura on the rocks. He drank alone until the bar closed, then went to his room.

Tapping a gram bottle on the dresser, the seven-foot Union director used a matchbook cover to scrape some white powder into two thick lines about two inches long. He quickly snorted the lines into his sinus cavities through a bar straw, wiped the white residue off the dresser top with a big bony finger and rubbed it on his gums.

He pulled a chair up to the window facing the dark ocean and, drinking from the tequila bottle in his lap, sat all night listening to the Caribbean, wondering about Bobby Hendrix and dreaming of being emperor of the Western Hemisphere.

KIMBALL AWASH

DRIVING back to his hotel, Taylor stopped at the harbor, turning the rented topless Jeep so the one pitiful headlight shone across the water to the big cruiser that A.D. and Charlie Stillman had been aboard earlier in the evening.

The weak yellow light of the headlight dribbled across the water's surface, fading quickly. Taylor pulled forward until the Jeep was at the breakwater's edge, the front wheels dangerously close to rolling off the concrete. It was a twenty-foot drop to the ocean. The headlight flickered at the back of the boat, the roll of ocean putting the black painted name momentarily in the yellow beam, then snatching it away again. The big cruiser bobbed up and down. Slowly the word on the stern rebounded in the light to Taylor Rusk's tequila-addled brain. It was such a simple name.

Momma, it read, *Corpus Christi, Texas.*
Momma. Corpus Christi. The body of Christ.

That night Taylor again told the two young boys about how he and Bobby had driven a tank from Texas to Germany to kill Hitler, stopping in Rome to kill Mussolini, then driving to New York and Washington to punch out the military-industrial complex.

Smiling peacefully, Bobby and Billy fell asleep as Uncle Taylor got to the part in the story where he and the boys' dad and mom came back from the war and decided to invent football.

Anytime that night, when Bobby or Billy would ask a question—like "Who was Mussolini?"—Uncle Taylor told them to ask their mother. Later.

Down on the dark beach, several hundred yards from the hotel, Ginny Hendrix was crying and screaming their father's name into the warm Caribbean wind. The slight breeze and surf drowned her cry completely. She knew she was screaming. She could feel the vibrations in her jawbone, the pain in her throat.

The next morning a hoarse Ginny Hendrix told the boys that their father was dead and gone.

Taylor ended up with a greater respect for the network guys by the time twenty-four hours had passed.

They showed up for Ginny and the boys at noon in the only clean black Cadillac four-door on the island. They wore business suits and took care of business. They knew how to be executives. They comforted the widow and orphans while every other son of a bitch in that hotel jumped when they snapped an order.

Overnight they had contacted Gus Savas in Houston and had taken him by private jet to Mérida, where he was with Bobby's remains, waiting for his daughter and grandchildren to join him. Then the private jet would depart immediately for Houston. Normal customs and INS rituals had been waived by both governments.

The network guys were great at getting a dead man quietly out of Mexico, Taylor thought as he watched them hydroplane away from the hotel.

On the other hand, Taylor couldn't get *himself* out of the country. So he went looking for Kimball Adams.

"It was your travel agency that booked these tickets," Taylor said to the ex-quarterback when he found him two days later in a rundown bar south of town. "They won't honor the ticket, Kimball. The airline says you paid with a revoked credit card." Taylor waved the plane ticket.

Kimball did not appear to be listening or, for that matter, conscious. Taylor Rusk knew from past experience that Kimball was both conscious *and* listening. Kimball Adams had been drunk and awake since he heard that Bobby Hendrix had fallen out of the very plane Kimball had talked him into.

Kimball Adams was glad to talk about anything that could take his mind off the awful vision he had of what his ambition had created and destroyed. Anything. Talk about anything else. The expired credit card or about a game when he shaved points or the time he threw the interception and then blocked Ox Wood. Kimball would talk about anything to get his mind off Hendrix . . . about how in the old days Ox always liked for him to put his cigarettes out on his tongue or about how, when he came to the Pistols, Red Kilroy picked Kimball out as a cheater and gave him two years to make Taylor Rusk the Franchise.

"You were sure Fresh Meat then, kid." Kimball laughed and smiled. "You had a real godfather in Red; in the Old League we'd a chewed you up and spit you out."

"It isn't the Old League anymore, Kimball."

"Don't I know it." Kimball grinned, his false teeth too white, too large.

"I want to go home," Taylor said, tapping his fingernail on the red and white airline ticket.

"Jesus, man," Kimball pleaded, "don't leave me here alone. Your pal Dudley is gone, Stillman and the network guys are gone. The sons-a-bitches. Don't leave yet. I want somebody to talk to." Kimball's face was dirty, unshaven, sweat- and tear-streaked. His eyes were red. Talking as fast as he could and smelling like alcohol, sweat, piss and fear. "The lousy bastards tell me it will be my big break in the travel agency business and then take my best friend up and drop him smooth out of the fucking plane. There wasn't even no door on the son of a bitch, Taylor. No fucking door. Your typical goddam Mexican operation."

Several dark-skinned men in the bar turned toward Kimball when he spit out the word *Mexican* with such obvious distaste. Kimball just glared back at them with the same crazed eyes that had frightened bigger, stronger, even smarter, men to that moment's hesitation that is life or death.

"Yeah, I said goddam *Mexican*!" Kimball spit the words again. Quickly now. No doubt. Live or die. Or mind your business.

The brown-skinned men returned quickly to their own pursuits. Perhaps it was the Indians' innate sensitivity toward madmen.

"There wasn't a goddam door on the plane!" Kimball seemed to be pleading. "If I had known they weren't gonna even have a door...I know how scared he gets....Goddam, man, I'm not stupid....I wouldn't have asked him to go....Are you crazy?" Kimball seemed to answer a private inquisitor. "Am *I* crazy?" Kimball was drinking from a quart bottle of gin and crying then, heavy tears running through dirt and stubble. He was wearing a filthy yachting cap with *Momma, Corpus Christi, TX* stitched on the front. "I shouldn't have let him get on that plane. He was so scared. He knew he was gonna die, but he went anyway 'cause I asked him to do it."

It was eleven in the morning. The sun was just beginning to get hot.

Taylor's skin felt clammy.

Kimball brushed at a fly crawling across his lip with the hand that held the bottle. He missed the fly and hit himself in the chin with the gin bottle. The fly flew to the ceiling.

"Why'd you take him to the airport?" Taylor winced at the sound of chin meeting gin bottle.

Kimball shook his head and gathered his thoughts. He had almost knocked himself out. He blinked a few times at Taylor. "Stillman told me the network guys wanted him at the airport and I should deliver him. There wasn't room for me anyway. Stillman took the copilot's seat and the big fat cameraman took up the whole port side of the plane. That left Bobby the seat right by the open door. They wanted him there so he would show up in the film of the Tulum ruins. Assholes, I hope they got their shot."

"You ever talk to the network guys or Terry Dudley?"

Kimball shook his head and sweat rolled from beneath his dirty hairline down the back of his neck. He coughed and hawked and spit on the floor. Then glared the room full of Mexicans down again.

"Nobody ever talked to me about anything except Stillman, and now he's gone." Kimball coughed. "I called his hotel this morning. He checked out yesterday."

"I guess we could call Stillman the producer," Taylor said. "He said he was the producer."

"Stillman gave me the crooked credit card."

"You already knew the credit card was no good?" Taylor asked.

"Fresh Meat"—he looked directly at Taylor—"don't you think I already tried to get off this motherfucking island myself?"

Kimball took a deep swallow of gin and some alcohol dribbled from his mouth, mixing with his tears. "Do I look like a complete fool? I can look in the mirror and see I ain't stupid." Kimball was arguing with his invisible interrogator. "What makes people think I'm so goddam dumb? Just 'cause I'm a football player?"

"It isn't *just* because you're a football player, Kimball." Taylor got up and left the ticket on the table. "But being one sure doesn't help much." Taylor pointed at Kimball's dirty yachting cap. "Whose boat is that in the harbor? *Momma* from Corpus Christi?"

"It belongs to the Cobianco brothers. . . . I don't know how it got here or who's on board."

"You don't want to know, Kimball."

"They trick-fucked me, Fresh Meat," Kimball said. He took off the hat and threw it out the window next to their table.

"I know. And they aren't finished." Taylor turned and walked out into the bright, hot Caribbean sun.

THE MOMMA, CORPUS CHRISTI

TAYLOR drove the rented Jeep north through town, back toward his hotel. The activity along the downtown waterfront had slowed with the midday heat. A few tourists wandered in their bright-colored shirts and shorts, their Japanese cameras strapped across their chests. At the harbor the replica of the Spanish galleon was gone, but the big white cruiser *Momma* was still moored, rolling slightly with the small Caribbean swells.

Taylor stopped and looked at the cruiser. Several people were gathered on the fantail. Taylor left the Jeep and walked across the breakwater to several rowboats. He paid a kid two dollars to row him out to the *Momma* and wait for him.

As they pulled alongside, Taylor could hear happy chatter and laughter. He recognized Wendy Chandler's laugh. There were seven people on the fantail, having drinks, enjoying finger sandwiches and light conversation.

Taylor climbed over the side and the gay chatter stopped. The people turned, staring openmouthed at the big quarterback. Taylor's eyes went from one person to the next until he had identified everyone assembled around the table. Wendy glanced at Taylor for a moment and then turned back to Lem Three, frozen in his deck chair, his mouth agape. On Lem's right was LouElla Burden, wife of the league commissioner, Robbie Burden, who sat at her right. A. D. Koster was next to the commissioner, and next to A.D. was Donald "Mr. C." Cobianco, owner of the *Momma* and the eldest of the three Cobianco brothers. Squirming nervously in his chair next to Mr. C. was Charlie Stillman. Taylor heard shuffling from the lower cabin and Tiny Walton suddenly filled the hatchway, his thick arms folded, his eyes dark and focused on Taylor. The outline of the butt of a .45 automatic stuffed in the waistband of his deck pants showed through his T-shirt.

"I guess you all heard about Bobby Hendrix?" Taylor's eyes moved from face to face but always returned to Wendy Chandler's. She acted like he was not there. Everyone else kept their eyes fastened on the big football player.

"Yes, Taylor." The commissioner found his eloquent voice first. That's why they paid him $500,000 a year to be the commissioner. "It was a tragic accident. Charles, here, was telling us all about it."

"He must tell pretty funny dead-people stories," Taylor said, his eyes still moving. "The way you all were laughing, someone could get the idea that you all were happy about something." He saw movement out of the corner of his eyes and stepped closer to the rail to keep Tiny Walton constantly in his field of vision.

"You come on my boat to make trouble, Mr. Quarterback?" Don Cobianco's voice was even. "I can arrange trouble if you want it." Cobianco's eyes flicked to Tiny, who dropped his thick, sunburned arms to his sides. "You still owe me money on an apartment you rented from me and my brothers when you was a chicken-neck college kid." Cobianco grinned slowly, exposing his big teeth.

"Talk to A.D. about that," Taylor said. "His name was on the lease."

"We already talk." Cobianco's thick fingers dug into A.D.'s neck. He shook A.D.'s head and laughed. Koster winced in pain and his face turned white. "We had a long talk about it, didn't we, A.D.?"

"Yeah." The new Texas general manager tried to grin. "We already had a long talk."

"He said you refused to pay your share." Cobianco looked at Taylor and let go of A.D., who rubbed his neck with both hands.

"Yeah, well, A.D. lies a lot," Taylor said.

"You call your new boss a liar?" Cobianco looked at Taylor in mock amazement and then ran the look around the table past Lem Three and the commissioner. "You don't get far in the world, you call your boss a liar. Isn't that right, Mr. Commissioner?"

Robbie Burden nodded his head slightly but dropped his eyes to the plate of finger sandwiches on the table.

"Yeah, well, the commissioner lies a lot too," Taylor said. "That's why he's the commissioner—"

"Now, see here, Taylor," Lem Three interrupted, "you can't just come aboard this boat and begin insulting people and calling them liars."

"Shut up, Lem," Taylor said. "I'd be real interested in what Tommy McNamara would write in the newspaper about this little meeting here. I'm sure it is just coincidence, but you know those reporters; they have to sell papers." Taylor shook his head. "Dick Conly would never have done something *this* stupid."

"You want I should have Tiny toss you over the side, Mr. Quarterback?" Cobianco said to Taylor.

"Just like he tossed Bobby Hendrix out of the plane?" Taylor shot back. The two women at the table gasped at the accusation. Tiny tensed himself to move; Taylor was watching him, waiting.

"Come on, Taylor, old buddy," A.D. finally said, "that's not funny."

"I'm sure Bobby and his wife and kids would agree with you, A.D.," Taylor replied, "but I wasn't trying to be funny. I was just trying to get things straight."

"You have worn out your welcome here, Mr. Quarterback." Don Cobianco looked over at Tiny, who started his advance on Taylor.

Tiny had to step up from the lower hatchway. He got his lead foot on the deck and was shifting his weight, his hands gripping the hatch side, when Taylor spun and kicked him in the mouth. The heavy man careened over backward into the lower cabin, banging his head on the bulkhead, knocking him unconscious. The blue-steel .45 automatic flew out of his waistband and clanked onto the deck. Taylor picked it up and looked it over. He looked up at A.D. and Cobianco, then to Charlie Stillman. "Was this for Bobby if he refused to believe he could fly, Charlie?"

Stillman squirmed and looked to A.D. for help. A.D. remained silent, his jaw muscles working visibly.

"You better leave while you can, Mr. Quarterback," Cobianco said.

"It's your boat," Taylor said. "Anyone care to go back ashore?" Taylor turned back toward the rail and ladder.

Nobody moved.

Taylor looked slowly around the table.

Suddenly Wendy stood smiling at Lem, who was embarrassed by the whole scene and his inability to deal effectively with it.

"I'll go," Wendy said to Taylor without emotion. "I have some last-minute shopping to do." Wendy looked to the commissioner's wife. "LouElla, come on." Wendy held her slender hand across the table to the small, mousey, foolish woman married to Robbie Burden.

LouElla looked at Robbie Burden. The commissioner looked at Donald Cobianco, who nodded slightly and closed his eyes.

"Sure, dear," Burden began hesitantly. "Yeah, sure, that's a good idea." The commissioner wasn't sure, but Cobianco smiled and nodded again.

Below deck Tiny Walton was moaning loudly as he regained consciousness.

"Well, ladies," Taylor said, "I hate to rush you, but I hear the sounds of Mr. Cobianco's muscle coming awake."

The two women gathered their purses and went over the side, down the ladder and into the rowboat. Taylor Rusk followed them. But first he tossed the .45 into the water.

CONVINCING LEM

"WAS any of what that idiot was spouting true?" Lem pointed at the rowboat carrying his wife, the commissioner's wife and Taylor Rusk.

"It wasn't far off," A.D. said. "But don't worry, nobody'll believe him."

"What do you mean, don't worry?" Robbie Burden, the league commissioner, said. "You didn't actually have Bobby Hendrix killed? Did you? Well, did you?" Burden's carefully nurtured tan began to fade as blood drained from his face.

A.D. rolled his eyes over at Don Cobianco. A.D. exhaled loudly, irritated at the commissioner's simplicity.

"Look, Robbie, we are pretty certain that Hendrix was supplying Tommy McNamara with a lot of the information for those newspaper articles." A.D. lit a cigarette and took a deep drag, pausing to pick tobacco off his lip. "Kimball Adams figured it was probably Bobby."

"Those articles didn't prove anything." Robbie Burden's eyes began to burn with panic. "You didn't kill that boy over those articles."

A.D. exhaled again with exasperation. "What are you complaining about? He was *our* player. Tommy McNamara was close enough to accidentally flip over the wrong rock." A.D. looked directly at the commissioner. "Like your numbered bank account in the Bahamas. So Mr. C. and I decided . . ."

Robbie Burden turned completely white, his lips suddenly looking dry and cracked. He seemed in shock. "Don't tell me any more. I don't want to hear it," the commissioner said. "I'm not involved." Robbie covered his ears and closed his eyes.

"Well," Lem interrupted angrily, "I sure as hell want to know what you two decided. Damn you, A.D. I told Cyrus about you. I warned him."

"Yeah, I know," A.D. sneered at Lem. "And Cyrus told Suzy and Suzy told me. Then I told Suzy some things about you to tell Cyrus, and that's how the cow ate that little turnip. I don't imagine you'll be with the Franchise for the Super Bowl or even the new stadium in Clyde. Damn shame. A guy like you that spent so much time kissing ass."

"Like you with this gangster here?" Lem shot back. "Well, they may not believe Taylor Rusk, but they will believe me and the commissioner. Right, Robbie?" Lem turned to see the commissioner still had his eyes closed and his hands clapped over his ears. "Isn't that right, Robbie?" Lem pulled at one of the commissioner's arms, uncovering an ear.

"I don't want to know. I said I don't want to hear." The commissioner then began humming at the top of his voice until the bewildered Lem turned his arm loose and Robbie clapped his hand back over his uncovered ear.

A.D. laughed. "The commissioner doesn't want to explain his numbered bank account in Freeport or how many Super Bowl tickets he scalped to get the four million dollars deposited and unknown to Internal Revenue."

"Well, ahh..." Lem was momentarily shaken—"they'll still believe me, goddammit. They'll believe me."

"You should think about it a little, Lem." Charlie Stillman spoke for the first time. "As your attorney, I advise you..."

"You are not my attorney, Stillman."

"You should listen to Mr. Stillman. He has advised lots and lots of people on a variety of subjects," Don Cobianco said to Lem without ever taking his eyes off the rowboat, which had reached shore. Taylor Rusk was helping the two women out. "Otherwise, maybe you would listen to Mr. Walton over there, putting the ice on his lip where that chicken-neck quarterback kicked his face in before he left with your wife."

Lem looked around the table. The commissioner's eyes were still closed and his hands were still clasped over his ears. A.D. puffed on his cigarette and looked at his white loafers. Charlie Stillman tried a sympathetic gaze and a nod of the head. Don Cobianco kept his eyes on the three people who had reached shore in the ancient rowboat.

"You can't threaten me," Lem said. "I'm not afraid."

"I was afraid you were going to say that," Cobianco said. He signaled Tiny, who was nursing his smashed face with ice water and a bloody cotton cloth. Tiny dropped the red-soaked cloth and snatched Lem by his long hair backward out of the deck chair and dragged him down below deck.

Lem Carleton III screamed for help. The commissioner kept his eyes closed and ears covered. Charlie Stillman continued to look sympathetic and nod. A. D. Koster puffed on his cigarette and flicked some dirt off one of his Guccis. Don Cobianco watched the three Americans on the beach split up and the commissioner's wife go off alone in the Jeep.

It was less than a quarter of an hour before Lem realized he was afraid after all. The issue was settled. Tiny Walton had not put a mark on Lem's face.

DIVING FOR PESOS

"LouElla, you take the Jeep," Wendy said as they walked up the breakwater. "I want to walk to the T-shirt place and get Randall some; he is outgrowing everything."

Taylor handed the commissioner's wife the keys, and LouElla Burden started the Jeep and rattled off down toward the *zocalillo*.

Taylor and Wendy walked along the waterfront, hot beneath the midday Caribbean sun.

Wendy wore khaki shorts, sandals and a short-sleeved khaki shirt, open at the neck and tied at her midriff. She was naked beneath the green shirt. A bead of sweat ran out of the hollow at her throat between her delicate collarbones and down the tanned skin that separated slightly the soft mounds of her breasts.

Taylor wiped his forehead and tried to tell Wendy the pain he felt without her and Randall, but her presence made language impossible; his sadness was incoherent.

He watched another droplet of sweat make the run down between her breasts. She looked up at him.

"Is it true about Bobby Hendrix?" she asked. "They killed him?"

"Probably doesn't matter anymore. There's no way to prove it." Taylor shrugged. "And not much to gain."

He watched the Houston *turistas* tossing coins off the breakwater for a ten-year-old Mexican boy. The boy dove to retrieve the peso pieces.

"I knew that Bobby Hendrix was always making Cyrus and the commissioner mad with all his union and clubhouse lawyer work," Wendy said, "but I can't believe they'd kill him. I can't believe he's dead," Wendy said slowly. She shivered. "Why would someone kill him?"

"Mistaken stupidity and panic." Taylor wiped his face with his shirt front. "I'll find Tommy McNamara as soon as we get back to Texas. We need to think about moving out." Talking to Wendy about the death was the first time it hit him; danger was quite near and they were in a powerless position.

"The Kinky-Headed Boy?" Wendy asked.

Taylor nodded. "Now he's a sportswriter and he just wrote a

five-part newspaper series called 'The League and the Mob.' My guess is that someone thought Bobby was the source."

"Why?"

"Bobby was in professional football for twenty years. He learned a lot about gambling and ticket scalping and tax dodging schemes. He paid attention. But it was never worth it to him to ever say what he knew. He never talked about it. 'What's the point?' he always said. 'What's the point?'"

Wendy began walking again. Sweat formed on her forehead and upper lip. Her tanned face showed new lines around her eyes as she watched Taylor's face. There were no soft contours any-more. It was a hard face; the years had changed it. It was not handsome but like a wild animal's. Furious eyes, nose flattened, nostrils flared, he looked tired, beaten down, yet somehow stronger, painfully tempered by his struggles.

Taylor rubbed his eyes and watched the brown kid diving for peso pieces thrown by the white-haired Americans into the deep blue water.

"You think Tommy will give you his sources?"

"He'll tell me who it *wasn't*."

He stopped and faced Wendy, studying her thin, straight nose and full lips, her hollow cheeks highly ridged with delicate bone and pale, almost transparent skin. His gaze stopped at her cheek-bones, afraid to meet her blue gaze. He was ashamed, embarrassed.

"What are you looking at?" Wendy asked quietly. "Really, what are you looking at?"

"You. I'm just looking at you. We've got to get off this island. Where's Randall?"

"With Junior and Pearl at their ranch in Kerville," Wendy said.

"How is he?"

"You'll have to look and see." Wendy's voice was gentle, encouraging, trying to guide a child through a frightening but essential experience. She gazed easily at Taylor, realizing how much he had changed in a few short years. "You're just like him," she said. "You change so much." She laughed. "I swear, he changes between the time I drop him off at school in the morning and pick him up in the afternoon."

"Listen, I think . . ." Taylor looked up into Wendy's pale blue eyes. His own eyes were dark and wet, divided by a deep furrow wrenched between his eyebrows. "We ought to be together." Taylor blurted it out, then his face drew tight and pinched with pain. "We've lost too much time already . . . we got serious trouble. We need to go back and see Red. If he's ready, we're still in the race."

Football season was approaching. If Red was on schedule, it could be a Super Bowl season.

It had to be. Things were going too fast. Time was running out. It was the only way to get control back.

Wendy reached out and touched the back of his hand. "You call the plays."

Taylor reached for her, moving them quickly away from the waterfront into the street. He flagged down a battle-worn black and white '57 Plymouth taxicab.

"Where are we going?" Wendy stepped into the battered old Plymouth.

Taylor slid in next to Wendy. "Off into the sunset."

"Get 'em all, son." At the harbor's edge, the white-haired man tossed a handful of coins into the deep dark water. The boy dove after the glittering wealth before it was swallowed by the darkness. A large silver coin flittered and glinted just out of reach, sinking fast. The boy kicked harder.

The *turistas* waited about ten minutes for the boy to resurface. They looked up and down the breakwater and then walked away shaking their heads.

"Well, I'll be damned," the old man said. "I wonder where the devil he went."

PART TWO

"To live outside the law you must be honest."

BOB DYLAN
"Absolutely Sweet Marie"

MY WAY OR
THE HIGHWAY

WHEN Red Kilroy heard Dick Conly had quit and moved off to the Pecos Mountains, the head coach dialed Cyrus Chandler. Suzy Ballard answered and told Red that any questions should be asked of A. D. Koster, the *new* general manager.

Red slammed the receiver down, realizing finally what Suzy's plan had been—ambitious for a carhop but apparently attainable.

Red had released A.D. after his rookie season when a report came through from the commissioner that Koster's name had been picked up on an FBI phone tap on a bookie operation that included Dallas, Houston, New Orleans, Park City and San Antonio. This particular tap also recorded the Texas Pistols' team doctor calling his bookie on Mondays with the injury report.

The commissioner passed that information to Dick Conly, then sat on it. In the meantime the doctor ruined Simon D'Hanis's knee and made $550,000 on the side from the bookie. The publicity of being the team doctor for the Pistols increased his orthopedic practice three hundred percent and he was elected president of the AMA.

Conly had hired A.D. for the front office after some particularly intensive sensual lobbying by Suzy. Dick promised Red that A.D. would be kept isolated.

Now that Conly was gone, Red Kilroy tried to find Taylor Rusk. The rumors of his number-one quarterback going to Los Angeles for one million dollars a year were in the news, along with the stories of Conly's abrupt departure and A.D.'s quick ascent to the general managership. A.D. had not stayed isolated long.

Red Kilroy did not panic. He waited until he could reach Taylor Rusk. He found his quarterback when the news of Bobby Hendrix's death in the Yucatán hit the wires.

Red Kilroy gathered up all the films of Texas's previous season's games and called around the League to his contacts on other teams for them to send scouting films of the Pistols' upcoming season's opponents.

The head coach loaded all the films in the back of his station wagon and drove home. He stayed holed up in his basement office for several weeks, watching films and plotting his season.

He considered his options. Time was even more precious than ever before. Stable management was a necessity in order to win consistently. Turbulence and executive churn made winning a Super Bowl almost impossible.

Almost.

Red's nostrils flared and he smiled in spite of his problem. He loved the rush of solution. There was a way. A one-time shot. No more thinking about *next*, only about *now*. Gamble it all on this season, he decided then and there. Bet the pot.

"Well," the head coach said, "I came to play, not to stay."

And play he did.

That season Red Kilroy decided he would cash all his chips. Now or never. Yes or no. Win or lose. Live or die.

Red Kilroy gambled correctly that the commissioner and the owners would never allow Taylor Rusk to move to Los Angeles.

Allowing the new owner, Richard Portus, to offer five million dollars ran counter to every obstruction the League had erected—from blacklists and option clauses to compensation agreements—designed to inhibit player movement and upward pressure on salaries that the second merger had not already stopped.

But Red now put his own upward pressure on Pistols players' salaries. Had Cyrus offered him the two and a half percent that Conly suggested, he might have had a reason to hold player costs down. But Cyrus didn't. So Red increased bonuses and salaries. High-dollar football.

This had to be the Super Bowl season, and the coach installed a cash-bonus system for each game. He paid players in cash at his locker immediately after each game for performance: yards gained running, catching, turnovers, tackles, blocks, injuries inflicted, many other categories. It was all illegal, but Red Kilroy had come to play, not to stay.

Red also guessed correctly that the commissioner would punish the new Los Angeles owner. Red watched the Los Angeles films over and over until he decided on the man he wanted. When the commissioner issued his ruling and sanctions against Dick Portus "for tampering with Texas property, i.e., Taylor Rusk," Red demanded Los Angeles running back Greg Moore—six foot three, 228 pounds and 4.56 in the forty-yard dash.

Also, Los Angeles had been forced to take Simon D'Hanis in a "nonconditional trade," and Portus had to give Texas two number-one choices in the draft. Portus had to trade two players for Phoenix's number one, then give the choice to Texas.

Red worked over his three-deep charts, moving Screaming Danny Lewis from running back outside to flankerback, replacing him at running back with Moore. Lewis would make an exceptional wide receiver, fearless going across the middle for the ball, a dangerous runner after he caught it. Screaming Danny Lewis's running ability made him dangerous on reverses as well as on pass plays. Speedo Smith and Screaming Danny Lewis made a dangerous pair.

After he had been moved out wide, away from the giant, crazed defensive linemen, Danny Lewis never screamed again.

Red Kilroy knew his defense was solid after days of looking at the films in his basement and planning for Texas's next season, but he would need at least two new offensive linemen. Simon D'Hanis was gone and Darryl "Ox" Wood was old and couldn't be expected to last the whole season going the full game. Ox would need spells of rest, more cocaine. Red knew Ox could get enough cocaine, but it was up to the head coach to provide rest for the ferocious lineman.

There were several good college linemen in the draft. Red figured he could get one starter. The first Los Angeles choice would be the third in the first round behind Atlanta and New Orleans, who were maneuvering for the big running backs that had finished one and two in the Heisman voting. Both backs were clients of Charlie Stillman and had signed contracts with him in August before their senior seasons. They had believed Charlie's promise to keep it quiet and appreciated the loans of cash that Stillman advanced them. Stillman would deliver them quickly to whoever drafted them. He would advise them to take big-bucks contracts with low base salary, long-term payments, deferred and contingent upon services performed after their playing careers ended.

Red decided he would take the two best offensive linemen available in the draft. He called Charlie Stillman; they were his clients.

"I have both of them," Stillman said, clutching the phone in his continually sweating palm. "Wilbur Wilkins I signed on the back of a check when he was a sophomore, and I signed up Leon Donat before he played in the Sugar Bowl. What do you want with them?"

"I want you to hide them," Red said, "until I can draft them both."

"It won't be easy," Stillman said, changing hands with the phone and wiping the sweat off his free hand on his pocket handkerchief. Charlie sweated heavily when he talked on the telephone.

"Bullshit, Charlie. If they're stupid enough to let you tamper with their NCAA eligibility for a few bucks and some Italian baby laxative stepped on with crystal meth and procaine, then passed off as cocaine, they'll do whatever you say about the draft. If they don't, explain to them how being drafted *could* resemble being taken prisoner.

"I'm going to draft Wilkins third in the first round using our early choice from LA, so he won't be much trouble. But we don't get LA's other pick in the first round until thirty-two. Last. Someone else might want Leon Donat earlier. So hide them and let out the rumor that they may go to Canada." Red paused for an idea. "In fact, take them to Toronto. Knuckles Nelson is still coach up there. I'll get Knuckles to meet you. Keep them hidden so nobody else can talk to them, and tell anyone who asks that they are going to Canada. Nobody will draft them without a deal in front, and that'll keep Donat free until I can grab him."

"What's in it for me?" Stillman's shirt was soaked with sweat.

"I won't let Ox Wood break your legs. How is that?"

Red hung up before Charlie Stillman could reply, but the head coach knew that the agent would deliver. He *had* to deliver. There was an endless supply of football players to be betrayed and sold out, but there was a limited number of franchises. As Red had told Charlie many times, "It's my way or the highway."

Red called Knuckles Nelson in Toronto. Knuckles met the two college boys and their agent, Charlie Stillman, at the airport. Charlie convinced them that the Toronto trip was a negotiating ploy.

"The Canadian league is our only *real* bargain chip," Stillman told the overgrown college boys. "It's our hole card. You guys got some international value."

Stillman then gave them each one thousand dollars and a half an ounce of heavily cut cocaine, which he had put in their baggage before going through customs.

Knuckles Nelson took them drinking and to a whorehouse full of French-speaking girls from Quebec. They were ecstatic the following day when Charlie Stillman told them he had managed to get the Texas Pistols to draft them both in the first round with contracts amounting to over a million dollars apiece for five years—

including deferred compensation beginning in the year 2020 and continuing until the year 2040.

They never did figure out what had really happened, but they both turned into Pro Bowl linemen. They had been doing steroids since junior high school, had testicles the size of marbles and had absolutely no sex drive. They played ten years and never caused a bit of trouble.

And that is how Texas managed to get both Wilbur Wilkins and Leon Donat in the first round of the League draft.

Red Kilroy believed a precise question produced exact answers. When he began rebuilding and rewiring, Red wrote down his specific goal: "The Super Bowl, this season."

After defining the goal, Red detailed his method.

One word.

Red's desperate, ingenious method.

Faster!

THE TRUTH

WHEN Taylor drove up under the live oaks behind Doc Webster's, Tommy McNamara was working in the bunkhouse.

The chatter of mockingbirds, scrub jays and McNamara's typewriter punctuated the white rush of water sliding along the limestone bed. Taylor heard the distant wet crash against the granite boulders where Dead Man Creek made its hard turn at the base of Coon Ridge to form Panther Hole.

Inside the stone ranch house by the cold fireplace, lying on the highly polished slab of oak table, Taylor found all five articles from McNamara's newspaper series, "The League and the Mob."

He stretched out on the overstuffed brown corduroy sofa, started with "Ticket Scalping at the Super Bowl," and read straight through.

It was late afternoon when Taylor Rusk finished the fifth and final article. The final piece was about gambling and the question of whether football games had been or could be fixed. Tommy used his source—called Deep Threat—to reveal that "one well-known quarterback" considered his finest moment in football when he threw an interception, then blocked his own teammate, allowing the defender to score. The quarterback's team still won but by

— 313 —

less than the point spread, which was how he had bet. Deep Threat also did the math on how much cash Super Bowl tickets brought via scalpers, explaining how thousands of tickets were sold through travel agencies in package plans. It involved millions of dollars and accusations of tax evasion. Deep Threat gave the percentage of tickets per Super Bowl that ended up scalped at up to one thousand dollars apiece and alleged that the large majority of the tickets came from the commissioner's office, certain owners and the host franchise. Deep Threat alleged "a conspiracy to scalp thousands of Super Bowl tickets for millions of dollars."

McNamara also quoted Deep Threat as saying, "The Super Bowl was fixed after the second merger in order to give Memphis and the American Football Federation teams instant credibility. They had to keep the image of the Super Bowl as the premier event in professional football. Besides credibility for Memphis, it produced several million dollars in gambling profit for those who knew the twelve-point underdog, Memphis, would win."

All the charges were denied by everyone involved.

The article noted that Commissioner Burden announced that "the Super Bowl will still be hosted by the Texas Pistols, provided they get finished with the Pistol Dome. It will be a tremendous boost to the local economy," Robbie Burden said. "The Super Bowl will bring in over one hundred million dollars to the merchants of Clyde, Texas."

"Do you believe it?" Tommy McNamara stood in the doorway, his skinny arms folded across a new red and black Santa Fe Opera T-shirt. His tanned, spindly legs stuck out of ragged cutoff jeans, his brown feet fitted into tire-tread-and-surgical-tubing sandals.

"Which parts?" Taylor tossed the last article on the high-gloss slice of oak.

"Pick 'em." McNamara crossed the room awkwardly, sandals flapping against the rock floor, the Santa Fe Opera T-shirt swinging from his collarbones like a nightgown. He fell into the wooden rocking chair beside the hearth and looked across at Taylor stretched out on the brown couch.

"Couldn't you get a smaller-size T-shirt?" Taylor studied the red shirt with the black lettering draped across McNamara's chest and shoulders.

"Smallest they had in men's and I didn't want to buy in the juniors' with all the Indians and Mexicans around."

"Who is Deep Threat?" Taylor decided he might as well get right to the point.

Tommy McNamara rocked faster. "Listen, man, I got everybody after me on this story. FBI, League Security, IRS, Investico, Justice Department. They all want my source!"

"So do I," Taylor said.

Tommy McNamara stopped rocking and looked ready to run. The tan slid off his face into his Santa Fe Opera T-shirt.

"I'm not going to do anything." Taylor continued to slouch into the feather-stuffed couch, his hands clasped behind his head, feet over the heavy brown corduroy arm. "I just need to know."

"Man, I can't tell you. I can't tell anybody."

Taylor watched Tommy McNamara's face and eyes closely.

"You know," Taylor said quickly, "Bobby Hendrix got killed in Mexico."

"I heard. Fell out of a plane. It came over the wire." Tommy looked at Taylor. "What happened? Were you there?" His eyes were wide, guileless.

Taylor nodded. "It wasn't an accident. Somebody killed him."

"My God." Tommy seemed surprised, startled, confused. "Who would want to kill Bobby Hendrix? What did he ever do?"

"He wasn't your source?" Taylor sat up and crouched over the oak slab.

"Bobby? Good Lord, no," Tommy said. "You know him better than that. He wouldn't say shit to the press if he had a mouthful."

"Well, somebody thought he was. Calling your source 'Deep Threat' didn't help."

"Why do you say that? He wasn't Deep Threat—too slow." Tommy resumed rocking at a slow easy pace.

"Well, somebody killed him," Taylor replied.

Tommy shook his head. "Why kill somebody *after* the story is out?"

"Is the whole story out yet?"

"It's not," Tommy said. "That's what I'm working on now. Another series. There's so much more, even *you* wouldn't believe it. But Bobby Hendrix wasn't my source, and that certainly wasn't why he died."

"He didn't have to be your source," Taylor argued. "Somebody just had to *think* he was your source."

"Well, if that's true..." Tommy stopped rocking again and his face turned hard; the brown color returned. There was fire in his eyes, a glint of anger, desire, revenge. "...and I hope to God it is not true..." His skinny body seemed suddenly dangerous, destructive. "...but if somebody thinks they solved their problems by throwing Bobby Hendrix out of an airplane in Mexico, they are going to find themselves sadly mistaken when they pick up next week's paper."

"There's really more?"

"A whole lot more, including the commissioner's numbered bank accounts in Switzerland and the Bahamas," Tommy announced. "And Cyrus Chandler, the Cobianco brothers, and the Anglo-Bahamian Bank..."

"Where did you get that information?" Taylor's eyes went wide. "Who told you?"

"*Everybody* wants the name of my source," Tommy said. "Well, you can scratch Bobby Hendrix." Tommy quickly looked up. "I didn't mean it like that. I meant... well, you knew Bobby, he just wouldn't say anything."

"He knew there was no point in it," Taylor said. "Who could write the truth if they ever got hold of it? Who knows the truth?"

"I got hold of it, buddy-boy," Tommy snapped angrily. He was like a rat terrier; he didn't back off even if he got hold of a hundred-pound rat. "And I'm writing it. Christ, it isn't the gangsters that keep trying to stop me, it's League Security, Investico. The goddamn US attorney general puts the FBI on me.... They search my house, tap my phone. They're trying to serve me with a federal grand jury subpoena." Tommy was vengeful. "Then they plan to immunize me and make me testify. That's why I'm hiding out here."

"Take the Fifth."

"You keep acting like we had a bill of rights. You can't take the Fifth when you've been *immunized*." Tommy ground out the word. "That's contempt of court. If I refuse to testify under a grant of immunity, they put me in jail."

"For how long?"

"A year or two," Tommy said. "No big thing. Just a year or two out of the middle of my life, not to mention the fact that once I'm immunized and they try forcing me to testify, certain interested and yet unnamed parties might decide that the best way to litigate this constitutional issue is with me dead. Did you hear a car?"

"Yes," Taylor said. "I'm expecting Wendy."

"Jesus, man! You got Chandler's daughter coming here?"

"Don't worry, Tommy, the two of us can whip her."

In the fading light Tommy McNamara could see a dust cloud growing behind Coon Ridge, heading for the low-water bridge below the ranch house. He ran outside to the big gnarled Spanish oak at the bend in the road. From beneath the fresh green canopy he could see down to the bridge. The newswriter was back in a few moments and collapsed into the rocking chair.

"It's Wendy," he sighed. "She's got the boy with her."

Taylor was off the couch and outside, waiting to meet the car. Randall was sitting on the seat next to Wendy.

His son.

CHOOSING UP SIDES

"LEM has agreed to a divorce." Wendy spoke for the first time since Randall had dropped off to sleep, curled up in her lap, his head on her breast. She stroked his thick black hair.

The clacking of Tommy McNamara's typewriter came from the bunkhouse. The creek whispered and hissed below the bluff, crashing softly in the distance against the granite at Panther Hole. "Lem's leaving the Franchise and going into business with his daddy. Reselling oil. They scared Lem off the boat in Mexico," Wendy said.

"They scared me off first," Taylor replied.

Taylor studied the sleeping boy, then watched Wendy's profile. She looked out the window into the darkness of the creek and cedar brake country.

"Lem's always known Randall was your child," Wendy continued. "I guess just about everybody knew."

"Except me."

"You never asked." Wendy looked as she did on the road to Hugo to marry Buffy to Simon. She still had the power to make Taylor see her when and how she chose . . . to conceal or reveal.

"Well, Cyrus can't stop us anymore," Wendy said finally. "Christ, he can barely zip his pants."

"What happens now?"

"We take over the Franchise." She turned her head slowly and deliberately on her long, slender neck until she looked directly at Taylor.

"Do I still have to play?"

"Absolutely. You *are* the Franchise." The hearth embers reflected in her eyes. The lean arc of her neck contoured into her delicate collarbones, the hollows and shadows. "It's funny, but now your idea of not confronting my father begins to make sense." Her pale eyes glittered with fire.

"Not to me. This is *my son* and I missed three years of his life."

"But you didn't want—" Wendy protested.

"You don't know what I wanted." Taylor cut her off. "You only know what *you* wanted. Now you know why I'm more scared of you than Cyrus."

"Can we begin where we are now?" Wendy asked. "Right now and from this moment forward. All forgiven? No grudges? No blame?"

Wendy lay the sleeping Randall on the wicker sofa, leaned over, pulled Taylor toward her and kissed him long and hard.

"Friends?" Wendy watched him, her voice soft and measured. Taylor nodded.

"Tonight my father marries Suzy Ballard." Wendy forced a smile. "They're getting married on the *All-American Evangelical Hour*."

"Well, Billy Joe Hardesty didn't get his own TV show without knowing a pigeon when he sees one drool on himself."

Taylor followed Wendy outside to the hammocks. They both stared silently off the stone porch, listening to the night sounds. A whippoorwill called from the oak motte behind the cabin. A bat dived at fluttering bugs drawn to the mercury vapor light. Tommy McNamara's typewriter rattled away in the bunkhouse, sounding like machine-gun fire from the moth and bat war.

"Red always said he would own a franchise or die trying. Looked like he'll get his chance to do both." They both sat on the hammock and it swung slowly. "Bobby Hendrix used to tell him that he had a better chance of being adopted by your father than being made a partner."

"He probably still does," Wendy said. "But if he's willing to go with us against A.D. and Suzy."

"Don't forget your daddy."

"I'm not worried about Cyrus. He's just confused... disoriented. Suzy has purposely kept him isolated out at the hot springs." Wendy began to lace her thin fingers together and twist them. "He's lost without Dick Conly. Once we make a move he'll sit down and listen to reason. He doesn't understand the danger he's in."

"Nobody does."

They watched the red lights of an airplane appear over the distand southern horizon and float soundlessly across the great sky.

Wendy hooked her thumb toward the bunkhouse. "How about him?"

"Tommy will help, but we need Tommy's source. Whoever he is knows more than he's telling." Taylor pursed his lips, tapping them with his index finger.

"If we can connect A.D. and my father's new wife to the gambling and ticket scalping..." Wendy began to plot.

"You might also connect your father."

Wendy nodded, her face a petulant scowl.

"There's one more thing," Taylor said. "I call the plays. We are in a real fight and we'll either end up on the boat or in the water, swimming with sharks."

"Man is born to strive for the heroic." Wendy glowered.

"You better decide, Wendy. It's a new game." His stare offered ruthless absolution. "Bobby Hendrix already guessed wrong. Nobody's going to get a second chance. Red will speed it all up and go for the Super Bowl this year, twice as fast with A.D. and Suzy trying to put us into the wall. There will not be time for second guesses or the brakes," Taylor said. "If I make a wrong decision, only going faster will get us out. You accelerate out of trouble in this race—the pedal to the metal."

"What if you're wrong?" She held her slim fingers to her lips. Her eyes avoided his scalding stare. "What if you can't save us by going faster?"

"Then we hit the wall," Taylor said, "still accelerating."

"Pretty limited choice you're offering." Wendy was hesitant, no longer sardonic. "What if you fail?"

"Then I fail."

"That's your answer?"

"There's no other answer to that question...except quit."

Taylor scooped up Randall, carried the small boy to his bed, covered him and kissed his soft, smooth cheek. He stared at the sleeping child and thought of all they had missed. Things that would never be understood. Times that had never happened.

Taylor stayed in Randall's bedroom, watching him sleep. The boy's breathing was even.

Time, Taylor thought, *begins by running out.*

LOUIE THE HOOK

WHEN Taylor returned from the bedroom, Wendy had the television on and was watching the electric preacher marry the carhop to Amos Chandler's baby boy.

Suzy Ballard and Cyrus Chandler faced the Reverend Billy Joe Hardesty, a short, fat man in a dark-blue suit, plain dark narrow tie, white shirt, ankle-length black socks and black alligator loafers with tassels. Suzy guided Cyrus Chandler's liver-spotted hand toward the solemn man's, whose great rolls of red flesh flowed over his shirt collar.

"God bless you, brother." Billy Joe grasped Cyrus's delicate hand, squeezing with the zeal of the crusader. "It is a great day for the Lord. Welcome to the fold."

Cyrus winced as the evangelist ground his knuckles together.

"I look forward with a great pride," Reverend Billy Joe continued, "to joining you two lovely people in holy matrimony before the Lord and the millions of faithful who support my electronic ministry." Billy Joe turned Cyrus's liver-spotted hand loose. With his other liver-spotted hand Cyrus rubbed the mashed fingers gently.

Billy Joe gripped his blue polyester lapels and rocked back and forth in his tassled loafers. The motion caused the thin dark-blue knit coat to ripple.

"How is your life, Brother Cyrus? Will you share with us?" A wide grin pushed Billy Joe's jowls back toward his red jug ears and pulled a large flap of fat up off his collar.

"Well . . . ah"—Cyrus continued to massage the thin hand—"ah, lately I have begun to feel . . ." Cyrus stopped rubbing his hands and gazed blankly at them. He was searching for the lost thought. ". . . ah, I guess, that's not really what I feel. . . . it's more like . . ." Cyrus twisted his wrinkled face into a scowl of concentration. A slight tremor jogged him and his emaciated body shimmied. The skinny fingers and brown-stained had trembled. He suddenly became an old man. Saliva ran in a slight trickle from the right corner of his pinched mouth.

"Abandoned? Brother Cyrus, do you feel abandoned?" Billy Joe Hardesty prodded.

Cyrus Chandler's eyes brightened. "Yes. I guess maybe that

is it." Cyrus spoke slowly. "I feel abandoned . . . by my friends . . . my business associates . . . and my family."

"Well, thank you for sharing, and fear no more, Brother Chandler"—Billy Joe smiled reassuringly—"because I am here to bring you to the family of Jesus Christ, the one and only Savior and Son of God."

"Praise the Lord." Suzy watched Cyrus, trying to judge his reaction. "Praise the Lord. Amen."

"Through me"—Billy Joe Hardesty thumped his own chest loudly, causing his tie to flap and his face to jiggle—"Cyrus Chandler will come to know Jesus Christ, the Son of God."

Then Billy Joe joined in holy matrimony the increasingly senile old man and the hard, young and beautiful woman. The one-hundred-voice All-American Youth Choir of blemish-free white teen-agers sang to the new Mr. and Mrs. Cyrus Chandler. Saliva dribbled from both corners of Cyrus's mouth. His body fluttered occasionally inside his tuxedo.

Suzy Ballard smiled and dabbed the saliva with a white lace handkerchief that matched her $125,000 wedding gown. Glinting in the studio klieg lights, the new Mrs. Chandler's flawless blue-white emerald-cut nine-carat diamond ring caused hot spots and streaks on the television screen as she gaily wiped and dabbed the saliva from Cyrus Chandler's chin.

Throughout the ceremony Billy Joe Hardesty admonished people to press their hands to their television sets "as a point of contact with the everlasting soul of Brother Cyrus and Sister Susan and your Savior Jesus Christ throughout this glorious hour of celebration."

As Cyrus nodded his head, a thin smile turned up the corners of his deeply lined mouth. "Momma would be proud of me," he said weakly. The saliva still trickled down the sides of his chin. Suzy dabbed it away while she and Billy Joe exchanged smiles.

Billy Joe Hardesty reached out and took Suzy and Cyrus into his arms. "You shall never be abandoned or alone if you believe in the power of the Lord and let Jesus come into your life and heart." He cupped Suzy's full, soft breast in one hand and rubbed his thumb across the erect nipple. It was the one over the heart. "Give of thyself unto the Lord and his servants. This is a Bible-preaching, God-fearing ministry—that knows His power and His miracles."

"Praise the Lord!" Suzy was enthusiastic and acutely aware of Billy Joe's thumb and fingers.

Cyrus was thinking about his golf cart. He could not recall if he had purchased and shipped one out to the Hot Springs Ranch or just thought he did. He trembled again.

"Praise the Lord," Billy Joe bellowed, rolling the hard nipple between his thumb and forefinger.

"Praise the Lord," Cyrus repeated, with less enthusiasm and considerable confusion. The saliva began to trickle from the left side of his mouth.

"Praise the Lord."

And pass the telecommunications.

A MISSTEP
IN DEAD MAN

THEY sat on the warm granite boulder and watched Randall splashing in the center of the creek upstream from Panther Hole. The thin sun-burnished boy wore red canvas sneakers and red swimming trunks. He faced the current, kneeling in the shallow limestone creek bed, and slugged the water with his fist. The water ran cold, fast and clear, bubbling and whirling around the soft giggling obstruction.

"Your career has ended, Penguin," the brown boy said menacingly, rising to a half crouch, hands curled into chubby claws; grappling momentarily with the Penguin, he fell forward into the fast-running white-blue water. Recovering, he sat up, sputtering and shaking his long wet black hair. "Run for the the hovercraft," he said, clamping his brown eyes shut and wiping his dark, lean face. The Penguin had escaped.

"What do you want him to be when he grows up?" Taylor asked.

"Besides Batman?" Wendy turned her shoulders and, closing her eyes thoughtfully, let the sun bake into her face.

Taylor watched as the boy leaped on another invisible archfiend, dragging him down to cold, wet justice in Dead Man Creek. Standing and dusting his tiny hands, hooking his thumbs in the waistband of the red swimsuit, Randall searched with his large, round, dark eyes for an as yet unimagined horror.

"Come on, Boy Wonder. We're finished here." Randall trudged upstream, leaving fully administered justice in his wake, a serious but satisfied look on his face. Leaning down, he picked up a flat piece of limestone off the creek bottom and popped the white rock in his mouth.

"Hey! Batman!" Taylor yelled, "Don't get too far upstream. There are holes. . . ."

Randall spit the rock back into his hand and yelled without looking back, "You can't tell me what to do. You're not my boss, or my father, or my mother, or anything."

"The kid is harsh in his judgments. What does he mean, 'or anything'?" Taylor turned to Wendy. Her eyes closed, she was smiling and thinking and facing the sun.

"Come on, Randall, I'm at least one thing," Taylor yelled back to the boy. "I'm *bigger than you.*"

"You're crazy. My momma even told me so." The boy turned back upstream and popped the rock back into his mouth.

Taylor turned and nudged Wendy. "You better give the orders. There *are* some big holes in the creek bed."

"Randall!" Wendy yelled as she turned away from the sun and opened her eyes. "Randall? Where is he?"

"Up there." He pointed upstream, his gaze following his arm, but Randall Ryan wasn't where Taylor's finger pointed.

"Where?" Wendy's voice trembled.

Taylor looked along both banks; Randall had disappeared. Vanished.

"Oh, shit!"

Taylor sprang feetfirst off the high boulder. Hitting the water, Taylor had misjudged his jump, skinning his leg on the upstream edge of Panther Hole. But the long leap had put him closer to the spot where he'd last seen the boy, and hitting the shallow edge kept his head above water; he never lost sight of the dark water he reasoned had swallowed Randall.

"Randall! Randall! Randall!"

Scrambling up the creek bed against the fast, shallow current, Taylor heard Wendy screaming somewhere in his mind, but all he saw was the dark hole. The crystal-clear cool water turned to glue; the creek's force increased; each step seemed interminable. *Don't panic*, he told himself, checking his landmarks to make certain he was heading for the right hole. Stumbling against a rock, Taylor slipped and fell down. Quickly he scrambled back to his feet. The force of the Dead Man was eroding his balance, his control, his strength, his courage. For an eternal moment the struggle seemed a stalemate, then Taylor broke free and staggered to the dark hole. The rushing water clutched at him like fear. He fought for control, pausing again, checking his landmarks. *Make certain.* He stepped back and studied the dark hole, the shoreline, the oak tree and the rock. *Was this the place?*

Wendy, frozen to the rock, knowing she was being punished, screamed and screamed. "Randall! Oh, God, Randall! Randall! Don't hide from Mother, Randall! Randall! Randall!" She was the shriek of the storm while Taylor kept looking and thinking.

Don't panic.

Trying to remember his emergency training, Taylor recalled only what to do for vomiting old ladies and emphysemic drunks. *Don't panic; he hasn't been under long. Make sure this is the right hole.* Taylor looked into the dark green hole, searching for forms, shapes, colors. His son.

Calling the boy's name repeatedly, Wendy's terrified cries turned into a pulsing, keening animal wail. Tommy McNamara heard her all the way up in the bunkhouse with his stereo playing. The haunting sound reached Bob, Wendy's bodyguard—who was never far away—and his partner, Toby, in their white Ford at the cattle guard behind Coon Ridge. They all headed for Dead Man Creek.

Taylor decided he had the hole that got the boy. He carefully studied it, sticking his head into the water and looking, walking along the edge of the green water, concentrating, considering, knowing once he made his move into the hole that there was no second choice. No second guess. No excuse. Fear clawed at his mind but he kept moving, letting the terror flow through him like water. He must take control, put the adrenaline to work for him, let *it* push *him.* Discipline. Execution. Concentration. Speed.

It was a deep hole, ground by water and time out of an upthrust limestone block. The boy had stepped off an underwater cliff, dropping fifty feet into the eroded hole.

"No! No! No!" Wendy knew this was to be her punishment for being happy, for loving her son, for loving Taylor; their son would become nothing. Control was again revealed to be futile reaction.

Taylor backed off, changing angles for the sun, continuing to look into the hole, trying to find a ray to the bottom; years of sediment waited to stir once he went down.

He began to breathe deeper—filling, stretching his lungs, gorging his blood with oxygen. He had one dive to find the boy. One lungful of air. He breathed deeper; the sound of his respiration echoed off the rocks, waiting, searching the dark green void. One chance.

A flash of red? The water wobbled and the red was gone. Was that a red shoe? A red suit?

Taylor made his decisions and sucked in his final breath of air. He would search all the way to the bottom, then scour the bottom. Finally, oxygen exhausted, he would not quit, he would search until failure brought Death. One trip.

As he dove Taylor saw clouds of black sediment billowing up toward him. The boy was down there, putting up a hell of a fight, judging by the size of the dark plume growing toward the surface. Taylor swam straight down into the black cloud. It burned his eyes and blurred his vision; he barely glimpsed his own hands in front of him. The water rippled and swirled up from below—the force of the boy's desperate fight to survive. Taylor swam straight down toward the eye of the struggle. Faster. Faster.

He never saw Randall, just a red blur as a rubber-soled shoe kicked his face. Taylor grabbed at the small ankle, but the boy kicked away, terrified and lost without the guide of gravity in the black swirling depths. The boy was swimming down, heading deeper, thinking he was swimming up.

Taylor swam after him, thirty feet deep or more, catching glimpses of red as the water turned colder. His ears ached. Taylor kicked and clawed, digging deeper into the cold water, searching into the black. He lost the red; he felt nothing, no turmoil or struggle. Deathly still.

Taylor stopped, turned in the black cloud, spread out his arms and legs and waited. And hoped.

Randall Ryan was motionless and weightless in the water. The small boy had given up the struggle for life and had settled for peace.

After a fifteen-second eternity the boy's head bumped gently into Taylor's foot. Another two inches and they would not have touched, floating inches apart in the cold black forever.

Taylor Rusk stuck the cold, thin body under his arm and kicked toward what he hoped was the surface and not some refraction of the sunlight in the churning black water, drawing them ever deeper. His lungs began to ache and he began to slowly exhale, relieving the pressure of the carbon dioxide buildup but also losing any residual oxygen left in his lungs.

The boy did not move. Taylor clutched him tightly. *Faster!*

Taylor had exhaled completely, his lungs exhausted; the surface seemed no closer. No matter how hard he kicked, the light seemed farther away. Out of reach, feeling a sharp pain in his chest and tasting blood in his mouth, Taylor kicked and reached out desperately toward the fading light. He kicked one last time. He couldn't keep the water out of his lungs.

The light faded. All black. Dead.

Bob Travers grabbed Taylor's hand as it broke the surface, snatching the man and the little boy out of the water like rag dolls, dragging them onto the shallow creek bed.

Prying Randall loose from Taylor's grip, Bob lay the boy stomach-down along his sinewy arm. The boy's once-red lips were deep blue, the beautiful soft face in cold sleep. Cradling the boy's head in his large hand, Bob thumped between the shoulder blades, then pried the tiny blue lips apart. No water ran out.

"He's still got a heartbeat." Bob pressed his ear to the boy's back. "But . . . he's not breathing."

Taylor was half-conscious, gulping air.

"He's not breathing!" Bob repeated, using his hands to try to force the lungs to breathe by pumping the little chest.

"He may have swallowed his tongue," Taylor gasped out.

Bob stuck a big finger into the blue mouth. Finding the tongue in place, he covered the small nose and mouth with his rough cracked lips. Bob tried to force air into the lungs.

The small chest did not rise.

Tommy McNamara came running down the bluff and splashing into the water. Wendy howled from the rock.

Taylor struggled to his knees and forced open the boy's jaws, looking down his throat. He barely saw the white stone lodged past the soft palate. His finger could not reach it.

"Something's stuck in his throat," he said to Bob. "See if you can reach it."

Bob dug into the boy's mouth while Taylor looked around wildly. Tommy McNamara stood beside him, his gold ballpoint pen hanging from the neck of his Santa Fe Opera T-shirt.

"I can't reach it," Bob said, turning the boy face down and trying to squeeze it out compressing the small cold rib cage with one hand while pressing up against the diaphragm with the other hand.

"Goddam son of a bitch! Come out of there! Goddammit . . . Goddammit!" Bob Travers was no longer calm and low-key.

"Stop! You'll break his ribs."

"He's dying! Better broken ribs than dead."

"Turn him over."

Bob flopped the blue-faced boy on his back. Taylor's hand palpated the hollow of the boy's cold neck, fingers feeling for the cartilage at the soft hollow between the collarbones.

Which was it, now? Above? Below?

He snatched Tommy McNamara's ballpoint pen, clicked out the point and plunged it into the boy's slender throat.

Wendy scrambled up just as he drove the hole into their child's throat. She screamed and lunged for Taylor, but Bob caught her, then Tommy held her away. Taylor pulled the pen out, leaving a neat red round puncture. Wendy kept screaming, but Taylor and Bob heard the whistling hiss. The boy had begun to breathe again. The cold blue color retreated from his face as oxygen filled his lungs and bloodstream. The small chest rose and fell; air passed through the bloody hole in Randall's throat below the rock, the tiny chip of the limestone land.

Bob's partner came scrambling down the bluff with the white Ford's emergency kit.

"Jesus, who made this mess?" With a pair of forceps he pulled a limestone rock from Randall's throat. "We have to get him to a hospital," the partner said as Bob wrapped his shirt around the cold little body. "Who stuck this goddam hole in him? Could have severed an artery."

"Forget it, Toby, you're second guessing. We don't do that in this business." Bob still cradled the boy in his arms. One big hand easily held the large head. The brown eyes flickered open.

"Hi, Bob," the little boy croaked. "My throat hurts." Then, he saw his mother sobbing and he began to cry too.

Toby ran splattering across the creek bed in his cowboy boots. Bob walked swiftly behind, clutching the crying boy. Wendy ran alongside Bob, soothing the boy and wiping her own eyes.

Taylor Rusk stood up, wobbly in the shallow creek bed. Tommy helped him to his feet. Taylor took one last look at the dark hole, now a churning mass of sediment, a cloud of death.

"Jesus!" Taylor, gasping for air, gazed into the swirling black green. "Blind fucking luck." Then he leaned over and vomited bright-red blood into Dead Man Creek.

MEN ON THE MOON

TOMMY McNamara held the pen in one hand while he kept the other around Taylor's waist. Taylor used Tommy's shoulder for support in walking back up the bluff to the ranch house, stopping several times to cough up blood. Taylor began to shiver. He was scared . . . frightened to his soul.

After putting on dry clothes and lying down on the brown couch, Taylor could still taste his own blood; something had broken in his chest when he was underwater. The dry clothes warmed him, the shiver stopped. But he was still scared. Not of the blood; he had done worse damage to himself on purpose. He was scared of some *thing*.

"Well, I'm retiring this baby from active duty." Tommy held up the ballpoint pen. "It's the best day's work it will ever do." Tommy hung the gold ballpoint on a finishing nail over the fireplace. "Best day's work you ever did, too, Taylor."

"There just aren't a lot of jobs open for Super Heroes." Taylor spat up some more blood and smacked his lips, sticking out his tongue, grimacing at the taste of his own vital fluid.

"Mortality, you confronted mortality," Tommy said. "Hendrix would have said it scared you."

"I feel like I'm on a roller coaster and the worst part is ahead." Taylor spat some more of his blood into the bucket Tommy brought from the bunkhouse. "But mortality doesn't scare me. I can't think about being mortal, I got this job to do." Taylor licked blood off his lips. "I'm scared of being out of work and unlucky."

"The one true god," Tommy said. "Good luck."

"It was the odds we beat today, Tommy, and I'm scared of going up against the odds. I don't know what the *real odds* are!"

"The odds are always with the house in the Big Casino in the Sky."

"The real odds aren't with anybody, and there is no Big Casino." Taylor watched the wretchedly thin man in the T-shirt and the beltless jeans that hung from his hips. The blue denim had faded almost white in the empty sagging seat. The only extra flesh on Tommy McNamara hung in deep brown bags beneath each eye. His face was cadaverous from lack of food and rest.

"You ever feel like you had your face in the wind for too long?" Taylor asked.

"All the time. I know too much," Tommy said. "And I'm not too smart. It is all so insanely simple and everybody is so frighteningly stupid. What do I tell them?"

"Don't tell them anything." Taylor coughed. "Not anything complicated."

"It's like a movie to people," Tommy said. "They just watch it go by and see how it ends while they build cars and pay their bills. It's not like real life."

Taylor shifted on the couch and spat some pink saliva in the bucket. "Real life is pumping gas and hoping to get lucky."

"Watch your life go by waiting on luck and Jesus." Tommy stared out the south window. His dark black eyes were bloodshot and painful.

"Why do you care?" Taylor asked. "Why do you waste your time? Finding out which owner knows what gambler? Is it fixed? Isn't it fixed? It's all so silly." Taylor spat again; the saliva had turned a darker pink.

"I do it because it's real. It happens. Right there in front of millions of people the American soul is laid bare, but all they see is the football game and the marvels of electronics, egomania and greed. My job is better than the car wash."

"But you can write, you have a craft. Write about something else. Football is the only thing I know how to do."

"You know how to think," Tommy said. "You've learned to survive. That's why you're on the field and everybody else sits and watches."

"Not everybody else." Taylor spat again and thought. "Wendy for instance."

"A hell of a lot of them," Tommy said. "Everybody who is not part of the game watches. From some perspective." Tommy thumped his bony chest. "I have been lots of places in the world, and people know two things about America: Western movies and American football."

"And I still say why bother?"

"People deserve to know. If they want to know."

"I'm people. I already know. The people in the stands and watching on television don't want to know. They watch that shit all week on the job with their union, their bosses, their presidents. They're not interested." Taylor was speaking hard, tense and straining, making his throat hurt. "The network knows, but they are delivering millions of buyers and get *big bucks* for something to happen each week. I can shoot the President and the only person to miss the game will be the President."

Tommy shook his head. "The spectator should understand the cost of the juice . . . the cost to produce this spectacle."

"They understand. They pay part of that cost, and not just for after-shave. The fan knows what part of himself he's surrendering and for how long and what feeling he gets in return. That's the spectacle. I watch them, so for that matter I'm a spectator too." Taylor leaned back and tried to relax. He was angry at Tommy. "Don't get news *as* entertainment confused with news *about* entertainment. That's as different as going to church and discussing religion."

"I wrote my articles for you to read just like I write for a fan. I only supply my half of the story; the reader supplies the other."

"Old news." Taylor spat in the bucket just for the hell of it.

"But news, and not old to lots of people. Wendy, to use your example."

"You don't have to risk winding up in the trunk of your car just to get that news to me. You see what good it did Bobby Hendrix."

"I didn't do it for you, I did it for me. But it's there for anyone who wants it!" Tommy's bony face twisted into a painful grimace. "Bobby Hendrix didn't tell me anything. It's not my fault!" Frustration filled his eyes with tears. "Goddam you, Taylor, I didn't kill him!" Tommy wiped his eyes.

"I'm sorry," Taylor spat, "it wasn't your fault. I shouldn't have said that about Bobby."

Tommy's eyes were sore; he was tired and unhappy. "Being casual conspirators operating on half truths will put you and Wendy . . ."

"It all seems so unreal," Taylor said. "The whole goddam mess is incomprehensible."

"When I was a kid," Tommy said, "I used to spend Saturdays with my grandfather. I loved my grandfather. He was big and happy, knew how to carve wood . . . make things. Told me stories about West Texas and how he was on a trail drive once." Tommy smiled at the memory, then rubbed the smile away. He kept looking out the stone ranch house window like a man expecting unwelcome company. "But every Saturday afternoon at four o'clock . . . I remember it was four o'clock because that was how I learned to tell time. I learned by hating a specific hour. I *hated* four o'clock on Saturday."

Taylor laughed and it quickly degenerated into a cough; he alternately laughed and coughed and spat bright red again.

"*Wrestling*. From Fort Worth at four o'clock," Tommy said. "It didn't matter what we were doing; no matter how much fun we were having, Grandpa would get out that old pocket watch, and if it was close to four o'clock, we stopped and went to the house, turned on the television and watched masked men and midgets and women and Indians and fags wrestle each other in some television studio in Fort Worth."

Taylor stifled his laughter and coughing.

"I never could get my grandfather to believe wrestling was fake." Tommy shook his kinky head. "He loved it. I tried everything I could think of to discredit wrestling. Old Grandpa always believed it was real. It sure fucked up a lot of Saturday afternoons. To this day I'm still not crazy about four o'clock."

Taylor was working his jaws and licking his lips. "Is that why you're going to all this trouble? It seems like a fairly straightforward case of overcompensation." He looked down into the red-splattered bucket.

"If you try and take over the Franchise"—Tommy looked to the red-cast ridge—"I'm going to write about it. And I want to be close to it."

"I don't want to be close to it. Where'd you pick up that rumor?"

"I never get tired of listening and I never reveal my sources," Tommy said. "And I don't get tired of writing. Maybe I can help."

"I'm tired of it all and I'm coughing blood," Taylor replied. "Who's Deep Threat? And how good is he?"

"I can't say. It's a truth you don't need." Tommy turned back to watch the sunset. "You know, it's funny," he said. "My grandfather always believed wrestling from Fort Worth, but you couldn't convince him that men walked on the moon. He believed wrestling and died convinced the *Apollo* missions were television fakery. But God! How that old man loved Wahoo MacDaniel."

JUNKIES
AND PREACHERS

"HE's gonna sign everything over to that goddam Billy Joe Hardesty and his electric church," Suzy Ballard Chandler told A. D. Koster. They were in the kitchen of the Hot Springs Ranch headquarters. It was ten P.M. Cyrus Chandler had doddered and drooled off to bed about eight-thirty. Suzy had the wetback woman tend Cyrus and give him his Lasix and Valium, which he took dutifully without question.

"I thought the idea was to keep Cyrus away from people," A.D. said. "How does he spend so much time with Billy Joe Hardesty?"

"Billy Joe's got his own plane."

"Jesus." A.D. whistled softly. "An air force."

"He flies in without warning. The preacher smells blood. I never should have let 'em marry us on television. Billy Joe brings a video tape of the ceremony and a video tape player. He had titles made up. 'The Son of Amos Chandler Meets the Son of God.' It did something to Cyrus to see it on television. I can't control him around Billy Joe."

"Tell Billy Joe Hardesty that you'll shoot his Bible-believin' ass off if he ever sets foot here again," A.D. said. "If he shows up, have the son of a bitch arrested."

Suzy laughed bitterly. "He's already got a taped sermon on how Sister Susan is keeping Brother Cyrus prisoner, is not allowing him to keep his pledge and is endangering his immortal soul. He showed it to me while Cyrus took a nap."

A.D. whistled. "He outsmarted you! I'll be damned."

Suzy's eyes flared and she punched the Texas Pistols general manager twice on the ear. A.D.'s head snapped from side to side. His ear went numb, then began to ring.

"Goddam, Suzy." He ducked into his shoulder. "Knock it off."

"That's what I'm tryin' to do!" Suzy bounced two hard shots off A.D.'s biceps, but he kept his chin buried and his hands up and she knew she wouldn't get another clean shot at his head.

She hit him two right roundhouses in the ribs and back, breaking blood vessels in the triceps.

"Smart preacher, you say?" She gave him a parting jab. "This guy has lawyers and time on the satellite. He isn't a virgin in getting money out of old people." Suzy gnawed at her thumbnail. "You know what I mean?"

"Yeah," he replied and relaxed, dropping his guard.

When she saw the opening, Suzy hit A.D. in the jaw, knocking him loose of his chair.

They stayed in the kitchen all night, trying to figure out what to do about Billy Joe Hardesty. A.D. was black and blue by the next morning; Cyrus Chandler got out of bed singing:

> *This story has a moral*
> *Like a song must have an end*
> *Junkies and preachers . . .*
> *A man don't need for friends.*

He had no idea how long he had been at the hot springs.

GOOD GUYS
AND BAD GUYS

TAYLOR returned to his apartment to pick up his mail and some clothes.

The answering service had several messages.

"Red Kilroy has called twice. He said it was urgent," the girl said. "The league commissioner's office called. And Speedo Smith. I was so sorry to hear about Bobby Hendrix. How's Ginny?" She knew all about Taylor's life and he had never seen her.

Taylor called Speedo first.

"I'll pick up my momma and fall by your crib," Speedo said. "A.D. just renegotiated my contract, gave me a big bump every year for three years and a fifty-five-thousand-dollar bonus. I got me a fine fur, a little toot and some new wheels. They got more money than even Dudley says they got, and he says they got a lot."

Taylor dialed K   Kilroy's private number in his soundproofe windowless office in the basement of his house.

"Can't talk on the phone," Red said. There was no need t remind the head coach where he was or who he was working fo and against. "Call me back in an hour from a pay phone." Re had every known security device, and Dobermans patrolling hi fenced yard. He was one of Major Jack "Pat" Garrett's first clients

"I can't, Red, I got people coming over."

"Okay, okay," Red said. The sound of a film projector rattle in the background. "I'll be here all week long. Day and night Until Saturday. I promised the old lady I'd take her to the movie that night. Can you believe she's making me go look at mor film? Sunday the coaches come over and we set plans for th rookies' mini-camp." Red paused. The sound of the projecto changed as the coach began running the film backward to reviev something he thought he saw. "You call from a secure phone late and come over," Red continued. "When you get here, don't ge out of the car—just honk. I don't want my dogs eating my quarter back. Get here quick. We have a lot to plan."

"Soon as I can, Red." Taylor figured Red had special offensiv plans for the coming season and counterintelligence for the Fran chise struggle. Or both.

"Sorry about Bobby. How you feeling?" Red asked. "You knov I look after *my* boys."

"I know, Red. The trick is to stay one of your boys. Why' you trade Simon to LA?"

"You know as well as I do." The sound of the film projecto changed again as Red slowed it to watch something in slow motion "You didn't help him any by signing for five million dollars wit LA."

"So it's my fault you trade a crippled guy? If Simon was on of your boys, you should have taken care of him."

"I can't talk on your phone, Taylor." Red's phone had a ligh that flashed if the line was tapped.

"Pretend I'm in a phone booth."

"Goddammit, listen for a change." Red's voice was almos drowned out by whirling sprockets and rattling film as he leane up to the projector and adjusted the focus. "You better just com over when you can." Red hung up.

Taylor looked at the receiver. In college Red had intercepte all the players' phone calls and mail, keeping any letters from professional scouts. Red's boys went to the pro teams Red chose and the teams paid Red lots of money to send them.

Red's boys. Only two criteria, Taylor thought as he put the phone back in its beige cradle. *None of Red's boys are crippled or dead.*

After drinking several ounces of tequila, his sore throat burning, Taylor called the commissioner's office.

"Taylor. Good to hear from you." Robbie Burden's voice was cheerful, buoyant. "How can I help you?"

"Commissioner, you *sound* like you have a tan," Taylor said. "I got a call from your office." Taylor drummed his fingers on the table. He disliked Robbie Burden. It was an irrational emotion bequeathed by Bobby Hendrix. Before Hendrix was killed, Taylor just thought of Burden as a harmless, skilled, highly paid lobbyist and public relations man. Now he resented Robbie Burden for being the commissioner and never having been a player. Burden, the opposite of Bobby Hendrix, joined the League as Cleveland's public relations man the same year Bobby was Cleveland's Rookie of the Year.

"Listen, Taylor, I think we need to get together and talk about the problems caused by your signing that Standard Player's Contract with LA." The commissioner purposely slowed the pace of the conversation, trying to gain an edge. "I've talked to our lawyers. We're not certain that the contract is legal. Contracting for your services without public notice like that. I'm just not..."

"You should have said something in Cozumel, Commissioner," Taylor interrupted.

"Cozumel? What are you talking about?" The commissioner was good at sounding genuinely puzzled. "I haven't been to Cozumel in years."

"You and your wife were there on the Cobianco's boat with A. D. Koster and Tiny Walton." Taylor left out Lem and Wendy Carleton. Taylor didn't have a light on his phone like Red Kilroy that warned of eavesdroppers.

"I don't understand why you would say that, Taylor." Burden's voice was smooth and soft. "But we still must meet and discuss this Los Angeles contract that you signed. There are certain problems with it."

"Yeah, right, Commissioner, but they're *your* problems." Out the apartment window Taylor saw a red El Dorado convertible creep into the lot. Speedo Smith's new car had a white top and wire wheels. "Look, I've got people at my door."

"I will definitely be back in touch with you, Taylor." Robbie Burden's voice hardened. "And when you have a minute, you might reread Paragraph Nine. It says I can suspend you without appeal for any goddam thing I please!"

The commissioner slammed down his phone. It sounded like a gentle click to Taylor.

He poured and drank more tequila and spat in the kitchen sink. He had stopped bleeding, but the expensive Herradura still burned his throat.

Taylor watched Speedo, wearing a full-length natural mink, slip out of his bright-red convertible. Another long fur followed him out of the car; inside the coat was a big, good-looking blonde. Taylor recognized Flawless Jade, a Texas exotic dancer. Flawless Jade's debut had been in Dallas at halftime. She had dropped her halter at midfield. Taylor had seen the replay. The Pistols were beating Oakland when it happened.

Speedo Smith rapped on the door and walked inside with his arms thrown wide. The big blonde stood behind while Speedo did a slow full turn to allow Taylor the full effect of the new mink coat.

"That real mink?" Taylor whistled in admiration.

"Turkey, it is genuine drape. . . ." Speedo pulled open the coat to show the bright red lining and the Neiman-Marcus label. "'Cept the label. Flawless took it off one of her coats." Flawless Jade was still outside, standing behind Speedo. Sliding by the smaller man, she stepped into the apartment, closing the door.

"I told him it had to have a Neiman's label," Flawless said. "It just should be from Neiman's. Don't you think?" She looked at Taylor. When he nodded, she hugged Speedo, tucking his head between her breasts, stroking his thick, woolly hair. Flawless wore a full-length coyote coat.

Taylor watched them hug, a beautiful sight. Speedo—with his small, muscular, fine-boned face and smooth dark, black skin—snuggling into Flawless—tall, full-breasted, fleshy but pretty-faced, white-blond hair. The two people entwined with the long, full fur coats. Speedo, Flawless. The Mink and the Coyote.

"I wish I had your style, Speedo." Taylor admired them and sipped his drink.

"You is too white and lower class—morally speaking." Speedo nuzzled the large breasts and Flawless Jade laughed. "Right, Momma? Even with your new wealth, look how you live."

"What you drinkin', turkey?" Speedo, Flawless and the furs tangled.

"Tequila. You know where everything is."

"I ought to know where everything is." Speedo shucked his

coat. "You ain't moved nothing or bought anything new since you moved into this dump. You are froze in time and lost in space." Speedo helped Flawless out of her coyote. "Now I see you got armed guards to maintain the status quo."

"I do?"

Speedo was rummaging through the cabinet for glasses and drink. "Accordin' to the sign."

"I didn't see any sign." Taylor took another drink.

"It's about five feet by five feet and is red and white." Speedo laughed a short, delighted screech. "It's right by the entrance to the parking lot."

"I never saw any sign." Taylor shook his head and drank his glass dry.

Carrying two glasses of Scotch and water, Speedo returned from the kitchen and went straight to Flawless on the couch. He pointed at Taylor as he handed Flawless a drink. "He has to find me and throw me the ball in a stadium full of people and he didn't see *that sign*."

"I just look for the empty helmet," Taylor said.

"I don't see how you could have missed the sign." Flawless's voice was a hard nasal twang. "It damn near kept us from coming in. *Warning: Armed Guards* in two-feet red letters. It stopped us dead."

"It wasn't till we got to the fine print," Speedo said, "that we decided to continue on this mission."

"Speaking of fine print," Taylor said, "what about your contract? Did you read yours?"

"I'll show you mine if you show me yours." Speedo patted his pocket.

"The top desk drawer over there." Taylor held his hand out. "Let me see how A. D. Koster compares to Dick Conly."

Flawless filed her nails and sipped her drink while the two men read each other's contracts.

"Well"—Taylor spoke first, holding up the SPC—"this really *is* a three-year contract, not three one-year contracts. And all the money is due in this century."

"It don't come close to this," Speedo said softly. "A million a year. . . . Will they let Los Angeles have you?"

"I was speaking to the commissioner when you drove up, and I can, with relative certainty, say no, they won't let LA have me. But I can also say with some confidence that *somebody* is going to have to pay that money. Otherwise I take 'em to Antitrust City."

"Poor folks just got regular hell. Antitrust City is only for the minorities, the rich and powerful," Speedo said. "What kind of country discriminates against the rich?"

"Only in America, and I'm proud to be an American," Taylor said.

"It's harder for a rich man to reach the kingdom of heaven," Flawless said, inspecting her nails, "than for a camel to pass through the eye of a needle." Flawless knew lots of scripture and sewing tips.

Taylor and Speedo exchanged looks of amazement.

"All right, Momma!" Speedo said.

"Why did A.D. decide to renegotiate with you?" Taylor asked his receiver. "You got another two years on your old contract."

"Why do you think?"

"The last surviving player representative to the Union?" Taylor replied.

"Straight sellout. A.D. wanted me to spy for him at the Union meetings. I told him I would, so he gave me the bucks," Speedo said. "Now, I'm resigning and nominating you." Pointing a spidery black finger at Taylor, he grinned with his perfect white teeth. "You need to do *something* to protect your five million."

"I don't want to be the player rep."

"Who does? Look what it got Bobby."

"Why are you doing this to me, Speedo?" Taylor pleaded. "Just so you can have furs, white women and big cars?"

"You got it, turkey. You can afford all four"—Speedo tapped the Xerox of Taylor's contract—"white women, fur coats, big cars *and* player rep. You're making so much money you have to care. I am making just enough so I don't."

"Well," Taylor snapped, "quit saying *toot* on my goddam phone, pork lips."

"Fuck you, I got mine," Speedo squealed with glee. "Welcome to Niggertown. You might develop some style yet."

Flawless and Speedo both laughed.

"I always liked you colored boys . . . but from now on expect lots of short routes across the middle. And don't complain if the ball hangs and draws a crowd . . . and don't expect the laces up."

By the time Speedo and Flawless Jade left, she was drunk. While putting on her coyote, Flawless admitted that her name was Emma Lou Richards of Selma, Alabama.

"Boy, they would kill me if they saw me now, wouldn't they?"

"Flawless," Taylor said, "they may kill us all anyway."

Half asleep on his couch, Taylor heard the phone ring several times, but he let the answering service take the messages. They were all from Buffy Martin D'Hanis calling from a phone booth. He tried to return the calls, but she was gone and Taylor ended up talking to a guy claiming to be pursued by a hit squad from the Church of Scientology. When he hung up, Taylor lay back on the couch, fell asleep and dreamed about the fight with Simon in the weight room. The big lineman staggered and stumbled, his face a mixture of pain, panic and killing rage.

"Hey, wake up." Taylor Rusk felt someone shaking him. "Hey buddy, you okay?" Lamar Jean Lukas kept shaking the quarterback's leg. "Hey, Taylor, did those two do anything to you?" Lamar stood by the couch in his uniform; the Smith & Wesson .357 Magnum revolver was holstered and belted snugly around his waist.

Taylor recognized the voice from somewhere and squinted one eye open. He didn't plan to move, but the six-inch blue steel barrel hung at eye level and brought him straight up. Wide awake.

"You okay, Taylor?"

"Hey, yeah, I'm fine, fine, buddy. How you doing? Long time no see. What you doing with that pistol?"

"I'm one of the security guards here," Lamar replied. "Security Services, Incorporated."

"We never had guards before."

"Lot of weirdos out there." Lamar peered out the window, looking for weirdos in the darkness. "Some big Canadian company bought this place and they want security. So a fake Green Beret major puts our lives on the line for the minimum wage while the fucking Canucks take the depreciation and then convert to condos." Lamar shook his head. "And the dollars go to Toronto."

"You do world-market economics too?"

"I just pay attention to what I'm doing."

"Where've we met before?" Taylor wiped his face and eyes, trying to recall Lamar.

"Training camp a few years back." Lamar stuck out his hand. "Lamar Jean Lukas. I had just bought one of the first Pistols season tickets when we met."

Taylor took Lamar's hand.

"I'm pretty well over that now," Lamar said as they shook hands.

"Over what? Buying a season ticket?"

"I had a chip on my shoulder for a while," Lamar said. "Left over from the war. You were rude, but I can dig it. . . . I just walked into your room and woke you up to talk football." Lamar looked around the apartment again. "You had every right to get a little pissed. I just walked in and woke you up because I had a season ticket. One of the first." Lamar nodded. "I just walked right in and woke you up and started talking football, giving you advice . . ."

"Just like you're doing now." Taylor, over his initial shock, was beginning to get bored.

"Hey! No, man"—Lamar held up his hands—"this is security business. I came in here to check on you. I saw some spade in a fur coat leaving here, looking like Superfly with a big blonde on his arm, getting into a red Caddy convertible. I got their license number and ran a Twenty-eight and . . . I kept waiting on the Twenty-eight . . ."

"What's a Twenty-eight?" Taylor was irritated by this guy in the blue uniform, shoulder patch and badge. The big pistol was losing its deterrent value.

"License number check. The computer's down and it still ain't come back. Decided I'd better come up, and when I found the door unlocked . . ."

"You just walked right in and woke me up."

"Yeah." Lamar frowned at Taylor's attitude. "You oughtta be damn glad it was me; there's a lot of weirdos out there. . . ."

"Right. Right." Taylor sensed Lamar's anger and refocused on the Magnum revolver. "I'm sorry. Look, thanks a lot. I'm fine and I'll keep my door closed and locked from now on, believe me."

"What about Superfly and the blonde?"

"Friends. Speedo Smith and . . ."

"No shit?" Lamar's eyes lit up. "That was Speedo Smith? Son of a bitch, I've always wanted to meet him."

"Well, next time I'll introduce you," Taylor said. "Now, exactly how long are we going to have security guards here?"

"From now on, man."

Taylor was glad he was moving. Soon.

"Did you ever see *Walking Tall*?"

Taylor shook his head.

"It was about this sheriff, and when the bad guys would piss off the sheriff, he took a big old slippery elm club and beat the shit out of them. God! I'd like to do that. It would be great."

"Well, you don't have to worry about me," Taylor said. "I'll keep myself locked up here."

Lamar was looking back outside, checking for bad guys and weirdos.

"I'll bet it's great playing ball for the Pistols," Lamar said.

"Not like being in the goddam Marines, getting shot at, or working for the Exxon or guarding asshole Canadians' property." Lamar shook his head. "I bought one of the first season tickets the Pistols sold. Did I tell you that?"

Taylor nodded wearily.

"Oh, yeah, I'm sorry, I woke you." Lamar began backing out of the room. "If that goddam computer hadn't been broken, my Twenty-eight would have come through. . . . *That* was Speedo Smith? Damn, I love to watch him run. I'll see you later, buddy. Keep her locked. And watch out for the bad guys." Lamar backed through the door and closed it after him.

Taylor sat on the couch, momentarily confused. Suddenly jumping to his feet, he walked quickly to the door and locked it. Then he checked the windows and the back door. When he got back to the couch, he was too keyed up, so he poured some more tequila. Taylor sipped it and stared out into the deserted parking lot.

The bad guys?

Who *are* the bad guys?

THE LONG-GONE GAGGLE

RED was walking back and forth in his soundproof basement. Taylor sprawled across several pink plastic classroom chairs and watched his head coach pace.

"Well, I guess you understand the kind of problem we face with Dick Conly gone to New Mexico, A. D. Koster as the new general manager and Cyrus Chandler married to that fucking carhop and pissing on himself?"

"Not exactly." Taylor tried to figure out what Red knew, what he expected to hear, what he planned.

"Not exactly? Not exactly?" Red's face turned crimson. It was the source of his nickname. "The hell with 'not exactly.' You've known that son of a bitch A.D. since he forged his dead grandmother's Social Security checks, for Chrissakes. What the hell do you mean? Not exactly?"

"I mean *not exactly*." Taylor leaned back and let Red rave. He would rave himself out, then they would talk.

"I'm talking about a goddam lying, sniveling cheat that has been made general manager of this football franchise," Red yelled. "We have got to figure out a way to keep him out of the practices and away from the game plans and playbook or we don't win doodley squat."

"Can you trust your assistants?" Taylor asked.

"They're *my* assistants, ain't they?" Red snarled. "If I couldn't trust them, they wouldn't bounce the second time till they hit the goddam Gulf of Mexico.

"Who we *can't* trust is your friend, A. D. Koster!" Red pointed at Taylor; his finger shook, his jowls quivered.

"He isn't my friend. My friend is Simon D'Hanis, the crippled guy you traded to Los Angeles."

"That was *your* fault." Red turned his back and walked to his blackboard, where he broke four or five pieces of chalk and ate them. "You and good old Doc Webster. I never trusted that son of a bitch when I was at the University." The coach crunched up a piece of chalk.

"He didn't trust you, either, Red. For that matter, neither do I. How is it my fault you traded Simon?"

"Simon's through. His knee joint is totally fucked. That idiot doctor really ruined it and the commissioner made that Portus kid at LA take him as partial sanction for tampering. I also got the two best offensive linemen in the draft, plus Greg Moore, a hell of a receiver coming out of the backfield. All that as punishment for signing you to that huge fucking contract. Don't worry, Los Angeles will have to pay Simon off; he passed their physical. But he won't play. You've seen him work out." Red kept his back to Taylor. "We've got the personnel, the system, surprise..."

"What if they don't pay him?" Taylor asked. "What if they just cut him?"

"They won't do that." Red broke some more chalk and ate it. "It's whether everybody delivers on Sunday. Your responsibility..."

"The hell they won't cut Simon; that's *exactly* what they'll do, and you know it."

"Our schedule is good," Red offered. "I figure you want to start fast, win five, six straight, then slump and hide for a couple games...sandbag these jerks...then burn the last four or five games, hitting full stride by playoffs, and hit 'em coming out of the bushes." Red smiled.

"At full speed," Taylor added. "Okay, now what about Simon? You know you're screwing him. . . ."

"Your union's got grievance procedures. That's why you pay Terry Dudley two hundred thousand dollars."

"That's a shitty thing to do, Red. Real shitty."

"So?" Red spun around. "I don't call plays and I don't like it. If you don't like this, tell your goddam player rep."

"I don't like it, Red," the quarterback said, and the two men faced off. "And *I'm* the goddam player rep."

"Aw, sheeit, *you?*" Red bellowed and collapsed into his swivel chair. "We don't have enough trouble?" The color drained from his face. "You think I want to screw Simon?" His voice turned to a whine. "But everybody trades off for what they need. We need help *this year*! We have to win the Super Bowl this year."

"Too fast," Taylor said, "too fast."

"This race isn't all straightaway. We'll show our stuff in the curves."

"If we don't hit the wall or blow up or burn out."

"That's your problem, Taylor. It's what you wanted. I can lay it out, but you have to do it. *You* are the driver."

"Too fast, Red."

"It's the only way. This franchise won't hold together one more season."

It was three in the morning when Red Kilroy and Taylor Rusk finished discussing strategy tactics and personnel in the coach's soundproof basement. Taylor used the secure phone to call Wendy.

"How's the boy?" he asked when Wendy came on the line.

"Sleeping." Wendy's voice was weak, whispering. "The doctor says he'll be fine unless that hole in his throat gets infected."

"I'm sorry I panicked. He didn't look too good, turning blue like that."

"It's over now," Wendy said. "I didn't get a chance to say thanks at the creek."

"I've been with Red all night. We've been discussing how to keep A.D. away from the players, playbooks and game plan."

"That won't be easy," Wendy said. "He's out at the Hot Springs Ranch with Cyrus and Suzy now. I called Daddy to tell him about Randall. . . . Suzy said he was already asleep. I think they're drugging him."

"I wouldn't be surprised; I wish somebody were drugging me. When can I see you and Randall?"

"Don't come here. Lem's coming over in the morning to discuss

— 343 —

the settlement. I'll meet you out at Doc's. We need to find a place to live." —

"Randall's okay? You're sure?"

"I'm sure, Taylor. I'll see you at Doc's." Wendy hung up without saying good-bye.

Taylor put the phone down. "A.D.'s out at the hot springs with Suzy and Cyrus, right now," he told Red.

"Well, at least, he's a long way away." Red's eyes stayed on the movie screen.

"Are we gonna be better this year?" Taylor stood staring at the screen. "Or just faster?"

"Both. I got you all the ingredients and I'll tune up your top hat. The rabbits are in there somewhere, but you got to yank out twice as many twice as fast as ever before. Come on, I'll take you back to your car." Red reached up and took his riot gun off the wall rack. He pumped a double-ought buckshot cartridge into the chamber. "Can't ever trust them dogs." Red shook his head. "In the old days I used to have geese. Best damn guards in the world." Red led the way up the stairs. "A gaggle of geese. Somebody killed every damn one of them after we lost to A & M your sophomore year. If I ever catch the son of a bitch that did *that*." Red shook the sawed-off pump shotgun. "My daughter found 'em. She was only ten. Feathers, guts and blood, all over the yard. Heads twisted off. Jesus, what a sight!" Red opened the door to the outside. "I don't think she ever got over it. She went off to school in Switzerland and never came back. She doesn't even speak English anymore. All her letters are in French. My wife goes there every summer while we're in camp."

The two giant Dobermans came growling around the corner of the house.

"Hold. Hold!" Red yelled at the sleek black dogs as he raised the shotgun.

"Hold. Goddammit. Hold!"

The huge snarling dogs slid to a stop and sat, quivering and growling, while Taylor got into his car.

"Pretty fast, Red." Taylor rolled down his window.

"Do what I tell you and you'll have us a Super Bowl."

"Or crash and burn." Taylor drove away. The coach never took his eyes or the muzzle of the shotgun off the dogs.

Stopping in the lot in front of his apartment, Taylor caught sight of Lamar Jean Lukas wandering through the complex, checking doors and shadows.

"Hey, Lamar!" Taylor felt sorry for the lonely guard in his ill-fitting uniform. "Come on over, I'll buy you a drink."

"It'll have to be a Coke, buddy." Lamar hobbled over, holding the big Magnum to his side. "I can't drink when I'm on duty. I don't drink much anyway. I get kind of crazy."

Taylor handed Lamar his Coke. "Well, Lamar, just because I live here, don't you mistake me for an authority figure."

"Worried about me having flashbacks?" Lamar Jean Lukas stood in the middle of the living room.

"I have nightmares just from playing football." Taylor watched the television screen fill with the face of Billy Joe Hardesty. The volume was off; Billy Joe's fat lips flapped and his eyes blazed silently.

"Don't worry about flashbacks, buddy." Lamar said. "I've had a few nightmares—flipped out once at a rock show when they started the flashing lights and colored smoke bombs—but I'm in pretty good shape now. Hell, I don't even limp near as bad anymore. My counselor says that the delayed stress syndrome is probably not my problem." Lamar sipped his drink. "I black out, that's all...just black out."

Taylor sat on the edge of the couch. "*Just* black out?"

"They caught one of the boys up in Dallas sticking up a bank, and a hot-shot San Antonio lawyer got the brother off; he claimed the war left him with the need for excitement that only sticking up a bank could satisfy. Billy Joe"—he pointed at the TV screen—"said God used the war to punish Americans for creeping humanism."

"'Creeping humanism'?" Taylor watched the soundless Billy Joe.

Lamar frowned at Taylor. "You read much?"

"Books," Taylor said, "not newspapers or magazines. I know how much bullshit is on the sports page; it spoils the rest of the paper."

"Bisexual." Lamar pointed to Billy Joe Hardesty. "I had a corporal in my outfit who was in the All-American Youth Choir. And he married a girl from the Chorale. On their wedding night the girl broke down and confessed she'd had sex with Billy Joe. She's begging my guy to forgive her for screwing Billy Joe and my corporal starts screaming and crying and the girl is bartering her eternal soul. If my guy won't tell and won't throw her out, she'll do anything. Anything! And she does—has for years now. I was at his house when we got back and she treats him like a king." Lamar hunched his shoulders as he laughed. "When I was

— 345 —

leaving, the corporal told me a secret that his wife didn't know and he hoped I wouldn't tell her, but since we'd been together a year, he would tell me the funny half of the story." Lamar wheezed. "When he was in the All-American Youth Choir, he'd screwed Billy Joe too."

Lamar laughed and limped to the kitchen to put his crumpled empty can in the garbage. "I got to finish my rounds."

"Watch out for the weirdos and bad guys." Taylor leaned forward to turn up the volume on Billy Joe Hardesty. "I'll keep tabs on the creeping humanists."

"I heard rumors about the new Dome Stadium they're building in Clyde." Lamar now stood by the open door.

"What rumors?" Taylor held on to the volume knob but turned to look at the security guard in the doorway.

"They're saying that us season ticket holders'll have to buy a five-thousand-dollar construction bond if we want to keep our seats." Lamar's face turned blank. "They promised me that I could always have my season ticket. I bought one of the first ones, you know?"

"I know, Lamar. You woke me up to tell me." Taylor left the volume down and leaned back on the couch. "I heard the same rumor. And next year, A.D.'s going to raise prices and make season ticket holders buy all the exhibition games—eleven games in all."

"Son of a bitch," Lamar whispered softly, amazed that he had been played for such a big sucker. "I feel so foolish. I sure wish they wouldn't do that to me. I should have been treated better; people deserve more courtesy. But it's my fault. I should have paid closer attention. Where am I going to get that kind of money?"

"Hell, Lamar, I'll give the money to you." Taylor finally looked back at the door but it was closed. Lamar Jean Lukas was gone.

Taylor watched Billy Joe Hardesty's *All-American Evangelical Hour*. Billy Joe formatted his show just like Johnny Carson, opening with a monologue sprinkled with both laugh lines and amens.

A fat guy in a wig laughed, amened, and joined Billy Joe on the dais. Billy Joe sat behind a Formica desk. The guy in the wig was on the couch.

"Just let us hear from you," Billy Joe pitched, "and we will send you a copy of my new book, *The Lord and Me*, absolutely *free*. But we need to hear from you if we are to continue our fight against Satan. You can make the difference. . . . Strike the devil a killing blow, send a check for five dollars or fifty dollars or five hundred dollars, we'll send you my book *The Lord and Me* absolutely free. So let us hear from you. Because *I* want to save *you* from eternal damnation."

Billy Joe clapped and rubbed his hands together. "Boy, have we got a show for you tonight. But first I want to send special word out to a dear, dear member of our flock—Brother Cyrus Chandler."

Taylor sat up at the mention of the owner's name.

"You all remember that a while back, right here on our show, we married Mr. Chandler and his beautiful bride, Sally...I mean...Suzy. It was...well, it was just a lovely, blessed event, and we rejoiced together in the Lord and joined two wonderful Christians in holy matrimony." Billy Joe tossed in a few amens. "Amen. And I really mean *amen*, because Brother Cyrus Chandler has truly given his life and wealth over to the service of Jesus Christ our Savior. Brother Chandler has pledged ten million dollars for our construction fund."

Amens were hot and heavy, then the crowd broke into loud gasps, cries, wails, cheers, plus more amens and applause, responding to the flashing applause and Amen signs hung from the studio ceiling. Billy Joe held up his hands. His manner was so similar that Taylor guessed Billy Joe studied videotapes of the *Tonight* show.

"Amen. Amen," Billy Joe said, and began tapping his desk with a pencil.

Billy Joe dropped the pencil and snapped open a legal-looking document. "We were just with Brother Chandler at his ranch recently and he signed this pledge agreement. So you can see we are well on our way to reaching our goal of one hundred million dollars. Now is the time for the rest of you to get out your checkbooks, break open that piggy bank, get out that money you were saving for a rainy day and send it to us, because there is no better use for that money than in service of the Lord Jesus Christ our Savior. We need to reach our one-hundred-million-dollar goal."

"One hundred million dollars!" Taylor said to the television screen. "What are you building? The space shuttle, for Chrissakes?"

"...You all send what you can." Billy Joe grinned. "We don't expect everybody to send ten million....Just send a million...." Billy Joe laughed; the fat guy in the wig joined quickly. Billy Joe Hardesty had made a joke.

Taylor flicked off the TV and stared at the ceiling until dawn.

The next day City Trust, a wholly owned subsidiary of the Chandler Bank Holding Company, was robbed by a lone gunman of five thousand dollars. He waved a large-caliber revolver and demanded five thousand dollars in small used bills. Running from the building with a limp, the man escaped on a stolen motorcycle.

The Stadium Authority bonds went on sale two days later.

The Dome was on schedule for completion in the late summer. Chandler Construction was the general contractor. Cobianco Brothers Construction had the subcontract for the cement work.

Lamar Jean Lukas, one of the first to purchase a five-thousand-dollar bond, got a seat on the forty-two-yard line. He was quiet and sullen while forms were filled out, his knuckles white as he gripped the ticket counter.

Lamar's behavior at the ticket office was not unusual for the early days. The bond scheme did not meet with immediate public approval, and several original ticket holders filed suit. One man was arrested for trying to hit the ticket agent; another took seventy-five stitches in his leg after kicking out a glass door.

When training camp began, some old fans were falling into line and new fans replaced the spaces left by dropouts. Each paid thousands of dollars for the right to buy a ticket for the Pistols games in the Dome.

It *was* the only game in town.

KILLING SNAKES

THE setting sun was squeezing the last drop of red from the sky when Taylor crossed the Dead Man Creek low-water bridge downstream from the terrifying dark green hole that had nearly taken Randall. Taylor shivered involuntarily as the car splashed over.

Up-country, rains had pushed water above the bridge and turned the stream dirty; twigs and small limbs were swirling along.

Once over the low-water crossing, Taylor watched the dirty brown creek. The water didn't seem to be getting any higher. But Taylor could see lightning flashing to the southwest and north. It was going to rain hard soon. He hoped Wendy would get across before it started and Dead Man Creek went on a big rise.

The dying light caught the rippling glint of a water moccasin weaving along the shoreline, trying to stay out of the fast current. The cottonmouth was about four feet long, thick and black.

Loosening up his arm and shoulder, Taylor picked up a baseball-size rock and watched the cottonmouth work its way downstream, swimming directly away thirty yards below the bridge. Taylor took a short windup and threw.

The rock hit just behind the head and broke the neck. Taylor's jaw fell open in amazement. Only the cottonmouth was more surprised; it thrashed against death.

Taylor Rusk watched as the snake sank in the boiling dark water. Thunder rumbled as he climbed back into his car, drove up to the hilltop, left his car in the oak motte behind the house and walked into the kitchen.

The light was on in the bunkhouse; Tommy McNamara's typewriter was clacking away.

The main house was dark and cold.

Taylor set about building a small fire, nursed up the flame, then tossed on a good-size mesquite log. In the kitchen, searching the old white refrigerator, he found a bottle of Carta Blanca, then walked through the living room to the porch and the wide net hammock made to hold two people strung between the naked cedar posts. Taylor stretched across it sideways.

It was dark. Lightning flashed, momentarily wiping out the shadows and illuminating the rocky yard, the gnarled trees, and bushes along the old fence line. Quickly it was black again, but the vision persisted in Taylor's brain as the thunder rolled down the canyon and bounced off Coon Ridge.

Taylor kept his feet on the porch stone and rocked himself slowly, gently, in the hammock. The breeze carried the scent of rain and honeysuckle. The lightning flashed frequently and the thunder came closer on the heels of the fire bolts.

Once Taylor saw a man moving up the bluff to the east, but the next fulmination revealed nothing but fence posts and persimmon. The man was just a figment of electricity, a persistence of imagination. A ghost.

A few big drops of rain thumped the tin roof of the porch. The lightning crashed nearer, louder, until the thunder and light became almost simultaneous. The rain picked up, hammering the tin roof, syncopated by the occasional bang of golfball-size hailstones.

The headlights of a car rounded Coon Ridge, crossed the low-water bridge and headed up the bluff toward the ranch house. When the car reached the bend at the big Spanish oak, lightning turned the night to day. Taylor watched Bob Travers's white Ford heading straight toward him. Inside the car Bob rode in the passenger seat; Toby, his partner, was driving.

Wendy jumped out of the backseat and onto the porch. Bob wasn't going to let a flash flood get between them.

She bent over and kissed Taylor on the mouth, then lay next to him crossways on the big hammock.

The rain drummed the tin roof, hailstones banging like rim shots.

Lightning flashed and crashed on all sides.

Taylor put his arm around Wendy, her head on his shoulder. "How's Randall?"

"Doing fine. Lem's with him tonight and asked me to thank you." She held a small walkie-talkie in her hand—a small red light glowed, showing it was on and working. She reached behind herself and set the black radio on an old apple crate. "And Randall asked me to bring you to see him. It looks like you've made a friend."

"Imagine that." Taylor rocked the hammock slowly. "It only took me four years and I had to nearly kill him."

"Lem cleaned out his desk down at the Franchise and moved back downtown in the First Texas Trust Building. The gas prices are going to make it worthwhile to reopen all those wells his daddy drilled and capped during the fifties, sixties and early seventies." Wendy yawned. "Lem and Junior will probably get rich again. Junior hasn't been doing much since the governor made him chairman of the regents."

"Just dabbling in the two-billion-dollar endowment fund," Taylor said, "up to his armpits." Taylor continued to swing the hammock gently. Wendy took the beer bottle from his hand and drank.

"Cyrus gave *me* stock in the Franchise." She handed the bottle back.

"Why?" Taylor replied. "The League frowns on franchises with more than one owner. The partners might squabble over their dirty laundry and the public would see backstage. The curtain protects the League's integrity."

"Integrity?"

"Yeah. Integrity—the final hiding place."

"It's better than *no* hiding place."

"But it's expensive. Integrity isn't cheap."

"Or easy," Wendy added. "After Lem and I got married. I think he was feeling guilty."

"Cyrus feeling guilty? I find that hard to believe."

"So did Dick Conly. It really pissed him off."

— 350 —

"Did he give Conly stock?"

"No. Nobody else got stock," Wendy said. "Except Randall. When Randall was born, Conly established a trust for Randall and put ten percent of the Franchise stock in the trust every birthday after that. Under the conditions of the trust, the principal can't be touched and only the interest or dividends can be spent," Wendy continued as the lightning split the darkness and the thunder rumbled and banged off the mountain and canyon walls. The rain battered the tin roof. The hail ceased. "Randall wanted toy cars, but instead the trust holds forty percent of The Texas Pistols Franchise stock."

"Who are the trustees?" Taylor was suddenly extremely interested.

"Me, my lawyer," Wendy replied, "my mother and Dick Conly. Conly created it as a shelter from inheritance tax—a charitable nonprofit trust. But if the Pistol Dome hosts the Super Bowl, the trust'll have so damn much money..."

"Unless A.D., Suzy and the Cobianco boys get it first," Taylor warned. "Once they get to the tickets..."

"I imagine that was extra motive for Conly to look for a place to shelter the Franchise from taxes. And from Cyrus—so Dick didn't bother to tell Cyrus that once the trust had fifty percent, Cyrus was odd man out. Conly puts the Franchise stock for Randall in the trust where even Cyrus can't touch it. So he finally keeps his promise to Amos through Randall."

"Dick is pretty clever. How much stock have *you* got?" Taylor asked. Another lightning bolt hit Coon Ridge with a sharp crack, like a giant pistol shot. Taylor and Wendy both flinched. It was a painful sound. A flash of fire.

"Ten percent." Wendy drank the last of the Mexican beer.

"That's the magic number—fifty percent. Your stock combined with the stock in the trust totals fifty percent on Randall's next birthday. You and the trust will have control."

Taylor eased out of the hammock, groaned and stood up. "We'd be a lot smarter, safer and happier if we followed Lem's example and got the hell away from the Franchise." Taylor walked toward the door. "Red's decided to put the pedal to the metal and blow past everybody before they see us in the mirror."

"The Super Bowl? This year?"

"Red's become a real go-faster." The quarterback stopped at the door. "A *too-faster*. I hope you've learned how my circuits work. You may have some rewiring to do by the time this season ends."

"I'll stock up on pennies for the burned-out fuses."

"Very funny. We'll probably all burn."

The storm crashed and rumbled around the old stone house. In back the light was on inside the bunkhouse. The storm drowned out the sound of McNamara's typewriter. Suddenly the wind shifted and swirled, lashing stinging drops of rain. Taylor held the door; Wendy ducked inside out of the storm to the warm glow of the fire.

"Speedo Smith quit as player rep and appointed me in his place." Taylor prodded the flames with an old branding iron.

"Can he do that?" Wendy found a blue wool poncho and sat cross-legged on the Navajo rug between the stone fireplace and the brown couch.

"He says he can." Taylor tossed on two small oak logs and a big chunk of mesquite. He dusted his big hands, put them on his knees and stood up, bending his head and shoulders backward, stretching his spine. Wendy could hear the vertebrae pop and crack. There was a loud snap. Taylor coughed and stopped his stretching. He coughed again, leaning forward, hands on his knees.

"What was *that*?" Wendy wrinkled her nose like he had done something distasteful.

"I'm not sure." He straightened up again. "Lately it's *always* the one that gets me." Taylor coughed again and pointed at his rib cage over his heart. "I knocked some ribs loose and I don't think they ever grew back. When they snap like that it knocks the wind out of me." Taylor frowned and shrugged. "It just got bad recently."

"Have you seen a doctor?"

"Not one I would trust." Taylor coughed and spat into the fire. He tasted blood. "Anyway, it's been this way since before we got the sting routes and pass-blocking straight; we kept missing the stunts and blitzes. Some guy from New York speared me between the shoulder blades with his headgear." Taylor's voice softened and slowed as he recalled the incident. He seldom reminisced. "I had set up wrong or I would have seen him coming. I paid for it and never made that mistake again. The team doctor said it was just a deep bruise. Any deeper and I'd have a hole in my chest. It gets bad at night and I think about the guy that did it." Taylor rotated his trunk, slowly, trying to loosen muscles and unlock frozen joints. "I heard he hurt his fucking neck."

The guy *had* hurt his neck smashing his headgear into Taylor's back. The big defensive lineman had stress fractures of two cervical vertebrae. *His* team doctor told him it was just a pinched nerve.

The cold rain pounded the tin roof.

"There's a Union meeting in Houston soon and I'm thinking about going. Maybe stopping off and seeing Ginny Hendrix."

Wendy nodded and stared silently into the glowing fireplace. She pulled her knees up to her chest and wrapped her arms around them. Wendy hugged her legs and rested her chin on her kneecaps. She was rocking forward and backward, a slight, slow motion.

Taylor stopped at the kitchen door and looked back at her. "I'm player rep by default and do have large and diverse interests in the game." Taylor was trying to be rational. "My contract is causing a stir, and now you and Randall control half of the Franchise. I *better* go; it would be foolish to miss it."

Wendy was now rocking harder, her gaze fixed on the flaming oak. She knew that Bobby Hendrix had died a violent death. The facts of his death had been horrifying enough. Wendy did not want to know the details. The details of Bobby's death in Mexico might dissuade her from the choice she had made.

Wendy Chandler listened to the rain, watched the fire and swayed on the black rug, woven white birds in the gray center, trying to shut out the pictures and thoughts of Bobby Hendrix. She thought of Randall and what she and Taylor both owed him. She did not want to know about the Union and she didn't want Taylor to get involved. She wanted the Franchise for her son; he'd paid for it. It was his by right of suffering. Suffering to come. She could think of no words that would not cause trouble between her and Taylor, so Wendy rocked and stared into the fire.

"Do you want to go?" he asked.

It was the question she had feared. She liked Ginny Hendrix and enjoyed her company, but she hadn't seen Ginny since Bobby's death. It was fact, but until Wendy saw Ginny and looked into her face, the horror of death was not yet reality.

"I don't want to go," Wendy replied. "I don't want *you* to go to the Union meeting especially. Let someone else——Screaming Danny Lewis, Margene or Ox Wood——be the player rep."

"If you plan to take the Franchise away from A.D. and Suzy and your father, you're going to have to deal with the Union and Terry Dudley."

Wendy huddled on the rug. The fire was flaming and sparking. "A.D. bought Speedo off with a new contract," Wendy said. "Why take the job just because Speedo Smith sold out?"

"Speedo deserves the money, the mink coat, the red convertible and Flawless Jade just for what he does on the field every Sunday from August to January. He shouldn't have to be player rep." Taylor shrugged. "Besides, there is power there somewhere, so I should see what it's all about." Taylor was tense and talking hard—not yelling, yet straining. He could taste blood again. "We have to decide who the game really belongs to. Rich promoters—men like your father and Dick Conly? Second-rate hustlers and swindlers like A.D. and Suzy?"

"I plan on it belonging to me," Wendy glared at Taylor. "For our son. I want to give it to him. He's your child too. Don't you want him to have it?"

Taylor shook his head slowly. "I wouldn't want him to have it even if it were ours to give. Which it isn't. It belongs to all the players who ever played anywhere who broke up, crashed and burned or were just whittled down to nothing, trying to make it and never did." Taylor relaxed. Talking was a cure for tension, confusion and fear. "It belongs to those players who made it and never recovered from the success and sacrifice. The families that were blown apart by fame or sucked under by fear. The old players, wrinkled old beauty queens. The drunks, the maladjusted, the beaten, the murderous. Everyone who left their humanity in the game." Taylor watched Wendy growing increasingly irritated with him. "Every player dies a little in every game. Win or lose..."

"The *players* are going to own the game?" Wendy's question was derisive. "They are all such *good* businessmen."

"Some are stupid and greedy, but many suffer from the fatal flaw of *trying* to be honest and fair without learning how. It makes them the perfect victims." Taylor paused. "The system has finally created the perfect player, right down to the brass ring in his nose. The problem is anyone, even Suzy and A.D., can grab that brass nose ring."

Wendy looked back to the fire.

Taylor watched her. "I want to see how Dudley and the Union use the players. Terry could drop a loop through the brass nose ring just like anybody else," Taylor said. "If he does, then we have more problems. If he doesn't, we got more help. And we are going to have to know what we've got and what we're going up against. This franchise is worth billions; we better know how to protect it or at least how to lose it and stay alive.

"Only players really know what happens out there," Taylor continued. "It's the guys you play with and the money you leave with. I want to see what kind of guys I'm playing against and what size nose rings they wear. And why twenty-two exquisitely skilled men between the white lines can't apply those skills outside the lines."

"Maybe they don't want to." Wendy faced the fire and spoke through clenched teeth. "Or maybe they know better."

"Maybe. But you're not a player," Taylor replied softly. "You want to be an owner. I am a player and I don't want my son to be a player *or* owner. I want him to have different, better, choices."

"The middle-class dream." Wendy was openly sarcastic, shaking her head and watching the fire. "The fucking All-American dream. Well, I want a little more than that in my life."

"That's what Speedo said. There's nothing wrong with that." Taylor remained calm. "But if you want more, you have to create it; you can't take it out of another person's hide. If a football game is created—truly created—each Sunday, who are the creators? The players? The coaches? The guy who owns the television network? When rich people want something, they peel some bills off their roll. When an athlete wants more, he has to peel it off his hide—a very expensive price. Does he deserve a reward for that sacrifice? That price? Or is the pain its own reward?" Taylor watched Wendy glare into the fire. "If the game is played for the audience and not the player, it is spectacle. And the ultimate spectacle is death."

"Please spare me the moralizing on the ultimate meaning of professional football," Wendy said. "The ultimate meaning to my old man was the tax shelter."

Taylor walked back to the kitchen and looked out at the bunkhouse. The light was on inside. He couldn't hear the typewriter. The rain was still heavy. He walked back to the doorway.

"If we start the Franchise takeover, never look back or question an order. Once the fight starts, if it hasn't already, we do it by the numbers and the book—my book and my numbers. We can't quit. Now, I'm going to Houston to the Union meeting and to see Ginny and her kids," Taylor announced with finality. "I wish you would come with me."

Wendy slowly shook her head.

Taylor walked to the kitchen. He gazed at the bunkhouse. *Women,* he thought, *they want everything, all the time, no matter what the cost. Fight her daddy, fight the League, the Mob, the Cobiancos. We'll take 'em all. Then she breaks a fingernail and the whole thing is off.* "Quit?" Taylor thought aloud. "It'll be a cold..." He stopped, his eyes drawn to movement in the lighted bunkhouse.

BATTLING MONSTERS

TOMMY McNamara was dead. His face was battered and bloody, featureless, the eyes, nose and mouth caved in; white bone splinters stuck through the chopped flesh. His fingers, cut off, lay in neat rows of five on each side of the typewriter. His Santa Fe Opera T-shirt knotted around his neck, he hung from an open beam, his bare chest and stomach covered with cigarette burns and razor cuts. His ears were cut off and a large strip of adhesive tape covered his mouth.

The bunkhouse was torn apart. His killer had searched for something, probably notes and tape recordings.

Taylor stood outside in the driving cold rain, looking through the screen door at the battered man dangle and twist, fixing his eyes on the bony naked feet and dangling toes, just inches off the floor, an eternity away.

"Taylor?" Wendy called from the kitchen. "Taylor? Is that you out there? What are you doing?"

Taylor stared at the ravaged meat hanging from the beam, a pop T-shirt for a noose.

A Santa Fe Opera T-shirt.

"Taylor?" Wendy called again from the ranch house kitchen. "What is it?"

"Call Bob." Taylor opened the bunkhouse door. "Tell him to get here quick. We just lost one of the guys on our team."

"Oh, God. No." Wendy said it softly, like God was there in the room with her and could be prevailed upon to change things. The radio was on the kitchen table and she called Bob Travers to the bunkhouse, then wrapped herself in her blue wool poncho and watched it all from the kitchen.

Whoever battles with monsters had better see that it does not turn him into a monster. The words were typed on the paper Taylor found in Tommy McNamara's Royal 440.

Bob was at the bunkhouse in two minutes. Toby went to the kitchen to stay with Wendy.

"It looks like they took a long time killing him," Bob said as they cut Tommy McNamara down. "They must have wanted some information, or they just enjoy their work."

"Why do you say *they*?"

"I don't imagine this young fella cooperated any." Bob studied the cut, burned and battered flesh. "And when you start doing this sort of shit, a fella will get plenty hard to handle. See." Bob pointed to large half-moon-shaped contusions on both shoulders. "Somebody was holding him here. Pretty big fella by the size of those bruises...fingers made them. He was keeping your friend still while his partner was working on him. It looks like he squeezed the shoulders out of the sockets." Bob's flat voice rose slightly. He was surprised by the dislocations.

"You seen stuff like this before?" Taylor was horrified, shocked, numb, calm.

"On the border and in Mexico and South America," Bob nodded. "And more and more frequently around here."

Taylor leaned over to peel the white tape off Tommy's mouth.

"I wouldn't do that," Bob said. "As it is they're gonna give us hell about cutting him down. And all you're going to find in there are his ears." Bob pointed to the ragged bloody stubble hacked off at the skin line. "Is this the guy that federal marshal had the subpoena for the other day?"

Taylor nodded. "They were going to immunize him, take him to the grand jury and make him name his source. They wanted his notes and tapes."

"Deep Threat?" Bob asked.

Taylor turned with surprise.

"I read the papers, just like real people." Bob began to run his eyes slowly around the bunkhouse. "So the feds put him between a rock and hard place. I wonder what got him? The rock? Or the hard place?" Bob continued to look over the room. "I wonder if they found what they were looking for. Or if the poor son of a bitch even had it."

Suddenly the wind changed, swirling through the bunkhouse and blowing the death and decay full into Taylor's face. The smell of a man rotting away. Taylor vomited, emptying his stomach onto the wooden bunkhouse floor. He retched and coughed and spat. Bright red blood mixed in with the foaming brown Carta Blanca. Bob brought him a wet towel from the bunkhouse bathroom.

"Chop a man up like that"—Bob looked at the body—"he'll turn bad real quick. You're spitting up blood."

Taylor nodded and wiped his face. He was soaked in sweat.

"When it's someone you know, that smell is too familiar." Bob picked up a blanket from one of the other four beds and covered

Tommy McNamara. "I have worked for Wendy since she started junior high school," Bob said, looking at the abstract dead form beneath the blanket. "But ever since her father bought that damn football franchise, my work has gotten harder and dirtier every day." He looked at Taylor. "What the hell is the matter with people in your business?"

"They get to keep changing the rules. So they have no respect for them. There's no rule book. For them, making the rules is the game." Taylor looked at McNamara's dead shape covered by a brown wool blanket. "How long you think he's been dead?"

"Not very," Bob said.

"Then, with the low-water crossing flooded..." Taylor tried to organize his thoughts.

"They may still be around." Bob reached into his coat and came out with the small transistor walkie-talkie. "Toby? Toby?" Bob spoke into the radio.

"Yeah, Bob?" The voice crackled back.

"It's Red, Toby, Bright Red."

Bob reached into his pocket and pulled out a white envelope. Inside was a radio crystal, a different frequency. Bob inserted the new crystal and waited on Toby, who was doing the same.

"If these guys are professionals," Bob said to Taylor, "they know about us and probably monitor our usual radio frequency. So we carry different crystals randomly. If they were scanning us, they just lost us." Bob put the radio back to his lips. "Kill the lights, Toby, and zip up to the house. I'll call on the radio before we approach. Shoot anybody else and apologize later. *We* are going for booger bears."

Bob turned out the bunkhouse lights.

"Lie down on the floor and close your eyes for a couple minutes," Bob ordered. "Let your eyes get used to the dark. I'm going to the car."

The door opened and closed quietly and Taylor kept his eyes shut until Bob returned, a binocular case around his neck. In one hand he held a metal case. Inside was his AR-15 with a Starlight Night vision scope cushioned against the foam rubber lining.

Taylor opened his eyes and sat up. He could see better; his eyes were adjusting. Bob handed him a long-barreled Colt Python revolver. "Let's hope they don't get close enough that we need it." Bob began checking over his assault rifle. Five fully loaded thirty-shot clips were in a covered pouch that hooked to his belt. A clip was already inserted in the gun. A second magazine was taped upside down to the first, so Bob had sixty rounds quickly available. Holding the scope up to his eye, he wrapped the leather sling around his arm for stability, fingers gripping the stock, the gun held steady. The AR-15 shot a fifty-five-grain slug at 3,300 feet per second, and when it hit, the slug tumbled like a tiny buzz saw, ripping and tearing awful wounds. Bob brought two camouflage rain ponchos and tossed one to Taylor, then filled the pockets with loose .357 ammunition—hollow-point, soft-nose lead, steel-jacketed Magnum cartridges. He showed Taylor how to release the chamber, swing it out and eject the spent brass to load fresh ones. One-hundred-and-twenty-five-grain lead slugs with a flat nose and a hollow point at 1,350 feet per second.

"Use both hands and point like it was your finger," Bob explained. "The muzzle blast kicks up and to the right and it is sighted for dead-on at twenty-five feet. Now, let's not shoot each other."

Taylor looked the massive pistol over and felt the weight of the cartridges in his pocket.

"I checked around and up behind the oak motte with the infrared glasses." Bob pointed at the binoculars hanging from his neck. "Didn't see anything."

"Earlier tonight," Taylor recalled, "I thought I saw someone off to the east of the house near that old fence line that follows the road." He shrugged. "But I don't know...."

"We got to start somewhere. How's your vision?"

"I can see you"—Taylor squinted—"not much farther."

"It'll be worse in the rain. I better handle all the gear and you stay close to me. I look far, you watch up close." Bob pointed at the pistol. "If you think it's time to shoot, don't think, *shoot.*"

"That must be them," Bob said.

They had been searching east of the house below the bluff in overgrown pastureland, creeping and slogging through the bottomland mud and rain for an hour. Taylor had fallen several times and they were about to give up, when the roar of a big engine reached them through the pounding of the storm.

Moving toward the sound, they found they were seventy-five yards from a big, solid black Ford Bronco.

The Bronco had brought the killers in overland along the canyons of Dead Man Creek. Now, going out, they had gotten mired in the rain-soaked bottomland. The high-riding Bronco slid and slipped along the edge of a hill, trying to get around the water that overflowed the creek and filled the pasture they easily crossed earlier. The Ford engine screamed and cried, but the Bronco made little headway; it was slipping sideways.

Bob watched through his infrared binoculars.

"I make out three of them," he said. "The driver is a guy called the Leech. Lennie the Leech. He works for the Cobianco brothers as business agent for the Laborers Union. The big guy riding in front is Tiny Walton." Bob took the binoculars away from his face. "I can't make out the guy in the back, but he looks bigger than Tiny Walton."

"Jesus," Taylor gasped, "bigger than Tiny Walton?" He patted at the heavy revolver in his poncho pocket.

"Well?" Bob was looking at Taylor. "What's your verdict?"

"What?"

"Your verdict?" Bob repeated, wrapping the rifle sling around his arm and fitting his eye to the Starlight sniper scope. "Did they do it? Or are they just out here on a mushroom hunt?"

"They did it."

"Okay," Bob said, "take these infrareds and watch that Bronco. Keep track of anybody who gets out. I can only concentrate on one at a time. I don't want any surprises."

Bob snugged the butt of the AR-15 against his shoulder. He was in the prone position, legs splayed, elbow on the ground, the sling wrapped tightly.

Taylor put the glasses to his eyes. The car was facing them but slightly angled down the grade of the hill, and the headlights diffused into the heavy rain. Taylor could see the driver and Tiny Walton through the windshield. The hulking form in the backseat was unrecognizable.

Pop . . . pop . . . pop . . . the rifle crackled hot death from its muzzle. Bob had barely touched the trigger.

Taylor's ears rang. He kept the binoculars on the Bronco. Bob had aimed directly at Lennie the Leech's sternum; the first shot shattered the windshield, deflecting the tumbling slug down into Lennie the Leech's bowels, ripping and tearing through his intestines and blowing a large portion of his ass off as it exited near his rectum, passed through the seat and buried itself in the floorboard.

Bob raked the car with three short bursts of fire as he searched with the scope for his next target. Just as the cross hairs found him, Tiny Walton dived out the door and Bob shredded the seat with six tiny buzz saws.

Tiny's open door turned on the interior light. The huge man in the backseat was a perfect target. Bob put three slugs into his chest, slashing the lungs and heart, shattering his shoulder blades and cutting his spinal cord.

"Where's Tiny?" Bob was swinging the gun.

Taylor had followed Tiny with the infrared glasses. He ran and slipped and fell and splashed across the open glade. Tiny was moving with amazing speed despite his size and the condition of the terrain.

"To the left, fifty yards from the car," Taylor said. "He's heading for that small ridge line."

"I can't find him in the scope." Bob continued to swing the rifle. "There he is. How did he get that far?"

Bob emptied the clip at the scrambling, crawfishing, running, stumbling fat man. Taylor watched the slugs kick up mud and water around Tiny. At Bob's last shot, Tiny fell out of sight into a small ravine.

"I think you got him with that last one," Taylor said.

"Keep the glasses on the spot you last saw him." Bob removed and reversed the magazine, slamming the other clip into the gun, emptying it at the edge of the ravine where the fat man had fallen. Dirt and mud and rock chips flew, but Taylor didn't see Tiny.

"Shit! He's gone. I missed the son of a bitch. Okay, quick, check the car carefully, then go back to the house and button up." Bob was nervous. "Move! He knows we're after him now. I ain't *that* anxious to kill him. Did you see him carrying anything?"

"No, his hands were empty."

Inside the gore-splattered Bronco, they found a package bound in heavy paper and wrapped in plastic. The killers had found something. Taylor wondered how long it had taken before Tommy told them where it was hidden.

While Bob scanned the ravine once more, Taylor stuck the package under his arm and stood there in the driving cold rain.

They were swimming with sharks.

THE ABYSS

TAYLOR dropped the package on the kitchen table. Toby locked all the doors and secured the shutters before turning on a light.

"Shouldn't we call somebody?" Wendy said. "Doc finally went to the trouble to put a phone in here—"

"Lines are cut," Toby interrupted. "Already checked. I can get on the car radio, but I doubt I can raise the sheriff with the storm."

"Never mind, Toby," Bob cautioned his partner. "Let's think a minute. Tiny Walton is out there somewhere. Scout around the house and make sure the fat bastard didn't circle back here."

Bob turned the light off. Toby opened the kitchen door and slipped out into the rain. The lightning and thunder had begun again.

Bob turned the small table lamp on again. The three people remaining in the kitchen looked at the bulky brown package.

"Should we open it?" Wendy looked first at Taylor, then at Bob.

"If we open it"—Bob looked intently at the package—"we can never tell the law that we found it. We got enough explaining to do."

Taylor touched the wet plastic and thought of the ravaged body hanging from the beam in the bunkhouse, flesh ripped, burned away, ears and fingers cut off. Taylor slowly tore the plastic wrapping away and then split the brown paper.

Inside the package were hundreds of copies of internal documents from Chandler Industries, Inc.; The Texas Pistols Football Club, Inc.; The Football League Commissioner's Office, the newly formed Domed Stadium Authority and Cobianco Brothers Construction, plus personal business correspondence from officials of the various companies, the commissioner, US Senator Thompson, Cyrus Chandler, Don Cobianco and various other people. Some of the names Taylor recognized, others he didn't.

Across the top of the stack was a small scrap of paper with the words "Tommy . . . This here is how it all works and why. You can't say I'm not a clever son of a bitch. D.T."

"Deep Threat," Bob said. "It's what they were after. If Tiny survives tonight and gets back to the Cobianco brothers, they will assume that *we* got the package."

"You think they knew what was in this?" Taylor shuffled through copies of letters to Kimball Adams's travel agency from the commissioner offering five thousand tickets to the Pistol Dome Super Bowl at $450 per ticket. Four hundred dollars over the face value. The letter explained how Kimball could then package Super Bowl trips by block-booking hotel rooms before the commissioner announced the Super Bowl location, then chartering airplanes from New York, LA and Las Vegas. Kimball would charge $100 more per Super Bowl ticket and $200 extra a room. He was to split that profit with the commissioner in cash and assume the tax liability.

League Commissioner Robbie Burden cleared $2,750,000 in cash just from the deal with Kimball Adams Travel.

Two other letters outlined similar deals with travel agents in Los Angeles and Las Vegas. The commissioner would walk away from the Pistol Dome Super Bowl with a total cash rake-off of $8,250,000. At the bottom of one of the deal letters was scrawled the name and numbered account in a Bahamian Bank.

The Bahama Freeport Bank Ltd. . . . Acct. #23765 . . . He will carry it aboard the Cobianco brothers' boat *Momma* in Corpus Christi after the game, straight to Freeport, drop the money, then cruise a few islands while planning next year's deal. I think the Cobiancos get a carrying charge.

The note was initialed "D.T."

"Eight and a quarter million dollars. My God." Wendy sat down heavily in the creaking wooden captain's chair.

"That's tax-free cash." Bob perched on the wobbly stool.

Taylor paced back and forth in the kitchen, then walked into the living room and tossed another mesquite block on the fire.

"Taylor. Taylor," Wendy called from the kitchen, "look what Bob found."

Taylor returned to the kitchen, where Bob was unfolding a large paper diagram of the interlocking connections between the professional football teams and the various organized crime families around the country.

"We should show this to League Security," Wendy said.

Taylor and Bob looked at each other.

"League Security is run by a company called Investico," Bob said, "which is staffed by guys from Justice, FBI, and CIA. One of those guys, J. Edgar Jones, is the liaison between League

Security and Investico. They are all scumbag hired guns who try to discourage overzealous lawmen and use their old agency contacts to cover up, short circuit or obstruct any investigations by law enforcement agencies. They keep the house clean by sweeping everything and everybody under the rug. Investico is owned by Casinos International, which is divided between Mob families from New Orleans, Chicago and California. They started it as a joint venture police and terror squad to protect their casinos in Cuba and the Carribean . . . nice little family business. The whole operation moved to New Orleans when Castro ran them out of Cuba. A Lebanese named Kazan is the Man. Cyrus and Dick did business with him—legitimate as far as I know." Bob paused and thought. "The story I heard was that Old Amos got the Man into the US from the Middle East through Mexico without a passport during World War Two. . . . It's just a story. The Mob families were into professional football because of the betting. In LA, Marconi would bet five hundred thousand a week at the end of the season when they had the division wrapped up. He would bet against LA, then leave star players at home. *That's* where the money was in those days. Fixing games. But Marconi was getting hard to handle, and several owners and the commissioner wanted him out."

Bob looked through papers to compare what he found to the chart Deep Threat made for Tommy McNamara.

"I guess calling the League office is a bad idea?" Wendy was confused.

"These are smart, thorough, mean sons-a-bitches who've been into this a long time." Bob scanned the bundle. "That boy lying out in the bunkhouse wasn't dumb, but sometimes you don't know you're holding a bomb until it blows."

"Bobby Hendrix wasn't dumb either," Taylor said.

"I can't believe my father would be part of all this." Wendy seemed about to cry.

"Who knows?" Taylor said. "Gambling wasn't what Conly saw in the Franchise. He saw an incredible tax shelter and ever-increasing TV money. Here's a letter to Senator Thompson from Conly urging antitrust exemption to allow the second merger and Cyrus didn't even have the Franchise yet. You think he had plans? 'For the good of the game,' he says." Taylor laughed. "And here's the letter from Thompson saying that it's in the bag. Here's another letter about getting complete antitrust exemptions. Thompson says that he'll need help with liberals and labor on the Hill. . . . Here's another letter about deregulating broadcast and pay-TV and abolishing the FCC. . . . Jesus! The foxes will be in the hen house after that!"

"They're planning to stamp out white-collar crime by making it legal," Bob added, and continued his search through the stacks of papers, stopping now and then to trace a name on a letter to a spot on the chart. "If this is right, there are more than a few teams in the League influenced by organized crime. The Pistols aren't listed; Conly saw to that. He knew you couldn't get in bed with those bastards and ever get out again." Bob shuffled through more papers.

"Conly's gone now," Wendy said.

"It used to be the gambling; hell, the Memphis franchise was won in a poker game. But now the legitimate money is so good . . ." Bob studied the chart. "The Kansas City Mob, the Chicago Mob, the Florida Mob, the New Orleans Mob." Bob pulled a two-page sheet out of the stack. It was a complete financial summary of the Texas Pistols' previous season. "Cyrus doesn't have to fix games and beat point spreads, not with these numbers."

"That doesn't mean A.D. and Suzy don't." Taylor tapped the two pages of figures that he held. "Look at the gross revenue for the Pistols for last year alone." His index finger hit right on the numbers. "Twenty-eight million, four hundred thousand. And the next TV contract will be double at least. A lot more from pay-television. Pay-television would mean billions of dollars. Billions! Dick Conly's whole operation is a work of art. Greed operating in the medium of creative accounting and government relations." Taylor handed the pages to Bob. "And the only hurdle left is one they'd hoped Charlie Stillman had handled years ago."

Wendy had her elbows on the kitchen table, her chin in her hands and her eyes glazed at the pile of documents, letters and contracts.

"What's that?" she asked wearily, as if in a trance.

"The Union," Taylor said. "Hendrix got Stillman out and Terry Dudley in. These guys are so greedy that billions of dollars still won't be enough to go around and they'll still be squabbling and killing each other, but in the meantime they'll want the Union back. They'll want big labor support if they're ever going to get these pay-TV and antitrust and deregulation schemes through Congress."

"*The Union?*" Wendy jerked up out of her trance. "Are you kidding?"

"I could take these papers," Taylor said, "show them to Terry Dudley, have him make the financial information public, and cause

— 365 —

all sorts of public reaction. Even Senator Thompson is ultimately responsible to the ballot box."

"No!" Wendy interrupted. "Absolutely not. They'll kill you too."

"We don't have lots of options. The fight has started and we don't have a choice," Taylor said. "Besides, I thought you wanted to take over the Franchise."

"The Union?" Wendy didn't know how to react to that information. "Terry Dudley will see all this?" She pointed at the stack of papers. "And will stop it?" Wendy sagged. "It has to stop. *We* are the bad guys."

"I'm glad somebody finally told me who they were." Taylor smiled. "I had about given up trying to decide."

The kitchen door squeaked open. Bob shoved Wendy under the table, snatched out his pistol and dropped, crouching, into a firing position. Taylor stood paralyzed in the middle of the room.

Toby stepped through the door, his eyes going wide as he looked down the barrel of his partner's revolver.

"It's me! It's me!" Toby squealed, his arms raised reactively.

"Goddam, Toby!" Bob lowered the gun, his voice quivering with emotion. "You should have more sense than to just barge in like that. I damn near shot through the door without even waiting to see. Christ!"

"Sorry, boss." Toby was shamefaced. "I didn't see anybody outside."

"I been rethinking this." Bob stuffed the blue steel Magnum back in its holster. "My suggestion is that once the storm stops and the creek goes down, we clean up our own mess and get out. Deny everything. We were never here. That way none of us ends up squeezed between the grand jury and the Cobianco brothers."

Taylor nodded agreement, half listening as he read a letter from Don Cobianco to A.D., promising "to take care of any labor troubles in return for the certain considerations previously discussed." Cobianco Brothers Construction got all the cement work on the new stadium. The brothers also contracted for laborers on the Pistol Dome, bringing them out of Mexico in trailer trucks, keeping half of their pay. Any troublemakers became part of the Pistol Dome.

"You go back out and stay with the car, Toby," Bob said. "Keep your eyes open and the doors locked. We'll stay in here and do the same.

"Get the three-fifty-seven out of the glove compartment and

keep it next to you on the seat. First, bring me the shotgun. The quarterback here can hit something with it."

Toby turned back to the door.

Bob turned off the kitchen light and Toby slipped out. In a moment he was back, slipping silently into the kitchen again. In his hand he gripped an eight-shot Smith & Wesson twelve-gauge sawed-off shotgun. Toby locked the door behind him and Bob turned on the light.

"Show him how to use it," Bob instructed. Toby showed Taylor the safety catch, the pump mechanism, the pump release and the loading procedure. Taylor took the vicious-looking gun, Bob turned out the kitchen light again and Toby slipped back out to take up his post in the car.

Taylor took the shotgun into the living room and propped it next to the brown couch. Putting another couple of oak logs on the glowing coals, he sat next to Wendy on the black and white rug. They both stared into the fire and said nothing while Bob moved from room to room, checking the outside with his infrared binoculars.

The rain let up around five A.M. and stopped completely by daybreak. The creek had dropped enough by afternoon to ford the low-water bridge. Wendy went with Bob and Toby. Taylor drove alone. Bob offered Taylor the shotgun but the quarterback refused.

"If they want to kill me," Taylor said, "I'm not very hard to find and I'm an easy target."

"Well, put that in a bank vault somewhere," Bob said, pointing to the package of documents that had cost Tommy McNamara his life. "Then write out your will and leave instructions that the safe-deposit box be opened with only the people you choose present. I would include Wendy and the chief judge for the western district, plus a lawyer you can trust. Do you know any?"

Taylor shook his head. "How about you?" he asked.

"If Wendy's there, I won't be far away." Bob clapped Taylor on the shoulder. "You got balls, kid, but I wouldn't show those to anybody and I believe you should get yourself a gun."

"My apartment building has security guards."

"What company?"

"Security Services, Incorporated."

Bob frowned. "I believe I'd get myself that gun. The guards SSI hires aren't any match for Tiny Walton or Investico, if they get involved. Keep your eyes peeled and your back to the wall; stay low and move fast." Bob walked to his car. That was his good-bye.

The white Ford drove off with Wendy in the backseat. She never turned around. Taylor followed them out to the main road. They turned in opposite directions.

Taylor followed Bob's instructions concerning the documents, with one addition. He made one more set of copies at the Quik Copy near the University. He spent days studying the documents. He planned to take them to the Union meeting in Houston.

Taylor watched the paper and listened to the news for days. There was never any mention of the three dead men they had left at Doc Webster's ranch.

Nobody *ever* mentioned Tommy McNamara again.

> *If you gaze long enough into an abyss,*
> *the abyss will gaze back at you.*

That was the rest of the Nietzsche line that Tommy McNamara had planned to type on his Royal 440 when he was so rudely interrupted.

A SMALL REVENGE

THE next morning Taylor called Wendy's house. Lem Carleton III answered.

"They're both gone, Taylor," Lem said, "I don't know where. She packed up and left in a big hurry. You know we're getting a divorce?"

Taylor said he knew.

"I was wondering how the boy was doing?" Taylor continued. "I damn near killed him sticking that hole in his throat. I'd just like to make sure he's all right."

"He's fine, Taylor. And I want to thank you for what you did that day. You risked your life for my . . . I mean, *our* son. You don't mind if I lay some claim to him, do you? I raised him some. He is a good boy, and it looks like you'll be the one to make a man out of him."

Taylor was embarrassed and saddened being told about his own child—times he had totally missed. He felt weak, ineffective, foolish. Helpless.

"They'll be back," Lem said. "Wendy said she just had to get away for a while. She seemed pretty shaken. I guess I'm taking the divorce better than she is. I hope we can all be friends. I always liked you, Taylor, even back in Spur. Come have a drink with me sometime. I'll tell you stories about your son. He's a pretty remarkable kid."

"Thanks, I'll do that." Taylor nodded his head and his feet shuffled nervously. "If you hear from Wendy, tell her I'm looking for them. And I'm sorry things didn't turn out for you."

"Oh, they turned out fine. I wanted out of the Franchise. It's a sick business. It makes the oil business look like social work." Lem laughed at his own joke. "You be careful. With Conly gone and old Cyrus pissing on himself, there's a new regime up there. A.D. has increased the front-office staff by double and brought in some real bad guys who don't know a football from a pick handle. He put Johnny Cobianco on the payroll at two hundred thousand dollars a year plus expenses as a scout."

"They didn't waste any time."

"Cobianco never came to the office while I was there; neither did the others. I just saw the checks," Lem said. "I called the commissioner's office about it and the next day somebody slashed all my tires and broke out the windshield of my car. I'm glad to get out without a major injury."

"A.D. could accomplish the impossible and *really* lose money this year," Taylor replied. "What does Red say about all the new people?"

"Nothing yet. He's still got all *his* coaches and scouts in place. If A.D. starts tampering with them, I imagine Red will put up a fight."

"Does Cyrus ever come in?" Taylor asked.

"Never. Suzy keeps him out at the hot springs. You wouldn't recognize him. I flew some papers out that had to be signed and all he did was sit there, picking imaginary lint off his bathrobe. Suzy's got some big Mexican to haul him in and out of bed. I imagine the second Mrs. Chandler will have power of attorney before long. He acts senile, but she's doping him, keeping him isolated and disoriented. The only time he gets unreasonable or even shows any signs of life is when he watches Billy Joe Hardesty's *All-American Hour*. Your pal Dudley was on the show the day I was there."

"Do you ever hear from Dick Conly?" Taylor asked. "You don't figure Conly would come back and help Cyrus?"

Lem laughed. "Only if he was helping five others carry the old bastard to his grave."

"Then, there really isn't anybody to keep Suzy and A.D. and the Cobianco brothers from looting the Franchise?"

"Not unless you want the job," Lem said. "My call to the commissioner didn't do anything but cost me a perfectly good set of radial tires and a tinted windshield."

Taylor hung up the phone.

Wendy must have taken the boy and gone to hide out, Taylor thought. It made him lonely, but he felt safer knowing that they were taking serious precautions.

He wished he knew how to take precautions.

He wished he knew how to be serious.

You can't take yourself very seriously when you spend your life playing games, he thought. It is a double bind: playing meaningful and meaningless games. The up and down drove men crazy if they didn't understand the difference between failing and quitting. That is the secret, Taylor decided: Failure was inevitable but quitting was choice. And guilt was the result of the misunderstanding.

But in the *real game* that A.D., Suzy, the Cobianco brothers and the commissioner were playing, the difference didn't matter because failures or quitters still ended up dead. Guilt was meaningless.

The real game.

Taylor looked over at the stack of copied documents that he had assembled for the Houston Union meeting.

I might as well trust old Lamar Jean Lukas to get me through tonight, Taylor decided, and stretched out on the couch in his apartment. He punched the remote control and turned on the television to watch the nightly news for word about the massacre at Dead Man Creek. The face of Harrison H. Harrison filled the screen and Taylor pushed up the volume.

"New York police could establish no motive for the brutal attack on Mr. Harrison, president of Venture Capital Offshore, outside Mr. Harrison's apartment, where at least five men assaulted him with baseball bats, breaking his arms and legs. Adding to the mystery was the burning of several Greek letters into Mr. Harrison's forehead. The assailants had what authorities claim was an electric branding iron. The police have not speculated except that the letters were Greek and spelled a slang vulgarity for a portion of the anatomy, but not the forehead. Mr. Harrison is in satisfactory condition at an undisclosed location."

The television picture cut from the full face of Harrison H. Harrison to the anchorman, who turned to the weatherman.

"Boy, Mario!" the anchor said to the small Chicano weatherman. "It takes all kinds, but New York is getting weirder by the day."

"Right, Bob, I'll take Texas any day," the Chicano grinned. "And especially tomorrow, because I have got a great day in store for all you sun worshipers. . . ."

Taylor clicked off the television. He wasn't a sun worshiper.

HARLAN COUNTY

TAYLOR followed I-10 eastbound for Houston. He would stop at Gus Savas's place in River Oaks and see Ginny and her two youngest boys. Jimmy had joined his older brother attending the University of Texas.

Taylor had the documents on his lap and constantly checked his mirror, pulled off at rest stops and made directionless trips on side roads, trying to see if he was being followed. For all his paranoid effort he didn't discover any trackers. Nor did he lose them; they had planted a small transmitter in the rear bumper of his car.

At dusk Taylor pulled up to Gus Savas's sprawling River Oaks home with a false sense of security.

"Uncle Taylor, Uncle Taylor, did you bring us a surprise?" Billy and Bobby Hendrix came running out to meet him and each grabbed a leg. They had grown and changed rapidly, as only children that young can.

"Let me look in the trunk, boys," Taylor said, trying to move to the back of the car with one clinging to each leg.

"Yeaa! Yeaaa! See, Mom, we *told* you Uncle Taylor would bring us a present!" A slight snottiness crept into the voices, berating their mother for telling them earlier not to expect presents just because Taylor was coming.

Ginny Hendrix stood smiling in the open doorway while Gus stepped out at his stumpy pace; like his grandchildren, he did not want to be left out.

Taylor popped open the trunk and pulled out a microprocessor electronic game.

"Yeeaaa!" the boys squealed. "A 'lectronic game." They immediately fell to arguing over who would get to claim ownership.

"Hey," Taylor scolded the squabbling boys, "this game is for your mother. If she wants to let either of you two play with it, you are going to have to ask her and say *please*. You get me, fellas?"

The two boys nodded, then turned and ran to their mother, yelling, "Me first"—"Me first"—"No, me"—"No, me."

Gus let the boys plead with Ginny while he helped Taylor unload.

"Taylor, my boy, how are you?" The greeting was effusive. Gus hugged the tall quarterback, and for a moment the two men seemed to clutch each other for security, safety. Taylor felt the hard bulk of the Mauser .380 automatic Gus had stuffed in his belt under his shirt.

"It's gotten pretty weird, Gus." They released each other. Taylor leaned into the trunk. "Somebody had Tommy McNamara killed. I guess the same people that did Bobby."

"The Cobianco brothers," Gus announced, then picked up a Texas Pistols equipment bag. "Tiny Walton was the cameraman on that plane in Cozumel," Gus said.

"I know. That's all Bobby's stuff." Taylor pointed at the bag Gus had pulled out of the trunk. The bag had *Texas Pistols #88* silkscreened on the side. "I went down and cleaned out his locker. Hide it away somewhere. Ginny and the kids might want it in a few years."

"I'll leave it in your trunk"—Gus dropped the bag—"and come get it later."

"Tiny Walton was in on the killing of Tommy McNamara," Taylor continued, "but there hasn't been a word about it." Taylor pointed to his own bag. "I got the documents that they took from Tommy. I guess they killed Bobby thinking he was Tommy's Deep Threat."

"Damn Tommy," Gus said. "He should have known that using a name like that would put the suspicion right on Bobby. But no, the dumbshit has to play Watergate. Stupid shitass sportswriter." Gus crouched down and unzipped the duffel bag to check the tools of one of the great wide receivers in football. Gus pulled out Hendrix's big jar of Nutty Putty. Bobby always had had the putty in his hands, squeezing and exercising, turning his fingers into the strongest and surest in the history of the game. All gone now, all that work, effort.

"I'll bet he wished he'd spent the time teaching himself to fly," Gus said. "He probably could have done it."

Gus opened the bottle and shook out the putty while Taylor pulled his bag out of the trunk. Gus dropped the wad of plastic under the yellow Lincoln. Stretching to reach the putty, Gus turned and saw the transmitter stuck under the bumper.

Gus stopped and looked closer. He had seen lots of bugging devices and electronic eavesdropping gear. In the oil business, espionage is much of the trade. "You got a traveling companion under here."

Taylor knelt down and looked under the bumper; the little black transmitter was attached by a magnet. Taylor reached for it, but Gus grabbed his arm.

Gus put the putty back into Bobby's old equipment bag and slammed the trunk shut. "I don't see them. Probably around the corner, out of sight, just listening to the beeper." He looked up and down the street. "You go on inside while I put your car in my garage." Gus's eyes blazed for a moment. "Did you hear about the terrible accident that Harrison H. Harrison had right outside his fancy-pants apartment?"

"It was on television." Taylor nodded. "What Greek letters did they brand on his forehead?"

"*Asshole* would be the closest translation in English, but it means more than just that." Gus walked around to the driver's side of Taylor's car, jerked open the door and slid behind the wheel. "That's the breaks in the oil business."

"While you're in the garage, take out Bobby's bag and stash it."

Taylor turned up the walk to the front double doors of the sprawling white brick mansion. He had his bag in one hand and the game under his arm. The two boys waited on either side of their mother, hopping up and down.

"Please. Please. Momma." They each pleaded. "Please. Please, Momma. Please. Please."

It took about twenty-five minutes to find a television set and hook up the game. Taylor had brought game tapes that simulated tank battles, an invasion by space aliens, baseball and spelling. Shortly the room reverberated with bleeps, bloops and roars of electronic battles punctuated by the screams and cries of the two boys fighting colored dots on the television screen and each other and themselves.

Ginny frowned at Taylor when the bleeping and squalling and screeching reached a particularly feverish pitch.

"Thanks, Uncle Taylor," she said. "At least maybe now they will forget about how you and their daddy killed Hitler and Mussolini and won World War Two."

"We may have to win World War Three before this is all over, Ginny." Taylor leaned over, kissed her cheek and hugged her. She wiped tears from her eyes when he released her.

"It's funny"—Ginny was sniffing—"when you called to say you were coming, I had this thought that when you arrived, Bobby would be with you and everything that happened in Mexico would have been a dream." She wiped her eyes. "But here you are all alone. It's hard to believe he's gone forever. Real hard."

A door opened and closed in the back of the house somewhere and Gus walked into the big living room. He had the transmitter in his hand.

"Your car is locked up safely in the garage." Gus sat down in his favorite leather chair. "I have one of my men on the way over."

The boys started fighting and yelling from the den. Ginny went in to referee the struggle with the alien invaders.

"I called the River Oaks security," Gus continued. "Whoever is following you won't be able to park around here all night; the security boys will keep them moving and off balance. When my man gets here, he'll take the transmitter into the bayous. He's got some kinfolks in Vidor that just flat don't like outsiders. And believe me, Vidor takes it all pretty serious."

Taylor watched the three people in the den arguing about whose turn it was to kill the alien invader.

"How have they been taking Bobby's death?"

"Okay, I guess." Gus stared at the door to the den. "I probably took it worse. They never saw Bobby; I wouldn't let Ginny open the casket. Maybe that was a mistake, maybe you're supposed to see the dead so you *know* that they're dead. But Jesus, he looked a whole lot more than dead; he was smashed to fucking pulp. Just sort of exploded when he hit those ruins. Some American there said pieces of Bobby flew all over. He hit near the top, directly on a sacrificial stone. The guy said Bobby never made a sound, not a scream. Nothing. He just fell and hit like a ripe watermelon." Gus looked at Taylor. "I couldn't let them open the casket, there was nothing in there but a bag of mush. Ginny was mad at me for a long time for not letting her see Bobby. But it's better that she remember him alive. Don't ever live long enough to bury your children." Gus turned his dark Greek face to Taylor. His eyes were blazing black coals of hatred. "A. D. Koster and Charlie Stillman and Robbie Burden were all there on Cobianco's boat when it happened. Stillman was in the plane and that goddam sleazy low-life son of a bitch Kimball Adams was the one who took Bobby to the airport. . . ."

"I don't think Kimball knew what they had planned," Taylor said. "I found him two or three days later, a blubbering, heart-broken drunk. They just used him."

"Yeah," Gus said angrily, "and they still use him. Being weak and stupid isn't a defense, Taylor. Don't ever forget that. If I live long enough, I'm going to settle the scores. Harrison H. Harrison was only the first, and that was just for fucking me and Bobby on an oil deal." Gus held up a clenched fist. Taylor was surprised by the size. It was a formidable weapon.

Gus continued to hold up the clenched fist. "I know it was Tiny Walton, but for who?" Gus hit the arm of his chair. "I'd like ten minutes alone with that little weasel and we'll find out real quick why he threw Bobby out. Did Tommy tell you anything?"

"Tommy didn't last long," Taylor said. "I don't know who his source was."

The doorbell rang. Gus jumped quickly from his chair and walked out of the room, holding the small transmitter. He returned empty-handed. "My man's got a Lincoln just like yours, maybe a year or two newer. Whoever was following you is going to find themselves at the end of a very long dirt road in the middle of the Thicket, surrounded by a lot of guys in white sheets, toting shotguns and pistols."

"You look okay financially." Taylor looked around at the opulent interior of the River Oaks mansion. "Still rich?"

"Naw, not since the VCO bust out. Now I am highly levered." Gus smiled and raised his bushy black eyebrows. "I'm into the banks for so much, they got to keep me afloat if they ever hope to get *any* money back."

The electronic war continued in the den until late that night.

The next morning, on his way to the Union meeting, Taylor's car radio told the news of two men arrested stark naked on the Eastex Freeway. He guessed they were agents of Investico sent by J. Edgar Jones.

Taylor Rusk was now certain that Robbie Burden had him listed as "off the reservation."

The first meeting had already begun when Taylor arrived at the hotel. He sat in the back of the big ballroom. Terry Dudley recited the history of the early labor wars in the League, invoking Bobby Hendrix as a classic labor martyr. In closing, one of the players who had been blacklisted himself for Union work pointed out that Bobby Hendrix had died under very mysterious circumstances.

"We are talking about serious sums of money here," the player said. "People have been killed for less. It may be time to pick up the gun."

The room fell silent, and the only sound was the squeak of the player's shoes as he returned to his seat on the dais. No one spoke. Nobody moved.

Time to pick up the gun?

The room full of men who had spent their entire working lives honing their exquisite skills of violence were struck dumb by the thought that they might have to use violence to gain their union goals. It confused some and frightened many, but the ex-player knew what he was saying and why.

So did Taylor Rusk. So had Bobby Hendrix.

"Think of yourself as a coal miner, Taylor," Hendrix had said. "And professional football is the Harlan County of your mind."

THE UNION

"*SOLIDARITY* is the word. We start to lose this battle when we are not unified," Union Director Terry Dudley said. "This will be a fight and we must be *ready* to strike, *organized* to strike, not *afraid* to strike. Solidarity." He hit the podium with a clenched fist. "Organize or Die. Strike or Die."

"They don't *own*, they *promote*, football games. The only people with the requisite skill to play the game are you people right here in this room." The tall man pointed out at the meeting room full of players. "You are the best, the finest, football players in the world, and without your skills there would *be* no football. But we are fast approaching the time when your exceptional skills will not be quite so necessary. Let me quote you some figures and see if you understand." The tall man in his blue blazer, gray pants and black loafers gripped the sides of the podium with his slender fingers. Strands of hair curled along his forehead. "Ninety percent of all seats to all professional football games were sold last year. Most teams sell out every game whether they have a winning or losing season. Some of the worst teams in the League have *no tickets* available for the general public. *None*. They have been sold out for years, although they haven't had a winning season since Ike was in the White House.

"The incentive to win, to compete, exists for players and coaches but does not exist for the promoter. You notice I call him the *promoter*. And he is often a *great* promoter. The League hypes the draft and idolizes the number-one pick and explains that by letting the last team pick first the level of competition stays even. That of course is pure bullshit perpetuated by Robbie Burden, our beloved commissioner, in order to keep the draft in place and players' salaries depressed."

The director wiped his hand across his creased forehead, pushing the hair back. Regaining his hold on the podium, he leaned forward.

"The truth is that the draft serves *no other purpose*, and if you aren't drafted in the first couple rounds, it's a much better deal *not to be drafted at all*. Because in reality you're not drafted, you're taken prisoner. The number-one pick has some leverage because the *promoter* will look stupid if he doesn't get his number one. But much lower than number one or two and your bargaining power disappears—and you learn the first reality of the game. The promoter has perpetual rights to you and perpetual is a long time. There is no other labor market. It is what economists call a monopsony."

Terry Dudley was beginning to work himself up. His was the final talk of the morning session.

"Canadian football? You can try it, but they only have eight teams and each team is only allowed fifteen Americans; and besides, the Canadian Football Conference is in bed with our league. The commonality of interests between rich-men promoters runs much closer than any fellowship they feel for *you*. They consider you *property*. You are their *tax shelters*."

The director of the Union stopped and looked around the room, letting what he had said sink in. His blue eyes scanned the upturned faces, more black than white.

"Competition?" Terry began again. "Oh, there's competition all right, but it's not between the *promoters,* it's between you guys for the fifteen hundred spots, the only fifteen hundred jobs in the world that are available to you. And you have to *break your ass* to get one of those jobs. The *promoters* don't have to compete. Winning and losing has little bearing on profitability.

"Network television pays each team *eleven million dollars a year* on their new ~ontract. The highest team expenses calculated on the sketchy figures they give us is only five million dollars. They are six million dollars in the black and they haven't sold a ticket at the gate yet. Add ticket sales of, let's say, five million dollars, on the low side. Now the team has thirteen million dollars gross before-tax profit."

Terry quickly scanned the faces of the crowd. He feared the numbers parts of his speeches—they always seemed to lose the audience a little—so he pushed through them quickly.

"Now, the promoters have other expenses. Dallas claims it costs them $150,000 to scout, draft, sign and train each member of its franchise, but remember, that's money that is really just moving from one part of the franchise to another. Stadium rentals? Most teams play in municipal or city stadiums that are tax supported and usually get a discounted rent. A few teams own their own stadiums, which allows them to charge whatever rent they please, depending on each year's tax situation.

"The Texas Pistols Dome financing scheme may be the most ingenious scheme I have seen yet. The fans must first finance the domed stadium before they can buy a ticket. And only a select few know what sort of tax break the city of Clyde, Texas, is giving the Pistols franchise to move a few miles south. Taxes that someone else will have to make up.

"I haven't even tried to list the other sources of income to the promoters, like parking, programs, concessions, licensing agreements through the privately held Football League Properties, Incorporated. They are substantial amounts, but the main income to a franchise is its monopoly rights on television and gate receipts. Its monopsonistic rights on labor allow it to control the Franchise's major cost: player salaries."

Terry Dudley, director of the Union, took a moment and stepped away from the podium. He was getting ready for the stretch run of his speech. He wanted to be ready and he wanted it to be right. He took his handkerchief and wiped the sweat from his face, then took one more look at his audience. They seemed receptive, they seemed to be listening, but then they could still be stunned from the previous speaker telling them they might have to *pick up a gun*. Terry worried about that but it was too late. It had been said, it was in the air. The tall man stepped back to the podium and again gripped both sides of the stand. He stared at his audience.

"Informed sources tell us that the next network contract offered to professional football will be well over three billion dollars.

Three billion dollars! Can any of you even conceive of three billion dollars?

"It will break out to approximately twenty million dollars per team per year. Now, with that kind of income, win or lose, what is the incentive to the promoter to pay high salaries to secure the best playing and coaching talent? *There is none.*

"The *promoter* is into *profit-maximization*, not winning silly games. He's a businessman, and so what he spends his time doing is not diagraming plays but figuring out how to cut expenses and hide profits to *avoid taxes*."

Terry Dudley's eyes flicked around the room, and for the first time he saw Taylor Rusk. Taylor's presence startled him. The big-money stars seldom came to Union meetings and were generally the ones who broke any attempts to strike by crossing the picket lines and going into camp.

The director quickly recovered from his surprise and went on with his speech.

"The promoter's tax avoidance schemes are too complicated to go into here and apparently too complicated for the IRS, because they continue to allow all sorts of weird schemes. For instance, last year a number-one draft choice was signed by New York to a contract that was reported in the press as $1.8 million for five years. Sounds like a lot of money.

"But after signing with his agent, Charlie Stillman, who took his ten percent directly from the New York franchise immediately on the total aggregate amount, the player had second thoughts and brought the contract to the Union. By the time he got to our offices in Washington and had our lawyers look the contract over, he had already bought his mother a house and himself a Rolls-Royce.

"First, of the total $1.8 million, exactly $800,000 was a one-time cash bonus, which serves several purposes. One, it reduces the actual size of his base salary by $800,000, so when he negotiates again—if he does—he will be negotiating from a four-year base salary of not $1.8 million but $200,000 per year. Second, of the $800,000 cash bonus, only $100,000 was paid immediately. The remainder was deferred until the year 2010, to be paid in yearly installments until the year 2025. The New York franchise, on the other hand, expenses the whole $800,000 immediately while they put the remaining $700,000 in the money market to draw interest. In five years minimum they have doubled the money at no cost to them. By the year 2010 they will have had use of the player's money for over twenty-five years *interest-free*. The agent, Charlie Stillman, advised the player to sign the contract because

Stillman got his ten percent immediately and it was in *his* best interest to get the biggest numbers—even if it wasn't in the player's. Also, the player's salary was carried on the Franchise books at $200,000 a year, but Charlie Stillman again convinced the player to defer half until the year 2010. It, too, would be paid out in yearly installments until the year 2020. The agent gets his ten percent immediately on the full amount. The New York franchise carries the player's salary on its books for tax purposes as a $200,000-a-year expense."

Terry Dudley looked again at the faces in the crowd; the wrinkled brows and low mumbling told him that for the first time several men finally understood their contracts.

"Needless to say, it was not very much fun to have to explain to the player that not only was he *not rich*, like the newspapers said, but he was actually broke. He couldn't possibly make the payments on his mother's house and his Rolls-Royce and meet his daily living expenses."

Dudley held up his hand.

"Now comes the real bad news. The player has learned his lesson and he's going to do better on his next contract—but more than likely there will be no next contract. The average career is *four years*. Right at this moment, seventy-two percent of all players in professional football have five years experience or less."

Terry gave the players a moment to wrestle and come to terms with all the numbers and schemes he had just thrown at them. He glanced again at Taylor sitting quietly in the back with a brown paper package in his lap. Terry recalled that Bobby Hendrix had always said that Taylor Rusk would eventually make a good Union man. The director had dismissed Hendrix's appraisal, giving more credit to Taylor's ability to be all things to all people. It was an ability that was necessary if not generic to all major-league quarterbacks. They not only had to lead and control a team of stars—giant men in suspended adolescence, spoiled, deceived, pampered—but also, like the head coach, the quarterback was the interface between the players and the promoters. To survive for long as a pro quarterback required quick wits and a selfish ruthlessness.

Terry Dudley took a last glance at Taylor Rusk and stepped back to the microphone.

"You, as players, will negotiate one, *maybe* two or three, contracts in your whole career," Dudley continued, "while the man you negotiate with will have negotiated hundreds, maybe thousands. Plus he will have access to the data on the salary schedules of the other League franchises. The promoters who call themselves owners meet three or four times a year to discuss the problems of their business." Dudley held out his hands. "What are the problems of the football business?" He paused for effect. "*You. You* are the problems.

"Your salaries are the major expense and the promoter-owners complain publicly about rising salaries destroying the game. Well, here is a figure you can toss back at the next newspaper man or TV sportscaster when he asks about 'high salaries': In the mid 1960's, *before the merger*, the salary was around $18,000 to $20,000 and accounted for almost fifty percent of a franchise's total revenue. Today, *after the merger*, the average salary is around $130,000 and accounts for *only twenty-eight percent* of a franchise's total revenue.

"It's simple math and even the sporting press can understand it, drunk or sober. I'm not saying they'll write it, or care about it, or even consider it, because they know that *you'll* be gone one day and the *promoters* will still be around, handing out free plane tickets and drinks and, most important of all, giving them *access*."

Terry turned to the last page of his text. He glanced around the hall. No one seemed to be fidgeting; the speech was going well. Taylor Rusk sat quietly and erect in the last row, holding his package, looking straight ahead.

"It has taken us a full decade," the director of the Players Union continued, "to get this far. We haven't set the world on fire, but we *are* a union, a *labor* union, and we have built a foundation for the eighties, at great cost both in money and in men's careers. Great athletes were traded or cut outright for Union activity, and there will be more reprisals and more players will be sacrificed. The promoters will tell you that the *Union* is the reason that you're being cut . . . that the Union is causing you all the trouble. But we now have a pension, a true grievance procedure, collective bargaining and several important court rulings in our favor. Now comes the real battle, because we are asking for true free agent status and an end to the compensation rule, which totally eliminates movement except when the promoter wants to sell or trade one of you, so he gets the profits on the sale of your bodies as assets. We want salaries and benefits that approximate what players were getting before the merger.

"If we fail to achieve these goals for the eighties, we will be broken as a union. Professional football will degenerate into a studio sport like professional wrestling, a spectacle that requires only average skill while the expert television announcers make large sums of money convincing the audience they are seeing pro football at its best. We must stress solidarity before the League gets its pay-television plan on line. If we don't, they'll be too powerful and will have broken this union." Terry paused, then finished his speech in a soft voice, ignoring the droplets of sweat that ran down his face.

"Know your enemy because they know you. Don't let them use your honesty and integrity against you. Remember that twenty-three percent of the players from last season will be gone next season. You could be one of them. Rookies are cheaper for the promoters. So be prepared to strike. We are fighting a conspiracy of rich, powerful men who are beginning to control *all* sports, not just football.

"They own pieces of basketball teams, soccer teams and tennis circuits. They own baseball teams and cable stations and communications satellites. The promoters grow more powerful by the day. We must fight back, strike back. Hit them where it hurts—in the pocketbook. Strike, stay unified. Solidarity of commitment." Dudley paused again. He looked slowly around the room at the simple, silly, brave, confused and frightened young men.

"Now comes the hard part," Terry Dudley said. "Strike or die."

The tall director of the Football Players Union turned from the microphone and walked slowly to his seat. For a moment no one made a sound; then at the back of the room a big black defensive end from Baltimore stood and began slowly clapping his giant hands together. The sound echoed through the room. Soon a white cornerback from Minnesota stood and joined in. Slowly, unsurely, throughout the room players, black and white, began standing and clapping their hands. It was a slow, rhythmic sound, like the tramping of feet. *Strike. . . . Strike. . . . Strike. . . . Strike. . . . Strike. . . .* Soon everyone in the room was on his feet, smashing his palms together in a slow, determined rhythm. It was loud and solemn and went on and on. *Thump. Thump.*

Taylor stood and listened, holding his package.

It gave him chills.

"Come on in, Taylor." Terry Dudley opened the door to his hotel room. "I'm glad you could come, but I must admit I'm a little surprised."

"I am, too, Terry." Taylor stepped inside, the package of documents under his arm. "I always paid my dues and I never crossed a picket line. But isn't it a little early to be yelling 'Strike'?"

Terry closed the door and followed Taylor into the room. It

was a standard Hyatt hotel room and could have been in Atlanta, Dallas or Rangoon.

"It's never too early to organize." Dudley had shucked his coat and tie and rolled his shirt sleeves up. Rings of sweat stained his white shirt at each armpit.

"Don't you think you ought to discuss the issues first? The contract has another full year to run." Taylor looked out the window at the Houston skyline. The brown-yellow petrochemical smog was held in place by an atmospheric inversion. "These guys will follow you but you should tell them where they're going."

"I explained my idea about residuals." Dudley sat on his bed. "Actors get them through the Screen Actors Guild. We'll pay through the Union a certain percentage of the gross revenue to each player. I can't get too specific or I don't have negotiating room."

"You better explain it now, because if you get residuals, you'll have fifteen hundred screaming niggers saying the Union isn't giving them their fair share," Taylor replied, still looking out at the yellow sky. Houston was growing at a phenomenal rate and falling apart almost as fast. "Because that's how it is with players, you know that. Why would you want the problems? The strain could split the Union." Taylor faced the director.

"You can be damn sure the owners hope it will," Dudley said. "But it's the only way to help the players help themselves. You heard those statistics, the percentages."

"Statistics are management weapons," Taylor argued. "The players can't win a fight they don't even comprehend."

"That's why I keep it simple," Dudley said. "Anyway, you're right that the contract isn't up until next year. They'll know the issues in plenty of time for small-arms training and to start our Take a Teamster to Lunch program!"

"A year may not be long enough." Taylor tossed his package of documents on the bed next to Dudley. "If you scare easily, don't read those."

"I always went for cheap thrills." Dudley opened the package. "I guess that's how I got into labor law. Although I certainly expected professional athletics to be a little higher class."

"You haven't heard the bad news yet." Taylor turned back to the window and the opaque Houston sky. "You know, there isn't anything wrong with this town that a couple of real good hurricanes couldn't fix."

The Union director searched through the documents, scanning, watching Taylor out of the corner of his eye. He went through the package quickly. Finished, he said, "Is that all?"

"Is that all? Isn't it enough?" Taylor turned back from the window. "That's my contribution to the next Collective Bargaining Agreement. Use them any way you want, but be careful. Bobby Hendrix died because somebody *thought* he had those documents. I have another set of copies in a safe-deposit box and a letter with the key in case I don't live through next season."

"Thanks, Taylor, but I'm not sure what we can do with these." Terry shook his head. "Who's gonna believe this?"

"Nobody with any sense. Maybe it *is* time to pick up the gun. Say," Taylor changed direction, "any retired players show up? They could help—"

"No," Terry interrupted. "The Union's charter restricts voting to active players. The Player Rep Board doesn't want them."

"But," Taylor said, "who's looking after their pension fund?"

"I appoint a pension board with two retired players on it," Terry replied. "It's easier that way. More centralized decision-making."

"Solidarity?" Taylor asked.

"Yeah, solidarity."

"I want a favor in return," Taylor said. "Do what you can to get the insurance and pension claims on Bobby Hendrix expedited. Ginny and the kids need the money. And check into the trade of Simon D'Hanis to LA. He's crippled and something stinks."

"That's two favors," the director said.

"Then I want two favors."

Taylor Rusk left Terry Dudley with his mouth hanging open, studying the documents.

VISITORS

AT four in the morning Lamar Jean Lukas limped up to the yellow Lincoln as Taylor stepped out at his apartment.

"Hidy, Taylor." Lamar Jean's eyes moved around, checking the shadows. "You had visitors while you was gone to Houston."

"How do you know I went to Houston?"

"Same way I learned about the visitors. The major told me that they were friends of yours and you had gone to Houston and had forgotten some papers and they were supposed to get them. Great security, huh?" Lamar smiled sourly; his eyes never stopped moving, checking the shadows. "The two gorillas looked like feds and picked the lock on your door quicker than you could open it with a key."

"Did you go inside with them?" They walked toward Taylor's apartment.

"No." Lamar kept his eyes moving. "Let's get out of this light. I checked out the plates and registration on their car. They work for another security company called Investico. It's headquartered in Las Vegas. They had photos of you in the glove compartment and notes on your comings and goings and who you come and go with." Lamar lowered his voice as they reached Taylor's apartment. "I would imagine they wired your whole place. Who are they?"

"Investico works for the commissioner's office." Taylor tried to remain calm. "I guess they're trying to see if I'm involved with gamblers or selling kilos of heroin to sixth graders."

"They were real wise guys," Lamar said. "The kind of guys the major would really suck up to. You ain't selling heroin to sixth graders, are you?"

"No, Lamar, I'm not. I have enough goddam trouble just playing the game."

"I didn't think so." Lamar frowned. "Damned wise guys. I got me one of them spectrum analyzers; you want me to check your apartment?"

Taylor looked in amazement at Lamar. "Who are you, James Bond?"

"It ain't *me* they got bugged." Lamar turned and limped off into the darkness, returning in a few moments with a square box with an antenna attached.

Lamar didn't find anything hidden in the walls or furniture, but when he took the telephones apart he found an infinity transmitter in each.

"All someone has to do with one of these"—Lamar held up the small transmitters for Taylor's inspection—"is dial your number and blow a special tone whistle and your phones broadcast everything that is being said anywhere in the room." Lamar dropped them in his pocket. "Well, the sons-a-bitches are out about $1,200 on these."

"Thanks, Lamar," Taylor said wearily. He sat on the couch. "Is there anything I can do for you? Money? Tickets? What?"

"Just one thing, Taylor. I bought my five-thousand-dollar bond,

I got my ticket on the forty-two, I bought my bus pass, I'm ready for the Pistols' first season in the Dome. I want the Pistols to go all the way to the Super Bowl. They promised us the same seats for the Super Bowl. If you want to do me a favor, take the Pistols to the Super Bowl this year. It'll probably be the only one I ever get a chance to see."

"Deal," Taylor said. "And thanks, Lamar."

"Just doing my job as I see it." Lamar turned to leave, then stopped. "Oh, here." He dug inside his Security Services uniform jacket and pulled out a letter. "It came special delivery three different times, and I knew the goddam postman was either going to throw it away or send it back, so I kept it."

Lamar handed Taylor the envelope. It was stamped Special Delivery and postmarked Santa Fe.

THE PISTOLETTES

It was A.D.'s idea to have cheerleader tryouts as the first event in the new Pistol Dome in Clyde, Texas.

There was still construction work to be finished. The decorators were just starting on the luxury skyboxes that leased for $150,000 a season. A hundred fifty thousand dollars for bare concrete floor and walls and the rights to buy twelve season tickets and twelve Insider's parking passes.

The majority of the construction was finished ahead of schedule, thanks partly to the cooperation of the Cobianco brothers and their ability to avoid labor trouble. The only work delay was a two-hour break on site to elect a new business manager for the Laborers Union after Lennie the Leech disappeared.

At first A.D. wanted to charge admission and have spectators watch the tryouts, but when they got four thousand applicants for the twenty spots, A.D. decided instead to just charge the applicants a twenty-dollar cash registration fee each. A.D. oversaw the registration fee collection himself. The Texas Pistols general manager accepted no checks and paid the Franchise secretaries with Franchise funds to work overtime on Saturday and Sunday to assist.

A.D. pocketed the eighty thousand dollars in registration fees and personally interviewed the forty semifinalists in private.

It took place in early April.

Even A. D. Koster was overwhelmed by the number of beautiful, talented, desperate, upwardly-mobile girls that showed up at the Pistol Dome that rainy weekend. Mobile. Hostile. Agile.

A.D.'s personal interviews of the semi-finalists took place in his luxury skybox suite. Some refused his sexual advances, others submitted reluctantly, a few cried later. A.D. picked the twenty most enthusiastic and chose another sixteen to be "alternates."

"It's a long season," the exhausted general manager said to the thirty-six assembled girls who had remained in the cavernous dome until the early Monday morning hours. "And just like the football team we need a certain amount of depth on the cheerleading roster. The alternates will participate in all Pistolette activities except those on the field during game day, unless one of the regulars is unable to perform up to snuff."

A.D. looked over the thirty-six women admiringly, though his tone was threatening.

"Your jobs will be just as demanding as those of the men on the football team, and anyone who thinks their personal life is more important than being a Pistolette better say so now, because you will be expected to do what you're told, when and where you're told." A.D. smiled disarmingly. "You are the *best* out of over four thousand applicants, but getting to this stage was the easy part. Now comes the hard work and selfless dedication that will help carry the Texas Pistols to the Super Bowl and make the Texas Pistolettes America's cheerleaders. You will be the best, the champions, *numero uno*. Purple and white pride."

"Purple and white pride!" All the girls squealed with delight, and even the reluctant alternates caught the enthusiasm, vowing silently to do better. "Purple and white pride!" Thirty-six tiny fists shot up in a power salute. "Purple and white pride!"

"Now"—A.D. held up his hands—"it's late and we're all tired. You will get a list of rules and regulations in the mail in the next few days. But there is one rule to keep from now on." A.D. glared at them. "Don't ever talk to, go near, wave at or even smile at any of the football players. That is an unbendable rule. No fraternization with the players. Understood?"

The thirty-six pretty little heads nodded up and down in unison.

"Great!" A.D. clapped his hands together. "You'll be hearing from us about practice schedules, dress codes and the rest. That's all. Good night, girls."

"Good night, Mr. Koster." Thirty-six lovely voices echoed through the empty dome, giving A.D. delicious chills while the

exhausted, elated, violated, confused, compromised girls bega
to pack away their dancing gear and wander toward the exits.

"Monique! Monique!" A.D. called to a statuesque brunette wit
clouds of dark hair piled on her head and raining down over he
creamy shoulders. "Come here, Monique."

"Yes, Mr. Koster." Her exquisite body covered by purple Dar
skins, a sweater and thick leg warmers, the tall brunette stalke
smoothly to the general manager's side.

"I want to talk to you about being the captain of the Pistolettes.
A.D. put his arm around her shoulders and led her back towar
the private elevator and up to his skybox suite.

Monique had developed an exceptional technique involving ic
cubes, toothpaste and a string of large fake pearls. A.D. late
described the experience to Don Cobianco.

"It was like a covey of quail flying out my asshole."

Monique got to be captain of the Texas Pistolettes.

THE CADILLAC RANCH

TAYLOR Rusk took I-40 west at Shamrock, after taking 83 nort
from I-20 at Junction. He was on the *llano estacado*.

It was a bright blue high-plains spring day as Taylor passe
Stanley Marsh's Cadillac Ranch rusting outside Amarillo. Goo
old boy, Stanley. Years before, Stanley had buried seven Cadillac
nose down about windshield deep in the high-plains dirt. It wa
a fine view to cruise past on a spring afternoon, the Intersta
shimmering ahead and behind for miles. The Cadillacs were slowl
deteriorating in solitary splendor, two rows of elegant, delightfull
expensive, useless metal fins pointing skyward.

Taylor Rusk gazed at the Cadillac Ranch jutting out of the re
plains. The full Texas moon was rising round and red, climbin
over the tailfins. The rising moon grew big, turning to yellow a
it crawled high in the east. The Interstate was a black glistenin
snake growing out of the side mirror, winding backward acros
the high plains toward the cutting edge of horizon, the bright fu
moon, the dark blue sky.

Ahead, the sun sank quickly into New Mexico.

Taylor was heading for the Pecos Mountains and Dick Conly.

The last game Conly knew was fixed was the third Super Bowl after the second merger. It was done to give the public the impression that the new leagues *were* evenly matched, thus maintaining national television interest in the Super Bowl. The newspapers and television handicappers made one fair football team twelve-point favorites over another fair football team. The underdog team then proceeded to play like they had been sitting in the favorite-team meetings all week. Which somebody had been doing. The losing owner bet huge sums against his franchise. He made a fortune to soothe his injured pride.

For his plan to work, Dick Conly needed the Texas Pistols in the Super Bowl that year. He wasn't sure he would live another year. It had to be that year.

Dick pushed a button on his armchair console and his seat back hummed to an upright position. Picking up the phone, he placed the receiver in his Datotek DV 505 Analog Voice Scrambler and began placing telephone calls.

It took him most of the day to reach the people necessary to guarantee that everyone could deliver. The Man in New Orleans promised to convince the Cobianco brothers to take the pressure off A. D. Koster during the regular season and allow the Texas Pistols, Red Kilroy and Taylor Rusk a chance to reach the Super Bowl.

"Tell them the big killing will be on the Super Bowl game," Dick Conly said into the Voice Scrambler while he made himself a bologna sandwich. "It'll be a big killing."

A big killing.

The Texas Pistols in the Super Bowl to climax the Franchise's first year in the Pistol Dome. It just had to be.

The Pecos River raged below with spring melt.

Taylor had to drive four miles up the winding private road after Gonzolo Martinez, the *pistolero*, let the Lincoln through Conly's main gate. As he drove the switchback road through the ponderosa pines and high mountain forest, Taylor never saw another person, but they saw him. That was the important part for Dick Conly.

"I want the Super Bowl before I die," Dick said when he opened the door.

Taylor stepped from the car and looked around the rock and cedar house hanging on the mountainside. "I always wanted a pony and a groom and an exercise girl."

"You boys've just got to win the big one." Conly held on t the door for support. He grinned at Taylor, pulling his mottle gray skin tightly across his death face. His stomach protruded pushing his shirt away from his belt. He carried his hard, swollen scarred liver like an unborn child to full term, and from the look of him it would not be much longer now. Dick Conly had pur posely, unrelentingly, gestated death in his vitals; it had grown t killing size.

"Can't win 'em all—or you'd still be general manager."

Conly plopped down in an oversize chair surrounded with but tons, gadgets and appliances. "I make sure I win enough of th right ones." He pushed a button on the console beside his chai and a motor quietly hummed. The chair gently changed shape elevating Dick Conly's feet while slightly lowering his head.

Conly pointed Taylor to a hard, straight-back wooden chair He nodded his head at the small white refrigerator between them "There's beer or whatever you want cold in there."

Taylor sat and slouched, uneasily trying for comfort or at leas balance. The chair seemed purposely designed to foil his attempts "I bet you don't have much company."

"I get lots of visitors, Taylor-boy." Conly grinned. "They jus don't stay long. Company and fish."

Conly was surrounded by an array of gadgets, books, remot controls, keyboards and consoles, a little hovel in the center o what was a forty by forty room with a pitched twenty-foot open beam ceiling and a spectacular view of the high mountains abov and the rushing white water of the spring Pecos flood below Taylor was surprised he had not noticed the incredible sight whe he first walked inside. His attention had focused on Dick Conl and his little technological hutch built in the center of the room Conly's chair faced away from the window.

"Why don't you turn your chair around, Dick?" Taylor asked gaping at the spectacle of the Pecos Mountain spring. "Some sor of personality quirk?"

"Most people are too polite to ask, Taylor, or observant enoug to understand or just don't give a shit." Dick pushed a button tha opened the wall and revealed a five-foot television screen. "I hav me one of those big-dish antennas that takes off the satellites. can even get dirty movies from Japan."

"Do you ever peek behind you, just for the hell of it?"

"What's the point?" Conly rattled his words out quickly. " know what's back there; that's where I have been. I keep my eye ahead, watching what's coming, so I can identify what rips my head off." Conly pushed another button and the chair moved to a slightly different position.

"You should take a last look, Dick," Taylor said, gazing out at the unbelievable mountains, the incomprehensible river.

"Why? I saw it when I first came here. That's why I built here." Dick pointed a finger to his temple. "It's all up here. I see it as clear as the day I brought that roller-skating cunt up here and asked her to marry me." Conly took his tall glass from the holder built into the chair arm and took a long drink of the amber fluid. "You ever see that river down there when it reaches the Horsehead Crossing in Texas?"

Taylor nodded.

"Looks like shit, doesn't it? I mean real shit, the color of shit. It smells like shit. Well, that's life. The dumb, mystical, sumbitch that said the river remains the same never followed the Pecos from here to the Rio Grande."

Taylor leaned over and opened the small refrigerator. Inside, bottles of beer, tequila, gin and Scotch filled the top two shelves and the door racks. The bottom shelf was stuffed full with stacks and stacks of bologna and loaves of Mrs. Baird's bread.

"You ever see the Ganges?" Conly asked.

"No." Taylor stared at the contents of the small refrigerator.

"I didn't think so. Or the River Jordan? Shit, no . . . you haven't seen anything." Conly squinted at Taylor, who was taking a beer but looking at the huge store of bologna. "You don't even know that everybody likes bologna sandwiches, do you?"

Taylor closed the refrigerator door. "It'll take everybody to eat all that."

"I hope to die with a drink beside me, the television on a dirty Jap movie, a bologna sandwich in one hand, jacking off with the other." Conly pushed a button; his feet went down and his head came up. "You should understand *this* without much trouble, Taylor. Didn't you once tell me that all that had motivated you since high school was the constant urge to lie down?"

Taylor nodded. "I'm thinking about fixing me a bologna sandwich."

"The Pistol Dome will be finished soon, thanks to the generosity and stupidity of the mayor and city council of Clyde," Conly said. "So the next Super Bowl will be played in Clyde, Texas, under the Pistol Dome. Now, wouldn't it be a wonderful thing if the Texas Pistols made their first Super Bowl appearance there?"

"Red already beat you to the idea. He expects to win the Super Bowl this year. Big deal."

"Red's on my wavelength. Good," Dick continued. "You'll be favored over your opponent by many points, maybe as high as sixteen. The ever-obliging sporting press will pound that into the heads of the willing fans and bettors."

Conly hooked a thumb over his shoulder. "Believe me, Taylor. Just as certain as I am that the fucking Pecos Mountains are still right behind me, that spread will be so big that it'll be irresistible. This is going to look so good to the Cobianco boys that they will want it all."

"What are you talking about?"

"The Cobiancos normally start laying off bets after about five hundred thousand dollars and keep their book balanced, but this time they will be *sure* they can clean up. The Pistols will be favored by thirteen to sixteen points, and the Cobiancos will try and control the Pistols through A.D. and Suzy. They will be convinced the fix is in, that they have a *sure* thing, and they won't lay it off. They will carry every bet on the Pistols they can get. A.D. and Suzy must make certain the Pistols lose."

"So?" Taylor stared blankly at Dick Conly. "A.D. and Suzy will make certain we lose."

"They'll try, God bless 'em, they'll try," Conly said. "But I have decided to stay alive long enough to make certain the Texas Pistols win the Super Bowl by *more* than the spread. And of course you will have to make certain you stay alive too. No better way to render a team less than effective than to kill the quarterback."

"The phrase has a familiar sound," Taylor said, "but it doesn't ring of homecoming floats and football mums when you say it. What do *you* get?" Taylor asked Conly. "I know you don't gamble."

"It's a reason to stay alive another year." Dick Conly's face showed slight desire to live another day.

"It's you." Taylor suddenly understood. "*You are Deep Threat.* You sent Tommy the documents."

Conly nodded. "I assume you're the one who has them now, judging from the bizarre places they appear. I wish you'd use them with more effect."

"Everybody denies or ignores them while Investico combs the League, looking for the source. If you want to accomplish something, tell somebody that they're *your* papers and you sent them to the missing and unlamented Tommy McNamara."

"I could do that if going to jail were what I wanted, but I have a certain result in mind: the Cobiancos betting several million against the Texas Pistols winning the Super Bowl and counting on A.D. and Suzy to deliver up the stunning upset. But instead you win and beat the spread. What I want is called *revenge*."

"If we win, and A.D. and Suzy have promised the Cobiancos that we will lose . . . and the point spread is so large in the Pistols' favor that the Cobiancos get greedy and don't lay any of the big bets off . . . they'll be wiped out; they won't be able to pay off. They'll kill A.D. I'm amazed they didn't kill him back in college, when he was just stealing the rent money." Taylor stopped and looked over into the red, watery eyes of the brilliant, vengeful man. "They might even kill Suzy."

"Oh, let's hope so," Conly said. "I plan to bet heavily on that result."

"You know they have the offices *completely* wired." Dick Conly fixed himself a bologna sandwich. Taylor stood at the window, watching the Pecos River flow out of the snowcapped mountains. "Voice-activated, the latest state of the art. Cyrus had the phones tapped, but A.D. and Suzy have gone even further. She even has herself wired when she goes to owners meetings. I have copies of all the tapes." Conly leaned back in his chair and took a big bite of bologna and white bread. He washed it down with Scotch. "I still have influence and people in the right places. The commissioner's office, for instance. Robbie Burden is scared shitless since A.D. and the Cobianco brothers had Hendrix tossed out of that plane in Cozumel. The commissioner knows they arranged for the death and disappearance of Tommy McNamara. He's up to his ass in tax evasion, scalping Super Bowl tickets. So far the only thing that saves him is failure of vision. The average person can't imagine a guy making five hundred thousand dollars a year being football commissioner would steal. They can't imagine five hundred thousand dollars but would kill to get it, as well as strike themselves deaf and blind." Conly chewed on his bologna sandwich. "It is beyond their capacities to conceive how much cash can be made scalping Super Bowl tickets. Cash! Millions! Six to ten million dollars for the game in the Pistol Dome. All sold to out-of-town high rollers and tour packages."

"I tried to use that secret bank account number in the Bahamas." Taylor still watched the river and mountains. "I'd leak it to one reporter after another and they would come up blank, or if they found something they would shortly lose interest."

"They either got bought or threatened off," Conly said, wadding the last of his sandwich into his mouth. "The bank is a CIA front. They established a bunch of those offshore banks to finance themselves secretly, which eventually made them bankers for dope and gun smugglers, gangsters, tax evaders and Communist revolutionaries in the Caribbean. They aren't going to give all that up just to catch the football commissioner stealing tickets and evading taxes. It isn't un-American to steal and evade taxes. They just take their cut."

"Does the commissioner know the bank is a CIA front?"

"I doubt it." Conly drank his Scotch. "He uses Investico as his security and information people, and the CIA infiltrated Investico years ago, when everybody was falling all over each other to kill Castro and make the Kennedys and the Mob happy. No. Robbie Burden is just another highly paid cutout man. He's expendable and they don't tell him more than he needs to know to look good in five-hundred-dollar suits and a year-round suntan. He'd rather face the Justice Department than end up in the trunk of his car. And he's smart enough to know that what he doesn't know won't hurt him nearly as bad as something he *does* know." Conly coughed and held his stomach; the spasm caused him internal pain. "That's where A.D. and Suzy are too smart for their own good. Jesus, can you imagine taping everything? Too much knowledge or too little, you can't get by on big titties and blow jobs forever." Conly took a deep drink. "But then, who wants to live forever?" Conly pushed a button and the chair began to vibrate. "The two of them won't even last long enough to see the real Big Money. The FCC is falling in line, the private companies are launching their DBS satellites, the technology is all in place and shortly professional football will go to pay-television: subscription, cable, direct broadcast. I'll bet *the League launches its own satellite*. You're talking about billions. Billions of dollars to each team. Each franchise. The Super Bowl reaches between fifty and seventy-five million households now. The Pistols will eventually reach a million households, at twenty bucks a game, twenty million *per game!*" Conly yelled; his face turned red. "Twenty games a season is four hundred million a season, and they'll still be fucking you guys with deferred contracts and incentive clauses."

"It wouldn't be pro football if they weren't fucking us, now, would it, Dick? I mean, *that* is the real game." Taylor never turned away from the mountains and cold rushing Pecos River that Dick Conly never looked toward.

"Taylor," Conly explained, as if to a child, "people *want* it to happen. It's the American Way."

"If it don't hurt, it ain't doing no good?" Taylor looked back over his shoulder at Conly.

"You'll be going pretty fast, but I think you'll survive the jump." Conly looked right at the quarterback. "Not the crash, though, so you are going to have to win by sixteen points or more, Taylor. We split fifty-fifty if I win my bets with Don Cobianco."

"Seventy-five, twenty-five," Taylor answered. "I plan to pay the taxes on mine, and besides, you won't live to spend more." He always told Conly what he thought.

"You might not either, boy," Conly stuck out his hand. "Okay. It's a deal." They shook. "A Super Bowl deal," Conly added.

Helluvadeal.

PART THREE

"I'm glad to see you've got religion,
I'm glad to see you've gone to God,
I'm glad to see you've straightened out your lines
and evened out your odds."

LOUDON WAINWRIGHT III
"I'm Glad to See You've Got Religion"

ARRANGING
THE EAGLE SHIT

BEFORE driving out to training camp, Taylor Rusk stopped by the team offices to talk to A. D. Koster about the schedule of payments on his Standard Player's Contract. The Pistols had been forced to match the Los Angeles offer on the SPC that foolish young Dick Portus had signed and offered Taylor.

The Texas Pistols agreed to pay sixty monthly installments of $83,333.33. No money was deferred and it was all guaranteed. No cut. No trade. All compensation was cash: no "free cars," no "incentive bonuses." No bonuses at all.

It was all salary. Taylor wanted A. D. to hand paychecks to him at training camp that year.

Previously the Pistols had mailed the checks to Taylor's apartment. With all his mysterious visitors, the quarterback didn't like the idea of $83,333.33 checks scattered on his apartment floor under the mail chute. Lamar Jean Lukas promised to keep a particularly close eye on Taylor's apartment, but he still didn't want to risk his paychecks.

A.D.'s secretary wasn't at her desk. Taylor knocked on the general manager's door and opened it quickly, hoping to catch A.D. and his secretary fucking on the couch. Instead he found Johnny Cobianco, the youngest brother, sitting behind A.D.'s desk, casually going through the drawers.

"What are you doing here?" Taylor asked.

"I might ask you the same question," Johnny mouthed back.

"You might, but you won't," Taylor replied. "I have an answer."

"I'm the new assistant general manager; I'm negotiating with all this year's rookies," the young Cobianco said. He had the same dark, hairy, square features of his brothers but he lacked their presence, their ferocity. Without his brothers Johnny Cobianco seemed incomplete.

"Find anything interesting in A.D.'s desk?"

"Nothing I ain't seen before." Johnny closed the drawer he had been rifling.

"Well, keep on looking, don't let me stop you. You might find an Easter egg or dirty pictures."

"Up yours, jerk."

"Hey, boy." Taylor closed the door. "You are all *alone* here. Your big brothers are off somewhere, shaking down crippled newsboys. You keep mouthing at me and I'll feed your lungs to the goddam pigeons." Taylor advanced on the dark man behind the desk. He felt an unreasonable anger. Fury.

Johnny Cobianco pulled a large blue steel automatic pistol from his belt.

"I ain't quite alone," he grinned.

Taylor kept moving toward him. Can't back up now—Kimball Adams had taught him that. Make a decision quick and move on it. Life or death. Move. Fast. Something irrational in him was already justifying the violence that Taylor knew would take place. Can't back up. Yes or no. Find the weakness and move fast. Gamble or die.

A pause, a hesitation, now could be painful, humiliating or fatal.

"You better put the fucking gun away, greaseball, or start looking for some spaghetti sauce, 'cause I'm going to feed it to you." Taylor was startled by his own reactions. He felt out of control, very dangerous. But he liked it. He justified it to himself, something Johnny Cobianco hadn't considered. Taylor was being shot through with adrenaline and he enjoyed the rush. It was stupid but he fell for it. And enjoyed it.

Young Cobianco blinked and jerked back. He had never had to go further than this. People usually stopped dead at the sight of the big Colt .45 automatic, but it just made this big football player madder. Johnny Cobianco tried to think: Had he ever shot anybody? It was his second mistake of the day; thinking takes too long. Taylor had reached the desk.

"I'll shoot," Johnny said, failing to draw back the hammer. "This is a forty-five. You know how big a hole I can blow in you?"

"Are we going to have a quiz on it later?" Taylor's jaws were tight, his nostrils flared, his eyes were wild, as he came around the desk after the wise guy sitting in A.D.'s chair, pointing the gun. "I hope Colt is your favorite flavor."

Terrified, Johnny decided to shoot, jerking on the trigger and discovering what Taylor had already noticed: Johnny Cobianco had forgotten to cock the single-action automatic. In a fight, noth-

ing is quite as disheartening as finding oneself unexpectedly un-
armed.

With the possible exception of not being chosen acolyte when
he was twelve, Johnny Cobianco experienced no greater distress
in his life than when that brand-new four-hundred-dollar Colt
Combat Commander .45 automatic lay in his hand and failed to
do a thing.

Lunging forward, Taylor snatched the heavy automatic from
Cobianco's hand and hit him across the throat with his forearm,
pinning the young brother to the chair back. Taylor Rusk jammed
the two pounds of blue steel square in Johnny C.'s mouth. Blood
and teeth splattered on A.D.'s big desk.

Cobianco went over backward in the swivel chair and lay half
conscious on the floor, choking and gagging on his own body
parts and fluids.

"My teeth! You knocked out my teeth!" Johnny wailed.

"Wait a second, I'm not finished yet." Taylor kicked at the
overturned chair, trying to scramble past it to reach the crumpled,
crying, bleeding man tangled in the drapes in the corner of the
room. The tortured body of Tommy McNamara hanging from the
bunkhouse rafters flickered through Taylor's brain. Bobby Hendrix splattered all over Tulum. The combat automatic in one hand,
Taylor tossed the heavy furniture aside easily with the other. The
swivel chair banged on the handcrafted desk, knocking out expensive divots of teakwood. He was over the edge, out of control,
and didn't care. He lost it and loved it, needed it. The crash of
the chair brought anger, hatred and revenge, surging adrenaline
hungering for more ferocity. The fury turned everything red. Shoving the pistol in his back pocket, then picking up the United Fund
golf trophy by the marble base, Taylor pounded the whimpering
Johnny Cobianco with the four-foot metal loving cup. The cup
wasn't particularly thick or heavy metal, but it had real nice sharp
edges and good balance.

"You got ribs to break, lungs to puncture, a spleen and kidneys
to rupture." Tightly gripping the base of the battered trophy, Taylor
hit the injured, terrified man with full baseball swings, knocking
out huge chunks of flesh, bruising muscle and bone. Cobianco
screamed and curled fetuslike, covering his head and neck with
his hands. He took a powerful beating.

Taylor looked around on A.D.'s desk for another weapon, a
blunt instrument to pound the hoodlum. The solid brass team
insignia paperweight was too heavy, the full-size replica Colt was
too lethal.

The creeping logic of the search for the appropriate weapon began to divert enthusiasm for inflicting damage on the seriously damaged man. So Taylor finally just gave him another halfhearted kidney fungo with the trophy. *Make the little shit piss blood for a couple of days.*

The door opened and A.D. walked into his office. Taylor threw the trophy against the wall.

"What the hell . . . ?" A.D. looked at Taylor, then at Johnny Cobianco, then at the gore splattered on his desk and papers. "Jesus! Taylor! Did you do this?"

"As much of it as I could." Taylor began gasping for air and sat down on the battle-scarred teak desk. "I tire easily lately."

Taylor's anger was gone as fast as it came, leaving him slightly confused.

"*Jesus!* Taylor!" A.D. was dumbstruck. "That's Don Cobianco's little brother."

"I know, A.D. Goddam, you think I did this by mistake?" On the edge of the desk Taylor sat heavily and nodded wearily. "A.D., you are so stupid . . . I can't . . ." He lost the words. He was unchastened, just embarrassed at losing control, losing to chaos.

Taylor found his voice. "I just came by to tell you to send my paychecks to camp and I find this Al Pacino look-alike going through your desk, playing Baby Godfather, and then I'm looking down the barrel of this." Taylor pulled the .45 automatic from his back pocket. "The little jerk-off forgot to cock it or you'd be scraping me off your padded and flocked wallpaper."

"Jeeesus! Taylor!" It seemed to be the limit of A. D. Koster's vocabulary.

The quarterback looked around the purple and white office. "Who picked out this wallpaper anyway, A.D.?"

"Jeeesus! Taylor!" A.D. was riveted to the floor.

Gasping, desperate, severely injured, Johnny Cobianco curled on the floor and bled into A.D.'s expensive white carpet.

A.D. took a wastebasket over for Johnny to bleed in. The beaten man knocked it away. The general manager of the Texas Pistols Football Club, Inc., walked back to his desk. Taylor's breathing began to slow. Control returning, he studied the visible damage on Johnny C.

"Will you send my checks to camp, A.D.?"

A. D. Koster nodded his head, still staring at Johnny. "Jesus! Taylor!"

"Wait till my brothers . . ." Johnny wheezed.

"Eat it, punk." With good snap Taylor threw A.D.'s autographed football at the bloody man's head, bouncing the point off his occipital bone and driving his face to the floor. Johnny curled up, whining and bleeding.

"Jesus! Taylor!" A.D. was horrified. Johnny's blood was an ever-growing pool.

Taylor showed A.D. the boots he had used on Johnny's ribs. "I got them at Rios in Raymondville. Cognac brown, French leather, hand-fitted. Prince Charles gets boots there. What do you think? Huh? A.D.? You like 'em?"

"Jesus, Taylor. They'll kill—"

"Sorry about your desk and papers. The blood and teeth are his." Taylor jammed the automatic back into his hip pocket. "Now, don't forget the checks; send them to me *in camp*. Don't send them to my apartment. All those goddam Investico agents you got running in and out of there will stomp all over them." Taylor Rusk studied the general manager.

"Jeeesus! Taylor!" A.D. repeated.

Taylor opened the door, then turned back.

"You know, A.D., you and your latest carhop have gotten us all in way over our heads. This is a lot worse than Doris and the Charros. We are in serious deep shit here. This is out of my realm.... You're breaking new and terrifying ground." Taylor looked over at the whining, bleeding youngest Cobianco. "Why, A.D.? Why?"

"Just lucky, I guess." A.D. watched his expensive white carpet become stained red.

Taylor started to close the door but again turned back, his face torn by confusion. "A.D., they kill people. Bobby Hendrix? Tommy McNamara? And God knows how many poor wetbacks ended up as part of the cement work in the Pistol Dome." Taylor pointed at the man on the floor. "He was already trying your chair on for size. They don't need you anymore, A.D., and they don't have a waiver list. They may need Suzy to front the Franchise for them, since Cyrus is a drooling fool, but *anybody* can be a general manager in professional football. *You* proved that. You're only really necessary to send my checks to camp." Taylor closed the door, leaving A. D. Koster alone with the whimpering Johnny Cobianco.

"Jesus! Taylor!" A.D. said.

Johnny Cobianco continued to bleed into the white carpet. He didn't move.

BABY JESUS MEETS
THE COLT COMMANDER

TAYLOR carried his bag and portable TV down the long dormitory hall to his room. He set the television on the small built-in desk and tossed his bag on his bed. He noticed someone had left luggage on the other bed, along with a white leather Bible. Taylor opened the book and found it personally inscribed by Billy Joe Hardesty to Greg Moore.

Greg Moore was the top-notch running back from Los Angeles who Red had finagled as part of the "tampering" compensation resulting from the five-million-dollar offer to Taylor.

Taylor called Red Kilroy in the other wing of the dormitory.

"Whaddaya want?" It was the way Red always answered the phone in camp. Red thought it put the caller on the defensive.

"I want Greg Moore out of my room," Taylor said. "I hate born-agains worse than coke heads."

"Taylor! Welcome to camp."

"Save the confetti and champagne and get this running back out of my room. I room alone in camp, Red—always."

"Well, Taylor," Red stalled, "I . . . ah . . . I sorta thought that if you two roomed together, he could pick up the system a little faster."

"That's your problem, Red, not mine. I need my privacy to deal with the system."

"Come on, Taylor, think about the team. This could be our Super Bowl year."

"That's fine, Red. But I can't share my time with a surfer for Christ."

"Taylor!" Red acted like his quarterback had suggested killing babies with baseball bats. "Taylor! Don't tell me you don't care; we're talking the ultimate football game."

"You said the same about the Cotton Bowl and I'm still waiting on the rapture. Now, I want Moore out of here."

"Taylor. Taylor."

Taylor hung up on Red Kilroy.

Greg Moore walked into the room, grinning and glowing as only "one on the true way" can.

"Listen, Greg, I'm Taylor Rusk. Nice to meet you . . . glad to have you aboard . . . but there's been a mistake . . . I always room alone at camp."

"This was my assigned room," Moore answered. Muscular, with a California tan, sun-bleached hair and perfect smile, he was the prototypical LA player. He was beautiful.

"It's one of Red's mind games," Taylor explained. "He could be doing it to you or me or both. But I need my privacy . . . quarterbacking for Red is peculiar. So if you could . . . ?"

Moore was sitting erect on the bed, doing curls with his barbells. He listened politely to Taylor while he did his curls.

"No. They assigned me the room. I like it." He had a pleasant smile.

"Please?"

Moore shook his head.

"I'm the quarterback."

Moore frowned and did curls.

"Look, Moore, you got to go. I room alone. I expect personal, career and life crises. You'll be in the way and could get hurt. Actually I would *like* to hurt you. Now, get the hell out of here."

"I was assigned to this room and I'm staying," Moore replied with calm confidence. "You can threaten me all you want, but I'm hardly afraid."

"You don't care what I want?" Taylor said, shocked. "Even though I have to run this team?"

"If you want to put it that way"—Greg Moore plopped down on his bed and began flipping through his white leather-bound Bible—"you're nobody special to me."

"What if I call Ox Wood to break your fingers?" Taylor Rusk watched him for a moment. Moore was about six feet four inches and 235 pounds. Taylor was six feet five inches, 225 pounds and had doubts, even though, while Moore was reading his Bible, Taylor would hit him with all of the furniture that wasn't nailed down. But Moore was young and powerful, and Taylor had been in one fight that day, with Johnny Cobianco. He didn't want to deal with all the blood, adrenaline and heavy breathing, especially if it was all his.

Taylor picked up the phone and dialed Red Kilroy.

"Whaddaya want?" Red said.

"I told you, Red. I want Moore out of my room *now*. I'll put him on the phone; you tell him to pack and move the manger or down the hall."

"Taylor, Taylor. Give it a chance. Come on."

"Does that mean no?"

"It just means give it a little time."

"I'll give it five more seconds. Do you tell him over the phone or do I throw his surfer ass through the window?"

"Maybe you ought to think about it. Moore is younger than you, Taylor."

"He isn't going to get much older if you don't get him out, Red."

"You sure you can take him, Taylor? He lifts weights year-round." Red was beginning to enjoy needling his quarterback. *The competitive edge will sharpen under this kind of strain*, Red thought. "I mean, *can* you take him, Taylor? Ask him what he bench presses."

Red *was* playing mind games. The certain realization helped Taylor decide on his action.

"You mean with God on his side, he also jogs and lifts weights?" Taylor looked at the fresh-faced kid thumbing through the white-covered Bible, a gift to him after an appearance representing Athletes for Jesus on the *All-American Evangelical Hour*.

"Partly," Red continued to push Taylor. "Greg Moore's in his early twenties, with a little seasoning, just hitting stride and driven by conviction. He's what I want at running back. He's perfect."

"Red, you can't win the Super Bowl by playing mind games and using this poor fool. We *can* use him." Taylor's voice quieted, his tone calculating. "But if you think causing me trouble is going to be one of his jobs, you're mistaken. We'll see how *cabin fever* affects him."

"What?" Red asked. "What about—?"

Taylor hung up the phone, cutting off the coach.

"You know, Taylor"—Moore kept his nose pointed into the Bible—"being a Christian athlete gives me certain advantages over non-Christian athletes. I put my life in God's hands and dedicate my life to Christ. Knowing God has a plan, I don't worry. I'm solid in my faith. You worry too much and will become a victim of anxiety."

"God's plan?"

"That's right." Moore turned a page. "When you get all worked up over room assignments, it proves that relying on your humanism will fail."

"'Creeping humanism'?" Taylor asked.

"You can call it that," Moore said. "It's replacing faith in the Almighty with faith in yourself, a human."

Staring at the ceiling, Taylor thought about R. D. Locke still playing defensive back at Denver. It was probably going to be Locke's last season too.

"Say, Greg." Taylor leaned over and dug inside his bag, pulling out Johnny Cobianco's .45 automatic. "What if I *am* the Almighty?" He flicked off the safety and thumbed the hammer spur. "In your case?"

The explosion was deafening, bouncing around the cinder block walls of the small dormitory room. The recoil jolted Taylor's arm to his shoulder. The slug knocked out a chunk of cinder block about three inches square, two feet above Greg Moore's head. The rock fragments cut up the smooth young cheeks and neck; fortunately the white leather Bible protected his eyes. The running back dived onto the floor, dropping the Bible and scrambling for the bathroom door. All asshole and elbows.

Taylor squeezed off a second shot that blew a dresser drawer to splinters as the scuttling Moore crawfished through the bathroom to the other room. He jumped to his feet, running for the coaches' wing. Explosions echoed down the hall as Taylor emptied the clip into Greg Moore's old bed and pillow.

Taylor tossed the pistol back into his bag and listened to the thunder of feet in the hallway. He was sorry the gun was out of ammunition; he liked the sound and smell.

Taylor Rusk roomed alone again that year. He bought more ammunition and, the last day of camp, shot up A.D.'s rented Cadillac. He considered it a good start for the Super Bowl season. Greg Moore did well that camp; he was the League's number-two rusher that season and was All-Pro. Greg understood perfectly about rendering unto Caesar or else. He and Taylor spoke only in the huddle and were not friends, but he ran like the wind, hit like a truck, was an excellent receiver and pass blocker, never made mistakes and could throw the halfback option with incredible accuracy. He also ended up as the punter with a forty-four-yard average.

"Different approaches motivate different players, Red," Taylor explained. "I spend a lot of time with football players, trying to influence their behavior. . . ."

"I can't fucking believe you!" Red ground his teeth. "You could have killed him!"

"Greg's the kind of player who needs a couple of shots across his bow to get going."

— 407 —

"I can't believe you shot up the dormitory."

"Does this mean I get traded to Denver?"

"I can't believe it!" Red stormed off. "My quarterback leads his team at gunpoint."

"We're in desperate straits, Coach." Taylor laughed and continued to fieldstrip the .45 Colt Commander.

SIMON/BUFFY

SIMON D'HANIS spent that exhibition season with Los Angeles. He was usually in such pain that he seldom practiced but saw lots of action. It was Thursday or Friday before the swelling reduced from the previous Saturday, often requiring aspiration of the joint and injections of cortisone. He took Butazolidin in addition to his normal daily intake of painkillers, anabolic steroids for muscle bulk and various vitamins and mineral supplements. For pain he was taking Percodan and used Seconal to sleep, depriving him of dreams.

Simon *needed* dreams.

On game day Simon added a hundred milligrams of Dexedrine in ten- to twenty-milligram doses starting four hours before kickoff and continuing on into the fourth quarter of the game. After an exceptionally hot early season game, he had to be packed in ice and rushed to the hospital. But Simon D'Hanis did not miss a game. And his leg did not improve; rather it was beginning to degenerate from abuse.

Buffy and the children stayed in Texas. The marriage was self-destructing under the traumas of Simon's knee injury and the Machiavellian machinations of surgery, rehabilitation and the trade to LA. Despite his brutal treatment of her, Buffy stayed with him. She would not listen to an unkind word about Simon.

"He was there when I needed him," Buffy told Wendy at lunch. "I'm going to be there when he needs me."

"He doesn't seem to need or want you around," Wendy argued. "I've seen the marks he's put on you, Buffy. He's dangerous. Taylor says he's capable of killing somebody. You might be doing the best thing for both of you and the kids if you all went and stayed in Kingsville while Simon took this whipping by himself."

"That's sure a nice way for a friend to talk," Buffy replied angrily, putting her fork down and folding her hands in her lap. "And you can tell Taylor Rusk for me that if he were a real friend, he wouldn't say things like that about Simon."

"Taylor only told me because he worries about you and the children."

"Oh, that's real big of him." Buffy crumpled her napkin and tossed it on the table. "I noticed how he jumped right to the front and claimed paternity on Randall when you got pregnant."

"I never told him I was pregnant." Wendy reached over and took Buffy's arm. "Come on, dear. I'm sorry. Eat your lunch and let's gossip and forget about football and football players."

Buffy cocked her head and gave Wendy a look of consternation. "That's a laugh, coming from you. You get knocked up by one football player, own about fifty others, and your father trades my husband fifteen hundred miles away with a shattered knee and you want to hold hands and gossip." Buffy jerked her hand away. "No, thanks."

Buffy left the table and restaurant quickly, sticking Wendy with the bill and two Caesar salads. Buffy picked up Simon Taylor D'Hanis at the baby-sitter's house and drove home. The two girls were still in school and wouldn't be home until around three-forty.

Buffy held the young boy to her breast and rocked him, telling him about all the things he and his father would do when Simon returned from Los Angeles.

"You know, Simon, to tell you the truth," Dick Portus said, "when the commissioner forced me to make a deal for you, I figured"—Portus rocked back in his leather and stainless steel chair, putting his Gucci shoes up on his massive desk—"this is no shit, I figured that Cyrus Chandler and Dick Conly and the commissioner were running a dead horse in on me. I saw your wreck in Miami in the Playoff Bowl. I didn't think anybody could come back on that knee." Portus used his thumbs and forefingers to frame an imaginary television screen. "It looked like your leg was torn off at the knee, all twisted around like that. Then, when I saw the X-rays and your knee, I was *convinced* they fucked us. I think they thought they fucked us too." Portus laughed and laughed.

Simon D'Hanis sat erect, wedging his massive body into the small cloth-and-steel chair. His hands were folded neatly in his lap. His body was coated with a thin film of sweat. He smiled slightly and nodded while Portus laughed.

"But"—Portus stopped laughing—"you came out here and did a hell of a job for us and you showed those deadbeats pride and endurance and how to play with pain. I goddam appreciate it." Portus hit the table with a tiny fist. He was a small man at five feet six inches and 130 pounds. He dressed in white slacks and tennis sweaters. Only in his twenties, he was almost bald. "You worked hard all through camp and exhibition season. You were an inspiration to the young guys. You taught them a lot. But, taking the long view . . ."

Simon felt his gut tighten and a chill ripple up his spine. The hairs on his neck stood up.

". . . we did pretty good in the draft," Portus continued. "And your teaching brought the younger guys in the line around." Portus grimaced and shook his head. "I just don't see where we are going to have a spot for you."

"But," Simon said softly, keeping his hands quietly in his lap, "I got one more year on my contract. I need that year for the pension and for the money. I don't have much put away. I worked out every day off-season and didn't make any money, and most of my salary is deferred. I'm broke. . . . Football is all I know. I got another year in me, Mr. Portus."

"Call me Dick," the tiny balding man said. "Well, that's why I called you up here to explain our problem. There just isn't going to be a place for you. We're going with the younger guys. The guys *you* helped bring along, and don't think we don't appreciate it. That's why I wanted to give you a chance to catch on with another club. We're putting feelers out now. . . ."

"But I don't understand, if you think I'm good. I don't know what else I got to do. I'm twice the ballplayer any of those rookies are," Simon pleaded. "I got three kids and no savings and no job prospects."

"You mean none of those rich Texas oilmen are football fans?"

Portus waved a hand as if batting Simon's plea out of the air like a fruit fly.

"I'm a lineman, not some glamour back," Simon said. "Besides, I spent all my time rehabilitating, not looking for work."

Portus began inspecting his nails and hands. "We just aren't going to have a spot."

"But I've got another year on my contract," Simon argued.

"That gives you the right to come to camp, Simon, that's all." Portus was tiring of the conversation. He swiveled back and forth in his chair and leaned forward to inspect one of his shoes. "If you'll *read* that contract, you'll see that you are required to report in physical condition to play football. That knee of yours is hardly what you would call in good condition."

"But I played every exhibition game, Dick."

"Call me Mr. Portus."

The tiny man pulled his feet off his desk and sat up, preparing to end the discussion. "I just figured to showcase you, maybe trade you, but nobody wants you. Nothing wrong with your game, but your injury is no secret . . . no secrets in this business." Portus paused and cleared his throat.

Simon sat dumbfounded.

"Look, Simon. Your knee is no good. You have violated your contract just by having a bad knee. Our doctor will say so. The Texas Pistols will say so." Portus snorted a laugh, "Christ, they should know, they fucked up the surgery. Anyway, there's no place for you."

"But . . . what about . . . ?" Simon's mind was chaos. None of this made sense. "What should I do? I didn't expect . . . I don't know what to do. I played hurt for you . . . I just thought you would respect that and . . ."

"Well, Simon, the Union might help," Portus continued. "You could sue, but it's expensive and you would have to sue Texas, then LA, then the League. You'd be in court forever. Besides, we have film of you playing, and Texas took film of you doing range of motion drills on the friction table. So go out with pride and style; quit the game before the game quits you."

Portus turned to his phone and snatched up the receiver, signaling the end of the conversation. "Diane, send those scouting reports in here, will you? And get the coach on the line." He signaled toward the door with his eyes for Simon D'Hanis to leave. "Go away, Simon, I'm through with you."

Simon sat wedged in the chair and looked at his sweating hands, twisting his thick fingers until they ached. Finally, slowly, he got to his feet and reached over the desk. With his right thumb and forefinger Simon D'Hanis grabbed LA owner Dick Portus by the nose, snatching him out of his seat. Portus howled, the blood vessels in the tip of his nose rupturing as Simon dragged him across the cluttered desk top, scattering contracts, letters and memorabilia.

The telephone clattered to the floor.

Simon raged and shook Dick Portus like a dirty mop. The little man's shoes flew off in separate directions. The young owner flopped around, his face white with terror and pain. Turning loose of the mashed nose, Simon got a grip on Portus's clothes, stretching his tennis sweater out of shape.

Then Simon D'Hanis decided to throw Dick Portus out the window of his twenty-second-floor office.

As the giant heaved Portus sailing toward the twenty-second-floor glass, the tiny man clutched desperately at Simon's shirt sleeve, tearing it enough to change the angle of his trajectory, and Dick Portus bounced off the teakwood credenza, smashing into a Picasso print.

The next day Simon D'Hanis was listed as officially retired on the commissioner's list.

Dick Portus's nose required restorative surgery where Simon's thumb and forefinger had crushed tissue and vessels.

Simon D'Hanis was now out of control.

And he was heading home.

MENTAL TOUGHNESS

RED Kilroy took a calculated risk that training camp. First, he successfully banned all Texas Pistols Franchise personnel except players and coaches. Even A. D. Koster, the general manager, was banned. He was the reason for the ban.

Second, Red immediately cut his roster down to sixty players. He only invited eighty to camp, and the physical examinations eliminated ten of those. After personal interviews with Red, ten more were released. The remaining players were guaranteed their salaries for the season, in return for a promise of complete loyalty to Red Kilroy.

Suzy and A.D. tried to fight both the ban and the guaranteed contracts, but Red unrolled his contract—negotiated years before with Dick Conly and Cyrus Chandler—and pointed out the clause that gave Red complete power of hiring and firing over coaches and player personnel. Violation of the clause was sufficient reason for Red to resign, at which time he had to be paid a lump sum of $1,500,000, plus additional payments of $500,000 a year for fifteen years, regardless of whether he accepted another job. A.D. retreated in the face of Red's overwhelming numbers.

A.D. retreated for another reason.

As Taylor Rusk had predicted, the more people the Cobianco

brothers moved into the Franchise, the more apparent it became that A. D. Koster was expendable. He was required to stay close to the office and protect his flanks and back.

A.D. spent his free time in his skybox luxury suite at the Pistol Dome with Monique. Together they designed the Pistolettes uniforms and drew up the Pistolettes' "code of conduct" to ensure they did not hurt the image or the integrity of the Texas Pistols Football Club, Inc.

A.D. often sent the Pistolettes to the Cobianco parties when the brothers were entertaining "associates" from out of town. A.D. hoped that those favors kept him in good stead with the Cobianco brothers. He didn't look at it as pimping but as public relations. At one of the parties a nude, drunken, nineteen-year-old blond Pistolette drowned in the swimming pool. It took a lot of money and fast talk to keep the story out of the news. A.D. complained to Don Cobianco about the trouble.

"Trouble? What trouble?" Don snarled over his breakfast. The two men were meeting in Don's hotel suite. "There ain't no trouble. That's why you got them alternates. Next time, send us some alternates." He waved A.D. off and went back to reading the Chandler Communications, Inc., newspaper.

A.D. called Suzy Ballard Chandler out at the Hot Springs Ranch.

"Don't complain to me, A.D.," Suzy yelled over the phone. "I have enough trouble out here. The crazy old bastard wants to either give all his money to that goddam Jesus freak Billy Joe Hardesty or support the Players Union director Terry Dudley for governor. I'll bet he's written five hundred checks to those two. If I hadn't burned them, we'd be dead broke." Suzy changed hands with the telephone. Her palms were sweaty. "And he seems to be getting *better.* The Valium doesn't seem to be keeping him under control."

"He's probably built a tolerance to the stuff," A.D. said. "Give him more."

"I'm giving him a hundred milligrams a day now," Suzy whined. "It keeps him drowsy and a little confused, but now he's talking about getting back to the city. I'm scared to death that the next time Billy Joe Hardesty flies in, he'll take Cyrus off with him."

"Put one of those cowboys at the airstrip with a shotgun and blow Billy Joe to Jesus if he steps out of his plane," A.D. replied.

"Really?"

"I'm serious. We can't fuck around anymore with that guy. I got a lot of trouble up here with the Cobiancos. They're taking

— 413 —

over the Franchise. Johnny is my assistant and they got all sorts of goons on the payroll."

"Shit!" Suzy said into the phone. "What are we going to do? I don't understand all this stuff. Most of the other companies seem to run themselves with presidents and boards of directors, but Dick Conly ran that damn franchise out of his head. You know what Cyrus has been doing?" she asked but didn't pause. "He's been transferring the Franchise stock into his grandson's trust. Ten percent a year on his birthday."

"Taylor and Wendy's kid?" A.D. asked. "Randall?"

"He doesn't have any other grandkids that I know about," Suzy said. "The kid has forty percent already. It was Dick Conly's idea, the bastard. I asked Cyrus to stop the trust and leave the stock to me, but he said he can't do it; he doesn't control it."

"Jesus!" A.D. was startled by their sudden precariousness. "If he does that much longer, the trust fund'll run the Franchise. I thought you had him under control?"

"That is what I have been saying, you jerk!" Suzy clenched her damp palms. She ached to hit A.D. one good shot in the nose, watch him bleed, his eyes water. "Since the Trust already has forty percent and Wendy Chandler's got ten percent, we already got a standoff."

A.D. whined. "I got trouble at both ends and in the middle. They will clean house. What the hell am I going to do?"

"They'll try, but you don't have to let them," Suzy condescended. "I got my tit in a wringer down here. I may just kill the old bastard. I'm tired of fucking with him. They want to fight, I'll fight."

"Jesus! Wait a minute, Suzy," A.D. cried. "Cyrus may not be ready to die—*taxwise*, I mean. You'll need a hell of a lot of cash to pay inheritance taxes on that old bastard, and as far as I know he doesn't have the cash or the insurance policies. Let's not go looking for trouble. Let's deal with it as it comes."

"Well, talk to Cobianco!" Suzy yelled. "Let's do something. I'm tired of this *shit*!" She slammed the phone down.

A.D. sat numbly at his desk and talked to himself. "A fucking roller-skating carhop got a covey of houses, maids, servants, a half-million-acre ranch with high-blood herds of horses and cattle, her own hot springs, God's most spectacular Rio Grande canyons, *and now she's tired of this shit*." A.D. laughed weakly. "*Shit*, she called it. *Shit*." He lay his cheek against his arms, folded on the desk top. "'Let's *do* something,'" he mimicked Suzy. "Fucking roller skates made her crazy. *Do* something? Do *something*? Goddam cunt, this ain't *nothing* I'm doing. I don't know what it is, but it's *something*." A.D. sat resting his head on his arms, wondering how it had gotten so complicated.

"Taylor was right," he whined. "Years ago. He's always right. I never did have no fucking luck with carhops."

THE LAST OF CYRUS/THE FIRST OF THE IRS

Suzy Ballard Chandler decided to double Cyrus's Valium dosage and see if that didn't reduce him back to the half-vegetable that spent his days doddering around the house, picking imaginary lint off his bathrobe. In the short term Suzy achieved her goal and Cyrus was quickly back to drooling and wetting himself.

Unfortunately, one Sunday afternoon, after a lunch of Froot Loops, Cyrus Chandler choked to death on his own vomit during his afternoon nap.

As A. D. Koster had feared, Cyrus Chandler was not ready to die.

Taxwise.

The Chandler Industries were protected; Dick Conly had seen to that before Amos Chandler died. But no provisions had been made to shelter Cyrus Chandler's personal holdings, including his remaining fifty-percent ownership of the Franchise; the Hot Springs Ranch with its buildings, fencing, airstrip, twenty-five thousand head of Santa Gertrudis, fifteen hundred purebred quarterhorses and miscellaneous vehicles; and his $2.7 million home in the city.

The will was simple, leaving everything to Suzy.

The only insurance was a $2,500 burial policy.

Two months after Cyrus died, the Internal Revenue Service presented Suzy with an inheritance tax bill of a little over sixteen million dollars.

SWIMMING
WITH THE SHARKS

Suzy Ballard Chandler had no idea how to raise that much cash. Nor did A. D. Koster.

Other than the fifty percent of the Franchise, the only assets with much liquidity were the purebred cattle and quarterhorses; even those showed the peculiar bind that Suzy faced. The ranch foreman had kept meticulous records of the high prices paid for the breeding stock, which the IRS used to compute the growing value of the horse and cattle herds. The actual distressed market price, however, was much lower, closer to the value of slaughter cattle and saddle horses. The foreman's careful records had been good for depreciation but bad for depreciation recapture upon inheritance.

The shelters for tax avoidance had not yet been created to pass Cyrus Chandler's personal wealth intact to the next generation. The taxes were staggering and pressing, since the Government was also in a liquidity crisis and the IRS insisted on prompt payment and preferred cash.

Sixteen million cash. Pronto.

It might take years to sell the ranch and the expensive mansion in the city.

Dick Conly could have extricated Suzy from the seemingly desperate cash-poor position with just a few phone calls. It wasn't even genius-level work. But A.D. and Suzy were swimming with the sharks, and Conly merely watched.

Quite soon the IRS began making threatening noises about property seizures and attachments, and their target of first choice was the Franchise.

Even at that late date, if Suzy and A.D. found an honest lawyer, they would have been all right. Instead they called Charlie Stillman. The lawyer, union organizer, player's agent, part owner in Cobianco Brothers Construction and counsel for the Laborers Union, said he would call back.

When the phone rang, A. D. Koster answered.

"It's set," Stillman said.

"What's set?" A.D. shrugged his shoulders at Suzy, who was chewing the polish off her nails.

"The meet."

"What meet?" A.D. looked to Suzy for some indication of what his response should be if he ever figured out what Charlie Stillman was saying. "What meet?" A.D. repeated. Suzy suddenly pulled her bare foot to her face and began chewing on a toenail.

"About the sixteen million," Charlie Stillman said. "I got it for you."

"Oh."

Suzy and A.D. went to see Don Cobianco. He was expecting them.

"I can have the money for you next week," the eldest brother said. "But first you will *both* have to take out life insurance policies in the amount of the loan, payable to me. We don't want this same sort of problem cropping up again. It won't cost you anything. My brother Roger has an agency that does business with one of those fast-track companies out of Detroit. They pay a hundred-and-fifteen-percent commission on the first year's premium. So we'll make your premium payment and keep the fifteen percent." Don Cobianco smiled. "Don't worry about the physicals. We got doctors." Cobianco reached into his desk drawer and pulled out two insurance forms. "Just sign here and leave the rest to me."

"I don't know...." A.D. said.

"Well, if you don't want the money..." Cobianco began to put the sheets back into his desk.

"Goddam, A.D.," Suzy snapped, "what else can we do?"

Cobianco pushed the papers back out in front of the two confused and desperate people. "It's just a precaution. You'll be able to pay me back easy with the cash flow that the Franchise will generate in the next few years. I'm charging you less than prime-rate interest. IRS charges more interest; they're the real sharks. Where else could you get a better deal?"

Suzy and A.D. had no answers.

Suzy snatched up the pen and quickly signed the insurance form. A.D. hesitantly followed suit.

Donald Cobianco slid the papers into the drawer.

"Now, of course we'll just fill out a simple loan statement. I'll want the ranch and the Franchise as my collateral."

When the paperwork was finished, A.D. and Suzy got up to leave.

"Now, remember," Don Cobianco said, "you check with me

on all fiscal matters involving the ranch and I will exercise a certain amount of day-to-day control over the Franchise."

The two people nodded.

"Let's see if we can get to the Super Bowl this year, *partners*. Since it's going to be played in the Pistol Dome, it means lots of tickets and a home-field advantage. We ought to make a killing. Give someone else a liquidity crisis."

"How does it feel to be so liquid?" Suzy asked A.D. when the money arrived.

"We've made room." A.D. finally spoke. His mood was low. "For bigger and bigger sharks."

LAME DUCKS
IN THE LINCOLN BEDROOM

"HOLD the line, please, sir." The female voice on the phone had a nasal clipped eastern sound. "The White House is calling."

Taylor Rusk pulled the phone onto his bed and lay on his right side, the receiver wedged between his left ear and shoulder. Motionless while the phone made clicking and buzzing sounds, he wondered what time it was, but was too sore to look for the clock radio.

It was dark.

Taylor Rusk had just crawled into bed. The team plane returned late from the Los Angeles Monday Night Playoff game and the sun was up when Taylor eased his aching body onto the king-size mattress.

Los Angeles blitzed the shit out of them. The Los Angeles linebackers, halfbacks and free safety kept coming all night; Taylor took some terrific blows to the ribs and back after he had released the ball. They called some roughing-the-quarterback penalties, but that didn't keep Taylor's bones and muscles from bruising or his rib cartilage from tearing.

Los Angeles's game plan was to "intimidate" the quarterback by attempting either to break Taylor's back and ribs or rupture a major internal organ. Failing that, Los Angeles figured that the Texas quarterback would begin to hear footsteps. The constant blitzing was a personal vendetta for Dick Portus. The young Los

Angeles owner wanted some retribution for the trouble his attempt to sign Taylor had caused him. Chastised and publicly embarrassed, Dick Portus exacted his revenge.

"I want you to kill him," he had told his defense. They didn't need much encouragement and battered Taylor all night. Speedo Smith and Screaming Danny Lewis made the correct pass-route adjustments every time, but the young offensive line missed a few blocking changes. Fortunately Taylor made up some time himself and had to eat the ball only once. Ignoring the pressure and finding the right receivers, Taylor picked the LA defense apart.

Texas beat LA 36–6 in front of a national television audience, but Dick Portus got his pound of flesh. By Taylor's reckoning, aching in his bed, the telephone against his ear, Dick Portus got maybe three to five pounds. But it cost him the Playoff, putting the Pistols one step closer. If they got by Washington, they were in the Super Bowl. It was exactly what Red had expected Portus to do, and he designed his game plan into it. Red offered the LA players the chance of doing their jobs and stopping the play or a free shot at Taylor Rusk.

"It's just for one game, Taylor," Red explained when Taylor figured out the reason for naked bootlegs and fake QB draws. "This is the year. This is the only way to beat them for sure. Try and protect yourself, but don't flinch."

"Hello?" a familiar voice came on the line. Taylor flinched.

"I'm ready with your call to Texas," the White House operator said.

"Taylor? Taylor, my boy?"

"Yeah?" Taylor groaned, too sore and tired to attempt to place the voice.

"It's me, Terry Dudley. I'm calling you from the White House."

"Good, Terry," Taylor said weakly. He didn't move from his side or open his eyes.

"Thought I'd call." Dudley's cheery voice irritated the sore, aching quarterback. "It's beautiful Foggy Bottom on the old Potomac River. Me and the wife are up here to meet the President. Pretty hard to believe, huh?"

"Naw. That son of a bitch will meet with anybody." Taylor kept the phone cradled against his ear. His lower back seemed welded tight with muscle spasm and he could feel something grinding in his rib cage with every breath.

"We're here for a Republican governors conference." Dudley's voice remained bouncy, cheery. "Last night, after we watched your game, I was lying here in the Lincoln bedroom. Milly was giving me some head and I thought, I got to call old Taylor. I told Milly that only you could appreciate your union director getting a blowjob from Miss America in the Lincoln Bedroom of the White House."

"Abe might appreciate it." Taylor's throat clogged with phlegm.

"Still the same old kidder, hey, Taylor?"

"Laugh a minute."

Dudley rambled gaily on. "I'm on the dais tonight and will talk about what our union can do for the Republicans."

"Self-destruct," Taylor mumbled. He could feel himself drifting off to sleep. A muscle spasm under his shoulder blade woke him. "How's Milly?" Dudley had married right after the Houston Union meeting.

"She loves it."

"I know *that*. You said that's why you married her, but how does she like the White House and being the wife of the *only* Republican labor leader?"

"That's what I . . . what?" Dudley was confused momentarily. "Oh, yeah. She also likes the White House, the President and his wife." Dudley laughed the harsh guffaw he had developed on the organizing trail. "These people will help us. This is a big step toward more power for the Union. We'll be solid, organized, ready."

"Well, give Milly my love. I don't want to know who 'these people' are . . ." Taylor yawned. ". . . unless it's the Beverly Hills Gun Club."

"Listen, Taylor, I need a big favor," Dudley said. "I can collect a few IOUs for the Union if you can get me tickets to your game here next week."

"Awwwww, noooo, you asshole. You mean that's why you called me from the White House? For fucking tickets? I just got in bed from LA!"

"What was in LA?" Dudley seemed slightly hurt.

"A playoff game," Taylor groaned.

"Oh? Oh! Oh, yeah!"

Taylor lay with the phone wedged against the side of his head. "You are the Union president who wants to be emperor of the Western Hemisphere and you can't get football tickets? What about Washington players?"

"No real solidarity on that team. Terrible, isn't it?" Dudley said. "Of course, that's why you'll kick their ass. I'll need about twenty. I have lobbyists and congressmen to consider. We're hav-

g a party afterward at the Mayflower. A.D.'s bringing the Pis-
lettes; they're performing at the game."

"*And* at the Mayflower?"

"They're coming to the party with A.D., if that's what you
mean." Dudley turned slightly defensive because Milly was in the
room. "Now, can you get me the tickets?"

"Why doesn't A.D. get them for you?"

"He says that he's used up all his; besides, he's bringing the
Pistolettes. Come on, Taylor. I need a favor."

"I'll see what I can do." Taylor was exhausted. "Things have
changed since Conly left. The Cobiancos seem to have a lock on
the ticket office and I did Johnny's dental work with his brand-
new forty-five automatic."

"I heard about that," Dudley said. "Well, say that the tickets
are for me. They supported labor during the campaign with lots
of money."

"Why don't you call them if you all are such big buddies?"

"Jesus, Taylor, I can't deal with people like the Cobiancos.
I'm the Union director. Direct favors like tickets..." Dudley let
the thought trail off for Taylor to fill in the blank spots. "I need
a *real friend*."

"Okay, okay. Lemme work on it." Taylor was sore and still
sleepy. He didn't want to talk more. "I have to pay for the tickets,
so send me a check. They're forty dollars apiece." Taylor stopped,
remembered. "Hey, you still haven't delivered on the two promises
you made at Houston. I want Hendrix's wife to start getting the
pension money that's due, and the Union's got to help Simon
O'Hanis. They really fucked him around. Portus cut him illegally
and Texas traded him illegally."

"I'm right on top of both cases, Taylor."

"All right, you do those things and I'll find tickets." Taylor
was slipping again. "Forty bucks apiece. They're *not* free."

"The check'll be in the mail today. Will you come to the party
at the Mayflower after the game? Lots of senators and congressmen."

"I'd rather hang out at the bus station. So mail me the money.
I'm always getting tickets and ending up having to pay myself.
Send me the money and don't forget about Simon and Ginny
Hendrix." Taylor hung up, took two Seconal and codeine number
four and went back to sleep.

Taylor arranged for Dudley's tickets. They cost the quarterba[ck] eight hundred dollars. He didn't see the Union director in Was[h]ington.

He *never* saw the check for the tickets.

LAME DUCKS INSIDE/OUTSIDE
THE WHITE LINES

IN a slow, cold rain, on a fourth-quarter split route, Speedo Smi[th] put the Texas Pistols in the Super Bowl. The Washington fr[ee] safety was running step for step with the Pistols' split end wh[en] Taylor launched the pass under pressure. He overthrew, Tayl[or] thought, but Speedo put on a burst of speed that was unbelievabl[e], blowing past the safety and running under the ball.

Speedo turned around and danced the last ten yards to the e[nd] zone backward, holding the ball over his head for the crowd [to] see. The gesture was met with a chorus of boos and howls; th[e] more deranged fans threw bottles and seat cushions. A whiske[y] bottle sailed from the upper deck, knocking a fourteen-year-o[ld] black peanut vendor into a four-day coma and permanent bra[in] damage.

A Grapette bottle shattered against the side of Taylor Rusk['s] headgear.

The commissioner, Robbie Burden, fined Speedo Smith fi[ve] hundred dollars for behavior damaging to the League's integrit[y]. "Inciting the fans" was the official charge.

The gun ending the game was fired directly behind Speed[o], scaring him so badly he was still shaking, his voice quivering [in] the locker room.

"That's the third Grapette bottle thrown at me since college[."] Taylor showed him the dent in his headgear. "Maniacs, fuckin[g] maniacs, all shot up on Grapette. Say, Speedo, where did th[at] burn come from on that split? I didn't think you could get there[."]

"Taylor, my leader turkey"—Speedo was still wired, his eye[s] sparkled black—"I hope this will finally put away overthrow. [I] call that move '*getting rubber in overdrive*.' As you walk out the[re] at QB on Super Sunday in the Pistol Dome, remember what yo[u] w today. Your split end can't be overthrown or outrun. You got he *Fastest Nigger Ever.*"

"Why did you wait till now?" Taylor was amazed. "There's st and there's *fast.*"

"We didn't need it before," Speedo said. "Now we need. A ttle advantage only you and I understand. Nobody's going to lieve Washington's safety."

At the Mayflower Hotel, Terry Dudley took great delight in e victory, making certain that every legislator that had placed a et with him paid publicly, enduring the kind of ritual humiliation at can only be inflicted by a seven-foot winner.

The Texas Pistolettes performed as A.D. had promised, alough A.D. was upset with the attention lavished on Monique y the majority leader from Pennsylvania. A.D. had even taken on Cobianco's advice and brought some alternates for the party, hich fragmented rather than ended.

Participants ended up in various parts of town, in altered states f mind, performing a variety of acts.

It required the Secret Service and the DC police chief to disngage without charges the Vice-President of the United States om the Chinese puzzle of naked male and female flesh that mbled out of the elevator into the lobby and lay pulsing and robbing at the feet of a trade delegation from the USSR.

The night manager, desk clerk and bellboys ran, while the ussians politely excused themselves and tiptoed through the tan-le of naked bodies onto the elevator. The cheerleaders, con-ressmen, an undersecretary of state, a microcomputer contractor ith CINCPAC, a CIA general and two hookers—along with the ice-president, who was the focal point—seemed to be inextric-bly tangled in a multidimensional carnality that reached new eights of bureaucratic obscenity.

The inability of the first arriving policemen to describe the calpolitik of the sexual act was the key in keeping the whole pisode quiet.

That the Red Chinese found out so quickly was considered dication that the Sino-Soviet split had ended.

In China several wall posters with intricate drawings explained e naked dialectical struggle, reminding the one billion or so hinese that the fellow in the middle wearing only a cowboy hat as obviously the victor and only "a heartbeat away from being resident of the United States of America." Thereafter the Chinese lways held the vice-president in higher esteem. This veneration d to the vice-president's many trips to China.

Terry Dudley used the Washington trip to test the political water and float a trial balloon for his candidacy as governor o Texas. He billed himself as a conservative Republican with soli credentials from organized labor.

Nobody even thought it strange.

The Pistols were in the Super Bowl.

That was strange.

SIMON HITS THE WALL

TAYLOR Rusk stayed in his seat until the charter plane was com pletely emptied and the crowd of fans had followed the team dow the concourse to the lobby. Taylor left the plane when the main tenance crew came aboard to vacuum up the chewing tobacco cigarette butts, snuff and vomit and gather the blood-soaked ban dages, empty bottles and crumpled beer cans.

At the turn in the jetway Wendy Chandler was waiting for him

"I wasn't sure if I had missed you." She leaned up on he tiptoes as he bent down to kiss her. Their lips parted.

"How's Randall?" Taylor's back was stiff and hurt.

"Sleeping." She watched his slow, careful movement. "Bob': with him back at the house. Toby's got the car right here."

Wendy opened the door out of the jetway onto the apron. The airport hit them like a blast of wind: jet engines, propellers, tow trucks, baggage tractors, roars and howls, catering wagons rattling food from plane to plane, tankers dodging around with high explosive jet fuel. The smell was almost as painful as the noise.

At the stair bottom the white Ford idled. Toby held the back door open. Taylor and Wendy slipped inside and Toby slamme the door, shutting out the cyclone. The car interior was warm an quiet. The tape deck was playing softly. Taylor slumped back against the seat and closed his eyes; the airport disappeared.

Wendy gently kissed his hand, seeing the flesh gone off three knuckles to the bone. He had knocked the divots in his finger hitting a Washington lineman's headgear after releasing the bal to Speedo for the final touchdown.

"Too much follow-through," he said softly as Wendy presse her lips against the wounds. The tape deck played:

...It isn't for the money
and it's only for a while
You stalk about the rooms
You roll away the miles...

Toby, a trained escape driver, put a red flasher on the dashboard
d quickly took them out of the airfield into the city traffic. The
r moved rapidly, easily.

When they passed his apartment, Taylor wondered what Lamar
an Lukas had seen in his absence? What had Investico done?

"We going to Doc's?" Taylor asked.

"No," Wendy said. "Do you mind running a little errand?"

"As long as I don't have to stand up." Taylor kept his eyes
osed. Wendy held his skinned and bandaged hand to her cheek.

"You know the way, Toby. I guess we better hurry." The Ford
aped forward, eating the pavement.

Taylor felt his sore hand throb. He could still see the ball arcing
the gray DC sky. He had put too much behind the throw; Speedo
uldn't get to the pass. The Pistol wide receiver had seemed to
eak stride, almost stumble. Taylor had thought he was falling.

"Where we going?" Taylor didn't open his eyes or lift his head.
re and exhausted, he really didn't care.

Each game, even though they kept winning, his beatings were
orse, while the roughing calls were fewer, farther between. In
C, Taylor had been speared twice, long after he released the
ll.

"That's twice," he yelled at the back judge.

"Maybe this business is too tough for you," the official replied
Taylor picked himself up.

"Go fuck yourself," Taylor shot back. "But first open your
es." That cost fifteen yards. Red Kilroy went berserk, starting
t onto the field after the official. Taylor had to cut off the coach
d explain or they would have gotten fifteen more.

Taylor sat in the fast-moving car, Wendy holding his battered
nd.

"This has to be the Super Bowl year," he said. "I couldn't last
other season. Red was right, this team is now or never. We'd
ver last two years at this pace."

"Buffy called."

Taylor nodded slightly, noticing that his neck hurt.

Since Simon returned to Texas, Taylor's attempts to contact
e big lineman had been unsuccessful. Buffy hadn't talked to

Wendy since stalking out of their lunch, leaving two salads an the check.

The last time Taylor called, Simon's phone had been discor nected.

Simon had tried other clubs, but the word of his attempt throw Dick Portus out the twenty-second-story window of the Lc Angeles offices went around the League at the speed of light.

Simon D'Hanis's football career was over.

Taylor wondered what Simon would do. He hadn't even com close to getting his degree, spending his University time on th football field or their apartment couch, memorizing the names c obscure old movie actors.

Recently Doc Webster had gotten Simon a job with a helme manufacturer selling headgear to high schools and junior colleges But the company went broke after a sixteen-year-old quadriplegi won a four-million-dollar suit against the company, claiming th headgear broke his neck. Actually the kid's high school coach ha broken his neck by teaching him to tackle with his headgear. Bi that didn't change the fact the company was bankrupt and Simo was out of a job.

Red Kilroy found Simon a high school assistant-coaching job that lasted only a week. The high school head coach made th mistake of yelling at Simon during practice. Simon broke th coach's nose, knocked out his front teeth and strangled him int unconsciousness before all the assistants and the whole first-tear offense could pull Simon off the poor, stupid son of a bitch.

Simon quit before the coach regained consciousness.

"How's Simon?" Taylor rubbed his sore neck with his fre hand.

"Not good." He didn't realize she was answering his questio about their destination.

"Buffy called me during the game," Wendy suddenly burs forth with explanation. The greeting—everything to this mo ment—had been an effort of intense self-control. The words tum bled out. "She said that Simon had locked himself in his troph room with his portable television and was still in there; she coul hear him screaming and breaking things. She begged us to com get the kids." Wendy, pausing to catch her breath, looked a Taylor, who had opened his eyes but kept his head against th seat back.

"Well," Taylor sighed, "I guess he's not pleased about us bein in the Super Bowl."

"Simon's in bad shape." Wendy looked ashamed, tears fille

her eyes. "I told Buffy I was on my way to get you and we'd be right over." Wendy wiped her tears on Taylor's sleeve.

"Simon was listening on the extension," Wendy continued. "He started screaming terrible things, crazy things."

"Simon was always a wild and crazy guy." Taylor slowly turned his head despite the pain in his neck, and he winced at the grinding in his ribs. "Just how wild and crazy is he this time?" Taylor felt all the reserve energy drain from him.

"He told me to make certain *you* came first. He said deer season was here and he needed to sight in the four-power scope on his two-seventy." Wendy looked at Taylor. "What's a two-seventy?"

"A heavy-caliber thunderstick." Taylor rubbed his undamaged hand across his face. "What the fuck kind of world is this?" He slugged the seat facing him. "The DC killer fans almost get us, but at the Mayflower Hotel, A.D. and the Pistolettes give global superpower blowjobs to congressmen, admirals and the whole State Department. Back at my apartment wait CIA agents on leaseback from the Mob, while I'm on my way to let my only friend use me to sight in his goddam deer rifle. The dumb son of a bitch! I told him to get his degree; I told him to lay off the steroids—always taking those Russian steroids. What the fuck do friends bring but trouble? *Russian* steroids. *Russian*, for Christ's sake—"

"I'm your friend, Taylor," Wendy interrupted the anguished rambling, brushing his cheek, "and congratulations for what you did today and all season"—she kissed him lightly on his neck—"and especially for who you are."

"That's my job."

"I'm beginning to understand how hard it must be."

"Not a lot of choice. The only game in town."

"You really made it all happen." Wendy's small, strong hands gripped his jacket tighter as she pulled herself tighter against him. "I've watched how hard you work, how much disappointment you swallowed all year long. . . ."

"I didn't do it alone. I got The Fastest Nigger Ever, Ox, Danny, Red, Margene . . . you, Randall . . ."

"But only you remember the bad news constantly."

"I told you, it's the job."

"When you and Red started laying all these plans for going to the Super Bowl"—Wendy nuzzled gently against his neck—"I kept thinking talk was cheap. But then I saw how much you paid— the discipline, dedication, pain, anger, fear, concentration and caring it took to back up those words." Tears wet his neck. "How much we all depend on you, your words, to keep us happy, believing in you. . . ." Wendy cried softly; he touched the tears on her cheeks.

"Just believe the words. Don't worry about the rest." He pulled her to him with his good hand. "The words are *I love you*."

She fitted herself comfortably on top, her warm thighs gently clutching him, her breasts softly pressed against his chest, her lips brushing the hollow of his neck. "I love you . . . I love you."

Taylor felt the depth of her fear. She wanted him to guarantee that he could save them all. Everybody. Everywhere. Forever.

He turned his head wearily and watched the town whirl past, a kaleidoscope of colors and shapes. All moving too fast. He felt dizzy, almost passing out, concentrating on his pain to stay conscious. Taylor let out a long, painful sigh, his ribs, neck and hand throbbing.

"Simon is going *too fast* and he thinks it's *too slow*."

"Turn here, Toby," Wendy said. "It's the two-story house on the left with the light on in front."

"Toby?"

"Yessir?"

"You have that rifle with the Starlight scope on it?"

"Yessir. It's in the trunk in its case."

"Any tape?"

"In the trunk."

"Then stop here and let's organize," Taylor instructed.

The car jerked to a halt a block from the D'Hanis house.

"Toby, you get the tape and rifle and get in the backseat. Wendy, you drive and I'll ride next to you in the passenger seat."

The three people changed positions. Toby retrieved the tape and the rifle with the night-vision sniper scope. Taylor taped down the interior light switch on his door, then told Wendy to drive past the D'Hanis house and through two intersections until reaching a cul de sac. Taylor's breathing was audible. Toby had checked his rifle and was quiet.

"Now turn around and drive back," Taylor continued, "but park across the street. Toby, you stay down when I open the door. I want him to think it's just Wendy and me."

Wendy eased the white Ford to a stop across the street from Simon D'Hanis's house. The tires squeaked against the curb.

The D'Hanis house was dark inside, but the yard and porch lights were on. Taylor could see an open window on the second floor. A figure moved at the window. It was Simon. He was holding his .270.

"Second-floor window." Taylor's heart pounded. "Don't shoot unless he does. He can't hit a bear in the ass with a bull fiddle."

"A two-seventy isn't a bull fiddle and you're no bear's ass." Toby rolled the window down and lay on the seat.

"Either way, don't shoot unless you have to," Taylor insisted. "Then just ruin his aim. Try not to hit him unless he shoots at the car."

"Don't *you* leave the car," Taylor said to Wendy. "Keep the engine running, and if he starts shooting, get out of here fast." Taylor stepped out into the street and closed the door. The interior light never came on.

"Taylor-boy, I was hoping you would make it in time," Simon yelled from the window. "Come on, I got something for you for getting in the Super Bowl. You aren't alone are you? Bring the little lady inside. Let her see what *pro*fessional football is all about. Let her see how her daddy's team builds character. I mean, I wasn't any *real* important football player, like you." Simon's voice came in rushes, pulses. Loud, then louder. "Even at the University it was you and that seven-foot faggot basketball player that got into Spur. Now the Super Bowl. Goddammit, must mean you'll be a general manager next, or an owner; just marry the boss's daughter. Come on, now, Taylor, tell her to come inside. We'll celebrate your Super Bowl success, all at my expense."

"No, Simon. She isn't feeling too good." Taylor's voice broke slightly. "I just thought I'd stop over and see if you wanted to talk about anything."

"That's a good one." Simon laughed harshly. "Yeah, I want half your goddam five-million-dollar contract, I want a new knee and I want to play in the goddam Super Bowl." Simon's voice continued to increase in volume. He shouted the last words.

"*And I want to be somebody again!* Goddammit! *I want to be somebody!*" Simon's voice echoed down the quiet streets; house lights came on down the block.

"You *are* somebody, Simon." Taylor talked softly. "You've always been somebody." He walked slowly across the street and started up the walk to the darkened house. His first fear was of being shocked and startled by the muzzle blast of Simon's .270. Taylor fought the urge to cover his ears.

"Oh, yeah? What was I?" Simon yelled. "*You* are the big shot. Goddam A.D. was a thief. Look what it got him: He's running the goddam Franchise. I was dog meat . . . Mr. Honest Guy. Mr. Sucker. I strained until I cried to get full flexion so they could videotape my knee working good and they used the tape *against me*. I fucking *posed*."

"You weren't a sucker, Simon. You got hit; you got wounded." Taylor kept walking slowly. "We were all so busy dodging bullets, none of us helped you." Taylor's neck was aching and the pain seemed suddenly unbearable. "It was all our fault—my fault."

"You hurt me!" Simon screamed back. "They told me it was your five-million-dollar contract and the Union that forced them to get rid of me. You and the Union."

The dark house loomed ahead. Taylor's stomach churned at the thought of what waited inside. His toe hit the porch step. "That's not true. I didn't hurt you. You are not a sucker for being honest, trying hardest, Simon. But you're still hurt bad and you need to get well." Taylor looked up at the window. "They lied to you, maltreated and abused you, with no concern for the health of your body. But that doesn't make you a fool. It makes them *criminals*." Fear had him by the neck. Taylor almost passed out from pain. He was terrified and it hit him at his weakest point.

"There is justice in the world, Simon, and honesty. You're the good guy. They're the bad guys, not you or me." Taylor tried to calm himself, take the ragged edge off his breathing. The still of the night was ominous. Nothing came from Simon's house but his angered screams.

"Simon? You're the good guy."

"Not anymore." Simon's voice was suddenly weak. "Not any-more."

"You just need time. Time to heal and rest. Time to slow down." Taylor listened for other sounds inside the house. "I got Terry Dudley at the Union working up your injury grievance...."

"Yeah." Simon's voice was flat, suspicious, angry. "Well, you're taking your sweet time getting anything done. I called Dudley once and he never called back because you hurt me and you told him not to help."

"I *didn't* hurt you, Simon." Taylor kept looking at the window, wishing he had prepared his eyes for night vision. He could only see a shapeless shadow in the frame. "I want to help. You can have anything of mine you want or need. Money, anything."

"I want your leg," Simon laughed.

"Can't have that. Anything else?" Taylor prayed there was. Toby was placing the cross hairs right on Simon's sternum, despite Taylor's instructions. Toby shot only to kill.

"Yeah, I want to be nineteen years old again," Simon growled from the darkened second-floor window. "I'd just watch movies all day."

"You don't have to be nineteen; you could do that now." Taylor stepped up onto the first stair. He heard the bolt work on Simon's rifle. "I'm coming in, Simon. Please don't shoot me." He could feel Simon sighting down from directly above him. He climbed the stairs and reached the front door. It was unlocked and Taylor was quickly inside, then a blast of pain shot through his neck, knocking him to the floor. At first he thought he was shot, but it was only fear that had hit him hard again in the neck. Taylor pushed off the floor; pain shot up his arm from his right hand. Trying to regain his feet, he had reinjured the fingers with the large divots of flesh missing.

Taylor leaned against the wall, trying to calm himself. His breathing was in gasps. Gulping oxygen desperately, he could feel the blood running from his fingers. Terrified, he started up the stairs. Each step seemed insurmountable. What was he climbing to reach? Why?

Finally the quarterback reached the open doorway of Simon's darkened trophy room. The roar and flash of the explosion of Simon's .270 blew Taylor flat on his back. He lay in the sudden stillness. D'Hanis had shot himself.

Taylor stood and slowly searched the quiet house. The quiet of the grave. He found Buffy fully dressed and sprawled on the floor, two neat .22 caliber holes behind her ear. Some dying reflex had caused her to kick one of her shoes up onto her dressing table and it lay in front of the mirror that Buffy faced every new day. A mirror that Simon faced less and less as he degenerated.

Each girl was in her bed, wearing a nightgown. They seemed asleep, except for the blood-soaked pillows and identical .22 holes punched behind their ears. Simon had shot his daughters as they slept. The sisters looked peaceful and content in their sleep, without dreams, without fear.

Taylor was not yet strong enough to look for the baby boy. Instead he returned to the god-awful mess in the trophy room.

Simon D'Hanis had used the .270 only on himself, fearing that a misplaced shot from the .22 Woodsman that he used with such cool efficiency on Buffy and the two girls would not have the same fatal effect. He didn't want to fuck up his own killing.

"You have to sacrifice your body," Simon always said. "Sacrifice your body. Destroy yourself."

Taylor found Simon amidst the wreckage that had been his trophy room. His arms were flung out, the rifle beside him, the remains of his head in a widening pool of blood. The room was destroyed: trophies, plaques, game balls, scrapbooks—all smashed, scattered, slashed, destroyed, strangely diffused, almost atomized. It seemed to be disappearing as Taylor looked. Decomposing. Decaying. The football career of Simon D'Hanis was as obliterated as he.

Simon had stuck the gun in his mouth and taken off most of the back and top of his head, turning it into so much red, gray and white mucilage splattered on the walls of his trophy room. Blood and chopped-up newsprint, brains and brass platters, bone chips and chunks of a game ball. Destroy yourself. Sacrifice your body. Leave it on the field.

Taylor looked at Simon for only a moment. He still twitched and gave off life, but Simon D'Hanis was dead. It was taking a while for the message to make the circuit. The aura would not last long.

The worst Taylor left for last: the baby. He would be in the nursery at the end of the hall, in his crib, all dressed as if to sleep, soaked in blood with two holes punched neatly behind his ear.

Taylor's neck pain drove him down; he didn't know if he could make the walk to the crib to find the inevitable. He was sick.

Then, from down the hall, the baby boy started to wail. Simon Taylor D'Hanis had slept through the entire ordeal of destruction.

Back in the nursery, Taylor's godson was screaming his lungs out and shaking the crib slats with his big hands. Simon Taylor D'Hanis was a large baby.

The note was in the crib:

Taylor . . .
    Take care of him. He is the only one who won't remember me. Thank God for that. I couldn't leave Buffy and the girls. What would they have done without me?

                                                                    Simon

"You should have asked, Simon." Taylor put the note back in the crib. "You big dumb bastard, you should have asked."

Picking up the screaming baby boy, Taylor walked toward the staircase, holding him against his shoulder, singing to him. He hummed "Yellow Submarine." When he reached the car, the baby had stopped crying. Toby opened the door and Taylor and the baby slid in next to Wendy, still behind the wheel.

Sirens were howling in the distant night, far across the old cotton fields. House lights flashed on up and down the street.

eople stood on their porches. They peered at Simon's house and he white Ford, staying close to their open doors, ready to beat a asty retreat.

"What about . . ." Wendy started.

Taylor continued the tune of "Yellow Submarine," inserting he words "The rest are dead, so let's get going before the police ome . . . the police come . . . the police come . . ."

Wendy drove them off into the night.

By the time the police car reached the street, the curious had eturned inside their own homes. The squad car cruised up and own the block twice. Nobody came out, so they returned to their ormal patrol. An hour later, after Wendy Chandler's lawyer called, hey were dispatched to Simon's house.

One of the patrolmen vomited all over his partner when they ound the mess Simon had made in the Trophy Room.

Wendy stayed at home with Taylor, the baby, Bob Travers and oby. Randall was sleeping undisturbed in his bedroom.

Taylor carried the sleeping baby to the old crib in Randall's oom.

He had left Simon's note for the police. One line burned his rain.

What would they have done without me?

Lived, Taylor kept thinking. *They would have lived.*

Taylor and Wendy, the older guys from the team and Buffy's nother and father were the only ones at the funeral. The Franchise ent a flower wreath in the team colors shaped like crossed pistols.

Perfect, Taylor thought, looking at the wreath. *Just perfect.*

As they lowered the four caskets Taylor kicked the pistol wreath nto the grave.

SIMON'S BODY FAT
GOES PUBLIC

HE day the medical examiner released the autopsy report on what ad remained of Simon D'Hanis, Ginny Hendrix called.

"The insurance company's refusing to pay Bobby's life insur-nce." Ginny talked fast. She was agitated. Bobby Hendrix being mashed into the ancient Mayan ruin at Tulum, Bobby being tossed out of a doorless airplane by Tiny Walton, Bobby five hundred feet up, free falling in blue Caribbean sky. These were *not* the things upon which Ginny Hendrix wanted to dwell.

"The insurance company has his blood tests showing leukemia so they say he killed himself, and *of course* the policy has a suicide clause. I keep telling them that they didn't know Bobby and that he wouldn't kill himself over the possibility of dying, which you would think any rational person could understand as a perfectly sane response. Wouldn't you? Of course you would." Ginny did not slow down. The words would not stop. "Bobby *knew*," Ginny machine-gunned her monologue into the telephone. "When he chose to play football, he *knew* that he would get hurt. 'Uncontrollable factor,' he called it. Like a motorcycle, or living on the river, or owning a horse. They'll get you. He *knew*."

Taylor held the phone away from his ear. He could imagine Ginny pacing that big Spanish kitchen floor, her black eyes glowing, constantly tossing her hair in fury. She howled in pain.

"Sooner or later... no matter how hard you plan... the son of a bitch is gonna get you! Bobby always accepted death as his companion; he *wouldn't* kill himself," she pleaded. "He couldn't. He always figured that they'd invent something or make an exception in his case. It was that way with the Butazolidin. He knew he took a chance. He always figured they would come up with some new miracle drug. When he learned about his blood count, the first thing he said was 'Now we'll find out what they got that'll fix *that*.'"

Ginny pulled at her dark straight hair. In the background was the distinctive sound of the electronic game and the two boys arguing fine points of Alien Invaders from Hyperspace.

"Look, Taylor, I can't stand this. I don't want to point out daily, justify daily. You're the rep. You've got to help me to explain what *really happened*." Ginny leaned forward, opening her free hand, thrusting it twice. "That somebody threw him out of an airplane." Ginny hit herself on the thigh with the open free hand. "He paid dues for twenty years. That's *twenty years,* Taylor. The guy says we don't believe you and don't believe Bobby was murdered and will recommend we fight your claim because Bobby Hendrix committed suicide because he was going to die. It's the *cost-effective thing to do*. That's what twenty years buys today. Now I know why people fear loneliness."

Taylor thought for a moment of four freshly dug graves, two large coffins and two small ones. He heard the creaking as they were lowered forever.

"What should I do?" Ginny slowed. "What? Tell me, Taylor, please."

Taylor washed away the thoughts of another family almost gone. He brought the phone closer to his ear. "Have you heard from Terry Dudley?"

"No." Ginny paused. "But I don't answer the phone very often; it's never good news. Terry may have called a dozen times. I don't know. It was the news about Simon that made me call." Ginny calmed. "They *published* the chemical analysis of his *fat tissues*. It just made me mad. They just put Simon's fat analysis in the newspaper like they were everybody's business. The chemical level of his fat. How would you like it?" She began to anger, almost like a child who catches sight of how sad she looks in the mirror and cries.

"Ginny, be calm." Taylor reached for her sense of outrage. "I try not to think about what they'll do or say about me when I'm gone. I mean, they already dissected Simon years ago. Christ, Simon dissected himself. He's probably glad they know about the chemical level in his fat. He probably always wondered himself."

"Jesus!" Ginny was not soothed. "They publish your urine count . . . your blood count . . . your sperm count . . ."

"My sperm can't count." Taylor kept at Ginny's outrage. "They can spell and make balloon animals but they can't count."

"Yeah, you are still a laugh a minute." Ginny slowed but the anger still poured out. "It *happened* to me. I work each day to strike that part of my mind dead, to erase it, wipe it out. I don't want to have to think about it ever. Now this damned insurance guy wants to talk blood counts and states of mind."

One of the two young boys won something on the electronic game and an immediate fight ensued. Ginny continued talking over the background noise.

"People are already beginning to talk about Bobby like he was crazed. And now, with Simon . . ." Ginny stopped and listened to Taylor breathe at the other end.

"I'll call Terry Dudley," Taylor said. "I'll get it all straight. Don't you worry about it."

Suddenly she asked, "Did he kill them?" She sounded like another person. She wanted the naked facts. Quickly. She almost couldn't. It was awful.

"Yes, he did."

"Why did he leave the boy?"

"He figured the kid wouldn't remember him."

"Really?"

"That's what I got out of the note." Taylor changed his tone. "Look, Simon's story isn't going to help. I'll contact Terry Dudley at Union headquarters and get him to take care of it. You try and forget about it," Taylor advised slowly and thoughtfully. "Terry'll tell me who at the Union can help and I'll call you later."

"In order to collect the insurance, I'm supposed to go to public court and prove my husband was not a suicide. Shit." She was angry. "Shit. Shit. *They killed him.*"

Taylor thought a moment. "He scared them. Bobby was always the thinker, always ahead of his time. His moral stance didn't make sense to them, and when documents began showing up in Tommy McNamara's pieces about the League and the Mob, they figured Bobby was McNamara's source. A mistake."

The line was quiet for several moments.

"A mistake," Ginny repeated. "I guess I could live with a mistake. Accidents, you know. Accidents happen. Like that?"

"Yes. Do it like that. I'll get Terry and the Union moving on it." Taylor spoke slowly. "Remember this phone *is* probably tapped. Let's not give away too many secrets."

"Well," Ginny yelled, "if you are really listening, you made the biggest fucking mistake of your lives. You'll pay. I mean it. You'll pay." She paused, listening while her screamed threats died away, as if she could tell whether she had been heard. Finally she said softly, "You'll pay."

"I don't see any point in threatening the tape recorder, Ginny," Taylor interrupted. "Whoever they are, they have made some mistakes. One day they'll make a big mistake and the world will get yanked out from under them."

"Promise me you'll get even for Bobby?" Ginny asked, dropping her voice a full octave. "Please, Taylor. You won't let them get away with killing him; you couldn't. You were teammates."

"We were friends, Ginny. Anybody can be teammates." Taylor was unhappy, reluctant, but he went on. "I'll do something someday, Ginny. Somehow. I promise. That's as specific as I can get."

"Thank you, Taylor. We all love you here. Be careful." Her voice changed suddenly. "Do you really think your phone's tapped?"

"I figure somebody is listening to everything. A wiretap is treading that fine line between paranoia and The One God."

"Taylor, when you came and stayed with us, did you take some documents and give them to Terry Dudley?"

"That was just the kind of question I didn't want you to ask when I told you my phone was tapped." Taylor sighed.

"Well, A.D. called the other day, offering to help with the insurance, and he asked me to ask you. I told him I didn't know."

"Be glad you don't," Taylor said. "Now I have to go call Dudley. He believes that vibrations on magnetic tapes are evidence of something."

Taylor called Union headquarters and left a message. The director failed to return the call until two days later, after Terry Dudley's house and office were burglarized.

"Nothing of value was taken except the documents and they're of limited value to us anyway," Dudley said. "After all, they *are* stolen. We can't enter them as evidence of anything at any forum."

"The damn things aren't even good insurance anymore," Taylor moaned. "If the Cobianco brothers were as certain as I am that television won't touch this shit with Tom Snyder in a wetsuit, they would drop Tiny Walton on me like a truck."

"Don't think that way," the director said. "As evidence in a murder trial, documents are powerful stuff. Now you are talking."

"I should get killed?"

"No. Well . . . wait a minute. No. I guess not you, but if you could tie the documents to the disappearance of Tommy McNamara . . ."

"Tommy McNamara is with Jimmy Hoffa." Taylor leaned against the wall. "I called about Bobby Hendrix. . . ."

"Bobby Hendrix didn't even know about the documents," Terry seemed to argue.

"But A.D. and the Cobiancos thought he had them," Taylor said. "They killed him, they were so certain. In their case it doesn't take much evidence. Anyway, what about Hendrix's insurance?"

"What about it?"

"Your guys on the insurance and pension board turned down the claim. His and Simon's."

"And?"

"*And* my ass." Taylor turned angry quickly. "You can't turn his claim down *or* Simon's."

"Oh? I can't?" Terry seemed slightly amused. "You're right, of course. I can't do *anything*."

"That's not what I meant and you know it. You promised me. We have a deal."

"There were the chemical reports on Simon and evidence that Hendrix may have killed himself. Besides, it's the board's decision."

"Fuck the board, Terry. My deal is with you and I plan on collecting. Tell *that* to the board."

— 437 —

"I'll *do* that, Daddy. Anything else?"

"Yeah, you roundheaded son of a bitch. You owe me eight hundred dollars for tickets to the Washington game. If you don't pay, I'll come wring it all out of you, *personally*. Now get your ass in gear. Go to work!"

"Taylor, calm down," Dudley said easily. "We can straighten this out. Don't forget we are *Spur*; we are *friends*. I get the message. These things take time, but I'll fix it. Don't worry."

"Fuck Spur! And if you don't get those pension and insurance claims to Ginny Hendrix and for Simon's boy, we aren't friends."

"Well, being your friend hasn't been easy," Dudley complained.

"If we end up as enemies," Taylor warned, "you are going to find your ass in a storm every day, all day long. And that'll be a lot harder."

NOTCHING EARS

SUZY Ballard Chandler summoned Red Kilroy. She had taken over Cyrus's old suite and moved A.D. into public relations. She kept the head coach waiting in Dick Conly's vacant office, checking her makeup and clothes, letting him daydream about his possibilities of filling Conly's shoes.

A.D. finally led the coach in to meet with the young widow. Red sat down in the low, cloth-covered chair across the desk from Suzy. He was looking up to her.

"Feel free to smoke," she said, dismissing A.D. with manicured, fluttering fingers. The ex-defensive back shuffled out angrily.

"Mind if I chew?" Red took his pocketknife and cut a thumbsize chunk off a plug of tobacco he kept in a Baggie.

"Not if you don't mind if I puke."

"Puke away." The coach popped the cud into his mouth. Chewing slowly, he watched Suzy with polite, passionless eyes.

"Well, as you know, since my husband's death I have begun to take a more active interest in the Franchise." Suzy smiled thinly. "The work will help keep me active and vital while mourning the loss of Cyrus. But I must also admit that for quite a while I have been thinking about certain changes in the structure of the club."

Suzy reached to the small silver cigarette box on her desk and withdrew a long brown filter-tipped cigarette. Red made no move to light it; he just chewed and watched. The wad of tobacco swelled out the right side of his face.

Suzy lit the cigarette with a miniature revolver, the Texas Pistols official lighter. Inhaling deeply, letting the smoke slip out of her mouth and nose, she looked about to breathe fire.

"I'm thinking of replacing A.D. as general manager." Suzy studied the whomper-jawed head coach, searching for a reaction. "Well? What do you think?"

"About replacing A.D. as general manager?" Red chewed slowly. He made certain to spit before, during and after he spoke. His lips were brown and runny, tobacco stuck between his teeth, juice sloshed around his mouth. Suzy choked back her gag reflex. Red spat again, then probed his mouth with his tongue, rearranging the chew—an extremely unattractive operation.

"Well..." Red probed thoughtfully. Suzy held both her hands to her mouth and closed her eyes. Red watched her pretty Adam's apple bobble. "A.D. ain't worth a shit." Red spat again. "But at least with A.D. we know what sort of an idiot we're dealing with...."

Suzy kept her eyes squeezed shut and both hands clamped against her mouth. She continued nodding her head.

"But"—Red spat, purposely leaving residue on his lips—"if we get some new yo-yo in here, anything can happen." Red licked the juice clean. "I don't know of any good general-manager material around for hire, do you?"

Suzy shook her head violently. Red watched her and chewed slowly. Suzy opened her eyes and dropped her hands, then took several deep breaths.

"Well, now, Coach"—Suzy was wobbly but was gaining—"actually I was thinking about somebody from inside the Franchise. Somebody like you."

Red grinned, showing his brown-stained teeth and mouth.

"I'll want an ownership position as part of my contract," Red demanded. "Say, five percent with options for five percent more?"

Suzy nodded, kept her eyes down and gulped great quantities of air, choking back the urge to vomit.

"What's the kicker?" Red chewed slowly, swallowing some of the juice. "What do I have to do?"

Suzy again took deep breaths; she was in a nauseous sweat. Finally she could speak. "You make certain we lose or at least don't win by more than the spread against Denver."

"What spread?" Red chewed calmly, betraying no emotion. "The Vegas line or the one in the Sunday paper?"

"The spread." Suzy belched. "You go by the biggest spread."

"I have been around football for most of my life, and I have seen and done some really incredible stuff, but believe it or not, this . . ." Red spat. ". . . this is the first time I have ever been asked to take a dive."

"Well? *Will* you do it?"

"Do I end up as GM and head coach with five percent of the Franchise and an option for five percent more?"

"You got my word on it," Suzy said. "We'll draw up the papers and make the announcement right after the game."

"I have your word on it?" Red asked again.

"May God strike me dead. What do you say?" Suzy stuck her small hand out. Red gripped it hard and grinned brown.

"I say we got a deal or God may strike you dead." Red pumped Suzy's delicate hand. "You got Red Kilroy's word."

Red went back to his office and sat, thinking about what had just transpired.

Red had always known Suzy would squeeze out A.D. sooner or later, but Red had never figured himself as the replacement. He was disturbed by her quick, almost desperate agreement to his demand for a percentage of ownership. Suzy Chandler knew that ownership was something that Red had wanted for years.

An owner. Not an employee but an *owner*.

Red Kilroy ached with desire to accept Suzy Chandler's offer, but of course the deal was worthless. Suzy's word was no good. For that matter, neither was Red's. The head coach decided to agree to Suzy's scheme because he knew that A.D.'s efforts would switch from attempts to steal and to thwart Red's Super Bowl game plan to A.D.'s own scramble for survival. Red was right. A.D. dropped out of sight quickly. Suzy emerged as the Franchise management. For the remainder of time left to prepare for the Super Bowl, Suzy paraded in front of the media and the team was left alone.

Red planned to win. To win *big*.

He knew, compared to the handshake and word of an ex-roller-skating carhop, a chance to win a Super Bowl was money in the bank.

TAKING SCALPS

"How many tickets do we get? Total?" Don Cobianco was asking A.D. Koster. "I mean the *full total*." They were riding around in the backseat of the black four-door Cadillac. In the usual way Roger Cobianco, the middle brother, was in the front passenger seat and Johnny, the youngest, was driving.

Johnny had lost his looks, along with his teeth and his brand-new Colt Commander, when Taylor hammered him with the .45 in A.D.'s office. Johnny's young face was now permanently pale, scarred and sunken. The false teeth were mismatched with the real ones and showed gold at the gum line.

But more had happened to Johnny Cobianco than losing a four-hundred-dollar gun and some teeth. He had been truly scared for the first time. He hadn't just lost, he'd quit. He had gotten whipped and realized his mortality with a terrifying, demoralizing clarity. It opened a tiny hole at his very center that never stopped growing until he was totally empty. Johnny C. had never felt so completely vulnerable, he had never lost so quickly and completely. He wondered if killing Taylor would blot out the constant dread that haunted him. His brothers thought he should take revenge, but Johnny refused to discuss it.

Johnny Cobianco was in a state of constant alarm, almost paralyzed by fear. It was killing him. His brothers saw his usual ebullient mood change to one of grim, sullen frowns, grunts and nods. The brothers noticed his skin color seemed bad, but if anyone had told Don and Roger Cobianco that their brother, Johnny, was being slowly scared to death, they wouldn't have believed it.

"A.D., I asked you a question." Don Cobianco's voice was soft in the backseat. "What's taking so long to figure? How many tickets do we control for the Super Bowl?"

"Including season ticket holders?" A.D. asked.

"Including everybody's, even yours," Don said. "Come on, give."

"We can't take *all* the season ticket holders' tickets," A.D. argued. "We've got some big corporate clients on that list."

"If they're big," Don Cobianco said, "they'll pay big. If they don't want to pay big, they're not the kind of customer you want

— 441 —

for the Franchise. We want spenders. High rollers. There's lots of stuff to sell at spectacle besides the spectacle. We want our share of all of it and we want the customer to pay the absolute highest price possible. Any other business technique would be un-American." Don looked at the square, dark, curly-haired heads of his brothers. "So, A.D., I'm asking again. How many tickets?"

"Twenty-seven thousand, five hundred," A.D. said.

"It's a seventy-thousand-seat stadium," Don Cobianco said. "We get at least half the seats. It's our stadium *and* we're one of the Super Bowl teams. It is *our* franchise. No. You tell the commissioner that we want thirty-five thousand seats minimum. Repeat: minimum. We have commitments." The thick-set man turned and looked at A.D. "Make Robbie understand what seventy thousand drunk fans would do if we shut Clyde, Texas, and the Pistol Dome down on Super Sunday. It wouldn't be super, believe it. You explain or I'll go see the commissioner and explain myself."

"I'll do it," A.D. said. "Robbie told me that I should carry on all contact with you. Since McNamara did the newspaper series on the League and the Mob, Robbie thinks a little distance wouldn't hurt deniability."

"No. It sure wouldn't hurt deniability." Don Cobianco grinned. "Tell him thirty-seven thousand, five hundred, and settle for no less than thirty-five thousand. You tell him that comes from me. If he has to give up some of his tickets, I still want thirty-five thousand bottom. Otherwise we'll come to his office and get them."

"Stop here, Johnny. We'll let Mr. Big Shot Pistols General Manager off three blocks of deniability away from his office. The walk will do him good." The car stopped and A.D. got out. They drove away.

A.D. stood for a moment, taking off his tailor-made silk suit jacket and loosening his tie, tossing the jacket over his shoulder. He began walking slowly toward the offices.

He had lied to Don Cobianco. The Pistols' share was thirty thousand, but A.D. had held out a few for himself. He had plans for two thousand tickets between the forties. Kimball Adams would give him $540 apiece for them and then make them part of a Super Bowl travel package from Las Vegas, New York or L.A.

A.D. planned to walk with a million in cash, tax-free.

Now he had to find an additional five thousand tickets for the Cobiancos. The commissioner would have to supply them, A.D. decided. Robbie Burden would have to take them from someone else.

The season ticket holders will go crazy, A.D. thought as he walked. The fans had just gotten settled down after the Franchise forced them to finance the Pistol Dome. And now their Super Bowl tickets were going to be scalped.

A.D. was worried; they had promised Super Bowl tickets to season ticket holders. There were going to be heavy negative vibes on this one. It was going to take real public relations.

A.D. walked in the warm January Texas sun. The heat penetrated his already sweat-soaked suit. In the heat of that afternoon moment A.D. decided that it was time for a new League rule absolving the Pistols Franchise of any blame on the distribution of tickets that would be done in the commissioner's office by a secret process. A.D. figured the people would buy it if the press would. The press would buy it if the commissioner stuck to the story. A.D.'s step became quicker, springy. A.D. had solved a problem and it made him feel good.

By the time he reached the Pistols offices, A. D. Koster had completely forgotten that solving the problem merely broke him even with the Cobianco brothers.

It was not until the middle of that night that A.D. sat straight up in Monique's bed and fully realized that the Cobianco brothers were taking *his million dollars*.

They would continue.

Soon they would take everything, as Don Cobianco had just done with the Super Bowl tickets.

"They want it *all*?" is what Suzy asked when A.D. told her the ticket demands. Robbie Burden said the same. Nearly. The commissioner had been expecting between six and nine million dollars.

"They'll ruin the game," Burden said.

"They're ruining it for me already," Suzy cried. "If we give in this time, they'll want more the next. I can't pay them back if they keep stealing my money."

"They were hoping we wouldn't notice right away," A.D. said.

"Well, I'm noticing," Suzy said. "They got to come way down."

"Absolutely," the commissioner agreed.

"And you have to give up some of your tickets," Suzy said to Burden. "These guys are friends of yours too. Maybe better friends? Maybe *you* are in with them? How do I know?"

"Now just a second . . ." the commissioner started to protest.

"Look," Suzy cut him off, "we have to stick together on this—*unless* you are in with the brothers. If that's the case, I think your secret Bahamian bank account can be proved. I believe they give jail terms for tax evasion, Robbie. The person who turns you in

gets ten percent. We can't afford to have people like A.D. i|
desperate straits where they are liable to do something that drastic.

"I was needing that million. I got debts." A.D. looked hangdog
"Commissioner, you're going to have to give us some of you|
tickets."

"Wrong." Robbie Burden watched Suzy file her long nails
"How do I know that *you two* aren't in on this with the Cobiancos?"

"You don't." Suzy lit a brown cigarette and exhaled a clou|
of smoke through her nose and mouth. Finally she looked righ|
at the commissioner.

Burden rubbed his chin. "I could cut some allotments, the|
use Kimball Adams to scalp the tickets back to the same people
They'll *still* get tickets; it'll just cost them more in the secondary
market. That'll free up other tickets that I had earmarked for th|
secondary market." The commissioner smiled. "Kimball sure ha
come in handy over the years."

"When you were a general manager, you always had a grea|
eye for talent, Robbie." A.D. smiled. "I thought your trade o|
thirteen players for a guy with a broken leg was genius."

A.D. cut his own throat by humiliating the commissioner. Righ|
then and there Robbie Burden decided A. D. Koster no longe|
served a purpose worth one Super Bowl ticket.

After the meeting with Robbie Burden, Suzy knew she neede|
money even more than she needed it before. So she called Re|
Kilroy into her office. "How's your coaching strategy comin|
along?" she asked pointedly.

"Super Bowls come every year, but the chance to own part o|
a franchise is once in a lifetime," Red said.

"It will be our secret until after the game." Relieved, Suz|
again shook hands with Red, sealing their bargain. Then she passe|
the word to Donald Cobianco.

The Cobiancos bet heavily against the Pistols. Their book quickl|
hit the million-dollar mark, at which point they usually bega|
laying off money around the country. But the Cobiancos continue|
to accept all bets on the Pistols, laying off only the bets agains|
them.

Later estimates put the Cobiancos' total bets against the Pistol|
winning the Super Bowl at between two and five million dollars
Some estimates went as high as ten million. Dick Conly suppos|
edly bet two million himself. Even Suzy Ballard Chandler bet fiv|
hundred thousand dollars she didn't have against her own team

On the *Tonight* show she predicted a twenty-one-point win. There was talk of her getting a Lite beer commercial.

The fix was in.

Only no one knew what the fix was.

THE LOUISVILLE
SLUGGER

THE fist was massive or somebody was beating his door with a Louisville Slugger. Unfortunately, when Taylor Rusk jerked open the door, it turned out to be both.

Instinctively dropping his left shoulder and ducking his chin into his rising right shoulder. Taylor pivoted on his left foot, bringing his right arm up to protect his face and head. The move kept the baseball bat from caving in the temporal area of his skull. His shoulder and arm absorbed the glancing blow. But while deflecting the bat, Taylor pivoted directly into Tiny Walton's short right hook. Two more quick hooks to the face with Tiny's massive fist—covered by a black leather, lead shot-filled sap glove—and Taylor was down.

A well-honed ability to take and roll with a punch, plus a small miracle, accounted for Taylor's cheekbone, jaw and teeth remaining intact. He hit the floor with the skin split wide under his left eye, another dislocation of the septum and a series of mouth lacerations. Not seriously injured, Taylor bled copiously.

Hymie, the large man wielding the bat, was uglier and taller than Tiny, with a bald anvil-shaped head and bad teeth. Fortunately he didn't have Tiny's wrist action, otherwise Taylor might not have ducked the bat quickly enough, and a *major* miracle would have been necessary to keep Taylor's skull intact.

The two men dragged Taylor to the couch and tossed him facedown.

"You dropped him like a sack of ashes, Tiny. You can still punch for a guy your age."

"Fuck you. My age." Tiny punched the unconscious man in the kidney because Hymie had pissed him off. Hymie went looking for a drink, coming back with the square Herradura bottle. Hymie took several quick drinks.

Taylor's whole body hummed; he felt peaceful and happy. His head tingled with flashes of disconnected color and sounds. He felt a spiritual connection with The Oneness: total loss of ego, complete confidence and fearlessness.

He was out cold.

Regaining consciousness took several minutes. It was quite painful but extremely fortunate. Taylor first wiped his fingers in the blood dripping from his mouth, nose and cheek. He rubbed the blood between his fingers, staring at it. His mouth tasted of metal. Slowly the harder pulses pushed their presence into Taylor's addled brain. Alarm reactions were going off. The brain stem had good news and bad news. The good news was that Taylor was not yet seriously injured.

"Huh," Taylor said. He was looking at the blood on his hands and shirt and all over the floor. "Kimball? Bobby? Is that *all* my blood?" He knew he was in his apartment, but he thought it was his rookie year, the night they moved in and got drunk. His battered head rang with throbs of pain. "Am I cut bad?" His tongue found all his teeth and began to probe the cuts.

"You got some blood left. How long you keep it is up to you." Tiny leaned down into Taylor's face and clutched it with his thick left hand. "Now, understand this. You *are* going to tell us where the documents are hidden."

Taylor couldn't yet place Tiny, but he remembered that his rookie year had been a while ago.

"You will return the documents, that is for sure." Tiny pushed the bloody glass-eyed face away. Taylor felt the burn of the fabric as his nose mashed into the cushion. "When you tell us, how much pain you stand, what kinds—those are all minor considerations, because you *will* give."

Taylor's recollections of Tiny Walton surfaced. Tiny spoke from experience. Taylor remembered the documents and Tommy McNamara's fingers lined up on each side of the typewriter in Doc Webster's bunkhouse. Taylor decided to give them everything and more.

Tiny took another small sip of tequila. He held it in his mouth momentarily before swallowing. "Then, even after you tell, Hymie's got to keep doing you and keeping you alive, just to make sure you ain't lying. A pitiful commentary on mankind when you can't take the word of a man whose nuts you just crushed with vise grips. Hymie, let's make this slow."

Taylor tried to separate the reality from the dream. Kimball Adams was a dream. The rest turned real quickly as Hymie left and returned with his black bag. It was an old doctor's grip filled with scalpels, needles, drills, pliers. Placing the grip on the counter, Hymie lit a stove burner.

"Hymie's going to heat up some stuff." Tiny pulled handcuffs from the bag.

Taylor had been handcuffed once by a Houston cop, who had then proceeded to work him over with a nightstick. It was a woman cop. The experience gave him the sense to know, even semiconscious, that once Tiny got the cuffs on him, Taylor would never live to see them off.

Lunging upward, Taylor drove his head directly into Tiny's face, breaking the nose but not crippling him nearly as much as Taylor had hoped. Tiny didn't seem to mind the broken nose at all. Hymie didn't even seem disturbed. They were old hands at this, few stood still for what they had planned.

But their underestimation of Taylor's size, strength and sudden reaction to handcuffs allowed Taylor to get free of Tiny and off of the sofa, stumbling into the doorway.

Unfazed, Tiny reached for the quarterback's throat to choke him down. But Tiny's vision was blurred slightly by his flattened nose. Taking a long step, his foot slipped off the carpet, onto the wooden floor and into a pool of Taylor's blood. Skidding in the blood, Tiny went down fast, hitting his head on the Heisman Trophy doorstop, which Taylor had moved from his bedroom. The trophy cut Tiny badly, punching a small hole in his skull. Blood and a clear fluid ran from the wound, which made him slightly woozy and very angry.

Hymie snatched up the bat and was in his backswing to hit Taylor, who was stumbling toward the stairs, trying to reach his bedroom and Johnny Cobianco's gun in the bedside table. Hymie was beading on Taylor's skull base when Lamar Jean Lukas barged through the front door, blazing away with his Smith & Wesson, just like he'd been taught. Lamar wasn't trying to hit them, only get them moving out and away. All he wanted to do was to make them somebody else's problem. He blew big holes in walls and door frames and hit both men with fragments of wood and hot lead, but he let them escape. Just like the war. Lamar seldom shot to hit anything over there—but when he did he hit it. Lamar passed up killing shots on both men. Just didn't pull the trigger. He chased the men out the back, reloaded for practice and fired again at their car as they sped away. Taylor could hear the slugs hitting the car body and shattering window glass. Lamar was an expert pistol shot. He had a medal.

"I knew they looked fishy walking across the lot," Lamar said, holstering his pistol as he entered Taylor's apartment. "I went around the pool, and when I got back I lost them. I should have figured they were in your apartment with the drapes pulled. You never pull your drapes. Make a hell of a target." Lamar pointed his thumb over his shoulder. "I scared the bejesus out of three girls next door. Dove headlong into a room full of naked titties and girls in panty hose. What did they want?"

"Conversation and fungo practice." Taylor wrung out a towel and blotted his bloody face. He kicked the bat Hymie had dropped. "They wanted some answers for *The Sporting News* before they killed me."

"Killers?" Lamar pressed his forefinger to his lips. "You ain't dead."

"My only good fortune."

"You know, the Major told me to take the night off tonight. Should I have shot to kill?" he asked.

"You didn't have to on my account." Taylor looked at his damaged face in the hall mirror. "They told me this was for starters. They work for Cobianco."

"The Major has the contract for security on the Pistol Dome. He got it through the Cobianco brothers," Lamar said.

Taylor put ice in the towel and placed it against his split cheek. "The stocky guy is Tiny Walton. He's their mechanic. I never saw the medical technician before." Taylor pressed the gash in his cheek together. "Get me that white tape out of my bag over there. I've got to close this."

"They won't be back tonight." Lamar dug through Taylor's canvas bag. "They'll regroup. But I'd be glad to look after you." He pulled out the tape roll. "I told you that a long time ago." Lamar tore strips of tape. "I guess you forgot or didn't hear." He quickly made butterfly-style tape strips. "I am your friend. Friends look out for friends. Lamar's Law." He handed Taylor the well-designed butterflies and helped him seal the wound.

"I feel like I'm in an episode of *The Godfather*."

"I should have killed them, huh?" Lamar watched Taylor.

Taylor washed out his mouth with golden tequila. He offered the bottle to Lamar. Refusing, Lamar pointed at his own head, making the crazy sign. Taylor nodded at Lamar's question, then drank Lamar's share of the alcohol.

"Those two guys going to keep after you?"

"Yep." Taylor wiped his lips gently with the ice-filled towel.

"It's been obvious for a while, but I just got convinced for the first time tonight. I didn't figure they would kill *me*."

"Nobody does," Lamar said, and smirked slightly. "I could've killed those two. The fat guy knew it. He almost went for his gun, then he looked at me. *Right here*"—Lamar pointed at his own eyes—"and *he knew*. I was hitting what I wanted to hit. If I decided on him next, he was stats." Lamar looked at Taylor.

"The fat guy has killed people, several up close and personal. He's a hard guy."

"*I'm* a hard guy," Lamar said. "The Major told me not to work tonight, which means he is involved."

"He got the Pistol Dome contract," Taylor repeated. "That makes him theirs."

"Whose?"

"I don't know for sure."

"You better find out quick before you are dead." Lamar's voice turned harder. He seemed less consciously submissive, apologetic. He assumed a military bearing toward problem-solving. "Anything they want, short of you dead? Something to bargain?"

"Documents maybe," Taylor answered, "but I'm beginning to wonder. They seem to bring violent death from Tiny but little interest otherwise." Taylor touched his purple, split cheek, bloodying his fingertips.

"We make a deal," Lamar decided. "Your life for the documents."

"What's to keep them from killing me after we give back the documents?"

"It would make your story more believable if they killed you."

"What are you? A literary agent? I don't care what anybody believes about *anything* if I'm dead." Taylor's head started aching.

"I see your point there."

"It is two weeks to the Super Bowl and we are a sixteen-point favorite," Taylor said. "So it's not just the documents they want, anyway. By killing or crippling the quarterback, the Cobianco brothers ensure the Texas Pistols do *not* cover the spread."

"What?"

"The new owners of the team do not want me to lead my teammates to a Super Bowl victory and to glory," Taylor explained.

"*What?*"

"They don't want the Pistols to win the Super Bowl."

"The Pistols *have* to win the Super Bowl! I'm countin' on it.

That's why I bought season tickets! To see you win the Super Bowl!"

"Makes you wanna keep me alive, don't it?"

Lamar nodded grimly.

"Good," Taylor said. "That's the kind of fans I like to hear from."

"But," Lamar said, "there is one thing I learned from the war, and it applies to this situation."

"What's that?" Taylor asked.

"If they want you bad enough, *they get you*."

Taylor decided Lamar was a mixed blessing.

"Look on the bright side." Lamar smiled. "Maybe they figure tonight was enough and you ought to be good now for a couple interceptions, some overthrows in the end zone and fumbles in your own territory. The usual stuff."

SKINNING LAMAR JEAN

"I'M not finished yet, asshole." Taylor recognized the voice on the telephone. It was Tiny Walton again. "They'll be picking you up with a bucket and a sponge."

"Tiny, why don't you just say dirty words or breathe heavy. Trying to string sentences together will hurt your head."

"Real funny, punk," Tiny grunted. "Next time you hear something funny, you'll have to unzip your fly to laugh. You got something that don't belong to you, punk."

"And," Taylor interrupted, "you are phoning in your objection. Okay, I got you down here for one 'No' vote, Tiny. But I have to tell you the truth. Yours is the only 'No' vote so far." Taylor hung up.

Shortly the phone started to ring again. Taylor ignored it and turned up a cable news story of a huge fire and oil spill from a well in the Gulf. The rig was a VCO semisubmersible, and company president Harrison H. Harrison said from his hospital bed that sabotage was possible. VCO stock dropped six points as soon as the market opened. Gus Savas was just starting the war.

Taylor answered the knock at the back door to find Lamar Jean Lukas.

"Your phone is ringing," Lamar said.

"Go ahead and answer it," Taylor suggested. "You won't like "

Lamar Jean strode over to the phone. He wore ragged jeans, black tennis shoes and the Texas Pistols sweat shirt Taylor had given him.

"Hello?" Lamar listened and his eyes grew wide, then his face grew red. "Who the goddam hell is this?" Lamar demanded. "Are you that fat slob I should have killed last night? The next time you are fucking *dog meat*! If I'd known *you* killed Bobby Hendrix, you'd be wall stains now. *You hear me?* You squirm, mother-fucker! I'll meet you any goddam place anytime and..." Lamar looked shocked and stopped yelling into the phone. He turned to Taylor.

"He hung up." He put the phone back in its heavy cradle. "I hate people like that."

"Apparently." Taylor popped a large brown-spotted B complex tablet in his mouth along with a green mineral tablet. He washed them down with water. "This city is one of the last in Texas that still uses underground aquifer water—water that is actually *good* for you. Every other big town in Texas has already ruined their underground drinking water. You ever taste Dallas or Houston water, Lamar?"

"Never been there." Lamar's eyes kept moving around the apartment and he paced. "Never been anywhere but here, Quantico, Camp Pendleton and the Highlands." Lamar stopped pacing and stared at the wall. He didn't seem angry, just agitated.

"The water in Houston and Dallas tastes exactly like insecticide. The bugs won't drink it."

"Goddam the Houston and Dallas bugs!" Lamar resumed his pacing, stopping occasionally to gaze out the window. His agitation was too obvious to ignore.

"What's bothering you, Lamar?"

"I went down to find out about my Super Bowl tickets and the woman told me that the Pistols didn't control the tickets." Lamar stared out the window. "The commissioner's office handles Super Bowl ticket disbursement secretly."

"So they fucked you again on tickets?" Taylor shook his head. "I would think you'd wise up to these people, Lamar. Why would they sell you a ticket for forty dollars when they can get a thousand scalping the same ticket?"

"'Cause I'm a *fan*," Lamar said. "I was one of the first. They promised me tickets to the Super Bowl when I bought that five-thousand-dollar Pistol Dome bond. They said they had too many

fans and too few tickets," Lamar said. "The same bullshit the
gave me when they broke their promise about guaranteeing seaso
tickets to people who bought season tickets when you guys ju
started and were shitty."

"We just hadn't gelled yet." Taylor was anticipating Lamar'
story, knowing what Lamar had done when the Franchise force
him to buy the five-thousand-dollar bond before he could buy
season ticket. "Tell me, what did you do?"

"Nothing. I was so shocked, it was like somebody had slappe
me with a dead skunk."

"Come on, Lamar," Taylor urged. "Last time you robbed on
of Cyrus's banks for the five grand to buy a Pistol Dome bond
I don't believe you just stood there."

Lamar frowned. "Well, I did throw a big marble stand-u
ashtray through the glass doors. But that's all. I was just to
shocked, you know what I mean?" Lamar seemed about to cry
"I just can't believe they fucked me again."

"Don't feel like the Lone Ranger, Lamar. Nobody that I knov
got any tickets. At least not yet. There are a whole lot of ticket
missing. You answer my phone for the next few days, you'll b
surprised the people who can't get tickets."

That information didn't seem to ease Lamar's discomfort. Hi
eyes darted glances at Taylor, then off to the wall or floor.

Taylor watched Lamar Jean and waited. He knew there wa
more bothering Lamar. Lamar finally burst forth with the news
"I got fired from my job at Security Services. The Major said
was insubordinate and overqualified."

"May the Major soon be eaten by his attack dog."

"He won't give me a recommendation for another job." Lama
stared at the floor.

"I'll give you a job." Taylor walked out of the kitchen. "You
can live here in the downstairs bedroom."

"What's the job?" Lamar asked.

"All you gotta do is stay here and pretend you're me. I'm
getting the hell out. You answer the phone and keep people from
finding me until after the Super Bowl. Tell 'em there aren't any
tickets. If Tiny calls back, use your discretion." Taylor walke
toward the stairs. "I'm going up to pack a few things. I don'
want to talk to anybody but Wendy or Randall. When I finish
I'm moving. I'll call you from time to time."

"We can do it," Lamar said.

And they did.

It worked out fine.

Though there were some rough spots.

SECRETS
FROM THE HIT MAN

R. D. Locke stepped out of the bright Texas sun into the dark of the Pressure Cooker Bar and Dance Hall.

It was eleven-thirty A.M. on a January Monday. A live band played, several couples swayed on the dance floor, shadows laughed and drank. Occasional bolts of daylight shot through the place when the door opened; otherwise it seemed like Saturday night. But it was Monday morning, late January. Super Bowl week in Clyde, Texas.

R.D. stepped to the side of the door and crossed his hard, muscular arms across the front of his tank-top shirt. His shoulder muscles bulged as he stood, the heavy, sharp cheekbones and square, solid jaw of his angry face thrust out, waiting for his eyes to become accustomed to the faint light.

Colored by the lights from the bandstand, cigarette smoke wreathed up into big clouds. The stand was caged off with chicken wire to protect the band from the audience. When someone out here in the vast dark didn't like the music, the service, his date or his wife, he would launch a beer bottle. Just about anything could cause a massive mad launch of missiles at the bandstand.

Red saw R.D. as soon as he entered the Pressure Cooker; the flash of daylight had pulled his eyes to the door. Red waited, watching R.D. adjust his eyes to the dark. The coach admired the man's physique: a natural athlete, mean, tough. Red regretted trading him off.

As the defensive back looked in his direction, the coach lit his team logo lighter and held it over his head. His eyes taking in the whole place, the black man glided slowly, carefully, toward the small corner table.

R. D. Locke sat down and Red Kilroy shook his hand.

"You got the stuff?" Red asked.

R.D. nodded. "You got the money?"

Red nodded.

"What about the job?"

"It's yours in July." Red took a thick envelope from his inside pocket and pushed it across the small table.

R.D. took a thick sheaf of pages from his back pocket and tossed it to the coach. The pages were covered with arrows and lines and X's and O's. It was a game plan, offense and defense. R.D. took the envelope from the coach and stuck it in his pocket.

"You going to count it?"

"Eventually." The muscular black man looked around the bar and dance hall at the chicken-wire-barricaded bandstand, the couples shuffling around on the scuffed floor, the strained and infrequent laughter. "Everybody's tryin' too hard in here. It's a dangerous place."

"That's why I picked it. Nobody's going to tell anybody they saw us at the Pressure Cooker before noon on Super Monday. How do they explain what *they* were doing here?" Red was pleased with himself.

"Well, I don't dance and it's too wet to plow." Denver defensive back R. D. Locke stood, towering over the table, then turned and walked for the door. Red looked at the incredible body as the man weaved through the table maze. Slide, step, glide. He moved like a cat.

Red shook his head. *I wish I looked like that when I was forty* he thought.

R. D. Locke was forty-one but had lied about his age when he first came into the League. Never mentioned the Army years. Or Vietnam. Just walked on. At six foot three, 225 pounds, a 4.6 in the forty-yard dash, and a nickname of "The Hit Man," who was going to quibble whether he was twenty-one or twenty-four years old?

Red Kilroy signaled the waitress for another drink.

"The boss says you gotta buy two drinks to sit and watch the housewives dance," said the red-eyed waitress in the white western shirt and black slacks. "Take my word for it." She wiped the table. "Just buy two drinks; the bartender only puts in half a shot anyway." She exchanged the dirty ashtray for a clean one.

The band started playing.

Glass broke somewhere in the dark vastness of the dance hall

> *The news is out all over town*
> *That you been seen runnin' round . . .*

The things a man will do to win a football game. Light exploded the dark as people came and went. The things people do. The things we will do to win or just to pretend we're winning. Ain't no second place. Ain't no second act. Ain't no second chance.

> *... You'll cry and cry*
> *and try to sleep ...*

Red smoked a cigarette, drank his watery Scotch and watched the housewives, the unemployed, the con artists, the night shift workers, the bored, the lonely, the mean.

It was straight up noon at the Pressure Cooker, and Red Kilroy was surrounded by losers.

> *Your cheeeaaating heart willll tail on yew ...*

THE END
IS NOT IN SIGHT

TAYLOR was up in the Penthouse suite, listening to records as E. Fudd, garment salesman, when Red Kilroy called.

"How did you know I was in here?" Taylor asked. "I'm down on the ninth floor with the rest of the team."

"I told the desk clerk to look for famous cartoon characters. Are you alone?"

"Just me and Elmer."

"I'll be right up. If anybody calls or comes before I get there, get rid of them," Red hissed into the phone. "This is urgent. I don't care if all your cartoon friends want to come over. That suite better be empty when I arrive. Just you and me."

"And Elmer," Taylor added. "Come on, say it. It'll confuse whoever is listening."

"And Elmer," Red said sullenly. "I'll be there in ten minutes."

"Bwing some cawwots, okay, Wed? Wed? What about the cawwots?"

The phone clicked dead at the coach's end.

"Dwat you, Wed . . . Wats . . . Wats . . . Wats . . ." He wondered if someone was listening. And if so, who? Why?

"There are no secrets," Dick Conly always said, "just shit you don't know yet. The two-hour head start. The news is always bad and you laugh because you haven't heard the news."

The news was that Bobby Hendrix had fallen out of a plane and was smashed flat on the Tulum Mayan ruins.

That's the news. It's always bad.

Tommy McNamara and his five-part series on the mob and the League. *That* was news. The fingerless, earless, bloody-raw Kinky-Headed Boy hanging from a bunkhouse beam, his Santa Fe Opera T-shirt knotted at his neck. *That*'s the bad news nobody heard.

Taylor Rusk planned to stay hidden in E. Fudd's penthouse suite until the game.

Come Super Sunday, Taylor Rusk planned to hit and run. He planned to win by seventeen. Or more.

Red Kilroy buying the Denver game plans from R. D. Locke for a future job in Detroit and an undisclosed amount of cash didn't hurt.

"He's promised two goal-line pass interference calls," Red whispered. They were out on the suite's small patio. The afternoon air was hot. "He promises to fall down the first time he sees you keep both your backs in. So the first time you call full protection, run Speedo at him on a straight outside fly."

Taylor nodded, looking through the Xeroxed pages of the Denver Super Bowl game plans. He read the scouting report on himself.

. . . doesn't like to get hurt . . . doesn't like pain. . . . The two phrases stood out.

"I'm supposed to *like* pain?" Taylor asked.

"Don't worry about it," Red replied quickly. "It's a psychological ploy to try and get those guys to hurt you."

"Then what?" Taylor argued. "I fool them by saying how much I enjoyed my ruptured spleen? I want hot routes back in the game plan. I want a dump-off man on every play. If a lineman misses a new audible call, I want a sting man to go to."

"Jesus, Taylor, that really complicates the offense," Red argued.

"I don't want them to have *one free shot*." Taylor held up his index finger. "*Not one*. They got at least two guys in that defensive line who could break my ribs with a hand slap, reach in and jerk out my heart just to psyche me." Taylor looked at his coach.

"They'd love a chance to get armpit-deep in my guts and play handball with my major organs. Okay, Wed? What about it, Wed?"

"Will you stop with the Elmer Fudd? All right, but we won't need hot routes if you read the defenses right."

"I'm not worrying about me fucking up and missing a defense, I'm worried about R. D. Locke fucking up and missing a defense." Taylor looked at the head coach. "Or have you forgotten exactly why you traded him to Denver in the first place?"

"I was going to trade him anyway," Red protested. "It just happened that he shot at you just as we were working the noodles out with Denver."

"Was his thirty-eight one of those noodles? Did you get compensation in caliber or muzzle velocity?"

"What we *got* is this here Denver game plan," Red said. "Now, you study it tonight and tomorrow. Give it to me at practice tomorrow afternoon. I'll make one more copy at the practice field. I'm going to call all our defenses Sunday."

"Margene know about that?" Taylor watched Red walk to the suite door. "Say, Red? You really going to get Locke a job?"

"I take care of my boys, Taylor. I have always taken care of my boys."

"Oh, yeah. You have them all over the League."

"I got them all over the world." The coach stepped out the door into the hallway. He turned, looked back at Taylor Rusk, his quarterback for these many years of college and professional ball. "I got them all over the world."

"I'm not one of your boys."

"I've known that since you played at the University, Elmer." The Texas Pistols head coach pulled the door closed and left Taylor alone with the stolen Denver Super Bowl game plan.

"Dwat!" Taylor flipped the stereo back on.

"Elmer Fudd wins Super Bowl," Taylor said aloud, picking up the Xeroxed pages. "Daffy Duck coach of the year."

Taylor looked out the window toward the sunbaked Pistol Dome hunched over Clyde, Texas, within pouncing distance of the city.

Red Kilroy's plan to call his own defenses from the sideline was unwelcome news to the Pistols' defense, because on game day Red Kilroy was always a raving lunatic. On the sidelines he was completely out of control. He would froth at the mouth, talk in tongues, go for whole quarters without pronouncing one identifiable word. In Taylor's sophomore year at the University, the whole game against Michigan, Red called him "Bobby."

Middle linebacker Margene Brinkley would talk Red Kilroy

out of calling plays by Sunday or, as he had in the past, woul
simply ignore him.

Red would not remember.

The stereo played.

> *...my soul cried out for rest*
> *and the end is not in sight...*

IMPOSTER

LAMAR Jean Lukas stayed around Taylor's apartment, reading
magazines and books, watching Chandler Cable and Chandle
Communications' new subscription Pay-Per-View channel, send
ing out for food and answering the telephone.

The telephone calls were the most fun, and whenever a calle
seemed gullible, Lamar pretended to be Taylor. He said all sort
of things to all sorts of folks. He gave consolation, advice o
encouragement on a variety of subjects, but lack of Super Bow
tickets was the nagging complaint. He heard many sad, urgen
tales about Super Bowl tickets not being available.

Taylor Rusk watched from the penthouse as Super Sunday
approached and Lamar Jean Lukas evolved into the Super Bow
quarterback. The Franchise. The object of millions of fantasies
idealistic, realistic, nihilistic. Lunatic.

Lamar's quotes began accompanying Taylor's photo in th
newspapers and on television. Lamar/Taylor would only gran
telephone interviews. Lamar was good copy. He expressed thought
about the condition of society.

Lamar made a fascinating Taylor Rusk, predicting in an early
phone call to Brent Musburger that the Pistols would beat Denve
by twenty points or more.

Robbie Burden called A. D. Koster, ordering the fast-fading
Pistols general manager to "protect the integrity of the League i
the public eye and muzzle any talk about point spreads."

A.D. told Red at the office. Red told Taylor at the practice
field. Taylor phoned Lamar that night.

"Taylor Rusk, Super Bowl Quarterback," came Lamar's voice on the line. "It's your quarter: Shoot."

"Taylor who?" The quarterback disguised his voice.

"Rusk, Taylor Rusk. Winner of the Heisman Trophy."

"Never heard of it."

"Taylor? Is that you?"

Taylor watched the clouds. "Any news? Good or bad?"

"There is no good news. Nobody in the world has any tickets to the Super Bowl. Ten jillion people have called for tickets; even the governor's office called. I told them I'd only talk to the governor."

"I know." Taylor nodded his head. "I read about it in the 'Capitol Grapevine' section of the paper. You've turned me into a pretty colorful guy, Lamar. Just don't tell where I am and stop talking about point spreads or betting."

"Understood. Maybe I'll talk about how poor I was as a kid, stuff like that," Lamar said. "Movie people are always looking for stories like that. Maybe I'll give myself a wooden leg."

"Terrific."

"Maybe invent some childhood tragedy. A favorite dog that died a long, suffering death; the cats ate your baby duck in front of your little eyes."

"Did I get any messages, Lamar?"

"Only requests for tickets and death threats. You are popular with a wide range of persons. I've talked to people who merely want to hear how you sound, to crying young girls who begged me to visit their junior high schools and to sportswriters who are so desperate for a daily story to file, they'll believe anything."

"Thanks. Anything else?"

"No, just that fat guy that killed Hendrix. Boy, he pisses me off. I need to shoot him."

"I think you better remember he may shoot back."

"Not the way I do it." Lamar chuckled. "Well, he calls in a threat or two a day. I'm sure he's got money down against you. How come no beautiful young chicks call up and come over or something?"

"They don't need Super Bowl tickets," Taylor answered. "They're the ones who have them all."

"Well, being you isn't all it's cracked up to be," Lamar Jean complained.

"It's sure not what you're cracking it up to be, Lamar. You have to stop believing your own stories."

— 459 —

"If I didn't make something up, you wouldn't get any puss or have any fun."

"I don't see how the war record you gave me in the *Sportin News* story will hold up against any scrutiny. You say I saved a ambassador's life?"

"Pretty good story, huh?"

"It read like 'Gunga Din,' 'The Knute Rockne Story' and 'Th Charge of the Light Brigade.'"

"I said it was a godless system that made people read anythin as boring as *Das Kapital*."

"All that's fine. Just don't talk about betting or Tiny or th Cobianco boys to the papers unless you got forty Montagnard fully armed and in the room with you."

"You mean in the room with *you*," Lamar corrected. "Can say you killed Hitler? Hand-to-hand combat with flamethrowers?"

"Fine."

"And you got to screw a lot of women?"

"Okay. Just don't talk about gambling, injuries or point spread Okay?"

Lamar hung up without a reply.

Taylor decided he might have given Lamar too much latitud and tried to call him back.

The line was busy.

LAMAR'S SUPER
BOWL TICKET FROM TINY

THE telephone rang five times before Lamar Jean Lukas coul return from the kitchen to the living room. He snatched up th receiver. "Taylor Rusk."

"Did that chickenshit come back there yet?" It was Tiny Wal ton.

"Hey, Fatso, he ain't back, but get your blubber on over her and we'll shoot some."

"I ain't got time to waste on fleas and ticks. I'm just going t kill the dog. Did you give him the messages?"

"I certainly did. He said you would probably get hit by a bus
ause you are so *fat*."

"Tell him he can't hide forever. He has to walk out on that
eld Sunday."

"But you won't be there, Fatso." Lamar's anger rose with the
ords in his throat. "Because, you scumbag slob, *I am the bus*
id you are a crippled fat cat in the express lane."

"Why don't *you* come to the Super Bowl?" Tiny asked. "I'll
: there in a skybox with the high rollers. You know what I look
ke, now you know where I'll be. I can get both of you on one
xpense account. Come get me."

"I ain't got a ticket."

Tiny began to laugh. "Big man Taylor Rusk can't even get his
ooge a ticket to the Super Bowl." Tiny laughed, wheezing and
ughing.

Lamar Jean Lukas was losing control. Being a Pistol season
cket holder was like Chinese water torture. After all the shit
amar had gone through, he still couldn't get a ticket to the Super
owl that was being played in the Dome he'd paid five thousand
ollars to help build. Tiny Walton had a ticket. A two-bit hoodlum,
ired muscle, he had a skybox ticket.

"I tell you what, dimwit"—Tiny stopped laughing—"I'll send
ou a ticket. I bet you don't show. The Pistols may not even show.
nd I'll bet that if they show, they lose."

"I don't have any money." Humiliated, Lamar spoke through
ghtly clenched teeth. "I'll just bet. No money. Just a bet."

"Jerk." Tiny laughed and slammed the phone down.

Tiny Walton sent Lamar Jean Lukas a ticket to the Super Bowl.
 courier service delivered it within the hour. Tiny provided op-
ortunity and victims to a man with many motives and methods
› commit murder. The Super Bowl ticket fused the furious ele-
ents of Lamar's badly scattered and scarred mind on Super Sun-
ay at the Pistol Dome.

MAYBE THINGS'LL
GET A LITTLE BETTER

TAYLOR Rusk wore the glitter T-shirt Randall gave him at Chris
mas to the morning meal.

"Taylor Rusk?" A short, bald writer from the Denver *Po*
stopped the quarterback in the hall outside the dining room. Th
small man had his pad and pen ready.

Taylor nodded and slowed almost to a stop, watching the wri
er's eye take in and his pen quickly note the glitter-T-shirt solutio
for world hunger blazed across his chest in six-inch Day-Gl
sequins:

EAT THE RICH

"Taylor?" The small writer seemed to be stuck on the fir
question.

Taylor stopped completely and looked down at the reporter
"Yes, Jerry?" He was good at remembering names and faces
Balding Jerry had covered the Bowl Game in Taylor's senior yea
Jerry had had more hair then. "Come on, hurry up. I have to ea
so I have something to throw up besides my stomach lining."

The small reporter rocked back slightly, looking up at the six
five quarterback of the heavily favored team. Sixteen points i
favor.

"I wanted to ask you about your article in yesterday's *Times*
You said that the commissioner has shown you all the indication
of a man who does not masturbate enough?"

"I said *that*? In print?"

"The *Times*," the writer said.

"Did I offer any disclaimers?" Taylor looked anxiously pas
the writer to the continual lobby crowd. He shifted his body weigh
from foot to foot. "Did I say the evidence is purely circumstanti
but based on stains or forearm size or anything like that?"

The writer glanced through his Xerox of the newspaper story

"I don't see anything in the story," the writer said. "It was
telephone interview. The reporter called you at home."

"But I'm not at home . . . haven't been for several days. I didn't give that interview; it's a mistake." Taylor watched the lobby as a crowd of young boys in official Pistols jackets welled up in the hallway, pointing at Taylor and the writer.

"Actually," Jerry said, "I'm more interested in the documents you talked about near the end of the story."

"Documents?" Taylor startled himself and Jerry. The boys in the Pistols jackets had broken away from the lobby crowd and were sinisterly moving toward Taylor like the Blob.

Taylor leaned down and put his hand on the writer's shoulder. He peered at the article. "Documents?" Taylor whispered. "What did I say? Where?"

The writer pointed out the already-underlined paragraph. His index fingernail had been chewed to the quick, then gnawed to death.

"You told the *Times* that you had documents proving a nationwide network of ticket scalping, game fixes, gambling and income tax evasion totaling millions of dollars. . . ." The writer squinted at the paper. Taylor's eyes glazed over in shock.

". . . You hinted at the involvement of political figures." The small writer looked up, readied his pen.

"That all I said?" Taylor had broken into a fine, cold sweat. The *Times* had obviously gotten Lamar at a bad time. Tiny Walton had probably phoned in the day's threats and insults and Lamar had lost it for a while. Taylor conceded to himself that it had probably not been a terrific idea to give so much responsibility to a man suffering from delayed-stress syndrome and attacks of acute paranoia.

"You refused to reaffirm earlier predictions that Texas would beat Denver by twenty points too. You said the commissioner threatened you, but you had crossed the line and it was a matter of honor and national security. You were a soldier, you said."

"I did? A soldier? For who?"

The bald man tapped the Xeroxed sheet. "I thought telling the *Times* you were vital to national security was great. The Imperial Quarterback."

Taylor thought back to the first training camp, when Lamar had shaken him awake in his dormitory bed to discuss his season ticket. Lamar Jean Lukas had always been half a bubble out of plumb.

"He's out the whole bubble now," Taylor mumbled. "Not that it matters."

"What?" Bald Jerry held up his pad and pen.

"Nothing." Taylor looked into the dining room; his teammates were eating at big round tables.

"Listen"—Taylor pointed at himself—"you recognize me, right?" Taylor kept his eyes moving.

The writer nodded his head.

"Okay." Taylor kept looking, hoping no other media people would show up. "You're the official spokesman on this." Taylor looked nervously toward the lobby. The bitter taste of panic rose in his throat.

"Now, this is the truth," Taylor whispered. "I haven't talked to the press *once* all week. That's the *truth*. That's *the scoop*."

The writer looked unconvinced but kept writing.

"I've been hiding out since last Friday, dodging the pressure," Taylor explained. "The guy who looks after my apartment has been giving all those telephone interviews. He gets a little carried away and pretends to be me. He's harmless. I have to have someone at my apartment to watch out for weirdos when I am so publicly away at the Super Bowl."

The writer stopped and looked up at Taylor.

"You're telling me that all of those interviews, all of those quotes"—he shook his small, discouraged bald head—"all of those stories, those miles and miles of column inches about Taylor Rusk—the man they call *the Franchise*—all those long explanations about how you audible without moving your lips . . ." The writer wearied of listing the frauds.

"'Taylor Rusk Saves the Ambassador'?" Taylor added helpfully.

"The war diary that ran in *The Sporting News*?" The writer showed a *new* capacity for shock. "You *made up* all those stories?" The writer began to show possibilities of outrage. Outraged sensibilities in a sportswriter seemed doubtful, but this was the Super Bowl—the ultimate.

"*I* didn't make them up. *This guy* did," Taylor argued. "I haven't said anything to anybody until I started talking to you just now. This guy makes up the stories. He enjoys it. What's the harm? It was okay with me until . . ."

"*Okay* with you? *Okay* with *you*!" The writer was furious; his pen was shaking against the paper, making tiny capillarylike scribbles. "Deliberate deception of the press and it's *okay* with you! I'm supposed to accept that?"

"You don't have to," Taylor whispered, "but I'm going with it. Now, if you'll excuse me while I disappear back into the woodwork to reappear refreshed and triumphant on Super Sunday . . ."

Taylor turned and walked quickly to the elevator, riding it to nine. He disembarked and used his key for the private penthouse elevator.

Taylor Rusk disappeared.

He no longer attended team meetings. Instead the quarterback would meet with Greg Moore, Amos Burns, Speedo, Danny Lewis and Ron Savage, the tight end, after curfew in Red Kilroy's room. They knew Denver's defense better than Denver, thanks to R. D. Locke. The backs and ends discussed routes—and studied automatic adjustments. He met with Ox and the line at Red's early in the morning before breakfast. The preparation was in quiet, patient exhaustive detail.

All practices were closed.

Major Jack "Pat" Garrett of Security Services, Inc., lost command of the practice-field security. Offensively Texas added nothing. They just practiced execution and mental toughness. They spent their time bringing plays to a high polish, planning for the unexpected.

Jerry from the Denver *Post* wrote a column the next day about his meeting with Taylor Rusk and how the Pistols' quarterback had explained that the press had been duped. It went out on the wire.

The media went wild. There were stories about "alleged meetings" and "an alleged man in a hallway." There were mathematical analyses proving that Taylor had not yet been born when he claimed to have killed Hitler. Taylor Rusk's imposter became *the* story of the Super Bowl.

Taylor stayed in his suite on twenty-five. He called the apartment, but Lamar Jean Lukas never answered. Taylor knew he was there, but Lamar no longer pretended to be Taylor Rusk. He was too busy planning his Super Sunday.

UP IN THE OZONE

TAYLOR took a long bath in the eight-foot-square black marble tub. Four whirlpool jets pummeled his tired body. The water was hot and deep, and the quarterback stretched out full length, floating in the primal warmth.

Breathing deep and slow, he concentrated on the small red spot that appeared when he closed his eyes, emptying his mind of all thoughts, watching the spot grow larger while muscle tissue released stored emotional and physical tension in twinges and twitches.

No longer embodied, Taylor drifted through this inner universe in a free-floating consciousness. A distant ringing slowly brought him back. He began to lose the rhythm of his breathing. The red spot grew smaller, the ringing louder. He finally opened his eyes to remember who and where he was.

And why.

The phone was conveniently mounted on the wall next to the tub. Taylor reached it, having to move only his left arm.

"Yeah?" Taylor answered on the fifteenth ring.

"What took you so long?" It was Bob Travers, Wendy Chandler's bodyguard, calling from the car. "Where were you?"

"Damned if I know." Taylor shifted slightly so one of the water jets pounded on his right shoulder. "A long way off."

"We'll be at the hotel in fifteen minutes," Bob continued. "Miss Chandler has a key to the elevator and we'll come right up. The boy is asleep. You might want to get his bed ready."

"Fine." Taylor still floated weightlessly in the hot swirling water. "Make certain no one sees you use the elevator. The press has the hotel staked out, trying to find us."

"Anybody sees us, I'll kill them." Bob hung up, leaving Taylor to wonder if he meant what he said.

Taylor put down the phone and picked up the playbook from the shelf next to the tub. He leafed through the book, looking for any plays that had been left out of the game plan that might be useful. He found no additional plays. The plan he and Red had designed was well thought out and now depended on Sunday's execution. Taylor only had to pull the biggest rabbits from his hat, faster and in greater numbers than ever before.

Taylor studied the interesting work that Randall had done with his felt pens and crayons all through the book. In some places the boy had merely tinted various colors on the X's and O's or added additional marks, more X's, O's, sometimes lines and arrows, even a couple of flowers.

On the backs of other pages Randall had drawn pictures: houses and cars, horses and cows, airplanes and clouds, several different-sized and -colored guns, cats and dogs and stick people of various shapes, sizes and questionable gender.

On the page illustrating the Power Sweep with pinch block adjustments for the tight end, Taylor found a green crayon drawing of three stick people holding hands: one small child, a medium-size woman and a tall man wearing what appeared to be a football helmet. It took the quarterback a moment to realize that he was looking at Randall's conception of his family and that he had included Taylor.

He got out of the tub, dried off, tore the page from the playbook and taped it to the mirror over the sink. The quarterback smiled at himself in the glass and walked to the adjoining bedroom to pull on a gray sweat suit.

He was a very happy man.

With his quarterback in seclusion, Red Kilroy refused to co-operate with anyone who wanted to find Taylor. Various threats of League sanctions, Franchise reprisals and bad press relations rolled off like rain on a tin roof. Suzy and A.D. threatened to fire him. Robbie Burden threatened to fine him and the press threatened to crucify him. But Red refused to make his quarterback appear for scheduled press sessions. He also told his other players to hide out as much as possible, promising to pay any fines. Daily threats were issued, trying to force the Pistol players to be more coop-erative in the week-long pregame carnival of hype.

"Distractions can lead to destruction," Red warned. Many of the players, while staying registered in the hotel, returned secretly to their homes and families.

Red took all the heat for his players, knowing it was vital to steer them safely through the week-long minefield.

Taylor waited for his family in the penthouse.

Earlier he'd ordered an avocado-and-bean-sprout sandwich but had only eaten half. Now, clearing the old glass, plates and soft-drink bottles, Taylor put them on the room service tray and set the tray in the hall.

The day the players arrived at the hotel, Bob Travers had convinced Red to put a man in the kitchen to check the employees and oversee the preparation of players' food.

"A little ptomaine goes a long way, Red," the bodyguard had warned.

Bob brought in a friend from the Bexar County Health Department as a dishwasher to watch the food service and pick up information.

A computer check uncovered a newly hired cook with a felony arson conviction who two weeks earlier had been a pizza chef at a Cobianco restaurant. Bob arranged to have the cook kidnapped and held in the Piedras Negras jail until after the game.

Dick Conly paid to put two more men and a woman in the hotel kitchen to secure the food supply Conly flew in fresh from New Mexico daily.

The Cobianco brothers never knew what happened to their pizza chef.

When the private penthouse elevator started, Taylor walked through the huge suite of rooms to the large bedroom on the west side. He pulled back the covers on the king-size bed, fluffed up a pillow, drew closed the drapes and lit a Snoopy nightlight.

Taylor returned as the elevator doors slid open. Toby carried Randall. Taylor pointed him toward the bedroom and Toby crept off with the sleeping child.

Wendy followed them off the elevator, giving Taylor a hug and a kiss, which he bent to receive, an awkward motion that was difficult because of their height difference and his increasingly weakened back.

Bob got off last, his eyes reading Taylor's face, then quickly glancing around the room. He followed Toby to the boy's room, then began his ritual search of the huge penthouse. Bob Travers was paid a large salary to be carefully observant.

Wendy brushed past Taylor and walked into the sitting room, carrying the evening paper. She stood at the window, staring to the south, looking for the dark shape of the Pistol Dome.

"It's still out there. I saw it this afternoon." Taylor understood her intense gaze. "It's moving closer but has yet to make its intentions known. It may have to be destroyed before it reproduces."

"Where are we?" Wendy kept her eyes searching south. "The Twilight Zone?"

"The Ozone." Taylor studied a page of the game plan shaded in blues and reds with *Randall* scrawled on the bottom in purple.

"The paper has the Pistols at fifteen while the Greek says fifteen and a half." She waved the paper at him. "How do you score half a point?"

"Concentration and execution. Kimball Adams may have been the last quarterback good enough to do it."

Wendy turned and looked at him, her pale-blue eyes wide; finally she blinked, gazing back outside. "How much are you paying for the Ozone?"

"Twenty-five hundred a day. It's got six bedrooms and baths, a three-hundred-and-sixty-degree view and its own elevator. What more could an American hero want?"

"You'll lose money." She looked around the room. "It costs more to stay here than you'll make for playing in the Super Bowl. Win or lose."

"Yeah." Taylor nodded. A frown tightened his face, his mouth a line curved down at the ends. The pull flattened his nose slightly. "I was never good with money. That's why Doc handles it."

"Do you know how much you have?"

Taylor shook his head. "I'm scared of the damn stuff."

Wendy slapped her leg with the rolled up newspaper. "Well, there is a certain Olympian quality about the view. Taylor Rusk, the greatest of the classical Hellenistic quarterbacks. Did you discuss the line with the gods?"

"We were kicking the spread around when Bob called." Taylor was straight-faced. "Zeus wants to bet the spread, but Athena will bring him around. She hangs out with the oddsmaker at Delphi. They'll bet on us, but whether they'll help . . ." Taylor shrugged. "Gods can be such vindictive assholes. Look what they did to Prometheus just for giving a guy a light."

Wendy looked out at the darkening blue sky and the sparkling city. "All pretty epic, Taylor."

"It beats the Armadillo Ranch."

"Yes, it does," Wendy agreed. "You do things in a truly heroic style."

"This is serious ritual."

"Well, keep yourself healthy and profound," Wendy said. "Spend time contemplating the Pistol Dome and stretching your Achilles tendon."

"Despite the nay-sayers among the gods and the doubts and teasing of my favorite goddess"—he glanced at Wendy—"I shall go forth on Sunday and fulfill the immortality fetish that all America has hungered for since God went on the nod. History will compare it to the parting of the Red Sea—"

"Or the parting of your hair," Wendy cut him off, tossing the newspaper at him. *"Read."*

The headline read:

BILLY JOE HARDESTY EVANGELICAL LIFE, INC., SUED BY CYRUS CHANDLER WIDOW

Taylor read the copy aloud:

The widow of the founder of The Texas Pistols Football Club has filed suit against BJHEL, Inc., claiming that Reverend Hardesty used lies and fraud to persuade her late husband, Cyrus Chandler, to sign over extensive property to BJHEL, Inc.

Charlie Stillman, attorney for Suzanne Ballard Chandler, filed the suit in the Ninety-seventh District Court. Mr. Chandler, Stillman said, "was a devoutly religious man, and Billy Joe Hardesty took advantage of his trusting Christian nature to swindle him. We will prove that in court."

"If Stillman can convince a jury my father was a trusting Christian man, anything is possible."

Taylor returned to reading.

Rev. Hardesty claimed that the Devil was controlling Mrs. Chandler and encouraged all his followers to pray for her soul. Hardesty quoted Scripture as his support and guide:

"For the Lord himself shall descend from heaven with a shout, with the voice of the archangel, and with the trumpet of God. And the dead in Christ shall rise first; then we who are alive and remain shall be caught up together with them in the clouds to meet the Lord in the air."

"Billy Joe is explaining sky diving?"

"If I know my Scripture," Wendy said, "that is First Thessalonians, fourth chapter, verses sixteen and seventeen, and has to do with the Rapture."

"It sounds like an experimental ballet company."

"It's amazing that people believe Billy Joe."

"In the Ninety-seventh District Court the alternative will be to believe Suzy."

"Which reminds me, I have been giving a little thought to the

— 470 —

issue of business. If we do business, we better *do business*. I'd like for us to meet with my lawyer."

"So he can cut himself a slice off me?" Taylor interrupted. "No, thanks."

"But . . ."

"End of discussion," Taylor said. "I don't need a lawyer to explain Sunday. I will do what is right and proper at the time. I *like* being a hero."

Taylor walked up and gripped her shoulders in his oversize scarred hands. She leaned back against him, resting her head on his chest. He could feel her warmth; the crushed-flower smell of her filled his head. She relaxed and gently fitted her soft contours against his body. He gathered her to him, his hands sliding across her back, her ribs. He bent, kissing the hollow at her neck and shoulder. Her supple, pliant body stiffened.

"What do we do with the Franchise?" she asked. "Can we take it and run?"

"I don't know," Taylor said. "It's not the price we pay," he mocked, "but the fee the lawyer earns."

Wendy Chandler disengaged and drifted away with grace and determination. She shivered, rubbing her arms with her slender hands. It was cool out; a front had pushed out of the panhandle, clearing the air. The dying sun cast a pink glow in the high blue sky.

Taylor grabbed the playbook. "These are pretty good field notes on the culture and the kind of man who survives and thrives in this system. We could research the problem all night." He pointed at the pages of *X*'s and *O*'s, arrows and lines. "I offer myself as your case study in athletic archaeology and anthropology." Taylor pulled off his sweat shirt.

"Can I use my rock hammer?"

"We don't want to contaminate the dig. It will have to be done totally naked and very carefully." He tossed the shirt onto the carpet.

"This has little similarity to hunting for arrowheads." Wendy frowned, then reached for the snaps at the back of her blouse. "But then, rock hunts never did blow my skirt up."

The next morning, in the penthouse living room, Randall was sitting on the floor, watching the television reruns of *Scooby-Doo, Where Are You?*, when the bedroom phone rang.

Taylor answered on the third ring. Wendy stirred but kept her eyes closed, trying to cling to a few more moments of sleep.

The operator told Taylor the time, date and outside temperature and wished him a good day. He had ordered the wake-up call to keep him from lying in bed too long.

Pulling on jeans and a Texas Pistols T-shirt, Taylor padded barefoot on the thick pile carpet into the living room.

Toby was watching Randall watch the early adventures of Scooby, Shaggy, Freddy, Velma and Daphne. Bob was reading a computer magazine called *Systems and Software*. He looked up from the article on recent advances in security systems that accompanied the piece on Major "Pat" Garrett. The Major elaborated on the security precautions and elaborate plans that Security Services, Inc., had designed for the Pistol Dome. "Crowd control will be the major problem of the eighties," he said.

"These reruns are better than the new shows," Toby said to Taylor.

"What?" Taylor was still groggy.

"Scooby-Doo," Toby continued. "These early shows had good stories and plot twists with character development. They were great for kids. Not like the new ones, with nothing but pie fights and car chases. You know?"

Taylor nodded dumbly.

"And now," Toby continued, "all the superfiends look like Koreans with congenital defects and pear-shaped heads."

"Uh-huh." Taylor stared at Toby a moment, then returned to the bedroom. Bob shook his head and continued to read.

Randall never took his eyes from the screen. He rode along with Scooby and friends in the Mystery Machine.

Wendy sat up sleepy-eyed in bed as Taylor drew the curtains and heavy drapes, letting in hazy morning light. Wendy picked up the five-dollar Super Bowl program and began leafing through it. Taylor gazed into the white light, trying to make out the distant form of the Pistol Dome.

"When Albert Speer designed the Nuremberg stadium, you know what he wanted the Nazi fan to feel?" Taylor asked, still searching the fog for the familiar form.

"Nothing." Wendy glanced at the beer ad on the inside cover of the program. "And I don't care."

"That's right . . . you're right." Taylor was surprised.

"I know." She thumbed past the disgustingly maudlin story "The Old Pro and the Kid." "I know lots of things."

Taylor finally saw the outline of the dome. "Speer said he wanted the spectator to feel *nothing*."

"I know." Wendy looked up. "I just told *you*."

"I wonder if he succeeded?"

"He did on you. Talk about going numb." Wendy tossed the Super Bowl program on the floor.

"Whiskey, cars, drugs and jocks," Wendy said, stretching and yawning. "What else could a person want? Or feel?"

Randall wandered into the room, carrying his *Star Wars* Light Saber. Sitting at his mother's side, he called room service, ordering everyone pancakes and Pepsi-Cola for breakfast. There was a small circle of scar tissue at the hollow of his throat, a constant reminder of life's precariousness. The boy hacked his way back through a forest of Imperial Storm Troopers to the living room and the end of *Scooby-Doo*.

"Let's start looking for a house and a preacher," Taylor said.

Wendy stretched, relaxing catlike, slow, enjoying the release.

"I want to be married by the bell captain."

Breakfast arrived with a scream and a crash. Randall, with his Light Saber, ambushed the room service waiter.

"EEEyaaaa!" The boy leaped from the hall closet and slashed the thin Latin man across the legs and buttocks with the whistling plastic sword. The terrified waiter, his escape blocked by the table he was wheeling, tried vainly to dodge the stinging hollow *thonk*s.

"Where's the Scooby Snacks, Hairball?" Randall continued to whip the man in short red jacket and black pants.

"Randall! Randall!" Wendy yelled from the bedroom. "Stop dismembering the waiter. And we don't call people 'Hairball'!"

The boy's face fell. He checked his backswing with deep disappointment; it was to have been a head shot.

The waiter pushed the table into the room and, without waiting for Taylor to sign the check, dashed back out the door before Randall resumed his attack.

Wendy entered the large living room, tying her blue floor-length robe. She had already brushed her hair and teeth and rinsed her face with cold water. She sat quickly and began soaking her pancakes in honey from a jar shaped like an anthropomorphic bear.

Randall pointed at Toby with his Light Saber. "Me and Shaggy are going on a mission."

"That right, Shaggy?" Bob Travers's eyes were still on his computer magazine.

"We're gonna go look for clues." Toby's mirthless voice and set jaw convinced Taylor that he took playing Shaggy seriously.

Wendy smoothed the boy's thick hair with her fingers. Randall twisted away, irritated.

— 473 —

"Stop it, Momma." He purposely messed his hair again.

Randall grabbed two pancakes and a canned Pepsi. Rolling the pancakes up, he put one in his shirt pocket and handed the other to Toby. "Here's the supplies, Shaggy. You all be Freddy and Velma and Daphne."

"I'll be Daphne." Taylor also rolled his pancake, dipping one end in a pool of maple syrup and eating it like a tortilla. Wendy ate her pancakes properly with an efficient but delicate dispatch.

"Momma, you be Velma and Bob can be Freddy."

Bob grunted and kept reading. Wendy nodded.

"You guys pretend that me and Shaggy are out looking for clues to help find the Abdominal Snowman."

"The Abdominal Snowman?" Taylor dipped his pancake in the honey on Wendy's plate.

"He's a fierce aminal," the boy replied.

"An-i-mal," Wendy corrected automatically.

"Come on, Shag, let's go." Randall ignored his mother and crept down the foyer to the door, then the hallway beyond. Toby followed obediently, eating his plain pancake like an empty burrito. The door slammed.

Taylor ate slowly while his mind automatically worked through another version of the coming game. He, too, was looking for clues. Keys. What ifs. He was gathering himself for the task. Not yet Super Sunday and already sixteen points behind, the quarterback withdrew into his mind and imagination to play the game over and over. Taylor played Sunday's game from each position all possible conditions, in every down and yardage situation against all of Denver's defenses. On Super Sunday nothing could happen during the game that Taylor hadn't already confronted in his imagination.

He imagined, therefore he could. He could do what it took to win by more than sixteen points.

He began, as always, by suspending disbelief.

"What is the town's most popular misfit thinking about?" Finished with breakfast, Wendy licked honey from her fingers. "You're frowning."

"Sorry, I was thinking about the game." Taylor smiled automatically, his eyes not quite reaching focus. "Fine-tuning my manic depression."

"Will you speed up or slow down by Sunday?"

"I never know." Taylor's eyes darkened. "That's what makes the horserace." He picked up the game plan sheets. Randall had added X's and O's where he chose. This time he had used purple

— 474 —

crayon. "I think we'll have a big element of surprise early in the game. They won't expect us to start the game playing like we're sixteen points behind. We'll start fast and speed up." Taylor began to feel the rush, the building of emotion. "Denver'll be expecting our regular offense with a few new wrinkles, but we are going to play the *whole game like a two-minute drill*. We'll gamble big *all day*. Gamble on third and fourth down. We'll line up without a huddle. Run when they expect pass, pass when they expect run. Onside kicks, fake punts and field goals. Sixteen points is a hell of a lot to make up. The defense has to force turnovers. We have to knock them down early, then pound them, blow them out. We have to find the big gun and shoot it over and over and over."

INSIDERS

THE Commissioner's Annual Super Bowl Party was held in the Pistol Dome on the Insiders' Level. Circling the stadium, the Insiders' luxury skyboxes opened off a wide hallway covered in white wallpaper and purple carpet leading to the south end zone and the Insiders' Restaurant, where the wealthy, influential, beautiful or just plain lucky drank and dined with a fine view of the field.

At the party there were League officials, team owners, staff media types, wives, celebrities, groupies, prostitutes, politicians, Senator Thompson, the mayor of Clyde, country singers, movie stars and several Latin American air force colonels.

The commissioner's five thousand closest friends gouged huge divots of caviar. Using everything from breadsticks to bare fingers, they quickly devoured a scale model Pistol Dome over six feet high.

Terry Dudley, the Union director, and two of the network guys from Cozumel stood in a corner, talking and nibbling an oversize goose liver football with anchovy laces; the commissioner's autograph was made from pimientos.

Monique led the Pistolettes through a nicely erotic routine. The girls also served as hostesses, pushing free drinks for the remainder of the evening while entertainment included two different country and western bands, the Texas Championship Square Dance Team, the Billy Joe Hardesty All-American Youth Choir performing

"Songs for the Apocalypse" and a jazz band from Prairie View
A & M.

Suzy Ballard Chandler sat at the head table with the Commis
sioner and Nick O. Brown, the Denver owner, an oil man an
real estate developer whose wife went down instantly with a mi
graine at the sight of the fresh young widow stuffed into her low
cut purple evening dress.

The Cobianco brothers had a table near the dance floor. A. D
Koster and Captain Monique joined them. The statuesque Pisto
lette sat next to Don Cobianco, leaving A.D. uncomfortably nea
Tiny Walton.

The Commissioner's Annual Super Bowl Party was a ritual o
cheap thrills. Payoff night from the League. Greed, gluttony
drunkenness, sloth, curiosity, a tab of half a million dollars, bu
it was not enough. The customers were never satisfied.

Wendy steered Taylor away from Terry Dudley to avoid a
incident over the Union pension board's refusal to pay claims t
Bobby Hendrix's and Simon D'Hanis's survivors. Since carryin
the documents to the Houston Union meeting and extracting
promise from Terry to help the Hendrix and D'Hanis cases, Taylo
had called the Union headquarters a dozen times without satis
faction.

"It was their body-fat tests, Taylor," Dudley said the last tim
the quarterback had called. "They were full of chemicals. Yo
know how the public is about that stuff. It wouldn't look goo
for the Union."

"What do I tell Ginny? What about Simon's kid?" Taylor ar
gued.

"Blame it on the League."

Strangely unnoticed in the rapacious scramble, Wendy led Tay
lor easily through the crowded, curving hallway, winding throug
the hoggish mass of people.

"I'd like to have urinalysis done on this bunch," Taylor whis
pered. "I'll bet some are legally dead."

Bob Travers walked about four steps behind, slightly t
Wendy's left, traveling in her difficult wake, moving at a stead
glide, projecting her path, quickly setting his course through th
mass of groundlings and stinkards. He studied parties and learne
how people moved, clumped, huddled.

Bob studied the crowd. Half the people were crazy, drunk o
alcohol or ego or cheap thrills; the others watched in stone-sobe
disapproval and envy. Bob Travers hated parties. People went t
parties to forget themselves—a very dangerous thing.

Wendy stopped at the back entrance to her skybox, digging through her small glittering diamond-studded purse for the key. She unlocked the door and Taylor followed her inside quickly. From the loud, smoky, oppressive atmosphere of the Insiders' Restaurant and the commissioner's party, it was a startling leap into the quiet of Wendy's personal luxury skybox.

Walls covered in a brown burlap fabric matched brown carpeting, which cushioned their walk into the trilevel luxury box. Twelve wood-and-leather swivel chairs were arranged on the two lower levels. The back level contained a wet bar, a leather-topped table with eight heavy captain's chairs and a color television stuck on the wall for quick views of instant replays of the network broadcasts. Facing the playing field below, the top half of the glass wall slid open. The skybox was heated and air-conditioned.

Taylor gaped at the too-green gridiron. He had never been in a skybox. The isolation, the height, the angle, made everything look odd, unreal. Or too real. "It looks like a giant doormat. We must look like mice on a billiard table."

"No, that's silly." Wendy walked behind the wet bar in the back. "Now, how about a drink, Mickey?"

"I'd like a piece of cheese." Taylor stared at the plastic playing field. "That thing is too clean for man's work. Man's work is a dirty, bloody business."

"What?" Wendy was pouring Dr Pepper into two long-stemmed crystal glasses.

"Something Ox said when we moved in here. He loved playing outside. Men fought wars outside; real football was *played* outside. Ox said you had to beat the other side, the weather *and* the field. He's proud that he lost two toes to frostbite in Minnesota."

"He's crazy."

"No, he's the perfect offensive lineman. He avoids the spotlight, shuns awards and publicity, never thinks about winning or losing . . . just plays recklessly, sacrificing his body to protect mine, hoping to wake from the delusions of daily life. He's been one hell of an offensive guard for twenty years."

"Do you agree?" Wendy topped off the crystal and tossed the Dr Pepper can in the trash compactor.

Taylor shook his head. "I am not Ox Wood. I have to think about winning and losing. I can never be reckless. I don't willingly sacrifice my body, nor awaken from my delusions. I need my devils and my angels."

Taylor continued to stare at the playing field. Muted sounds crossed from the skyboxes on the west side.

"Who owns those?"

"Junior and Three lease that one with the chandeliers and the blue and white French provincial furniture."

"All they need is a guillotine."

"The Let-Them-Eat-Cake Suite." Wendy carried the long stemmed crystal down to Taylor, who was staring over the edge. You don't get down in it like the old stadium," she said. "You don't get any of man's dirty, bloody business *on* you."

"Are you sure?"

"No, I'm not. Maybe up here it just doesn't leave any stains." She held out the Dr Pepper. "How about a drink?"

"I better not." Taylor was preoccupied. "It's Thursday." He looked into the seats below, then back to the bright-green-and-white-striped field. Taylor carried chronic burns and bruises from hitting the plastic-covered asphalt. "Damn painful turf."

"But cost-effective." Wendy handed him the stemmed crystal.

"For who?"

Taylor held up the expensive wineglass. "What's this?"

"Dr Pepper." Sitting down in a brown leather swivel chair, she slung a leg over the soft chair arm. She wore jeans, a tailored western shirt with ivory snaps and chocolate-brown kangaroo-ski boots.

Taylor took a drink. "It must be strange up here during a game."

Wendy pointed at the bright green and white grid. "I bet it gets stranger out there."

He waited a long time before saying, "I don't think so."

"Red Kilroy came to my house a couple of days ago," Wendy said. "He told me that Suzy had offered him the GM's job and five percent ownership with an option on five percent more. She wanted him to throw the game." Wendy looked at Taylor for reaction. She got none.

He was looking out at the field, watching the artificial ground crew and drinking Dr Pepper out of $175 crystal.

"Well?" Wendy asked finally.

"Well, it means that A.D. is out. A definite lame duck."

"That's all you get out of that?" Wendy stood and walked to the glass wall.

"That's all I see on the surface."

"Will Red throw the game?"

Taylor shook his head. "Not on Suzy's word. Red knows power and how to deal with it. Winning the Super Bowl *is* winning the Super Bowl. To Red, Suzy is a fart in a whirlwind."

— 478 —

"I want to get the Franchise back from her," Wendy said. "After the Super Bowl I'm moving against them."

"I thought you wanted out."

"I changed my mind."

"Okay"—Taylor held up a hand—"but I am getting tired of this relentless exercise of your rich girl prerogatives and by Sunday there is going to be some sort of shakeout. Why don't we let things take their course, relax . . . come along later, picking up the pieces."

"Why?"

"Because my job is winning, not losing. I can't be reckless and risk beating myself. I have the means and am responsible for the end. Only the *end* counts for the quarterback." Taylor gazed down at the bright-green plastic arena, the straight white lines, the neat, exact angles, the definite set of rules. "Football was fun because it used to be so unlike life. But now the game *is* life. This Sunday the world turns upside down and we have to be incomprehensible . . . *bigger* than life."

Wendy sat back in the wooden-and-soft-glove-leather chair. "What if you can't do it? What if you can't win by more than sixteen."

Wendy's negative questions and flights of future fancy were slightly irritating.

"I *can* do it. And I can convince my teammates *they* can do it. Convincing Denver'll have to wait until Sunday." Taylor was struck by the unreality of the ground crew that was now zooming around on the field in a golf cart. Out there on the turf, even the grounds keepers looked artificial, nonhuman. "On Sunday we will be *bigger than life*."

"Bigger than life is quite an order," Wendy said.

"That's why being a hero isn't all penthouse." Taylor walked away from the edge and sat in a brown swivel chair next to her. "Lots of times it's the shit house. Most of the time . . . maybe even all. You can see why I cling to my delusions; I need them for a while longer. I'll deliver."

"We only control fifty percent of the Franchise," Wendy said.

"A rich girl's complaint; half isn't enough." Taylor stared at his new boots, studying the six-row stitching, checking for loose ends. He found none. "Give Red ten percent and watch the fur fly."

"Give up a share and then just wait it out? Waiting seems to be your solution to everything. If I wait, there may not be a Franchise left."

"Not if you give Red ten percent. He'll start kicking asses and taking names. No sense planning past Sunday. It's wasteful and distracting."

"We have to protect Randall's interests. It *is* his trust income that's being threatened." Wendy slugged down the last of her soft drink like it was rotgut.

"For Chrissakes, he isn't going to starve. He doesn't *need* a professional football franchise," Taylor protested. "*Nobody* needs a football franchise."

"If I let that bitch and those hoodlums bleed the Franchise," Wendy argued, "it's just like I'm helping them."

"Who cares? I don't recall one game you played," Taylor said. "Without Dick running the Franchise, it's already a leaky boat. I don't think it's worth the effort to toss the other passengers overboard. We'd still have to plug the holes and bail water. Not to mention all the bloodstains on the deck." Taylor dropped his feet to the thick carpet and sat up in his chair. "Besides, I'm gone after the Super Bowl, and I *am* the Franchise."

Taylor looked across the field at the commissioner's guests drinking, dancing, eating and necking in the west skyboxes. "A.D. and Suzy can't deliver; the Cobiancos have bet the farm *and* their pizza chain. Red will keep leading Suzy on while Conly makes certain the Cobiancos do not lack for takers. Sunday night they will all be broke. The ultimate football game for this season will be decided by a strategy based on the oldest, motivation in the world," Taylor said. "Revenge. Revenge for making Dick Conly look like an old fool. Just plain old revenge."

"I don't want revenge, I want the truth known," Wendy said.

"If you wanted revenge or blood, I'd feel better," Taylor said. "You just want what you *think* is yours." He began to anger. "In another year you'd be calling plays from up here."

Wendy stepped down from the top level and stood next to Taylor. Lifting his battered right hand to her gentle, exquisite face, she pressed the aching fingers to her soft, smooth cheek then turned the hand over and kissed the palm, closed the fingers into a loose fist and replaced it in his lap. She didn't deny it.

At midfield a grounds keeper was staring up at the Insiders boxes, looking into each skybox, slowly turning a complete 360 degrees, his jaw slack and his mouth hanging open in salacious shock. Finally he shook his head and returned to work, painting the Pistols logo on the turf.

Wendy watched the man lay out the stencils, then spray two purple Colt .45 Peacemakers, crossed and cocked against a circular field of white.

"And Samuel Colt made men equal," Taylor said. "While the infrared sniper scope made them all the same color."

There was a sharp rap on the skybox door. Bob stepped into the skybox. "He's here."

"Send him in," Wendy said.

The door opened wide for a smallish, well-dressed man in a three-piece suit and carrying a slim attaché case. In his mid-thirties, he wore a full head of prematurely gray hair. He was Wendy Chandler's lawyer and adviser, Samuel Biggs Rice of the law firm of Rice, Rice, Rice & Rice.

Wendy introduced Taylor. The two men shook hands.

Competitive senses told Taylor the lawyer was his adversary. Taylor had no time for new enemies or outside interference. "Which Rice are you?"

"The last," the lawyer snapped.

"You should have said the first," Taylor sparred. "Who would know?"

"I would," the attorney said. "It's not a ranking in order of ability."

"What's it by?" Taylor had to dispose of the lawyer immediately, returning the focus of his concentration to Sunday's job. "Height?"

The small man's face flushed.

"Please, Taylor," Wendy said. "I invited Sam to meet with us to discuss future plans. He thinks we have a good case for moving against Suzy and the Cobiancos after the Super Bowl."

"Please spare me this. All lawyers think you have a good case until you get to the courtroom." Taylor turned to Wendy. "Then they tell you that the law is a funny thing, juries are undependable and we got a bad judge. I have more important things to do than watch his high-dollar tap dance at my expense." He studied her eyes, trying to plumb the depths of her conviction. "You *really* think you know more about what's happening here than I do?"

Wendy's face was slightly flushed.

"You and lawyer Smurf don't have the vaguest idea of what has to be done."

The lawyer's face froze in a grimace. He turned to Wendy.

"Taylor, the least you could do is listen to Sam. There are other matters besides the Franchise to resolve. We're getting married and . . ."

"I don't have the time, desire or ability to listen now." Taylor stood and stretched. "Let it be. We can get married without Mr. Rice as flower girl."

The attorney stiffened, his tiny heels clicked together invol untarily, his face purpled. He struggled for self-control.

"As I told you earlier, Miss Chandler"—Samuel Biggs Rice attorney-at-law, found his oversize voice—"we should not wait Those people could be draining assets that rightfully belong to you and the trust."

"Let's have a footrace to the courthouse," Taylor looked a Wendy. "Get rid of this clown, because the problem with shit i the more you stir it, the more it stinks."

"Please, Taylor." Wendy was confused. "Just listen. Wha harm can it do?"

"As much as you can afford, starting with me and Mr. Rice here will defend you to your last dollar." The quarterback pushe by the small attorney and started up to the door. "He don't eve know about the Cornpicker."

"It is still my opinion, Miss Chandler," the lawyer began again "that it is a mistake to wait. And"—he spoke to Taylor, whe stopped and looked back—"I'll want those documents you have Mr. Rusk. I would like to go over them tonight."

"And he put his foot right in it." Taylor looked at Wendy ir disbelief. Narrowing his eyes, he cut them to the lawyer.

"Mr. Rice, *I* would like to go over *you* with a fungo bat Unfortunately I left mine at home." Taylor turned to Wendy. "You understand what you are doing?" Taylor looked back to Rice "Look, jerk, these people you want to slap silly with bench war rants have a cement overcoat for you in their junior department.' Taylor grabbed the doorknob. "I don't know what document: you're talking about and neither does she. If you pursue the issue I'll make it a point to drop by your office with my bat and use you for infield practice around the law library." Taylor looke over to Wendy. Her face was ashen. "I'll meet you downstairs There is only one driver in this race. It's my way or the highway.'

"I must say, Mr. Rusk, you are an exceedingly rude and coarse man." Samuel Biggs Rice cocked his head back and looked dow his nose.

"So sue me, you little cocksucker." Taylor jerked open the door and lunged into the hallway, almost knocking Bob Traver: down. "You better get her away from him," he told the bodyguard "I'm going downstairs."

Taylor picked his way through the gorged, besotted crowd.

Terry Dudley and the network guys were still standing by the buffet, finishing off the remains of the goose liver football and discussing the ex-basketball player's aborted fishing show.

"I would have been great." Dudley popped one of the anchovies that had laced the goose liver ball into his mouth.

"You had a real presence and knack for television," a network guy said. "It was a damn shame."

"No sense looking back." The Union director reached for another anchovy. "I am committed to labor relations and helping the football player. I understand athletes, their strengths and weaknesses. Sports law is why I got my degree."

"That fishing show would have led to bigger things," the network guy injected. "A bigger platform to build on and speak from. Of course you would have to be careful . . . we've got a standards and practices department."

"I know." Terry nodded thoughtfully. "I know. It would have been interesting . . . to say the least. My public image helps the Union, so for that I'm thankful."

Taylor slipped past the buffet without being noticed. The director was talking on his favorite subject: himself and everything he had done for the Union.

Waiting at the service elevator, Taylor Rusk wondered if the coming Sunday would help resolve his constant dilemma of wanting to be a part of it all, yet knowing that salvation lay in being the outlaw.

The elevator arrived and Taylor climbed in, riding to the garage level with three blacks in busboy white.

"You guys work here?" Taylor asked idly.

The three men laughed.

"Naw," said the tallest, fingering the collar of his short white bus jacket. "We didn't get an invitation to the commissioner's party"—he smiled—"so we done made ourselves *invisible*."

Surprised by the reply, Taylor began to laugh loud and hard— a true fool. The doors slid open. The three men in busboy white stepped off and walked away, giggling. Taylor Rusk staggered and convulsed with laughter. It was the perfect joke.

The black men heard his laughter long after they had walked to the street. It echoed from the bowels of the Pistol Dome like wails from a madhouse.

The service elevator returned as Taylor regained composure and tried to recall where he had parked his yellow car and the best route to it. The door *shoosh*ed open, disgorging Wendy Chandler, Bob Travers and Mr. Rice.

The lawyer glared at Taylor, furious that a football player had interfered with his role. The plans that he had spent time and money formulating destroyed by a jock. A jock! The next day

Rice bet five thousand dollars against the Pistols and prayed for Taylor Rusk's public humiliation on international television.

"Bye, Sam." Wendy's voice lilted sweetly.

The lawyer waved as he walked off; he kept his back to them.

"Don't take it so hard," Taylor yelled after him. "Learn to add long columns of numbers and you can be an orthopedic surgeon."

"Shush." Wendy slipped up next to Taylor and slid under his arm.

Bob stood back about five feet, his eyes moving constantly, checking the corners and shadows.

"Okay, so we don't need lawyers." Wendy clutched his arm. "I'm sorry I told him about the documents. I should know by now that Sunday is enough problem."

"Right now I'm just trying to remember where I parked my car." Deep furrows dug into his brow. "I think it's this way."

"You didn't drive." Wendy laughed lightly. "Bob drove us over. Take us to the car, will you, Bob?"

The bodyguard looked at Taylor, shook his head, then pointed in the opposite direction Taylor had picked.

"Oh. Yeah. Right . . . I . . . ah . . ." Taylor's voice trailed off as he followed Bob. Wendy clung to his side. On the way to the commissioner's party Taylor had been running plays in his head, reading defenses, considering adjustments. He did not remember the trip at all.

The white Ford was parked next to three matching Rolls-Royce Corniche convertibles. As he and Wendy crawled into the Ford's backseat, Taylor purposely banged the door into one of them, gouging out paint down to the bare metal.

"Where's Randall?" Taylor asked once Bob got the Ford moving.

"At the hotel where we left him," Wendy said. "Watching television with Shaggy—I mean Toby."

"Oh . . . yeah . . . ah . . . I forgot. It's all in my head," Taylor mumbled. "Somewhere."

THERE'S A
MUDDY ROAD AHEAD

MAJOR Jack "Pat" Garrett's company had the Pistol Dome contract for "security and crowd control." The Major also was supplying security dogs to Investico. He was dealing with J. Edgar Jones.

J. Edgar had risen quickly through Investico's ranks. It was his responsibility to cut the "dog deal." For Pat Garrett the Super Bowl dog deal was frosting on the SSI cake—and all the Major had to do was kick back five percent of his gross to J. Edgar Jones.

The Major still procured his dogs through his contact at the Air Force base. They were canine washouts from the security school—incorrigible and marked for extermination. Major Garrett bought them cheap and leased them dear to Investico, recouping twice his investment.

The day before Super Sunday, J. Edgar and the Major went to see a couple of the dogs that SSI was letting Investico use for sniffing out explosives, drugs, illegal aliens and for crowd control. J. Edgar was awed by the terrible size and visible fury of the sleek black Dobermans. Unchained, so the handler could demonstrate a few simple commands, the enormous dogs went right for J. Edgar, ripping him ragged.

In the growling, slashing, screaming confusion, the Major drew his pistol and shot the dogs off the agent. One shot blew off J. Edgar's right kneecap, costing SSI the "dog deal."

The Major covered his own ass by immediately calling the commissioner and telling him of the kickback scheme. He sent Robbie Burden copies of incriminating tape-recorded conversations with J. Edgar.

The commissioner turned down J. Edgar's claim for disability and fired him the day he was released from the hospital.

Lamar Jean Lukas spent that Saturday, the coldest day of the year, getting ready. A certain snap returned to his life; he moved with command and purpose. He felt alive, exhilarated, alert to the world; learning, seeing, smelling, moving with the lean, quick economy that got him out of Vietnam alive.

His SSI uniform would be perfect camouflage for his mission at the Pistol Dome. The high turnover of minimum-wage security guards made it doubtful that he would be recognized.

Picking up his uniform at the cleaners, Lamar Jean then stopped at the hardware store for aluminum powder, a gallon of kerosene, and an empty two-gallon paint can. At the Target store he bought two bicycle inner tubes, a pair of surgical rubber gloves, a two-gallon gas can, and an official Texas Pistols duffel bag. He filled the gasoline can at the new self-serve Exxon that replaced Louie Deal's Crockett Street station.

He hauled all the gear back to Taylor's apartment, into the private patio with the barbecue grill and eight-foot stockade fence.

After starting the charcoal fire, he pulled on the rubber gloves and went to work cutting up the inner tubes into sleeves six inches long, sealing them at one end. Then, sitting down at the small table with a pair of pliers, he pulled the slugs from several of his .357 Magnum cartridges, dumped the gunpowder in a bowl with the aluminum powder from the paint store and mixed them. He poured the mixture into packets of thin paper and sealed them with wax, then placed the packets in a manila envelope inside the purple and white bag.

While the charcoal burned down to glowing red coals, he returned inside to get a long wooden spoon and a cookie tin.

Lamar placed the empty paint bucket on the grill and poured in about two inches of water. Letting it come to a boil, he shaved a bar of soap into the water with his pocket knife, stirring with the wooden spoon until the mixture cooked to a paste. Then he began adding and stirring, very carefully, a fifty-fifty mixture of kerosene and gasoline. The gasoline would burn hot; the kerosene would keep it from burning too fast. The soap paste would make it stick. Several times the mixture flared into flame; Lamar quickly smothered the fire by placing the cookie tin over the mouth of the paint can. He removed the can from the grill when he had an approximate twenty-to-one ratio of gasoline-kerosene to the water-soap combination.

After cooling, the mixture turned gelatinous and Lamar proceeded to pour it into the rubber sleeves cut from the inner tubes, sealing both ends tightly, placing them in the vegetable bin of Taylor's refrigerator.

Lamar dug in his coat pocket for some cherry bombs and firecrackers left over from New Year's Day. He tossed them into the bag, along with some old rags, two new disposable lighters and three railroad flares.

From the broom closet, he pulled the small .22 automatic rifle and a box of .22 shorts. The small rifle fit neatly into the purple and white bag with the crossed Walker Colts on the side.

Lamar poured the remaining gasoline and kerosene into two empty quart bottles, capping and placing them in the duffel bag, wrapping them heavily with industrial toweling he stole from the gas station where he'd filled his gas can. Lamar carefully cleaned up the mess, ditched it off the Red River Bridge, returned to the apartment satisfied with his work and fell asleep on the couch.

Lamar Jean Lukas had adeptly used a skill taught to him by his government. Finally he'd found military training that was adaptable to civilian life.

Lamar Jean Lukas had spent the day making napalm.

Around one in the morning at the commissioner's party in the Pistol Dome, John and Roger Cobianco had four hands inside Monique's Pistolettes uniform, leaving little room for Monique and none for A. D. Koster, looking on helplessly.

At Taylor Rusk's apartment Lamar Jean suddenly awoke and sat straight up, listening and waiting, his eyes probing the darkness. Lamar gradually returned from the central highlands of Vietnam.

Carefully making his way back to the kitchen, he opened the silverware drawer and removed the envelope containing the Super Bowl ticket from Tiny Walton. Lamar handled it like fine china, padding catlike to the purple and white bag, he placed the ticket carefully inside and zipped the bag shut.

Returning to the living room, squatting cross-legged, arms folded, back against the wall, Lamar Jean Lukas slept with one eye and an ear open. It all came flooding back. He finally understood the trade his government had promised to teach him and a few good men. He was on a mission. A mission with the few and proud on the muddy road ahead.

INFILTRATION

AT daybreak Lamar Jean Lukas donned his SSI uniform, strapped on his pistol, checked his official Pistols' duffel bag, carefully filled with his handicraft and set out for the Texas Pistol Dome.

The parking lot was nearly empty when Lamar, wearing reflector lens aviator sunglasses, arrived. The fat SSI guard at the gate waved him through without looking up from his television set.

The network had started nonstop coverage of the game the night before. It was cheap, highly rated programming that commanded exorbitant advertising rates of over $500,000 a minute.

Lamar walked completely around the dome, checking the security areas, communications centers and television trucks. The TV technicians had been in the dome all night, checking the cameras and making final decisions on their broadcast strategy.

On his second trip around the parking lot, Lamar picked his spot: a twenty-eight-foot Winnebago with Colorado plates parked directly opposite the exit from Insiders' parking.

It was perfect cover.

The Denver fans were drinking Bloody Marys and fixing breakfast beneath a canvas awning that extended out from the side of the giant RV. They had a camp stove, tables and chairs and plenty of liquor; most important, they were already drunk. The van owner, a real estate developer, was a red-faced, friendly man in a denim outfit and a black wide-brimmed hat. Lamar walked up and began a conversation about alcohol and allowable behavior in the parking lot. Eager to befriend a uniform and large sidearm, the Denver fans fixed Lamar breakfast and treated him like kinfolk.

He lounged in a low canvas chaise in the shade of the awning with his duffel bag by his side, his pistol holstered and his eyes on the Insiders' lot. "How about letting me borrow that hat?" Lamar asked. The man hesitated, then tossed Lamar the hat.

After breakfast Lamar mentioned it was chilly and was instantly given a red and green plaid flannel shirt. Lamar was now unidentifiable and indistinguishable from the rest of the Colorado people enjoying their pregame party in the Pistol Dome parking lot across from Insiders' parking.

Having successfully infiltrated, Lamar waited calmly in ambush, his duffel bag at his feet.

Slowly the lot began to fill and Lamar was a fish in an ocean of football fans. The Denver fans left him and went to their end zone seats to drink screwdrivers.

Just before kickoff, the Cobianco brothers arrived in their black limousine. Monique was with them, still in her Pistolette outfit; she'd been their "guest" since the commissioner's party. The captain of the Texas Pistolettes looked like someone had wrapped her in a wet sheet and beat her with a garden hose. Tiny and the driver had to help her from the car. The three brothers were laughing, having the time of their lives.

Lounging back in the canvas chaise, the big black wide-brim hat tipped forward, hiding his face, absently patting his duffel bag, Lamar watched them through his reflector-lens aviator glasses.

BE TRUE
TO YOUR SCHOOL

IT was predawn Sunday morning. Taylor lay next to Wendy, going over possible alternatives to draw and delay trap calls on his quick count. If he keyed a blitz with the line ready to go on the first sound, he couldn't audible. Yet, he had to come off the play. The QB sneak was the simplest adjustment, requiring only Taylor and the center. The quarterback's signal would be a slap on the lineman's hip; then, instead of setting back and faking a pass block, the center would fire straight out on the snap with Taylor right behind. Taylor decided to tell his center in the locker room before the game about the adjustment.

In the pregame morning darkness of the penthouse master bedroom, Taylor ran the adjustment to precision in his head. He ran the play more times with slight variations, depending on the type of blitz.

Just in case.

Bob rapped lightly on the door.

"You got company," he said. "Red Kilroy's in the sitting room, trying to have a stroke. He said he had to see you, said it was urgent."

"For him it is." Taylor opened his eyes. "What time is it?"

"Four in the morning."

"Not bad." Taylor stretched and twisted as he rolled out of bed, his bare feet sinking into the carpet. "Before we played Notre Dame, he woke me at two and tried to change the whole game plan. He thought we were playing LSU in the Sugar Bowl. I'll be right out. Holler if his pupils dilate, his lower lip quivers and his asshole snaps shut."

Taylor stood in the middle of the room, looking out at Park City's lights. It was that short moment between dark and daylight where nothing seemed to move. No one was going anywhere. It only lasted a moment, then a blue and white police car rolled south on the freeway toward Clyde.

It was game day and Red was going nuts again.

"Sleeping kind of late, aren't you, Coach?" Taylor had pulled on a gray sweat suit. He was still barefoot. "I called down to the kitchen for coffee and rolls."

"Good, Jimmy. Good idea." Red sat on the edge of the couch, staring at the carpet between his feet while his knees pumped up and down so hard it caused the coffee table in front of him to shake.

"Taylor." The big quarterback picked up the glass ashtray from the table to keep the clatter of vibrating glass against the tabletop from driving him nuts.

"What?" Red looked up from the floor, his feet still nervously pumping. "What did you say?"

"I said *Taylor*. My name is Taylor."

"I know that." The coach looked slightly irritated.

"You called me Jimmy."

"I did not!" Red stood suddenly and began pacing the room. The swiftness of the movement startled Taylor and he stepped back. "Quit fucking around here, Taylor, goddammit! It's almost game time and you are fucking around."

"Red." Taylor sat in the beige corduroy wing chair by the glass wall. "It is twelve hours until kickoff." Looking into his coach's wild eyes, he wondered why he took the effort to explain.

"Can't be, just can't be." The coach continued his pacing. "I left a wake-up call. I distinctly remember leaving a wake-up call."

"I don't doubt you left it, Red." Taylor watched the worried man walk in tight circles and figure eights, weaving around the furniture in the large room. "Are you sure you got called back?"

The question stopped his pacing and lifted his eyes from the blind stare into the carpeting. It lasted only a moment.

— 490 —

"Certainly. Certainly." The coach resumed his desperate travel. "Of course. I wouldn't be here if I hadn't got the call, now, would ?" Red looked at Taylor for reassurance.

"I guess not. Are you here for any particular reason except the oadwork?" Taylor watched his coach wander to the far side of he room. His shirttail was out and his pants hung baggy in the eat.

"Reason! Reason! Goddammit, boy, where's your head?" Red whirled and strode directly at his quarterback, eyes blazing fire and fear. "It is goddam *game day*! We got things to discuss, noodles to work out of the offense, adjustments to make, some new wrinkles for the game plan."

"Why don't we make some trades?" Taylor leaned back. "Nobody else but Denver needs their players today."

A momentary flicker in Red's eyes betrayed the depth of thought ne gave his quarterback's suggestion; then it was gone and he saw Taylor watching him. "I thought you ordered some coffee? Where he hell is it?"

The phone rang.

"That'll be it now. I've got to go release the elevator." Taylor started for the phone, then looked back at Red, haggard and disheveled, sinking deeper into the madness of the Super Bowl. "By the way, Red, how did you get up here? The elevator's locked."

"I used the fire escape."

"Jesus, you're lucky Bob didn't shoot you." Taylor continued on to the phone.

"The son of a bitch wasn't very polite, I'll tell you that," Red began his pacing again.

"He isn't paid to be polite." Taylor replaced the phone and walked over to unlock the elevator door.

"Where do you meet people like that, Jimmy?"

"Taylor," the quarterback again reminded the coach.

Red ignored Taylor's correction. "The thing to remember about these guys today is they put their pants on the same way we do—"

"But later in the day," Taylor interrupted. "And they tuck their shirts in."

"Fuck their goddam shirts," Red said. "Fuck their pants too."

The doorbell rang.

"That's the coffee." Bob was already there with his right hand in his coat pocket. It was the same waiter Randall had attacked earlier in the week with his Light Saber. The man looked nervously

around the room as he set down the tray and then scurried bac
out.

"What the fuck is wrong with him?" Red asked.

"You look like a border patrolman."

"He was running like it was Judgment Day. Hey!" The coac
looked down at his bare wrist to check the time on a watch h
hadn't had since his last year at the University, when he ha
skipped a flat rock on the river, then stood slack-jawed, watchin
his six-thousand-dollar Rolex chasing the rock into the swift wate

"It must be getting close to time for pregame chapel." Red ke[
looking at his bare wrist.

"It's early yet. Have some coffee, get *really* nervous." Taylo
saw no reason to remind the coach that he had not had a pregam
chapel since the year Red beat up the team chaplain for performin
oral sex on a sophomore defensive tackle from Houston. By day
light, Red would forget he forgot and also remember he no longe
had a watch.

Red sat back on the edge of the couch, but his legs continue
to jiggle and his hand shook, spilling his coffee on the low table
staining the pages of the visitor's guide with the cover shot of th
Pistol Dome. Red pointed at the magazine. "By God, one da
we'll have a domed stadium like that."

"It wouldn't surprise me, Coach."

"How do you think Hendrix'll do today?" Red asked in a
seriousness.

The question hit like a fist, sinking Taylor down into his chair

"I was thinking that if we concentrated on getting him dee
while the defense is doubling and tripling Speedo . . ." Red's voic
trailed off in confusion. Something was amiss, a basic truth tha
even in his game-day madness would not be denied. The coach'
face went white. Suddenly nauseous, he jumped to his feet.

"The bathroom?" Red gagged.

Taylor pointed across the room, but the coach was alread
hurrying down the hall toward Randall's room, hands over hi
mouth, shirttail flapping.

"No. Red! No! This way!"

It was too late. Red burst into Randall's bedroom. Taylor wa
on his feet, chasing his coach.

"Toby! Toby!" Taylor yelled. "It's all right, don't hurt him
He's just lost! Boy, is he lost."

Toby had spent several years as a cattle ranger and slept o
the floor across the entrance to the boy's room. When he felt th
footsteps coming down the hall, he was instantly awake.

Red Kilroy came sailing backward out of the room as fast as
went in, slamming against the opposite side of the hallway and
ding slowly to a sitting position on the floor. Toby came out
hind him with a trench knife in his hand and his revolver shoved
his belt. Toby preferred the knife; a wild shot could accidentally
ike the boy.

"I'm sorry, Taylor." Toby stood over Red as the quarterback
n up. "It all happened so fast. I didn't hear you until it was
ver."

"Holy Christ!" Taylor's heart began to hammer. The quarter-
ck knelt beside his coach, searching for the knife wound. "Did
u stab him?"

"No. But I don't think hitting that wall did him a whole lot of
od. I think I felt his arm break when I tossed him."

Red Kilroy's eyes fluttered open and he looked at Taylor.
immy! Jimmy! I'm glad you're here." The coach smiled and
en threw up all over himself.

Taylor jumped away. "He's all right. Puking is a vital sign for
m."

Toby slipped his fingers out of the brass-knuckle grip and slid
e knife back into its leather sheath.

"Who's Jimmy?"

Taylor shrugged and watched his coach heaving on the floor.

Randall stirred in his bed and mumbled in his sleep. Taylor
ent to the boy's bed, untangled him from the bedclothes and
ondered at the soft unlined face. He ran a hand across the sleep-
ssed hair and kissed his son gently on his soft, pink lips. The
ght Saber stood against the bedstead, at the ready.

"Red was lucky he didn't get past you," Taylor whispered to
oby when he returned to the hallway, where the bodyguard was
ouched, checking Red for broken bones and making certain he
dn't strangle on his own vomit. "If Randall had gotten his Light
aber this man would look like a Salisbury steak."

"No broken bones as far as I can tell, but he may have a
oncussion, the way he was vomiting."

"He always vomits that way."

"You tell 'em, Jimmy."

Toby looked at Taylor, then down at Red. "Jimmy?" He stepped
ack into Randall's room and closed the door.

Taylor helped Red to his feet and into the bathroom.

"I'll get another sweat suit from the bedroom, Red. You are a
ess."

"I'm fine. I'm fine." Red stuck his head in the shower cabinet

— 493 —

and turned the cold water on full, soaking his head and shoulde and splattering the mirrors and walls.

"You stink. I'll get you one of my other sweat suits."

"So we can look like goddam twin faggots? This is *game da* buddy-boy."

"And you want to look like a wino and smell like a dead cat' Taylor walked out of the bathroom. "You might as well piss your pants while you're at it."

"Thanks, buddy-boy, I goddam just might do it."

Taylor returned to his chair, drank coffee and looked out th window. The southeastern sky was beginning to color.

"Every day is Judgment Day, but Super Sunday comes onl once a year," Taylor said.

"Usually the Sunday after Robert E. Lee's birthday." Red walke out of the bathroom, drying himself with a towel. His face wa red and his hair plastered flat from the cold water. His shirt ar pants were horribly stained.

"You ought to send those clothes to the laundry with you them."

"Taylor, let us not waste our creativity on trite jokes. I expe some magic from you today. We're going to need it."

"If you can remember my name, Red, the least I can do is pu a few elephants out of the old headgear."

"That's my boy." Red smiled and looked around. He was different man since Toby bounced him off the wall. It would t short-lived. Game day was Red's hell. "Now, where's the rol and coffee?"

Taylor pointed and Red attacked the food.

"Okay, I figure you'll have up to three and a half seconds throw on certain types of protection: straight dropbacks with bo backs in, half rolls with the offside seal and even cup protectic with both backs out, as long as they don't blitz." Red started c his second roll. He would vomit it all back up on the way to th game. "You got one hell of a line. They don't make 'em like C Wood anymore, and the younger boys are real Nazis. They d what they're told and they enjoy it. What kind of drugs do the use?"

"What kind you got?"

"What kind do they need?"

"Fuck them, what about me?"

"You don't need drugs. You are a magician, remember?"

"Who says magicians don't use drugs?"

"What do the linemen need?" Red started his third roll an

— 494 —

aylor resolved to stay clear of Red the remainder of the day. "I now Ox uses amphetamines and cocaine," the coach continued, ut what about the baby Nazis?"

"They do everything Ox does except fuck Ox's wife."

"God, is that a great-looking woman?" Red followed the weird ngent. "You think they want to fuck her? I think about fucking er all the time. It's hard to believe she's forty and they been arried over twenty years," Red rambled. "Hey. Now, don't go lling Ox."

"Don't worry, I live in the same huddle with the man."

"We got to beat their pass rush, so keep them off balance with uick counts and don't set too deep. Let the tackles push their efensive ends past you." Red paused. "Are you sure they have verything they need?"

"Who?"

"Your pass blockers, asshole."

"If they don't, I'll help you find it for them."

"The Butazolidin Blues," Red said slowly, absently. He was eginning to drift again. "Listen," he suddenly snapped back. "I eed a favor. I kept those media scumbag slime off you *all week* nd I'm taking a lot of heat for it. You could get me off the griddle you'd do a pregame interview with the network's greaseball ookie."

"Will *you* leave me alone at the stadium?" Taylor asked. "No st-minute suggestions?"

The momentary battle raged on Red's face. "Completely alone?"

Taylor nodded. Red hesitated. It was a painful, humiliating ecision.

"Goddammit, all right!" he said finally. Red's eyes unfocused nd he leaned back, wet hair plastered down and his clothes stained ith vomit.

And there on the couch in the penthouse sitting room with aylor Jefferson Rusk watching the sun rising, Red Kilroy slipped way again into the personal purgatory that was his mind on game ay.

The sun was well above the horizon when Wendy walked into e room and found Red and Taylor.

They sat at opposite ends of the couch; Red leaning foward, ringing his hands, tapping his feet to some infernal silent pulse; aylor laid back, slouched down, with his bare feet up on the low ble.

They both stared silently out at the Pistol Dome, the two men

— 495 —

whose lives had been joined for a decade of treacherously exhilarating guerrilla warfare against the powers of established authority and corruption.

They now studied the Pistol Dome, the final Bunker.

When Wendy entered, Red spoke, his voice quivering, his control tenuous.

"What do you think it will be like when we win, Taylor?" The coach's voice broke on the last three words, ending in a rasping squeak. His legs still jiggled, his hands shook.

The coach's whole body quivered like a cowed dog. He resumed wringing his hands. Taylor looked through the morning haze to the monument celebrating welfare for the rich and corporate socialism.

"It'll be like winning the state championship at Park City High," Taylor said. "When I was eighteen years old, you told me you were recruiting me for the University because I was a champion, a proven winner."

"Well, by God, you were," Red defended the lie that seemed true, a lie that had worked itself out.

"State champions." Taylor pronounced it thoughtfully. "You took Simon D'Hanis that year, too, remember?"

"You made me take him," Red replied, slightly irritated. "But Simon turned out to be a good one." His mood improved as he ascribed Simon's unexpected success to himself.

"Simon compared the national championship at the University to the state championship at Park City High School." Taylor pointed out toward the dome. He purposely seemed to lose track of the conversation because he knew how much it irritated Red. Particularly on game day.

"Well?" Red was exasperated.

"Well what?"

"What did Simon say? How did it compare?"

Taylor pushed up from the couch. "It was almost about the same." He walked away. "It'll be almost about the same today."

Taylor disappeared into the bedroom and closed the door. Red gazed after him in quaking confusion.

It'll be almost about the same.

Wendy returned to the bedroom and, while Taylor lay on the bed, called the defensive coordinator to come take Red away. The man arrived to find Kilroy still staring silently at the Pistol Dome.

Red left without a word. Taylor remained on the bed, lost somewhere deep in himself, his eyes dull, flat, face slack. He was searching for the horror.

It was that time again.

The plans had been laid, the deals made; they had polished their skills, honed their instincts and intuitions, executed the plays to perfection and were bound as a football team by respect forged in pain and fear and joy.

Now it all depended on Taylor's struggle with the horror of the void. It was his job. The hard part.

Wendy had seen him like this many times as he hunted the beast inside to confront the awe of nothingness. His facial muscles no longer formed a mask of flesh. Taylor appeared a stranger—impassive, expressionless, unfamiliar, absent, empty.

Gone away.

His eyes suddenly flared; he had again found nothing. Thin creases sliced down from his mouth. He winced in pain, trying not to turn from the terror. His face no longer slack, panic drew a mask of heavy lines. His whole body stiffened, he flinched slightly, his eyes sparkled sightlessly, black with fear. He began to flush and sweat. A violent tremor shook his shoulders and a facial tic jerked at the corners of his mouth.

His eyes watered and it was over.

He had his game face.

The rest would be easy.

Whatever it was.

A GOOD SONG
TO DANCE TO

BEFORE leaving for the stadium, Taylor placed a call to Ginny Hendrix. One of the boys answered.

"Bobby?" Taylor asked.

"Naw, Billy."

"This is Taylor. Is your mother around?"

"MAAAAA!" Billy squalled into the mouthpiece. "MAAAAAAA!!!!!"

Gus Savas's huge house absorbed the screams and wails of his grandchild.

"Hello?" Ginny came on the line, breathless.

"Hi, Ginny, this is Taylor. I thought I'd call and say hell« Billy didn't seem too pleased to hear my voice."

"Oh, he's waiting on a call from a boy down the block. The have a big Super Bowl party planned with a six-foot televisic and two VTR units for their own instant replays."

"And I'm on the phone interfering with the planning of tl party?"

"You got it. You shouldn't be calling now just before the gam You need to be psyching yourself up, don't you? Bobby alwaʸ puked his guts out."

"I know, I roomed with him," Taylor replied. "Don't worr I've done the hard part. I'm just going to the stadium for the rᵒ call and make sure everybody else does what they are told. It easy for me from now on."

"Mr. Automatic," Ginny teased. "Oh, Taylor, thanks for tl rings for the boys. I'll give 'em to them today. Maybe Billy wⁱ forgive you for bothering him on game day."

"Those are exact scale duplicates of the rings we picked. They' the least gaudy Super Bowl ring ever designed. Actually those aᵣ the only two in existence, plus mine; everybody else has to waⁱ I already played the game and we won. I just have to go to tl Pistol Dome and convince the rest of my teammates and the world.

"Taylor?" Ginny turned hesitant, embarrassed. "I can't tal this check. I appreciate it, but...."

"That's just until we get the Union pension problem workeᵈ out. I haven't had the time during the season. Now I know wʰ Speedo quit this job; there's so much to do. How did Bobby ᵈ it?"

"He worked his ass off. He believed in it." Ginny's voiᵈ dulled. She was not a believer.

"I told Terry that after this game I'd come to the office or tal to the pension board or whatever it took. I'm doing the same thiⁿ about Simon for the kid."

"Where is he?"

"Down in Kingsville with Buffy's people."

"In a minute, Billy," Ginny said. Taylor could hear the bᵒ telling his mother to get off the phone. "In a minute, dear. It Uncle Taylor."

Taylor heard the boy say he didn't care.

"Taylor...I..." Ginny stammered; the boy was badgering hᵉ for the phone. "Taylor, I have to go...but I...just a minutᵉ Billy....Taylor, I just wanted to thank you for caring about ᵘ

d ..." Her voice broke. Billy kept his verbal assault. "I have
ot to go. Good luck and we all love you."

The line went dead. Billy had been hovering near and pressed
own the disconnect button.

Taylor looked across the bed at Wendy. She was wiping tears
om her eyes.

Taylor smiled at her. "Billy made her hang up on me so he
ould call his friends and plan their Super Bowl party."

Bob Travers rapped on the door.

"Anytime." Bob had already taken Toby and Randall to the
xybox.

Taylor picked up his playbook and followed Wendy out of the
edroom door. They followed Bob to the private elevator.

In the parking garage two uniformed policemen stood by the
ord. Bob left the elevator first, then signaled Wendy and Taylor
follow him into the car. They sat quietly in back.

Bob stuck the flasher on the car roof, waved off the police and
it his siren.

At street level in front of the hotel, about fifty Denver fans
ere holding a pep rally hanging Taylor Rusk in effigy. They
ere drunk and loud and all were barechested. Men and women.
was twenty-eight degrees. They were chanting, "Die ... Die
.. Die ... Kill ... Kill ... Die ... Die ...
ill ... Kill ... Kill ..."

Taylor watched Wendy, who had turned pale at the up-close
adness.

"I don't like the words," Taylor said, snapping his fingers,
ut I like the beat. It's a good song to dance to."

Bob hit the siren and hurtled into the gathering storm of traffic
ooding toward the Super Bowl at the Pistol Dome.

Wendy turned for a last look at the mob.

"What would they have done if they'd seen you?"

Taylor thought a moment.

"I don't think they meant *everything* they were saying."

Bob laughed and hit the accelerator. With a sucking, roaring
ound the car leaped ahead and slid through the traffic like a fish
rough water.

Kill. Die.

ON THE ROAD AGAIN,
SORT OF

ON the freeway south of Park City, the traffic slowed and th
lanes congested. Since the enthusiastic welcome of the Pistol Dom
to town, things had deteriorated, and the city council of Clyde
Texas, lacked the political savvy or clout to convince a majorit
of voters to pass bond issues necessary to build the exits to g
the high-volume traffic off the eight-lane freeway into Clyde an
the Pistol Dome.

The construction costs and interest rates were astronomica
and the public learned the price of the tax-free deal Dick Conl
had negotiated for the dome.

Dick Conly could have handled the Clyde problems accordin
to the usual pro-growth formula. They were sheep and God mad
them to shear, but the shepherd, Dick Conly, the architect o
Clyde's healthy business climate, had moved to New Mexico.

So on Super Sunday the eight-lane freeway tried vainly t
funnel thousands of cars into Clyde through only two exits an
access roads.

"We'll never make the dome." Bob Travers shifted dow
"This'll be gridlocked in another hour."

"Do what you have to," Taylor said.

Bob nodded, hit the siren, cranked the wheel, pushed the ac
celerator to the floor and crossed three lanes of traffic.

The freeway cut through Chalk Mountain and the Pistol Dom
was behind Chalk Mountain, but the first exit was another mi
south. Bob figured they needed ninety to a hundred miles an ho
to climb the grade that would lead them, without a road, to th
dome.

"Grab the roll bar and hang on," Bob said calmly as the ca
launched itself into the air. The wide, billowing trail of chalk du
looked like rocket exhaust. There was some minor sideslippin
and a couple of bumps; otherwise it seemed a relatively simp
achievement.

Or so it appeared to the dozens of motorists who tried to follo
the white Ford up the hill.

It was a major catastrophe when measured in dollars. Eighty-
e cars were seriously damaged or totally destroyed.

The three people in the white Ford were too busy searching
r the quickest way to the underground entrance to the dome
rking lots, unaware of the mass destruction going on in their
ake.

The lots were jamming up with cars and buses and motor
mes. There were tailgate parties everywhere. Crazies and drunks
andered the parking lot yelling "Kill" or "We are number one."

The SSI guards were adding to the confusion because of their
familiarity with the stadium grounds. Even though SSI had the
owd and traffic control contract for the whole season, the Major's
gh rate of personnel turnover and his own inability to administer
e contract made every Sunday a Chinese fire drill.

Bob spotted the underground entrance that led right to the locker
om door, but cars, buses, RVs and souped-up pickups jammed
ery drive leading toward the players' entrance.

"Miss Chandler, if you don't mind, I believe I am going to
ive to tear up some more real estate," Bob said. "Personally I
n't think either of you should try to walk through those parking
ts."

"Let's go," Wendy said. "That's why God created insurance
mpanies."

"Yes, ma'am." The expert escape driver downshifted and crept
owly toward a four-lane, two-way boulevard leading straight
ward the entrance. The median was about twenty feet wide,
anted with two rows of young pecan trees. A white clapboard
ard shack commanded entry to the boulevard.

All the traffic lanes were gridlocked.

The people were leaving their cars, wandering around with
inks in their hands. Four Mercedes stretch limos full of Arabs
d Houston lawyers were surrounded by bodyguards in Hong
ong suits carrying Israeli submachine guns.

The SSI guards had lowered the gates to the boulevard. A fat
an in an ill-fitting uniform and reflector glasses began shaking
s head and waving Bob away. A cheap .38 in a cheaper leather
olster flapped at his hip. He had bought the whole outfit from
e major on time.

"Move it, mister; nobody comes in here."

"I can see that," Bob said, "but I wanted to ask you how I'm
ping to be able to get to the players' entrance? It's straight down
ere."

"Hey, that's your problem. Don't tell me your sad story."

"Well"—Bob continued talking while his eyes studied the gua
shack and the layout of the median and the brand-new pec:
trees—"I have Taylor Rusk in here, and if I don't get him i
side . . ."

"Taylor Rusk, huh?" The fat guard looked into the back.

Taylor nodded at the rude, coarse man.

"Yeah, you're him all right, but it still don't cut no ice wi
me." He stepped back. "Get it out of here, pal," he smirked agai
"Besides, I bet a whole month's pay against you guys. Ain't ▪
way you'll beat Denver by sixteen points."

"It's guys like you that make me believe in God." Taylor look:
at the fat man who was trying to hold power. "A whole month
pay? I love it. You look like you could afford to miss some meals

"Wait a minute, buddy." The fat man moved toward the ca
"You can't talk to me like that."

"He didn't mean it, Officer," Bob interrupted, knowing t
guy loved being called officer. "We'll be moving on." Bob studi:
hard on the guard shack.

"Well, goddammit, git before I run you all in." He hooked
fat thumb on his gunbelt.

"Is there anybody in the guardhouse?" Bob pointed at the wood:
shack.

"Naw, the dumb son of a bitch I'm working with came in dru:
and is off trying to find a bathroom."

"You don't have a bathroom?"

"Or heat! Not a damn thing in there; they just set it down
the grass. Four walls and a desk. Now, get that goddam car ou
here."

"Thanks, you've been a great help." Bob put the Ford in ge:
Bob hit the gas and the car leaped forward. The fat man was t:
clumsy to move and fell over. Anticipating the fall, Bob swerv:
around the terrified scrambling fat man, drove right through t
guard shack and straight down the median, mowing down pec:
trees and dodging drunks who failed to hear the siren or see t
flashing lights.

At the Cyclone fence separating the stadium from the parki:
lot, the median stopped. The white Ford didn't, tearing throu:
the fence with amazing ease.

"I figured the Cobianco Brothers Construction Company wou
use subspec fence," Bob said, cranking the wheel to miss a corn
dog stand and three guys selling Super Bowl programs. Steeri:
toward the entrance to the locker rooms, Bob had to tear throu:

another fence. He shut off the siren and started to slow as they came around a curving runway.

"Oh, Jesus!" Bob said. "Look at this!"

Ahead was the network crew shooting coverage tape for use if the game was the yawner the point spread promised. The three personalities in front of the camera wore big cowboy hats on little heads. The talent—in network jargon—were making extemporaneous remarks written on giant cue cards.

"I can't stop," Bob said calmly.

"Hit the talent." Taylor wasn't even looking; he was watching off to the side into the parking lot, craning his neck back at a big Winnebago motor home. He thought he saw Lamar Jean Lukas laid out on a chaise longue. Taylor decided it couldn't be Lamar and turned back to see if Bob was steering for the talent.

Wendy's eyes were wide; her grip on Taylor's arm was pure-white knuckle. Bob was doing some fast calculating on the distance between the technicians and the talent.

Taylor had taken a quick look and figured it himself. "You got six inches to a foot to spare."

"They haven't seen us yet. If they do, they'll react. And if anybody moves, I lose my six inches and up go my insurance premiums." Bob hit the accelerator.

"Pour it on," Taylor agreed. "Go faster to get out of trouble."

The white car shot foward toward the crew.

Taylor heard the word *Hornung* or *horny* as the white Ford shot between the camera and sound crews and the talent with eight inches to spare, two on the driver's side, six on the other.

Bob pumped the brakes hard, downshifted, setting the car up into a drift, then slammed the accelerator to the floor. The tires screamed and smoked, biting into the concrete, plunging the car straight down the ramp. A crash dive beneath the stadium.

Taylor could still smell the burnt rubber as Bob pulled up next to the locker room door.

"Leave it here a minute," Taylor said. "The bus with the rest of the team isn't scheduled to leave for another thirty minutes. Wendy, you're going to have to find them a helicopter. I'll call Red."

"I have more helicopters than I have cars." She stalked into the Pistols' locker room and on through to Red's private suite.

"You better get one for Denver too," Taylor suggested. "But try and find them an ex-Air Mobil pilot from Vietnam who's been crop dusting and drinking ever since."

Wendy arranged for off-shore crew helicopters from Chandler Well Services. The Pistols got a civilian pilot who was a Baptist deacon with a wife and five kids. Denver got a twice-divorced ex-MEDEVAC pilot who had three tours in Vietnam and was still carrying shrapnel in his back. He loved to fly under power lines and bridges. His hangover was killing him but he promised to deliver. Wendy told him to be certain he gave the Denver players a demonstration.

The choppers brought the teams. The ex-MEDEVAC pilot had so enjoyed the Denver players' screams when he dove under the Chalk Mountain Overpass that he couldn't resist a little joke at the end. Hovering at about fifteen hundred feet, checking the markings on the makeshift landing pad, he suddenly cut the motors. The giant helicopter dropped like a stone, as he screamed. "We're all gonna die!"

Then he back-rotored the big chopper and gently delivered the Denver team—safe if not completely sound.

THE HALF STEP

THE game was the easy part, as Taylor had imagined and Red had planned.

Everybody knew their steps and angles.

Only Texas's young offensive linemen made any mistakes, failing to pick up a couple of pass-rush stunts. But Speedo and Danny Lewis made uncanny route adjustments and caught balls thrown early under pressure, while Amos Burns and Ox Wood often blocked two pass rushers at once, knocking them into each other like billiard balls.

Denver sprung no big surprises, and the Pistols' defense did not give up a first down until the second half.

Red Kilroy's game plan had been well thought out. It was basic, solid and well constructed, depending on execution and superior personnel plus tricks and brand-new wrinkles. The Pistols were the better team and continued doing what they had done best all year. Plus, *they gambled.* From the Pistols' opening onside kickoff, which they successfully recovered, Texas pulled trick plays. Taylor gambled all day. Favored by sixteen points, he had to gamble or die.

Taylor read coverage quickly and correctly, his teammates did the same and together they made the necessary adjustments, continually confounding Denver's defense.

"We've got the half step on them," Speedo Smith said early in the game. "I can feel it. I can hear their brains clankin'. They're already guessing."

"There is no man in football can outguess me," Taylor said, "'cause I just change my mind on the spot. Speedo, I'll want overdrive." The quarterback asked, "Can you give me some?"

"I got whatever you need. I'm held back only by your lack of faith. You name it, I can do it."

Taylor hit Speedo on a first-down fly route. The cornerman guessed wrong and stopped dead at twelve yards, expecting a breaking route. Speedo flashed by him and the back was so shocked, he just stood there watching the play go for seventy-six yards. The ball was in the air less than twenty-five. Taylor let it go as soon as he saw the cornerback set up, expecting a break. The ball was less than ten yards away, coming down on the money, when Speedo looked. He grabbed it and ran with an easy grace and speed that had never been seen in professional football before and would probably never be seen again.

Taylor stood in the pocket and watched in awe long after he had released the ball.

Speedo's next touchdown was spectacular, but only Taylor understood his receiver's astounding athletic skill. Speedo beat a double coverage and broke open up the middle, running straight away with two backs in pursuit. The free safety was dropping straight and deep and Taylor put too much on the throw, making certain the free safety didn't get to the ball. Taylor knew he had overthrown badly. He was starting to cuss himself when suddenly Speedo put his stride into the overdrive Taylor had never seen before the Washington game.

Overtaking the ball, leaving the defenders in the dust, as promised, Speedo had done the impossible.

To everyone but Taylor Rusk the play seemed perfectly timed.

Taylor found Speedo on the bench, heaving oxygen into his lungs, his face twisted in pain.

"You okay?" the quarterback asked.

Speedo nodded, his chest heaving, rolling his head back in agony. He could not speak yet.

"What's the matter?" Taylor began to look for a trainer, certain that his best receiver was injured. Speedo grabbed his arm with small, strong hands and held Taylor there on the bench while he continued to gasp and writhe in pain. Finally he began to breathe easier and released his grip.

"You all right, Speedo?"

"Sure, man," he gasped, "it just *hurts* to run *that fast*."

"That was faster than Washington. I figured I had overthrown by twenty yards."

"You did." He pointed at his powerful legs. "These babies don't lie."

"I am the only person in this stadium that knows it was impossible to run under that ball." Taylor shook his head. "Nobody is that fast."

"You *can't* overthrow me."

"I've overthrown you lots of times."

"Not today, turkey." Speedo's breathing eased, but pain still creased his face. "Not today . . . so put it up as far as you can and relax"—Speedo closed his mouth; his nostrils flared to allow more air to his lungs—" 'cause you're throwing to The Fastest Nigger Ever!"

Speedo Smith's third touchdown reception came on a third and four quick out. As Taylor took the snap, the outside linebacker turned and ran straight for Speedo. The halfback laid off, depending on the linebacker for the short route. The weak safety started moving up to take the short inside. It was a peculiar defense but instead of coming off to an alternate, Taylor just dropped the ball over the linebacker to Speedo up against the sideline.

The quarterback would have been satisfied with the five yards and a first down. They had Speedo tripled against the sideline surrounded with no place to go. But instead of just stepping out of bounds, Speedo ran straight back at the linebacker, who made the mistake of trying to tear the small receiver apart instead of just grabbing him. Speedo ducked, cut upfield past the weak safety in the same movement and was running free.

"We got the half step," he yelled back at the Denver defense strung out behind him.

Taylor threw eight touchdown passes in that Super Bowl, a record almost certain never to be broken.

He threw five to Speedo Smith, one to Screaming Danny Lewis and two more to his backs.

Taylor gambled constantly. The fourth touchdown pass to Speedo

me on a third and one on Texas's twelve-yard line. A dive fake
Amos Burns and a naked bootleg gave Speedo time to get
ehind everybody for an eighty-eight-yard TD. Speedo's fifth
ouchdown came on the first play after middle linebacker Margene
rinkley had knocked a Denver back loose from the ball, re-
overing it on the Pistols' two. Taylor then caught Denver blitzing
nd flipped the ball to the hole in the short secondary where
peedo's sting adjustment would put him. Speedo wasn't there
et, but Taylor knew he would be, and the blitzing Denver line-
acker was grabbing the quarterback already. Taylor never saw
hat happened, the Denver defense buried him. Speedo scored,
e could hear it.

Red Kilroy outcoached Denver in every stage of pregame prep-
ration. During the game Red, of course, lost his mind and spent
our quarters looking for it. He ranted and raved on the sidelines,
uggesting plays years removed from the playbook. He even called
ut defenses from college.

All day long he called Ox Wood "my man Bluto" and twice
e called for Bobby Hendrix to get in the game and "run some
hort stuff across the middle—make those linebackers stay loose."

As usual, nobody listened.

EVENING
OUT THE ODDS

r became painfully apparent early in the game that Red Kilroy's
romise to Suzy Chandler and A. D. Koster to throw the Super
owl game was as ephemeral as the promises he made recruiting
ighteen-year-old blue chippers for the University.

Suzy and A.D. had been fed bad dope.

The promise of five percent of the Franchise failed to sway
ed, and by halftime the Pistols had a thirty-six to seven lead.
enver would never get closer.

The Pistols' game plan that Red had passed through Suzy and
.D. to the Denver coach was fraudulent. It only confused Den-
er's preparation and confounded them during the game.

By the middle of the second quarter Don Cobianco was con-
inced he had been betrayed. By whom he did not know yet.

It was a fix, Cobianco was certain. He was partially right.

He never saw the magic. Nobody does, except the magician

As the game progressed he was more and more certain th Dick Conly was involved. When Conly had placed his huge bet Cobianco had laughed to himself and made jokes to his brothe about the senile old fart who had been outsmarted by a carho Don was happy to book the enormous bet.

"No fool like an old fool."

R. D. Locke, the Denver cornerback, fell down on a simp set-backfield up route and Danny Lewis had six points. Then, third and goal from the five, Locke was called for interferenc bumping Amos Burns in the end zone with the ball in the air.

After Denver's first score there was a late flag and the sco was nullified. Denver's right guard was called for holding. La the films showed Denver's right guard was the only man in t line who *wasn't* holding. Denver cut him the next year anywa explaining that his early penalty was the turning point of the gam

The official picked up his flag and stuffed it into his hip pock He loved football. In high school they were winners. Distri champs. He had played running back for an unknown coach nam Kilroy.

Red Kilroy had co-conspirators everywhere; he'd spent yea placing them. Red and Dick Conly understood the game: build winning system, infiltrate the entire game, dictate the rules, t regulations, the winners, the losers and the television schedul fine-tune the show, the team, the circus, the spectacle, the ganization, the system. Control the delivery *and* the content.

Starting the second half, the Denver quarterback threw thr interceptions in a row, and by game's end had tossed five. Tv were on purpose. The old fool Dick Conly had protected his t by purchasing $200,000 worth of the quarterback's markers fro an Atlantic City casino. Conly paid fifty cents on the dollar a Denver's quarterback came as a bonus. Conly got one more bonu The Man from New Orleans made him an offer he couldn't refus The Man would, for twenty-five percent, make certain the C bianco brothers paid Dick Conly his winnings.

Cutting up money. And people.

Word of the Denver quarterback's problem had come to Di Conly from J. Edgar Jones, Investico's ex-agent and professio snitch. Gathering information and misinforming the players abc drugs and gamblers, J. Edgar spent off-seasons dealing the pri ileged intelligence to the high bidder. Actuely aware of the val and power of information, he traded it constantly without restra

r concern. All it cost him in the end was his kneecap and his
.b. He was one of the lucky ones.

By the close of the third quarter, Donald Cobianco realized the
normity of the fix. Dick Conly was still a man to fear. Donald
.. learned the lesson too late: Dick Conly would always be a man
to fear.

The Denver quarterback threw his fourth interception—this
.ne an accident. On the first play of Pistols' possession, Taylor
usk hit Amos Burns sneaking down the sideline for a touchdown.

It was play action. Speedo Smith, in motion, faked an end
round. Amos dived into the line, losing himself in the tangle of
.odies, then snuck out to the area just vacated by the Denver backs
.hasing Speedo and screaming, "Reverse! Reverse!"

Taylor took the snap, faked Amos into the line, held the ball
gainst his stomach, faked the pitch to Speedo racing deep through
.e backfield, then drifted slowly away from the line, his back to
.e action. The play was timing and counting steps. Taylor never
.oked downfield until he threw the ball. Planting his right foot
.n his fifth step, Taylor turned, found Amos where he expected
.nd threw the ball. Burns never broke stride. The ball spiraled
.own, landing light as a feather with the laces up.

Donald Cobianco fell back in his luxury-box chair and began
.o gag and choke in fury. "Goddam nigger!" were the only words
.e could get out. His face turned bright red.

"Well, that's it," he said finally, after choking and coughing.
.e mopped the sweat off his forehead, face and neck. "What the
.ck else could possibly go wrong?" Mr. C. was not expecting
.n answer.

Roger Cobianco reluctantly put down the telephone installed
.ext to his chair. "Kimball Adams disappeared with our share of
.e Super Bowl excursion money. He didn't catch his flight out
.f New York. He never checked into his hotel room and he was
.ue here before the half."

"Goddam! Motherfucking cocksucking jockstrap assholes!" The
.lder brother turned completely purple. His screaming could be
.eard clear across the Pistol Dome.

"It could be he got caught in that god-awful traffic," Johnny
.ied to placate his brother. He was terrified by his rage.

"The traffic jam don't go all the way to New York," Roger
.aid quietly, warning his brother with his eyes to just shut up and
.t still. Big brother was in a killing rage.

Tiny Walton sat at a back table and played double solitaire.

— 509 —

"He had six thousand tickets plus our split on the hotel room we block-booked." Don turned from purple to white, looking suddenly exhausted and old. He knew he had to regain control. His situation was deteriorating with every second and he needed to be alert. "Almost four million dollars."

"We'll find him, Don," Roger said.

Tiny Walton smiled his mean little smile. He loved to see big operators get outsmarted, played for the fool. A sucker in a hand-made suit. Soon they would have to ask him to solve their problem. All their big-time schemes and dreams reduced to nothing, ash and smoke. Then Tiny would be asked to do a favor. *Man's work, bloody business.* All the rest was as phony as the Pistol turf. They should have let him kill Taylor Rusk in the first place, but they had been scared that all the "suckers" would quit betting on the Pistols with the Franchise blown in half. They should have been so lucky.

"I should have known when the Man from New Orleans asked to lay off *his* book," Don snorted. "A favor, he says ... too much coming in on the Pistols in spite of the spread. He likes to keep his book balanced. A favor, he says. I tell you, one day I'll return the favor. Maybe you'll return it for me, Tiny?"

The killer nodded and played a red queen on a black king. *A cold day in hell is when I try to clip the Man from New Orleans,* Tiny thought.

"Why did they pick on me?" Cobianco complained in a whine. "It ain't fair, big guys picking on little guys. It just ain't fair." Donald rocked and swung in his heavy reinforced chair. He was thinking, scheming desperately. Tiny peeked at the cards left face down and waited. It wouldn't be long now. The genius brothers were almost out of options; if Donald didn't make up his mind quickly, they would be completely out.

"Tiny," Don said, still rocking his chair, "you better go down and pick up our share from Suzy Chandler and that asshole Koster."

Tiny nodded and played another card. There would be further instructions.

"You might as well get their share too."

Tiny nodded, slowly lay down his cards and reached for the small leather fleece-lined bag.

"And dissolve the partnership."

Tiny never changed pace, unzipping the bag and removing the blue long-barreled military-style automatic pistol, working the action and checking for lint or dirt, anything that might cause it to jam. He left the breech open and looked down the barrel, making sure it was clear. He unfastened a side pocket on the zipper bag and pulled out two ten-shot clips, checking the spring tension and their fit in the gun. From his coat pocket he removed a small box and slid it open to reveal forty rounds of .22 caliber hollow-point bullets. He carefully loaded ten rounds in each clip, sliding one into his pocket and the other in the gun, depressing the slide lock with his thumb. The breechblock slammed home, stripping a shell from the magazine and seating it in the barrel.

Tiny glanced at the idiot brothers, jammed the automatic into his belt, closed his jacket and walked out.

He followed the purple and white curving hallway to the door of Suzy Chandler's luxury skybox. The door was unlocked. He slipped quietly inside and turned the lock. Sitting alone, abandoned, behind the one-way glass, A.D. and Suzy never heard him enter.

Tiny looked around the skybox. Everything was made out of animal parts; the walls, floors, ceiling. Skins, horns, hooves, heads, teeth. Suzy had designed it with help from a Dallas fag who had something against animals. The luxury box made Tiny's skin crawl. He liked animals.

Two briefcases sat on the chair next to A.D. They were made out of alligator skin.

Suzy Ballard Chandler and A. D. Koster, both drunk on twenty-five-year-old private-label Scotch, had come a long way from the Sonic Drive-In. They'd come too far too fast and were too drunk to understand how badly things had gone wrong. There was to be no second chance. And it wasn't even their fault, only their misfortune.

"I come for the money," Tiny said.

Suzy twisted quickly in her seat at the sound of Tiny's voice, but A.D. stayed slumped in his seat. The sight of Tiny's face sobered Suzy considerably and she tugged at A.D.'s shoulder.

"It's Tiny." She kept jerking at her general manager's shirt. "He wants the money." Her eyes grew wide with fright. "It's Tiny for the money," she repeated.

"So tell him to pick a bag." A.D. pushed her hand away. "I'm watching the game."

"I want both bags,".Tiny said flatly.

"Now just a goddam minute." A.D. whirled around; Tiny had gotten his attention.

"The deal was..." A.D. focused abruptly when the automatic with the Dallas-made silencer appeared in Tiny's hand.

"The deal's changed. The partnership is dissolved."

"You won't get away with this. . . ." A.D. stopped when he realized how many times he had heard those lines on television.

"Let him take the money," Suzy pleaded.

"Jesus." A.D. grimaced and shook his head. "After all the shit, this is all? One fucking Super Sunday in a luxury box."

"Yep." Tiny nodded. "You wanna watch or . . ."

"Let him have the money, A.D.," Suzy kept repeating. "Let him . . ."

"It isn't just money he's here for."

"What else is there?" Suzy looked from A.D. to Tiny. The two men looked at each other.

"The insurance. The sixteen million dollars in policies we signed to get the loan from Cobianco."

"Yeah, honey, but that's just if we . . ." Suzy realized as she spoke, the word frozen on her lips.

"No options?" A.D. asked.

Tiny shook his head. "You wanna be first? Or do you wanna watch?"

Suzy's breathing became labored, her eyes went wild, the beautiful young face contorted in terror. She looked desperately at A.D. to do something.

"Here, honey." A.D. handed her the bottle of Scotch. "Don't worry. Have a couple of drinks while Tiny and I discuss this."

She took the bottle in her tiny trembling hands and held it to her lips. Her eyes closed involuntarily, as they did whenever she drank.

A.D. looked up at the shooter and nodded toward her.

Tiny put three slugs in her delicate ear before she took one sip. Suzy dropped the bottle and looked in shock at A.D. Blood spurted from her ear. She thought he had slapped her and confusion spilled from her eyes across the beautiful, treacherous face. Parting her soft lips in an attempt to speak, only a mewing sound escaped. Suzy slid to the floor.

A.D. faced Tiny with a cold stare of hate that unnerved the killer slightly.

"Come on, you fat pig. Kill me. The sooner I'm dead, the sooner I can start back after you." A.D. glared down the muzzle of the pistol. "I won't close my eyes. I won't even blink."

Tiny felt the slightest twinge of awe, then pulled the trigger.

A.D. took five forty-grain slugs in the forehead and cheek. He never moved; his eyes stayed open. Tiny started to shoot him again when Suzy twitched on the floor and he put the other slugs in the back of her head. Her body convulsed in the ever-widening pool of blood.

A.D. was still erect, staring at Tiny. He was dead where he sat, but his eyes never closed. Tiny slipped a new magazine into the pistol, picked up the empty shells and grabbed the two briefcases. At the door he looked back. A. D. Koster still sat there, staring furiously at him with cold, dead eyes.

Tiny was frightened by A.D.'s eyes. Dead eyes that watched him with hatred and promised revenge.

Tiny locked the skybox door and joined the brothers at the insiders' private elevator. He rode down with them.

"Tomorrow," said Don, "American Imperial Insurance Company is going to have the Prudential's whole rock dropped on them. They're the reinsurers on the sixteen million dollars in policies we took out on A.D. and Suzy."

"You think they'll pay?" The elevator hummed, descending slowly.

"Let 'em try and get out of it." Don clamped his jaws on the cigar stub and chewed violently. "They'll take a long time paying, but they'll have to eventually."

"We'll get Kimball Adams. I'll call New York tonight." Tiny looked up at the ceiling. "We'll have that money by Tuesday."

Don listened and didn't care. He had enormous bets to cover with very dangerous people.

"We lost serious money today," Don said as the elevator continued its descent. "We got to figure out who else to squeeze to pay Dick Conly."

Don Cobianco frowned. He hated to lose. It was going to cost him more than money. It was going to cost him respect, and that could be fatal.

"Fucking Dick Conly," Donald C. complained. "No goddam decency. This country would be in one hell of a fix if we was all like Dick Conly." Don paused. "I guess we better make some sort of deal."

"Tell Conly to go fuck himself," Johnny said. He maintained his imaginary nerve. "What's he gonna do?"

"You tell him," Don said to Roger, despairing of his baby brother.

"Johnny"—Roger's tone was friendly but patronizing—"what would you do if some real tough son of a bitch owed *you* millions and refused to pay?"

Johnny grinned. "I'd get a *tougher* son of a bitch to go collect for a percentage."

"You think Dick Conly is smart enough to figure that?" Roger said. "There's some real tough sons-a-bitches in Dallas and Houston. Besides, we took other bets. Kansas City. San Antonio laid off Pistol bets on us."

"So did one very bad boy from New Orleans," Tiny added. He should know. He often did wet work as a favor to the Man.

Don furrowed his brow. Where would he get more money? Who could they squeeze? It would be months, maybe years, before Prudential paid off. Conly wouldn't wait. Neither would KC nor New Orleans. Not long. Don didn't have the money.

"*You mean* . . . ?" Johnny looked shocked. "Well . . . but . . . they . . . ? You? You wouldn't help *him* against *us*?" Johnny looked from face to face in the sinking elevator. His own face sagged in despair. There was no Santa Claus nor honor among thieves. It *was* every man for himself.

The elevator stopped on the ground level.

"Well, we got a little time." Don was upbeat. "I think we may have to squeeze that prick that gave us the sixteen million. I was hoping to save him until he got hold of the big money, but . . ."

The sun was gone, and the eerie flat glow of the Mercury vapor lights reminded Lamar Jean Lukas of star shells when the elevator door shooshed elegantly open, delivering the Cobiancos and Tiny to the Insiders' parking lot.

Johnny's disappointment with crime became moot and Don was wrong about time.

Lamar had some due bills of his own to collect.

FREE MOVIES

It was the middle of the fourth quarter when the fire broke out in the end zone seats.

It was a small fire. Few noticed, nobody left and the only person to panic was the girl who was set afire by the people free-basing cocaine in the seats behind her. The peanut vendor had knocked over the ether bottle.

The people around her cheerfully ripped the burning clothes from the flaming girl and threw beer and soft drinks on her head to quench the fire in her hair. One man, claiming he was a smoke nper, kept throwing lighted matches on her naked body. He d he was trying to start a backfire.

The referee called a $500,000 time-out for TV commercials.

"Take a break and sit down," Taylor said in the huddle. He sn't certain why the official time-out had been called, the girl rned clean, without much smoke. "It's in the bag, boys, just down and suck it up. Enjoy the win. We couldn't lose now if t Red start calling the plays."

"Don't go talking crazy." Amos Burns spoke his first complete tence of the game. Mostly he communicated with nods and ints.

Ignoring Red Kilroy's frantic signals to come to the sidelines, ylor pulled off his headgear and stepped away from his teamtes. For the first time since stepping on the field, he looked o the Pistol Dome Super Bowl crowd. Until then he hadn't red look. Like always he had played the game from within nself. The audience was a distant noise, which, if really heard, uld draw him from his concentration, wake him from the dream it he had spent so much time and effort creating: his angels, vils and delusions.

The quarterback looked up into the bellowing inverted monr's mouthful of people, the animal roar vibrated his skeleton. s nostrils flared as he drew deep drafts of air, controlling the nic and continuing to watch those who watched him. His shiny es were black, the pupils so dilated that the thin brown rim was perceptible.

Running on pure adrenaline, concentration and imagination for arly four quarters, he had danced on the edge of the void. One sstep and he would fall forever into the deep dark hole overhead d all around. If he fell, it would be *up* into the mouth of the ast to be devoured and forgotten, a tasty morsel fed to the void.

He could never create enough. The fan could chew, taste and allow, but he remained forever empty, hungry. Hungrier. Who re these people, arriving empty to be force-fed, to gorge themves for hours on the spectacle and leave emptier than when they ived?

Fans in a feeding frenzy. It was a frightening vision and his art began to hammer. His mouth went dry; he choked back the ter taste of fear and the urge to run for the tunnel. If he broke d ran, they would smell blood, and blood was what they wanted. *What if I had failed*, he thought. *Would they have devoured* ? The roar continued, momentarily seemed to increase, then led. The crowd was still screaming for more, but he was re-

gaining control, even if they weren't. He pulled on his headgear
What if you can't? Wendy had asked. *But I can* was his reply
Few understood.

He wouldn't quit. He hadn't failed. They had won the Super
Bowl. The crowd had gorged itself the whole game. He'd kep
their plates piled high with something created out of nothing.

Loaves and fish.

He was their messiah.

But now he was leaving.

Before the crucifixion.

ALMOST ABOUT
THE SAME

THE handlers brought out the Dobermans with about two minute
left in the game. They stood five yards apart, completely aroun
the field. Another group of them formed a double phalanx leadin
to the locker rooms.

Denver had possession and was still vainly putting up an a
battle, throwing outs and ups, always angling for the sidelin
trying to kill the clock.

Sensing that their time was also running out, the crowd bega
its own two-minute drill. Brushfire wars between bands of drun
broke out in the upper deck. Seat cushions, rolls of toilet pape
bottles, cans, red-hot coins, sailed out of the stands. The playe
on the sidelines put their headgear back on. A dead calico c
flung out of a luxury box hit a Pistolette in the back, knockin
her unconscious.

"What the hell?" Ox Wood turned to Taylor when he saw th
dead cat fly through the air and knock the full-breasted brune
flat on her face. "Why would anybody do something that sick"

"Maybe it's tax deductible."

Two men jumped onto the field and started to run for the Pistol
bench. One carried a gun in his hand. The dogs had both men
seconds. The gun turned out to be an official Texas Pistols pist
made of purple plastic.

It was at that point that Taylor Jefferson Rusk began to si
toward the double row of dogs that led to the locker rooms. H

ked slowly with apparent unconcern but in dead earnest and a
ight line. He had just reached the dogs when someone in the
wd lit a Roman candle and began launching fireballs at the
d linesman. Keeping his head down, protecting his eyes, Taylor
eded up his walk and broke into a jog. Something clanged off
headgear. It was a Grapette bottle, but he didn't slow up.

As he ducked through the door into the tunnel, he thought he
rd gunfire or firecrackers. He slowed to a walk and was im-
diately accosted by the network girl.

"Say"—she pressed what looked like a hearing aid into her
—"you owe me an interview. Red Kilroy promised that you
uld talk to us before the game."

"Oh, yeah." Taylor smiled politely and kept moving toward
locker room. "I drove right past you before the game and you
er said a thing."

"When was that?" She looked puzzled, then suddenly cocked
head and pressed the small earphone farther into her auditory
al. "*What*? I can't hear you."

Taylor kept moving and she walked along, yelling to the di-
tor in the truck.

"*What*? I can't . . . oh . . . oh, all right. . . . That's better. . . . I
him right here." She reached over and grabbed Taylor's arm,
if to prove what she was saying. "No, I don't know where the
w went. . . . The sound man got hit in the eye with a hot
ie. . . . *What*? . . . I can't. . . . Okay. . . . Okay, you're coming back
d and clear. Are you sure there's a camera? . . . I'll ask him."
e turned to Taylor. "There's a camera set up in your locker
•m. Could we do a quick interview right away? They've had
stop the game and clear the field of chickens."

"Chickens?" Taylor tried to sound unsurprised. "How many
ckens?"

"How many chickens?" She repeated the question into her
crophone, then tilted her head, waiting for an answer. She
dded her head several times and listened. She looked back at
ylor. "*Lots* of chickens."

"How long will it take?"

"Not long. I just have a couple questions."

"I mean, how long to clear off the chickens?"

"How long to clear off the chickens?" she yelled into the mi-
phone. She waited a moment, then her head snapped up. "There's
reason to use that kind of language. *He* wanted to know, so I
ed you." She listened but looked up at Taylor and rolled her
es.

— 517 —

They were rapidly approaching the locker room.

"We're at the Pistols' dressing room now," she said into mike.

Taylor grimaced.

"*No kidding?*" She turned to Taylor, "The dogs have sta killing the chickens. They have to cut to something else quic She picked up her pace, her heels clicking on the concrete. ' want to ask you about the strike that Terry Dudley mentioned then of course all about the drug situation."

They reached the Pistols' locker room door.

"Well, first, it wasn't a strike at all, the pitch was low outside." Taylor opened the door for the broadcaster and let walk into the dressing room. "And you'll have to get your c drugs." He closed the door, continued down the hall and aro the corner and ducked into Red Kilroy's private suite.

When the network girl looked around, she was alone in locker room with a camera crew and two boys whose job wa: pick up jocks, socks, dirty clothes and old tape.

It was almost about the same.

Once inside Red's private suite, Taylor locked the door fr the inside and turned on the television. The game had not en yet, although the dogs had just about cleaned up the chickens

The network girl was on the screen in the empty Pistols' loc room.

"I had Taylor Rusk, the Pistols' sensational quarterback, v me just a moment ago."

It sounded to Taylor like something from the *Park City H Yearbook*.

"I'm certain he'll be right back." She pressed her fing in her ear. "Unofficially we have him passing for over six h dred yards, which is certainly a new Super Bowl record. He he . . ." Someone was talking into her earphone and confound her. ". . . threw for a touchdown eight times. . . . I mean . . threw for eight touchdowns, not the same touchdown ei times. . . ." She snorted a giggle. "But of course you know . . . w any . . ." She pressed against the earphone again. "*What*? . . right. . . ." She looked back into the camera. "Play is resum with fifty-eight seconds on the clock and we are returning to field." She held her smile until the director cut to the midfi action camera.

Denver still had the ball and was running plays withou huddle. They had no time-outs left. Feathers coated the field :

wirled in the air like snow, a blizzard of down and fluff. The layers were coated, covered from head to toe with plumage, and occasionally a surviving chicken would dash across the screen.

"Well, I tell you, Pat," the announcer said, "it's been a long ime since we've seen a game like this."

"You can say that again," the color man replied.

"There have been others?" Taylor asked the television as he ndressed, pulling his jersey over his head. He unsnapped his houlder pads and the flak jacket he had had custom-made after watching one quarterback play in Houston without a rib cage. He ot booed and generally publicly humiliated for his trouble. Near he end of his time, the quarterback was taking twenty-four Xyocaine shots a game in the ribs and finally had his lung punctured. le gurgled a little but that's all.

"Well, you've got to give this Denver bunch credit," the television droned. Taylor looked up to see a close-up of Denver's quarterback picking feathers off his lip. "They haven't given up." The camera angle changed to a shot down the line of scrimmage. Half a chicken lay next to the tight end.

Taylor unlaced his shoes and kicked them off, then rolled down is knee socks and took them off simultaneously with his sweat ocks, unbuckled his purple belt, and unzipped his satin pants, tepped out of them and pulled off his sweat-soaked T-shirt and ock.

Standing naked in the middle of the room, digging his bare eet into Red's deep plush carpet, he watched the blizzard of infeathers and plume continue unabated on the television.

"It sure looks cold down there, Pat."

"Well, maybe that will satisfy Ox," Taylor looked around the elaborate, elegantly appointed room that Red Kilroy demanded as he head coach. "Red, you always had style and you could always pend other people's money. I guess that's what Dick Conly liked bout you." Taylor looked back at the television: the whirling eathers *did* make it look cold. "Turn up the air-conditioning, naybe Ox could lose a toe."

Taylor turned off the television. He didn't want to know. He idn't care. It was over. The high-speed ride had taken a large art of his life, gone in a split second.

"Warp factor eight Mr. Chekov. It has been a long, strange rip," Taylor continued talking to himself. "I would probably do t again, but I will *not* do it *anymore*."

The locker room would be chaos for at least two hours after he game ended. The network insisted that the hour-long postgame

show originate from the locker room of the winning team, whic
would add to the length and intensity of the postgame madnes
Taylor Jefferson Rusk saw no reason to participate any longer.

He was finished. He had delivered. It was over. There woul
be no more.

The dirty, sweaty, smelly, naked quarterback walked ginger
to the purple refrigerator; his feet were always sore after a gam
on artificial turf. The softness of Red's expensive carpeting mi
igated the tenderness.

Opening the door and grabbing a quart bottle of Red's privat
stock of well water, Taylor took a long drink. Standing by the ope
door of the refrigerator, Taylor felt a slight chill. The sweat wa
drying on his skinned and bruised body. He took another long drin
as he closed the door and walked to Red's closet, grabbing a swe
suit and towels and hobbling over to Red's big leather swivel chai
As he took a long gulping drink of the cold spring water, a shootin
pain blazed behind his eye right through the top of his head.

"Goddam, goddam, goddam." He pressed his hand into his ey
and fell forward against the desk. "Goddam, goddam." He ha
drunk the cold water too fast and was now paying the price. H
might also get sick as a dog; he did it all the time. The paralyzin
blinding pain finally passed and he raised his head and leane
back in Red's chair.

Taylor Rusk spent the next two and one-half hours alone an
quiet. For the first time since high school, he enjoyed the day'
victory without thought of tomorrow. Because it was *not* by th
next game that he would be judged. It was *this* game. His last.

Today.

Not tomorrow.

He did not have to pay the horrible price of living in the future
He rushed nothing into the past; he relished the moment, th
memory of today. He no longer dismissed his greatness or dwelle
on his mistakes, for there was nothing to prepare for. No future
he could think about the joy of the game just finished, the gam
just created. *Something from nothing*—and he was no longer re
quired to destroy the masterpiece in order to keep it from inte
fering with the next masterpiece. He was keeping this one. Thi
one was the last.

"*I am here now*. Finally." He smiled and drank the water
"Price paid and the privilege earned."

He sat there sipping water and easing his nervous system o
the adrenaline overload. The familiar depression set in, the au
tomatic fright, the built-in system that made certain he would b

ble to confront the horror of the void the next time and the next. The specter of the dreamless sleep, the melancholy that warned of relaxing, dropping too far, leaving him without the quickness of resource to create and recreate, spinning gold from straw, pulling elephants from headgear. Life in gear, the engine running, the clutch engaged. He had built his engine for speed. The fast track. No time for warm-up or tune-up, just hit the accelerator, pop the clutch, blow out the carbon and run and run and run.

Taylor Rusk had spent years developing the system that was his body and its component parts. Just as he knew how fast to run it without blowing up, he knew how slow to idle without shutting down completely, maybe never to start again. He wasn't even sure he *had* a starter: He had never shut completely down before. He had no idea what would happen.

There was only one way to find out.

And there in Red Kilroy's plush suite in the Pistol Dome, in a confusion of joy, melancholy, excitement, fear and exhaustion, Taylor Rusk, for the first time since he had left Two Oaks, shut himself down completely.

He felt it drain from him, the force, the hydraulics slipping away, losing the prime, certain he could never pump it up again. He fought panic as the pressure drained, then he felt peace. After the damage of a lifetime riding the clutch, waiting for the flag to drop, he let go completely, fully, shut down cold.

Taylor Jefferson Rusk leaned back and smiled, took himself down off the cross and put himself up on blocks.

THE TAILGATE PARTY

THE Colorado fans had decided to go inside the Pistol Dome forty-five minutes before kickoff. They filled several large military canteens with vodka and orange juice on a one-to-one basis: one bottle of vodka for every orange.

The man wanted his black cowboy hat returned, but Lamar said there was a state law against wearing hats inside domed stadiums. The man was disappointed; the fantasy of himself in the big black hat was a sustaining motive during the long drive down, but he reluctantly agreed that it would be unwieldy anyplace else but on his head. Lamar assured him that once he entered the dome, his head was the one place he would not be allowed to place his huge black hat.

The wife wanted to lock the Winnebago, but Lamar suggested they leave the van open and he would just sit right there and protect it and would not have to go off in search of a bathroom.

The Denver fans exchanged hesitant glances.

". . . but if you all would feel better locking her up, that's fine with me." Lamar began to remove the big lumberjack shirt they had loaned him, making certain they saw his SSI badge and got the full effect of the man in uniform.

"Oh, come on, honey," the man said. "If we can't trust Bobby Ray, here, who can we trust?"

"It's a fair question, ma'am," said Lamar Jean Lukas, a.k.a Bobby Ray Collins. "If you can't trust the law, who can you trust?"

The answer was nobody.

Lamar would let them learn that on their own. Besides, he wasn't going to steal anything, and if everything went according to plan, the Winnebago would be safe and sound.

Lamar watched the Colorado people weave toward the stadium and listened to the cacophony of the growing traffic jam that eventually turned the access roads, side streets and a large portion of the freeway into a parking lot.

Lamar Jean Lukas lay back on the chaise and studied the Insiders' lot, deciding on a simple plan of action.

The exit from the lot ran along the dome wall. When a car exited the lot, the driver was required to insert a special plastic card in the automatic gate opener. The theory was that having to use the card not only to get in but to get out doubly protected the wealthy and privileged. They could enjoy the game relieved of the constant worry that roving car-theft rings of Negroes, Mexicans, Cubans or Haitian boat people would make off with their limousines the moment their drivers went to piss or snort cocaine.

Paranoia was highly marketable.

When a car stopped at the exit gate and the driver opened his window to insert the card, the right side of the vehicle was no more than a foot from the dome wall, making it impossible to open the doors on that side. If at that moment for any reason anyone wanted to leave the car, they would have to use the door on the left side—either the driver's or rear passenger door.

And that led them toward Lamar.

After the game kickoff Lamar moved the card table to the back just beneath the awning that shaded the entire side of the van

cing the Insiders' lot exit, he put a green and white webbed
wn chair by the table. He picked up the purple duffel bag with
e cheap silkscreen on the side and stepped inside the Winnebago.
tting in the booth, which folded down into an exceptionally
comfortable bed, he placed the bag on a red table. Outside,
ople continued to arrive, walking from cars long abandoned.

Opening the bag, Lamar removed the surgical gloves, pulled
em on, then checked the contents he had so carefully prepared
rlier at Taylor's apartment.

The Super Bowl ticket from Tiny Walton lay elegantly oversize
top. The ducat was beautifully printed in four colors with the
ction row and seat numbers on the bottom. A schematic line
awing of the stadium was printed on the reverse side. Lamar
rned the ticket over in his hands, cherishing the feel of it, study-
g the design, remembering all that it would have meant to him
those years ago when he first became a Texas season ticket
lder. One of the very first and very few. The heavy coated paper
ade the colors shine, and Lamar considered the ticket a minor
ork of art.

"I'll be damned," he said softly when he checked the numbers
the bottom against the schematic on the back. "Fifty-yard-line
ats. Fifty-goddam-yard-line seats for a cheap thug killer."

Removing the gin bottles filled with the fifty-fifty mix of ker-
ene and gasoline, he carefully unwrapped the stolen toweling.
e tore the towel into strips, which he would use as wicks for the
olotov cocktails in the gin bottles.

Then he lifted out the rubber sleeves filled with the homemade
palm. Using gaffer's tape, he attached to the inner tubing the
memade fuses of gun and aluminum powder. Beneath each of
ese homemade fire packets Lamar slipped a cherry bomb, fas-
ning it with tape so that the bomb would explode *after* the
memade fuse had ignited the gelatinous mixture of soap paste,
soline and kerosene, hopefully blowing the burning gel over a
ider area—about the size of a stretch limousine.

Rummaging through the drawers, he found several T-shirts,
hich he tied off at the neck and sleeves, putting one bomb in
ch with the fuse exposed through a small hole punched in each
irt.

He kept one tube of napalm separate with no fuse.

He checked his pistol and the speed loaders, then checked the
all .22 rifle.

The railroad flares were his final backup in case none of his

homemade fuses or wicks worked and the timing was off on ▌
cherry bombs.

Near the end of the third quarter Lamar refilled his bag a▌
stepped out of the van, walked back to the card table and plac▌
the heavy bag beside the green and white webbed chair.

He sat and studied the grade at the Insiders' lot exit; it hac▌
slight downslope toward the dome wall, which meant if he fai▌
to hit the target with his Molotov cocktails, he should try a▌
throw short, allowing the flaming liquid to flow down under t▌
car. Then he took the single unfused sleeve of homemade napa▌
and walked over to the gate, laying it against the fence. The bla▌
rubber blended perfectly into the asphalt.

Back at the table, while he waited and watched the eleva▌
door, he taped the Super Bowl ticket to one of the gin bottles.▌
seemed like the best way to return it to Tiny.

Lamar was startled by a couple of false alarms as the end ▌
the game drew near and people began to exit the elevator that f▌
into the Insiders' lot.

When the Cobianco brothers and Tiny did step out into t▌
gathering night, Lamar Jean Lukas was calm and ready to perfor▌
He remained remarkably collected as he set out the contents ▌
the bag and prepared for Tiny and the Cobianco brothers' li▌
ousine to try to get out of the Insiders' lot.

He lit a long cigar and puffed up a large red coal at the en▌
Then he lay his lighter on the table and checked the wicks in t▌
gin bottles to make certain they were soaked. The T-shirts we▌
stacked on the table, next to his pistol, the speed loaders, t▌
railroad flares and the small .22 rifle. He still wore the surgic▌
gloves.

Except for the red spot of the glowing cigar, he was complete▌
hidden in the shadows of the awning.

He checked the area once more for people who might acc▌
dentally wander into the firefight and had the small firecracke▌
ready to toss at them to drive them off. There was no one arou▌
as the limousine's lights came on, and it wheeled out of its parki▌
place up to the gate.

Lamar picked up the small rifle and drew a bead on the driv▌
as he approached the automatic gate opener. His window humm▌
down and he shoved the car into park. When he leaned out ▌
push the plastic card into the small orange box, Lamar squeez▌
off two shots, hitting him below the left eye, scattering lead fra▌
ments through his sinuses and prefrontal lobe.

The small pops were lost in the sounds inside and outside t▌

r. The driver jumped slightly, dropped the card and sat back in
 seat. Johnny C., sitting beside him, never noticed; he was
oking and listening to the discussion in the back.

Lamar drew a bead on the rubber tube of jellied kerosene and
soline, blowing holes in it with the small .22 rounds. The gel
gan running slowly down the slope. He lay down the rifle and
cked up his lighter and one gin bottle. He lit the wick and tossed
underhand at the car. The bottle sailed through the air, bounced
f the leather top of the limo and failed to break, rolling onto
e trunk and catching in the bumper. The wick came loose and
nt out. Lamar quickly grabbed the second bottle and flicked
 lighter without success, getting only sparks.

Nobody in the car saw the first Molotov cocktail, but they
ard something bump the roof. When Johnny looked around, he
w the blood running down the driver's face.

"Son of a bitch! Donny," he cried, "look at Mort."

Lamar finally got the second wick lit and tossed the bottle hard
 the limousine, overthrowing and hitting the wall on the far side,
ning it into a sheet of flame. It wasn't what he wanted, but the
cklight from the flames outlined the occupants of the car clearly.
Johnny tried his door several times in panic before giving up
d trying to crawl out the window over the dead driver.

Lamar picked up a T-shirt and touched the exposed fuse to his
gar. It ignited, hissing and sputtering. He tossed it high, hoping
 attached firecracker would explode in the air; it didn't, and
 napalm-filled tube bounced harmlessly off the hood. He lit
d tossed a second before Johnny could complete his attempt to
wl out the window. It, too, failed to explode. Lamar reached
wn on the table for his combat .357, squeezing off one shot,
ting Johnny directly in the crown of his head and knocking him
ck into the passenger seat. Lamar grabbed and lit a third home-
de bomb, tossing it just as the rear passenger door opened and
ny dived out, carrying one of the alligator attaché cases filled
th A.D.'s money.

The gel-filled rubber tube bounced off the fat man's back di-
tly into Donald Cobianco's lap, where it exploded, blowing
ming gelatin all over the inside of the car.

Momentarily the other bombs began exploding and the car was
gulfed in flames, and Lamar watched the two brothers in the
ckseat screaming and flailing around hopelessly.

It always amazed Lamar how long it took to burn to death.

He pitched his remaining napalm and the railroad flares into
 inferno, calmly puffing his cigar, watching Tiny scramble away

with the bag in one hand, the other digging in his belt for [his]
pistol. Tiny had his pistol out and was heading straight for [the]
van, raising the gun, moving fast for a fat man. Lamar chew[ed]
his cigar and thought about the Captain. He got killed the nig[ht]
they were overrun in the highlands. That night, too, there h[ad]
been gunshots and explosions, fire and screams, terrifying a[nd]
glorious.

"All the heroes are dead," he told Lamar the day he joined [the]
outfit. "I need live soldiers and all the heroes are dead." T[he]
Captain said that and then went right on ahead and got hims[elf]
killed, trying to pull two guys out of a burning MEDEVAC cho[p]-
per. They were *his* men.

The whine of lead cut through the air fairly near Lamar Jea[n's]
head. The big fat guy was getting closer, firing his automa[tic]
pistol and carrying a satchel.

Everything began to slow down as Lamar concentrated on ki[ll]-
ing Tiny Walton. The napalm explosions no longer sounded, th[ey]
were just hot winds blowing. Lamar let the fat man get close, [he]
puffed his cigar and stayed calm. He had been in lots of the[se]
firefights. How many times you fired your weapon was meanir[g]-
less; what counted was how often you hit your target.

He heard the deadly song of lead as he waited on the fat ma[n]
who was tiring, his shots increasingly wild, off the mark.

Everything began turning red, as it did in those firefights [in]
the war, and then, as the fat man, gasping air, carrying the satc[hel]
and shooting, reached the point Lamar had chosen, Lamar poin[ted]
the heavy pistol and fired three quick rounds, placing the slu[gs]
within a 3-inch circle centered on the bridge of Tiny's nose.

After that the blackness rolled over Lamar Jean, as usual.

THE LAST ZEUGLODON

WHEN Taylor finally returned to the locker room, it was alm[ost]
empty. The game had been over more than two hours. The la[st]
of the television equipment was being hauled out. The two you[ng]
boys were picking up old tape and jockstraps and socks befo[re]
sweeping the carpet.

"Where you been, man?" Speedo Smith was checking hims[elf]
in the mirror one more time. A thin film of sweat covered [his]

mooth black forehead. "They was all looking for you to show your dick on television. I showed them mine instead."

"I was hiding in Red's whorehouse." Taylor sat in front of his locker and tossed all the gear he carried. "I am not *ever* wearing that shit again."

"Yeah. Everybody says that in January, but then when the eagle don't shit and April fifteenth comes round, they all come back." Speedo took a towel and blotted his face. "Everybody must have been off fucking. A.D. and Suzy Chandler didn't show up for the presentation. The commissioner gave the trophy to Red."

"I'll bet Red loved that." Taylor felt calm and relaxed, drained but buoyant. "Did he recite the Gettysburg Address as his thank-you and acceptance speech?"

"No. He just gol'danged and gee-whizzed his way through." Speedo laughed. "He kept calling Commissioner Burden 'Commissioner Gordon.'"

"*Batman's* Commissioner Gordon?" Taylor was too tired to smile.

"You got it," Speedo cackled. "The commissioner didn't like it. Ol' Robbie Burden was white as a sheet and shaking like a leaf. The man will have to get better to die."

Taylor stared into the bottom of his spacious, perfectly engineered locker filled with free shoes. Each day Jack the Equipment Man stacked his twelve pairs of different brands and colors. The shoe companies paid Jack to do it.

"Speedo, do you remember the mouse that lived in my locker that first year in Colony Stadium? He ate my chin strap, the earpieces and webbing inside my headgear. The mouse had a good life, ate good and got to hang around with pro football stars."

"It's too bad he couldn't be here today," Speedo mocked, "but he missed the bus."

"The mouse couldn't live here." Taylor was listening to the sound of the showers and smelling the antiseptic. "Too clean, neat, orderly..."

"Right, man, right," Speedo said. "We should have voted him a share...taken his ring size...a share along with D'Hanis and Hendrix."

Taylor nodded.

"Well, leader turkey, I gave it to you, the best game forever. No receiver will ever be as good as I was today, and only you know it." Speedo shook his head.

"No one else would believe it," Taylor sighed. "Thanks, Speedo...for everything."

Speedo pressed a dry towel to his face once more, checked himself in the full length mirror. The sign above the mirror said

REMEMBER, THE GUY LOOKING AT YOU
REPRESENTS THE PURPLE AND WHITE
PHILOSOPHY.
LOOK LIKE A TEXAS PISTOL.
BE PROUD.

"The purple and white philosophy," Taylor said. "How do you look like a Texas Pistol?"

"You do white," Speedo said, "I'll do purple." He walked out the door. The door sign said:

HAVE YOU FORGOTTEN ANYTHING? ZIP YOUR FLY.

Ox Wood came limping out of the training room, where he had spent over an hour with his knees packed in ice to keep down swelling. He did it after every game and most practices. The ancient body was worn out.

"You the last one in the training room?" Taylor watched him in the mirror by the exit door.

Ox nodded. "First one in, last one out. Where were you?"

"In Red's hideout, jacking myself off."

"I don't blame you. It was a circus here." He was still sweating and breathing hard. His face looked tired; dark half-moons lay beneath his eyes.

"You were great, Ox, you know that?" Taylor began recalling bits and pieces of what he had seen Ox do that day. "You always kept them out long enough. Without you and Amos picking up the slack for the young guys, it would have been a long day. That one touchdown of Speedo's had to take five seconds to get off. That's a long time. I saw you grab a lot of slack today. You played the whole game."

"First time this year. But it isn't as tough to pass-block, since the defense can't handslap and it's legal to hold. They still knocked you around today. I don't understand it. Those young kids are faster, smarter and stronger than me, but they lost their men. You got hit!"

"Not until too late. They kept them off me long enough, that's all that matters."

"That's all *they think* matters," Ox said. "But you know it's

— 528 —

ot. It's like they're doing a job, not protecting the quarterback. 'here's a difference—a big difference."

"They're young—" Taylor said.

"But they act old," Ox interrupted. "They don't understand bout duty, loyalty, pride, teammates. . . . They're your teammates nd they let you get hit. In the Old League you would have some oles in you, but because we win big, these young guys think ney played good enough. One good shot in the Old League and ou would be just a memory."

"This isn't the Old League," Taylor said. "Thank God."

"The name of the game is protect the quarterback, and those uys didn't protect you, they just did their jobs. The rules protected ou. And it is still the Old League, it's just a different game now. could still beat the shit out of someone if I got permission from ne referees, but I never know if I got it until *after* the play."

"New rules for new fans, Ox. We are on a constant search for udience . . . counted every fifteen minutes." Taylor felt his aches nd pains. "Today, for instance, the referees let them work me ver late, like they have all year. Then the commissioner checks ne Nielsen overnights. Change the rules and build ratings—or o current theory holds."

"The rules make new kinds of players too. You got hit a dozen mes today and these baby Nazis think they played great. Nice oys. Clean-cut, with a career rap for seminars and TV talk shows.")x unwrapped the towel from around his thick waist. "You should ave seen training camp in LA in 1968. The highway from Oxnard ooked like the Indy 500." Ox smiled. *"The rules? Fuck the rules. Ve broke all the rules. We fought the law.* That year three players rashed and burned trying to make curfew. A glorious death when ou consider Oxnard and the world in 1968.

"Fuck the rules, fight the law." Ox took his boxer shorts from is locker and pulled them on. He was sad. Dressing for the last me. "These young guys, the baby Nazis, got everything: size, peed, technique. The colleges are building right to spec, including naking them afraid to break the rules . . . putting rings in their oses. There are no longer any football players allowed without ose rings. Basic equipment. Fear of *the rules* comes in their gene ools. Not the law but *the rules*, the ones printed in the front of ne playbook. *These rules.* They don't even know about the law. Jnion law, contract law, entertainment law. They want to get long, not cause trouble. Be friends. Friends? Why the fuck do is if you can't break the rules?"

"Some people like to go through life in step." Taylor shrugged. "Christ, it's a team game. From goose liver to goose step."

"A man who has never broken a rule"—Ox was frustrated—"is a dangerous man. The baby Nazis are all hormones and motor functions."

"Why don't you show them how to break the rules?"

"Why don't you?" Ox pointed at Taylor.

"'Cause I'm finished."

"Me too." Ox wiped his face with his towel. "Besides, they don't want to know. I ain't playing with guys who don't love the game between us and them. They think that being a pro football player makes you important. Well, I play ball to be me, no assbackwards. They follow the rules, so they're allowed to stay. What happened to all the guys with tattoos? Where are all the real crazies? The sickies?"

"They broke the rules and the law." Taylor took Ox's towel, mopped his own forehead. "Break my mind and their rules." He tossed the towel on the bench.

"I will, but whose rules? These guys aren't ashamed when you get hit. I don't understand a football player who wants to be normal and then hires some agent to hold his wallet. These guys hug too much. How about a little heckling and motherfucking, for Christ sakes?" Ox stopped dressing. "You know who holds my wallet?"

"Your wife."

"And what does she have in her other hand?"

"Your balls."

Ox nodded. "And, my friend, that is how you last twenty years."

The zeuglodon, the prehistoric whale, the last of his kind, the scarred and tattooed giant, dressed awkwardly, his knees causing him great pain and imbalance. Ox Wood was the personification of the brutal pride that kept Taylor Rusk safe. Even when the referees gave a man permission to tear the Pistol quarterback's head off, he had to get past Ox Wood, who made them pay the price and seldom gave them the privilege.

Taylor headed to the showers, singing: "Take it back, oh no. You can't say that. All my friends are either dead or in jail . . ."

"You know," Ox interrupted, "you never once put a cigarette out on my tongue."

"I don't smoke, Ox."

"That's what I mean."

Taylor nodded, continuing: "Sweet revenge will prevail . . . without fail."

When Taylor returned from his shower, Ox Wood was gone. The trainers were draining the whirlpools and closing down the training room. The locker room was dark and empty. Taylor dressed slowly, taking a long last look, enjoying the satiated feeling that came at the end. He checked himself in the mirror, looking at the dressing room behind, then left.

In the hallway he noticed the new paint was peeling. Water stains streaked the ceiling, and it was cracked and sagging in spots. There was a sour smell; damp, moldy. It was already coming apart.

His boots slipped on the concrete, the promised carpeting was still not installed and wires dangled through holes in the ceiling and walls, marking unfinished electrical work.

When he reached the underground parking lot, he heard sirens in the distance and wondered if the gridlocked traffic would ever be cleared.

Taylor recognized the deep roar of the engine before the white Ford drove up out of the darkness.

Wendy jumped out, smiling, and ran over to Taylor. "You did it!" He lifted her up and she kissed him hard. She stopped for a moment, leaning away to look at him. "You actually did it! Unbelievable!"

"I was out there alone with lots of other guys." Taylor pulled her toward him; she kissed him hard again, throwing her arms around his neck and squeezing, hugging him tightly.

"God! I do love you! I never knew how much I loved you until now."

"Front-runner." Taylor's ears rang from the pressure she put on his neck. She had never shown him this desperate sort of affection. "I apparently showed a side of me recently that has caught your attention."

She kissed him again.

Randall walked up with his Pistols pennant. "Come on, Mom, knock it off, quit the kissing. Taylor's had a rough game. Right? Haven't you, Taylor?"

"Yeah." Taylor bent and scooped up the boy. "But not so tough that I can't kiss you." He began nuzzling the boy's neck and kissing his soft face.

"No . . . no . . . no . . . no . . ." the boy squealed with glee.

Taylor carried him to the car, following Wendy into the back-seat.

Taylor *had* created a miracle. He was carrying him in his arms.

"I'm done," Taylor said. They were still driving. Randall had fallen asleep at the edge of town. Wendy told what she knew about the carnage at the Pistol Dome.

"This Super Bowl was the first time I played for *real* stakes." Taylor cradled the sleeping boy in his aching arms; he loved the feel of holding him. "The real game. Your basic human struggle ... greed ... hatred ... revenge ... stupidity ... pride ... vanity ... your life-and-death issues. I could only do that once. I got through this thing without getting killed and I am finished. That was my last and best game. It was amazing, but I'm not going to invest another fifteen years for more. We'll move to Doc's until we buy our own place. Just take up sunbathing where we left off."

"I'm delighted." Wendy sounded skeptical. "If you think you really can quit."

Taylor laughed. "Quitting is easy; *everybody quits*. I contracted for the Super Bowl, a hopeless bargain, but I delivered. That's why I'm worth one million. Now it's adios."

"You *are* serious." Wendy watched approaching headlights; she wondered what he would do if he weren't quarterback.

"*They* are serious," Taylor replied.

"You just decide today?"

"I've always known, but I decided right after the game." Taylor smiled. "It's easy. I am just not going to do it anymore. I don't want any more training camps or late-night neurotic phone calls from Red Kilroy. I got hit by another Grapette bottle today." Taylor sighed. "I wish I had the deposit money on all the Grapette bottles I've been hit with."

"What are you going to do?" Wendy asked.

"I don't know. Don't care." Taylor drummed his fingers on his knee. "I have to straighten out the problems with the Union benefits for Ginny Hendrix and Simon's kid, but that's all, and then I just quit chuckin' 'em." Taylor shifted Randall.

"I want us to be a family," Wendy said. "It will be wonderful for us to have all the time we want."

"Nothing but time together."

They rode in silence for several minutes. Finally Taylor spoke. *I can* quit, just like I've done everything in my life that everyone tells me I *cannot*. Nobody wants anything to work for anybody else. . . . They don't want to hear or see my good idea. They're hustling their own good idea. I can do anything, Wendy, but only *you* believe I'm right. Only if you understand why and who I am."

"You're a misfit," Wendy said. "A freak. Savvy?"

"Savvy." Taylor nodded. "Why go to all this trouble and not be allowed to be a freak? Ox Wood makes that point exquisitely."

They drove out to Doc Webster's Ranch.

He carried Randall into bed. Taylor kissed the soft cheek and lay the sleeping boy down, the gentle, unlined face framed by the yellow pillow. He went to the kitchen and then out on the porch, searching for Wendy. She was lying in the new double hammock and listening to the night sounds. Taylor lay next to her. The gentle sway of the hammock and Wendy's reassuring presence helped ease the coming down.

All the way down.

The night was cold, clear and still. Dead Man Creek gurgled and splashed; animals moved along the fence row; a doe dashed through the yard after grazing almost to the porch before Taylor's cough spooked her. The deer bounded off into the darkness, its white flag still visible as she cleared the fence and headed back to the cover of the creek bottom.

Several times in the stillness Taylor would sip tequila and stare into the sucking vacuum of the billion-star sky—no up or down, right or left, just on or off. Dead or alive. Do you get what you deserve? Or merely what's left? Wendy's even breathing told him she was asleep.

Sometime before dawn Taylor thought he heard typing. He knew it was something else, rationally explainable if he made the effort, an insect or the wind or a chaparral suffering from future shock. A coyote preparing for the endless chase. Taylor never made the effort and drifted off to sleep in the hammock as the sun came up. He was fully dressed, wearing a heavy coat and bundled in quilts, clutching Wendy desperately in his arms.

It was over and he was glad.

THE OUTHOUSE

TAYLOR and Wendy and Randall Rusk made their home in th
main house for a while. They had to remodel the bunkhouse t
accommodate Bob and Toby and leave room for Doc, should h
want to use his own ranch. Taylor also requested an outhouse fo
perspective. The contractor started work immediately.

"God, it's cold this morning." Wendy led the way out of th
back of the house toward the rain barrel. "Are you sure this is
good idea?"

"Sure . . . it'll be good for us." Taylor carried Randall out th
kitchen door on his shoulders. "Duck, bub."

The boy squealed as Taylor squatted down and waddled unde
the lintel. "Stop . . . stop . . ." The small boy laughed and dug h
little fingers into his father's hair. "Look at me, Momma. Momma
Look at me. I'm riding a bucking bull. Momma?"

Taylor snorted and swung the boy. Wendy watched them whil
she stood by the rain barrel and listened to the hammers knockin
out the wall next to Tommy McNamara's old desk. She shivere
involuntarily at the memory of the horror in that bunkhouse.

"Come on, I think it's too cold," Wendy protested, still shakin

"Momma? Watch me ride the bucking bull. Momma?"

"Oh! That's wonderful; you are such a good cowboy. Taylo
it is too cold!"

"No it's not. It's fresh. I'll go first." Plucking the boy off h
shoulders with his huge hands, setting him on his feet next to h
mother, Taylor plunged his head in the cold water.

Real cold water.

The frigid jolt made his ears ring, his eyes ache, his soft tissue
instantly contract in shock and squeeze his skull. It felt as if h
had set his face on fire. Taylor jerked backward as fast as h
could. The cold water had stunned him as effectively as a hit
the head.

"Aaaahh! Yeeahhhh! Haaahh!" Taylor's head throbbed. Ey
still closed in shock, he clutched at his face with his hands. Gaspin
in pain, he sat down on the crate next to the barrel. Wendy laughe
and tossed the towel at him.

— 534 —

"Maybe it is a little too cold." His ears still rang. Spots swam in his eyes.

"Say, Wendy," the contractor called from the bunkhouse. He always talked with Wendy, who understood his task and information requirements much better than Taylor. "Could I show you something?"

Wendy walked toward the fat, middle-aged carpenter who did all of Doc's work. Taylor wrapped the towel around his frozen head.

"I'm next," Randall yelled. "I want to jump all the way in the rain barrel."

"Wait a minute, Randall." Taylor was trying to recover. "I think I miscalculated."

"You promised! You liar, you promised!" Randall began in a singsong, "Taylor is a liar, Taylor is a liar . . ."

"I'm not a liar. I made a mistake."

"You *lied* . . ." Randall pointed at Taylor in disgust. "Liar, liar, pants on fire . . ."

"I didn't lie, I made a *mistake*," Taylor was pleading as Randall was trying to crawl up the side of the rain barrel. "Wait."

"Don't touch me," the boy howled, as though he had been stabbed. "You got to let me do it."

"An honest mistake." Taylor tried to placate the boy. "Everyone makes mistakes, why can't I? Huh? Get down from there . . ." He grabbed the boy's arm just as Randall was about to dive headfirst into the cold water.

Wendy finished talking to the contractor and returned to where Taylor and Randall's argument had degenerated into scuffling.

"Not fair, not fair!" the boy screamed as Taylor tried to pull him away from the rain barrel edge. "Liar! Liar!"

Wendy slapped Taylor on the back of the head with a thick manila envelope. He turned the boy loose and she stuffed the envelope in his hands.

"Randall! You stop!" she said, swooping the boy up against her breast and taking him into the house.

At the back door she stopped and turned to Taylor.

"They found it in the wall next to Tommy's desk. He had it hidden there, I guess." Her face was drawn and white; she looked frightened.

Randall stuck his tongue out at Taylor.

Wendy carried him into the house and Taylor sat down by the rain barrel.

Inside the manila envelope was a file folder marked *Bob Hendrix*.

He sat with a towel around his neck and read through the fi̶ It was one of Tommy McNamara's that hadn't been found th̶ rainy, murderous night.

There is always a secret.

Bobby Hendrix *had* uncovered one after all, and it had ma̶ him madder than anything the owners had ever done.

Mad enough to get him killed.

From the penthouse past the outhouse.

SAWING WOOD

LAMAR Jean Lukas opened his eyes with a start, crouched in t̶ corner of the living room in Taylor Rusk's apartment. A rush terror clutched his stomach; he felt the uncomfortable shiver his skin tightening, quickly squeezing and compressing his enti̶ body into a small size.

The instant panic was painful yet absolutely necessary, mai̶ lining enough adrenaline to snap him to full consciousness.

He had been *unconscious*.

Not just resting the muscles and bones, not just asleep whi̶ dreaming a dream of pure reality—hearing, seeing, smelling̶ but *out*. Blackness. Remembering nothing. He tried to go bac̶ to recall. But he had broken the chain of continually connecte̶ randomness that, since the highlands, was the life event know̶ as Lamar Jean Lukas, and now he could not recall.

Lamar Jean Lukas had experienced a good night's sleep.

It was the first of many to come.

THE LOOSE END

NOBODY was on the street yet. The Lebanese man leaned forward, drawing the red velvet away from the tall eight-pane glass, and hung the heavy drape on the horns of the antique bronze Devil's head. It was morning.

The rain thrashed. The Quarter was black. Water ran in the street; great falling pearls exploded against wood, brick, wrought iron, tin, glass, buildings, buses, cars, light poles and hydrants, filling the air with a rising mist that threatened to overwhelm the ancient city and sink New Orleans into the mire without a trace.

The hammering rain was a peaceful soothing sound to the Man, a furious rhythm that matched his internal pulsing drives, desires and needs. The Man was at one with the storm and the sodden morass of the Quarter.

Cisco knocked on the door but did not enter.

"The phone, sir. Charles Stillman calling from Texas about the Cobianco brothers."

"That is none of our affair, a jurisdictional dispute. We are not involved. Kindly tell Mr. Stillman to stop bothering me."

The janitor from Louie's on Rampart Street walked up Royal after turning off Iberville. The Man checked his watch. The janitor was right on time. He would proceed up Royal past Bienville, Toulouse and the rest up to Esplanade Avenue to catch his bus. Every day for nineteen years he walked up Iberville, turned at Royal and walked to Esplanade. Six-thirty-four on the dot he turned the corner at Royal. Why did the black man never walk to Esplanade down Rampart Street?

"Sir," Cisco explained through the door, "I have already explained that to him. This is the fourth time he's called since midnight. He says there is a loose end you might be interested in hearing about."

"Loose end?" The Man leaned forward and lifted the heavy red drape off the grinning demon's horns. "We are always interested in life's loose ends." He dropped the velvet drape.

The storm slashed the Quarter with renewed fury.

BR'ER RABBIT
HITS ONE DOLLAR A SOP

THE Cadillac arrived outside the airport. The flight from Ne
Orleans had just been announced. The driver was waiting on t
two shooters.

It hadn't been an easy deal to make. The driver was flyi
blind, grabbing his ass and hoping the wind kept up with hi
Stillman had put him in touch with the Man from New Orlean
Finally.

It had taken all night before Charlie Stillman handed him t
phone.

"Care to dance?" the lawyer asked.

It was a long shot but his only shot, so he talked and he talke
He explained that the favor needed now was insignificant wh
considered against the gain of maintaining power and control.

"What we need to buy here, sir, is just a little time."

"Do you know a more precious commodity," the Man replie
"especially for a man in your predicament?"

"It gets less valuable as it passes, my friend," he replied. The
covering the mouthpiece, he whispered to Charlie Stillman, "T
fucking greaseball sounds like dialogue from *Casablanca*."

"I'll tell him you said that." Stillman stared coldly. "I'm su
he'll think you quite droll. The Lebanese have an intriguing sen
of humor."

Returning Stillman's stare, he spoke into the phone. "Be certa
of one thing: I've spent years pursuing this particular prize a
have grown strong with adversity."

"That is brave, defiant talk. I like that in a man—if that pr
cious commodity time does not prove him a fool." Suddenly hea
raindrops hammered the green roof of the Royal Street house.
squall was blowing through the Quarter, cheering the Man u
making him generous. He took the rain as an omen, advice fro
his lover. "What is it you want from me?"

"I let Donald Cobianco have twenty-five million dollars wor
of bonds to secure a sixteen-million-dollar loan from you. It w
to be a short-term loan and then they were to be returned to m

he Cobiancos were to use the sixteen million to secure control
the Franchise."

"The Franchise?" The Man played dull. "What kind of fran-
ise? I'm not aware of any loan or any bonds. Are you certain
your information?"

"Look, let's just pass on the *Tom and Jerry* routine. You wouldn't
ave taken the call if you didn't know about the bonds. Now,
ear me out. I don't want the bonds back."

"If I had the bonds—which I don't"—the man signaled for
isco to pull the drapes so he could watch the rain—"you would
ot get them back until the debt was paid. Sixteen million dollars
twenty-five percent interest."

"I told you, I don't need them back yet. I just need a little
ore cash to stretch this thing out through probate. If you cash
ose bonds, you'll never get the sixteen million, and if I can't
eep my end together, you won't ever recover your losses."

"Why? Have you done something illegal? Did you give away
onds that weren't yours to give? The government frowns on that."

"No. It's all legal. I have the right to assign the bonds, but the
eople who gave me the right assumed if I did it, it would be
ght and proper. If it was to become public that . . ."

"It all sounds right and proper to me." The rain pounded harder
nd the sky turned black. Cabs and cars splashed and honked and
ared along the street. Everything was shiny, wet, renewed. "Why
re you so worried about public exposure?"

"Because the Cobianco brothers are dead and so's Suzy Chan-
ler, and by the time this is all dragged through probate . . . a man
my position . . ."

"Ah, yes. A man in your position can't be seen associating
ith people like the Cobiancos. But you can call me for a favor."

"This is not just *my* problem. The interest on the bonds was
ssigned to you for the loan, and in the meantime I was to receive
onetime payment *today* of three million dollars from the
obiancos."

"And they are dead."

"Precisely."

"And you need the three million and hope that I might be
ersuaded to lend it to you?"

"Exactly. I have to replace that interest income from the bonds
order to cover normal costs and two very expensive, trouble-
ome, extraordinary expenses."

"Why don't you just eliminate the costs. And the trouble."

"Some of the cost is *because* somebody tried to eliminate
trouble."

"What am I to gain?"

"You'll get your sixteen million and interest, for starters."
was sweating, just as the Man from New Orleans wanted. "E
we have to wait and let the probate take its long, long process
inventory and disbursement, let the banks enter our claims quiet
If we do that, we'll all come out of this with as much, may
even more, than before. Now, do you want to help me or not
He was beginning to panic and his tactic became bluff and thre

The Man from New Orleans grinned. He could sense the blo
and fear through the telephone.

"Three million dollars is what you have to have. How will y
explain where it came from?"

"I'll only have to explain if it doesn't arrive to meet expens
That's why I have to have the cash *now*."

"Three million is more than the quarterly income from
bonds."

"I have large expenses," he replied. "I'm a big tipper."

"I can see that." The Man paused. "Well, *if* I had the bon
which I emphasize I do not, and *if* I were to lend you the thr
million to protect the sixteen million that I supposedly loan
against the bonds, I would have to have a man of mine watchi
the books and cutting down on your tips to yourself and yo
cronies."

"Now, hold on. I didn't put all this together to hand over
you."

"You would still have your title and position, but I'd have
man handle the money. I will not find myself in the squeeze y
are in. Your other choice is to watch it all fall down. On you.
would be a shame, but I have much more money than time. Y
have too much time and no money. I will think about it and ha
my man advise you. Now, would you put Mr. Stillman back
the line, please?"

"*Wait*, who is your man?"

"You are supposed to be handing the phone to Mr. Stillma
Please do. We will have no further need of contact. Good-bye

Charlie Stillman took the phone and listened for several m
ments, then hung up.

"You got a deal," Stillman said. "He takes half of your h
of the Franchise when you get it. I'm to be immediately hired
counsel and chief financial officer and you don't spend one di
I don't approve."

"Is that all?" he said sarcastically.

"No. You got some wet work to do," Stillman said.

"Wet work?"

"Yeah, asshole. Wet work. The Man is sending in a couple of shooters. One is a guy named Hymie that Mr. C. used every now and then after Lennie the Leech got clipped."

"You mean they're going to kill someone?"

"Don't act like I busted your cherry. It was you that got Bobby Hendrix his flying lesson in Mexico and sent Tiny and Lennie out after Tommy McNamara."

"I just figured all of that was over now."

Charlie Stillman laughed. "Over? It ain't *ever* over. You got to pick these guys up at the airport this afternoon. Two shooters from New Orleans."

"*I* have to? Why me?"

"Because you are going to help eliminate some problems and the people that go with them."

"I'm not killing people for him."

"You got it backward. These people are *your* problems and you have to get the shooters up close." Stillman shook his head. "Why do you need the three million?"

"Expenses—you heard me. The bond income may not cover operating expenses, and if Taylor Rusk keeps forcing the issue . . ." He stopped and looked at Stillman.

"Bingo."

"But why? If he gives me the three million, that ought to . . ."

"*Ought to* ain't good enough," Stillman said. "Besides, it removes potential opposition down the road."

"What? How?"

"Simple. You kill Taylor Rusk, Wendy Chandler and the boy."

"Why? In God's name, why?"

"The same reason you asked for Hendrix and McNamara."

"I didn't ask you guys to kill them. I just wanted to know if there was any sort of file on me. I began to get suspicious of Hendrix. I thought maybe he and McNamara were up to something they weren't."

"How do you know?"

"I saw the documents."

"You saw *some* documents. There could be more. What if there's a file on you?" Stillman's voice was cold, his eyes slits. "You do what you're told. Pick the shooters up, drive them out to Doc Webster's ranch and help them with the killing. *Then* you get your three million dollars." Stillman clapped him on the shoulder. "Now,

write out that executive order making me counsel and chief
nancial officer. I've got to go look over the books. You seem li
the kind of fellow that can't be trusted with other people's money

Stillman read and folded the letter when it was finished. I
started to leave.

"You know"—he stopped and turned back—"I asked Wen
Chandler for a little work once, right after her daddy died. S
said, 'You'll get work from me when Br'er Rabbit goes to a doll
a sop.'"

Stillman laughed and shoved the letter into his coat.

THE SHOOTERS
FROM SWAMP CITY

THE driver sat outside the baggage claim, waiting for the tw
shooters from New Orleans. It wasn't an easy thing to do, but
was his problem. There was no one else.

"Every problem presents opportunity," Stillman had said. "T
tragic deaths at the Pistol Dome could be a golden opportunity
increase power. It seems to me that Taylor Rusk, the woman a
the child are the only problems left. Their removal will leave t
trust fund without purpose or direction."

The woman and the child. He had not expected that.

"What if there is a file?" Stillman had said. "If you clip h
and she's seen it, she's not likely to back off and let us screw t
trust set up for her kid or the Franchise her daddy built. Do
leave witnesses. Little kids are smart. Can't trust 'em. Got six
my own. You do as you're told or we don't have a deal. The M
doesn't need you to pick up the pieces. Make it too tough, I
you loose." Stillman warned. "The Man in New Orleans does
need this deal, so shut up and do what you are told."

The two shooters came out of baggage claim. The driver re
ognized the giant, Hymie. Patch, the other one, was small a
ferret-faced.

He drove them toward Dead Man Creek, Taylor, Wendy a
Randall.

"This guy is a friend of mine," the driver said impulsively

"Aren't they all." Patch, the small guy, was assembling a Browning .22 automatic, Woodsman model.

The Cadillac climbed into the hills.

"Lot of fucking rocks in this country," Patch said.

The Cadillac turned onto the caliche road and across the cattle guard.

"How many people?" Patch asked.

"Three, maybe four. I don't know for sure."

"Terrific." Hymie spoke for the first time. "What kind of clown re you? You contract a hit and don't know how many?"

"Well, I don't do this stuff too much, you know."

"Neither do we, asshole, but we try to get it done right. They said you were a professional and could stand the heat. What the ell is this?"

A pickup truck came toward them on the one-lane caliche road. hree men sat in the front seat. The Cadillac and the pickup passed owly. The three men waved. The obligatory gun rack in the ickup window held three shotguns.

"Who are they?" Hymie grabbed the driver's seat back with is huge hands. "They act like they know you? That's three fucking itnesses, you jack-off!"

"They don't know me. Everybody waves around here. We're the country," the driver said. "You saw the sign on the truck; ose guys were carpenters, probably doing work at the ranch. 's five; they'd be quitting now. Don't worry: People trust each ther out here."

"We'll cure them of that," Patch laughed.

"I don't like this," Hymie said. "This should be planned better. ew Orleans can't wait?"

"If somebody wants to call him," Patch mocked. "I'll put up e quarter." The small man slid a magazine of mini-mag hollow oints into the automatic.

"Somebody killed the Cobiancos," Hymie said. "Fucking wiped em out. I would like to know *who* before we go charging in."

Patch shoved the long-barreled pistol into a scabbard inside his elt.

"The big man at the wheel is the key. Ask him. We got a job do."

"Who killed the Cobiancos?" Hymie asked the driver.

"Not me, for Chrissakes. I don't know. I thought you guys . . ."

"Shut up and drive, asshole." Patch, the small man, opened ne of the bags and took out and assembled a nine-millimeter

— 543 —

submachine gun. "And don't act like a fag choirboy. The Ma
says you order hits like most people do pizza." Two long clip
fully loaded were taped together with gaffer's tape.

"Stillman said you had Bobby Hendrix tossed out of a plane.
Hymie was assembling a Winchester 1200 police riot shotgun.
looked small in his huge hands.

"He did?" Patch looked at the driver. "That right, asshole?"

"No. It was a misunderstanding."

"What? Hendrix think he could fly?"

Patch and Hymie grinned and nudged each other.

"Well, this one ain't no misunderstanding," Patch said, "We'
gonna kill three people and you are here to help. It's your hi
now tell us about the layout at the ranch house up ahead. We
figure out how to do it." Patch looked out the side window. "Th
guy played a hell of a Super Bowl Game, I got to admit, even
I lost my ass on the spread. Kind of hate to clip a guy like that

"I bet on him." Hymie slid the green three-inch Magnum triple
0 Buck cartridges into the sawed-off shotgun. "Made twenty-fiv
grand. There's something magic about that guy. I've seen him u
close. He could do it. He got away from me and Tiny one nigl
after I hit him with a baseball bat and Tiny busted his nose. He
going out on top . . . going out a winner . . . not like these bun
you see hang on to the end and then sell beer to the kids. Disgustin
what ex-jocks do for money. I feel kind of proud."

He pumped a shell into the chamber.

THE FILE

TAYLOR Jefferson Rusk sat out by the rain barrel and read throug
the file several times before setting it down. He stared out towar
the back field and the ravine beyond where he and Bob Trave
had caught up with Tiny Walton, Lennie the Leech and the b
guy in the four-wheel drive.

Until now Taylor had assumed Tommy McNamara had tol
them everything and had suffered the terrible desecration and mu
tilation in vain.

But Tommy McNamara *hadn't* told everything. He hadn't even told Taylor and Wendy.

The thugs killed him without learning what he knew. He was killed by uncertainty, the same reason Bobby died. The lack of information. Maybe. Maybe not. Kill them both and remove all doubt.

Kill 'em all, let God sort 'em out.

Information poor vs. information rich.

It wasn't what was *in* the file. It was the fact that the file existed. There appeared to be evidence for misappropriation of funds, questionable loans to the staff, letters to owners that hinted sweetheart deals and secret protocols designed to mousetrap the players. And, of course, the millions of dollars in loans from the Laborers Union. Local 666. The Cobiancos' union. Interest-free loans that kept the books balanced—as long as no one pushed too hard, probed too deep or cared too much about other players.

Bobby Hendrix, for instance.

The Cobiancos had killed Hendrix *and* McNamara. Not for the owners. Not for the League. But for the Union.

For Terry Dudley.

It was for Dudley that they had died. Dudley's thirst for power, his hunger for fame and reputation, his all-consuming desire to sit at the head table with big guys. The Ten Top Onions.

Terry Dudley was not a player.

He hated players.

In a world that Dudley insisted must be split into *us* against *them*, Terry Dudley was not *us*.

Terry Dudley was *them*.

But why?

That was the question Bobby had asked in his letter to Tommy:

Why would the League allow Dudley to go undetected? The players have little time or inclination to involve themselves in the Union. It's the kiss of death. The blacklist. But if *I* know, the League knows, and Dudley knows they know, which means *conspiracy*. We're right back where we were when Charlie Stillman was director. Except the stakes are bigger. We are the software and he is selling us out. They are all in this together: the League, the Union, the networks, big business, big labor. The only person left out, *as usual*, is the working stiff. They'll scream and holler and ritually sacrifice players in the name of collective bargaining, but *suddenly* we'll look up and they'll be sitting side by side taking turns sucking off the Congress for antitrust exemption, promising wage freezes and no strikes.

It's just a guess, but I'm close.

Look over the enclosed papers. The LM-2 forms from the Labor Department show the loans from the Cobiancos needed to balance the books. Check the notation I made on his personnel sheet. He spent six months in the Bahamas—Freeport, where Casinos International has the training school for Investico agents.

Let me know what you find when I get back from Cozumel.

Good luck on your piece on the League and the Mob. Be careful.

As Ox always says, they can kill us and they can eat us, but that don't mean we have to taste good. We can still stick in their craw and make 'em sick as fucking dogs.

Keep on.

B.H.

Taylor read the note from Bobby several times and still came back to the Cobianco brothers' union local. Why?

Why did they loan the players' Union all that money? What did they get or expect to get?

The builders had stopped work on the outhouse and were getting ready to leave when it finally hit Taylor right between the eyes.

The players' pension fund!

It wasn't big now, but if things kept on like they were going and they began talking *residuals*, *percentages* and minimum bargaining agreements instead of free agency and collective bargaining agreements, the pension fund would be monstrous. The Union would control hundreds of millions of dollars, not the players...the Union.

And soon the players' pension fund would be lending money to the Cobianco brothers to build gambling palaces for Casinos International—all to be protected by Investico. Paid for by players. Generations of players. Everyone would get rich but the players. Those were the rules. That was the game.

"If we know, the League knows," Bobby Hendrix had written.

They were letting Dudley do it. He was theirs.

It was a Punch and Judy show while they picked the players' pockets. And judging by the figures on the LM-2, Dudley was careless, felt so invulnerable, that he could misplace three million dollars in three years and nobody noticed.

Maybe, Taylor thought, *the laborers local 666 didn't really end the money at all. Dudley was cooking the books.*

Or maybe, just maybe, Dudley couldn't keep his hands off the ension fund either.

"He went through all those millions a year in dues and needed ore. Maybe he just lifted it out of the pension fund, expecting pay it back shortly." Taylor began talking out loud, listening how it sounded.

"That's why he refuses to pay the claims for Hendrix and imon. He is *broke*. The Union is *broke*. The pension fund is *roke*, and since the killings on Super Sunday, the Cobianco broth-rs can't help bail him out!" Taylor began to pace. He was hy-erventilating. "Maybe . . . maybe Terry Dudley is in a box and unning short on air!"

"Holy shit!" Taylor jumped straight up in the air. "Holy shit!" e grabbed his head, pulling his hair in confusion. "I'm the one itting on the boxtop, screaming, '*No more air* until you come up ith pension money for Hendrix and Simon!' He ain't got it and an't get it."

Inside, the phone was ringing.

"Holy shit . . . holy shit . . ." Taylor started wandering blindly the yard, holding his hand across his mouth so his spirit didn't scape and make a dash for safety. "No. No, no, no. Wrong. an't be." He stopped dead in his tracks and stared down at a corpion digging in under a rock, hiding from the sunlight, waiting sting some poor fool.

"It's for you." Wendy was at the back kitchen door. "He says 's urgent."

"Okay, I'll take it." Taylor looked up at Wendy. "Did you read is?"

She shook her head. "You said you quit all that shit."

"I quit a season too late."

Taylor walked inside and picked up the phone. It was Lamar ean Lukas.

"Say, Taylor. I found a briefcase here in your apartment in the itchen broom closet that I never saw before. The initials on it e A.D.K."

"A. D. Koster?" Taylor said.

"I was hoping you would tell me."

"Why?"

"Well, I woke up feeling kind of funny this morning. I mean, felt great . . . sort of real good for a change, but I just felt restless l day and got to pacing around." Lamar paused and thought.

"Maybe I'm just coming down from the whole week of pretending to be you, but anyway, when I found this briefcase, I opened without thinking. I swear, man, whatever you do is fine by me but I wanted you to know I looked inside."

"And?"

"Well. It is full of money. Cash money. I quit counting after a while, but it's got to be a million, maybe millions. I never seen this much money."

"Millions? *Of dollars?*"

"They look real to me."

"Have you told anybody else?"

"Man, I told you I felt weird all day. I ain't turned on a radio or a television or opened the door."

"Okay, okay, okay." Taylor tried to hold his mind together. "That *is* mine, but part of the money is yours."

"Naw, Taylor, I can't take...."

"There ain't no *take* to it. It's a... it's a... it's a... a... fund, yeah, a *fund* that Doc and I are setting up for Ginny Hendrix and her kids, but Doc and I both felt you ought to have some say and control over the funds, since you were such a big help last week."

"Taylor, this is silly. I don't know about money."

The carpenter's truck pulled off and the caliche dust blew through the open window.

"I know, but Doc does, and he'll be right over to pick you up. Now, don't you leave until he gets there, you hear me? That's an order. Fair?"

"Okay, Taylor. Fair."

"Good. I'll get him over. Don't open up for anybody but Doc."

Taylor hung up and began dialing Doc's number.

"Wendy! We got to get out of here! Get Randall. Hello?... Doc. Just listen. Go to my apartment, pick up Lamar Jean... yeah, the lunatic. Take him and his briefcase somewhere safe. Pretend you know all about whatever he says and don't be surprised by what's in the bag. He thinks it's mine. Bye."

He slammed down the phone.

"There's a Cadillac crossing down at the low-water bridge," Wendy said, walking back from the front of the house. "I'll get Randall from his room. Are we still leaving?"

Taylor Rusk felt the bottom drop out of his stomach.

"Not right away."

Taylor Rusk stood on the porch and watched the Cadillac climb from the low-water bridge. He could see two men in the backseat

"Wendy"—he spoke through the closed door—"you and Randall hide and I'll come find you."

The idea was to make Randall think it was a game. He could ar the boy giggle and scramble around inside while his mother ushed him desperately. The noise quieted. They already had the athtub and mattress ready.

The Cadillac nosed slowly up the hill and coasted into the ade of the big live oak.

It was getting colder. The wind had turned around from the orth. They were predicting snow in the panhandle and sleet in e hill country. The first norther of the year.

"Stop here, asshole, and walk up to him." The short, dark man oked over the stone house. "Find out the layout . . . who else is re. . . ." He kept his small round eyes moving over the out-aildings and the lay of the peaceful limestone bluff overlooking ead Man Creek. "Might as well ask who those guys were in the ckup. We may have to kill them too."

"Jesus!" the driver whispered.

Patch's eyes snapped up to the rearview mirror, catching the iver's gaze. His voice was flat and steady, low and controlled. is stare screamed of death and rage.

"Hey, asshole! This is *your deal*! These people are getting ipped for you. So lay off the heavy breathing. Don't become a ef; everybody's expendable. Especially people who *make* them-lves useless or get in the way. Now, get out there and get us vited right inside that rock house." Patch kicked the driver through e seat, then turned aside to Hymie, who held the sawed-off amp shotgun. "If it's rock *inside* we better be careful we don't oot ourselves. Fucking lead will bounce around in there like nballs."

Hymie nodded thoughtfully as he readjusted the batting gloves wore. Patch kicked the driver's seat again; the driver was still nsfixed in the mirror.

"Go, asshole. Make small talk like an old friend. Tell him you t two fans who would just love to meet him." Patch tightened s thin smile. "A couple of big shooters from New Orleans got little post-season award for him and his family."

The small man kicked again.

"Do what I tell you. You are barely necessary, so don't become problem. Being ten foot tall don't make a shit to a good machine n."

He kicked the seat a final time.

Terry Dudley broke his stare into the rearview mirror and stepp‹
out of his Cadillac in the shade of the big oak.

"Hey, Taylor. *Surprise!* I'll bet you didn't expect to see me‹

BACK
AT THE CROSSROADS

TAYLOR stood on the porch and watched the seven-foot-two-in‹
gangling, loose-jointed basketball player – turned – union poli‹
cian move around the back of his Cadillac.

Taylor was baffled by what ritual formalities to observe. S‹
utation? Handshake?

Taylor watched Dudley approach.

"If you touch me, I'll kill you, I swear."

Taylor was moved to speech by the sudden clear breeze th‹
ruffled and rustled the live oak's leaves. The sound shook hi‹
awake.

"Let's get this shit over with," Taylor said. "I have been waiti‹
for guys like you my whole life."

Taylor decided to take a strong offense because he had litt‹
defense. He certainly was not going to let this giant man get mu‹
closer on the basis of his shit-kicking grin.

"Taylor, old buddy? You pulling my leg?" The tall man co‹
tinued moving. The day was cold and he was in shirt sleeves,‹
brown and black pullover with horizontal wide stripes. He wo‹
expensive slacks and high-top black tennis shoes. Freedom-c‹
movement clothes. The Emperor's clothes.

"The Emperor of the Western Hemisphere's new clothes la‹
substance and style," Taylor said. "You're naked, Terry, but I s‹
you brought a couple new tailors with you."

He kept coming, a sick smile on a pasty face—the look of t‹
overmatched, searching no longer for a way to win but a mea‹
of escape. He didn't want to go the distance. His nerve gor‹
Terry Dudley kept ambling toward the porch. The grin paralyze‹

"Stop, goddammit!" Taylor put out his hand and moved slight‹
up the porch to keep his vision clear to the Cadillac and the tv‹
shapes in the back. "Stop or I'll kill you where you are." Tayl‹

rowled just loud enough for the Union director to hear. "You
motherfucker."

Dudley continued moving until Taylor spit the very last word;
then, the seven-foot-two-inch, 250-pound frame hit the invisible
shield.

Taylor Rusk never thought profanity was useful in gaining
important results in serious disagreements, but it stopped Terry
Dudley as effectively as Ox Wood.

"Taylor, what's troubling you?"

"Just stand there and don't move for a second." Taylor had
Johnny C.'s .45 stuck in his back pocket, locked and loaded,
cocked, ready to fire. If he reached for it, events would assume
momentum of their own.

He was stalling, but he didn't know for what.

"What's the problem here, Taylor?" Dudley changed his tack.

"Things are fine; let's keep them fine by everybody standing
still for a minute."

"Come on, Taylor..." Dudley tried to take a step forward.

"Too fast! Talk slow and don't move." Taylor kept his voice
low, his eyes flicking from Dudley's pale face to the car under
the live oak tree. His accusation was unwavering. "*You* had them
killed. *You.*"

"No...it wasn't..." Dudley faltered. He could not keep all
the balls in the air, could not maintain enemies to the front and
car.

"They were told to find a file, not kill anyone." Terry Dudley,
the giant among men, regained himself, his command, his conviction. "It was unfortunate, but the information that we thought
they had was official Union property. It was confidential! The
owners would have ruined the Union with it. Broken us, the rich
bastards. Fortunately, the file didn't exist. Tommy and Bobby
were unfortunate victims, martyrs for the Union."

"Knock off your solidarity rhetoric, Terry. There *is* a file."

Taylor was exasperated, embarrassed, not angry. The monu-
mental stupidity of it all. "They're going to kill you too. You
know that, don't you?"

"What are you talking about?"

"Hey, look me in the eyes. Notice anything different?" Taylor
pointed with forked fingers at his own face. "I don't believe you,
me?" Taylor blinked. "Look around you. Hear the birds, smell
the air...listen to the wind in the oak tree. There's weather
coming. Okay, now, look at the two stooges in the back of your

car. Get it? It's a brand-new world," Taylor said. "You *lose.*
you *really* believe that *you* are using *them*?"

Dudley was a fish being quizzed about the water. He did
remember way back before the means became ends and the e
became an inside joke. A great believer in basic techniques,
became a creature defined by techniques. He'd learned how
compete, how to play and how to win. He'd learned what to s
but he never knew why. Terry Dudley knew a game was be
played: he'd planned to win.

"I don't know what you're talking about."

"Players really *want* to be heroes! Not technicians, not godd
organized labor or the head nigger of the League. Heroes do
build bureaucracies. You've spent their money, lives and care
organizing the same union over and over. You surround and
sulate yourself with greedy ass-kissers. You have a staff kept lo
with a million-dollar payroll. That is *players' money*!"

"I want to help the players."

"Just like you helped Hendrix out of the plane in the Yucat
You want to help *you.* You." Taylor looked over at the two sha
in the car; they seemed to be getting restless. He yelled and wav
"How you all doing? I'll be right on over.

"If you think that whoever replaces the Cobianco brothers nee
you, I refer you to A. D. Koster's mute testimony on the secur
of being in the middle. You are a dead man," Taylor said. "Y
just ain't got the word."

"They have no reason to want to kill me."

"That's not the issue. Do they have any reason to want y
alive?" Taylor replied. "You're dirty now. Looking clean w
your only quality."

"What do you mean?"

"Obviously you put this deal together quickly. Hymie, the
in the back of your car, who I met over a Louisville Slugg
works out of New Orleans."

The wind began picking up and the live oak rattled and groane
The men in the car were tired of waiting. They had a plane
catch. Taylor sensed their discomfort and dangerous impatien

"Think back. . . . What kind of deal did you make?" Taylor w
sliding down the porch, slowly trying for the corner of the ho
before all hell broke loose. "What were the terms?"

"You wouldn't understand. You're against the Union. Y
superstars always help the owners more than anybody! Hero
Stars? *Assholes*!"

"Question too hard?" Taylor eased slowly away; the men w

— 552 —

tting casually out of the car. "Okay, what did you actually *sign*?" aylor kept on. He could see the two men's weapons clearly now.

"Just a letter making Stillman Union counsel and chief financial ficer." The director seemed genuinely mystified. The look struck aylor as perfectly ironic.

"What do they need you for, Mr. Director?" Taylor laughed. You put Charlie Here-Let-Me-Hold-Your-Wallet Stillman right ack where he was before Hendrix went after him. You just be- me an extra ball to keep in the air and you're supposed to be e juggler."

"But I helped them get the sixteen million to get Suzy's half the Franchise."

The wind began to roar through the trees, the temperature opping fast, the sky turning rapidly gray.

The two men, Hymie and Patch, moved around the car, and aylor mistimed their movements badly. They were good at what ey did. No wasted motion. He couldn't make the corner of the ouse before they started shooting. Taylor Rusk was quickly flanked d trapped.

Terry Dudley still had his back to them in confusion; he didn't e the activity in Taylor's eyes. It was when Taylor reached back d pulled the automatic from his back pocket that Dudley seemed sense any activity separate from himself or his wishes. The ents quickly achieved the awful unstoppable momentum generic high-level violence.

Taylor crouched with a two-hand grip, trying to get a bead on e small man with the submachine gun.

"No, Taylor—now, that's silly." The tall, eternal organizer ached out. "This can be worked out."

He was right. He was just wrong about how and why.

The first burst from the Uzi tore across the man's long back, ocking his huge body into Taylor, crushing him to the ground, e twitching, jerking, dying body pinning the quarterback down. he warmth oozed from Terry Dudley's body, soaking Taylor and e dry, hard plateau ground. Dudley's jaw was slack, his eyes ide in surprise and confusion.

The wind was howling, the storm closing fast. The two shooters om New Orleans had to shout above the wail of the northwest ind, screaming down from the Arctic Circle. The live oak whis- ed and cracked. Kicking ass and taking names. Texas weather.

Taylor's right arm was free and he still held the .45. He lay ill, watching the two shooters approach. Shitting, pissing, bleed-

ing Terry Dudley shivered and died on top of him. Oozing aw
leaving the stench of decay and death.

Hymie moved toward the two men heaped in the bloody p
He planned to pump a load of buckshot into each man's head

Taylor saw him coming. He lay still, *let the big son of a b
get close*. The .45 was cocked, safety off, ready to fire. Tay
watched Hymie with one eye and waited.

Too long. He mistimed again. He had let himself run do
stop completely. It threw off his timing and execution.

Taylor was just raising the .45 when Hymie snapped up
shotgun quickly and fired his first blast, shredding Terry Dudle
head and Taylor's shoulder.

Even from the hiding place inside the cast-iron bathtub, r
to the rock shower stall, Wendy and Randall heard the sud
wind. They had a mattress pulled over them.

Randall giggled when the sudden wind banged open the kitc
door.

"Sshhh!" Wendy brushed his soft cheek and smiled, keep
up the illusion of a hide-and-seek game. In her other hand
gripped her pearl-handled snub-nosed revolver. A useless fet
If the shooters got this far, they would shoot through the mattr

The sound of the wind almost covered the first bursts of f
but the second explosion was so close to the house that the
iron vibrated with the shock.

Taylor had time to return since the last explosion. He was
coming.

"Momma, I'm getting hot," the boy complained. "Let's
and get out."

"Shush. Stay here." She clutched him against her. "Ta
wants us to wait till he finds us." She didn't know why
whispered. It hardly mattered.

"I don't want to wait." He began to struggle. "I'm scared. .

Wendy grabbed the boy, firmly holding while gently talk
She hoped they shot through the mattress.

She could feel the footsteps vibrating up the clawfeet of
old cast-iron tub.

It was so hot.

Hymie saw Taylor's right arm coming up as he blew off
back of Terry Dudley's head.

The Union director was doomed from the moment the Man om New Orleans decided to take the call from Stillman. Charlie illman was a businessman who would never be as grasping as a ambitious man like Terry Dudley. That was the problem with cks, the Man knew: they all thought they were special, immortal. eroes.

Dudley was dirty and the Union was dirty, so the director came the cutout man who would solve both problems. The Man lled it "housekeeping."

Charlie Stillman would make the players' pension fund avail-le to New Orleans when the big money started rolling in. He ould keep better books and cut better deals. The more things ange...

Hymie blew off the head of the cutout man. He planned to do e same to Taylor Rusk, but the hand with the .45 never slowed, en after the first shotgun blast. Hymie knew he didn't have time r a pump. Hymie knew his tools and he didn't have time. He atched the blue automatic flame and buck, the breechblock slam-ing back and forth, ejecting the empty cartridge and cleaving other live shell into the barrel, all in a flicker. Two shots. For aylor Rusk, better late than never.

Hymie ran completely out of time.

Beneath the dead weight of the deposed director of the Union, lattered with bits of his skull and gray matter, Taylor struggled antically. He was beginning to get dizzy, sick; his left shoulder as no longer numb. The pain rolled over him in black waves. e was losing blood, lots of blood, mixing with Dudley's in the liche.

"Goddam you, I'm bleeding to death!" He slugged the dead an. "Even dead, you screw up...even dead." He gasped and egan to feel cold.

Falling back, he looked up into the gray sky. The clouds stretched t, running in front of the wind. Runaway clouds, stampeding verhead, chased by the cold that was seeping into his body. The ld and the damp.

He knew he was dying, but he didn't care.

He watched the cattle running overhead.

"Cowboy...change your ways," he groaned.

He didn't want to look surprised dying like Dudley. Or tor-ented like Tommy McNamara. Or crazy like Simon.

"Or...forever you...will...chase...the Devil's herd..." e was so cold, so sleepy. His shoulder didn't hurt anymore...

— 555 —

"forever...across...endless...sky." He had gotten most of t
words.

He heard the shooting inside the house as he fell into the blac

He felt himself falling upward to the endless, endless sk
Forever.

It wasn't so terrifying.

Patch, the small man, stepped into the house from the por
just as Hymie fired the first blast into the two men on the groun
Patch could see almost the entire house from inside the front do
Except the bathroom.

The bathroom door was closed.

Patch quickly glanced at the other rooms. It seemed pre
obvious the woman and kid were in the bathroom. Patch w
amazed how many people end up in the bathroom. He walk
over to the bathroom door. Inside, Patch heard voices. He look
out the front window.

Hymie was hurriedly jacking his pump gun. Patch watch
impatiently.

More muffled sounds in the bathroom caused Patch to lo
over the heavy oak door and check the knob. No lock. Deadbo
Maybe.

Outside, the muzzle blast sounded sharper—not the hea
boom of Hymie's shotgun, but two quick bangs. Patch looked
to see Hymie and his shotgun sailing backward; somebody h
jerked the big shooter clean off the world.

Patch was stunned, taking a deadly moment deciding wheth
to bust into the bathroom, finish off the woman and the kid or
kill the goddam quarterback first.

It didn't matter.

Patch didn't own a moment.

Bob Travers owned every moment since Patch came throu
the door of the house.

The bodyguard was crouched cross-legged in the back bedro
closet.

All six rounds .38 Special hollow points hit Patch.

Not one slug went completely through his body, although th
made an awful mess of the insides.

Taylor Jefferson Rusk fell from the endless sky after a sho
romantic, painless pursuit of the Devil's herd. He fell with mu
more pain and fright than he had risen.

Toby had begun the replacement of the blood as soon as

t him on the couch. He increased Taylor's oxygen supply with
nasal cannula.

Taylor's brain stopped its dreaming as the oxygen brought the
rve centers to full consciousness of the awful damage Hymie's
otgun had done to his shoulder.

The pain jerked Taylor awake.

"I'm not dead?" He could see Toby over him, shaking his head.
nybody dead?"

"Not on our side."

"Hurt?"

"Nope."

"What about me?"

"We gave you up on points at the start, then played the spread."

Taylor looked at the bottle of whole blood and the tube leading
his arm.

"O negative," Toby said. "Your favorite flavor, right?"

"Where'd you get it?"

"We carry everybody's flavor. We are professionals."

Pain shot through Taylor's left shoulder and arm. "I liked it
tter dead."

"That comes plenty soon."

"How about something for the pain?" Taylor whispered.

"Naw. Thanks," Toby said. "I had a couple of drinks right
er all the shooting. That's enough."

"I mean me," Taylor said.

"Geez, I don't know, Taylor. You been shot. You sure you
ould do drugs so soon?"

Toby laughed and left the room. When he returned with the
ringe, Taylor was asleep.

EPILOGUE

THEY lay on Panther Rock above the swimming hole.

Below, their three children splashed in the slow-running cre[
It had been a dry spring and the Dead Man was low. Randall v
swimming in the hole while two-year-old Matty Ellen Rusk pla[
with Simon Taylor D'Hanis Rusk on the shallow limestone botto[

They had adopted Simon Taylor D'Hanis just before M[
Ellen was born.

"Ginny Hendrix is bringing Billy and Bobby up in the morni[
They're going to stay the summer." Wendy rubbed oil on [
white furrowed scars on Taylor's left shoulder. "I hope these d[
burn. They always burn." She applied more sunscreen while [
watched the children.

Wendy stopped rubbing but kept her hand on his shoulder

He looked up at her.

She was staring off to the east, where the creek sparkled in [
morning sun.

"What is it?" Taylor squinted down the creek.

"It's at the low-water bridge," Wendy said. "I can see the he[

ABOUT THE AUTHOR

ⲧⲉⲣ GENT was born August 23, 1942, in Van Buren County, chigan. He attended Michigan State University on a basketball olarship. Upon graduation, he joined the Dallas Cowboys and, a wide receiver and tight end, played for five years on their t winning teams. He was then traded to the New York Giants. nt has published two novels, NORTH DALLAS FORTY and XAS CELEBRITY TURKEY TROT, and coauthored the eenplay for the film of NORTH DALLAS FORTY. He has tten for *Esquire, Rolling Stone, Panorama, Sport*, and the *LA* ɪes. Peter Gent has a daughter, Holly, and a son, Carter Davis, currently lives in the Texas hill country with his son.